A DAY AT THE THEME PARK

PART 2: SPRING SEMESTER

RYAN WAGNER

Ryan in 2012

Cover design by Ryan Wagner and Chorfia Meliantha
Cover artwork by Chorfia Meliantha

Paperback ISBN 9798999005519
Ebook ISBN 9798999005533

First edition: September 2025

For the genderqueer communities, particularly trans folk,
because what's being done to you pisses me the fuck off.
The T is not—and will never be—silent.

A DAY AT THE THEME PARK has a soundtrack!
(Movies and games have one, so why can't a book?)

The first playlist is a compilation of all the songs the story mentions by name that are meant to go along with that particular scene, while the other five playlists are simply meant to set the vibe for certain stretches of the story. Keep an eye out for the headers as you read! (Not that anybody's telling you what to do.)

Search 'ryan_the_wagner' on Apple Music or Spotify!

▶ 1. POV: You're reading "A Day at the Theme Park" and don't wanna look up the songs

▶ 2. POV: College isn't as scary as you thought so now you're just vibin'

▶ 3. POV: It's cold and it's dark at 6 p.m. but it's just you and baby blue

▶ 4. POV: You're turning up at 370 Rock and you just connected to the speakers

▶ 5. POV: You're at 'some loser concert' and it might be your favorite one ever

▶ 6. POV: It's summer break and you're trying to enjoy it but you don't know what to do with your life

3. POV: It's cold and it's dark at 6 p.m. but it's just you and baby blue

January 23

In a world that isn't trying to constantly cockblock us, Ethan and I would've both gotten back to campus in the early afternoon—but he didn't get here until after 5, and then his mom and stepdad took him out to eat. I dined alone at Patnick since neither Tylor nor Kade nor Victor were back yet, and I didn't wait for them because I wanted to get the Wrath of Patnick over with as soon as possible without anybody in my room to hear, and it's a good thing I did. You'd have thought I caught dysentery in the trenches.

I felt like a dick for turning down my Axworthy friends when they asked me if I wanted to hang when they finally did make it onto campus, but I wanted to spend some time alone with my boyfriend. That's what I straight-up told them. I was in my boots as soon as Ethan texted me that his mom and stepdad were gone. I was too hyped to see him to even notice the cold drizzle or my backpack heavy with books for him weighing me down, and the sight of him through Kessler's front doors had me running. His face lit up like a sunrise as he broke through the doors to meet me. We crashed into each other, squeezing each other, kissing to make up for the weeks of not being able to. "I've missed you so much," I said instead of breathing.

"I missed my baby *so fucking much*," he said into my mouth. I don't know what happened over Break that made him go from *I-don't-want-people-to-know-I'm-gay* to kissing me up against a wall out in the open, but I'm not complaining. Doesn't isolation lead to self-discovery and realizing what's important when it's not depressing the shit out of you?

"Get a room!" somebody in Timberlands said on their way out of the building.

"I like the way he thinks," Ethan said just before pulling me into the building. *This new confidence of his is getting me all hornt up.* He caught me staring as I followed him up the chilly stairwell. "What?"

"Nothing," I smiled. "Just how much you've changed over Break."

"After being apart from you for that long and wanting nothing more than to be with you, I realized I don't really care what people think anymore. You're worth whatever hate I get for it," he said, loading my heart into Kade's water balloon launcher and sending it clear across campus.

He led me by my hand up the stairs and down his hall without caring who saw. "Nate's not back yet, is he?" I asked as he punched his code in at 341 Kessler.

"Nope. And I'm not sure when he's coming back, so let's not waste any time." I slid my backpack to the floor so we could pick up where we left off. As much as I wanted to just lay there with him afterwards, we made ourselves presentable so Nate and his parents wouldn't walk in on us naked from the waist down.

"So, don't be mad at me," I grinned as I took his belated Christmas gift from my backpack, "but Merry Christmas!" I whipped it out and held it out to him.

"Oh, babe! Thank you!" He got up and took it with a kiss. "Why would I be mad though?"

"Because you might feel bad about not getting me anything?"

"Who says I didn't get you anything?" He opened his wardrobe and took a small present from the bottom of it. "Ignore my amateur wrapping skills."

"I actually don't think I'll be able to accept it," I laughed. "Thanks babe. You open yours first." *But what if he never wears it?* I thought as I watched him peel away the paper. *What if he hates it? What if—*

"Oh. My god," he said once he'd unrolled and unfolded it. "I love it!" He loved it so much that he tore off the shirt he had on to try it on. "It fits perfectly!" he said to his reflection in the mirror before collapsing into me with a hug. "Thank you thank you thank you!" I stepped back to admire it on him, creased words and all.

☒ SINGLE
☒ TAKEN
☑ MENTALLY DATING DYLAN MINNETTE

"I thought of you as soon as I saw it," I grinned. "Even if you don't wanna wear it out and about, I figured you'd still like it."

He furrowed his brow. "Of course I'm gonna wear it out and about. I'm done giving a shit what randos think about me. Your turn now." I tore open the paper, and not in a hundred years would I have guessed it would've been a box of perforated words. "It's a magnetic poetry set. I figured you could keep it on your memo board, and you can make poems when you need to take a study break or whatever," he said like he was trying to convince me it wasn't useless.

I opened it to skim the tear-apart sheets of words. "Thanks babe. I'll *definitely* be using this. And now for the second part of your gift."

"You already gave me your cum!" he laughed.

"Get your mind out of the gutter," I chuckled as I started setting the books I brought for him into a pile on the floor. "I just meant these. Which I *do* expect back at some point." He leafed through their pages before lining them up on his shelf without even trying to put them in any order.

I hung around to help him unpack, and I got a closer look at his pre-NHU life from the photos clipped to his wire memo board when I wasn't passing him things from a tote. I picked him out in a photo of his baseball team back home in their orange jerseys. In another, he and some other guys stood in tuxes and freshly cropped hair before their prom night. *Was he the only one whose date wasn't somebody he truly liked? The only one who didn't have a happy ending?* A much younger Ethan gleefully held up a puppy. A face-masked selfie of him and his friend Chante from back home holding iced drinks and flashing peace signs. He didn't bring any pictures of his family. And even after we were done, Nate *still* wasn't back. "I guess I should head back," I finally said. "The longer I'm here, the more likely we are to get walked in on."

"That's just how college works," he shrugged. "Sometimes you just get walked in on."

He held my hand all the way to the front door, where he let me go with a kiss. I took four steps and almost ate shit on the sidewalk.

"Holy shit," I breathed. "It was *not* icy on the walk here." I should've just said fuck it and stayed with Ethan all night, because it was a legit treacherous walk back. And shit must've gotten spicy overnight, because I woke up to an email from the university telling me and the rest of the student body that classes were canceled due to the weather. I looked out to see the roads and sidewalks were glistening sheets of ice.

"What are we even supposed to do if we can't go anywhere and we don't have anything to work on yet?" I asked Tylor once he was awake.

"Edge and see who can nut the farthest," he said without skipping a beat. "It's supposed to warm up though, so it should be fine in a couple of hours." His eyes fell on my steaming mug of tea. "What's the first drink of the semester?"

"Chocolate orange pu-erh," I said, feeling massively cultured.

3

"Poo air? Is that what you're supposed to say when you smell a fart or something?"

I don't think there could've been a better day to sit around and do nothing but drink tea and get reacquainted with French press coffee. *I wonder how long our provisions would last us if the dorms got buried beneath a blizzard of biblical proportions?* I thought as I bit into a PopTart. *How long would it take before we started eating each other?* "Would it weird you out to see Ethan and I doing couples stuff together?" I blurted out to Tylor. It's annoying when I come back to the room and see him and Amina cuddling in bed and watching something and I'm supposed to think nothing of it, but then I have to worry about what he'd think about seeing me and another guy doing the same thing—not that I think he'd be disgusted by it or anything.

He paused his new *Sonic* game to turn to me. "Dude, not at all. You two can do whatever you want. Forreal," he said in a way that made me feel as if I was being scolded for asking such a stupid question. "If there's anywhere where you should be able to feel comfortable, it's your own room. Got it?"

I nodded. "Yeah."

"And when I say do whatever you want, I mean *whatever* you want," he went on. "I was in a frat—I've been in bed with people having sex." I couldn't tell if he was joking or not, but I doubt that'll happen since I can barely even take a piss in a public bathroom if there's somebody in there with me.

Once the ice looked like it was mostly slush and pockets of people started venturing out, I asked Ethan if he felt safe making the walk over. I signed him and his sopping wet shoes in 20 minutes later, greeting him with a kiss. "So how's your morning been so far?" I asked him.

"Pretty boring, actually," he said. "I started reading *Heartstopper* and watched Straight guys do Straight-guy things like try walking on the ice and falling on their asses." His hand found mine in the hallway. "So Nate *still* isn't back yet. I guess his hometown got the ice before we did and they couldn't go anywhere."

"Ugh, I wish he would've told you that last night! I could've slept over in your room!"

Ethan rolled his eyes. "I *know.* We'll just have to wait for him to go home some weekend." *Yeah, like that'll happen.*

"Oh, and just so you know," I said as we got to my door, "Tylor said we don't have to act like we're just friends if he's in the room with us. So don't be afraid to be my boyfriend, mmkay?"

He smiled like we had the room to ourselves. "Okay."

"Whattup, E!" Tylor hopped off the bed to greet him with a fist bump. "Did you have a good Break?"

"It was as good as I expected it to be," he said as his eyes fell on Tylor's new 3-in-1 charger for his phone, AirPods, and Apple Watch. "You didn't use your poetry set yet?" he asked me when he saw it still neatly packed in its box.

"I only got it last night!"

"You've had all morning!"

"Well, now you can help me with it!"

"Goddammit mom," Tylor exclaimed, "quit fighting with mom!"

Ethan and I sat on my bed and tore apart adverbs and nouns and participle fragments into confetti. "You're a peach," I told him as I held up 'peach' for him to read.

He searched through the pile of words. "And you're a 'sad'—'monkey'—'butt.'" I threw 'peach' at him, which is how we ended up throwing words at each other. Ethan snapped selfies of us lying on my bed afterwards, posing and making faces.

"So remember how I said I don't care what you do in the room?" Tylor said suddenly. *Uh oh.* "Well you're being too cute, and I'm gonna have to ask you to stop." He shot us a sideways glance before laughing through his nose. "I'm kidding. Please continue."

I was swiping through all 21 pics Ethan sent me when a text banner from Victor reading **You think Kade'll get up if I fart next to his face?** came through. The answer is apparently yes, because a few minutes later he told me the two of them were getting ready to head over to Patnick. Tylor left to meet up with Amina and Jaxon, leaving Ethan and I to tread over NHU's premier dining hall ourselves. I recognized the two figures who exited Axworthy together ahead of us, and picked up my pace to slap the shorter one with glasses on the back. "What it fucking *do*— OH MY *GOD* I am so sorry!" I blabbered as the person who was most certainly *not* Victor stumbled in surprise. "I *totally* thought you were somebody else!"

Not Victor clutched his chest. "I thought I was getting fucking *robbed*, bro," he panted.

"I am so fucking sorry. I'm gonna leave now," I said as my face burned. Ethan was howling with his hands on his knees, joined by the real Victor and Kade. "Oh my god, was that embarrassing," I said from behind my hands.

"What the hell was *that?*" Victor asked in an ushanka complete with a red Soviet star on the front.

"I fucking thought that was *you!* I saw the hat and the glasses and I thought—"

"So what, you see somebody wearing glasses and a hat and you assume it's me?" he laughed. They all dragged me about it until we were past the dorms.

"Real talk though," Kade said as he hooked an arm of his fleece-lined bomber jacket around Ethan's neck and the other around mine, "I'm *hella* glad to see you guys again. I was starting to get sick of him." He shot a sideways glance at Victor.

Patnick was banging, I guess because nobody had any leftover pizza or wings yet. Patnick Paul probably got a kick out of watching students race out of the building before they could get hit by the welcome-back shits. "If *you*"—I pointed to Kade as Paul's eyes pushed us out—"get back to my room and say that you need to take a shit—"

"I was actually gonna go in my own room when I stopped to grab a game for us to make love to, but I think I might hold it now just for you," Kade smirked.

"Wow, you're so thoughtful."

"Aren't I? And I didn't go at all yesterday, so it's gonna be bad. So until that happens, you guys can legitimately say that I'm full of shit." Despite his threat, he took care of his business in 239 Axworthy. I put on some Panic! at the Disco for courtesy noise as my own toilet got violated again and again.

"Imagine having an entire day to ourselves," Ethan daydreamed as he rested his head in my lap while Victor took his turn. "Just us. Not having anything to do or anywhere to go."

Five of my fingers laced with his while the other five petted his hair. "At least we don't have to be secretive about it anymore, thanks to *you*." He propped himself up to meet my kiss even as the bathroom door opened.

"Please don't stop on account of me," Victor said when he emerged, wearing a look of profound relief.

"Oh, we won't," Ethan smiled. I didn't take my arm off him until Kade's text telling me that he was about to be out front pulled me off the couch to go sign him in. He kicked off his wet shoes and made a home for his hulking backpack on my desk.

"Tylor has a desk too, you know," I said.

"You know," Kade said as he unzipped his backpack to take out a game called *Scythe* that's so bulky you could construct a building out of enough copies of it, "when we were coming back up yesterday we passed an NHU billboard advertising over 150 undergraduate programs. Why isn't squirting on people one of them?" He fished out a small metal canister. "Because of woke, *that's* why." He popped the lid off and took a deep whiff before shoving it under my nose. Its harsh and smoky aroma was unexpected, but not unwelcoming.

"Oh damn, what is *that*?"

He closed his eyes to inhale it again. "Lapsang souchong." He slapped his hand over his face and pretended to sob. "Grandpa used to lapsang souchong!" He looked back up and chuckled. "Not like grandma though. That woman could swing her ass in a circle."

Victor played his new chakra bowl he'd gotten over Break for us while Kade unboxed what's probably my new favorite board game. The chakra bowl's calming, ringing voice made me wonder why it's not an instrument that Music majors can major in. Learning *Scythe* was pretty rough, but I stuck it out for the premise and the artwork and the mech figurines. Between the weather, the tea, the game, and the soundtrack for the game that Kade put on on YouTube, the vibe couldn't have been more on-point. None of us wanted to go back to Patnick for dinner, so we ordered Domino's—we wrote in the instructions for them to write a joke on the box —and had movie night since it'd been a while since we'd had one. "You just wanna put on a movie so you two can smooch," Kade accused Ethan and I, though Kade was all for watching a movie once he saw *Donnie Darko* on Netflix.

"Here's to hoping we like *Donnie Darko*," I murmured to Ethan. He and I sat on my bed against the wall together and made Kade's accusation come true a few times. I wasn't planning on putting a pic of our pizzas on my Instagram and Snapchat stories until I opened one of the boxes to read *'How do you save a dying pirate? By giving him C-P-ARRRR!'* Sharpied on the inside.

We were split 50-50 on the movie by the time the credits rolled, with Ethan and Victor making up Team *What-the-hell-did-we-just-watch?* "Are you gonna head out soon?" I asked my boyfriend with a stretch. "Do you want me to walk back with you?"

"No, you don't have to," Ethan said a little wistfully. "I have to get ready for tomorrow. Back to work, too."

My hand slapped itself over my mouth when I realized I never showed up to *my* job. "Oh *shit*. I *totally* forgot about work." I looked around at them like they were supposed to have an answer for me. "Hopefully I didn't get myself fired."

"I thought I was gonna get fired from my old job at Panera because I kept telling people their totals in years," Kade laughed. "I'd be like, 'your total today comes to the year Columbus sailed to America' or something."

"Hashtag too soon," Ethan said. *"Did* you end up getting fired for that?"

"Nah. I got fired for fucking the bagel slicer."

Ethan and I traded horrified looks. "What the *fuck?!*"

"Oh my god, I'm gonna throw up!"

"How do you even fuck a bagel slicer?"

"It's easy," Kade smirked. "You just spread his cheeks and you stick it in."

Spending time with Ethan is like Summer vacation—the longer it lasts, the harder it is when it comes to an end. "Don't worry, we'll take good care of him," Victor said with a grin as he put an arm around Ethan. I pulled him into a hug and kissed him right there, waiting for whistles that didn't come.

"Not gonna lie," Kade said, "you two are actually hella cute together."

I couldn't help but smile and giggle as I swiped through the pics Ethan and I took earlier of him in his crimson Gryffindor sweatshirt and me in my royal-blue Ravenclaw one against the backdrop of my comforter—our mouths and eyes open in exaggerated thrill, our entwined arms, our hands making a heart together, our

7

tongues sticking out, me licking his cheek, his lips on my cheek, our lips on each other's lips. But the one I made my background looks so candid, like it was taken by accident—my chin is in the crook of his neck and we're looking into each other's heavy-lidded eyes like we're moments away from drifting off to sleep in each other's arms. We look so natural, like it's not possible for there to be anything more natural in the world.

I actually hate you m lolol, Logan replied to the pic on my story of the pirate joke.

January 24

Three shootings in three days. Can we chill the fuck out, America?

So I didn't get fired. I guess half of the student workers just assumed they didn't have to go in and the library let it slide because the only people in Rosenberg anyway were Gamer's Guild people playing *Magic: The Gathering* or whatever.

And I remembered the first rule of the first day of class this time: *Don't forget your class schedule, you wet sock.* Dr. Davis told us that although her class is technically called 'African American Literature' she just calls it 'Black Literature' since we'll be reading works by both African and American authors and poets. "But calling it 'African and American Literature' just doesn't sound right," she shook her head.

I made a beeline for the bookstore after Dr. Averescu let us out and took my poshly-priced books back to 222 Swafford, where I hung around for a while before heading over to Bubble Up to see my boyfriend. *I still can't believe I get to call him my boyfriend.* "Did you have a good first day of class?" I asked Ethan. He's done with his Tuesday/Thursday classes by noon again, so he's able to keep the same work schedule he had last semester.

"As good as going over syllabuses—syllabi?—can be," he shrugged as he took my order. "Are you done for the day?"

"Nah, I have Macroeconomics at 3:30. I might just hang out here until then and check out this one cute guy who works here," I winked.

My playful mood had disappeared by the time I was trudging towards Ebersol Classroom Building in the far corner of the Quad. *Economics? What the hell was I thinking?* I couldn't shake the image of the professor being some boring, balding, heavy-set retired accountant who doesn't even attempt to give the class a good time. If that wasn't enough to make me think about just dropping the class, then the TV right inside the main doors showing market trends and graphs and conversion rates and red arrows and green arrows all changing in real time did. I forced myself to go to at least one class though just to say I tried. I passed like five people on my way up to the third floor, and I wasn't even early or anything. *Am I in the right building? Did they dissolve the School of Business just today and I missed the email?* I found the room a little more than half-full without a professor in sight, and took an empty desk in the middle. *Pat yourself on the back, Trevor.*

"Do you always look like you're trying to hold in a shit when you walk into class?" the person beside me said. *Wait, are they talking to me?* A lump caught in my throat as I turned to see Tylor trying to stifle a laugh.

"What are you doing here?" I laughed in relief. "I thought you had this the period before?"

"Yeah, so did *I*. Somebody in the academic-whatever office must be smoking crack cocaine, because the one I signed up for was at capacity." He shook his head with a smile. "This is the next most convenient time slot for me, even though I wasn't thrilled about taking it later in the day. But it works out though since my fam's in it with me!" *I can't drop the class now, I just made the boy's day.*

I hadn't seen a professor I'd ever describe as 'cool,' but that was the only word that came to my mind when ours walked in—and yes, the Hawaiian shirt had a lot to do with it. Between that and his tan, he looked like he was ready to go on vacation. "Afternoon folks," he said like he was out of breath. "Sorry I'm late—we just got back from Doha on Sunday and I'm still screwed up from the flight. I'm Dr. Jurado, and this is...what class is this again?" he asked a girl in the front row. I could feel the whole class tense up. *How funny would it be if everybody was in the wrong class?*

"Principles of Macroeconomics?" she replied timidly.

He ran his hand down over his gray Freddie Mercury mustache. "Oh good, that's what I was hoping you'd say." He wrote and underlined *ECON 102* on the board before turning back to us. "Okay. Can anybody tell me what happened in 1776?"

The room stayed quiet.

"Nobody knows anything that happened in 1776?"

"America happened," somebody answered. *Yeah, maybe in a History class. The Wealth of Nations was published.*

"Yes, but Adam Smith also published *The Wealth of Nations*, which helped lay the foundations for our modern economics theories," Dr. Jurado said as he wrote and underlined 'Wealth of Nations' on the board. "Next question: why are you here?" Some guy slouching in his seat muttered something. "Speak up, please."

"Because we have to be," he mumbled a little louder.

"That's fair," Dr. Jurado said with his hands in his pockets. "But *do* you? Yes, I *know* you need the credits to fulfill your requirements to graduate. But you don't care about this garbage. You just figured you'd breeze through some 100-level class to fill an easy requirement, am I right?" A handful of us nodded. "I'm not judging. You think *I* didn't try to take the easy road when I was in undergrad?" he laughed. "But I don't just mean this class though. Why are you here *at school?*"

"To get a degree," Girl Who Confirmed What Class It Was sucked up.

"Okay. How about you?" he asked the person behind her. He went down each row and asked every student the same question. Degrees were the most popular reason. My chest pounded as he looked me in the eyes.

"To discover new things," I said.

"To smell the roses," was Tylor's answer.

"All fair answers," he said after everybody disclosed their reasons for indebting themselves to the system. "But you know they're mostly bullshit. You're not here for a *degree.* You're here so you can get drunk and sleep in and sleep with people and do what *you* want for a change without anybody telling you otherwise! You've lived under your parents' roofs for long enough, and you're ready to make your own decisions, right?" He sat us up straighter as he spat fire. Even Slouch was at attention. "If making good money is your endgame, then getting into some illegal trade or playing the stock market are much more lucrative options."

Tylor and I exchanged keen glances.

"I'm going to let you in on a little secret," Dr. Jurado went on. "I've been around the world dozens—literally *dozens*—of times. I've been to every continent. I've worked in Hong Kong, Morocco, Brazil. I spent a couple years on a boat in the Mediterranean. And I only got to do all that stuff because I *knew the right people.* That's what it all comes down to," he said simply with his hands in his pockets. "Your degree won't land you your dream job or make you money." He paused to let us absorb that. "You don't believe me? Say you're a manager and you're hiring for a position—are you gonna go with some person who has the education and all the qualifications, or are you gonna go with somebody your best friend has known for years? I'm sorry, but that's just the way it works," he shrugged. "The sooner you realize that, the more of a head start you'll have. But by being here and by doing all this—hell, maybe even from taking this class—you're giving yourself the opportunity to meet and connect with the people who can help get you there."

"But wouldn't it make more sense to network with stock traders and drug dealers?" Slouch asked.

Dr. Jurado gave him a smile. "We're gonna be good friends this semester."

"Holy *shit*," Tylor said in the hallway 40 minutes later. "He's already my favorite instructor I've ever had."

I grinned. "*Right?*" And from what I overheard as the class filed out, that's pretty much the consensus. And to think that I wasn't even going to give it a try.

January 25

So Zukoff *doesn't* have any Indian food options, believe it or not. Retweet if you cried every time.

My first class of the day, American Military History, was unremarkable except for the fact that Dr. Kotek is an actual lieutenant in the Army with a torso as big and as sculpted as a battleship. He looks like Mr. Incredible in a golf polo. I waited by the vending machines for Victor's own history class—Civil Rights Movements— to let out so we could walk across campus to French together. The most direct route from Shaver to Abernathy is across the running track next to the Field House, which is like walking through a wind tunnel. There's nothing like an unrelenting gale of wind against your face on an already-16-degree day to make your tears freeze to your face. Like you know how it gets so cold that it makes you mad? *That's* how cold it was. My scarf and hat didn't do jack-fucking-shit to keep me warm. The wind blew in our faces no matter which way we faced. We even tried walking backwards and it was *still* blowing in our faces.

"*That*," Victor chattered in the vestibule of Abernathy, defogging his glasses, "was some goddamn fucking bullshit."

"Holy *fuck*," I breathed. "I'm no stranger to lake-effect weather, but that was just unnecessary."

Victor, having a brain in his head, snapped a pic of his class schedule in case he lost or forgot it. "It's in...D-107?" He looked up and down the hall. "Does that just mean *room* 107?" He poked his head into room 107 to ask if it was French I. "That's not it," he muttered.

"Maybe it's on the second floor?" I suggested.

We climbed the steps to look for any rooms that started with D. The third floor didn't have anything either other than two flustered boys, one because it was 11:02 and I wasn't sitting in class yet, and the other because he thought the room numbering system was bullshit. Back on the ground floor, we knocked on the open door to the staff lounge as a last resort.

"Hello," Victor smiled at a professor stirring her coffee. "We're a little lost. Do you know where we might find room D-107?"

"D? D is in the basement." She pointed over to a staircase separate from the main stairwell that only went down. *Why not name it B-107 then, for basement?* Because, as we soon found out, 'dungeon' is a more accurate term for it. The basement passage—passage, not hallway—was narrow, uneven, and lifeless. Sure enough, there was a D-101, but the door looked like it hadn't been opened in years. D-102 had no door and nothing but blackness beyond the frame. *There's no way*

11

they have classes down here. Abrupt angles broke up the corridor's short, straight stretches. The ceiling was a desolate highway of pipes and dim lights hanging by a cord. I could only think of all the horror movies I'd ever seen. A mouse scurried along the wall into D-104. I kept my distance from a random, rebarred hole in the wall in case a hand shot out at me as I squeezed past. Finally, a single solid door lay waiting for us at the very end. D-107. Light spilled from beneath it. *What in the living shit are we about to walk into?*

A large sinister pendulum swung uncaringly through what used to be the waist of a tied-down body. Its lifeless eyes stared into mine, forever stuck in wild horror. A cockroach scurried from the mouth.

"Ah, *bienvenue au Français un!* Come in, come in, find a seat," the professor leisurely ushered us in. The natural light bathing the room from the wall of windows was a shock to the eyes. All eyes were on Victor and me as I shut the door behind us and took some neighboring desks towards the back. "Don't worry, I even had trouble finding the room at first," Dr. Le Marque, who kind of reminds me of Seth Rogan, went on. "Pro tip for next time though? The door behind you is *way easier.*" He pointed to a door at the back of the room. We went over *être* and other ankle-deep stuff after the syllabus before getting sent back out into the cold.

"I was hoping he'd let us pick out French names for class," Victor whined as we bundled ourselves back up. "I spent all night coming up with Jean Parmesan."

I let Ethan and Kade know we were on our way to Patnick so they could grab us a table, since they were coming from Ebersol and would get there first. We brushed past people and tramped down sidewalks and steps with squinted eyes. Paul swiped us in with a grunt.

"So how were everybody's classes?" Victor asked musically once he and I returned with our cauldrons of soup.

"Okay, *listen,*" Kade said passionately as he set down his fork. "If you ever take an economics class, you gotta take it with Dr. Sutcliffe. I just had Sustainable Economics with him and I legit can't wait to go back. He's the realest professor I've ever had."

"Well *I* say that if you ever take economics, you gotta take it with Dr. Jurado," I said from behind folded arms.

"Yeah? Well *my* economics professor can beat up *your* economics professor."

I threw my hands down on the table. "Oh yeah?"

Kade stood up. "Yeah!"

"I'll throw a tantrum right *now* if you two don't stop fighting," Victor threatened.

"So either Sutcliffe or Jurado," Ethan nodded. "Noted."

"*Jurado,*" I coughed. Kade shot me a warning glance.

"So sell me on these profs," Victor said. "Give me your elevator pitch."

Kade was speaking before I could even open my mouth. "So the first thing he tells us is how once upon a time we were the purest forms of ourselves—optimistic, hopeful, curious, carefree. And then life started happening to us and we had to adapt to it, hiding that purest form of ourselves. Basically, we lose ourselves as we get older, and the meaning of our lives is to tear down those walls, to embrace who we truly are and to follow our passions regardless of what anybody else thinks. Show your true self off to the world. Success isn't worth it if you lose who you are." *Yeah, I'm totes taking this guy next year.* "And then he started talking about conscious capitalism, which I'd never even *heard* of. And this is all before he even hands out the syllabus."

"And here I thought *my* Economics professor was great because he told us that selling drugs pays better than whatever job a degree could get us," I chuckled.

"*Mmkay*, I'm listening," Kade nodded as he rubbed a finger around the edge of one of his pink tunnels that are so iridescent they could be LED.

"My Accounting professor sounds like she's saying 'turd' when she says 'third,'" Ethan chuckled in his Dylan Minnette shirt.

"My profs are all boring," Victor said. "And I'm pissed that my Astronomy class isn't in the planetarium."

"You know, I think I—" Kade said as he patted his pockets. "Nope, I'm actually all outta fucks to give."

"You should see where our French class is," I said. "You have to go down through this old windy basement hallway to get to it."

"Holy *hell*," my classmate swore. "I thought we were gonna get killed. It's so creepy."

Kade took my hand with both of his. "Trevor," he said in an eerily sincere tone, "I'm so sorry that you had to go through that." He let go of me to spin on Victor. "Who the fuck's even talking to you, you whiney little sub?" he barked at him as he swiped the air in front of his face. "Go suck an egg."

January 26

life	is	like	a	sordid	symphony
pounding	my	head	with	the
ugly	bitter	petals	of	time

January 28

Tylor introduced me to an EP of lo-fi remixes of songs by The Story So Far, as oxymoronic as such an album sounds. If I ever have a kid, those will be the lullabies I put on for them to fall asleep to. Hell, they might be the lullabies that *I* start trying to fall asleep to.

Since our first classes of the day start at the same time, Ethan and I get to have breakfast together every day before we part ways in the Quad with a kiss. And even better, he's done with everything on Fridays by 12, so we kicked off the weekend by taking some Zukoff rice bowls back to his room and playing Switch and sharing my AirPods. There's no way Nate can still think that Ethan and I are just bros.

"So what's the move tonight?" my boyfriend asked us over a dinner of Patnick meatloaf that was more spongy than anything.

"Tylor mentioned something about going over to Amina's—I can ask him if that's still on offer," I said as I pulled out my phone.

"Kelsey hooked us up with some ambrosia before we came back," Kade said. "She was gonna try to get me a fake ID for Christmas, but her PennDOT friend wasn't able to come through."

"I'm telling your parents about all this," I chuckled.

"Go ahead," Kade chuckled. "They already fucking know."

I raised an eyebrow. "And they don't care?"

"*Please.* When you have as many issues as I do, all you have to do is tell your parents you're feeling depressed and they'll do whatever you want. They know I'm being safe. Where do you think I get my cigarettes from?"

"Um, you take Patrick Paul into the bathroom and show her a good time?"

"Oh my *god*, I'm gonna throw up," Ethan heaved.

My phone buzzed with Tylor's response. "It looks like we're getting saucy in Amina's room."

The night saw us playing Kings in 348 Walcott, though I was hoping we'd play Drunk *Jenga*. Amina went over what each card means, but I was too busy zoning out at the can of unflavored sparkling water that Kasey had set in the center of the table, thinking about how the last time I'd played Kings was at the prom after-party, and how my date would break up with me less than a week later. I finally shook myself from my thoughts when I realized that everybody else was pointing at the ceiling and watching me. I forced a laugh with them as I took my penalty drink.

I still think Drunk *Jenga's* more fun though since it's more than just 'you drink' and 'they drink' and 'I drink', even if the Categories round of naming different candies in Sean Connery's voice had us weak. I always enjoy 'Never Have I Ever' because that's when you *really* learn about your friends. Kade's never had a Big Mac. I'm the only one who's never been to a haunted house. Kade's the only one who's had a night terror—"Yes, there was a demon, and *no*, it wasn't shitting on my chest." Tylor and Victor are the only guys who've never jerked off to their bare ass before. Tylor and Ethan are the only guys who've never accidentally creamed in their pants. Victor's the only one who's given himself blue balls or crowd surfed. Ethan and Kade are the only two who've used a butt plug. Everybody but Ari and I have been to a Disney park. Ethan's never whistled.

"Not on purpose anyway," he explained. "Sometimes I'll accidentally whistle when I'm blowing on my food."

"That's why they make whistles, you know," Kade pointed out. "So you don't have to."

"Never have I ever had COVID," Tylor said. "Or, I guess I should say never have I ever *tested positive* for COVID."

"Of course you haven't, you germaphobe," Amina said as she put down a finger.

"Never have I ever been to California," I said. Kasey looked me in the eye as she put a finger down, as did Kade and Victor. "When the hell did you two go to California?" I frowned.

"Like…2018? We spent a week with my aunt and uncle who live out there."

"And you never *told* me?"

"I didn't know we were *supposed* to."

"Never have I ever gotten a piercing," Ethan said. Everybody but Victor put down a finger.

"Never have I ever eaten a girl out," Kasey said. Tylor, Amina, Ari, and Kade all put down a finger.

"And I've been on a seafood diet ever since," Ari laughed. "Never have I ever been to a drive-in." Everybody put down a finger.

"Never have I ever *had sex* at a drive-in," Victor said. Tylor, Kasey, Kade, and I all put down a finger.

"Does it still count as sex if I didn't orgasm?" Tylor asked.

"If that's the case then I didn't have sex until like four months ago," Kasey laughed through her nose.

"Never have I ever had sex with a guy," Tylor said. Everybody but Victor put down a finger.

"Never have I ever had sex with a girl!" I said, down to my last finger. Tylor, Kade, Ari, and Amina each put down a finger. Victor blushed and kept his hand under the table.

Ethan looked around at us and our remaining fingers. "Never have I ever gone to a Pride parade," he smirked, making Victor and I run out of fingers.

"Mother *fuck*," Victor swore.

"We're gonna have to fix that," Kade said to Ethan.

In the end, Ari's card was the one to crack open the can of sparkling water. "Oh god, I'm burping!" she exclaimed from behind her hand after chugging it with a hearty belch.

We took a refill/bathroom break before we started the next game. "Hey Kade," Ethan said, "out of curiosity, how did you get your gauges? Like, how did you make the holes in your ears that big?"

"I just got a hole-puncher and just—" Kade pinched his earlobe and made a *click* sound.

Ethan lurched forward in his seat. "Oh Jesus, I'm gonna throw up! Are you forreal?"

"Of *course* not," Kade chuckled. "They just started off as regular piercings and then I used tapers to gradually get them to be this big. And I mean *gradually*. We're talking *years* in the making."

"Does it hurt to size up?"

Kade's finger found his earlobe. "It's like what they say about bottoming—you just have to take your time and use lots of lube."

"He did them himself you know," Victor said as he returned to his spot on the floor. "The piercings, I mean."

"Really? Wasn't it hard to do it yourself?"

Kade shrugged. "Not really."

"Have you ever pierced other people's ears?"

"Yeah. I've actually done a few people on my floor for a little extra cash." Behind him, Victor jammed his index finger in and out of the OK sign he made with his other hand. "Why, are you thinking of getting pierced?"

Ethan thought for a moment. "Maybe." He lifted his cup and stopped it at his lips. "Yes."

"Well, just lemme know if you want to. I'd be honored to do it for you."

I gave Ethan's earlobe a gentle squeeze, picturing studs in them. "I think they'd look hot."

"Who said anything about my ears? I was thinking of getting a Prince Albert," he almost said without cracking up.

By the time I had to chug the next can of sparkling water, we were so sauced up that I for sure thought we were going to get a knock at the door. The DA watched us stagger past the front desk with arms around shoulders and drunk smiles on our faces when we left to head back to our own dorms.

"Just so you know Eth," Tylor almost slurred, "I told Trev that you two don't have to act like bros when I'm around. I don't have a problem with you staying over—not like you need my permission or anything. Just saying."

Ethan turned to me like he was upset. "You didn't tell me I could stay over!"

"Yeah, because he didn't tell me either!" I said to Tylor. "Forreal?"

"*Yeah?*" He rolled his eyes. "Didn't I just say you don't need to ask me?"

I smiled at Ethan. "Do you wanna sleep over then?"

Ethan thought it over. "I think I'll just head back to my room tonight if that's okay," he sighed. "I don't wanna sleep in my contacts, and I don't wanna make the walk to my room and back." He gave me an apologetic look. "Will the offer still be on the table in the future?"

"Nope," I smiled. "Offer valid for tonight only."

I wonder if the bookstore has any contact cases and little bottles of solution I could get to keep here for him, I thought as I laid in my bed, waiting for sleep to carry my drunk ass off. And then Tylor dropped a bomb that I could've never learned from a game of Never Have I Ever.

"Hey Trev?" His quiet voice broke the silence of our dark room. "You still up?"

"Yeah?"

"Remember how you asked me a while ago why I don't like frats?"

I frowned in the dark as vague memories of the Club and Organization Fair so many months ago trickled back to me. "Yeah?"

"After they officially let me in, I was at a party, and the job they gave me was to stand outside a bedroom door and let people go in one at a time after the person who went in before them came out." I squeezed my eyes shut as I tried to follow him. "I thought they were just taking turns taking hits of something, but I saw somebody passed out on the bed with their pants off." He said it like it doesn't haunt him anymore, but insomnia and I are such good friends that I can tell when people's ghosts still keep them up at night. "I hope you know what I'm getting at, because I can't say it."

I closed my mouth to swallow, not remembering when it fell open. "I think so."

"So yeah," he struggled to say. "*That's* why I don't like frats."

I wasn't about to try telling him that he shouldn't let a one-off thing determine his thoughts about something, but isn't that all it ever takes? *Was it even a one-off thing though?* "Why are you telling me? Why now?"

"Because I'm drunk and I'm thinking about it and I needed to tell someone."

I almost bolted upright. "I'm not the first person you're telling, am I?"

"Unh uh. Jax knows. I wanted to tell Amina, but I know something bad happened to her at a party once, and I couldn't live with myself if I ever found out it was her." *Jesus fuck...*

I rolled to face his bed in the dark. "It wasn't your fault. You know that right?"

"I've tried to tell myself that over and over, but I've never been able to believe it," he said like he was trying to not cry. "I'll *always* feel like it's my fault."

"But you didn't *know*. You didn't *do* anything."

17

"Exactly—I didn't *do* anything. All I did was leave, but that didn't put a stop to it. I was afraid of what would happen to me if I ratted on them."

I didn't say anything, because I know firsthand what it's like to see something happen and know that maybe you could've done something to stop it or change it. "It wasn't your fault," I said again through teary eyes either minutes or an hour later. He didn't say anything back, whether because he refuses to stop blaming himself, or because maybe for the first time he did stop blaming himself, or because he was just asleep, I don't know.

January 29

I have a new favorite 'awake at 2 a.m.' artist, and his name's King Krule.

I still can't get over what Tylor told me. I know we all have skeletons in our closets, but actually finding out what they *are*? It reminds me that nobody's ever just an NPC.

Ethan and I blew off our friends to drive to the nearest town with a movie theater to see the new *Avatar* movie that we each held off from seeing over Break so we could see it together. I wanted to be cute and make out in the theater, but Ethan wasn't having any of it. "I'm trying to watch this," he whispered as he pushed me away. "We can smooch whenever we want." The movie made him crush my hand in his grip when it cruelly reminded us that humans are pieces of shit whenever anything gets in the way of our greedy asses. I really hope we go extinct before we're able to make it to another planet and shit all over *that* one too.

Back in 222 Swafford, we tangled ourselves on my bed and stole kisses while we finished the last couple episodes of *Heartstopper* and played our own Switches. Tylor hijacked Ethan from me for almost an hour to talk about *Breath of the Wild* while Ethan explored Hyrule Kingdom for himself. Although Tylor said he was fine with us doing anything in the room with him, I waited until he left to go grab dinner with Jaxon to abandon *Pokémon* and start planting kisses on Ethan's neck. We made out until we were poking each other through our underwear, which didn't stay on for too much longer.

"That was *hot*," I said after I swallowed the taste he left in my mouth.

"We're *so* going to hell," he smiled wickedly. "But it'll be so worth it."

Half-dressed, we held each other on top of my covers. "Do you believe in heaven or hell?" I asked.

"Yeah, back when I was a looney-tune conservative."

"Yeah, samesies." And then after a moment, "So do you think we won't ever be reunited with people who've died? Like family members?"

"I don't know. I'm not religious, but I like to think we still have spirits." He shrugged a small shrug. "But even if there *is* a heaven, I wouldn't wanna go."

"Why not?" I asked just to hear his reason.

"Well, if it's faith and not works that gets you in, then that means that Hitler and the Stupid Orange Fuck will be there, along with all the church-going politicians who restrict human rights and make people's lives harder, and all the Catholic priests who tortured people to death for not being Catholic, all the slave owners who whipped their slaves while reading bible verses about slaves being obedient to their masters. I don't wanna fucking spend an eternity with *them*. Would you?"

"*Fuck* no."

"Yeah, exactly."

We laid together, staring up at the ceiling and listening to music without speaking until I heard him sniffle. "It doesn't matter though, because I'd never be allowed in anyway," he said as he wiped away a tear.

January 30

You know what fucking sucks? When you hear a song that slaps the shit out of you but then it ends before you can Shazam it. It's like in *Indiana Jones* when the treasure they'd been chasing falls into the bottomless chasm.

After French let out—we were practicing making the French r sound over and over and all I could think about was how ridiculous we sounded, like a panel of people with sticks up their asses scoffing at artwork—Victor and I and our Zukoff rice bowls decided to check out the French Conversation meetup that Dr. Le Marque gave a pitch for in class. It's not the *official* French Club—it's like a more structured Lit Club, but without muffins or pastries. The student running it went over color names in French, asked us why we were taking French, and then if any of us had ever been to France. And then we just talked about whatever. It was pretty low-key, and everybody seems nice. I wouldn't mind making it a regular after-class thing since it's easy extra credit, but I only have an hour between French and work, and I can't afford to buy lunch from Zukoff three times a week.

Making good on my promise to try going to Proud as Halle with him, I waited for Ethan in one of the nondescript armchairs in Bixby's atrium after dinner, sipping on a bubble tea that I got so nobody would think I'm a Starbucks gay. I saw Ethan approaching through the front windows, beaming as soon as his eyes landed on me. My stomach soared at the sight of him, a feeling that I hope never goes away.

"Thanks for doing this with me," Ethan smiled after greeting me with a kiss.

"Of course," I forced a smile as we climbed up to the third floor towards the wing of conference rooms where big university budget meetings happen behind frosted glass walls. I felt eyes looking us up and down as we walked in, but I just followed Ethan to some chairs near a girl sitting by herself. He's so calm and confident that you'd never guess he's newly out.

"Is anybody sitting here?" he asked the girl as he took his coat off.

"Nope! They're all yours," she said with a genuine smile. Maybe she could sense how uneasy I felt, because she went on, "I'm Zoe. Is this your first time here?"

"Yeah," Ethan nodded. "I recently just started coming out and I wanted to check this out."

Zoe put her hands together. "Yay! I'm so happy for you!" She turned to me like I was supposed to have an answer too.

"I'm just here to support my boyfriend," I said as I patted Ethan on the thigh.

"Aww, that's so sweet of you," she said as another girl dropped into the seat next to her and swung her legs onto Zoe's lap.

"What's sweet?" she asked as she sucked on a Tootsie Pop. "Other than me, of course."

"Ethan here wanted to come to one of our meetings, and his boyfriend Trevor came along to support him. Folks, this is Luna."

Luna gave me an up nod. "She/her. Nice to meet you, Ethan."

"Oh no, I'm Trevor," I said. "He's Ethan. He/him for both of us."

Ethan looked at me. "Did you just assume my gender?" he asked, which made me lighten up a little.

We talked, by which I mean the three of them talked while I listened and scanned the room. It felt like the cafeteria at an all-queer high school—there were the assertive masc girls sitting together, the face-masked femboys, the quiet girls who look like they're authors, the obnoxiously loud queens who are too gay to function. It would've been nice if there was a group of people who came off as overthinking, music-loving introverts that I could've felt at ease with. I wasn't too surprised to see Branden, the guy Miles brought along to Lit Club that one time, stride into the room. He made a beeline for the queens to give them hugs and say hi, and by 'say hi' I mean loudly calling each other 'girl' and 'bitch' and 'honey.' *I can see what Miles meant about clashing personalities.*

Another guy grabbed a seat on Zoe and Luna's other side. "*Ladies,*" he greeted them with a nod.

"*Alex,*" Luna nodded back.

Alex turned to us. "How's it going, guys? Kade didn't wanna come?"

Ethan and I traded confused looks.

"You don't remember me, do you?" We shook our heads. "Kade Oakley introduced us at the last Open Mic Night? My housemate's the guy who always plays acoustic songs?"

"Oh yeah, Alex! I remember now!"

"Yeah, he told us to call you Alejandro because you don't like it!"

Alex rolled his eyes. "Whatever it takes, I guess," he grinned. "What are your names again?"

"Trevor."

"And Ethan," Ethan waved.

"I'll try to remember," he smiled. "Is this your first time coming?"

"Uh huh," I nodded. "First for both of us. Have you been here before?"

"I come every now and then," Alex said. "I figure it's a good way for me to show my support for the community."

"And to meet guys," Luna muttered.

"Oh my god, I'm *not* gay. When have you ever seen me leave with a guy?"

Luna shrugged. "You text them later and meet up with them." Alex rolled his eyes.

Ethan nodded over to a big coffee dispenser on one of the tables. "I'm gonna go get some coffee. Do you want one?"

"Nope, I'm good," I said as I swirled around my bubble tea. "Thanks though." I don't even know why they have a big thing of coffee when like most of the people there had their own Starbucks.

One of the queens with judgy-looking eyebrows checked Ethan out from behind as he went by. Luna must've seen me scowl because she yelled over, "Hey Bradley! He's off-limits!" Bradley stuck out his tongue and gave her the finger. She returned the gesture. "Guys are such dicks—no offense."

"Oh no, we are," I said as I sipped my tea.

Bradley flicked his eyes at Ethan as he made his way back over. "I thought there'd be a little more people here," he said to our newest acquaintances.

"There usually are," Zoe said. "The cold weather keeps people away, and there really isn't anything going on this time of year. The actual meeting was only like five minutes long, and then people just hung around."

"What do you mean when you say there's not a lot going on? Like what exactly do you do?"

"We do community outreach and activism on campus. We do stuff for National Coming Out Day, Trans Day of Remembrance, International Day of Trans Visibility, Day of Silence, IDAHOBIT if the semester hasn't ended by then. We have movie showings, and we feature a book or movie each month. You might've seen the fliers around campus."

"I just assumed the Gender Studies department put those up," I said.

"Nope, that's us. But most importantly, we try to be a safe space for people. We let people open up if they need to, and we're here to listen." That's the kind of stuff I can get on board with—not making hole jokes and accusing each other of being in throuples, like some of the other members enjoy doing.

"I remember there were people holding up flags when that homophobe was here in the Fall yelling about people like us going to hell," I recalled. "Were they Proud as Halle members?"

"Oh, *that* fucking prick," Luna growled, so triggered that she sat up. "Of all the people that get killed in shootings, why can't fuckers like that ever—"

"Yeah, that was us," Zoe cut her off.

"Nice." I turned to Ethan. "Did I ever tell you I saw Victor shouting that guy down?"

"No?" Ethan frowned. "Really?"

"Victor's a good egg," Alex said. "I'm so happy that Kelsey and Kade's parents made him a part of their family." It took everything in me to not ask him the details.

Like Zoe said, it was a pretty uneventful meeting. The five of us just sat and talked. "We're always open to taking book recommendations for our monthly features, if you ever have any," Zoe told me after I said I was an English major. Ethan and I were low-key underwhelmed and didn't hang around for super-duper long.

"My housemates and I are probably gonna have a party this weekend," Alex told us before we left. "You two and Kade and Victor are all more than welcome to come if you want. It's been years since I've really seen them, and you both seem pretty cool too." *Maybe this is what Luna meant by picking up guys.*

"Yeah, maybe," I said noncommittally. We gave Zoe our email addresses to add to the group's distro list on the way out. "Well that wasn't a total waste of time," I said optimistically.

"Yeah, it wasn't bad," Ethan agreed. "I'd like to come back again. How about you?"

I nodded. "Yeah, I would." We hugged each other goodnight in the atrium before we left through different doors. "I'll see you tomorrow for breakfast?"

"Tomorrow for breakfast," he said before giving me a kiss to keep with me.

January 31

I did that thing in class today where I started choking on my own saliva and caused a scene. Every eye in Black Lit was on me when I came back in from the hallway, so now I'm thinking about dropping the class. "You'd think that for as many times as I've swallowed that I'd know how to do it by now," I laughed when I told Kade about it at lunch afterwards, making him spit out his ginger ale.

Ethan and I actually weren't able to get breakfast today because he forgot that he and the other House Council Presidents were getting breakfast together like they're supposed to do once a month to foster 'togetherness.' "Macro might actually be the class I look forward to the most," I told him when I stopped to see him for my twice-a-week—since nobody's still figured out if 'biweekly' means twice a week or every other week—bubble tea fix.

"I'm glad you're enjoying it more than you thought you would," he smiled as he shook up another customer's drink. "I wish I could say the same thing about my Social Media class. That was the one I was the most excited about."

I stuck out my bottom lip. "I'm sorry it's not living up to your expectations." *Trevoring 101: expect the worst and you won't be disappointed.*

"That's actually a really cute look on you," he giggled.

"I'll make it a meme and just bombard you with it," I smiled.

"Go ahead. You won't do it," he dared me. "You have your Lit Club meeting later, right?"

"Nah, this week's the off week."

"Oh, okay. Are you gonna go to your House Council meeting then?"

"*Maybe,*" I said, knowing what was coming next. "It'd be my first time."

"Then you *really* should! You can ask Tylor or Nikole if they'll go with you," he suggested, knowing me well enough to know that I'm more likely to do something new if I'm not doing it by myself.

"Yeah. I don't think I have a whole lotta work to do, but I'll see how I'm feeling later on."

"They usually don't take that long," Ethan tried to convince me. "You know how you had to pay a House Council fee as part of your admissions fee?"

"What?! No? How much was *that?*"

"I think only like $20," he chuckled. "But don't you wanna have a say in where that money goes?"

"Yeah, I guess so." Being one of those people who takes without doing their part—especially in a democracy, even one the size of a residence hall body—isn't a vibe I'm going for.

"Trust me, it's discouraging as fuck when the House Council members put in the time and effort to get residents to come and only have the same few people show up. Most residents don't care, but it's more important than you think."

"Okay, stop!" I laughed. "I said I was gonna go!"

"I don't think you actually *did,*" he smirked.

"Yes, I'll go to my House Council meeting tonight," I smiled.

"Thanks," he smiled back as he passed me my drink. "They'll appreciate it. I know I would."

"Of course you would," I laughed. "If you saw me walk into your meeting, you'd be in the bathroom with your pants around your ankles."

His jaw dropped. "Come here you—" He grabbed me by my coat collar and pulled me across the counter to plant a hard kiss on my lips. We laughed as he pushed me away without caring if we looked like cringey freshmen. "Now get out of here, you studmuffin," he winked as he blew me another kiss.

Nikole was on DA duty in another building, and I didn't want to knock on any doors, so it was just Tylor who joined me down to the multi-purpose room, a.k.a. the MPR. Residents peppered the stackable chairs set up in rows. I smiled at Becky as we found spots in the second row, and Theo took the seat in front of us. Once the apparent House Council members were all seated behind the table that the rows of chairs all faced, the guy with cochlear implants sitting in the middle gave the table two short, loud taps with a gavel.

"Welcome everybody," he said, giving off the same bossy, power-bottom vibes as the gay guys who take your order at the drive-thru. "Do we have a motion to start tonight's forum?"

Theo put his hand up.

"Do we have somebody to second the—"

A girl at the end of our row put her hand up.

The person who I assumed was the Secretary typed up the minutes on his laptop before taking roll call. "President Westley?"

"Here," Power Bottom said like he didn't want to be there.

"Vice President Aimee?"

"Here," the girl sitting to his left said.

"I am here," he said to himself. After the other two girls declared their presence in turn, he noted the representation from each floor. Even with only the four of us, 2 East had the most people. The members went over old and new business, upcoming hall events, and where the budget stood. It was like starting a series mid-season, but I managed to piece things together: they'll be buying new games to sign out at the front desk—which I never even knew was a thing—and February's hall event is going to be a party for that football thing that everybody loses their minds over. It was boring, but it's nice to feel a little more involved in something. There were so many motions to adjourn the meeting that you'd have thought they were asking who wanted some free money.

I was surprised to see Westley approach us before we could leave. "Excuse me, but are you Ethan's boyfriend?" he asked like he was upset with me over it. "Travis or something?"

"Trevor," I frowned. "And yeah, I am. Why?"

24

"No reason. Ethan showed us a picture of you two, and I thought you lived in my building."

I furrowed my brow. "When'd he show you a picture of me?"

"At our House Council Presidential breakfast. We meet up and talk about presidential stuff." I just nodded, not sure if he was trying to be funny or not.

"I'm not sure how to take him," I muttered to Tylor once the two of us were back in the lobby. "Westley, I mean."

"Up the ass," Tylor said without skipping a beat.

February 1

the	milk	&	honey	thing
is	an	enormous	lie
you	could	say	the	same	about
all	the	bittersweet	days	we
trudged	lovelessly	through	our	gorgeous
yet	deliriously	quick	garden	of	life
never	stopping	to	smell	the	dying	roses

February 2

To anybody who can't comprehend how there are countries out there who could possibly hate the United States, look no further than Groundhog Day. Don't even get me started.

We got our first writing assignments for Creative Fiction back today. Mine was about astronauts who returned to Earth to find themselves hundreds of thousands of years in the past, only to be hunted down by their distant ancestors. I couldn't help but smile when I saw Dr. Averescu's note saying 'You are a _really_ _good_ _writer_' next to her red 'A.' So needless to say, I've been in an unstoppable kind of mood for most of the day.

Dr. Jurado makes Macro so enjoyable that I don't even mind having to make graphs or getting called on. Every class he does this thing where he'll ask a real-life question and have everybody answer. Like today, we each had to give an example of a time when we bought more of something because they were cheaper if you got more than one. I said how I'd buy shirts because they were buy-one-get-one-half-off. "A couple of times," I lied.

Ethan's been vacillating—one of those SAT prep words that nobody ever actually uses—back and forth since last weekend over whether or not he wants to get his ears pierced, but he told me that he "for sure" wants to do it. "Kade said he can do it later on after I get off work," he said while he spent his break at a table with me. "Will you be there with me when he does it?"

"It's Thursday—I'd be with you regardless," I said as I bumped his foot under the table. "Not gonna lie though, I'm not sure how I feel about letting some weirdo penetrate you." He almost sprayed me with his drink.

"Why not? I've been letting a weirdo penetrate me since December," he shot back. "Did it hurt when you got yours done?" he asked my onyx-black studs.

"I cried," I nodded. "People were staring." He raised an eyebrow at me. "It just felt like a pinch, kinda like getting a shot."

"I hate getting shots though!"

"It doesn't really *hurt.* It's more just the thought of a piece of metal going through my body that makes me queasy."

"But that's *exactly* why I hate getting shots!" he whined. "When did you get them?"

"Last March, right after I turned 18."

"I keep forgetting you're younger than me," he said as we stood. "I think it's the height difference."

"It's like *an inch* difference."

He looked one inch up into my eyes before I lowered my lips one inch to taste the strawberry tea on his. "Whatever you say, tall and handsome."

The evening saw Kade and I in 239 Axworthy drinking tea out of the iron tea set he got for Christmas and discussing what the best superpower would be. We agreed that the power to control probability would be the ultimate one since it would cover all the others. Chance you'll have super strength at will? 100%. Chance you'll be able to fly at will? 100%. Chance you'll be able to turn invisible at will? 100%. Chance you'll be able to make that super-hot person thirsty for you at will? 100%.

"How are things going with you two, by the way?" he asked as he cut out pictures from a magazine for his collage art. "You and Ethan, I mean."

"They're good," I said. We're like a month-and-a-half in so we're still giddy at the sight of each other, but we're also not one of those Instagram couples who show themselves off and pretend that everything's perfect. If *that* started happening, *then* I'd worry. "I can't believe how nervous I was over what you guys would think of us when you found out that two of your best friends have been hooking up. I guess I was just overthinking."

"*You?* Overthinking something?" he laughed. "But real talk though, I'm happy to hear it. Honestly, I think friends make the best partners, since they pretty much already know what they're signing up for. You already know all the good things that you love about them and the bad ones that make the good ones worth it." I love how Kade and I can have some deep talk in one breath and then crack penis jokes the next.

"Yeah, that makes sense." I was so in love with everything about Ethan that I'm surprised it took me as long as it did for me to admit that I love him. "Is there anybody you've been interested in since last semester?" I asked, by which I meant 'since Will.'

He looked up from his magazine pages. "Actually...Nikole and I were talking a little over Break."

My head cocked on its own. "Forreal?"

"Yeah," he grinned. "Though I can't help but feel that she'd be better with someone like Victor."

"What? Why would you think that?"

"I dunno." He shrugged. "I just can't see how she could like me back. I mean, she knows I'm quirky and shit, but there's no way she'd wanna actually *be* with somebody as fucked-up as I am. At least Victor's mentally stable and has a filter."

I scoffed at him. "Don't say that! She could be thinking the same thing about you, and be afraid that you won't like *her* back for all you know." Maybe love is just finding that person who's the same level of fucked-up as you, and that's what makes two people perfect for each other—although if Ethan's as anxious and depressive as I am, then he needs to give me some pointers on how to hide it. "But if you *are* serious about her, then you should be honest with her. It'd be better to be up-front with her about it instead of springing it on her later."

He started shaking, and I thought he was going to start crying. "That's what the actress said to the bishop."

Ethan brought his dinner of a wrap, some baby carrots, and a cookie from Percy's with him, since Kade told him not to be on an empty stomach. Kade went over the aftercare as he pulled piercing supplies from his clear plastic drawer unit. "These are the only ones I have," he told Ethan as he showed him a pair of clear studs. "Is that okay?"

"Yeah, sure," Ethan nodded like he had a choice.

"Perf. Do you like Mountain Dew?" *God, how I love a good non sequitur.*

"Yeah?"

"Good, because that's all we have. You'll need it to keep your blood sugar up." Kade pulled on a pair of nitrile gloves with a *snap*. "Now, prepare your anus."

"You're not gonna use one of those guns?" I asked.

"Nah. Needles are cleaner and more precise," he said as he took a hollow one from a sealed package and held it over the flame of a contraband tea light. Everything seemed professional and clean—I expected the corks to have wine stains on them, but even they were sterilized and individually wrapped. If there's any one thing you can say about Kade, it's that he takes his shit seriously. He dabbed Ethan's earlobes with an alcohol-soaked cotton ball before marking each one with a dot. "Do these spots look good?" he asked as he handed him a small mirror.

Ethan turned his head from side to side. "Yeah, I guess."

"Are you sure? It's kind of a permanent thing."

"I think they're good spots," I told Ethan with a smile.

Ethan nodded. "Yeah, they look good."

"Good. You ready then?"

Ethan played with his hands like a Trevor. "Uh huh."

I kept my eyes on Ethan's because seeing needles going into people makes me physically sick. I gave his sweaty hand a squeeze. "It'll be over in a few seconds," I smiled. He tried to smile back.

Kade pressed the cork to the back of his earlobe. "Okay, take a deep breath." Ethan inhaled sharply with his eyes locked on mine. They grew wide as he crushed my hand. "Halfway there," Kade said. "You doing okay?"

"Mmhmm," Ethan nodded through tightly-closed eyes. Kade and I switched spots. Ethan's fresh piercing had a dot of blood around it.

"Alright, you're all done!" Kade handed Ethan the mirror again. "What do you think? You have to say you like them though."

Ethan stared at himself. "I think...I think I need to get to the bathroom." He lurched up and out of Kade's chair. *I mean, he does always say how he's gonna throw up.*

I listened to the sound of my boyfriend not throwing up for a minute before going over to the cracked bathroom door. I knocked before pushing it open a few more inches. "Are you okay in there, babe?"

Kade shoved a can of pop into my hand. "Here, give this to him."

I crouched beside Ethan as he sat up against the wall, gulping it down. "Are you okay?" I asked him again.

"A little," he said before letting out a burp. "I felt fine and then I just got super lightheaded all of a sudden."

"It's honestly nothing to be embarrassed about," Kade said from the doorway. "It happens all the time." *How many of his floormates have puked in here?* He pointed to Ethan's pop. "Finish that before you try standing up again."

I looked from Ethan's ear to the other and back. "I think they look good," I smiled.

"You think so?" He pulled up his phone's front camera and swiveled his head from side to side. "Oh shit, I like them," he grinned. "How much do I owe you?" he asked Kade.

Kade waved him off. "I do friends for free."

"Do I get my money back then for that time we met up in the bathroom after class?" I joked as their door *beeped* open.

"What it do!" Victor said as he kicked off his shoes. He narrowed his eyes at the sight of us all in the bathroom and Ethan sitting on the floor. "Wait, what *do* it do?"

Ethan pointed to an earlobe. "This is what it do."

Victor stooped down to get a closer look. "*Dude*. Did you just get those done?"

"Yep. What do you think?"

"Spank my bottom with a wet fish Batman! They're dope as hell!"

February 3

They'll never let me inside of heaven
Because I've been inside of you
And I'll gladly burn for it
I don't care

February 4

Whichever WXNU DJ has been on an early-'80s U2 kick knows what's up, because it's some *killer* music for these snowy, overcast days.

"So Alex sent me this this morning," Kade said as he slid his phone over to me at lunch. "What do you guys think?"

> **Hey, it's Alex! We're having a party at our place tonight**
> **You and your friends are welcome to come if you don't have anything else going on!** ☺

"Yeah, he mentioned that when we saw him at Proud as Halle," I said as I pushed it back.

"I've never hung out with him before though," Kade said to the ribbons of noodles twirling from his chopsticks. "He was friends with Kelsey, not me."

"He always seemed pretty cool though," Victor said as a piece of tofu fell into his lap. "Not that I'm trying to influence anybody's decision."

"I'd be down," Ethan said as he forked up his noodles like spaghetti.

29

Three sets of eyes were on me. "Sure, why not," I shrugged.

We piled into my car to make an Aldi run for snacks and mixers for Kade's liquor. Victor and Kade both insisted that Ethan should have permanent shotgun privileges in my car, though my boyfriend was happy to share the metaphorical aux cord with them. We hung out in 222 Swafford when we got back onto campus, where we played *Super Smash Bros.* and blew through most of our snacks before I sent our Axworthy friends back to their building so Ethan and I could have some alone time. We made ourselves presentable again afterwards in case Tylor showed up, listening to music and taking selfies on my bed. I swiped through the pics and held down my favorites to see the live photo.

"Can I put us on Snapchat?" I asked him.

"I was wondering when you would," Ethan smiled.

"Forreal? You wouldn't mind?"

He shrugged. "Go for it. It's not like any of my family or anybody back home is gonna see it."

"Joke's on you," I chuckled, "I actually have a streak going with all of your hot cousins." He slapped me.

"No, joke's on you—they lure all the gays in and then electrocute them. It was nice knowing you," he said casually. I slapped him back on the butt.

"*No*, joke's on *you*—I turned them all gay in the process."

"I don't blame them," Ethan smirked.

Madi was the first to respond to the pic of us. "*You two are so cute together!*" she wrote, wearing a closed-eye, ear-to-ear grin.

"*Ah, the post-coital selfie,*" Kade captioned his look of smug satisfaction.

After dinner—the Patnick special was shepherd's pie, which I'm not convinced wasn't just all the food scraps they took from the sink strainers and stirred together —we chilled in 239 Axworthy until we stuffed our backpacks with liquor and mixers and Drunk *Jenga* for a walk across campus. It was so cold that I couldn't feel my face by the time we were passing Old Main towards the side streets of town.

"So where are we going?" Ethan asked with his arm looped around mine.

"To hell if we don't change our ways," Kade said without skipping a beat. "To Alex's place."

"No *shit* we are," he chuckled. "I mean what's the address?"

Kade numbed his hands to check his phone. "Uh, 370 Rock Hill Road."

"Rock Hill Road?" Victor asked. "Like the ice cream?"

Number 370 belonged to a two-story, kind-of-Victorian house that I figured was split into two different units. Muffled bass grew louder as we stepped onto the covered wooden porch. "Should we knock?" I asked as I tried to make things out in the green light through the windows on either side of the door.

"And wait around in *this* bullshit?" Victor said as he bulldozed past us to push the door open.

It was the least crowded college party I've ever been to—there was actually room to move around without having to squeeze between people. *Nope, this is one whole house.* We stood around gawking like we were lost. I was looking around for Alex among the people who all looked like upperclassmen when a girl holding a seltzer drifted over to us. "Hi boys...can I help you?" she asked in some kind of European accent.

"Yeah, we're friends with Alex," Kade spoke for us.

She looked us up and down like a bouncer. "Really?"

Alex materialized from around a corner just then, looking *way* too happy to see us. "*Yo!* You guys came!" He gave each of us a hug. *Yeah, he's hammered.* "Let me show you the coat closet," he said as he led us around the corner into the dining room/kitchen.

"Sorry," the girl apologized. "You looked like freshmen."

Victor just shrugged. "We are."

The 'coat closet' was a table in the corner with a pile of coats on it. Kade and I took the Coke and middle-shelf rum from our bags before stowing them under the table. In the kitchen half of the room, we poured ourselves drinks while trying to keep track of the people Alex introduced us to. "This is Eren"—a guy wearing a sweater who smelled really good lifted his glass of blood-red wine to us—"Sonia"—a girl with big glasses who kind of reminded me of Elisha smiled warmly at us— "Cameron and Chance"—two guys who I guessed were boyfriends waved at us— "and Charlotte, who you already met." The doorkeeper, who's actually really friendly, laughed when she caught our eyes. I've never felt so at ease so quickly at a college party before. I didn't feel pressured to be anything other than my generally-introverted self. Ethan and I could kiss out in the open without worrying about somebody having a problem with it instead of stealing one when nobody was looking. Everybody seemed to be friends with each other, like they've all been coming to the same party all year, yet they still made us newcomers feel as welcome as possible. But the *music* is what I couldn't get over—it wasn't your typical college-party grinding music. Sure, almost anything sounds better the more you have to drink, but the stuff there sounded good before I was even tipsy. There was some rap that I didn't hate, some heavier stuff that Victor fucked with, some '60s rock, some post-punk, some new wave, some techno that wasn't EDM, a song by Foster the People, and a song that sounded like *Scooby-Doo* chase music. There wasn't a *single song* that I didn't like.

"Hey Alex, who's this?" I'd shout as I pointed to the ceiling.

"The Drums!"

And then a little while later, "Who's this?"

31

"Crocodiles."

"What about this?"

"Crystal Stilts."

"Alex, who's—"

"Goddammit, don't you have Shazam or something?"

I Shazammed an album's-worth of songs while I made conversation with strangers. *These people have gotta be Art majors or something.* The only thing that could've made it feel more like the kind of college party that I always hoped I'd find myself at one day would be if some English or Film Studies or PoliSci professor was there too. And then everything made sense to me—the music, the fact that it wasn't jam-packed with people, the overall atmosphere: *these are people who've never sold out.* These are people who looked at SGB, the football team, the Heteros who keep tallies of their body counts, the people who think they run the university, and anybody who has a problem with them not fitting into the mainstream, and they gave them all a big middle finger. They can shake the house with noise pop and drink wine from wine glasses and burn bundles of dried herbs and talk about economics and art and philosophy because they *don't give a shit* what the mainstream thinks about them. They're not trying to please anybody or trying to be popular—they're just doing them, and if like-minded people find their way to them, then good for them. It's like a reaction against the typical college party scene. "It's like all the other parties are 18th Century Europe, and this is the French Revolution," I said without realizing Kade wasn't still standing right beside me.

We migrated to the living room, where we found Alex's housemate Matt and a handful of people sitting around what looked like some kind of antique lamp with flowers painted on it. Somebody sucked on a tube that ran from it and exhaled clouds—and I mean *clouds*—of smoke. "Oh *shit!*" Kade exclaimed in a moment of pure excitement. "You guys have a *hookah?* Can I get in on this?"

"Sure thing boss," a guy said as he passed Kade a box of individually-wrapped mouth tips. Another guy with a forearm tattoo made room on the couch for Ethan and I to sit close to Kade, who gave us a brief rundown of what hookah is and how it works from his spot on the floor. I half-listened as I took in the room and the mismatched furniture that gave the place an eclectic vibe. People played pong on a pool table in the back half of the room.

"So why not just vape then?" I asked as I watched smoke fill the glass base of the hookah. The whole thing sat on a Lazy Susan so it could rotate as the hose made its rounds around the circle of smokers.

"You fucking *churl*," he squinted. "Who the fuck even *vapes* anymore?" Kade took the hose from the girl on his other side and inhaled deeply. Smoke zoomed through the clear plastic hose on its way to his hungry lungs. He closed his eyes and exhaled through his nose, looking like a content dragon. "Oh yeah." He took another drag. *"Oh, is that good."* He offered it to me. *"Do you wanna give it a go?"* *If you don't try smoking something new in college at least once, then why even go?*

"Yeah, why not?" I unwrapped a mouth tip and did what Kade did, only to *violently* start coughing as soon as the smoke hit my throat. Kade grabbed the hose from me and somebody else jumped up, though they were more concerned about the hookah getting knocked over than they were about me choking to death.

"You okay?" Ethan asked as he patted my back.

"Have you never *smoked* before?" Kade asked me like I was supposed to have.

"Smoked what?" I hacked out.

"I like him already," a voice laughed.

I wiped my eyes. "I tried a cigarette once, and weed another once."

"Maybe *don't* breathe it in then," Kade advised me. "Like, just take a little hit and hold it in your mouth." I just passed it to Ethan instead, who took short, gentle puffs. His smoke was an ethereal wisp compared to the fog-machine-spew that Kade and a few others produced.

"Ooh. What flavor is *that*?" he asked as he inhaled again.

"Two apples, or double apple as it's more commonly called," Forearm Tattoo answered in a British accent. He sipped what I figured was whiskey from a rocks glass. "It's popularly infused with anise flavor"—*flavour?*—"which is why it carries a black licorice taste."

"This guy knows his shit," Kade said.

"I'm quite familiar with hookah," Forearm Tattoo said as he took the hose from Ethan. "I'm Henry, by the way." He shook hands with us before taking a hit as big as Kade's before another guest plopped down on his lap. "Hello love," Henry said. He kissed him on the mouth and passed him the hose.

"Don't do that," Love told him in a total American accent. "People are gonna think we're *gay* or something."

Henry rolled his eyes. "Gentlemen, this is Luca. Luca, this is Ethan and this is Trevor. I don't know who this is," he said to Kade.

Kade looked him dead in the eye. "I'm the Christian right's worst nightmare."

People joined and left our circle as the hookah hose made its halting rounds like a hand of a malfunctioning clock. Matt moved to Henry and Luca's recently-vacated end of the couch next to us. "What'd you put in there? Rum? Vodka?" I nodded to his can of Arnold Palmer.

"Nothing," he smiled. "I don't drink, or take anything else for that matter. I like to enjoy life as soberly and as clearly as possible. I wanna experience it as it is, if that makes sense."

"No, totally!" I waved my paper cup at him. "I can respect that."

"I make an exception for hookah though, obviously," he said before taking a puff from the pipe.

"I gotcha," I nodded. It sounds like the kind of lifestyle I can see Victor aspiring to—and if so, then he has a long fucking way to go.

"*Guys*. What is *up*," he said passively when we spotted him leaving the bathroom with a bored smile. He put out his fist for a bump.

"Is dollface feeling—oh my god," Ethan laughed, "you're fucking zooted as *shit!* You should see your eyes!" What little I could see of Victor's eyes were glossed and red.

"Who the hell were *you* smoking with?" Kade laughed.

Victor shrugged, oblivious to the portrait of JFK torn from a magazine taped to the wall beside him. "I dunno. Just some people. Alex. Some girl named Linguine or something. Downstairs." He nodded back towards the basement stairs.

"I can *promise* you there's nobody here named *Linguine*," I said while the other two cracked up.

"Whatever," he said indifferently.

Kade threw his thumb towards the living room. "They have a hookah going out there."

"No way," Victor said as he shambled down the hallway.

Ethan and I held hands as the three of us descended the dark, steep stairs to the basement, where the tang of weed swamped us. *Now* this *is a college party.* The room to the right of the stairs was so heavy with blue light that it felt like the air itself was dyed. Flags and road signs and beer memorabilia decorated the brown paneled walls, and blacklights mounted above the pong table brought the designs tattooed on it in highlighter to radiant life. Lowercase-s straight guys sat and talked on some dingy bar stools. A girl riding an exercise bike held up her drink and flashed a peace sign for her friend's pic. We didn't see Alex or anyone who looked like they might be named Linguine, so we sauntered over to the other side of the basement, which practically begged you to get high in it. Christmas lights and a lava lamp bathed the room in red. Blacklight posters and a tapestry hung above a shabby faux-leather couch patched with duct tape. A smaller hookah—the exact kind that the store with glassware products for 'tobacco use only' sells—three different ashtrays, a stack of poker chips, what looked like a tiny glass dildo, and an incense holder covered most of the stains and burn marks on the coffee table. And on one of the couches sat Alex, sealing a freshly-rolled joint with his tongue.

"Guys!" he said at the sight of us. "Welcome! Take a seat." He gestured to the loveseat across from him. The three of us had to get intimate to fit on it. "This is Linh," he said, nodding at a girl sucking on the hookah. The light reflecting in her glasses made it look like she had lasers for eyes.

"*So not linguine,*" Ethan whispered with a smile.

Alex flicked back a Rolling Stones Zippo to light the joint, and took a few tokes to get it going. The lit end flared like a lightning bug. "Any of you want some?"

Kade hit it a few times before handing it to Ethan, who did the same before holding it out to me. "I'm good for right now," I said. *God's smiling on you right now, Trevor—which, shame on him for not worrying about more important shit that's going on.* He passed it back to Alex since Linh was content with the hookah. "I only ever tried weed once," I felt the need to explain. "I'd already been drinking that time though, so I couldn't really feel it."

"You do whatever you feel comfortable doing, babe," Ethan smiled. My back muscles relaxed as I watched the joint pass between the other three. I half-listened as Kade and Alex caught each other up on the last three-or-so years of their own lives. People popped in and out to take a quick few drags of the hookah. A guy and a girl emerged from a door at the back of the room. Alex dropped the unholdably-tiny roach into one of the ashtrays before dissecting and emptying another cigarillo to roll with weed. Kade went off somewhere, leaving Ethan and me with Alex and Linh, who scrolled on her phone without saying a word. *You know what? What the hell.*

I nodded to the joint. "I'll actually give it a try after you," I said to Ethan.

He raised an eyebrow at me. "You sure?"

I nodded. "Yeah." It tasted mostly burnt, with a hint of white grape. I didn't really feel anything, even after hitting it on its next go-around.

"How do you feel?" Ethan checked in on me.

I vibe-checked myself and shrugged. "Still more drunk than anything." *Though I wish I could feel the same way Victor's feeling.* "So who else do you live with again?" I asked Alex, who was staring straight up at the drop ceiling.

"Other than Matt, there's Andrew. He's not here because he picked up a bartending shift," he said like he had to think about it. "And June, who went home because her great-aunt or somebody died. You'll get to meet them next time, assuming you ever even wanna come back."

"Are you kidding? This is my favorite party I've ever been to." I didn't try to explain my reaction-against-other-parties theory.

"I'm glad you're liking it," Alex smiled. "You should've been here for Halloween." He laughed to himself. "I knocked over the jug of mead my friend from home brought. It took him like, *months* to make it."

"Can I RSVP to the next one now?"

"Oh, how I wish there'd be a next one," he sighed. "We all graduate at the end of this semester. But I don't even wanna think about that right now. Anybody wanna fuck up the pong table with me?" And as if the place couldn't get any more college, the pong table turned out to be a door, with the hole for the knob acting as a cupholder. Up close, I made out the words and images in highlighter—eyeballs and serpents and serpents twisting out of eyeballs and eyeballs growing on plants and flowers and stars and geometric designs and all kinds of shit. I tried to take some artsy pics of it between throws, but they all ended up being shitty.

Ethan and I went back upstairs and almost had to shield our eyes from the kitchen light. Kade, Henry, Luca, and Sonia were sharing the hookah and having a lively conversation about what the effects of everybody having infinite money would have on inflation and the cost of living. Victor was slouched in an armchair, eating popcorn out of a colander. We made ourselves another drink and made a space for ourselves on the floor behind the couch to enjoy some us-time, Ethan's head resting on my shoulder. "Have I ever told you how much I love you?" he asked me.

I shook my head. "I don't think you have."

"Stop! Yes I have! I love you. You know I love you, right?" he pleaded with the most adorable eyes.

"Okay, I believe you." I gave him a kiss. "I love you too."

He sandwiched my hand between both of his. "I'm so lucky to have you."

"No, *I'm* the lucky one."

He nuzzled into me. "No, *I* am." We stayed like that for so long that he could've fallen asleep. I sipped my drink and listened to the music and the voices and the front door without moving so as to not disturb him. After what could've been any amount of time, I eventually nudged him and helped him to his feet.

"Have you been back there this whole time?" Luca practically shouted.

"Yeah," I stretched. "Why? How long were we back there? Where'd the skinny kid and the stoned guy go?"

"They're gone. They thought you left already."

"Oh shit," I mumbled as I checked my phone. "I guess we should head out too?" I asked Ethan.

"Yeah," he yawned. "Especially if we want omelets for breakfast."

"*Ugh*, a Ginny's omelet sounds *amazing* right now," Luca said. "Ham, cheese, and mushroom. Mmmm." Ethan's look told me he didn't know what the hell Luca was talking about either.

"A Ginny's omelet? What's that?" *An omelet made with Guinness beer or something?*

"You know, a Ginny's omelet," Luca said like it was obvious. "An omelet from Ginny's? The breakfast diner?" We just stared. "Don't tell me you've never been to *Ginny's* before."

Ethan shook his head. "Never heard of her."

Luca fell back in his seat. "I'm fucking *dead.*"

"Go easy on them, love," Henry said. "They're only in their first year."

"It's an NHU tradition!" Luca said before turning back to us. "Where do you go for omelets? Fucking *Patnick?*"

"We'll have to give it a try sometime," I said in the same way I tell people I'm going to watch the movie they just finished telling me about. We bid everyone who was still there goodnight and thanked Alex and Matt for having us over. We walked down Rock Hill Road hand-in-hand, probably looking as drunk as we felt. "Do you wanna sleep in my room?" I asked Ethan.

He looked at me with apologetic eyes. "I really want to," he squeezed my hand, "but the alcohol and the weed made me sleepy-eepy. I don't know if I can make it."

I tried to make a puppy-dog face he couldn't deny. "Just say it. You hate me."

He playfully tried to push me away but just pushed himself away. "Oh my *god* are you cute," he laughed. He pulled himself back to me and kissed my cheek. "How about this? How about we spend all day tomorrow together and then I stay over tomorrow night? Mmkay?"

"I'm already looking forward to it," I grinned. I left him off at Kessler's front doors with a kiss and told him to text me when he got back to his room so I wouldn't have to worry about him passing out in the stairwell. He must've already been conked out by the time I let him know I'd made it back to my own room, because he didn't respond to my goodnight text.

And we didn't even play Drunk Jenga either, I thought as my bed cradled me.

February 5

So I guess Victor was yesterday-years-old when he learned that the vagina and clitoris aren't the same thing. Kade gave him *massive* shit for it, but Victor was more mad about it than he was embarrassed. "*See?*" he shouted. "This is *exactly* why men shouldn't be trying to make decisions about women's bodies!"

While we breakfasted on some freshman-grade omelets, Ethan—looking *extra* cute in his glasses and puff-ball beanie—mentioned how he hadn't gone sled riding in a while, and how it would be a good day to do it. And since I'm a guy who can take a hint sometimes, I drove us to Wally World for some foam sleds, along with a colorful spinning disco light that might be fun to take to a party someday, and two cinder blocks of PopTarts. We swung by Kessler on the way back so he could grab his pillow and whatever else he needed to spend the next 24-plus hours in 222 Swafford. We carried our foam sleds over to the Ski Hill on the periphery of campus, which they should just call 'the Hill' since there isn't even a ski lift or anything. But what it lacks in facility it makes up for in size—it took us like five minutes to slog up to the top, where we beheld the view of the forest before us.

"Do you wanna be cute and go down holding hands?" I asked Ethan.

"Nope," he smiled as he ran and dove onto his sled stomach-first. I watched him rocket down before going after him, *immediately* wishing I'd gotten some ski goggles at the store too. It was like I was getting hosed down with snow. I couldn't see anything, and I felt snow going down my back, but I couldn't stop laughing because I felt like a kid again. "Holy *shit* can these things go!" Ethan laughed as he brushed off his glasses.

"I know! Let's go again!" I nodded, though my enthusiasm had waned by the third time we stumbled our way to the top.

"Oh my god," Ethan heaved. "This is what Syphilis must've felt like."

"Don't you mean *Sisyphus?*" I laughed.

"Whatever," he panted. "You knew who I meant."

My legs ached as we trudged back to Swafford, our bodies cold with sweat. "That was a good idea, babe," I said as I threw my arm around him and planted a kiss on his cheek. The treads of my boots tracked snow all the way up to 222, where I set them and Ethan's shoes on an upside-down tote-lid-turned-shoe-tray. My damp clothes landed in my laundry basket. "I'm gonna get a shower real quick."

"Can I grab one too when you're done?" Ethan asked.

"Go for it." I paused at the doorway. "But why sit around in wet clothes when you could just take one with me?" I slid down my underwear. "It might not be a quick one though."

"I'm fine with that," he grinned.

He took a mirror selfie of us afterwards, wrapped in towels with wet hair, my arms around him from behind. "That was hot," I said as I kissed his neck.

"Longest shower I've ever taken," he smiled as he swabbed his ear with a Q-Tip. "Why haven't I gotten to fuck *you* yet?"

"Why, are you complaining?" I smiled uneasily.

"*No.* But I wouldn't mind getting to clap *your* cheeks sometime," he winked.

I swallowed. "Can I lie?"

"Sure."

"I don't have a butthole."

He laughed out loud. "*Oh* yes you do. I've smelled what it can do after you have some garlic parm wings."

My fingers found my stud. *It's nothing to be embarrassed about.* "I've...only ever topped before," I winced.

"*Really?* Even with your ex?"

"Oh yeah. He was a total bottom."

"Sheesh, you gotta try it sometime," Ethan grinned. "And I'm not just saying that because I'd like a turn. It feels *amazing* when the guy knows what he's doing." I'm sure it *does* feel amazing—why else would he do it for me? And while moaning profanities the whole time?

38

"I'd like to, but I'm just nervous about doing it for the first time," I said.

He put his arms around my neck. "You do what you're comfortable with. If you ever wanna give it a try though, I know a guy."

We laid on my bed, playing our own Switches with our legs in a tangle. I was so engrossed in my gauntlet against the Elite Four that I hadn't realized that he'd stopped playing and was staring off into the room. "What?" I asked. "Do you have homework you forgot about?"

He put his screen to sleep, setting it down to sit up with crossed legs. "Something's been bothering me, and I need to get it off my chest," he said to my comforter. I sat up with him and rubbed circles on his back, though I was scared shitless. *He doesn't love me anymore. He met somebody else. He doesn't think we'll work out after all.* "So I wasn't totally honest with you," he finally said, "when I told you that you were the only person I was with after our first kiss." Fear stopped my hand. *Oh my god. Please no. Please tell me you didn't. Please say something.* His eyes started to well up. "We weren't actually *together* yet so it's not really *cheating*, but it still kinda feels like I did." He sniffled. "The day after we first hooked up, I went to tell this guy who I used to sleep with that what we were doing had to stop because I was seeing somebody else, somebody who I could see myself having a real relationship with. But then things happened, and we ended up hooking up again." He took off his glasses to wipe his eyes. "I didn't tell you because I didn't want you thinking you were getting yourself tied up with some fuckboy."

My hand resumed its motion while I chose my words. "I'm not *mad* at you. More than anything, I'm relieved that it was months ago and not last week," I said with a small smile that he didn't see. "But I'm glad that you felt comfortable telling me. And you're right, just because we were together one time didn't mean—"

Wait a second.

"Hold on," I said sternly. "So you're allowed to get mad and walk out on *me* just because you *suspected* that I was sleeping with somebody? But then you *actually* sleep with someone else and I'm supposed to just be okay with it?"

"No! No, I just wanted to be open with you! But this is why I was afraid to!" he said as he buried his face in his hands.

I launched myself off my bed to try to go pee so I could get away for a moment, but I just ended up standing over the toilet with a scowl and a pounding chest. The sound of him sniffling and pulling tissues from the box made my heart soften. I washed my hands anyway while purposely not looking at him, but one teary-eyed glance from him was all it took to make me realize that I might've been a little too mean. *It was months ago, Trevor, not yesterday.*

I walked over and held out my hand. "Here. I can throw those away," I said to the tissues in a soft voice. I dropped them in the trash and hopped back up onto the bed, where he just stared into the room and sniffled. He didn't recoil when I gingerly started to rub his back again. *Do I wanna be one of those people who hold their pride higher than the person they love?* "You know I'm not mad at you," I tenderly said a few minutes later. "I was being dramatic, and you didn't deserve that. I'm sorry."

Instead of saying anything back, he just laid his head in my lap. He ran his sleeve across his eyes and rolled to look up at me, looking so miserable that I felt my own eyes getting wet. "I'm sorry too," he swallowed, "because it's making me think about how I stormed out on you at the end of the semester—"

I was surprised to feel myself smile as I put a finger to his lips. "Not talking about that anymore, remember?" He chuckled, and held his arms open. I leaned down to let him embrace me, and to let him feel my love for him. I breathed in his hair, upset with myself for lashing out at the guy I used to daydream about.

He eventually let me go and sat up to put his forehead to mine. "I love you, Trevor."

"I love you too, Ethan," I sniffled. *What the hell's wrong with you, Trevor? You don't treat the guy you love like that. What were you even trying to prove?* I kissed his forehead and we squeezed the hell out of each other with the box of tissues between us. He broke our embrace to get off the bed, holding his hand out to me with a knowing smile. I took it with a curious look, and he pulled me to stand with him. He scrolled on his phone and tapped a song to play—"love song" by YUNGBLUD—before setting it down to hold my hands with both of his. I held onto him and followed his lead as we slow danced to the words he wanted to play for me.

Here was a boy, kind and happy and carefree, who was never allowed to be his pure self and who never knew love—or rather, only knew love when it was conditional, a boy who the world tried to shape into something he's not. And here was another boy, the one he chose to open himself up to and give himself to—a boy who he trusted enough to let himself be loved by, even though he'd never done it before. *I'll show what love's supposed to be like, Ethan. And if I don't do it well enough, then you don't deserve me. I want you to have the life you're meant to have, even if it's one that I don't get to be in.* I didn't even try to stop the tears.

We circled in place well into the next song. "And where there used to be pain, there was now only love," I said into his neck as I wiped my eyes. "Two people who used to just share words became each other's reason for living."

"What's that from?" Ethan asked.

"Probably the most romantic moment of my life."

He pulled back to furrow his brow at me. "What do you mean?"

"I mean that was probably the most romantic moment of my life."

"You mean you came up with that just now?"

"Uh huh," I smiled.

He gave me a back-breaking squeeze. "I love you so much," he breathed.

"Je t'aime beaucoup aussi." I opened my eyes to look at my room from over his shoulder. "I don't know what's wrong with me. Sometimes a thought will pop into my head and I just start thinking irrationally and I can't make it stop. I'm sorry I'm like this."

"There's nothing wrong with you," he said softly. "There might be some things that you can't help, but they're all part of what makes you the person I love."

We moved to my bed to hold and appreciate each other. I didn't plan on dozing off, but I guess walking up the Ski Hill three times and having shower sex tired me out that much. *I forgot what it's like to wake up next to the guy I love,* I smiled as I came to, throwing my arm over Ethan. I opened my eyes to see Victor's looking back into mine just before I pushed him right off the bed. The others were howling from their prank.

"What the fuck?" I swore as I sat up, which only made Ethan and Kade and Tylor laugh harder. "Where'd you come from? How'd you get in here? What time is it?"

Ethan hopped up beside me and gave me a hug that I didn't return. "I'm sorry babe, but you should've seen your face."

"Wait, wait, here it comes," Kade grinned at his phone while the others crowded around to watch. Me yelping followed by a *thud* was sending them all over again.

"Did you let them in?" I asked Tylor, who was too busy cackling from his chair to hear. "What if we would've been naked or something?"

"Then they would've seen us naked," Ethan pinched my cheek. "It's nothing they don't already secretly touch themselves to the thought of."

"Secretly?" Kade chuckled as he let me see. It actually *was* pretty funny—my eyes popping out of my head, the way I jumped back like I was avoiding lightning, Victor whacking his arm off my dresser on the way down.

We had an impromptu movie night and got wings delivered for dinner, which I guess Victor also didn't know was a thing. "That should be like the *first* thing they tell you in orientation," he fumed. Tylor picked out *Harold & Maude* for the night's feature—"Is that the one where they go to White Castle?"—which got Kade so pumped up that you'd have thought somebody whipped out some fresh rosemary in front of him.

"I forgot how much I love this movie," Kade said when we paused it to fetch and divvy out the clamshell containers once they got delivered. "Maude would be my patronus, although Frank Reynolds is a close second."

"Lewis Black would be *my* patronus," I said.

"The pope's *my* patronus," Victor said. "No he's not, that's just the first person I thought of."

"If you're the pope, then I'm a little boy," Tylor said impishly.

We debated whether the mascot of Catholicism would be the pope, Jesus, or the Virgin Mother after Victor said that he used to think that The Vatican was a Catholic-themed theme park when he was younger. "Has anybody ever tried those Hiroshima wings or whatever they're called from Percy's?" Victor asked us after the movie ended. "The hottest ones they have?"

"You mean the Double Nuclear wings?" Ethan corrected him.

"Did you deadass just make a fucking *Hiroshima* joke in front of the Japanese kid?" Tylor said threateningly.

"Too soon," Kade shook his head unsympathetically.

Victor shrunk into the couch. "I—I mean, I *did*—but—" he stuttered, making Tylor crack up.

"I'm *joking* fam," he patted Victor's shoulder. "Why, are you thinking about trying them?"

"Yeah, but I don't wanna do them by myself." He looked around at us, his eyes resting on Kade.

"Wait, you're asking *me*?" Kade said. "No fucking *way*."

"Don't look at me," Ethan shook his head.

"Yeah, no," I laughed. "I've had hot sausage that had me sweating."

"No comment," Kade smirked.

"I'll do it with you," Tylor shrugged like eating something with Double Nuclear in its name was no biggie.

"Oh," Victor said like he didn't actually think anybody would. "I mean, yeah, if you're sure."

"So when do you guys think we should go over?" Kade asked.

Victor shrugged. "I was thinking maybe on Monday, after dinner maybe—"

"Not the *wings*," Kade groaned. "When do you wanna go over to Alex's place?"

I spun on Kade. "Go to Alex's place when? Tonight?"

"No, next week," he rolled his eyes.

"I didn't know we were going over again tonight!" I said as I traded glances with Ethan. "We were just planning on staying in," I said like the idea sounded lame to him all of a sudden.

"Yeah," Ethan nodded. "We could've fit it into our plans if we'd had more notice."

"I wonder what those plans could be," Kade muttered. "What about you?" he asked Tylor.

"I would, but I'm already going out with Amina and Jax."

"You people suck *ass*. How are your ears doing, by the way?" he asked Ethan.

"I actually keep forgetting they're there until my shirt catches on one," he said as he went to touch one before stopping himself. I like them, but I don't like how I can't nibble on his earlobes anymore during sexy time. I almost kept accidentally doing it later on when the two of us had the room to ourselves.

"I just remembered Valentine's Day is coming up," I smiled as we laid together afterwards, gently making out with handfuls of each other's jawlines.

"That's right!" he grinned. "You'll be my first valentine."

"No pressure then," I chuckled.

"I'm guessing I won't be *your* first?" he asked like he already knew the answer.

I grimaced the way I grimace when somebody's watching me walk across the floor they just mopped. "No, you're not."

"That's okay," he smiled. "You're allowed to have been in love with somebody before me. And if there's ever somebody after me, then I hope you'd feel the same way about them."

"Don't say that!" I frowned. "Why would you say that?"

"Because *everything* comes to an end someday. Even if we never break up, one of us is still gonna die before the other," he said like he was telling me how class was. "I'm not trying to be depressing or anything. That's just the way it works. There's a Latin phrase—*hoc quoque transibit*—which means 'this too shall pass,' and it applies to everything." As much as I don't like to think about it, he's right. And then I remembered what he told me when I was still trying to make sense of the fact that he actually wanted to be with me: *'If I didn't have forever in mind, then I wouldn't be wasting my time.'*

We brushed our teeth and climbed back into bed, but we didn't go to sleep just yet. We looked up at my twinkling Christmas lights and just talked about things— our favorite *Pokémon* games, if we had Vine, what classes in school we hated, when he started playing piano, how I used to play tee ball, first crushes, the first bands we got into, the last movie that made us cry—'dimensional small talk' as I like to call it. When we were spooning, about to fall asleep, I whispered into the back of his head, *"You know you're in love when you can't fall asleep because reality is finally better than your dreams.'"*

"Is that a Trevor original too?" he asked.

"Nope. Dr. Seuss."

I felt him smile as he nestled himself into me. *"He isn't wrong."*

Between the fire he dropped about us coming to an inevitable end and the fact I finally got to fall asleep next to Ethan, it took me *hours* to fall asleep. I pretended to be conked out when Tylor got back, promising myself to do whatever it takes to make every day of the rest of my life end with my breathing matching Ethan's gentle snores until they lull me to sleep. I woke up thinking about what I must've done right in my life to be able to wake up next to him—yes, it was actually Ethan this time—and sidled up to savor the moment, because moments like that shall also pass. He blinked up at the ceiling like he forgot he wasn't in his own room, stretching with a sleepy smile that I wish I had a live photo of to replay over and over. *Is this what it's like to have it made? To always wake up to his bedhead, his morning breath, to have coffee together in bed on weekends until death do us part?* I made us French press—"rich people coffee," as he calls it—that we sipped in my bed without either of us reaching for our phones. We had PopTarts for breakfast and then each did our own thing on my bed, whether it be reading or playing Switch or working on an assignment or journaling.

"Out of curiosity," I asked like it was taboo, "who was that old hookup of yours?"

He raised an eyebrow at me. "Why do you wanna know?"

"I *said* I was just curious," I said defensively.

I figured he wouldn't indulge me until he handed me an Instagram profile. "This is him."

"You don't still follow him, do you?" I asked without trying to sound judgy.

"Oh no," he chuckled, "he just has it public."

He plays on the club baseball team, which is probably how they met. "He kinda looks like a dumb jock," I said as I scrolled, though that's not to say he wasn't unattractive.

"He might've been, but he actually treated me like a person instead of just a way to get off."

"Well that's considerate of him," I said as images of post-practice locker room porn filled my mind. "I wish I could sleep with a baseball player," I accidentally mumbled out loud.

"Oh *really?*" he laughed. "Well I have some good news for you then."

"Do you think you'll play again this semester?" I tried to off-ramp.

"Probably not," he shook his head. "I'd like to, but with all my other commitments, I don't think I'll have time for it while still having time for myself."

"That stinks," I frowned. "I wish I could have seen you play."

"I'll just have to fit it into my schedule next year," he vaguely promised. "And when I say commitments, I mean you too."

February 6

Here's a math problem and don't pop a vessel trying to figure it out: how many people with brown skin need to die in an earthquake before white people start giving a shit about it? If you said 3,500, keep going.

I'm still fucked-up over *Harold & Maude.* Who's to say that your soulmate—not the person you end up spending your life with, but I mean your *soulmate,* your Greek mythological other half—has to be the same age as you, or has to be somebody you cross paths with, or identify as the gender you're attracted to? How many people are settling for less than who they're *meant* to be with because we accept what's before us? Imagine if there was a way to *know* when you met your soulmate, like you'd literally start to glow or something when you'd get close to them. Would Ethan and I glow around each other? And if not, would we settle for each other knowing that there's someone out there who's better than either of us could ever be for the other, perfect even? Or what if we're together for 20 years and one of us starts glowing when somebody else walks by?

Anyway.

My possible-soulmate and I accompanied Tylor and Victor up to Percy's, where their certain demise awaited them in the form of incredibly hot wings. The Double Nuclear challenge isn't eating a certain number of wings within a time limit or anything—you literally just have to eat them. It sounds easy on paper, but how few names there are up on the wall of people who've done it and the look the cashier gave Victor when he ordered his tell a different story. He and Tylor even had to sign waivers. Ethan and I, fucking hard with self-preservation, ordered wings on the greener end of the menu's thermometer. The four of us found a table and sat, staring at their baskets of wings. My eyes felt spicy just looking at them. Tylor and Victor figured cutting them into pieces—you can only get boneless ones because somebody probably choked on a bone in their hysteria—and scarfing them down as fast as possible before they passed out would be the best way to do it. Tylor bought three bottles of milk from the cooler to help numb the burn. Ethan and I tore into our worry-free wings while the other two diced up their chicken and cauliflower.

"You know," Tylor said to his pieces of wings, "I'm starting to think this might not be a good idea."

"Yeah, same," Victor admitted. "But I don't wanna just throw them away." His determination gave Tylor the motivation he needed to uncap his milk and grab his fork.

"Okay, let's do this," Tylor said in his *here-goes-fuck-nothing* tone. Ethan and I started recording as he counted them down. They attacked their food like they were on a Japanese game show.

"These aren't as bad as I thought," Victor said. "Okay, wait, never mind. Yeah, these are hot."

Tylor, who loves even spicy Indian food, gasped. "Oh my god. Holy *shit* are these hot."

Victor pulled indiscriminate handfuls of napkins from the dispenser to wipe his sweat and his tears. "My mouth's on fucking *fire* right now."

Milk ran from the corners of Tylor's mouth like he'd gotten a shot of Novocaine. "Are we eating *lava*? My lips won't stop burning."

Even after they'd finished their wings, Victor's face glistened pomegranate-red like he'd swiped an experimental piece of chewing gum from Willy Wonka's factory. "I can't even fucking *see*," he wept. He tore off his glasses and accidentally knocked over what was left of his milk, pressing the sopping napkins to his eyes. "Is this what it feels like to *die*?" I ran to get them more milk—*Dr. Jurado would use this as an example of price inelasticity*—that they immediately slammed down. Tylor emptied the napkin dispenser to try to dry his face and forehead.

"I can't thtop thweating," he cried.

Victor pushed his chair back and almost fell as he jumped up. "I feel like I'm gonna puke."

Tylor headed for the bathroom after him. "And I feel like I'm about to thit mythelf." Other students watched them go, some smirking.

I almost tried a drop of sauce on one of my fries, but then figured I have too much to live for. "I feel bad for those toilets," I laughed.

"I feel bad for whoever's in there with them," Ethan said. A guy came out with a smile and laughed with his friends when he sat back down with them. "Oh shit," Ethan laughed from behind his hand. "That feeling when Aiden Fuentes hears you having fiery poops."

"Who?"

"Aiden Fuentes? The SGB President? Like the most popular guy on campus? Gets his tuition waived on top of getting a stipend? Has dinner with the President of the university? President of his frat? Has probably bred half the guys in his frat?"

"Nope, don't know him," I shrugged as I thought about the alternate universe where Trevor's the president of a fraternity and has a harem of boys at his disposal. "Oh wait, did he speak at the Freshmen Welcome Weekend rally?"

"Yep, that was him."

We watched the videos we took of them eating their wings—**See what you missed nerd** I texted Kade, who was in his Studio Sculpture evening class—while we finished our own. "I guess I should go check on them," I said after several minutes passed. I pushed the door open like I was about to walk in on a massacre. "Guys? Are you okay?" A toilet flushed and Victor emerged from the stall wearing a look of pain, holding onto each side of the doorframe for support.

"If you're ever thinking of trying that," he groaned like it hurt to speak, "don't."

"Yeah," Tylor said from a sink behind me, "*zero out of five thtarth*." I guess he forgot that there aren't paper towels in the bathrooms until after he splashed his face with water and had to dry it under a hand dryer.

I walked out with them because I'm a good friend, ignoring the eyes that followed us. "How do you feel?" Ethan asked like it was funny, which it kind of was.

Tylor drained his last drops of milk. "Like we juth got mouth-fucked by Thatan." Victor nodded as he reached for my pop to take a gulp.

"Now what if I have strep throat?" I protested.

"I wouldn't even care at this point," he breathed.

46

"Just think about all the pussy you'll get now that your names will be up on the wall," Ethan smirked.

"*Ew!*" I scowled in disgust. "Why would you say that?"

"I just wanted to gross you out," he laughed.

Nobody watches you eat the wings to make sure you don't just throw them away and say that you ate them, but I guess looking like you just got mouth-fucked by Satan is all the proof they need. The two of them got 'Double Nuclear Survivor' t-shirts that they threw on over their shirts for a mirror pic that promptly went on Instagram. Anybody who says it's fake only needs to look at their faces.

I went back to 222 Swafford with Tylor instead of going to Proud as Halle because I'm a good roommate. I let him know I was putting my AirPods in so he could carpet bomb our toilet without having to be shy about it. And then I kept making him say things that sounded funny, like SpongeBob SquarePants.

"ThpongeBob ThquarePanth," he chuckled.

I thought. "Say...she shells—*goddammit*—she sells seashells by the seashore."

He looked at me like he wanted to strangle me before he started cracking up. "Thee thellth theethellth by the thee thore."

February 8

The death toll from that earthquake is up to over 11,000 people. I heard somebody talking about it in Patnick, saying how those people 'probably deserved it' because they were Syrian, so fuck *that* guy.

I went over to 239 Axworthy last night for a State of the Union watch party that Victor printed out bingo cards for. We all got to put down a chip for 'an awkward George Santos moment' before the speech even started, and I shouted "BINGO!" maybe a little too loudly when Biden talking about semiconductors won me the first bingo of the night and a knock at the door.

I can't believe I wasn't even going to give Macro a chance. Aside from the fact that I actually participate—I know, right?—Dr. Jurado's been spitting fire pretty much every class. "I think they need to totally revamp school district funding," he told us today. "You have schools in low-income areas that never get any money because school taxes are so low. So then property values fall because the school district isn't good, which then lowers property values, which then lowers taxes, which then brings down the quality of the schools, which then makes people not wanna move there—you get the idea. And then on the other hand, you have good school districts that just keep getting more and more money because the reverse happens. So poorer areas keep getting poorer, and richer areas keep getting richer. And if that's

47

not capitalism at its finest, I don't know what is." He legit had us on the edges of our seats. "I think they need to put all the school taxes into one big pot that gets evenly distributed between all the schools in the state if we ever want to break the cycle and change the paradigm."

Proud as Halle had their first movie showing of the semester, *Boy Erased*, which I'm sure will be another one that'll stick around with me for a while. I almost couldn't stop tearing up. "As sad of a movie it is, it reminds me that things can get better," Ethan told me as we filed out of the theater in Bixby. "Even when I feel like I'm trapped."

"Yeah," I nodded, wishing I had that kind of encouragement when I needed it. "Didn't you make a video of you playing that one song from the movie?"

"The Troye Sivan one? Yeah." So that's how I got a private performance of the song in 341 Kessler. Even though he's not at war with himself anymore, Ethan's voice still cracked and his eyes were still glossy when he finished playing.

We were taking the kind of mirror selfies bros don't take in his wardrobe mirror when Nate came back from the gym, making me whip my hand off of my boyfriend like he was a hot stove. "He knows we're together," Ethan said after Nate got in the shower. "So we don't have to act like we're just friends around him anymore."

"What'd you do, straight-up tell him we're together?"

"I told him I was going to see a movie at Bixby with my boyfriend. And then he asked if you were my boyfriend, and I said yeah, and he said 'oh, okay.'"

"He doesn't have a problem with it, does he?" I asked like I give a shit.

"I don't *think* so. I've never heard him make any gay jokes or use the f-word, but I don't know if he'd be okay with you spending the night though."

"That's okay, you getting to be yourself in your own room is still a big win!" I hugged him. I gave Nate a smile and a up-nod of thanks that I hope he didn't take as me trying to hit on him.

"Which of these would you say is the most Instagram-worthy?" Ethan asked me as we swiped through the pics we took.

"Why? Are you gonna post one?"

He ran the backs of his fingers down my jaw. "Yeah. I think it's time we went Instagram-official."

"Good, because I've been waiting to show you off," I smiled. *But not flooding my profile with you like I did with Dillon.* "Do you want me to tag you in it?" I asked after I typed up a caption for my own post. "What if somebody in your family sees it?"

"Do you really think I'm friends with any of my family?" he asked with a raised eyebrow. "And even if I was, I don't give a flying fuck what they'd think."

"I'll take that as a yes," I chuckled as I posted it. "Done. I will warn you though, I have lots of connections, so don't be surprised if you start getting all kinds of follow requests."

"Oh, shut up," he laughed as he gave my butt a slap. "Wait, do you have Tinder?" he asked my home screen.

Oh fucking shit. "No! I mean, yeah," I stammered, "but I haven't used it since the Summer! I just never got around to deleting it!"

"Calm *down*," he chuckled, "I'm not *accusing* you of anything. Open it."

I hesitated, nervous all of a sudden. "Why?"

"Just open it," he repeated. "Now keep swiping until you find me."

"Swipe which way?" I joked, earning myself a hard flick to the back of my neck. I rejected guy after guy, a lot of whom I recognized, wondering how many of them I might've matched with and hooked up with. *But I'm with Ethan now,* I told myself to distract myself from missed opportunities. *Speak of the devil and he shall appear.* It was a pic from an Instagram post that I'd stared at countless times already, though I don't know why he made it the first one you'd see of him on Tinder, since his sunglasses hide his gemstone eyes. I swiped right, and—like we didn't already know it—a celebratory message told me that Ethan and I had matched.

"I liked you on here back at the beginning of September," he smiled. "I always hoped to see that you'd like me back, especially once you started coming to get Starbucks."

"So when you told me I should try using Tinder again at that party, that was your way of trying to see if I liked you back?" I chuckled. "So are you telling me that if I was into casually hooking up, then we would've gotten together a while ago?"

"That's *exactly* what I was trying to do," he smiled. "And I dunno, maybe we would have." But *would* we have? Would he have been as special to me if he was just another conquest, somebody who I wouldn't have been interested in getting to know any better? Or *would* we be celebrating our five-month anniversary?

I try not to measure the worth of something by the number of likes it gets, but I couldn't help but keep checking on my post to see how many it got. Currently, 17 people—I see you, Chris Burkhart, and I hope you're jealous—showed their support for two guys hooked around each other's waists and facing each other with one's finger under the other's chin.

wallowing_tbh There are a lot of names and words I can use to describe him, but I'm just going to leave it at 'wonderful'—I am *beyond* lucky to be able to call this wonderful guy my boyfriend 😊 I love you babe #sappy #dontcare

madzzzz FINALLY 😄 😵 😎

EthanE16 no I'M the lucky one 😊 😊 Love you too!!!!

oakley_dokey dad and dad you better stop fighting rn

morozov_cocktail 😊😊

hayashi_photography I can't with you two 😍

February 10

POV:

Friday afternoon. 27 degrees out. Big, hypnotic snowflakes. Warm in your boyfriend's bed. He's playing "Arabesque No. 1." Wishing he had stuff to make tea.

February 11

'February 8—Emergency services responded to a call in Patnick Dining Hall about a student who was squirted in the eye with hot sauce. The student said they were shaking the bottle when the lid came off and several drops of hot sauce landed in their eye. The student was transported to Armstrong County Memorial Hospital.' It's a good thing it wasn't Double Nuclear sauce, because that's literally how superhero villains are born.

Since we had more than an hour's notice, Ethan and I found ourselves making the journey to 370 Rock Hill Road last night alongside Kade and Victor. Tylor and Amina actually came too, and I had to stop myself from building it up for them in case they found it disappointing. It was the same party as last week with most of the same crowd, except I was comfortable before I even stepped inside. Alex greeted Tylor and Amina with a warm smile like he hadn't just met them. "Wine coolers and malt beverages are in the fridge, of course," he told them as we went to make ourselves drinks. "We have liquor, wine, and saki this time too, if that's your thing."

"Ooh!" Kade exclaimed. "Saki is *absolutely* my thing."

"My man," Tylor fist-bumped him. The two of them each threw back little decorative shot-glass-sized cup after cup of it. I tried some red wine because it seemed like the artsy-kid thing to drink, but it was like drinking rubbing alcohol. *I guess I'm just an uncultured little shit,* I thought as I poured myself some coconut rum and orange juice into a cup that they must've stolen from the bar in town.

I led Ethan to the living room, and we almost walked into Andy Warhol with pink-tinted hair as he turned the corner from the stairs. He looked around like he was seeing walls and ceilings for the first time, wearing a turtleneck, pants—not jeans, but like actual *pants*—and round mottled sunglasses. Alexis Rose from *Schitt's Creek* came down the steps behind him in her own enormous sunglasses. "Oh shit, I'm sorry, I—".

"Everything is good," he said like he was dazed. "Everything. Is. *Good.*" He reached for Alexis Rose's hand and they carefully stepped past us.

"If *those* people aren't high," Ethan giggled, "then *nobody's* high."

Tylor watched us trying to stifle our laughter as we circled around to some empty spots on the floor around the hookah. "What's so funny?" he asked us.

"Would you believe me if I told you that Andy Warhol's here?" I chuckled.

"Probably not."

Matt laughed through his nose from the legless armchair beside us. "That would be our other roommate, Andrew. Was there a girl with him?"

"Yeah? Big sunglasses?"

"That's June," he nodded. "They're both Art majors, if you couldn't have guessed."

"What *is* it with Art majors always being so fucking weird?" I asked as I shot Kade a glance. He slowly sucked on his finger before flipping me off with it.

It turns out that Amina not only knows her way around a hookah, but knows her way around it so well that Kade—*Kade*—called her an expert at it. "I don't ever remember there not being hookah in my house," she said mostly to Kade and Alex. "My dad and uncles and older cousins would always fire it up after dinner." She gracefully de-ashed the coals with a *clang* in the silver tray. "They wanted to open up their own lounge but my mother always talked them out of it. 'We already have one store to run!' she'd remind them."

"Oh nice, so did—" Victor started to say before abruptly shutting up. "What kind of stuff did they sell?"

"Sold," she corrected him with a plume of smoke. "COVID did them in. But just imported trinkets and stuff. Shisha," she nodded at the hookah. "Some spices and food items. Nothing too fancy."

"That's cool," Kade nodded. "Anybody wanna see the Five Dollar Hookah Trick?" He took a five from his wallet, rolled it up into a straw, and blew hookah smoke through it. We stared at him, waiting for him to go on.

"Wait, was that it?" Victor asked him.

Kade nodded with a proud smile. "Yep."

"That was the dumbest fucking thing."

"That could've been in a stripper's ass crack," I laughed as I took the hose from him. I started out with small puffs so I wouldn't cause another scene, and carefully worked my way up to deeper drags, overcoming the fruit-flavored tickles in my throat. Amina tried to teach us how to make smoke rings, but I couldn't do anything other than blow it out in a stream like an angry steam pipe. It only took Ethan a few tries before he managed to breathe out a flawless donut of smoke that traveled a good two feet before turning into a skimpy onion ring and dissipating.

"Did you see that?!" he asked as he tugged at my sleeve. "I did it!"

"Yeah, because you've had a lot of practice with how to position your mouth," I smirked, earning myself a backhanded slap.

We joined in on a game Luca brought called *Same Same But Different* that's all about double entendres. Somebody flips two cards with different scenarios on them and you have to come up with something that fits both, like Ethan writing 'what a log!' for something you can say while shitting in the woods and also when you have an erection that won't go away. Kade and I were the only two not howling over it because we were too busy staring at each other with horrified looks, like we'd been playing with a Ouija board just for fun and the stone actually started to move.

"The *triple* entendre!"

"*It's never been done!*"

We got up to refill our drinks, passing Andrew and Henry talking about Huxley's *Heaven and Hell* as June listened from Andrew's arm, and Victor grabbed me just as I was about to pour myself more rum. "I'm gonna go see if anybody's smoking downstairs," he said in a low voice. "You wanna come with?" I was about to say that the hookah was in the living room before I realized what he meant.

"Oh, *that* kind of smoking." I turned to Ethan. "Do you wanna do *that* kind of smoking?"

"Hell *yeah*," he grinned. "Do you?"

"Yeah, I'll give it another try," I said, determined to see what being high felt like, though I was low-key nervous about it. Victor led us downstairs into the red room, where we found Eren leaning over the blemished table, pinching fingerfuls of weed from a small, airtight jar and into the stack of poker chips that turned out to be a weed grinder disguised as a stack of poker chips. You know how they have that show called *Is It Cake?* They should have a show called *Is It a Stash Box?*

"Is it okay if my friends join?" Victor asked him after they gave each other an up-nod. "I have my own stuff." He produced a Post-It Note-sized baggie of small green buds from his back pocket.

"Where the fuck did you get *that*?" I muttered as we dropped to the couch. "Since when have you started buying weed?"

"Okay, *one* of us needs to calm the fuck down," he said. "And today was *literally* the first time."

"From who?" I asked, hoping he'd say Patnick Paul.

"Somebody in one of Kade's classes. I think he lives in your building."

Eren pinched some ground-up weed into the little glass dildo before holding a lighter to the bowl end of it and sucking on the other. "Oh, *that's* what that thing is," I said.

Ethan gave me a look. "What the fuck did you *think* it was?"

I put my mouth to his ear. *"Bend over and I'll show you."*

Victor hit it next before passing it to me. It tasted even more burnt than the joint, though not super harsh. I held it in for a few seconds like they did before letting it out, but I didn't really feel anything. I might've felt it a *little* after the second time, but then after the third time...

"How are you feeling?" my boyfriend checked on me.

"My head feels like if a ball sack was a balloon," I said to a spot on the wall across from me. "With flannel sheets on the inside." I felt like if I stood up I would've floated to the ceiling like a helium-filled sex doll if I hadn't somehow gotten nailed to the couch. *I am crucified upon this couch.* I didn't get a chance to think too profoundly about that though, thanks to Ethan and Victor giggling uncontrollably.

"This is like the second time he's ever gotten high," Victor explained to Eren.

"The first," I corrected him. *"High* high, I mean."

"Woah—I'm honored to be here for it." Victor shook my hand, as did Ethan, and Eren even leaned over to congratulate me.

"Didn't you say you smoked weed once before?" Ethan asked me.

I nodded. "Last week."

"No, before that."

My head rolled at him. "Before that what?"

"Last week you said you smoked before. I'm asking *when.*"

"Ohhh. I dunno. Last year sometime. I took a hit of a joint once, but I didn't get *high.*"

"See what happens?" Victor said. "You do the weed once and then it turns you gay."

"You're not gay."

He cheesed up. "I bet you wish I *waaasss though,*" he said in a sing-songy voice. He emptied the bowl into one of the ashtrays and started grinding some of his own stuff. "I ever tell you about the first time I bought weed and it ended up being oregano?"

"No?" I laughed.

"Whaaat?" Ethan smiled.

"Yeah," he chuckled. "I went to smoke it and it was just nasty. I let Kade make pizza sauce with it. Most expensive pizza sauce *ever.*"

The songs changing was the only way I knew that time hadn't stopped. And the music sounded *so fucking good.* I thought music sounded good anyway, but when you're high? Holy fucking *shit.* I legit almost can't even. It all makes sense to me now—and I mean like, *everything.* Eren disappeared like a magic trick. I didn't like the void Ethan left around the back of my neck when his arm left it, like a notch had been taken out of my back. I got up to get a drink, counting down from ten like

I was launching a space shuttle before lifting myself up off the couch. "I'm thirsty," I announced.

"Yeah you are," Victor smirked like twenty minutes later.

The blue room lured me in with its encompassing ultramarine aura, making me feel like I was in a fish tank. Going up the stairs was like a spelunking expedition, and everybody who saw us *had* to know what we were doing. Alex met my eyes and gave me a *that's-what's-up* nod. Sonia filled our right-where-we-left-them cups with water for us—"What a nice lady," Victor remarked—and I gulped it down like I couldn't get enough of it. Back in the living room, Ethan sat across my lap and we shotgunned smoke into each other's mouths. I only half-paid attention to the others flinging shit on the British monarchy and then the Repubes while the music kept trying to kidnap me. I couldn't go more than a few moments without smiling at Ethan, even when he wasn't looking.

Are you high rn???

I looked up to see Tylor watching me from across the hookah circle, and smirked back at him. Typing out a response was like defusing a bomb.

Bitch I might be

Go the fuck ahead!

The rest of the night played out like a movie that lost you that you're fighting to stay awake for. My mind felt numb, and a little jittery. *Adult Swim makes so much more sense now.* "Guys, I really wanna eat something," I whined without caring how busy Sheetz would be as we were about to leave.

"Yeah, I'm down to get some foodles badoodles," Kade said as Victor's head nodded loosely.

"Samesies," Ethan said like he was about to fall asleep.

We stood among students whose parents would be ashamed of them if they saw them like that for what felt like all night, but holy *shit* were those the best mac and cheese bites I've ever had—and the best popcorn chicken I've ever had—and the best bag of white cheddar popcorn I've ever had. If there'd been a box of chocolates on the table that two of The Skeletons sat at, romantically looking into each other's eye sockets, I would've been tempted to go check that shit out too.

"I think you missed your stop fam," Victor said to Ethan as he shambled past Kessler with the rest of us.

Ethan shook his head with a dumb grin. "Nah, I'm staying in Trevor's room tonight." He threw his arm around my shoulder to pull me smack-up against his side.

"Oh go 'head," was all Kade said instead of making the innuendo he's conditioned me to expect from him.

I *swear* we were teleporting across campus, because one moment we were passing Zukoff and then all of a sudden we were outside of Bixby. "Guys, let's all be roommates next year," I said before we ended up in the woods next.

Kade stopped in his tracks, making the rest of us almost trip. "*Fam.* That'd be fucking *sick!*"

"Yeah!" Ethan enthusiastically agreed. "We can get one of those four-person rooms like Amina has!"

"That'd be fun," Victor said. "I think I'm gonna try going for an RA position though."

I grabbed his shoulder and turned him to face me. "Dude! You should! You'd make a badass RA!"

"Oh god," Kade snorted. "Trev's saying 'dude.'"

"You think so?" Victor asked me like he didn't believe it.

"Hell yeah! I dunno what the qualifications are, but I'm sure you have 'em!"

"*I'd* want you for an RA," Ethan said encouragingly.

"Thanks," Victor said, though he still looked unconvinced. "I guess it's *super* competitive though. You get free room and board—"

"Well *yeah*, that's why," Kade said.

"But if I got it I'd have to live in just a regular double room. So you'd have to find somebody else to take my place."

The only person who came to mind was Tylor, but he already signed a lease with Amina and Jaxon for an apartment in Oakwood. "We'll worry about that if it happens," I said.

"He meant to say *when* it happens," Ethan encouraged him.

I've already fantasized about the four of us as seniors with an apartment or a house in town where we'd throw our own parties, 370 Rock-style, for all our friends and the newest like-minded generation of New Hallians. But I know that a lot can happen in three years though. Will we all even still go to school here? Will we even still be friends? Will what we have right now have passed?

I watched a video I only vaguely remember taking last night of Ethan lighting the bowl for me as I hit it, with the red-tinged tapestry and a song about getting medicated playing in the background, which says 'stoner' even more than Victor's diptych on Snapchat of him hitting and exhaling a joint. Maybe I should start smoking every night before bed though, because I was out within *minutes* of my head hitting my pillow. I *cannot* tell you the last time that happened. Middle school maybe?

February 12

Over 33,000 people are dead from that earthquake. *33,000.*

And does nobody else care that the war with aliens just started? The Air Force shooting down two mysterious objects and not saying what they were is how *War of the Worlds* or something starts off.

It's funny what can happen when you get the stick a little more out of your ass —a lot of the songs I have on the playlist I put on when I'm with Ethan are ones I would've never listened to even a few months ago. One will come on in the car and we'll exchange glances, remembering how it played the evening before when we were in bed together in the biblical sense. Another will be the only sound in the aftermath as I hold him close to me, recalling when I first heard it from one of his own playlists or on his YouTube channel in those early weeks when I literally couldn't stop thinking about him. I'll smile at him bouncing to one in the middle of one of our rooms and laugh as I let him pull me into it with him.

"So you're okay with being roommates with Victor and Kade next year?" I asked him at breakfast.

"Yeah, I think it'd be fun," he said as he scooped some of my blueberries into his yogurt. "Although I wouldn't mind just the two of us being roommates either."

"Yeah, until we get sick of each other," I laughed as I spooned off-brand Froot Loops into my mouth. Forreal though, I can't wait to make a home out of our room with him and start every day beside him in our pushed-together beds. "I don't know who we'd make our fourth if Victor does get an RA position though. I mean, I hope he *does.*"

"It'd be so nice to be an RA," Ethan said to his yogurt as he stirred it. "Yeah, you have duty shifts and have to tell people to behave, but getting the cost of the room waived *and* getting a stipend would be a *huge* help."

"Why don't you apply? You'd make a good RA!"

He just shook his head. "Not gonna happen."

"Why not?"

He picked up his phone and scrolled through his photos before finding the one he was looking for. It was a screenshot of a section of the police blotter from the September 23rd issue of *The New Halle Herald.* '*Sept. 16—David Kaufmann, 19, Ethan Eastwood, 19, Jada Adelson, 18, and Nathan Bowser, 18, of Kessler Hall were charged with possession of alcohol by a minor.'* Short, succinct, and factual—delinquents for others to shake their heads at over their Friday lunches.

"It was my own RA who caught us too," he said. "He was quick to tell me that they wouldn't even consider me for an RA position because of that when I told him I was thinking about applying for one."

"What a fucking dick," I said as I thought about how badass it would be to have 'Bowser' for a last name. "Did the school tell your parents?"

He grinned like I told him he could top me. "Oh my god, you should've heard my mom on the phone after she found out," he laughed. "Thank god she'd already sent me my birthday card," he laughed. "I can't even *imagine* what her reaction would be if she ever finds out I do drugs or sleep with guys."

The two of us hung around in 341 Kessler before migrating to 222 Swafford for a game of *Scythe* with our Axworthy friends. "So what's the move tonight?" Victor asked when we took a break to order pizza. "Do you guys wanna go out somewhere? Is Alex having another party?"

"You just wanna get high again," Ethan said. "You wanna get high as a fucking kite."

"You probably do too!"

Ethan pulled the neck of his shirt up over the bottom half of his face like a femboy. *"It's possible,"* he said from behind it.

"I wouldn't mind it again either, actually," I said as I hugged my knees. "Can I just say that I can't wait for us to all be roommates next year?"

"You may not," Kade said as he shot Alex a text.

"Okay," I said.

"Are we actually gonna do it then?"

"Yeah. We all want to, don't we?"

"So what, do we just tell the Residence Life people that we want each other as roommates?"

"I *think* so."

"Guys, it's gonna be fucking *lit.*"

"Alex says no party tonight, but we're still welcome to go over and smoke with them," Kade read off his phone.

"Smoke *what?*" Victor bounced his eyebrows.

"Ham," Kade rolled his eyes. "We're gonna smoke ham."

We stopped at Sheetz to pick up some snacks for when we got the munchies later. None of us knew what to expect as Kade knocked on the front door of 370 Rock. *Are they gonna be sitting around in their pajamas watching Hulu? Should I have brought some snacks as a gift for the house?* I was glad to see that Matt wasn't in pajamas and still had his hair tied up when he let us in. The house has a totally different vibe when there's not a party going on—the basement steps were dark and silent, the green light bulbs had been swapped with normal ones, and the music played from large wooden bookshelf speakers instead of from the bass-heavy network of Bluetooths. A sober Andrew filed through a crate of records in his washed jeans and Joy Division t-shirt, while June looked on from the couch in white overalls. "Alex is in the kitchen packing the bowls," Matt told us as he bent down to fan the still-black hookah coals on a hot plate. It smelled like car exhaust. I had a guess as to why the smaller waterpipe from the red room was upstairs beside the dignified-looking one we'd typically smoke out of, and seeing Alex layering green flecks in with the shisha into only one of the glazed hookah bowls confirmed it.

"The little one's reserved for weed," he explained when I asked him why. "We don't wanna contaminate Anubis with the devil's lettuce."

"You can smoke weed out of a hookah?" I asked like that wasn't what I thought it was for the first time I saw it.

"You can smoke weed out of *anything*," he said as he poked crop circles into the tightly-wrapped pieces of foil with a discolored toothpick. "I've smoked out of a beer can before. I've smoked out of an apple before."

"Ha," Kade smiled. "I get it. Anubis is the god of *death*. Smoking *kills*."

We cracked open our teas and pops from Sheetz as Andrew decided on a record like me deciding on a shirt to buy. "Anybody opposed to The Beatles?" he asked us as he held up one with a cover that looked like it was sliding off the sleeve.

"Go for it," Kade said as I shook my head. *If The Beatles are what the artsy, wine-drinking, turtleneck-wearing elements of the student body listen to, then by all means.* I fingered the burn marks in the Oriental-style rug and took in just how many houseplants they have as the speakers crackled with needle-on-vinyl pops. An unbroken tendril of smoke flowed from the tip of an incense stick.

We nursed the hookahs to '60s pop until we were making thunderclouds. "Now *that's* baby-making music," Alex smiled.

"Why have Yuengs and wings when you can have bowls and coals?" Kade said as he took Anubis' hose.

"You're telling me that this *sounds better than if I streamed it on my phone?"* Ethan said to me in a low voice and with a sideways glance at the turntable, but I was too busy proving Kade wrong to answer him.

"Hold on—this says that *Osiris* was the god of death, not *Anubis*," I read off Wikipedia. "Anubis was the god of funeral rites. Who's the uncultured shit now?" I said to Kade as I took a puff from the weed hookah, which actually didn't taste as horrible as I was expecting it to.

"Well shit," Andrew said. "We can't just rename it."

"No," Kade said as he read off his own phone. "This says that Anubis *was* the god of death during the Old Kingdom before Osiris got popular! So to answer your question about who the uncultured shit is," he glared, "not me."

"Oh, good," Andrew breathed.

"Well neither am I!" I said.

"Does anybody smell that?" Victor asked as he wrinkled his nose. "I keep getting little whiffs of a warm spot in the pool." He'd somehow missed the memo that there was weed packed into the bowl of the small hookah, even after taking hits of it. To be fair though, if I didn't see Alex packing it I probably would've just figured it was a different kind of shisha until I found myself more and more entranced by the music. "And speaking of which, I have my own stuff for whenever we *smoke* smoke." Victor patted his pocket.

Alex just smirked. "We'll get there."

I leaned back on my elbows with a content smile. "I've gotta say, The Beatles don't sound at all like what I was expecting. But in a good way."

"They were the first band I got into," Andrew said. "And I mean like, *obsessed.* Everybody in 7th grade was all about "Thrift Shop" and Fall Out Boy and Miley Cyrus and Imagine Dragons, and there *I* was playing the fucking *Beatles,*" he laughed. "Everybody thought I was weird, but I think I was just ahead of my time."

"I was the same way in school!" I said as I sat up straighter. "Not with The Beatles, but everybody else was all about whatever was popular, even if it was shitty. I listened to stuff that was actually good."

"And then I came along and corrupted you," Ethan said with a pinch. "I was all about whatever was popular. I knew there was something different about me long before I knew I was gay, so liking what everybody else liked was a way for me to feel like I fit in."

"Okay, that's valid," I admitted. *Is one of us more right than the other? Is it better to sell out if it means doing more, or to stay true to yourself? Do I just have that big of a stick up my ass still?*

"Weren't The Beatles a boy band once?" Victor wondered aloud.

June shot him a look. "You can't say shit like that."

"I was listening to The Beatles and Led Zeppelin and Jimi Hendrix and Pink Floyd and all that stuff long before I tried drugs," Matt said. "And then when I did, it all made sense to me."

"I thought you said you didn't take anything?" I asked him.

"Not anymore," he smiled. "There was a four or five-month period last year when I spent every day either high or worse. I learned that there *is* such a thing as overindulging, and it comes at the price of just existing instead of living."

"Didn't Oscar Wilde say something like that?" I asked, knowing full-well that he did. "Something about how most people just exist instead of live?"

"If he did, he wasn't wrong. Those months were the lowest point of my life. I only stopped existing and started living again after I OD'ed." Across from me, Victor's eyebrows jumped up alongside mine. "I saw how fragile my life really is, but the fact that I did it to *myself* is what I couldn't get over," Matt went on. "So I said never again, because I'm worth so much more than that."

Alex reached over to pat him on the knee. "And I'm so fucking proud of you, dude."

"I *will* say though," Matt went on, "that once you do psychedelics, it's almost like they permanently change something inside of you. Like music—it never goes back to the way it used to sound."

Kade sighed. "*God,* do I wanna try psychedelics."

The seniors were trying to convince us freshmen to give The Smiths another try after we'd said we didn't see what the hype was when Victor narrowed his eyes at the little hookah. "*Wait a second*—is there weed in this?" The rest of us busted out laughing. "You're all turds," he said as he took extra hits of it to make up for lost medication. "Big, steaming shit turds."

I fully expected June to put on a Smiths record next, but the one she took was from a totally blank white sleeve. "Excellent choice babe," Andrew said as the sound of an airplane landing filled the room. The album was so all over the place that I would've thought it was a playlist if I didn't know any better.

"What are we *listening* to?" I asked on the fourth song like I couldn't believe it.

"The Beatles," Alex said.

"Forreal? We were just listening to The Beatles though and they sounded *nothing* like this."

"Who said they had to? You don't become the most legendary band in rock music by doing the same thing over and over and over again."

"The Ramones did the same thing over and over and over again," Victor said, "and *they're* one of the most legendary bands in rock music."

Kade pointed to the door. "You need to *leave.*"

"Have you guys ever heard the rumors about Paul McCartney being dead?" Andrew said like a camp counselor telling a ghost story.

We tuned into him. "No?"

He held the tip of an incense stick to a glowing coal to light it. "The story goes that Paul died and the band left behind clues about it," he said to the strange cursive letters he wove with it. My mind flashed back to a 4th of July once upon a lifetime ago, when Ryder was waving around a sparkler to spell out a name that wasn't his own. The four seniors explicated every breadcrumb in the 'Paul is dead' trail, fervently showing us album covers and pictures and reading lyrics like it was *The Da Vinci Code.*

"Okay, this'll freak you the fuck out," June said. "Somebody record this in Snapchat and then play it backwards."

Kade got up to hold his phone to the speaker and what sounded like senseless murmuring. He listened to it backwards and almost dropped his phone. *"No fucking way!"* He held it to Victor's ear, and Victor scooted backwards to get away from it.

"The FUCK dude?!" he said. Ethan and I leaned over to hear what had them shooketh.

"Paul is dead man, miss him, miss him, MISS HIM."

I fell back onto my palms and my ass. *Ryder's dead man, miss him, miss him, MISS HIM.* I grabbed Ethan's hand to line up my fingers with his, and paid attention to each gentle acoustic guitar note of the next song as much as I paid attention to the lungs in me that made every wonderful breath possible.

"I *told* you it'd freak you out," June laughed.

It wasn't too hard to find a distraction from my thoughts when Alex started talking about all the homemade dinners he misses back home—*tostones* and *mofongo* and *pasteles* and *arroz con gandules* and other things that made Kade and I groan longingly for. "I love me some good Mexican food," I said, "but I've never tried anything farther south, gastronimal—gastromonic—gastronom—"

"You've never eaten anything from Central or South America?" Kade offered.

I nodded dumbly. "Yeah." I was thinking about quesadillas when I remembered something so earth-shattering that I startled people when I stood up. You know how sometimes you stand up too fast and you accidentally travel to another dimension? Now imagine doing that when you're as baked as a Black Forest cake. *"Guys,"* I grinned, "we have snacks."

I watched Alex and Kade pack fresh bowls while Victor and I lazily munched on a 'family-sized' bag of Bugles without leaving any survivors. "Oh yeah, you stick your fingers in that shisha, dad," I said with a face-splitting grin. Kade grabbed my shoulders and pushed me against the wall. "Oh *dad*, pin me to the wall and—"

"Okay, you high *as hell* right now fam," he said right in my face, making me crack the fuck *up.*

We inaugurated the second record of the album with a snack pack of cheese, pepperoni, and tiny pretzels, each slice of convenience store charcuterie a eucharist wafer on my tongue. Andrew, the chef of the house, talked cooking with Kade instead of the deep and experimental things I would've expected from a couple of Art majors. "I just like to *create* things," Kade gesticulated. "I don't even care if I never get rich or famous for it. I just need to do it." I didn't have anything to contribute, which was okay because I was too busy getting seduced by The Beatles. *I get what Matt meant about it all just 'clicking.'* The seniors said they're Vonnegut fans after I told them that he and Adam Silvera, who they'd never heard of, were probably my two favorite authors. Andrew tried talking to me about On the

Road even after I'd told him I'd never read it, but all I could hear was "*number nine, number nine, number nine*" and the cacophony of sounds and voices

"What the fuck even *was* that?" Victor asked once the 'song' was over.

"Art," June smiled.

"Art my *ass*," Victor muttered.

Matt put on yet another Beatles album that was easily the most eye-catching of the three. It would almost be an insult to just call it music—it was a kaleidoscopic stained-glass window of sound, entrancing me with its carnival of color and an India drone that left me craving some chicken tikka masala. The last song legit scared the hell out of us, which we took as the universe telling us to go get the hell to bed.

The lack of music made it feel like we were at a party and were the last ones to leave. "You guys are welcome to come chill any weekend you like," Alex told us as we sleeved our arms through our coats. Matt and June nodded behind him, while Andrew laid on his back on the floor to have a staring contest with the ceiling. "Seriously! And I'll let you know whenever we're turning up!"

The air outside felt like it was frozen in place. I couldn't look away from the starry sky. "Does anyone think it's kinda weird that some seniors wanna hang out with some lowly freshmen like us?" Kade asked us. "I know Alex was Kelsey's friend, but it's not like he was *my* friend."

"I mean, I guess it *is* a little strange."

"Maybe they're trying to win our trust so they can drug us and kill us, or lock us up as sex slaves."

"I mean, I'm pretty sure Alex *is* bi, so…"

"They're probably tryna make the most of the time they have left before they graduate so they're just partying with whoever," I offered. "Okay, maybe not *whoever.*"

"*Thank you,*" Kade said.

I went on a side quest to try sliding down The Railing, but frozen metal is somehow less smooth than thawed metal. "Do you guys wanna get breakfast at Ginny's tomorrow? That place in town Luca was telling us about?"

"*Ugh,* breakfast sounds so *good* right now," Ethan whined.

"I'll take that as a yes."

"You know how I love me a good pancake," Victor said.

Kade walked like he could barely stand. "Does the pope…play Parcheesi?"

I fell asleep feeling proud of myself, because I don't think you can get any more college than getting stoned out of a hookah with the artsy kids while listening to The Beatles on vinyl and playing it backwards. *If I'm doing that as a freshman, then what's there left to do here?* I thought as I snuggled into Ethan. *Just give me my diploma now.*

What scarce people there were out walking on a frigid Sunday morning hurried down Main Street and Quincy Street with purpose—no stopping for selfies, no looking in shop windows, no waiting for the walk signal to cross the street. Brew 22 was dead because everybody was at Ginny's a few doors down, where servers carried carafes of coffee and sides of toast between tables of students who were boisterous from the night before, though a lot of people looked like they were still waking up. The chintzy pendant lights made me think of a tavern that serves beer and lots of beige food.

"The place must be good if it's this busy," Victor said as he defogged his glasses.

"Dammit, they're cash only," Ethan said as he nodded to the paper sign taped to the register. "I don't have any cash on me."

"They're gonna have to stop being cash only once we get to a robot economy," Kade said like he was disappointed in the place. He opened his wallet to pull out four crumpled ones that were all facing different ways. "I can cover it as long as it doesn't come to more than a dollar per person."

Ethan braved the cold to run over with me to the ATM stuck into the side of the lifeless bank. "I'll be asking for a tip for having to go back out there when you Venmo me," I told my Axworthy friends when I returned with a few folded twenties in my pocket.

"Sure you will," Victor said as he nodded over into the dining room. "Tylor and Amina are here." I looked over to see Tylor, Amina, and Jaxon sitting with two other people I didn't know in the last booth along the wall.

"What's up fam!" Tylor greeted me with a smile like we don't live with each other when I popped over to say hi. He couldn't believe that it was my first time there. "It's an NHU way of life," he said like the college guru I've always thought of him as. And I can see why it's a way of life—on top of the food legit being good, it basically is a dollar a person. An omelet, a breakfast burrito, a stack pancakes, the Uncle Happy Time Breakfast Special, three sides of toast, four coffees, two orange juices, and the tip all came to like $30.

"Shit," Kade said as licked the rest of his strawberry jam out of the little plastic tub, "we might have to start making this a thing." *Going out to the local diner for breakfast the morning after with the boys? Yes fucking* please.

I looked into Brew 22's windows as we passed it on the way back, thinking about how we'd be watching Ethan perform again in a week's time. "Have you guys thought any more about playing together for Open Mic Night?" I asked.

The three of them traded looks. "We were actually going to, but then we decided against it," Kade finally said.

I spun on him. "What? Why?"

"It just wasn't working out," Ethan said. "We couldn't agree on anything. I guess being good friends doesn't mean being good bandmates."

"Besides, we figured Eth sounds good enough on his own," Victor added. "He doesn't need us dragging him down."

I frowned. "That doesn't even make sense. I've heard you all play and you're all *fantastic*. How would you sound bad together?"

Kade shrugged. "Why fix what isn't broken?"

"You sound like a conservative," I spat as I stuffed my hands into my pockets. "I assume you won't tell me what you'll be playing?" I asked Ethan.

"Nope. But the one we agreed on is one of your—" He stopped walking and stared at me with wide eyes. "*Scheisse.*"

"So wait, you *are* playing together?"

He looked at the other two. "Yeah," he laughed. "We've been practicing together over Break."

My feet actually left the ground. "I didn't know that!"

"Because it was *supposed* to be a surprise," Kade shot Ethan a sideways glance.

I hounded them with questions the whole way back. "Did you play over Zoom or something?" "You won't even give me a *hint?*" "Do you have a band name?"

"We don't have a band name because we're not a *band*," Victor insisted.

"The definition of a band is 'a small group of musicians and vocalists who play pop, rock, or jazz music,'" I read off of Google. "Are you playing pop, rock, or jazz music?"

"We're actually gonna do the '1812 Overture,'" Kade said. "I'll be playing the cannon." *The money I'd pay to see him rolling a cannon into a coffee shop.*

"Whatever. You can't just introduce yourselves as Victor and Ethan and Kade."

"Don't fucking tell me what I can't do, *mom*."

I went back to 341 Kessler with Ethan, where he let me watch him record a video of him playing a song by a band I'd never heard of called Vansire. "It's only fair, since you let me read one of your stories," he said as he adjusted his ring light, although I would've seen the end result of his work whether I would have let him read one of my stories or not. I didn't hang around for too long though since we had our own stuff to catch up on. I explored The Beatles' catalog while I worked on my assignments, though I kept getting distracted at the thought of my friends and boyfriend playing music together for a live audience.

The boyfriend in question persuaded me to go to my own building's event for that football thing that everybody loses their minds over, even though I give negative-zero shits about football. The event ended up being a projector and like 40 pizzas set up in the MPR, which I guess all the buildings did because it's an easy box to check. I didn't want to stay to watch any of the game, and apparently neither did anybody else—sure, all you have to do is whip out a pizza and suddenly you're

Moses to the student body, but why would anybody want to stay and watch it there when they could take some pizza up to the comfort of their own room and watch it there? I hung around out of pity though for a little longer than I otherwise would have, wondering if Kessler's own event was going any better.

Let's just say that I'll be set on food for the next couple of days 😆😆

February 13

So Dr. Kotek dropped the Realest Shit of All Time™ in class today. I was kind of zoned out though thinking about what he said about our ancestors telling themselves that the Native Americans were subhuman to justify genociding/ethnically cleansing them, so I'm not really sure how it came up.

"Every decision you make is rooted either in fear or in love," he said like it was something we should all know by now. "You look at everything and everyone through either a lens of love or a lens of fear, and *that* determines what kind of person you are." He caught me staring with my mouth hanging open. "I just blew your mind, didn't I?" *Um, yeah?* Because hate never starts out as hate, does it? Who wakes up and says, '*You know what, I think I'm gonna start hating today?*' It comes from ignorance—as refusing to accept or understand people and ideas that are different or unfamiliar, and when that ignorance gets fostered with an attitude of fear or in a climate of fear, then it turns into hate. And it doesn't take a fear-mongering dictator running the country for it to blossom either—the fear and hate was already in people's hearts and he just told them that it was okay to hate out loud. But choosing love over fear isn't a one-and-done thing—it's a conscious choice that we have to make every day, multiple times a day. Maybe it's the immigrant family who just moved onto the street, or two people of the same sex kissing, or a sidewalk of Jewish people just getting out of synagogue, or the Black kid with his hood up handing something off to another, or the Asian tourists who seem like they're always in your way, or people watching you from their porches and stoops as you drive through their low-income neighborhood, or even just being around somebody with politics you don't agree with, but every person we encounter is an opportunity for us to condition ourselves to see things through a lens of love. Do you think the people who shot up schools and gay bars and Black churches and synagogues and all the other places that were supposed to be safe havens viewed the world through a lens of love? And yeah, it's easier said than done, and no, one person making the effort to change their mindset might not seem like it could make a difference, but it has to start somewhere. Like Dr. de Conto told the kid last semester who said his vote wouldn't matter, *"If everybody thought the way you did then nothing would ever get done."* Hate isn't something any of us are born with—it's something we acquire. And I think it's something we can un-acquire too.

Anyway.

"So I finished all the *Heartstopper* books," Ethan told me as we climbed up the stairs in Bixby to the Proud as Halle meeting.

"Oh go 'head! That didn't take you too long."

"I almost couldn't put them down," he grinned. "Do you know when the last one comes out?"

"I dunno. I think sometime later this year?"

"Ugh, I don't wanna wait that long!"

"It could be worse," I shrugged. "Imagine reading the *Harry Potter* books as they came out and having to wait years in between them."

"Oof. That'd be *torture."*

That football thing that everybody loses their minds over actually came up a few times in Proud as Halle if you can believe it, but only Rihanna's Halftime show. Bradley, Jared, and Branden were going on about her performance like it was the greatest event on Earth. They're so loud when they get going that they legit hurt my ears. I'll be the first to say that my life isn't exciting, but it's not so boring that I have to occupy myself with the lives of celebrities and internet personalities. I think that the Halftime show should be a live stream of drone strikes against a children's hospital somewhere in the Middle East instead of a musical performance, because I think that says 'America' more than a concert.

"I kept looking at her like, *is she preggo?"* Bradley squinted. "Or is she *not?"*

Jared looked like he was projectile vomiting when he said, "She *slayed* though!"

"Love that for her," Branden said.

"Period."

"She released *Renaissance,* right?" I said to Ethan to try to show him that I know at least something about pop music. "The one that almost won Album of the Year?"

And then Bradley legit turned away from their conversation to look me in the eyes like I'd called him the f-word. *"Excuse* me? Did you just say that you thought *Rihanna* put out *Renaissance?"* He put his hand over his chest like he'd just gotten harpooned. "That would be *Beyoncé,* thank you very much."

I felt my face redden. "Oh yeah, I just got them mixed up," I shrugged. *Hashtag not sorry.*

He looked at me like he couldn't believe it. "What kind of gay *are* you?" *Hashtag triggered.*

"Um, one who doesn't know their pop artists too well I guess?" I said more sheepishly than I would've liked. He gave me an *and-don't-you-forget-it* glare before turning back to his friends and forgetting we were even there. *So that's how it's gonna be?*

"Don't worry about him," Denver, another member who was sitting nearby, said. "I'm not too big into pop music either, so I would've gotten them mixed up too," she smiled. *Don't let Bradley hear you say that,* I thought as I smiled back.

___

February 14

You know who's a sneaky fucker? *Snow.* You go to bed and there's nothing, not a *flake* to be seen. And then when you wake up? Boom. There's snow fucking *everywhere.*

The Residence Life office started grouping together upperclassmen—apparently sophomores are considered upperclassmen—for rooms today, so you can bet your ass I made sure the others had their room requests filled out with all our info like a Mom. It's basically a lottery, and I'm low-key nervous we won't get one since there are probably more groups of friends who want a four-person room than there are four-person rooms. Hopefully we'll at least end up on the same floor if we don't all get the same room.

Ethan and I exchanged our "Happy Valentine's Day babes" and kisses and "I love yous" this morning at breakfast, but we're going to wait until later this week to go out to dinner since he's busy literally all day on Tuesdays. I still wanted to do something special for him to make it an extra-memorable day though, which is how I found myself at the store buying pretzels and chocolate to make him chocolate-covered pretzels, since as he himself once put it, "It's chocolate and it's pretzels—you *literally* cannot go wrong." An older woman at the store saw the card and balloon I also picked up for Ethan and said something about how there's a lady who's lucky to have such a thoughtful and handsome young man like me for a boyfriend. Unfortunately for her and her heteronormativity, the young man in question was starting to not stay quiet and just let the moment pass anymore.

"A very lucky *boy,*" I corrected her as I held up the card so she could see the *'To the boy I love'* on the front in big blue letters.

Since I'd never covered things in chocolate before—ha—I enlisted Nikole's help to make the pretzels, because all I needed was for the building to get evacuated in the middle of fucking February because some idiot burned chocolate and set off the fire alarm. I left for Macro 20 minutes early with Ethan's card and balloon and a zippy bag of pretzels so I could swing by Bixby to see him before class. There were some stuffed animals and boxes of candy and even a bouquet of flowers earlier in the day, but by mid-afternoon I was the only one who looked like a high schooler and I didn't even care, because I couldn't wait to make Ethan's face light up. I was too focused on him instead of where I was walking and slipped on an icy patch, but at least the pretzels broke my fall.

"No, goddammit!" I swore as the balloon came loose and floated out of reach. The card just got bent a little in one corner, but most of the pretzels were broken. *"Goddammit to fucking hell."* I felt dizzy, so upset that I wanted to cry. *It'll be a memorable first Valentine's Day for him, that's for sure.* Since I knew it was the only thing that had a chance to calm me down, I trudged onward to see Ethan and to give him what was left of his gift. The smile I put on his face changed to concern almost immediately, and he came around the counter to take my shoulder. *Do I really look that sad and sorry?*

"Babe? What's wrong?" he asked.

"Are you able to get away for a minute?" I asked in a low voice while trying not to cry. He went over to the counter to say something to his coworker before turning back to me.

"I told them I'm taking my 15, but I'll stay as long as you need me to," he said as we walked over to the lounge area. I planted my elbows on my knees and crossed my arms, debating if I should just make something up and throw the pretzels away on my way out.

"Happy Valentine's Day, again," I sneered more than I said as I held out the baggie of sad-looking pretzels. He saw the card and put two and two together.

"I thought we were waiting until Thursday to give each other our gifts!" he said with a genuine smile.

"I wanted to surprise you since it's your first Valentine's Day," I explained, "and I know how you like chocolate-covered pretzels so I made you some, and I had a balloon too, but then on the way here I slipped and fell and lost the balloon and broke the pretzels and—" I stopped to take a breath. "I just really wanted it to be special for you, but I ruined it. I ruined your first Valentine's Day." He was too busy reading the card and the message I'd drafted and revised 100 times in my Notes app to hear me, and set it down to pull me into a tight squeeze. If you ever need your priorities realigned, let yourself get hugged by the person you care about the most.

"Oh Trevor, thank you, *thank you,*" he looked me in the eyes. "How is this not perfect? You *made* me my favorite candy yourself and—"

"Well I had Nikole help me, so technically—"

"And then you came to surprise me at work with them? Trevor," he said like he was almost at a loss for words, "this is the best valentine I could ask for. Granted, it's the *only* one I've had, so it's the best by default. But it's the kind of valentine I always imagined." He turned back to the bag of pretzel pieces. "Besides, just because these are smaller now doesn't mean they're *ruined*. I don't think it's *possible* to ruin a chocolate-covered pretzel." He popped a piece in his mouth to savor the salty sweet crunch, holding the bag open for me.

"Nuh uh! They're for you!" I protested.

"Shut up and take a pretzel," he said as a crumb fell from his mouth. "You could use one." I picked out one of the uglier ones to save the most intact ones for him. They weren't *bad*, but the chocolate-to-pretzel ratio was off.

"I probably could've gone with thinner pretzels," I admitted.

He bit into another one. "Okay—I didn't wanna say anything, but..." he trailed off. We looked at each other and started to giggle. "No! They're still good! Just very pretzel-y." We sat there and munched on the biggest pieces.

"I definitely owe you one," I said. "Maybe we can try making them again this weekend? And hopefully I won't destroy them this time."

"I'd like that," he beamed. "It's a date then." *Yep, seeing him did the trick.* I sat in Macro with a dopey smile on my face, in love with how Ethan can see the good in just about anything, even when his mopey boyfriend tries to convince him otherwise.

Fast forward to an hour ago, when the sound of something small hitting our window made me jump. I just figured it was a stray snowball or snow sliding off the roof or something until it happened again. I stood up to peek through the blinds with my hands cupped around my face to try to see anything.

Tylor pinched an AirPod from his ear. "What's up?"

My eyes lit up. "It's Ethan!" He waved up at me from the sidewalk, nothing but smiles. I jogged down to find him already waiting in the lobby for me. "What are you doing here?" I beamed. "Don't you have your House Coun—?" He shut me up when he pulled a card and a box of candy out from behind his back and pushed them into my hands. "I thought we were waiting until Thursday to do this!"

He rolled his eyes. "Yeah, so did I, *mister*," he grinned. "I figured you deserved a surprise too since you went out of your way to surprise me, especially since you seemed kinda frazzled earlier," he chuckled. I hugged and held him tight for a good 10 seconds.

"I don't know what I did to deserve you," I said sincerely. "But it's too bad that there aren't any cute boys around to share this with," I said, looking around and making awkward eye contact with the DA.

"Well, it just so happens that I know—oh, hey Westley!" He waved at Westley, who was just leaving the rec room with a bottle of pop to swipe himself into the wing of the building opposite mine, and who waved us a small wave back. "But it just so happens," Ethan went on in a low voice, "that I know a guy, *and* he lives in this building."

"I think you just missed him," I said as I nodded towards the doors Westley disappeared through, earning myself a smack. "So why didn't you just text me that you were outside or had something for me?" I asked Ethan as I took him up to 222 Swafford.

"Because throwing snowballs at your window is more fun and more romantic than sending a text," he said as his hand found mine.

I didn't want Tylor thinking I was trying to kick him out so Ethan and I could spend Valentine's Day night doing sinful things with each other. "Don't worry," I said to him before the door even had a chance to shut, "you don't have to leave. He's not staying for too long."

Ethan raised an eyebrow. "Aren't I?"

"Stay all night," Tylor shrugged. "See if I give a shit."

Ethan's heartfelt note in his card to me had me welling up inside. "And I love you so much too," I said as I leaned over to kiss him after reading it.

"You two," Tylor shook his head. "I just can't."

Either Ethan just happened to get me peanut butter chocolates, or he's good at picking up hints. "Please don't tell me you went out to get these after work just because I surprised you with those pretzels," I said as we sat on my bed and shared candy.

"Oh no, I got these last week when we went to get decorations for our House Council event," he smiled. And then we got into a debate over whether chocolate-covered pretzels were considered candy or not.

"They're mostly pretzels, and pretzels are *not* candy," I explained in the simplest of terms.

"But peanut M&Ms are mostly peanuts and *those* are candy, are they not?" he countered.

"Mom, stop fighting with mom!" Tylor pleaded with us. He said that candy is something you shouldn't get full off of, which leaves a lot of gray area.

Ethan's card's been finding itself in my hand over and over since he left. I'll trace my finger along his handwriting and imagine him writing it at his desk, connecting his *t*s to his *h*s with a little loop at the top. And then I remembered the card that somebody else had given me on another Valentine's Day, and I prayed that Ethan's never causes me as much hurt as that one did.

February 15

Here's a temperature check of how things are going in the United States: three people died in a shooting on a college campus in Michigan and I didn't hear a single person mention it.

February 16

The groundhog and its acolytes are all full of shit. Six more weeks of Winter my *ass*—it was 56 yesterday, 53 today, and there's not a day in the forecast that dips below the upper 40s. In *February*. I'm all about warmer weather, but we're *fucked* if this isn't a fluke.

Ethan and I agreed that November 19th—the day I taught him how to longboard, the day we went to the outlets to get him a new pair of shoes, the day he both ended and started my life as I knew it with a single kiss—was our first date, even though we weren't actually together yet. So why did it take me half an hour to pick out what to wear to dinner like we were going on our first date?

I suggested Forest Ridge Taproom since it's the nicest place in town, but he counter-offered with a link to a cozy-looking Italian place in the next town over. It wasn't that far of a drive, and the muted lighting and checkerboard tablecloths that the website showed gave it a romantic vibe—more so than a deer skull mounted on the wall, anyway. Next Town Over feels a little like New Halle but without a university, which is to say it's basically a shithole. Ethan and I hurried into the restaurant even though it was barely raining, and found it to be as warm, welcoming, and delightfully intimate as the pics made it out to be. Ethan—dressed for the occasion in black jeans and a light gray button-down—helped me out of my coat like a gentleman. *And here I thought he couldn't get any more handsome.*

"Dinner will be on me," I smiled, since the prices were pushing boujee by our standards and I know that money's tight for him, but he wouldn't hear any of it.

"Absolutely not," he shook his head resolutely. "If I wasn't prepared to spend the money then I wouldn't have suggested it." In the end we decided to pay for each other's meals, which made me conscious of what I ordered despite him telling me to get whatever I wanted. "Why are the candles on all the other tables lit?" he asked me after our server brought us a carafe of water and a basket of herbed bread without lighting our candle.

"Because lit candles are only for heterosexual couples," I said like it was obvious.

"That's bullshit," he said indignantly, though he made me proud by asking for it to be lit when they came back to take our orders. I didn't look around to see if two guys having a candlelit dinner upset anybody because I physically could not peel my eyes away from the dancing flame glittering in his own eyes and earrings.

"If this isn't nice then I don't know what is," I smiled. "Good suggestion, babe."

"Thanks. And yeah, it is," Ethan smiled back warmly as his foot tapped mine under the table.

We tore apart the bread to sponge up the seasoned oil, commenting on how nice the place was and making small talk until Ethan asked me pretty much out of nowhere, "Have you ever thought about moments in your life that seemed insignificant when they happened, but they ended up changing everything?" *Now this is my kind of conversation.*

"I think about them all the time," I smiled. "I call them 'swerves.'"

"Like, 'swerve bitch?'" he chuckled.

"Yes, *that's* what I mean," I rolled my eyes. "What brought that up?"

"Nothing," he shrugged. "I was just thinking about it."

"You just started thinking about that all on your own out of nowhere? Nothing to do with how we met and how we're now having Valentine's dinner together?" I asked as our salads came out.

"No, but that was a pretty nice swerve," he smiled. "But like when I was signing up for last Fall's classes, I made myself take something I normally wouldn't take, just to see how it would go."

"Sounds like my Macro class," I said. "And did you?"

"Uh huh. Philosophy. I had a feeling it'd be boring, but I took it anyway."

"Was it?"

"It was *so* boring," he laughed. "I was *not* sad when I handed in my final exam." *Sounds like Brit Lit.* "But anyway, the one day before class, this girl gets up and gives a pitch about how any students living in the dorms should consider getting involved in their House Councils."

"Just some random girl?"

"Well, random at the time. It ended up being Ciara, the RHA President. She didn't say who she was though, so I didn't know until the first RHA meeting." He laughed to himself. "She's great. At the first meeting she told the room that if anybody has a problem with a Black woman being in a position of power then they're in the wrong damn meeting."

"I like her already," I smirked.

"But anyway, I asked my RA about it, decided to try running for President, and somehow won."

"Did you have to campaign or anything?" I asked as I crunched on a crouton.

"Yeah, I went around and knocked on open doors and told people my name and that I was running for House Council President," he said like going around and knocking on strangers' doors is something anybody can just up and do. "I was a little intimidated about it all at first, but once things started happening it became just another part of my life. I've met so many people through it. I've had fun and I've gotten stressed out. It's been fulfilling and it's been defeating. My other House Council members and I joke that it's like *The Breakfast Club*."

I dabbed dressing from my mouth and tried to think of something to say other than that I've never seen it. "So what made you think of all this again?" I asked.

"Oh, I'm thinking about running for RHA President," Ethan said casually. "I wouldn't have been able to if I were applying for an RA position since it's a conflict of interests, but since *that* won't be happening..."

"You should do it!" I encouraged him. "I think you'd win! People know you from House Council, RHA, work, Open Mic Nights, baseball—"

"It's not a *popularity contest*," he chuckled. "And even if it was, then I have my work cut out for me."

"Why?" *Who'd you be running against, Patrick Paul?*

"This is all just a rumor, so..." He looked around like the guy in the trucker hat at the next table over might be a spy. "So RHA is the only organization that doesn't get its funding from SGB, and SGB low-key hates us for that."

"Where does RHA get its money from then? Fundraisers?"

"Oh my god no, they'd have like a $50 budget," he laughed. "No, it actually comes from the washers and dryers. They have a contract with the laundry provider, and they get a certain cut of the money that goes into them. So every time you do laundry, you're funding RHA. And fun fact: Gladby Hall does the most laundry because that's where the Exercise Science majors live."

"I'll have to remember that for trivia night," I said as they brought out our food. My chicken scallopini immediately had my mouth watering. "But why's SGB upset about that? Wouldn't that be more money they get to keep in their own pocket by *not* funding RHA?"

"Maybe they just like having all the power?" he said as he twirled his fettuccini alfredo. "I don't know why though, because their events through CPB—you know, Campus Programming Board—"

"I know what CPB stands for," I smiled.

"But their events are *way* more popular than anything RHA could ever do on its own since they're not limited to catering only to on-campus students. And they have an *asinine* amount of money. I'm talking like *hundreds* of thousands of dollars. Probably over a million at the start of the year."

"Is that rumor or fact?"

"That's fact. Ciara went to one of their meetings when we co-sponsored the haunted maze with them back in October and she saw their budget. The *rumor* is that they want somebody who's in with them to run for RHA President so they can try to change things from the inside, so that either their funding *does* come from SGB, or the whole thing just flat-out gets absorbed by SGB and becomes just another club that has to petition them for money and accreditation." *Thus the plot thickens.*

"So there's more at stake here than just you wanting to get more involved," I said.

"Yeah," he nodded. "Is it likely? Probably not. Is it impossible? No. But either way, I'm sure you don't wanna listen to me talk about that all night."

"No, you're fine," I half-lied. "How's your food?"

"It's *really* good," he said like it had just called him gorgeous. "Do you wanna try some?"

"No thanks, I'm not a seafood guy."

"Not even *shrimp?* Everybody likes shrimp."

I shook my head. "Not me. I don't do fish."

"Says the guy who just ate a Caesar salad," he said as he poured himself more water from the carafe. He met my confused look. "You know those have anchovies in them, right?"

"I wish I didn't," I said into my napkin.

"But anyway, that Philosophy class is also where I got introduced to Stoicism and the idea of *hoc quoque transibit*—the idea of everything only being temporary."

"Yeah, I remember you mentioning that," I bobbed my head. "I'd say one of my biggest swerves was when I bought Blink-182's self-titled album. In terms of making me who I am today, it's right up there with when I read *The Catcher in the Rye* for the first time."

He folded his hands to give me his attention. "Oh? How so?"

I leaned over the table. "Are you sitting down?" He checked to make sure he was indeed sitting. "Back in middle school, the only music I listened to was whatever was on the radio or whatever my classmates were into."

"Shut the f...*front door,*" he caught himself. "How the hell did *that* change?"

"Their album *California* had just come out and the radio played the shit out of the same few songs, which I low-key *liked* but was getting tired of. So I figured I'd give another one of their albums a try, and I went with that one because I recognized the logo on the cover. And then from there I discovered Green Day, New Found Glory, Neck Deep, The Story So Far, West Coast alternative, and everything in between. I was so proud of myself for liking music that almost nobody else was into. The popular stuff sounded more and more like garbage to me." I crossed my arms. "I'm *still* pissed that Warped Tour stopped being a thing before I could go."

Ethan just nodded. "Thank you for telling me all that," he said after a moment.

I cocked my head at him. "Why? It's not like it's private or anything."

"Maybe not, but most people probably don't get to hear that story," he smiled. "I like being able to understand you better—not like in the sense that there's something *wrong* with you or anything—"

"Which there *is*, and a lot of it."

"But I just like getting to know *you* better. Learning about the things that make you you."

"The things that make me a grotesque," I said.

"*What?*" he chuckled.

"I'll explain later," I said as I spotted our large, decadent square of tiramisu to share coming our way.

We swapped checks when it came time to pay, though I wonder who they would've given it to if it was just one check, because when it's two guys they give it to whoever they think the top in the relationship is. Back in the relative warmth of my car, Ethan gave me a deep kiss on the cheek. "Thanks for giving me a wonderful evening. It was everything I imagined."

"It's only as wonderful as the people you share it with," I said as I kissed him back.

He unplugged his phone as we pulled up to Kessler, leaving the car silent except for the engine and the wipers. "Park in one of the 15-minute spots," Ethan told me. "I have one more gift for you." With thoughts more curious than they were dirty, I parked and put on my flashers. "You have to come *inside*," he laughed when I didn't move. He didn't take me up to 341 or into the House Council office, but through a wide open study area, and into a smaller room with the same ceiling-high windows as the rest of the ground-floor rooms that look out into the inner courtyard. And in front of the windows was a grand piano that almost looked out of place, like they just randomly had one and didn't know where to put it. "I was worried it wasn't gonna be tuned," he said as he took a seat on the bench, "but it sounded okay when I practiced on it earlier."

"You're gonna play something for me?" I asked as I watched him flex his fingers.

He nodded, looking more nervous than any of the times I've seen him perform for a coffee shop full of people. His hands rested on the keys like he'd never played for an audience before. "You know," he said to the piano's insides, "it's funny to think how I thought I knew what falling in love would be like." He turned to meet my eyes. "Trevor, I've been waiting a long time to be able to play this for somebody, and I still can't believe it's you. This is for you babe." He pushed down on the keys and slowly started to sing a song that I recognized right away, thanks to him getting me hooked on Troye Sivan—"The Fault in Our Stars."

The notes resounded through the empty room, heavy, slow at first, like awakened ghosts. Yeah, he's played for me before on his keyboard in his room, but not on a real piano after just getting back from a real dinner for Valentine's Day. Against the rainy windows, he sang with an emotion in his voice that the patrons of Brew 22 have never heard. The songs he performed for them were nothing compared to the nocturne he played for me, like we were the only two people in the building. I may not be the first person he's given his body to, but I'm the only one he's given his *self* to. And then I thought of the day that will come when one of us will have to watch the other one die, and he'll sing it for me and I'll sing it for him, so sad that the day will have arrived, but so, *so* happy that we'll have made it there together. *Dear god do I hope we make it that far.*

His hands danced across the keys as the last notes wafted out into the chilly courtyard, up and away into the misty night. I leaned down to wrap my arms around his chest from behind. "Correction to what I said after we went sled riding that one day," I said as my eyes welled up. "*That* was the most romantic moment of my life. I wish I knew how to play something so I could serenade you back."

Ethan held me by my wrists. "Trevor, you loving me after I've spent years telling myself that I'm unlovable is music so sweet, I can't even begin to describe it."

"I don't think you need to," I said into his hair.

He nestled his head into the crook of my neck. "You know that line from *The Fault in Our Stars* about how falling in love is like falling asleep? How it happens slowly, and then all of a sudden?"

"Uh huh?"

"I think that's how I fell in love with you," he said tenderly.

"Yeah, me too," I smiled. If it wasn't the most romantic moment of my life, I'd have said how falling asleep is like peeing—the harder you try to do it, the harder it is to do.

And then just when I was sure there wouldn't be any more Valentine's surprises, Tylor dropped another one on me. "Oh, FYI," he said as he dragged a razor under his chin, "I'll be going home this weekend."

My head shot up so fast I don't know how it didn't pop off. "Oh? What's the occasion?" I asked without trying to sound too eager.

"It's my sister's birthday. She doesn't know I'm coming, so it'll be a nice surprise for her," he said, though I was barely paying attention because I was too busy relaying the news to Ethan.

February 17

POV:
You walk out of your bathroom to find your boyfriend lying on your bed in his baseball jersey and a backwards hat. He slides off his pants to reveal royal-blue baseball socks and a bulging jockstrap. "Didn't you say how you'd like to sleep with a baseball player?" he smirks.

February 18

> boys
> fawning after
> thoughts
> beliefs
> identity anew
> heretical
> run astray
> sin
> vindication
> not hidden
> not ashamed
> lust
> bedsheets twisted
> dominated
> in ecstasy
> nude
> breathless
> fulfilled
> overwhelmed
> at his mercy
> powerless
> desire repressed
> expressed
> quaint caressing
> mouths
> again growing

February 19

So I was yesterday-years-old when I bottomed for the first time.

Passion wrapped my legs around Ethan, desire rocking his body against mine. He sucked on my neck as I met his unbroken movements, moaning for him. He pulled away to look down at me, his eyes telling me *I want to, but only if you do*. I nodded, my own eyes telling him *I want you to have me*.

He said that me being on top might be more comfortable for me, but I stayed on my back for him because I wanted to give him total control over me. I wanted to know the feeling of trusting another person with my body in every carnal sense. He talked me through it—what to expect, asked how I was feeling. I cried out through clenched eyes, my hands grasping for something to squeeze. How could I relax when I felt like I was being split in half? *Is this what it feels like to die?*

"We don't have to keep going," he said. *"I can stop if it hurts."*

My teeth held my lip. I shook my head.

"It'll feel better, I promise."

How did Dillon and Devon give themselves to me so quickly and so eagerly? How could Miles have expected me to do the same for him? Forget the pain and discomfort—it's the submission and the intimacy that frightened me. Elio was spot-on in *Call Me by Your Name* when he said that your asshole is the window to your soul.

Ethan took his time to let me adjust to him, each reentry becoming gradually more painless until almost all of a sudden I felt nothing but ecstasy from feeling him massage me. *"Oh my god,"* I gasped.

"Does it—"

My hand grabbed his wrist. *"Don't stop."*

He knew exactly what to do, and he did it well. He carried me off to an unthinkable, overwhelming paradise. I whimpered as he pinned me to the bed, our fingers laced together. I made sounds I never knew I was capable of making. I didn't know how I'd be able to live without the sensation of feeling him moving inside of me. I think I might've had an out-of-body experience. I craved for him to fill the cavity he left me with afterwards, like his dick was an organ vital to my body's ability to function. Even when he was just spooning me, I itched for it. He awakened a hunger that I didn't know lived within me. He didn't protest when I initiated again and again. Being able to please him in a new way—whether I did the work or let him have me however he wanted—was a gratifying new turn-on for me. His own ability was the only thing keeping us from going at it non-stop. His back would've been raked red from me clawing at it if I didn't bite my nails.

"You were lying when you said it feels amazing," I grinned after round two. "Amazing doesn't even begin to do it justice."

My jeans and his joggers landed on the floor again and again. We fucked on the couch, on my chair, against the wall, in front of the mirror. I let him have me in his jockstrap. We even recorded ourselves. He fucked me so good that he could play a song out of me by hitting the right spots. The only two times in my life I ever came without anything wrapped around my dick were in the last two days. Sometimes my meds keep me from getting in the mood, but this weekend was not one of those times.

It was cold and shitty out, so I didn't feel bad about us staying shut in 222 Swafford basically all weekend except to grab food and to get stuff for chocolate-covered pretzels, which we fed to one another and did suggestive things to with our tongues. We had to repeatedly turn down Kade and Victor's sometimes lively requests to play a game or just to hang, even though I gave Victor the heads-up after French on Friday that we were going to be unavailable all weekend. I felt kind of bad for shutting them out, but it's not like they can't turn up without us. We can turn up at 370 Rock any time, but Tylor doesn't go home every weekend.

"Vibe check?" I replied to Victor's Snap to me last night of him sitting in the red room at 370 Rock with his hat sitting askew, eyes heavy with vice and contentment.

"Eleven."

February 21

First thing's first—we got a room!

The four of us all got the same email telling us to log onto the housing portal and select a room while supplies lasted, which is how we ended up on our Macs and Chromebooks at a table in Patnick, talking out which dorm and which room we thought would be best. I didn't care where we lived—any suite that I'd get to share with my boyfriend and best friends would be perfect. Only after rooms started to gray out did we finally make a decision: Novak Hall, room 115.

"I'm so fucking *pumped*," I grinned as we gave each other congratulatory fist bumps, though not as pumped as I was for Open Mic Night. It was just a single song, but I couldn't wait to hear Kade and Victor perform alongside Ethan. They insisted that they didn't need any help transporting their instruments to Brew 22, so I braved the biting, omnidirectional wind over to Quincey Street alongside Tylor and Amina. I went up to order our drinks so they could ward off anybody looking to steal some chairs from the table we'd claimed, and couldn't help but smile as I heard some of Ethan's other fans talking him up.

"I hope Cute Keyboard Kid plays something again!"

"I wonder if that guy who did that Chainsmokers song that last time will be here?"

"I haven't seen him at Starbucks in a while. I *guess* he still goes here."

Though they'd told me they didn't need my help, my boyfriend and friends didn't protest when I offered to help carry their equipment in from Victor's shithead car. "Did you happen to bring your light?" Ethan asked me after we'd gotten everything. I unzipped my bag to grab the little disco light that I bought at Wally World that he'd asked me to bring along.

"It'll cost you one kiss," I smiled, selfishly hoping that I made people jealous when he leaned in to pay.

I watched the three of them set up, interested in the regular guitar that Kade was tuning. "You're not gonna play bass?" I asked him when they joined us at our table.

"Nah, I figured guitar would be better than bass for our song," he said. "If we had another person to play, then yeah, I would've fucking slayed on my bass."

I turned to Amina. "*You* play guitar," I said with a bounce of my eyebrows.

"I mean, I could if they'd ever needed me to," she shrugged.

I jokingly apologized to Alex and Matt and June and Andrew for not saving them any seats when they stopped over to say hi, though I would've tried to get some extra chairs for Nikole and Elisha if I'd known they were going to come. I gave them a wave, and the person talking with Nikole waved back too before making his way over.

"Trevor! What's new?" Miles smiled. "Haven't seen you in a hot second. How was your Break?"

"Hey Miles," I greeted him. "Not much, and it wasn't too bad. I'm happy to be out of that Buffalo snow though, *that's* for sure," I laughed.

"Oh I *bet*. That storm was even on the news back home!" he said as he warmed his hands. "So when are you coming back to Lit Club?"

"Hopefully soon. My boyfriend convinced me to start going to my building's House Council meetings, and it's at the same time as this," I said, though I could easily hit up both if I really wanted to. I wished he would've asked me more about my boyfriend so I'd have an excuse to talk about Ethan.

"Don't worry about it," Miles said instead. "I don't make it all the time either. *It can be kinda boring sometimes, Trevor Bentley Huffman*," he said behind his hand, making me smile, and also making me think of the alternate universe where Trevor and Miles are together because Trevor put in the effort. I didn't have to think about it for too long though, because the guy who puts all others to shame came back from the bathroom.

"Is this guy trying to hit on you, Trev?" Ethan sternly asked as he let his arm fall across my shoulder. "Because I can beat his ass if I need to." I just gaped at him, lost for words.

"Oh hey!" Miles smiled at Ethan. "It's been even longer since I've seen *you!* How've you been? How do you two know each other?"

"Uh, he's the boyfriend in question," I said a little territorially. "How do *you two* know each other?"

"He was a Starbucks regular," Ethan answered before turning back to Miles. "I don't work there anymore, in case you've been wondering why you haven't seen me." The fact that it had apparently been a while since they'd spoken put me at ease, but I couldn't stop myself from going down the rabbit hole of Miles going into Starbucks for the same reason I did—which turned into thinking about them matching on Tinder, them meeting up for coffee outside of work, Miles taking him back to his apartment. But even if they did, why should I care? I say that like it doesn't bother me.

"I don't think I've seen you at one of these before," I said to Miles as I nodded into the room.

"I couldn't come last semester because my PoliSci class on the Holocaust was on Monday nights," he explained. "The professor told us that"—he let his voice become airy and awestruck, like an electronic toy with dying batteries—"*all the professors who have taught this class have killed themselves. The rest of us are on drugs,*" he said with a creepy smile. "But anyway, I'm gonna try to get a drink before this starts. It was good to see you both again!" He gave us a wave before heading off into the room.

"Small world, huh?" Ethan smiled from behind crossed arms like we're living in New York City and not Bumfuck, PA, population 2,000 during the off-season.

"Did I ever tell you that I asked him for advice about you?" I asked Ethan, knowing full-well that I hadn't. "It was before I told you I was gay, and I was so nervous how you'd take it."

"You asked him for advice about *me?*" Ethan asked me like he couldn't believe it. "How nervous were you?"

"Have you met me?" I chuckled as the lights dimmed.

Most of the acts were first-timers, though the regulars still performed—Matt playing an acoustic song that I recognized as a Beatles one we got high to, Fedora Guy doing some kind of cringey freestyle rap, a few Improv Club members doing a skit that had most of the room dead. "Why don't you do an act with them?" I asked Victor as they left the stage. "You're good at stuff like that!"

He just shrugged. "I'm just not that passionate about it."

A sock puppet telling dirty jokes followed an actual juggling act—"What the fuck is this, *America's Got Talent?*" Kade scowled from behind crossed arms. "I wanna hear music!"—and then they were up. The three of them moved their instruments into place and plugged themselves in. I don't know when my leg started bouncing. "How's everybody doing?" Ethan asked the room as he adjusted his mic. The response was legit kind of enthusiastic. "I know *I'm* glad to be back, and I'm *hella* glad to be playing here tonight. And I have friends with me this time!" he said as he gestured to Victor, who looked at him dumbly until he realized he was supposed to be introducing himself.

"Oh shit—hi, I'm Victor," he waved, almost dropping his drumstick. "He/him."

"Kade," Kade said with a two-finger salute.

"And I'm Ethan," Ethan said. "And together, we're Three Les—" he started to say until he started hissing with laughter. "We're Three Lesbians in a Wheelchair," he managed to say as the other two and some of the audience cracked up. "Anyway, here's a song," he said as he readied himself. He flicked on the disco light perched beside him and nodded to Victor, who clacked his sticks together to count them in. Their muted, almost reluctant notes brought the song—"OK" by Wallows—to life. I almost leapt out of my chair when I recognized it.

Just like the recorded version, Ethan's digital *eeps* triggered my ASMR and pumped acid into my veins, sending delicate notes of color raining down on the room. Nothing but the bass parts weren't played live—Ethan even somehow played the keyboard parts and the synth part at the same time on the same keyboard. Kade's so good on guitar that I'm wondering why bass is his instrument of choice. He did a little dance in place when he got a break during the bridge, when Ethan rapped in a low voice with both hands on the mic and his eyes locked onto mine, making me giddy. But it was Victor who blew me away—I was worried that the song would've been boring for him since the drum part isn't too crazy, but he took it and made it his own. He kept the basic beat and rhythm, but added in his own fills and accents that took the whole thing to another level. My little light lent to the atmosphere more than I thought it would, sending tricolor dots spinning around the room. The song came to an abrupt end, erupting the room in cheers and applause that I haven't seen for any other act, even Ethan's solo performances. A few people actually gave them high-fives on their way back to our table.

"Those are my residents!" Monique cheered Kade and Victor on.

"That was fucking *amazing!*" I said before they even sat back down. "You were *all fucking amazing*. I fucking *loved* that. Please tell me you're gonna play at the other ones this year. Did you get to practice together in person? Who the *hell* came up with that name? Did—" Victor put his hand over my mouth.

"*Woah*. Woah," he grinned. "*One of us* needs to calm the fuck down."

I was so high off their performance that I don't even remember the ones that were up after them. Miles and a few others came over to congratulate them, and not just the unofficial frontman. "That was as good as the actual song!" June said.

I gawked at her. "You like Wallows?"

She looked at me like that old meme of the confused-looking girl holding her hand up. "Who the fuck doesn't like Wallows?"

"I didn't even know you guys played instruments," Nikole said with a stunned look. "Besides you, obviously," she said to Ethan.

"We thought about going with The Strudels for our band name," Victor told her. "And then we thought about Affluent Spiders, and then Umami Tsunami, and then Insulted Butter, and then Venn Diaphragm, and then Depression Cake, and then Drastic Park, and then Chemical Bidet—"

"We really liked Molly Ringworm," Ethan cut him off, "but I guess there's already a band with that name somewhere."

"I came up with Three Lesbians in a Wheelchair," Kade said proudly.

It's crazy to think that was just yesterday. I know that life can change in a moment, and always when you least expect it. It's not like anybody died or anything, but being locked up in here for the rest of the week still sucks *ass*. I just figured that my cough was a sinus thing—because let's be real, it's *always* a sinus thing—until it started to hurt to speak a little. I remember how scared I was the first time I had to take a COVID test that it'd be positive—since I actually took the global fuck pandemic seriously—so I guess it's a good thing I got my positive result now instead of back then. A student worker escorted me—looking like a duck with a KN95 mask strapped around my face—to the car the Health Center uses to transport students to take me back to Swafford so I could gather up whatever I'd need for the next few days, only half-listening to what they said. "You can retest on Sunday." "Meals will be delivered to your room." "Your professors will be notified." I shamefully avoided the eyes of anyone I passed as I carried a tote packed with stuff back to the car, and then up to the top floor of one of the wings of Wooster Hall, where all the rooms are refurbished into single studios for isolation rooms. The doors are locked from the outside.

Bro you coming to class?

What if there's an outbreak and there are more sick students than there are rooms? I guess they'd have to put two sick students together. *There's a premise for some porn.* They certainly don't do anything to make you not feel miserable. Other than the naked furniture, bed linens, towels and essential bathroom items, a single cup and a dinnerware set for one inside one of the cabinets, there's *nothing*. It felt like back when I moved in, but this is as good as it gets this time. I wish I could even just talk to the person in the room next door just so I wouldn't feel so alone. And it's so quiet too—no muffled music, no far-off voices, no sounds *at all*. Why isn't everybody singing together like people used to do from balconies during the height of the pandemic?

Am I the only person on the entire floor? If I screamed, would anybody hear me?

February 22

Fun fact: when the Black Death ravaged Europe, Milan was one of the areas that didn't get hit as hard by it because I guess any infected person along with their entire family was just boarded up inside their house and left to die. And then sometimes the townspeople just burned it the fuck down.

Nobody else tested positive. I was worried that Ethan or Tylor might have gotten sick too since I'd been around them the most. I'm sure Tylor's wiping down the entire room. He actually put together a care package of soup and crackers and Powerade and medicine to give to Jaxon to have brought up to me since he lives in Wooster—which, what a nice roommate. I'm extra grateful for it too, since the meals I'm provided are just Patnick food in a to-go box. Maybe they have Paul spit in it as an extra fuck-you.

I talked to Mom and Dad twice in the last two days, which brings the total number of times I've talked to them this semester up to three. It's sad how you forget about the people in your life until you need them, even if it's just to listen to you wallow in your self-pity. They always took the pandemic seriously, but they still think it's "ridiculous" that I have to isolate. Like, what else would the school do with me, just let me go and infect the whole student body?

My professors emailed me what to work on—"If you're able to"—which won't take very long since there's nothing here to distract me. I mean, I have my Switch and some books, but those only keep you busy for so long. I may or may not have accidentally read *Real Life* all in one sitting even though Dr. Davis only just had us start on it. I liked it so much that I sent it to Zoe from Proud as Halle as a recommendation for their featured book of the month. It's too bad I'm not still into *Minecraft*, because these five days would've been up last week. I'm actually embarrassed by how much I used to play *Minecraft*—yeah, it passed the time, but how many people are on their deathbeds who would do anything for more time? And here I am trying to make it go by. I wish I knew somebody who could get me some edibles so I could put on some Beatles or Angels & Airwaves or *Rick & Morty* or something and think silly, arcane thoughts instead of all these self-mutilating ones.

February 23

Another fun fact: solitary confinement was actually first used as a punishment in the U.S. in Pennsylvania. Those Quakers. I guess they just locked people in a room with a bible until they reformed themselves—never mind the psychological effects it had on them, and never mind if they were as mental as I am. The UN actually considers it a form of torture if it's for more than 15 days.

How is this even allowed? Is this *really* the best the university could come up with—the same university that always talks up its mental health resources? I don't know how students aren't furious about this. I feel bad for the sick kids at the Christian college down the highway because they probably get beaten out of the belief that the virus can be expelled through prayer and bodily harm like it's 1400. At least there's a window I can look out of. It's nice to know that the world is still out there and that students are going to class or to eat or to the gym or whatever, but it sucks that I can't be a part of it. Other people who were locked in here before looked down and saw me living like everything's a given, like I'll be young and healthy forever, like nothing will ever come to pass. How was I so stupid to think that?

Dr. Jurado taught us the term 'ceteris paribus' last week, which is basically the assumption in economics that everything will continue as it is, which is bullshit because change is the only constant. I'm only just now realizing that I've been living ceteris paribus-ly—that I've let my life continue as it always has without trying to do anything about it. It sucks how it always takes something unfortunate to realize that.

Ethan's been calling me at least once a day, which has helped keep me somewhat sane. I don't have much to say, so I ask him about his day, small things that have never crossed my mind to ask him. I sounded like a deck of motivational prompts. "Who was your most memorable customer today?" "What made you smile today?" "Do you need to do your laundry?"

"Why are you asking me weird questions?" he laughed.

"Because you'd miss everything too if you got locked in a room," I snapped. "I'm sorry. It's just...this is *really* starting to suck."

He gave me a sympathetic look. "I know babe. I'm sorry this had to happen to you."

"It has to happen to *somebody*, so why shouldn't it be me? But this too shall pass." *Hoc quoque transibit.* If I ever get a tattoo, that'll be shortlisted for one.

Tylor's been checking on me every day too to see how I'm feeling or if I need anything. I could always ask for more books, but why do that when I can stare up at the ceiling for hours and think about all the people who don't worry about everything all the time, who are confident, who are never sad, who are popular, who have thousands of Instagram followers, who have never laid awake at 2 in the morning wondering why they just can't be *normal,* whose lives are better and more interesting and more fun than mine ever has been, who are being better versions of themselves than I can ever hope to be of me? It's scary how effortless it is to fall down that rabbit hole, like how effortlessly it would really be to kill yourself.

But Kade and Victor? I haven't heard from them at all today. They can't be so busy that they forget to text me. And then there are all the texts I didn't get from people whose days are no different whether I'm in them or not. Am I just being needy and craving attention? It's possible.

Ethan cheered me up by sending a link to a video he recorded just for me. It made me think happy thoughts for a while, but then I started thinking about him and Miles and the way they looked at each other, like they had a secret I wasn't in on. There's no way they didn't sleep together, maybe more than once. Is it bad of me to get off to the thought of that?

I actually feel okay right now, but I'm sure they wouldn't let me out.

What if I didn't actually test positive and this is just some experiment the Psych department is conducting? I can't prove that the Health Center worker wasn't just someone gathering research for their dissertation. I never actually saw the test result, so who's to say they didn't lie to my face and now they're watching me on camera to see how long it takes before I start peeling off my own skin? They'd see a ton of masturbating, *that's* for sure.

I wish I'd grabbed the Teddiursa stuffie from my room. I wish I could just fall asleep for the next 72 hours. It'd pass the time and let me get away from my thoughts—assuming my dreams wouldn't torture me too.

Holy *shit.* Imagine if my meds ran out while I was in here.

February 24

POV:

June 16, 2022. 8:14 p.m. Your boyfriend tells you with tears in his eyes that after everything and all the things you said to each other and all the dreams you had with each other and all the promises of "forever and always" that the two of you aren't going to work out after all because going to two different schools will be too hard and even after you tell him you'll switch schools to be with him whatever it takes he tells you that it's for the best which is when you start to cry because he used to tell you that you were always his best.

The bad thoughts started again after Victor asked me if he could borrow my sled. Nobody ever wanted to go sled riding when I wasn't locked in a room and now all of a sudden they do? It's like middle school all over again, when my friends would hang out with each other but never with me unless I asked them to. I think I wasn't their friend as much as somebody they tolerated when they had to. Was it because I wasn't as loud or as outgoing as them, because I wasn't into sports or girls or wanted to stay up all night playing *Call of Duty?* Did they know something was different about me before I even knew it myself? Maybe I really was just a nerdy loser who nobody wanted to be around, and being gay never even had anything to do with it. Are the friends I have now no different? Do they only hang out with me when it's convenient for them? Am I being irrational?

They're probably going out to 370 Rock tonight, and I'm sure it won't make any difference to them that I'm not there. Victor will still get high, Kade will still get to smoke hookah, and Ethan...I don't know what Ethan will do. Maybe when he's buzzed and without me at his side, his phone will slip itself out of his pocket, and Tinder will open itself up for him. *No, stop that.*

POV:

June 17, 2022. 12:57 a.m. You're sitting stunned after you drive into a telephone pole because there's as much tequila in your veins as there is blood and only then do you realize how loud your music is playing and how fragile your life really is but it doesn't matter because you're apparently disposable anyway.

I was today-years-old when I learned there's a music genre called grungegaze. I've been listening to Citizen and Movements and the other stuff that Ryder used to listen to all the time, which I *get* now. You can be utterly alone with a mind that won't stop, but music is *always* there for you. It *understands* you. Why isn't there a religion of music? Why did it take me so long to give this stuff a try? I mean, I *know* why, but at least I would've had something to turn to. God, how different would things have been if I'd been open with Ryder? We could've just listened to emo together and been there for each other like we should've been doing all along.

You know what it was? It was jealousy. Jealousy and a lack of consideration. Jealousy and a lack of consideration and choosing fear over love.

POV:

June 22, 2022. 6:45 p.m. Your classmates are accepting their diplomas while their parents cry happy tears for them but you're still sitting on your bed in your shirt and a tie crying sad tears because you can't bear to see your ex again or even hear his name and you don't understand how people can possibly be happy when your world's fallen apart again.

POV:

February 24, 2023, 11:31 p.m. Your heart warms and you can't help but beam when your shitfaced boyfriend calls you, because the people you love are the people you call when you're drunk.

February 25

I saw on Kade's story that they're at the bowling alley. I guess it's Charlotte's birthday and Alex invited them along. I actually feel sick. I wish I had a box cutter, but at least I have my music, and at least I have Instagram and the profiles of people whose lives are better than mine and who are having more fun than me and who have friends who actually like them. What color would my blood run if I sliced my wrists open? Wouldn't it be a vibe if the Blue & White Society was right this whole time and we actually *do* bleed blue and white? Maybe it wouldn't even be blood. Maybe it'd be hoisin sauce or music notes or alphabet soup but all in French. I'd put my lips to it and suck and suck, letting it run down my chin and stain my shirt as I savored the taste of my own life. What if I sawed through my wrists with the butter knife just so I could see what a severed hand or the stump of a wrist looks like? Or if I smashed my head through the window and ran my neck back and forth along the jagged rock candy mountain range of glass? My blood would run down the side of the building and it'd look like the people in the room below just have a Halloween window cling up year-round. And once I knew it was too late would I have a moment of regret? I like to think that Ryder had a moment like that. I almost want to try it, just so Ethan and Tylor and Victor and Kade will feel bad for living it up and stuffing their faces with pizza slices and hookah hoses and joints and dicks without caring about their boyfriend and friend who'd been lying dead in this room the whole time. Haters would say it's a cry for attention and they'd be absolutely right.

Ethan answered on the second ring. "Trevor! My *baby!*" It was loud where he was and he sounded drunk, again. "Why'd you regular-call me instead of FaceTiming me?"

"Because I've been sleeping even worse than I usually do and I look like shit," I said truthfully.

"I *doubt* that." I could hear him smiling. "Besides thinking he looks like shit, how's my baby?"

"I'm okay," I lied. "I just wanted to call you so I could say I love you."

"Why? What's wrong? You never call me just to tell me you love me." The noise around him got quieter until I could barely hear it.

"I know, and I'm sorry that I don't," I said through closed eyes. "You've been nothing but good to me and I feel bad about the times I've hurt you, whether I meant to or not. I just want you to know that I'm sorry for that."

"Trev, you're kinda scaring me," he said, and he sounded it. "This is like the kind of phone call someone makes when they're talking to somebody for the last time."

"I've just had a lot of time to think about things and what's really important in my life, and my mind keeps coming back to you." I wasn't just saying it to be romantic—it's true. "Like, I think about how if I would get hit by a car, my last thought would be how I never told you enough that I love you. So that's what I'm doing. I'm telling you that I love you while I'm able to, because someday I won't be able to. We both know that. Life's too short. I love you, Ethan," I said like tears weren't running down my face. "I love you so much."

"I love you so much too Trevor," he croaked. "I love you so fucking much. You're gonna be outta there soon, and we're gonna spend so much time together. I'm gonna tell you I love you every day, because you're right, I don't do it enough either, and someday I won't have the chance to."

We were silent for a few moments as he sniffled. "That was pretty much it," I said as I ran my sleeve under my eyes.

"I'm glad you said it, because I needed to hear it."

"So how's your night going?" I asked after a moment. "Are you at Alex's again?"

"Yeah. We're just smoking hookah and other things. You should've seen Victor," he laughed, the laugh I'd taken for granted. "Just before you called, he was asking if crab apples were the ones that grow on trees." I laughed with him, happy to know that they were going out and living life, upset with myself for selfishly expecting them not to.

I'm thinking about that scene at the end of *Don't Look Up* where they're having dinner and chatting like they weren't about to all get wiped out by a meteor, instead of hugging and telling each other how much they meant to each other. Because it's all the little, ordinary, insignificant things that make up your life and make you into the person you are. It's the sum of the parts that's greater than the whole, not the other way around.

What that has to do with being locked up in here, I don't know. I just really hope that I test negative tomorrow.

February 26

Today it finally came to pass.

The most welcoming sound I've ever heard was a knock at the door and someone asking my name, even if I wasn't in the clear yet. And then once I was, I noticed everything, felt and appreciated *everything*—the give of a door's push bar yielding to my force, the shock of chilly winter air on my face, the blades of grass poking through the snow. I don't want to take any of it for granted anymore. Having to wear a mask for a few more days is a price I'm more than willing to pay if it means getting to experience the world again and be a part of it. And the most welcoming feeling in the world was falling into Ethan's arms. I'm glad he's understanding of me wanting to stay masked up, even though nobody can really *make* me wear it.

"Please," he told me with a derisive chuckle, "I was the only one in my family who ever wore a mask when we'd go out during COVID. My family would always pull the civil liberties card." Which, isn't it funny how people only ever cite their civil liberties when they're trying to justify shitting on other people's freedoms? And by 'funny' I mean 'you can go fuck yourself.' I think the whole anti-masking thing was just white people finding out they don't like being told what to do despite having spent hundreds of years telling everyone else what to do.

"I'm gonna guess they aren't vaccinated then?" I asked.

"What do you think?" he rolled his eyes. "And of course when my stepdad *did* catch COVID it was super mild, so he kept saying how getting the shot is more dangerous than the virus." Even if COVID vaccines turn out to be dangerous and everybody who's gotten one *does* just up and die all at once, the only people who'd be left are the ones who think the 2020 election was rigged, and I think I'd rather just be dead than live in *that* kind of world.

We celebrated my release with lunch at Zukoff, where we tried to convince Ethan how splitting up the country—like how some of the more fanatical Repubes want to do—would only be beneficial for the more progressive states. "Imagine how nice it would be to take all the shitty-ass, backwards-fuck things out of this country," Kade said as he moved the invisible basketball he held from over his plate to over his cup, "and to put them in a different one."

"If fucking *only*," Tylor said from behind his own mask.

We spent the rest of the afternoon in 222 Swafford, chilling and drinking tea and playing games. I listened to the highlights of my friends' weeks like I couldn't get enough of them. *I'm never taking this for granted again,* I thought as I laid in my own bed. I remember how dead and empty my room felt the day I moved into it, but now I don't think there's any place that feels more like home to me.

February 28

My second test came back negative too, so I can be mask-free again, guilt-free.

"Look at this loser," Kade narrated the video on his Snapchat story from the POV of his window of me walking to Macro with my chin buried into my chest to try to keep the wind out of my face. *"Have fun walking across campus in this shit, nerd."*

Spring Break is only three weeks away, but I figured I'd go home this weekend for my birthday. I asked Mom if Ethan could come home with me too, even though I already knew what the answer was going to be.

"And also, I wanted to ask," I said, suddenly aware how stupid it sounded even after all the times I rehearsed it in my head, "what the chances are that my friend could come up with me and stay for the weekend?" Her silence made me start making things up on the spot to try to convince her. "We wouldn't be in the house the whole time. We'd be going out and doing things, hanging out with Logan, going out to eat."

She answered an eternity later. "I'll have to see what your father thinks," she said like I'd just asked her for $1,000 but it somehow wasn't an automatic 'no'. "Where would he sleep? I'm guessing this friend's a boy, right?" *Yeah, but why the fuck should that matter,* I didn't say.

"I can get the air mattress out of the attic!" I said.

She let out a long exhale. "I don't know, Trevor, I—" I heard the oven timer go off. "I have to get my roast out of the oven. We'll talk about this later." *Translation: no.*

"Okay," I sighed. "Last week was just really crappy for me, and I just—"

"We'll talk about it later."

I threw my phone down onto my bed after we hung up without caring how immature I was acting for not getting my way. I don't even want to go home if he can't come home with me—I'd rather just stay here and celebrate my birthday with him and my friends and wait until Spring Break to see Mom and Dad. I'm sure it wouldn't have been an issue if I hadn't come out yet or if I was straight. Hell, I'm sure if I *was* straight and asked if my theoretical girlfriend could come and stay for the weekend, Mom would say *Of course!* and *I can't wait to meet her!* and *What does she like so I know what to make for dinner?*

March 1

I learned a new phrase at work today—*ichi-go ichi-e*, which can be loosely translated as 'for this time only' or 'once in a lifetime.' Basically, it's the idea that every single moment of your life is unique and unrepeatable, which is a thought I've had before. I guess it's the same concept as that saying about not being able to step in the same river twice but better, because anything Japanese is automatically cooler.

Ethan was tied up with RHA, Tylor had his European Film class, and Kade was working on a project in Arrowood, so it was just Victor who joined me at Percy's for dinner. "Why do I get the feeling you just wanna see your name up on the wall of Double Nuclear challengers?" I smirked on the way there.

"So what if I do?" he smirked back. "And don't you mean the wall of...*victors?*"

I pointed down the hillside. "You need to *leave.*"

"I'll be *pissed* if we get there and it's not—*hold the fuck* up." He stopped to gawk at a poster in one of Bixby's front windows that made my jaw drop right alongside his.

"You're *actually* shitting me right now," I gaped. "Reel Big Fish? *The* Reel Big Fish?"

The concerts that CPB sponsors are usually country or rap or pop, so I was thrilled to learn that I'd have the chance to see one of the foremost names in third-wave ska on Friday, April 7th at Overholt Gymnasium for only $10. "How *the fuck* did they get Reel Big Fish to play here?" Victor asked as we made a beeline for the info desk.

"Fuck if *I* know. Do you think Kade would wanna go?" I asked him as I texted Ethan about it.

"He—I—yes," he stuttered. "The short answer is yes."

Do you wanna see reel big fish?

"I would've never pegged you as a ska guy," Victor said as the girl at the info desk took our payments. "I don't think I've ever heard you listening to it."

"I haven't in a while, but I used to listen to the shit out of them when I went through my ska phase."

If getting handed a ticket to see Reel Big Fish wasn't enough to put him in a good mood, then seeing his name on a list of last month's Double Nuclear Challenge victors did. "Look at that," he smiled as he zoomed in on it to post it to his story. "I know you're jealous."

I rolled my eyes. "Oh yeah, because I'm so jealous that I didn't get to cry and shit and puke all at the same time." I sent Tylor a pic of his name spelled 'Tyler Hayoshi.'

*real big fish?
You don't even like fish lol

Too bad I already got you a ticket

"So now what?" I asked Victor after we'd set our empty trays in their spot. "I don't wanna head back to my room just yet, I don't have any new bands to make you listen to, and I'm not sure if I'm in the mood to play anything."

"We could go see a planetarium show!" Victor suggested. "They have them on Wednesday evenings!"

The planetarium is a big, circular room right in the middle of Devlin that's only two rooms down from where my Physical Science class was last semester. It's smaller than I expected, but the domed ceiling plastered with stars still caught my breath. "Did you say this is where your Astronomy class is?" I asked him as I reclined my seat back almost horizontally like I was about to get my teeth cleaned.

"I *wish*," he said as his own chair tilted him back. "It's just in a regular-ass lecture hall. I found this by accident when I was trying to find my Chem Lab class last semester." I forgot that he and Ethan had class together, and thought about how they went from being just NPCs to some of each other's best friends. Wouldn't it have been a vibe if Victor knew that Ethan liked me too and just kept both of our secrets to himself? I'd legit be pissed.

I didn't really have any expectations for what a 'show' would be, so I can't exactly say I was disappointed when the student facilitating it just played YouTube videos on the ceiling instead of waving around a laser pointer or something. After the Liberty Mutual jingle assaulted us from all sides, we zoomed backwards and away from Earth, passing the sun, passing the other planets, the dots that are other stars, the arm of the galaxy, other galaxies, dots that are other galaxies, dots that are clusters of galaxies, dots that are clusters of *those* dots. I know the universe is big, but Jesus *Christ*. I was relieved when we started shooting forwards again, all the way back to our own Pale Blue Dot. *There's no way we're alone in all this.* And everybody who *does* think we're alone in all this better wise the fuck up and start taking care of this thing, because it's all there is. Isn't there a bible verse about being good stewards of god's creation? You wouldn't know that though because I guess it's not one of the important ones, like the 'god doesn't make mistakes' one that people use to try to justify transphobia.

"That was pretty cool," I said as we left the planetarium a handful of videos later. "It really does put things in perspective."

"Exactly," Victor said, wrist-deep in his pockets. "I wish that more people—"

"Hang on, my dad's calling me," I cut him off once I saw the name on my buzzing phone. "Hold that thought."

Rude," Victor frowned.

"Hello?"

"Hey Trevor, how are you?" Dad answered. "You're not busy, are you?"

"Hi Dad. I'm not bad. And not really—my friend and I were just about to do a line off the toilet seat." Victor snorted.

"On a *Wednesday?"* Dad chuckled. "We only ever did that kind of stuff on the weekends." *Thank god at least one of my parents has a sense of humor.*

"Pics or it didn't happen," I laughed with him. "Nah, I was actually at the planetarium they have in the science building here. They have a projector and show videos of stars and the universe and stuff on the ceiling."

"Well that sounds interesting," he said like it wasn't. "I don't wanna keep you then—I just wanted to call to let you know that your mother and I are fine with your friend coming home with you for the weekend," he stopped me in my tracks.

"Wait, *really?" Did you hit your head? Did Mom hit her head?*

"Yeah, it won't be a problem. It's your birthday, and you had a rough week last week."

I didn't know what to say other than, "Thank you, really." I knew Victor wouldn't pry, so I had to spill it to him. "I asked them if Ethan could come home with me this weekend for my birthday and he said that he could!"

"Go 'head!" he smiled. "I didn't know you were going home! But that's *two* weekends in a row now that we won't be able to hang with you!" he said like he was legit upset about it. "When are we supposed to turn up for your birthday?"

"The weekend after that, I promise!" I said, though I know that 'next weekend' isn't something I can promise him.

March 2

2 a.m. saw me lying awake in bed, thinking about the universe and our place in it. I remember how the beginning of *Independence Day: Resurgence* said how the nations of the world gave up war and conflict to build each other up and worked as one human race to make Earth the best Earth it could be after the alien invasion in the first movie. I thought that in a time of division that COVID would be what

would bring us together as a country, and holy fucking shit was *I* wrong. I hope the people who made *Don't Look Up* knew how fucking spot-*on* they were.

Ethan was today-years-old when he listened to ska for the first time. "Isn't it like screamo with trumpets or something?" he asked me on his tea-and-me break. I got taro milk tea after overhearing someone telling her friend that it tasted like the milk leftover from a bowl of Lucky Charms cereal, which is 1,000% accurate.

"You didn't look it up?" I asked. "You're pretty good with looking up new music."

"I know," he said almost apologetically. "Last night was kind of stressful, and I guess I just forgot."

"I didn't know you had a stressful night," I said sincerely. "Was RHA stressful?"

"Yeah. Some of us introduced legislation that would allow for gender-neutral housing in the dorms." His eyes fell to the table, looking both annoyed and disappointed. "You'd be surprised at how many people are against it."

"Forreal? Why?"

He laughed mockingly. "For any reason. The most popular ones were guys and girls having to share a bathroom, and a couple who'd have to keep living together if they broke up." He rolled his eyes. "Like, we made it clear *multiple* times that people would have to *request* it. It wouldn't be two random strangers just getting thrown together."

"How's that any different from any other unfixable roommate issue?" I asked, getting into it. "Don't they just make them both move out? And what about two boyfriends or two girlfriends getting a room? That's *literally* what we did."

"My point exactly," Ethan said. "It's almost like straight people are being discriminated against for being straight." *No comment. No fucking comment.*

"And the Housing Office doesn't even know who's in a relationship! We're just besties for all they know," I said as I gestured between the two of us.

"Trust me, we spent all night arguing about it," he crossed his arms. "All I know is that we have a long road ahead of us."

I sipped my tea, worked up over something that doesn't even affect me. But what would society look like if people only cared about the things that affected them personally? "So how'd you get involved in that? Did somebody ask you if you were on board with it or ask for your signature or something?"

"The opposite, actually," Ethan said as he rubbed the back of his neck. "I had to find other people to get on board with the idea."

I stopped sucking and let my boba pearls slide back down into my tea. "What do you mean, *you* had to find people?"

"It was my idea in the first place."

"Forreal?"

He gave me a small smile. "You sound surprised."

"I—I mean—I'm more proud of you than anything," I said, feeling a Victor-level of respect for him. "What made you wanna do it?"

He hesitated for a moment. "It's not really my place to tell, but..." he lowered his voice to a whisper. "My bathroommate Hunter started transitioning, and they'll eventually have to move to a different room, which I think is pretty fucking stupid. So I figured I'd try to do something about it. And if it doesn't happen, I'll make it my number one priority if I end up becoming RHA President."

My chair pushed itself out so I could get up to give him a hug. "I'm actually *super* proud of you right now." *Gryffindor all the fucking way.* "Can anybody who's not in House Council do anything to help get it passed?"

"I guess it's like how any representative government works—they can petition their House Council members to support it and vote for it."

"Consider it done," I said as I sat back down.

"Thanks. That means a lot to me," he smiled. "Oh! And remember what I said about SGB wanting somebody who's in with them to run for RHA President?"

"Uh huh," I nodded.

"I found out that Westley—who's in the same frat as Aiden Fuentes and who's buddy-buddy with the SGB people—is planning on running too."

"Well isn't that convenient for them?" I said as I wondered if Aiden's ever left Westley with a cream pie. I hadn't mentioned anything to Ethan about coming home with me yet because I didn't want to get him all stoked and then let him down in case Mom and Dad said no. "Do you have any plans for this weekend?"

"Some guys on my floor asked me if I wanted to be on their team for a dodgeball tournament on Saturday, but I think that's it. Why?"

"How big of a deal would it be if you missed it?"

"Not *that* big of a deal," he shrugged. "I guess they'd just have to find somebody else to take my spot. Why?"

"*Well,* I'm gonna be going home for my birthday this weekend, and—"

He slapped a hand to his mouth. "Oh *fuck!* I totally forgot it's your birthday!" He grabbed the sides of his head. "Shit fuck double fuck! I won't get to see you for it either!"

I took his wrists and lowered them. "Well, I was *gonna* ask if you wanted to come home with me for the weekend," I chuckled.

"Forreal?" he asked. "But what about—"

"I already asked them and they said yeah," I smiled.

"Wow, how'd you convince them to let your *boyfriend* stay for the weekend?" he grinned.

My smile faded. "Uh...I just asked them if my *friend* could come and stay."

His face fell a little. "Oh." He looked down at his tea. "So I guess they don't know about us?"

96

"No," I winced.

"Well, I haven't told my parents about you either," he chuckled. "So I guess that's fair. When would we leave?"

"You wanna come?"

"Of *course* I wanna come," he squinted. "Why *wouldn't* I wanna spend my boyfriend's birthday with him? I'll just have to hang back tonight though to make up for the work I won't be doing." He sat back in his seat with a smile. "So what kind of stuff are we gonna do while I'm home with you?"

"I'm not sure. I haven't thought about it yet." I laughed. "I mean, I know what I'd *like* to do, but my parents will be right down the hall, so I don't know if we'll be *able* to."

March 3

POV:

You and your boyfriend just discovered the best way to throw pope hat paper airplanes and you're having *way* too much fun doing it, like a scene from a coming-of-age rom-com movie where the characters are laughing through face-splitting grins, having the time of their lives while some upbeat '80s alternative song drowns everything out.

March 4

I like how instead of straight-up saying they're targeting 'the LGBT groups'—which they *are* doing, just to be clear—the red states are claiming the laws they're trying to pass to ban drag shows are to 'protect the children.' Why the hell do people feel the need to protect kids from drag shows and Pride parades but not church? Is indoctrination okay if it's at church, even though church is *way* more damaging? I guess a kid not seeing a drag show is more important to them than a kid being able to go to school without getting gunned down. And what 'LGBT groups?' Queer people?

Showing Ethan an entire side of my life separate from the one he knows at NHU had me feeling antsy, but not as antsy over how Mom and Dad would react once I tell them he's not just a friend. It's not like seeing their son with another boy will be anything new to them, but still. "This is the farthest north I've ever been," he said from my passenger seat as the bland, highway-green 'Welcome to New York' sign zipped by. At least the 'Welcome to Pennsylvania' sign looks like a wine-tipsy aunt who's happy to see you. "Will I get to meet any of your friends?"

"Madi, the one with a crush on you, is away at school. Logan just goes to community college though, so he'll be around."

"Community college would've been the smarter choice for me financially," Ethan said, "but I wanted a *real* college experience. Besides, I had to get away from home." He sighed. "Who knew that being gay would be so expensive?" he chuckled. "I shouldn't complain though. I wouldn't trade the experience for anything, and I've met some pretty cool people too." He smiled and gave my hand a squeeze. "Have you ever gotten road head before?"

"Do you *want* us to crash?" I laughed.

He gave me a pouty look before turning back to the window. "No fun."

As if going home doesn't already get weirder every time I do it, trying to see it all through Ethan's eyes was even weirder. I couldn't tell what he thought of West Seneca as he watched the side streets and the houses pass by as we headed up the main drag, which seems kind of rural once you really notice it. *Is it just like you pictured it?* I wanted to ask when we pulled into my driveway.

Ethan's mom probably loves taking him places to show off how well she raised him. He took his shoes off right away, and his compliments were sincere. "You have a beautiful home, Mrs. Huffman," he said. "Thank you so much for letting me stay." He even addressed them as "sir" and "ma'am."

"Maybe I should start making *you* call me 'sir,'" Dad joked with me. I shot him daggers with my look. Mom asked me why I didn't bring home any laundry to wash.

I watched Ethan take in my room, nervous that he was underwhelmed at what he saw—like when you finally see the *Mona Lisa* in person, according to Dr. Le Marque, or when you realize that the Tinder match's pics are at least a few years old. He moved from my pictures and posters to my records to my books.

"Holy *shit* is this heavy," Ethan swore when he picked up *The Count of Monte Cristo*. "And you've *read* this?"

"Nope," I admitted. "I'm not sure if I'll ever even get around to it."

He put the tome back on its sagging shelf. "You should Marie Kondo what you won't read if they're just taking up space."

"I like the way they look! This is my vibe!" Or at least it used to be—they *do* seem kind of extra now.

"That's how hoarding starts," he laughed. "So I assume I *won't* be sleeping in your bed with you?"

"All I told them was that I'd blow up the air mattress," I smirked. "I didn't actually say either of us would be *sleeping* on it."

He ran his finger up my neck and up my chin. "What a deceitful young man."

"They're gonna think we're gay if they see you doing that," I chuckled.

"Oh my *god* do I wish you were gay," he smirked. "The things I'd do to you."

I showed him Dad's office and Mom's craft room from their thresholds. He took a sightseeing tour of pictures of me as we circled the first floor. Misha boredly let him pet her before disappearing behind the couch. There was a bowl of candy on the living room table, which was weird because there's never a random bowl of candy just sitting around unless we're hosting Christmas or Thanksgiving. I ate one and offered him one that he politely refused. I kept asking him if he wanted any until I just tried forcing one into his mouth. "Stop—I don't like coconut!" he said through pursed lips as he wrestled me away from him. I popped it in my mouth just as Mom poked her head in.

"Don't eat too many of those," she said like I'd blown through half of them. "Dinner will be ready in a few minutes, so you can come and take your seats. I hope you like lasagna," she said to Ethan.

"Lasagna's one of my *faves*," he smiled.

I sat across from my boyfriend so Mom and Dad wouldn't think we're gay or anything. "Why don't you sit beside Ethan?" Dad said more than asked as he cleared the mail off the table. I eyed up the chair like it was booby-trapped. "Ethan, what would you like to drink? We have iced tea, Pepsi, ginger ale, moonshine..."

"I'll have Pepsi, please," Ethan chuckled.

"I'll take some moonshine," I said.

Mom walked in holding a silverware caddy that I've never seen before. "Ethan honey, would you mind helping me set the table? And Trevor, go see if your father needs a hand." I got up and left an eager-to-help Ethan with my lobotomized mother to go clomp down the basement steps. *What, he can't carry up some Pepsi by himself? He's not 80. And 'Ethan* honey?' *Where the hell'd that come from?*

"Mom sent me to help you," I said to Dad's turned back. And then after a moment, "Why are you both acting weird?"

He straightened up to give me a look. "Weird how?"

"You're both acting like—like there's—" My hands fell to my sides. "You know he's my boyfriend, right?"

"Of course we know," he chuckled. "Nobody brings home just any old friend with them on their birthday weekend to meet his parents."

"And you're *okay* with that? You're acting like there's nothing wrong with that."

"There *isn't* anything wrong with it—which yes, I suppose us acting like this *would* make it weird for you."

"I guess I'm just..." I let my eyes wander around the basement. "I mean, why now? You acted like Dillon and I just had a really strong bromance when we were together. So what changed?"

He set the drinks down on the washer to face me. "You not being here is what changed, believe it or not." The breath he took told me shit was about to get deep. "If you ever have a kid someday, you'll understand when they move out. The house is silent, and you start to think about all the things you missed out on and the opportunities you passed up and the things you could've done differently." And I know he didn't mean just me. He leaned his hands on the table reserved for containers and stray hangers, swallowed, and met my eyes. "Trevor, I'm going to be honest with you, and with myself. Your mother and I...we failed as parents. Everything we believed, everything we thought we were doing right—none of that meant anything if it meant that you, or your brother..." He pressed his thumb and forefinger to his eyes. "I just want you to be happy now. Whatever that looks like for you, that's all I want for you." My own eyes started welling up. "After everything we put you through, whether it was intentional or not, we owe you that at the *least*. And if you resent us for the rest of your life because of what we did, I'll understand. If my parents had done to me what we'd done to you, I know that *I* sure as hell wouldn't have forgiven them."

I was at a loss for words as our impromptu father-son heart-to-heart tore mine apart. I found myself forgiving them right there in the basement—after all their ignorance, their denial, their anger, their bargaining, and everything else that made my journey of self-acceptance and self-love more difficult than it ever needed to be. But I do think he's right about one thing: a small part of me does hate them for what they did, and I'm not sure how long it'll take for that to go away, if ever. I hugged him and he held onto me, both of us fighting to not sniffle too loudly.

"Is there anything else that gave us away?" was all I asked.

He chuckled after a moment. "I caught him looking at your butt a few times." *Way to be discrete, Eth.* We laughed and sniffed. "Try to get yourself together before you go back up," he said as he patted my shoulder. "You know how your mom gets when she starts asking questions." I laughed and dabbed my eyes with the paper towel he offered me just as Mom called down to ask if we were ever coming back up.

"Dad?" I said at the bottom of the steps. "Thanks." One word—one simple word that meant a thousand more.

Ethan beamed at me as I helped him carry salad bowls to the table. *"They know about us,"* I whispered when it was just the two of us.

His face fell. *Is that good or bad?*

It's good, I grinned.

Mom and Dad tag-teamed him with questions while we ate, hitting him with all the basics—*where are you from, how are you liking college?* "So Ethan, what are you studying at New Halle?" Dad asked him.

"I'm majoring in Communications," Ethan said. "I'd like to work in the music industry someday."

"That sounds fun!" Mom said. "Trevor *loves* music." I just rolled my eyes.

"Dad was hoping you'd say you're majoring in History," I told Ethan. "He's a history professor at the University of Buffalo."

"No way!" Ethan said genuinely. "That's *way* cool!"

"A school that Trevor could've gone to for next to nothing, I might add," Dad said to his plate as he dabbed a napkin to his mouth. I gave him a bored, *we've-gone-over-this-before* look.

"So how'd you two meet?" Mom asked. "Do you live on the same floor?"

I let Ethan answer for us. "Oh no, I live on the other side of campus."

"We didn't meet until, what? A month or so into the semester?"

"Yeah, he came in for coffee. I worked at the Starbucks on campus."

"I said how good you were at Open Mic Night! There's an Open Mic Night at this coffee shop in town that he plays at."

"You *flatter* me."

"And then we started hanging out—"

"I think he came in for coffee just to see me."

"I mean, that was part of it."

"I was always happy to see him walk in."

So that's how my parents came to be laughing with my boyfriend and I over dinner. They recounted anecdotes about me when I was younger, nodded while listening to him tell them about himself, smiled at his remarks of my idiosyncrasies that they're all too familiar with, and treated him like he's already a member of the family. *Where were these people two, three years ago?* I thought as I watched Dad compliment one of Ethan's videos I convinced him to show them. Mom glowed after Ethan described her getting free products from work as 'dope.'

"So do you have any plans while you're home?" Dad asked mostly me.

"Not sure," I shrugged. "We're gonna meet up with Logan in a bit. And then I'm not sure what we're doing tomorrow yet."

"Don't forget we're going out to dinner tomorrow," Mom reminded me.

"Oh, yeah. Ethan too?"

"No, he has to stay here and fend for himself," she said. I blinked. *Wait, did Mom just make a joke?*

We ferried dirty dishes back to the kitchen before we attacked Mom's banana cream pie. "I thought you might wanna look through this," Dad said to Ethan as he set my yearbook down in front of him.

"Dad!" I protested. "He doesn't wanna see that!" *Although, they wouldn't try to embarrass me if they didn't like him.*

"Says who?" Ethan smirked.

"Here, let me show you his senior picture," Dad said as he flipped through the pages. "Here he is," he pointed.

"Wow, look at you," Ethan smiled. It was September, but you'd have thought Summer was just starting with my sunglasses hanging off my shirt, my longboard just behind where I sat, and the unscuffed white Vans. And my smile was genuine too, because a boy was sweeping me off my feet.

Once the table was cleared—"Thank you again for dinner, everything was really good!"—Ethan headed for the living room with my yearbook tucked under his arm. "Where are you going with that?" I called after him.

"I'm not done looking at it," he turned back to smile.

"Just remember there are some things you can't unsee!" I said, and I didn't just mean an unattractive candid shot of me. I turned to the kitchen, where Mom was putting away leftovers. "Do you need help with anything?"

"No!" she whispered, nodding towards the living room. "Go be with him!"

I plopped down on the couch beside Ethan and draped my arm over his shoulder, looking at him looking for me among the pictures of people I didn't care about and groups I wasn't a part of. "Oh there you are!" he said as he pointed to a picture of me, not having a clue that the person wearing an identical fit for Twin Day wasn't just some friend, or that one of the seemingly most popular guys in school was my world at the time. My teeth clenched my tongue as he got to the prom pages. The largest picture—a photo of two elated boys wearing matching tuxes and crowns, one of them literally in the arms of the other—brought him to a halt. 'Prom Kings,' the text beneath it read, 'Dillon McKay & Trevor Huffman.'

Ethan stared, and swallowed. "Is that…?"

"Yep." I gulped. "That was actually the first time a gay couple was ever crowned prom kings. Or queens for that matter. Not queens like that—I meant two girls hadn't been—"

"I know what you meant." He stroked the picture longingly, gently, like it was yellowed newspaper ready to flake apart. He ran a finger under his eye.

"Shit—here," I stammered as I reached for the book. "I'm sorry you had to see that."

"It's not that," he said indignantly as he held onto my yearbook. "I told you, you're allowed to have a history. It's—" I caressed his shoulder and let him find the words. "It's just that…I used to dream about asking a boy I liked to prom, or getting asked. Something cute and cheesy, with balloons. And I never got to have that. I'll never get to have it. Watching other people get to have a real prom experience, with…" he trailed off, his voice carrying the same resentfulness that Dad gave me permission to harbor. "Everything that contributed to that—my family, my upbringing, religion—I don't think I'll ever be able to forgive them for never letting me have the chance to be myself, to let my teenage years be my own. And now that chance is gone," he said with a bitterness I'd never heard from him.

"Trust me when I say I get what you mean," I tried to console him. "But that was high school though. None of this stuff matters anymore," I said as I jabbed my finger into the asscrack of the open book.

He closed it and set it on the coffee table. "I need to use the bathroom," he said as he opted for the upstairs one.

I mentally cursed Dad as I put the yearbook back on its shelf. "Is the air mattress still in the attic?" I asked him. "I can go bring it down now."

Dad slung the damp dish towel over his shoulder. "Don't worry about the air mattress."

I blinked. "But—I thought—what about—"

"I think your bed's big enough for two people. We're not going to treat you like you're a teenager anymore," he winked.

I furrowed my brow. "But I am a teenager."

He flicked me with some water. "You know what I mean."

I walked up to my room in a daze and fell face first onto my bed. *What is happening?* "What's wrong?" Ethan asked when he found me. "Are you dead?"

I spoke into the comforter, my words too muffled for even me to understand.

"What?"

I rolled myself over. "They told me I don't need to get the air mattress and that they're okay with us sleeping in the same bed." I folded my arms on my stomach. "I don't know what's happening anymore."

"I mean, *I'm* not complaining."

"Neither am I." I sat up to meet his eyes. "Are *you* okay?"

He sat beside me. "Yeah, I just...I haven't totally come to terms with my past yet, and sometimes I start thinking about it too much, and...yeah."

"I told you, overthinking things is my job!" I said as I patted his thigh. "I used to struggle with my past too, and who I used to be, and the things I didn't do." My foot swung in circles, knocking against his. "But you know what? If you compare yourself to anybody but the person you used to be, then you're wasting your time. Besides, weren't *you* the one who told *me* how college is our chance to do what we want and be who we want?"

"Probably." He frowned for a minute before a smile crept across his face. "You know what? You're right. You're right," he chuckled. "Fuck the past. I'm who I am now, and I can do whatever I want. And I have you with me too." His squeezing my hand turned into full-on hugging me. "Thanks babe. I needed to hear that." He squeezed me, and we took turns squeezing each other back and forth. "Prom king though, huh?" he said. "*That* had to have been pretty cool."

"I guess," I tried to downplay it. "I didn't like all the attention."

"Did your school try to do that weird outdoor prom thing junior year too? With the tents and shit?"

"Yeah, but I didn't really know what to expect since it was my first time going." He gave me a confused look. "I didn't go freshman year," I explained, "and we obviously didn't have it sophomore year."

"Why didn't you go?" he asked me like he couldn't believe it.

"Um, because I was even more introverted then than I am now?"

"Oh, I couldn't *wait* to go. I felt like such hot shit going to prom," he smiled before changing the subject. "So what exactly are we doing tonight? You said we're meeting up with Logan?"

"I figured we'd just go over to our one buddy's place. But we don't have to if you don't want to," I quickly added. "I wouldn't mind staying in if that's what you wanna do."

"Nah, let's go out. We can stay in any weekend."

"Until one of us catches COVID," I muttered.

We walked to Logan's since it wasn't freezing and since I had a feeling we'd probably be drinking. "This is where I used to play tee-ball for about five seconds," I told him as we cut across the park. "I spent *a lot* of time at that playground when I was little. That's the ice rink. There's the library."

"Why do you own so many books when you can literally *walk* to a library?" Ethan frowned. "Why not just borrow them and save yourself the money and the clutter?"

"I told you—it's my vibe," I said with finality.

I'd forgotten how long the street that leads to Logan's is when you're not traveling it on wheels. I shot him a text and he emerged from his house on the corner, greeting me with our usual handshake before turning to Ethan. "And you must be Ezra," he said as he gave him a normal-people handshake. "I'm *joking*, I know it's Ethan."

"It's good to finally meet you!" Ethan grinned. "Trev talks a lot about you."

"Oh really? He's told me everything about you too," Logan smiled. "And I mean *everything*."

I don't know why I was low-key worried that Ethan would be turned off by Logan's geyser of playfully inappropriate comments when he's friends with Kade, but the two of them hit it off with each other right away. "Does this other friend live in the woods?" Ethan asked as we left the paved road behind and made for the grassy path through the trees.

"Nah. We're actually going to his grandparent's house," Logan said instead of answering with a witty Logan comment.

Ethan gave me a confused look. "Why his grandparent's?"

"Trust me, it's not as weird as it sounds," I assured him. "He stays there like half the time anyway." Logan and Ethan only had about a minute to get to know each other before we found ourselves on the dead-end side of Parker Tam's grandparent's street. Logan led the way past the cars parked in front of the house and up to the front door, which opened on its own as soon as he reached for it.

"Coming through guys," Parker said in an annoyed voice as he pushed past us, holding a tied-up plastic bag at arm's length. "I'll be right in." The three of us traded looks and headed inside. There were a dozen or so people there, most of whom were either still seniors or went to community college, and only one of whom I was genuinely happy to see.

"Oh, hey Ian!" I said as I gave Ian Umoh a fist bump. "This is the friend whose place I was at on New Year's," I explained to Ethan. "Ian, this is my boyfriend Ethan."

"Wattup Ethan?"

"How's it going?"

"Are you back home for the weekend too?" I asked Ian.

"Nah, it's Spring Break for me," Ian smiled. "Just got home today."

"Already?"

"Dude," Logan said as he cracked open a PBR. "I don't know *what* the people who come up with your guys' academic calendar are doing. You're like a week or two behind literally *everybody* else," he said as Parker returned. "Do we wanna know what was in the bag?"

"It depends," Parker said. "Are you in the mood for a poop story?"

"Ew, what the fuck?" Logan laughed.

"Let me guess—you're gonna throw up?" I said to Ethan, who dry heaved.

"Please don't," Parker pleaded. "I'm done cleaning up bodily...things for the night."

I introduced Parker and Ethan after Parker washed his hands. "Are your grandparents gonna get turnt with us?" Ethan asked him.

"*That'd* be a vibe. Nah, they're actually at the hospital."

"Oh shit," Ethan apologized. "Is everything okay?"

"It's eh. My grandpa's always in and out of there, and my grandma goes to stay with him."

"Is that why you're able to have friends over?"

"Nah, they don't care. My grandma tells me I just can't have any girls over."

"Which is funny because he's gay," I smirked.

"Lucky for me," Parker bounced his eyebrows. "Here, help yourself to some bevvies." He motioned to two 24-packs of beer that I get the feeling Grandma Parker didn't leave for him. "There are some wine coolers out in the garage too, if piss water isn't your thing." I led Ethan out to the detached garage and got lost in the sudden, painful thoughts about Parker taking a friend up to the room he has there to 'study' or 'hang out.' I twisted the cap off a bottle and let the boozy flavor of artificial strawberries wash down my throat and tried to keep myself from thinking about it for too long.

A few people who were at Ian's New Years party asked me if I'd brought Drunk *Jenga* again, and I kind of wish that I had instead of letting it watch Tylor and Amina take advantage of having 222 Swafford to themselves. It would've been more fun than the Kings and *Cards Against Humanity* and the actual cards that we played. It wasn't a total waste of a night though, because I got to get tipsy with Ethan and Logan and Parker and Ian and a few other people I don't hate. Ethan struck up conversation with total strangers in a way that I could never do. He and Ian talked about Penn State since that was one of the schools he was considering. I didn't say anything about it being my birthday this weekend just to see if anybody remembered. Nobody did.

We stayed until just after midnight before we left to make the walk back. "Well I hope you enjoyed that at least somewhat," I apologized to a fairly-drunk Ethan. I'd be running behind a bush to piss every five seconds if I'd had as many wine coolers as he did.

"Yeah, I had fun," he smiled. "Everybody seemed nice."

I watched us take the shortcut back through the trees from the POV of whatever creature with a hunger for human flesh lurked just out of sight. "Don't hate me, but I still haven't gotten your gift yet," Logan winced as we left him off at his house.

"You don't have to get me anything," I waved him off. "What are you up to tomorrow?"

"Work, and then I'll be with Sara in the evening."

"So you're saying you can't hang?"

He shook his head with a glum smile. "I cannot hang."

"So I won't get to see you again before we go back?"

"Don't worry about me. Just show your boyfriend a good time." He shot me a wink.

"Oh, he will," Ethan laughed.

"I'll be back in two weeks for Spring Break," I said. "And then we'll have to figure out when you can come down and visit!"

"Yeah, I've been waiting on *that* invite for a while," Logan said, making my stomach pang with guilt.

We all hugged goodnight—"See ya later *dad!*" "*Love you!*"—before Ethan and I walked down the middle of the street hand-in-hand. "I feel like he and Kade would get along," I said.

"Oh my god, *yes*," Ethan laughed out loud. "So who's Sara?"

"This girl he's been seeing."

Ethan stuck out his tongue. "Ew, girlfriends."

"A subject you know nothing about," I joked.

"I know more than *you* do!"

"Oh? How so?"

It took him a few seconds to say, "Remember how I said I lied about having an ex-girlfriend?"

"Yeah?"

"I kind of *did* have a fake girlfriend in high school."

"Like, so people wouldn't think you're gay, or what?"

"Yeah. Including her. And me."

I screwed up my face. "Wait. Start over."

He sighed. "There was this girl who I was kinda friends with who liked me, and I pretended I liked her back because I thought that having a girlfriend might make me straight," he said stiffly. "I still feel bad for making her waste her time on me when she could've been with someone who legit liked her back. She was even willing to wait until marriage to have sex after I told her that's what I wanted so I wouldn't have to do it," he said to the pavement. "She was so hurt when I told her we wouldn't work out. She didn't believe me when I told her it was me and not her."

"Wow, that's..."

"I did it to protect myself," he said defensively. "Don't tell me you've never said or did something hurtful to keep your sexuality a secret."

"Oh no, I have." *Oh, I have.*

Our living room window was the only one on the street with a glow peeking out from behind the curtains. "Okay, you gotta act like you haven't had anything to drink," I said as the curb caught the toe of my shoe.

"Like this?" He let his arms hang down and swing loosely as he zigzagged up the sidewalk.

"I'll give you all the money in my wallet if you go in like that," I said as I double-checked that I had the right key ready so we'd look sober, though Mom and Dad were both already asleep on the couch under a blanket with the Netflix screensaver on the TV. Quietly, we draped our coats over dining room chairs and sipped glasses of water in the kitchen before sneaking upstairs with a box of Cheez-Its. Sitting on my floor with the door shut, we talked and laughed and scooped crackers. *I wonder what the person at the post office would do if you tried to mail a letter with a Cheez-It taped to it for a stamp?*

"Do you still miss him?" Ethan asked out of nowhere. I didn't have to ask who he meant.

"No, not anymore," I said truthfully. Even if Ethan wasn't in the picture, I really think I would've made peace with the fact that Dillon didn't want to be with me anymore.

"Why'd the two of you break up?" *Break up, like it was a mutual understanding.*

"He wasn't willing to try to make a long-distance relationship work," I said simply. "But he never told me *why* though. And I guess he got tired of me begging him to tell me what it was about me I could fix and what I could work on if it meant we could stay together, because he finally just ghosted me. Blocked me on everything. Never heard from him again."

Ethan moved the box out of the way so he could sidle up and embrace me. "There's nothing about you that needs fixed. You know that, right?"

"I know that *now*," I said as I squeezed him back. "He told me that being with me would hold him back from meeting other people, better people. But I never thought that the same could be true for me too."

Ethan's eyes lit up. "You mean I'm better than he was?"

I just laughed. "You're *infinitely* better than he was."

"Then thank you Dillon," he smiled. And then, probably because he was drunk, "Do you still love him? Like, what if he messaged you and said he made a mistake and wants you back?"

"Then I'd tell him that's too fucking bad," I said seriously. "I have too much self-respect to go back to anybody who'd hurt me like that, even if I was still single."

Ethan just nodded. "What was he like?"

I gave him a look. "Why do you wanna hear about my ex?"

"I don't wanna hear about your *ex*," he said as his fingers grabbed mine. "I wanna hear about the people and things that made you into the guy I'm crazy about."

Where would I even start? He used to help me with my Chemistry homework, and I'd help him with his History. We'd spontaneously go out to eat or to the mall or bowling or mini golfing. Sometimes we'd drive just to drive. I used to think he was the most talented guy when I'd watch him perform in the school's musicals. This one time he chased me around the cafeteria with a Brussels sprout. Would you believe that he actually got me to go to a Sabres game with him? I always used to feel so alive when I was with him.

But instead, all I said was, "You know how I say 'mmkay?' I started doing that because of him. There were a few other Dillons at school—"

Ethan sat up so fast that he scared me. "Was Dylan Minnette one of them?"

"Yes, Dylan Minnette, who's in his mid-20s, went to high school with me."

He fell back into me. "I knew it."

"But anyway, people would always just call him 'McKay,' and when we started talking I'd say 'okay McKay' to try to be flirty, which turned into 'mmkay McKay.' And now it's just something I say," I half-apologized.

"Don't be sorry for it—it's a part of who you are now," he said as he looked up at me with those thoughtful blue eyes. "I was gonna tell you this earlier but I forgot—but earlier when you were downstairs with your dad, your mom was telling me

108

how you seem happier now, and how that makes her happy. I'm happy that you're happier now too."

We blew each other, and my bed sighed under us in satisfaction, having forgotten what it was like to offer itself as a place for two boys to fulfill each other. "It'd be nice if we had bigger beds down at school," I said as we made out afterwards.

"This extra room *is* really nice," Ethan smiled. "We just have to get Nate or Tylor to move out, and then we can make one big bed."

"That'd be *so* nice."

We fell asleep in each other's arms, even though there was room to spread out. *"You didn't deserve what he did to you,"* Ethan whispered as I was on the verge of dreams I don't remember. *"You didn't deserve to have to feel like you weren't good enough, because you're more than enough."* And then he said the one thing I swore I'd never say to anybody even if they begged me too, even if not saying it made me look like an asshole—something that made me remember that it only takes a moment for a life to never be the same again. *"I would never do anything like that to you."*

There's a universe out there somewhere where unpopular, introverted, alternative-music-loving Trevor and popular, extroverted, pop-music-loving Ethan go to the same high school and meet and fall in love and have the kind of senior year you see in movies—where Ethan shows Trevor what it's like to be alive and carefree, where Trevor has friends and goes to parties and never has to eat lunch by himself because of Ethan and the people he's met through him, where they end up on Homecoming court and wear matching fits on spirit days that land them on the school's website, where their parents have the other over for dinner and are nothing but supportive of them, where they break curfew to go to a late-night movie or cosmic bowling and don't get home until well after midnight—where, after everything they experienced with each other and because of each other, one doesn't dump the other a week after the most magical night of their lives. And present-universe Trevor is happy for them—as much as it hurts to think about them —because present-universe Ethan is right there beside me when I wake up, and ex-boyfriends and chances not taken and missed opportunities and lives not lived don't mean a fucking thing anymore.

March 5

You know how some bibles have Jesus' words highlighted in red? Why isn't that the whole bible? What's even the point of the rest of it? Call me a woke, agnostic leftist, but if Jesus' teachings are what Christianity is all about, isn't the rest of it pointless? Or are people just that into the fandom that they need thousands of years of backstory and secondary characters? Anytime anybody uses Christianity to make somebody else's life harder, it's never the words of Jesus they cite, it's almost always some shit from the Old Testament. Like, wasn't the whole point of Jesus coming to Earth to do away with the Old Testament by establishing a new covenant? The New Testament isn't big on oppressing people who are different from you though, so I guess I answered my own question.

As much as I wanted to just lay there and cuddle with my sleeping boyfriend, I pulled myself out of my bed to make coffee for the two of us, which turned into making a whole pot so it'd be there for Mom and Dad. *I should really get a French press when I'm home for Break*, I thought as I took two mugs up to my bedroom. "Wakey wakey, eggs and bakey," I said as I opened the curtains to a cloudy morning.

Ethan stirred without lifting his head. "Is there really?"

"No. But I made coffee though."

He rolled over and sat up, blinking as his glasses unfolded onto his face. "Thanks babe," he said, making kissy faces at me until I met him with a real one. I crawled back under the covers beside him and watched him sip his coffee. "What?"

I looked from his glasses to his bedhead to his *what's-so-funny?* smile. "Nothing," I said, by which I meant *'this is perfect.'*

We worked on the Mini Crossword and the Wordle together, staying in bed until we finally decided to make an appearance downstairs. Dad was making a clamor with pans and Mom was watching the local Saturday morning special on TV, both of them with a mug of coffee left by the coffee fairy—emphasis on 'fairy.' "I'm making some pancakes," Dad said as he set a bag of flour on the counter with a *thud*. "Do you want me to make you some, or are you gonna go out for breakfast somewhere?"

Ethan and I traded looks. "Yeah, we're down to fu—*I mean*," I chuckled, "yeah, we're down for some pancakes. Chocolate chip?"

He dug a half-bag of chocolate morsels out of the cabinet. "They can be."

We listened to the pancakes sizzle from the kitchen table, watching Dad work them like a hibachi chef. "I used to call pancakes 'flappies' when I was little," Ethan recounted.

"Why don't you still?" I smiled.

"I will," he said adamantly. "I'll ask Patnick Paul for a flappie the next time I see her."

I snorted as I tried to come up with what the Urban Dictionary definition for *that* would be. *"Pretty sure you won't be getting a pancake,"* I said in a low voice.

"Have you thought about where you'd like to go for dinner yet, Trevor?" Mom called over.

"Not yet, but I can," I said. "Actually, you know what I'm feeling?"

"*Yourself?*" Ethan muttered under his breath like a Kade.

"Hibachi. I can't remember the last time I had that."

Mom and Dad and even Ethan all exchanged glances. "Sure, if that's what you'd like."

Ethan thanked Dad for breakfast, and even offered to rinse off his own plate. "So what's on today's agenda?" he asked me.

"I'm not too sure. I figured maybe we could start at this cafe-slash-bookstore that's kinda nearby? And then figure it out from there?"

Ethan nodded. "Yeah, I could go for more coffee."

I pointed out places of interest on the way there—my school, the places Logan and Madi and I used to hit up for food on Thursdays when we'd get to leave school early. "Holy *fuck* is your school close," Ethan swore. "Let me guess, you used to longboard there?"

"Less than you'd think," I admitted. "I drove most of the time because I liked feeling like a senior." *And because it was a little tough to pick up your then-boyfriend on a longboard.*

"How unsustainable," he said out the window. "Although I probably would've done the same thing if I had a car then," he chuckled.

"Do you have one now?"

"*Pfft,*" he blew off the idea. "I can't afford a car. And then insurance? Nuh *unh.*"

"So you'd take the bus to school as a senior? Didn't you hate that?"

"It wasn't as awful as you'd think."

"And what about getting to work?"

"Also the bus."

"The same bus?"

"*Yeah,*" he rolled his eyes, "my *school bus* dropped me off at work."

"But you have your license though!"

"That just means I know *how* to drive," he smirked.

"You're one of the few," I muttered.

"So did your parents buy you your car?"

"I...actually inherited it."

"Really? I wish one of *my* relatives had left me a car," he chuckled, sending my mind to a bad place until he started asking me about my school again.

We browsed the books at Dog Ears, but I didn't buy anything because I knew he'd judge me. "Out of all the books we had to read in school, this was the one I hated the most," I said as I held up *A Separate Peace.*

His jaw dropped. "No *way!* I hated that one too!"

111

I gave him a look. "Did we just become best friends?"

He took a step towards me. *"I don't know,* did *we bro?"*

My hand found his face. *"Bro, I like,* really *wanna kiss you right now."*

"Well then do it, bro."

"I will, bro." I pecked his lips.

"Is that the best you can do, bro?"

"Wait until later, bro."

"Oh dad."

I would've suggested taking our coffees for a walk around the park if the weather wasn't shitty. "There's a game store nearby, if you'd wanna go check that out," I suggested instead. "I've only ever been there for video games before, but they have a shit-ton of board games too."

"Sounds good to me," he smiled. "I'm just here for the ride and the cute boys," he said as his eyes stole a glance at the cashier's bubble butt.

I could tell Ethan was enjoying the game store more than the bookstore by how many things he picked up to check out. "Did you ever collect *Pokémon* cards?" he asked a display stand of packs of cards.

"Collected them, yeah. Played the game, no," I said as I turned over a starter box in my hands. "I still have them up in my closet."

"At least *one* thing made it out of the closet," he chuckled.

Ethan convinced me to go halfsies with him on a cute game called *Everdell* about woodland animals building a city in the forest—"Yeah, but is it $70 cute?" I asked when I saw the price—by selling it as a gift for our room next year, and after I checked with Kade to make sure he didn't already have it. "And also because it's your birthday," he said with a kiss to my cheek.

"Whatever you need to tell yourself," I smirked. "Maybe we can crack it open later on?"

"I'll crack *you* open later on," he laughed.

From there we headed to the mall, where Ethan learned that there's almost nothing that infuriates me more than a car that comes to a complete stop at a green arrow. "Ooh, let's take some cute couples pics!" he said when he saw the photo booth near the vending machines and the trucks you can pay a quarter to ride. I followed him into it, not telling him that once upon a time I took cute couples pics in the very same booth with another person who meant the world to me, but that didn't stop me from trying to make the moment any less special for the two of us. We took our photo strips of us cheesing it up and kissing and just being goofy into BoxLunch, FYE, the Vans store, Five Below, American Eagle, Hollister, and the Lego store, where I learned that Ethan might not have grown up as well off as I did after he told me that he always asked for Legos for Christmas but never got any. "My Mom would tell me that Santa didn't make enough and that's why I didn't get any," he said forlornly to a giant roller coaster display. I almost bought him a set to try to put a smile on his face, but I knew he'd protest me spending that kind of money on him, even for a smaller set.

As much as I wanted to devour some Indian food—"Doesn't it taste like eating ass?" Ethan chuckled—we just got some pretzels at the food court so we wouldn't be full for dinner. "Hypothetically, would you rather do an escape room or go to Dave & Buster's?" I asked him.

"Hypothetically?" Ethan considered it. "Dave & Buster's. I'm not really in the mood to possibly get killed at the moment."

I stopped mid-chew. "Killed?"

"You know how you said you don't do haunted houses because they'd be the perfect place for somebody to get away with murder?" he asked. "Same goes for escape rooms. Who's to say that the people who are literally *locking you in a room* aren't psychopaths, and that the ceiling or walls won't crush you or something?"

"*Sheesh,*" I gasped, shocked that nobody's made a six-installment horror movie series about people dying gory deaths in escape rooms yet. "I never thought of that!"

"You're welcome," he said as I let Kade know to avoid escape rooms at all costs.

Good looks fam
Self preservation

Ethan and I agreed that the initial tokens we bought at Dave & Buster's were all we were going to buy, because that shit can get *expensive.* The marked-up dollar store—I mean, prize room—didn't have anything that I wanted other than *maybe* some shot glasses. "You can have my tickets if you want," I said as I held my card out to Ethan.

"Nuh unh, they're yours!"

"What am I gonna do with any of this stuff?" I asked as I gestured around at some of the same things I saw in Five Below.

"You don't want another coffee mug? Or underwear!" He grabbed a pair off the hook. "Look, there's little sushi rolls on them! You can wear them to dinner!"

"Nope. They're all yours." I stuck the card in between his fingers.

He walked around the place twice without picking anything up. "What if I don't want any of this stuff either?" he finally chuckled.

"Just get something," I shrugged. I looked around for ideas for him, and my eyes landed on a nearby kid looking up longingly at a *Pokémon Monopoly* game on one of the upper shelves. "We don't have enough tickets for that, bud," his dad was telling him.

"That's a pretty cool game, isn't it?" Ethan said to the kid, who looked up at him and nodded shyly. *That'd be my gay awakening if I was that kid.* "I'd get it, but I already have it at home."

"Is it fun?" he asked Ethan.

"It's so much fun," Ethan smiled. "I wish I had it back when *I* was a kid." He flashed him his ticket cards. "You think you'd have enough for it if I let you have my tickets?"

The kid's dad put out a hand. "Oh no, we couldn't—"

"It's not a problem. Really," Ethan insisted. "Somebody did something nice for me earlier, and now I'm just paying it forward."

The dad looked like he wanted to refuse so bad. "What do you say?" he told his son gravely as he took the cards from Ethan's offering hand.

"Thank you," the kid said simply and quietly.

"Now just make sure *you* do something nice for someone else, okay?" Ethan smiled.

"Well that was nice of you," I said as we headed across the arcade floor. "You should bring your copy of the game back to school with you when you come back home from Break."

"Oh, I don't actually have it. I just said that to hype him up."

"Oh, okay." I furrowed my brow. "Who did something nice for you today?" I asked as I turned to see the employee getting on a step stool to grab the game.

"Nobody," Ethan said. "But it has to start somewhere. Although, I guess your dad *did* make me pancakes."

"He kinda *had* to," I laughed as I slid my phone out to ask him what the plan was.

Your mother wanted to stop in the garden center at Lowe's just to 'look around' 😑

Better him than me, I thought.

We beat them to the restaurant even though Lowe's is practically across the street from it. We ordered some edamame and dumplings to share while Dad got some sashimi for himself. "Well I know what gene Trevor *didn't* inherit," Ethan smirked.

"There was a time when I wouldn't have touched this stuff either even if you would've paid me," Dad recounted. "It was actually my roommate in college who got me to try it." *Maybe that's what college roommates are for—to introduce you to new things*, I thought as my teeth squeezed an edamame bean from its pod.

Hibachi is always fun because you get a show with dinner, even if the strangers sitting next to you inevitably try making small talk. Like, where else can you watch someone blow a train whistle while they set fire to a ziggurat of onions? I never actually *try* to catch the chef's serve because I'm low-key afraid it'll go straight down my throat and I'll choke, but I did it to look cool for Ethan—which was how nine people watched a piece of broccoli bounce off my face. But even that wasn't nearly as bad as the staff singing "Happy Birthday" to me in two different languages. Ethan must've told them it was my birthday because Mom and Dad *know* that I hate being the center of attention. I got a bowl of green tea-flavored ice cream out of it though, so there's that. Ethan looked like he'd just gotten slapped when Dad said it would all be on one check.

"They didn't have to pay for my dinner!" he told me afterwards in my car. "I was planning on paying for myself!"

"Trust me," I told him with raised eyebrows, "there was a time when they would've *never* paid for the dinner of the guy they knew I liked."

"Well," he said after a moment, "I guess I should be honored then."

Our last stop of the day was the ice rink, which we just walked over to after changing into some thicker socks. "Somebody in my class lost a finger while ice skating here once," I told Ethan as we came upon the rink.

"Oh my fucking god, I'm gonna throw up!" he heaved. "Forreal?"

"Well, *part* of their finger. But yeah, they fell and somebody skated right over their finger." It's too bad it wasn't Kyle Brewer's wrist or neck that got skated over though, because that's what he deserves for being a fucking asshole towards me and Dillon and probably all the other queer kids.

"Maybe we *shouldn't* be doing this," a shooketh Ethan said.

"Just don't fall," I shrugged like it was that simple.

We traded our shoes for skates and clumsily plodded across the floor. We hugged the wall for support before we held onto each other's hands, even after I almost slipped and took us both down. I didn't even think anything of two guys holding hands like only couples do until another skater had something to say about it.

"What's up, fags?" some kid in a hockey jersey said as he zoomed past us with his hands in his pockets.

"*That's* the best you can do?" Ethan called after him with a smile before I could say anything.

"That didn't upset you?" I asked him.

"Sure it did, but I don't want him to know that he got to me," he grinned. "Stoicism 101: either roll with the insults or ignore them, and they lose their intended effect."

I chewed the inside of my cheek. "You've mentioned that before. What is it exactly?"

"An insult? That's when—"

"Not *that*," I laughed. "Stoicism."

"I know. I just like to get you worked up," he smiled. I took off my beanie to slap him with it. "It's a school of philosophy, but more of a training-your-mind philosophy instead of dichotomy paradoxes and that kind of shit." I nodded like I knew what he meant. "Tylor at least knows about it. That skull poster he has with 'memento mori' on it? That's a Stoic thing. 'Be mindful of death.' And I know he owns a copy of *Meditations* too. You should ask him if you can borrow it. I can see you getting into it."

"Yeah, maybe once Midterms are over and once I'm done with the book I'm on now," I said, though I know I'll have to get a start on *Invisible Man* for Black Lit soon.

A Harry Styles song came on, and Ethan took off like he was racing. "This always sounded like a good skating song to me," he smiled when he slowed to stay with me after lapping me twice.

"Where'd *that* come from?" I practically shouted. "Were you hustling me when you said you were bad at skating just so I'd agree to it?"

"I swear I haven't done it in years!" he insisted. "Maybe it's muscle memory? You just gotta get a good rhythm going." He coached me on copying his wide strides, and it wasn't long before I was gliding at a good speed, though nowhere near as quickly as him. After an hour on the ice, we turned in our skates and left the rink, walking awkwardly in our flat-soled shoes.

We showered after we got home—separately, since we weren't alone in the house and actually wanted to get clean—and unboxed *Everdell* at the dining room table. Dad tried to make sense of our game before telling Ethan how he used to play *Axis & Allies* with his college buddies and how he's happy he's able to break it out with his son sometimes. Mom threw us a curveball when she told us they were going out to the movies to see a late showing of the new *Winnie the Pooh* movie, which she apparently didn't know is a slasher. Ethan and I did what any two teenagers in love do when they have the house to themselves—we sat on my floor and listened to music. Ethan browsed my records and slid out the ones he recognized to admire their physical manifestations. "Yeah, they almost *do* sound better on a record," he said with a squint a few songs into *LP3*.

"Did you not believe me?" I smirked.

We laid in opposite directions with our heads together, feeling the music's weight as we talked about hometowns and childhoods and innocence lost until he asked if he could see my *Pokémon* cards. We picked through a tin of cards and flipped through a binder of cards to Waterparks' *Greatest Hits*, tilting the holographic ones to make them shimmer, and pointing out our favorite pocket monsters from the games.

116

"I kinda wish I *had* gotten that *Pokémon Monopoly* game from Dave & Buster's now," Ethan said as I put the cards back on the shelf in my closet. "Do you have a *camera?*" he asked as he pointed to the box next to it.

"Yeah? You do too. Open your phone and I'll show you," I smirked.

He gave me a look. "I mean a *real* camera, like a Polaroid."

"It's actually a Fujifilm, thank you very much," I said as I reached for it.

"Whatever. It prints photos right from it though, right?" He turned it over in his hands like he'd never seen anything like it, which I guess he *hadn't.* "How do you take a picture?" he asked as he looked at me through the viewfinder.

"First you press *this*"—he gasped as the lens popped out—"and then this is the capture button. But it's out of film, hence why it's up in my closet."

"You should get more film and bring it back to school with you! We can take pictures like how they used to take instant pictures at parties and stuff! Do you have any that you took with it?"

I grabbed the Vans shoebox with 'open for nostalgia' Sharpied on it to sift through the trinkets and mementos for the envelope of the pictures I'd kept for myself. "That's the treehouse Logan has in his backyard." "We went out to get food later that night and my fries were so greasy they almost made me sick." "That night was the first time we tried wine coolers and I thought they were so gross." If Ethan had been hoping to see any pictures of Dillon then he was disappointed, since those went into the fire along with his cards and love notes the day after he told me to stop trying to talk to him. It's too bad it wasn't as easy to empty my head of all the memories, our favorites, our firsts. *Have I been giving Dillon too much credit this whole time? Aren't these pictures proof that I had a life outside of him?*

I left Ethan to go pee and to fetch something for us to snack on, returning to my room to find only the Christmas lights on. "Why'd you put those on?" I asked, though I had a feeling.

"Because it's 12:02," he grinned. *It's March 5th.*

My last few birthdays didn't excite me the way they used to when I was little, but you know what? You only turn 19 once. And some people don't even get to. I'm pretty proud of the person these last 19 years have made me into. I've just been one-upping myself this whole time, and I don't just mean in the number of years lived. What kind of person will I be at 29, if I live that long? What will future me think of the person I am right now?

Ethan waited until I finished reading his heartfelt yet naughty card to me before he started unbuttoning my shirt. "Hap-py birth-day, mis-ter *pre-si-dent*," he whispered/sang seductively.

"I should be the one singing that to you! You're the President!"

He pushed my shirt to the floor. *"But it's not my birthday now, is it?"* Naked from the waist up, I put on *Peripheral Vision* before he took his time in undressing us both. We became one under the gentle shoegaze twinkle of the Christmas lights, though I did make us stop so I could flip the record to side B.

Maybe because it decided to cut me a break for my birthday, my brain let me sleep in...until almost 10. The time jolted me out of the bed that Ethan wasn't in, and I pulled on my clothes like I was late for something. I found my boyfriend downstairs with a mug of coffee, talking and laughing with Mom and Dad.

"Sorry babe," he smiled. "I was gonna stay in bed with you, but I smelled coffee."

"Wow," I chuckled as I went over to give him a kiss. "On my birthday too."

"It's weird to see you getting up this late," Dad smirked as he got up to give me a hug. "Happy birthday, Trevor." Mom washed her hands of the breakfast strata she was assembling to come over and wish me the same. Ethan just watched, beaming at me.

The only thing stopping me from stuffing myself silly with strata was knowing that we'd be having Grandma's pasta sauce recipe—impeccably replicated and already simmering—and cake for an early dinner. "What time do you think you'll be shoving off?" Dad asked as he put the rest of the strata in a container for me to take back.

"I'm not sure yet." I turned to Ethan. "How much studying do you have to do?"

He tilted his head from side to side. "Not that much. Accounting's the only one I don't really feel ready for. This week's Midterms week for us," he explained to my parents.

Mom spun on me. "You have *tests* this week? Have you studied enough? I didn't see you bring any notes home with you. Do you feel prepared?"

"Oh my *god*," I rolled my eyes. "*Yes*, I'll be fine."

Ethan and I listened to more records while we played *Everdell* again, and then the four of us played *Scrabble*—"You'd think the English major would've won"—as the pasta sauce's aroma permeated the house. "This might be my new favorite pasta sauce, but don't tell the Italians in my family that," Ethan said when we finally dug in. "And by 'Italian' I mean their great-grandparents were Italian." A plate-and-a-half of pasta and two pieces of raspberry-almond cake later, I felt ready to burst.

In my room, Ethan looked through my books to pick out more to take back with him in exchange for the ones I let him borrow at the beginning of the semester. "I don't think I've ever read so much on my own before," he said happily as he eyed up the stack of his new reads—*We Are the Ants*, *I'll Give You the Sun*, the rest of the ones I have by Adam Silvera, *Fans of the Impossible Life*, and *The Song of Achilles*.

"I've gotta warn you though, Adam Silvera will probably fuck you up," I told him as I added *History Is All You Left Me* to the stack. I made sure to grab my camera too so I could be that guy at parties with an instant camera like Ethan said.

We packed my car with bags and books and leftovers before saying goodbye. Dad gave Ethan a handshake, but Mom went in for a hug. "You're welcome back any weekend," she smiled.

"Keep an eye on Trevor for us," Dad smiled.

Old Main's clock faces glitched through the bare tree branches as we drove past it and pulled into one of the 15-minute spots outside of Kessler. "You know, you're welcome to study in my room if you want," I told Ethan.

"Believe me, I'd love to, but I need to get *some* work done," he said with an apologetic smile. "I had a great weekend though. I'm really glad you asked me to spend it with you."

We kissed goodnight like we wouldn't see each other the next morning. "Promise me one thing, babe," he said as he looked me dead in the eye. My breath caught in my chest as I prepared myself for whatever deep or romantic thing he was about to say. "Please don't ever take an Accounting class."

March 6

I learned a new word that's perfect for today: 'apricity,' which is the warmth of the sun in Winter. Late Winter is so much better when it's sunny. Charcoal-gray skies are for November.

My exam for U.S. Military History was basically a quiz, and our test for French was just Dr. Le Marque recording Victor and me reciting a pre-rehearsed conversation—I say that like being recorded didn't make me nervous enough to misgender at least one noun—so I had the easiest Midterm Monday out of probably anybody, although Kade's Sculpture class apparently doesn't have tests, and Ethan's Critical Reading class didn't meet so they could have a study period instead. "I'm pretty sure I bombed Accounting though," Ethan grimaced.

"You got a free period for Critical Writing?" Kade's hands slapped the table. "I didn't get a free period!"

"Oh boo hoo," I said.

"I will *eat* you out," Kade jabbed a finger at me.

"You won't fucking do it," I taunted him. "Come at me, bro."

"Why come at you when I can cum in you? No offense," he said to Ethan.

"But just think though, the harder this week is for you, the better it'll feel when we turn up for my birthday this weekend," I smirked.

"You entitled. Little. *Shit*," Kade squinted at me. "Just *expecting* us to go out for your birthday with you?"

"*And* it's St. Patty's weekend too," Ethan grinned.

"We gone get fuckin' turnt!" Victor said as he danced in his seat, though he'd just spent this past weekend getting fucking turnt if his Snapchat story was anything to go by.

Kade burped into his napkin. "Okay, you convinced me."

A shift at Rosenberg later, I found myself in 341 Kessler, where Ethan and I each worked on our own things until heading over to Proud as Halle. "Can you believe it's already Spring Break next weekend?" I asked.

"I know, right?" Ethan said to his laptop. "It feels like the semester just started."

"And then only six or seven more weeks after that until the end of the year."

"Oof, don't remind me." He dragged his hands down his face. "Can I come stay with you over Break? Your mom *did* say I'm welcome any weekend."

"Yeah, *weekend.* Not the entire *Summer*—not that I wouldn't want you to. But who knows?" I shrugged. "They're full of surprises anymore."

"Maybe they'll just let me move in. My mom and stepdad won't miss me." He turned back to his Chromebook. "Hell, they probably wouldn't even miss me if I killed myself if they knew how much I like dick," he chuckled. My insides tripped even though I wasn't moving, crashing into each other and sending glass flying. *He didn't mean it. He doesn't know what he's saying.*

"Please don't say that," I said after a moment, my voice coming out tiny and weak. "You have no idea how much they'd miss you."

He gave me a concerned look. "It was just a joke."

I knew I was going to cry before my vision even started to get blurry. I slunk down onto his bed next to him, holding onto him as if letting go would let him go, unable to stop myself from picturing Nate or Hunter or his other bathroommate whose name I don't even know calling the police after finding his body collapsed by the toilet next to an empty pill bottle, with foam on his cold lips and his joyful blue eyes forever lifeless because they were determined that not being alive is better than living a life that isn't his own. "You can never understand how much of other people's lives they let you take up," I paraphrased that line from that F. Scott Fitzgerald book while I could still speak. I didn't even try to stop the tears. "They'd miss you so *much*—" And then I was sobbing. *Sobbing.*

He held me, caressed me as I wept. "I hope you know I'd never actually do that," he consoled me. "I shouldn't have even joked about that."

"No, I know *you* wouldn't," I sniffed. "It's not that." He let me have as much time as I needed, cycling between collecting myself and not being able to even get a word out without crying. Even after the therapy, the pills, my last journal, I guess the pain never really goes away, because that's just part of what it means to be human, isn't it? I swallowed, dabbing my eyes with the tissues he'd set beside me. "I never told you about my brother, have I?" I asked, knowing full-well that I hadn't.

Because if college is the chance for me to shape myself into what I want people to see me as, then what good would it have done to tell people about Ryder?

Ethan gasped. "I didn't know you had a brother!"

"Well, I...I don't anymore. He...killed himself two years ago."

Ethan probably would've fallen over if he wasn't already sitting. "Oh my god," he said in a small voice. *Mom's craft room? It used to be his room. And the pasta sauce we had? He used to rave about it.* "I didn't know. Oh my god Trev, I'm so sorry."

"It's not your fault."

"No, but here I am making jokes about that, when..." His eyes welled up, and overflowed. "Do you wanna talk about it?" he asked after a few minutes of quiet sobbing. *You know what? Yeah, I think I actually do.*

With my knees hugged to my chest and my back against the wall behind his bed, I started to open up about Ryder for the first time to somebody who didn't already know what happened. The more I talked, the more I was able to more or less keep it together. "My brother used to be—for most of my life, really," I swallowed, "my brother was my sister—to me anyway." I could see Ethan's puzzled look in the corner of my eye. "To my parents, they had a son and a daughter. And then one day he told them that they in fact had two sons." The look on Ethan's face told me he understood. "And they couldn't comprehend it. I had a hard time making sense of it then too," I said with a scornful laugh. "Of course my parents thought it was just a phase, but then it became sinful. It became, *'how could you do this to us? How could you do this to yourself? How could you distort the body that god gave you?'*"

Ethan wiped the tears from his face. "Really? They don't strike me as religious."

"Good. That shows how much progress they've made. They used to be super Christian and conservative, and we were both raised that way too—prayers at meals and before bed, church every Sunday. Ryder was the first to see that it was all bullshit. He wasn't afraid to be different or to speak up. He wasn't afraid to call them out for supporting the Stupid Orange Fuck and for thinking that that piece of shit was god's chosen one. *'God must be pretty shitty if I have a better moral standard than him,'* he'd tell them."

"He wasn't wrong," Ethan said.

"They never saw him as their son while he was alive, never called him by the name he wanted, never used the pronouns he wanted. They do now, not that it really matters. I mean, it *does*, but it *sucks* that it took his death for them to do it. They threw him out more than once because of his 'choices.'" I tried to blink away my tears. "And then between not finding acceptance at home, being told over and over that he's going to hell, the Stupid Orange Fuck and how he brought out the worst in people, COVID, lockdown, and thinking that things would never get better for him, he...well, you know how the story ends," I swallowed. "Logan was actually the one who found him." Ethan's hand found his mouth. "It was my mom's birthday," I said, sneering at Ryder's cleverness. "His note was only one sentence long. *'You always say how you want me to stop being who I am, so here you go.'*" I rubbed circles on Ethan's back as he sobbed. "It's okay now," I lied.

"It's *not* though," he cried as he pulled tissues from the box. "I have no idea what it must've been like for you to watch that happen. And I can't *imagine* how *he* must've felt."

"I used to think I knew how he felt just because I wasn't allowed to be myself either, but it doesn't even come close." I stared at the same spot on the wall across from me until it started to warp. "And my parents...I mean, how do you handle the suicide of your own kid? Your kid who you were so proud of, who then all of a sudden was everything you didn't want them to be? At first they tried to forget all about him—they threw his things out, took down family pictures. They wanted to erase him, forget that he existed. But then the opposite happened—they tried to hold onto everything because their child was gone, and they were to blame. I guess it hit them that there was so much more to him than just an identity they didn't agree with."

We sat silent for a minute as I thought about the facets of people we never think about, all the things that would make main characters out of NPCs if only we stopped to understand and celebrate them. "So those pictures in your house of you when you were little with that girl," Ethan started to say. "*Shit,* I mean—"

"I know what you meant." *He probably thought it was a cousin or a neighbor.* "But yeah. And in those months between his death and me coming out, I spiraled. I fucking *spiraled.*" I didn't tell him how when I'd cut myself, I'd think that all I had to do was drag the knife a little deeper and a little farther and be free from everything that kept me from sleeping for more than two hours a night—how not existing at all sounded more appealing than existing with the pain. "And then one day I just couldn't take it anymore. Like you said, I felt like I was suffocating. I guess after one of your kids comes out as trans, the other coming out as just gay is nothing. But it's not fucking *fair* though," I said through gritted teeth. "I feel like it was only easy for me—relatively speaking—because it was so hard for him. I feel like I'm only able to be myself now because he was never able to."

"No," Ethan said sternly. "You can't think like that. You can't blame—"

"*Don't* tell me what I—" I started to say. *You wouldn't say that if you knew that I used to be a fucking transphobe back then, that I used to say the most repulsive shit about queer people like a fucking coward just because I refused to accept my own queerness.* I took a breath and cupped his cheek. "I'm sorry."

Ethan took my hand. "Don't be. You have a right to be upset."

"I don't *want* to blame myself, but I can't help it. But I guess my parents figured that the best way to keep me from removing myself from their lives—whatever that would look like—was to change their mindset, however slow they were to do it. The whole thing was kind of like a mid-life crisis for them, for lack of a better term." *The Tower in their own Fool's Journeys.* "They stopped going to church after the pastor told them that Ryder was in hell for the very thing they themselves told him that he'd go to hell for. They gave up religion altogether, or at least organized religion. And how could they stay loyal to a political party that has so much fun telling people they're going to hell for who they are? So they severed themselves from that too, and they've been figuring themselves out ever since. I think they've been doing a good job at it."

"Yeah, I'd say so, seeing as they didn't drive me away with pitchforks and torches," Ethan awkwardly chuckled. And then instead of trying to talk to me about the grieving process like all the other people who don't have a fucking clue what they're talking about, he said, "Tell me about him."

I told him about how into music Ryder was, how he called it his 'therapy.' "I never understood how music could ever help anybody like he said it helped him, but I guess that just goes to show that life hadn't happened to me yet," I said as Ethan's hand caressed mine. I told him how he would keep me company when I needed it, whether playing a game with me, or listening to and talking me through whatever was bothering me when I was nervous or anxious. I told him how he stood up for the bullied, the marginalized, and how he never let *anybody* walk over him. I told him how his dream was to play in a band. I told him how we'd take turns speed-running *Mario* and *Sonic* games. I told him how the people he thought he could trust distanced themselves from him once he told them who he really was. I told him how he slid from the top of his class to failing grades. I told him how he tried to find an escape in substances when music started to not do the job anymore. I told him how he'd be away from home for days at a time, and come back only to get screamed at before slamming the door and leaving again. "So yeah," I concluded. "The more you know."

"I'm sorry you had to talk about all that," Ethan said somberly. "I didn't mean to ruin the evening."

"No, it's good for me to talk about it," I shook my head. "It's easy for me to get trapped in the 'could've, would've, should've' rabbit hole, but thinking about it won't change it," I told him as much as I told myself. "The best I can do now is just try to help other people from ever feeling like it's hopeless for them. I know how tough it is though—a hundred people could be there for you, telling you how worth it you are, but then that *one* voice that tells you that you're *not* worth it and that you'll *never* be good enough is always louder than the others."

He clasped my hand with both of his. "You know I'm always here for you, right?" he told me with big, sincere eyes. "I'll do whatever I need to for you to never have to feel like you're not enough. Isn't there a Dr. Seuss quote about that?"

"You know, I actually don't think there is," I said as I wiped away the last of my tears for the night.

March 7

So I don't think I'll be going to Proud as Halle—which I think they should rename Prideful as Hell—anymore. I mentioned in passing that I've never watched *RuPaul's Drag Race* and Bradley spun on me like I'd just fired a gun before asking me yet again what kind of gay I am.

"A fucking *unconventional* one, apparently," I spat as my nostrils flared.

An Unconventional Gay: An Autobiography by Trevor Huffman.

I legit just got up and walked out, and nothing Ethan could say when he came after me could get me to go back. You're going to have a group that's all about inclusivity and supporting one another, and then you're going to try to invalidate my identity? Get the fuck lost. Bradley was probably telling the others how he felt "attacked" after I'd left, because you know, everything's about him.

Since paying for half of *Everdell* apparently wasn't enough of a gift, Ethan surprised me with a book I'd never heard of called *All That's Left in the World* when I stopped to see him at work and to try a new kind of tea on the menu. If taro tea tastes like the milk from a bowl of Lucky Charms, then royal milk tea tastes like the magically delicious cereal itself.

"I saw an ad for it on Instagram," Ethan said as he watched me skim the book's inside flap. "It's about these queer boys in a post-apocalyptic world, and they're trying to—"

"Stop," I cut him off with my hand. "Stop. You had me at 'queer boys' and 'apocalypse.'"

He said he wanted to read it after I was done with it, which will probably be tomorrow since I legit cannot put it down. You know how some people go to Lit Club and just read? That was me tonight. Marvin Bostwick was reading fucking Marcel Proust with a regretful look like he was serving a prison sentence, and then there was me, flipping through young adult pages faster than anything since *Deathly Hallows*.

I brought up gender-neutral housing in House Council during open forum and only like two people knew what the hell I was talking about. "I heard that some other House Council members were trying to move it forward in RHA to make it a thing," I said to Westley, who looked kind of bored with the topic, even as a few other heads nodded.

124

"Well I'm happy to hear that you're keeping up with what we go over," Westley said, knowing that I knew that he knew that I only knew because Ethan told me about it. "It's currently in discussion, but I don't really see it passing," he said matter-of-factly, which tells me he's either against it or he just doesn't care—either of which are pretty shitty if you ask me.

March 8

Are you still at work? I need to see you rn

...is the kind of text you do *not* want to get from your boyfriend. My chest throbbed as I waited by the circulation desk until I saw him approaching through the windows. I went out to meet him and he hugged me before I could get a word out. "I love you Trevor," Ethan said like he'd start crying if he spoke too loud. "I love you and you mean so much to me, and I don't say it enough."

"What happened?" I asked without trying to sound too alarmed. *Is he about to break up with me?*

"Remember how you said Adam Silvera would fuck me up?"

I relaxed, so relieved that I almost laughed. "Let me guess, *History Is All You Left Me?*"

He nodded into the side of my head as I let him love me. *"History Is All You Left Me."*

March 9

Here's a thought and don't lose your mind over it: no taxation without representation, right? So since people of color are being gerrymandered out of their due voice and shit like that by certain political elements, they shouldn't have to pay taxes, right?

Dr. Averescu told class today that when we write, we're really just combining all the best parts of all the things we've read, which is definitely something I've seen online somewhere. "So the more you read, the better your writing will be," she encouraged us.

In Macro, Dr. Jurado asked us if people still use the word 'stoned.' "You know, like 'let's go get stoned?'" We giggled and murmured that people still use it sometimes, though not as much as baked, fried, or zooted.

"Were you ever stoned, sir?" someone a few seats up and a row over asked him.

"No," he answered like it was ridiculous before flashing a peace sign. "I was beautiful."

March 11

You know how sometimes you hear a story that just leaves you with more and more questions as it goes on? *March 7—Campus police responded to a call about a man indecently exposing himself in a restroom in Bixby Student Center. An officer arrived on the scene to find the man giving himself a sponge bath.*

Kade and Tylor and I do this thing when we meet up to eat where we tell each other what our Economics professors said in class. Since Kade's Sustainable Economics class is MWF and we have Macro on Tuesdays and Thursdays, Ethan and Victor have to hear about economics basically every day of the week.

"So Sutcliffe pulls a dollar bill out of his wallet and holds it up for us to see," Kade told us as he yanked a napkin out of the dispenser to hold up as a substitute. "And he says, 'This is your vote. Every time you buy something, you're voting with your dollars.' Like, when you buy chocolate from some big asshole chocolate company that has toddlers in Ghana or somewhere harvesting cocoa beans for three cents a day, you're essentially casting a vote of approval and support for child enslavement and child labor. Ben & Jerry's though? *Not* an asshole company."

"Ooh, that makes me want Ben & Jerry's now," Ethan smiled.

"That's why I don't buy just any coffee beans," Tylor said with a look my way like he was reprimanding me, even though I've been getting fair trade coffee ever since he told me about it back in September. "But Jurado was telling us about the law of diminishing marginal utility," he went on. "The example he used was, 'if I tied you to a chair and shoved slice after slice of pizza down your throat, you'd enjoy each one less and less.'"

Kade slid down in his seat with closed eyes, biting his lip and rubbing his nipples. "Oh, *papi.* Sit on my face."

Tylor and I exchanged grossed-out scowls. *"Ew!"*

"Forreal though," Kade popped back up, "research where your chocolate comes from." I actually did, and let's just say I won't be buying chocolate from the vending machines or the bookstore or Sheetz anymore.

The film I ordered for my instant camera got delivered today, along with a small package from Logan containing a bag of dick-shaped gummy candy and $10 gift cards for McDonald's, Taco Bell, and Subway. I guess he peeped the town on Maps to see what places there are to eat. I reacquainted myself with my camera by snapping a photo of Tylor in a towel when he emerged from the shower. "I guess you got film for your camera then," Ethan said when he saw it on my memo board

"*No*," I rolled my eyes, "I've just always had an instant picture of Tylor in a towel."

"Oh, okay. How'd you clean the cum off of it?" he asked, earning himself a slap. I snapped one of him before letting him take some of me and the other things that looked artsy to him all of a sudden. We were critiquing each other's shots when he asked me somewhat reluctantly, "Are you doing okay?"

"Yeah?" I raised an eyebrow. "I mean, we're done with Midterms, so—"

"I don't mean that," he said as he rubbed the back of his neck like a Trevor. "It's just that…I've been reading about coping with a suicide victim, and I…I just wanted to check in on you. Make sure that you're okay. I know it was a couple of years ago, but still."

I laid down my pictures to hug him. "It was, but thank you for asking. Really, I mean it," I smiled. "I can't remember the last time anybody checked up on me about it." I know everybody grieves in their own ways, but I still felt like I was doing it *wrong* somehow. Like, was I supposed to have gotten over it after a year? Was it normal to go an entire day without eating? Was it normal to sleep for 10 hours a week? Will I ever stop blaming myself?

"Of course." He gave my shoulder a little shake. "Like I said, I want to be there for you."

I swallowed, feeling the need to say more on the subject. "I got tons of messages from people—people I didn't even *know*—telling me how sorry they were for what happened, how are you doing, things will get better, we should hang out. Most of them were probably just saying things so they'd feel like decent people," I laughed through my nose. "I'd keep going back and forth between being really sad and really angry, sometimes both at the same time. And then I got depressed. Like, *really* depressed. I'd lay in bed for hours in the middle of the day. Sure, I could still laugh and smile, but I was just numb to *everything*. Nothing made me happy. Not video games, not my friends or my family—not even being *alive*. Everything just felt so pointless."

"You never thought about…?" Ethan asked cautiously. *Of course I did, I was clinically depressed.*

"No," I shook my head. "My parents got me a therapist after I told them about all the bad thoughts. She found a support group for me, which I was kind of embarrassed to go to, but it ended up being pretty helpful. It was nice to be around other people who knew what it's like. Sometimes I envied the ones who weren't left with any reasons or explanations or apologies, and at other times I was grateful that I knew why Ryder did it. Dr. Valentino was also the one who suggested I try journaling. I thought it was stupid at first, but sometimes you get to a point where you're willing to try anything. I ended up liking it, if you couldn't tell."

"Whatever helps," Ethan patted my leg. "Life can be too hard to face on your own sometimes."

I nodded. "She helped me come to terms with my sexuality too. She was the first person I came out to. Well, actually my old journal was."

"Well, actually your old journal isn't a person," Ethan smirked.

I kissed his cheek. "You're lucky you're cute."

"And if I wasn't?"

"Then I'd probably shoot you with a rubber band." So that's how Kade's text found me with a rubber band wrapped around my finger gun and Ethan hiding behind a notebook. "Finally," I said as I let the rubber band leap pathetically from my hand as I got up to go sign them in.

Kade came into Swafford bearing a 24-pack of toilet paper with a big red bow on top. "Happy birthday fam," he said as he shoved it into my arms with enough force to make me stumble.

"I told him it doesn't count as a gift if it's repayment," Victor said.

"Like Stalin said, 'he who controls the toilet paper controls the people,'" Kade said before leaning in close. "*Because it's a toilet paper-based oligarchy.*"

We introduced the two of them to *Everdell*—Kade won of course even though he'd never played it before—before we headed out for my birthday dinner of Taco Bell, with a pit stop on the way back for Shamrock Shakes. I got extra food to-go since I had the feeling I'd be in the mood to destroy me some Taco Bell later on if we planned on going as hard as The Skeletons were, in their sparkly green bowler hats and shamrock t-shirts. Nikole threw us a curveball when she invited us to go out with her to a party at her friend's apartment at The Commons, which nobody was opposed to. I'd heard that St. Patty's weekend is second only to Halloweekend in terms of debauchery and people-watching, and I wanted to experience it from somewhere other than the basement of 370 Rock.

As if our green shirts or hats or jeans or socks or shoes weren't enough, Victor gave us each a beaded shamrock necklace that he picked up on their latest trip to Wally World. "And you have to wear this too," he grinned as he handed me a plastic crown.

"But—"

"*Shhh,*" he hushed me with a finger to my lips, getting so close that I legit thought he was about to kiss me. "*Just let it happen.*" I thought about all the drunk girls I've ever seen when we've gone out wearing plastic crowns for their birthdays, and how I was about to be that drunk girl.

I knew The Commons was swanky, but I didn't know *how* swanky it was. Tall rows of classist, colonial-style apartment buildings surround an open grassy area the size of a football field. You feel like you're at the kind of colleges you see in college movies. They weren't the kinds of parties you just wander into, either—one apartment we passed had a bouncer stationed outside the door, and by 'bouncer' I mean 'a freshman frat boy who was probably wearing a penis cage.' There were so many people with green clothes and hair and painted skin that it was like we were going to see Ireland play in the Quidditch World Cup. I had to make a concerted effort to not stare at all the appetizing guys as Nikole led us past the volleyball court, past the pool, and past the fitness center to her friend's building. *So this is how the upper echelon of the student body lives,* I thought as we followed her up to the top floor, and into the nicest apartment I've ever been in. Partying in a cookie-cutter unit with all the lights turned on almost didn't feel right compared to the cramped, dimly-lit dungeons that the peasantry gets drunk in.

"I like your crown, birthday boy," Nikole's friend Hayley said when Nikole introduced us. She kept being flirty with me and couldn't take a hint.

"*She wants to put your penis in her mouth,*" Kade whispered after she finally figured she wasn't going to get anywhere with me.

My friends/boyfriend and I drifted between games, from pong to Drunk *Jenga* to Flip Cup. Kade must've sank the last cup in pong from the way the table exploded after his shot. Victor went everywhere Nikole went. Ethan made easy conversation with everyone and anyone. I learned that Irish whiskey is *not* my thing. I wanted to strangle Victor with my necklace when he got up on a chair and bellowed "HEY EVERYBODY IT'S MY BRO TREVOR'S BIRTHDAY!" through cupped hands, which was how I ended up taking like five shots with strangers wishing me a happy birthday. I didn't tell anyone it was last week.

I was sipping on a Guinness—which actually isn't *horrible* as far as beer goes—when I caught sight of Victor from across the room, looking like he was about to start freaking out. He downed a shot and took something from Kade before disappearing from the apartment, and like a good friend, I went after him to make sure he was okay. Three endless flights of steps later, I found him outside, smoking a cigarette and muttering to himself.

"Hey, are you alright?" I asked. "What's up?"

"I'm smoking a fucking *cigarette*, do you *think* I'm alright?" he snapped. He took a drag like he was out for revenge on it.

"*Sorry for asking,*" I muttered. "Can I have one of those?" He shook one out of the pack and passed me Kade's lighter. I know that taste isn't what they have going for them, but holy *shit*. I smoked it anyway.

Victor took off his hat to run his hand through his hair. "I just really thought I might've actually had a chance with Nikole tonight."

I let my beer wash my tongue. "I didn't know you liked Nikole."

"How could anybody *not*? Somebody who likes girls, I mean," he corrected himself. "I mean, she's *beautiful*, but I just like everything *about* her. She's smart, witty, easygoing. She's just so *cool*."

"You've never mentioned anything about wanting to hang out with her or anything," I said. I know that his way of speaking to girls can be mistaken as being flirty, but I guess with Nikole it was legit all along.

"I mean, I've asked her if she wanted to meet up for coffee or dinner a couple of times, but she always says she has desk duty or has to study." He sighed. "Honestly, I feel like she's just out of my league."

"So why are you all hot and bothered about it tonight?"

He shot me a look. "What do you mean *tonight*? It's happened before with other girls," he said like I should know. "And *every time* there's always some excuse for them not to. And the *one time* I did meet up with a girl from class, she didn't wanna do it again. And the fact that I'm pretty drunk right now probably isn't helping. Not with the Nikole thing, but the me-talking-about-it thing." He took a swig out of his can and pushed air through his nose. "Since you told me one of your secrets, I'll tell you one of mine."

I gave him a look. "What secret did I tell you?"

"That you're gay."

I laughed out loud. "Okay, *one*, that's not even a secret. And two, I didn't even *tell* you, you just overheard—"

"Okay, whatever. But I'm still a virgin," he said with a flushed face.

"Oh, I knew that," I said, low-key disappointed that that's all it was.

"How? *I* sure didn't tell you."

"I figured it out the one time we played Drunk *Jenga*. Never Have I Ever. But so what? That's nothing to be ashamed of."

"You don't think that's sad? That I'm in college and haven't had sex yet?"

"I don't think so. There isn't a rule that says you *have* to."

"No, but I *want* to," he pined. "I *really* want to. It's not like I'm waiting for the right person or anything. Forget the act itself—I'm missing out on something that all my friends get to do. Like you and Ethan probably do it all the time, and—"

"Stop," I put a hand up. "We do *not* have sex all the time, so get that idea out of your head right now. Relationships are *way* more than just that."

"Whatever. You still *do* it though. Do you know what it feels like to see your friends and brother all get what you want so badly but can't have?"

"Um, as a formerly-closeted gay boy who had to watch straight couples in school holding hands and kissing and everything, I actually *do*."

"*Shit*, I'm sorry," he apologized.

"You gucc." *But not really.*

"But do you know how many times I've had to go to bed with my earbuds in so I couldn't hear what was going on in Kade's room? And even then, I couldn't sleep because I still *knew.*" He scraped his cigarette against the brick of the building. "It felt like Nikole and I were really hitting it off, but then she left with somebody who she like barely even talked to all night. Is there something wrong with me? Am I trying too hard? Am I being too nice? Do I need to start being an asshole? Am I ugly?"

"No to all of the above," I laughed. "And even if someone *did* sleep with you because you *did* play the asshole, you'd feel bad about it later." *'Oh, you're in a band? What do you play?' 'I play the asshole.'*

"True story," he chuckled.

I threw an arm around his neck. "So what I'm hearing from all this is that we just need to get you laid!" I said like it was that easy. "Have you tried hooking up with a guy? Maybe you're gay and in denial."

"I'm not," he said. "I let a guy kiss me at a cast party once, and it didn't do anything for me." *Woah, respect.*

"Maybe it just wasn't the right guy," I joked. "You said Nikole's smart and witty and cool, right?" I put my hands on the wall on either side of him. "Aren't *I* those things?" *I kinda wanna run my fingers through his hair.*

"Don't even think about it," he laughed as he pushed me away. "I'm ready to go back in when you are." My empty bottle swallowed our cigarette butts, and we headed back into the building—or at least we tried to, since you can't get in unless you either lived there or went in after somebody who did. "Sorry for making you listen to all that," he said almost sheepishly as we made room for a line of guys stampeding down the stairs.

"No problem," I waved him off. "It sounds like you've been needing to say that out loud to someone."

"I have. But I wouldn't have told just anybody all that though."

"I'm honored," I said sincerely, even if it sounded sarcastic. "Real talk though, if you ever need me to play wingman for you, just let me know. Don't know how good I'll be at it, but you're my bud and I wanna help you get that peen wet."

"Oh my *god*," he laughed. Back on Hayley's floor, he stumbled over his green Vans as he turned to face me. "Okay, so I'm *100%* only asking this because I'm drunk," he said as he looked around to make sure nobody was right there, "and please don't feel like you need to answer."

"Okay?" I said, high-key curious.

He chewed on his lip. "God, I can't believe I'm asking this," he laughed. "Have you ever taken a dick before?"

My cheeks puffed out as I held in my laugh. "I have."

"What does it feel like?" he tried not to crack up.

I looked up at the fluorescent ceiling lights. "You know how"—I hissed with laughter—"you know how when you take a really big shit? Like how it's kind of uncomfortable, but it feels *really* good at the same time?"

"Yeah?"

"Kinda like that." *Maybe taking a big shit feels good because it massages your prostate on the way out? Hashtag just drunk thoughts.*

March 12

So I met Ethan's bathroommate, Hunter, today. I say 'met' like I didn't accidentally walk in on them, and I say 'walking in on' like they were doing something other than just washing off their face mask. They scared the shit out of me because I'm so used to nobody ever being in there, but probably not as much as I scared them. I 180'ed and closed the door like I *had* walked in on them doing something naughty, and now I'm nervous to use the 341/343 Kessler bathroom again.

It'd been a full month since I was at 370 Rock last, which is to say it'd been a full month since I'd smoked the devil's lettuce. "The jazz cabbage," Kade called it while he sprinkled it into the bowl of shisha he was packing, which ignited a debate over whether calling it 'the jazz cabbage' is racist or not. We played poker at the dining room table in the same fits as the night before—yes, even my crown— while we passed around the hose of the small hookah.

"Does a full house trump a flush?"

"Hey, watch your language."

"Do you think our thoughts manifest the universe? Like you know how when you're thinking of a song and then it comes on?"

"The King of Spades is looking daddy *AF* right now."

"We used to play poker in the elevator in our building back in freshman year."

"Aces are high, right?"

"Asexuals?"

"Not as high as *I* am."

"I wonder if meditating gives the mind power, or if it lets the universe reveal itself?"

"I got a straight, no offense."

"You feel that tingle right above in between your eyes? That's your *third eye!*"

"You can't go Jack off of that!"

Fuck, I forgot how good this feels," I said as my eyes and mind meandered around the room without actually moving. I didn't know who had my camera, nor did I care. I didn't take it out to The Commons because I didn't want it to get lost, but I trusted the 370 crowd with it. My little disco light cast a carousel of light around the room, the hookah's metal and glass catching and reflecting it like a gemstone.

"Hey Ty," Kade elbowed Tylor once we were at cruising altitude. "You think he'd fuck with Wiz, or nah?" he asked him with his reddened eyes on me. The Wiz, *like the musical?*

"Khalifa?" Tylor said like he couldn't believe it. He stared at me like he couldn't figure me out. "Nah. Maybe? I don't know. Put it on and we'll find out."

Victor, wearing sunglasses over his glasses, sprang from his chair. "I gotchu fam. Yo Alex!"

"I'm curious to see how this goes," Ethan said like he had money on it.

The walls pounded with a synth drone and took me away to a place I never even knew existed. *Oh yes. Oh hell yes.* Linh whooped, and a few people waved their drinks in the air. The rooms were hazy with music. It felt like everybody was vaping, but the only smoke was from the hookahs. My light transfixed me like I was watching the womb of the universe in action. *This—this is what a college party should be like.*

"I think he likes it," I heard Tylor's amused voice say.

The song ended, and the music went back to the night's mix of clubby-sounding stuff that artsy kids who are high out of their minds have lights-on sex to.

"I fucking *love* Wiz," Chance said as he exhaled laced smoke through his nostrils. "Good looks, man."

Tylor and Kade and Victor and Ethan watched me like I was a zoo animal. "Well?"

I met their eyes individually, torn between not wanting to prove them right and wanting to share the euphoria of a new discovery with them. *"I fucks with it,"* I smiled. They high-fived and fist-bumped each other.

"Go the fuck ahead!"

"We did it boys!"

"It's fuckin' *lit,* fam."

Trying to participate in two separate conversations—one about the seniors' upcoming Spring Break trips, and the other about how fucked the country is if we can't even make Daylight Savings permanent when it's the one thing that literally everybody agrees on—meant that I just kept turning my head back and forth. The whole house counted down the time change like it was New Year's Eve. It was nearly 4 in the morning by the time Ethan and I finished mindlessly devouring the Taco Bell I had in my fridge like zombies pulling apart a short-winded person. I could almost hear it screaming. The people you love are the people you share your Taco Bell with.

The only pictures I have from the weekend were the ones from my Fujifilm that I kept for myself. I don't know who took any of them—Victor and Tylor on the couch trying to get playing cards to stick to their foreheads, Ethan tugging me towards him by my necklace with my crown catching the camera's flash, most of Kade's head obscured by the cloud of smoke he'd just exhaled. I wish I had copies of the other ones, but that's what makes instant pictures so special—each one is unique and as once-in-a-lifetime as the people and the moments they encapsulate. *Ichi-go ichi-e.*

I was putting away my laundry later on when Tylor asked me in a serious tone if he could talk to me about something. "You're the only one who I feel would understand," he said.

I turned away from my clothes-strewn bed to prop myself up on the edge of it. "What's up?" I asked, high-key curious.

He walked over to make sure nobody was standing in the hallway before saying in a low voice, *"I think I was abducted by aliens last night."*

"Really?" I asked with wide eyes. "Why? What happened?"

He swallowed and adjusted his glasses. "Well...I woke up last night at like 1:50-something to go take a piss, right?"

"Uh huh," I nodded.

"And I *swear* I was only in there for a minute, but then when I got back into bed it was somehow already after 3," he said as he backed towards the door. "Don't people who've been abducted by aliens say they experienced unexplainable lapses in time?" he said as he ran down the hallway, narrowly avoiding the balled-up pair of socks I yeeted at the doorway where he'd been standing.

"I HATE YOU!" I yelled after him, earning myself a glare from Sunita as she came around the corner.

March 13

You're like music to me, I told you,
Just when I think it can't get any better than this,
Something new makes me fall in love all over again.

March 14

I kind of had a feeling something was up today when I left for class and there wasn't anybody at the front desk. And then on the way to breakfast, it seemed like most of the students were just wandering around instead of going to class. *Did we get the day off and I missed the memo? Is Pi Day as big of a deal as the first day of hunting season around here?* I felt a buzz in the air as I got closer to the Quad, like electricity. *There's definitely some kind of demonstration going on.* And from all the Pride and Progress and Trans flags I saw being waved from makeshift poles and being worn as capes, I doubted it was just some kind of Blue & White Society thing.

"What the *hell's* going on?" I asked Ethan, who'd also left his backpack behind.

"You didn't hear?" he said like he'd just witnessed a car crash. "The people who attacked Denver aren't going to be charged with anything. Everybody's walking out over it."

I'd heard murmurings yesterday about a student who'd been assaulted on their way back from a party over the weekend, but I didn't get the whole story until today. Denver from Proud as Halle, who was never nothing but nice to me, was the student who'd been assaulted, targeted simply for being trans. An early-morning runner came across her lying near a dumpster behind the Field House, bruised, bloody, unconscious, and half-naked, with 'TRANNIES ARE FREAKS' Sharpied on her chest. The perpetrators weren't smart enough to do it in the woods or somewhere not in sight of any cameras, so it didn't take long to figure out who they were. If anybody other than members of our glorious football team had done it, then that would've been the end of them. But since they *were* members of the football team, they can apparently do whatever they want without getting anything other than a slap on the wrist.

My hands reflexively clenched into fists. "Are you *fucking kidding* me?" I spat in a small, rageful tone, like atoms about to be split. My body shook like glass near a passing train. I started to walk away, only to just pace back and forth. My teeth nearly ground themselves into powder. I grabbed my head and almost slammed my backpack to the ground before remembering my Mac was inside. "ARE YOU FUCKING *KIDDING* ME?" I bellowed through watery eyes. I think Ethan—the only person at NHU who knows the personal chord it strikes with me—was actually afraid of me in that moment, but he didn't flinch as I threw my arms around him to let his tears run with mine.

The bookstore was already cleaned out of supplies, so Kade led us into a deserted Arrowood building to mark our cheeks with blue, pink, and white paint, and to make signs—Victor wore his around his neck so he could carry a shower curtain rod with his Progress flag attached to it—to carry to the Quad, where we got lost in the sea of people and signs and flags.

'BOYS WILL BE ~~BOYS~~ HELD ACCOUNTABLE'

'TRANS LIVES MATTER'

'THE FIRST PRIDE WAS A RIOT'

'GAY PROUD AND PISSED OFF'

'CRASH THE FUCKING CIS-TEM'

'PROTECT TRANS KIDS'

'YOU ARE LOVED'

'WE WILL NOT BE PUSHED ASIDE'

'LET QUEER KIDS BE QUEER'

'PROTECT MY STUDENTS'

'I ♡ MY TRANS KID'

And it wasn't just students either—there were professors, workers from the dining halls still in uniform, administrative faculty, even people from town. Campus and borough police were there too, though I'm sure the students weren't the ones they were there to protect. I saw Drs. Gallagher, de Conto, Le Marque, and plenty of others who I don't have for class but recognized. The solidarity overwhelmed me to the point of tears. *I wish you could see me now, Ryder.* I picked out other members of Proud as Halle, and made eye contact with Bradley for just a moment. I didn't expect him to say anything to me, but I also didn't expect him to give me a nod. Sure, he and some of the others might be off-putting and have personalities that I can't stand, but his head and heart are in the right place. Zoe shouted through a megaphone before passing it on to another student who also preached revolution. Victor pushed his way through to take it next, and the crowd repeatedly met his tirade with cheers and applause. *I can't believe I'm one of this guy's best friends,* I thought. It's people like him who are going to change the world, and I can't wait to see them do it. I was so caught up in the moment that I don't even remember what he said—something about the future not being binary.

"Have you ever thought about running for President?" Ethan asked him when he made his way back to us. "Like, of the United States?"

"I have," Victor said. "But we've had enough straight white men be president."

The megaphone ended up in the hands of Dr. Gallagher, who urged us not to return to class until the university pursues the "morally appropriate action." I can barely sit in class on a normal day, let alone when there's a campus-wide rebellion going on. Being a part of it filled me with a new kind of fervor, like my life felt *meaningful* for once. People setting couches on fire and trashing the streets makes a lot more sense once you find yourself caught up in a protest with a fire in your heart.

President Norwood sent out an email to the student body full of the kinds of bullshit you'd expect from her—how she's 'seeking the proper course of action,' and that we students should 'uphold the reputation of our esteemed institution by maintaining the status quo.' "Oh yeah," I scoffed, "because I'm sure that sweeping transphobia under the rug when real people are victims of it is great for the school's reputation."

"And what the fuck does she mean, 'seeking the appropriate course of action?'" Kade angrily asked. "Expel and arrest the fuckers, how hard is that to do?"

"I wouldn't be surprised if they're some of Aiden's friends and he managed to keep them from getting in trouble," Ethan said bitterly.

No board game or video game or movie could've held our attention. We spent the entire day outside, joining Tylor and his friends at a sit-in in front of Old Main before heading to a protest at the bottom of the road to President Norwood's house, where police placed barricades and stood in a row with their guns very visible. "What are you gonna do, fucking shoot us?" Victor yelled at them. We marched our signs and Victor's flag all around campus and town, finding camaraderie in and giving camaraderie to the other pockets of protesters. If any of the campus Christian groups were counter-protesting, we didn't see them. And the funny thing is that 16-year-old Trevor would've been content to just go back to his room and let it happen without him, but I *wanted* to be a part of this—I *had* to be a part of this— even if it means just showing up and being seen. We didn't get lost in the sea of protesters—we helped make the protest what it was. I thought it just sounded inspiring when Dr. de Conto said last semester how if everybody decided to not do anything that nothing would ever get done, but I *get* it now.

March 15

Happy Ides of March.

Classes are still unofficially suspended, and news crews were on campus today. One of the reporters actually spoke with Kade, and I wasn't horrified to see myself clearly visible standing beside him—with fresh paint on our faces—when I watched the clip later, because protesting for human rights is exactly what I want to be seen doing. *His parents are gonna be so fucking thrilled if they see him on the news.* I wonder if it'll be on the news back home too? A lot of people are just up and leaving to start their Spring Breaks early, and I probably would too if it wasn't for Ethan—not that I'm complaining.

I got to spend a Wednesday evening with him today for the first time, since Ciara sent out an email to the House Council members cancelling the RHA meeting. He and I wandered around and did our own thing instead of going with Kade and Victor to another demonstration in the Quad, but I didn't let myself feel too guilty for not going since we'd done our duties as protesters by not going to class. I didn't even go to work. Go ahead and fire me, see if I care.

"Have you ever been up on the roof of Bixby?" Ethan asked me later on like it was something that people just do.

"No?" I furrowed my brow. "Have *you*?"

I half-expected him to scale up the side of it from landing to landing like somebody from the rock climbing club, but we took the stairs instead. I'd never seen Bixby so empty before. I think I saw maybe five people as I followed him up towards a maintenance door near Bubble Up. He looked around as he held it open for me.

"Aren't there any cameras back here?" I asked in a low voice. It looked like a back hallway used for deliveries to Percy's and Bubble Up, with chain link fences cordoning off food storage areas.

"Probably," Ethan shrugged. "But anybody who'd be watching probably has bigger things to worry about."

"So what you're saying is now's the time to do crimes?" I chuckled.

After rounding a corner, climbing a staircase, and then climbing another staircase, he pushed through a door that spit us out into the dark chill of a mid-March twilight. We stepped over the low partition enclosing the HVAC units, and found ourselves in a sea of gravel with rows of solar panels turned towards the sky like they were waiting for Christ to return. I peered down into a skylight, and the sight of the ground floor of the atrium however-many stories down pushed me away from it to join Ethan near the edge of the roof. A lower tier of the roof lay over the edge, so I'd probably just break my bones instead of flat-out splatting if I fell. "What do you think?" he asked me.

The hill behind the football stadium is nice for a good postcard panorama of campus, but the view from the top of the Student Center puts you in the middle of it all. The rooftops of the buildings sat like platforms in an open-world game just asking to be bounded over to. The demonstration in the Quad was still going strong, like a between-songs moment at a concert that was just out of sight. Old Main watched from afar, perhaps disappointed to see its home putting itself before its students. *How many other students have seen campus from up here?*

"Is now a bad time to tell you I'm afraid of heights?" I chuckled.

"Oh shit, forreal?" Ethan turned to me.

"Yeah, but I'm okay right now with you here with me."

He put his arm around me as we took in the view. "Well, I know how you like new perspectives." My eyes were picking out the first stars of the night when an idea hit me.

"I know somewhere I wanna show *you* after this," I smiled.

I was surprised to find Devlin's doors unlocked, and extra surprised to find the planetarium doors also unlocked. There wasn't a show since there was nobody working it, but dust-particle cosmos circled overhead like a screensaver. We found seats right in the middle, reclined all the way back, and let ourselves get lost in the pre-programmed heavens to Angels & Airwaves.

"I could look up at the night sky all night," I said contently.

"I used to stare out my window and look up at all the stars when I was little," Ethan told me, his eyes nowhere but above. The occasional streak flashed across the ceiling. Improbable clouds formed and transformed before disappearing. "Why do you think we're here?" he broke our silence.

"I don't know," I swallowed. "I had a panic attack thinking about it once. That, and the concept of infinity and eternity." Everything else aside, I wouldn't want to go to heaven simply because it would *never end.* "So I don't really think about it."

He gave me a look. "That's not an answer."

I sucked my teeth. *Why* are *we here?* I thought about Victor's "Pale Blue Dot" poster, and how coincidental and insignificant we really are. "I guess if I had to come up with an answer...I'd say that maybe we're just here to experience it? If this is all there is?"

He bit the inside of his cheek. "Yeah, I can get on board with that."

"Why, what about you?"

"I think we give each other meaning. Not just us, but people in general."

"How so?"

"Like, I think being together and interacting with each other is part of the human condition and the human experience. We make memories with each other and leave impressions on each other and shape each other. To me, life's only as good as the people you get to share it with. Like, if you lived in paradise but you were the only person there, would that be enjoyable?"

"Un unh," I shook my head. *And that's coming from an introvert.* "I think I see what you mean."

Kade told me once how Dr. Sutcliffe had told his Sustainable Economics class that sustainable business is all about "people, then planet, and then profit." But I think the planet comes first, because with or without people, the planet will exist on. What would the planet be without people, aside from an *actual* paradise? Do we then give meaning to *the planet* too? Are all the uninhabited planets meaningless then? Am I just being anthropocentric?

The closest spiral galaxy spun like an hour hand. "I can't believe this has been here this entire time," Ethan said. "*Literally* right around the corner from my Lab class."

"Yeah, I would've never known about it unless Victor told me about it."

139

"It sucks that the shows are at the same time as RHA, because I'd be here every week."

"Well then," I said as my hand found his, "let's do what we may or may not be here to do, and just experience it together."

March 16

    | come | sleep | with | me | boy |
    | make | a | mess | in | bed | with | me |
    | let | me | undress | you |
    | worship | you |
    | run | my | tongue | over | you |
    | please | you |
    | blow | me |
    | milk | me |
    | your | pole |
    | my | peach |
    | make | me | moan |
    | pant |
    | scream |
    | until | we | run | wet | together | with | the | frantic | juice | of | desire |

March 17

The walkout made it onto *Nightly News*! They didn't air the clip with Kade though. How fucking wild would *that* have been?

We spent most of yesterday demonstrating again, which has actually been getting low-key boring. President Norwood sent out another email saying that charges *will* in fact be brought against the perpetrators and that we should all 'finish the week with dignity'—which is good and all, but maybe she shouldn't have waited until Thursday, when just about everybody had already gone home for Spring Break. Ethan's probably one of the few people who wasn't looking forward to leaving, and I don't blame him. *I'd* rather be at school too, and I'm *allowed* to be myself here at home.

We took advantage of Tylor leaving a day early to make messes on and in each other. I pulled myself off my bed while Ethan showered to crouch in front of Tylor's bookshelf to look for *Meditations*, the book that Ethan mentioned when we were ice skating. I turned it over in my hands, opening to a page at random. *"It never ceases to amaze me,"* I read, *"we all love ourselves more than other people, but care more about their opinion than our own."*

"Holy *fuck*," I gasped. *If that's not me:*

Ethan found me with my nose so deep into the book that I didn't even notice him come back in. "I see you finally decided to give that a try," he nodded at the book.

"This," I said as I held it up like it was my first time seeing a book, "is fucking fire."

"I had a feeling you'd be into it," he smiled the same smile that I smile whenever somebody ends up liking something I recommended to them. I tucked it into my bag to take home for some Spring Break reading, which gave my inner kleptomaniac a glee it hadn't felt since I used to tear out pages of poetry to tape into my personal anthology.

As much as it killed me, I didn't see Ethan off when his mom and stepdad picked him up, because it would've been torture to say goodbye without holding and kissing him. My own drive home was a lonely one—Ethan's almost always been in my passenger seat this semester, singing along or dancing in his seat to whatever song was playing that made him light up. But putting those same songs on and seeing the empty seat beside me only made me miss him more and made me realize how much I've been taking him for granted—and just how much of my life I've let him take up.

March 18

I wonder if anybody's ever murdered somebody with a weighted blanket. Like some psycho caretaker lays a weighted blanket on their 90-year-old client and just leaves them like that?

I'm starting to wonder if Mom and Dad *would've* been okay with letting Ethan stay for Break. I wish I would've at least asked and pretended I was joking to see what they'd say. "At least you can have a week off from work and homework," I told my boyfriend when I called him. "And you'll have plenty of time to practice for Open Mic Night," I bounced my eyebrows.

"Oh no, I'm still gonna work," he laughed. "I'm gonna try to spend as little time at home as possible. But yeah, we still haven't decided on a song yet."

As much as I miss NHU, I was stoked to see Logan again. Madi's Break was last week, of course. We met up for a dinner of appetizers at Applebee's, where I played third wheel to him and Sara, which was probably a nice change for him after always having to sit across a booth from Dillon and me. "So am I ever going to get to come down and visit you at school?" he asked over a plate of loaded nachos.

"I've been waiting for you to let me know when's good for you!" I said like it was up to him.

"I'm not gonna just *invite* myself down!" he said.

"Well...what about the weekend after I get back?"

"We have tickets for that thing at the Albright-Knox," Sara nudged him.

"Oh my god!" I slapped the table. "Speaking of having tickets for things, I forgot to tell you that RBF is coming to campus on April 7th! What about that weekend?"

"RBF, like resting bitch face?" Logan laughed.

"*No*, Reel Big Fish!"

Logan's smile vanished. "Reel Big Fish?" he blinked. "Like, *the* Reel Big Fish!"

"Yes, *that* Reel Big Fish!"

Anybody watching him probably thought a jalapeño slice went down the wrong pipe. "You're *literally* shitting me right now. How do you just fucking *forget* to tell me that?" He turned to Sara. "Please tell me we don't have any plans for that weekend," he pleaded.

"Other than you going down to spend the weekend with your friend, no," she laughed. *At least she's not one of those controlling girlfriends.*

I mentioned to them how I'll have to stuff my face with some Indian food while I'm home, and not only does Sara love it, but she even got *Logan* to try it. He'll do it for her, but not for his ride or die since elementary school? I say that like I never used to do the same thing.

Victor's Snap story was a video of a thoroughly-zooted Kade munching on a chicken and cheese bagel sandwich at their kitchen counter. *"Bruh out here taking himself to Chick-fil-A,"* he laughed as Kade slowly gave him the finger.

March 19

So I think *Under the Whispering Door* might be my new favorite book, given the number of times it had me tearing up.

> **wallowing_tbh** A book—like music, like a movie, like any art done properly—
> does its job when it sticks with you even after you're done with it. You
> approach things with a new perspective, asking yourself the questions you've
> consciously been ignoring because you've been afraid of the answers. Have I
> been living my best life? Have I been taking all this for granted? Will I be

ready to die when my time comes? And why shouldn't today be the day I die?
oakley_dokey okay okay we get it, you liked it. Jesus
hayashi_photography dad quit yelling at mom
oakley_dokey I will throw a tantrum rn

March 20

I wish that tapes and tape players were still a thing, because it'd be really cute to make a mixtape for Ethan of all my favorite songs. Sure, I could just make a playlist and share it with him, but it wouldn't be the same.

I was today-years-old when I bought my first pair of Nike skate shoes, as a late birthday gift for myself. They're white with a mint-green swoosh, which is to say they're fresh as fuck.

I also had to buy my own copy of *Meditations* since I didn't want to highlight all over Tylor's. I read the whole thing in a day. I took it with me everywhere—my bed, the bathroom, the park, work. I guess it's just a journal that the Roman Emperor Marcus Aurelius kept that somehow survived and got published into a book. And the guy knew his *shit*. Listen to this—*"The things you think about determine the quality of your mind. Your soul takes on the color of your thoughts."* And *"You have power over your mind—not outside events. Realize this, and you will find strength."* Now I know where the fuck Tylor got his sage training from and why Ethan never seems to really get upset over anything, at least not to the point where it bothers him like how I let things bother me. *Hoc quoque transibit, memento mori.* It all makes sense now. Where the hell has this book been my entire life?

Imagine if somebody found *my* journals and published them. Dear *god*.

March 21

> Did you know in French instead of saying "I miss you" they say "tu me manque," which means "you are missing from me"
>
> That being said, tu me manque ♡

♡♡♡
I love you so much 😭😭😭😭
Tu me fucking manque too

Je t'aime aussi, mon petite pomme de terre

March 23

It's day 6 of Indictment Watch.

My Instagram is full of Spring Break posts of places from around the world and I'm *high-key* jelly. I might have to take a break from it until we're back at school.

I was laying on my bed, playing Switch for the first time in a hot second, when I looked up to see Dad standing in my doorway. "What are you *listening* to?" he frowned. It wasn't A Day to Remember. It wasn't even Wiz Khalifa or Kid Cudi.

"The Beatles?" I answered like it was the wrong answer. "And how long have you been standing there?"

His face broke into a smile. "I think the better question is how long have you been listening to The *Beatles?*"

I bit the inside of my cheek. "Maybe a month? And why'd you ask what I was listening to if you already knew?"

"Because that's what I do," he smirked. "I used to listen to them all the time when I was in college. I still have my old records of theirs up in the attic."

So that's how we ended up sitting cross-legged on the attic floor, looking through his old records—The Beatles, The Who, John Coltrane, Pink Floyd, The Smiths, U2, The Cure, and a bunch of names I recognized but hadn't listened to. "I forgot you even had these," I said as I examined one after another. "Why don't you listen to them anymore?"

"I still listen to the *music*, just not *these*. And I don't know," he shrugged. "I always said I was going to get a new turntable but just never got around to it."

"You could always use mine," I offered.

"Nah, that's okay," he waved off the idea as he flipped over the albums like they were pages of a book, reading the memories they hold for him. "Everybody was into grunge and rock when I was in college—which, don't get me wrong, I *liked*—but I barely knew anybody who listened to this kind of stuff. I figured it was what the artsy kids listened to." *Like father like son I guess.*

He sat them back in their crates by the handful, lining up the edges. "You can go ahead and take any of these that you want," he knocked me out of my seat.

"Forreal? You don't want them?"

"If they've been boxed-up up here for this long, then I think I can live without them," he winked. "It's funny how you outgrow things as you get older. You'll see."

"I feel like I might have an idea already," I muttered.

So that's how my record collection almost doubled in size. I had to rearrange things to make room for my newest acquisitions. Some of them unfortunately popped and crackled to the point where I just took them back up to the attic, where I found myself going down a rabbit hole of boxes of my stuff that Mom and Dad insisted on keeping—school projects and pointless awards, like the one I got for coming runner-up in the 5th grade spelling bee. Maybe I should submit that with my future resumes? The inside covers of my school yearbooks are scrawled with signatures and notes from teachers and people I haven't spoken to in years. My fingertip traced Aaron Froninger's *"Have a great summer!!"* with a smiley face, and I thought about how the kid who wrote it all those years ago wouldn't live to see junior year. I flipped back to stare down at his picture, three before me in a gray Reebok t-shirt. *It could've just as well have been me.* How many ordinary things do I complain about having to do that some people never live long enough to get the chance to do, like doing my laundry or paying my phone bill?

I opened another yearbook to find the only other Huffman in school, which is how I ended up going through a box of Ryder's stuff. My things were neatly packed away and organized, but Ryder's things were thrown together almost like it was salvaged—*grab it now before you lose it, before it's gone forever.* And not just school stuff, but his old CD player, his first phone with its shattered screen, a wristband with a skull sewn into it, a rolled-up water-damaged poster, his digital clock, old GameBoy Advance games I remember him playing—stuff that bore testament to the fact that he existed, evidence that he too walked this Earth. He never kept a diary or journal, but aren't his things themselves a kind of journal? His body may be in an urn, but his life is laid to rest in our attic. What things he did write down though—the paper he held with his own hands and entrusted his secrets and thoughts with—I took for myself. Call it nonsense or call it free verse poetry, but I'm keeping them forever.

Victor's Snap story was of a candlelit meal of some breaded tofu and furikake rice, complete with chopsticks and fancy dinnerware. *"When you get the munchies and accidentally end up taking yourself on a date."*

March 25

I can't stand these fucking Floridians. You don't want kids to learn about gender identities or sexual orientations in *any* grade now? I'm sure that heterosexuality somehow doesn't count though.

I think the enlightened states should pass laws prohibiting teachers from talking about god in school. Because if kids and teenagers are supposedly too young to understand gender and sexuality and who they truly are, then they're clearly too young to be making soul-binding pacts with some supreme being.

March 27

Today's one of those perfect March days here in New Halle—the whole sky is gray but it's sunny at the same time, and it's flurrying while things are just starting to bud. I love it.

After I picked up a Reel Big Fish concert ticket for Logan, the four of us grabbed copies of *The Herald* at lunch—"Peep those new shoes, fam!"—to read its take on the events that rocked the school just before Break. Let's just say that I doubt President Norwood will be eager to pick up a copy again anytime soon.

"Has anybody heard anything about Denver?" Kade asked mostly Ethan, since he's the one who knows people.

"I heard from Zoe that she's gonna finish the semester remotely, and then probably transfer to another school," Ethan said glumly.

My nostrils flared. "That makes me fucking *sick*." The perpetrators were expelled and pressed with charges, but I still shake with fury when I think about what they did to her. Do you know how damaging that is to a person? "Maybe we should beat the shit out of the guys who did it so they can see how *they* like it."

"No comment," Victor said without looking up, while Ethan and Kade exchanged glances.

"When has answering violence with violence ever solved anything?" my boyfriend asked.

Alone in my opinion, I silently went back to my food. "Do you guys need help getting your stuff to Brew 22 later on?" I changed gears.

"I don't think so," Victor said to his plate.

"What about my light? Do you want me to bring that again?"

"Nope," Kade said. "Just that cute ass of yours."

I'm not sure if it was because they brought the house down the last time they played, but Brew 22 was *packed* when we got there, and we got there *early*. I saw Nikole playing third wheel to Elisha and her new girlfriend Bethany at one table, Miles and who I guess is his newest boy toy at another, and the 370 Rock crowd at another as Tylor and Amina and I made our way over to the seats Kade guarded for us at the band's table.

Whoever's responsible for the order of the acts smartly put Three Lesbians in a Wheelchair last. The cheers that met them as they took the stage—Ethan in a shirt with a popped collar and Kade's Clubmasters, Victor in the tweed blazer he got at the thrift store last semester overtop of his 'PROTECT QUEER KIDS' shirt, and Kade in a pair of brown corduroy pants I'd never seen before—told me that their act was the one the crowd was there to see. "Hi," Ethan smiled. "We're Three Lesbians in a Wheelchair." He gave Victor a look, and Victor counted them into "Weather" by Ginger Root, a band that Tylor had only recently introduced the rest of us to. Ethan did some voodoo with his keyboard to make it repeat what he played so he could play something else over it, and Kade played his bass like he was in The Beatles, joining in on the chorus with his one-word vocal part. It had a very city pop vibe—a genre I'm proud of myself for even knowing—like I was taking in all the neon lights of 1980s Tokyo from the window of a cab.

"Thank you, thank you," Ethan smiled before taking the band right into *another* song as soon as the applause died down. My chest almost took off, *that's* how stoked I was to hear more of them. I couldn't stop smiling. The energy of their second song, also by Ginger Root, was more muted, but their performance wasn't any less captivating. They turned Brew 22 into the finest nightclub in western Pennsylvania.

"We couldn't narrow it down to just one song," Victor told me as I helped them carry out their equipment after the show. "We finally just asked Vanessa if we could do two and she told us to go for it."

"Well *yeah*," I laughed. "You guys are the reason for the turnout." *At this establishment in March 2023, Three Lesbians in a Wheelchair played their first show together as a band*, the future plaque on the front of the building will read.

Victor and Kade drove their stuff back to Axworthy in Victor's shithead car while I walked Ethan's stuff over to Kessler with him through pool after pool of lamplight. "It's a nice night," Ethan said to Old Main's eggshell clock faces.

"You know what'd make it even nicer?" I asked. "Listening to you play something for your boyfriend, right here." I was mostly joking, but he met me with a smile.

"As you wish, *mawn pumb-duh-tare*." He dropped to one of the benches lining the sidewalk around Kessler and laid his keyboard across both of his knees and one of mine. "Any requests?"

I tapped my chin in thought. "How about...one of the other songs you guys considered playing?"

He shook his head. "Nah, not the right vibe for this." His finger scrolled through his music library for one that did fit the vibe. "Well, *actually...*" He turned his volume up and he played a song with a tap, joining in live after the first measure. He didn't use an amp and he talked more than he sang, but it was perfect. People passed by, and one even recorded him for a moment, but I was the only one he sang for.

"That was perfect," I said as I laced my fingers with his and rested my head on his shoulder. *How did I end up with such a talented guy?* I planted a kiss on his neck. "So...I usually don't ask this of guys I just met, but would you wanna go back to my room?"

I felt his face smile. "I'm flattered, but I'll have to decline." He turned to plant a kiss on my mouth before whispering, *"My room's closer,"* his breath hot on my ear.

March 28

You know how there will be an album you don't care for, but then you give it another try and you're like *and I didn't like this* why? Yeah.

It's professor/course evaluation season again, which means we get to sample the other professors in whatever departments the class is in. Some of them make you *so* happy you don't have a class with them, like Dr. Russo from the History department, who gave us Dr. Kotek's evaluation. He's gotta be a million years old. He was barely able to pass out the papers without dropping them. Everyone in Jurado's class was murmuring about how awesome Dr. Kershaw seemed after he'd left the room because of his three-piece pinstripe suit and cool confidence, but he just seemed arrogant to me.

I guess somebody posted a clip of Three Lesbians in a Wheelchair's performance on Twitter and it's gotten hundreds of views, and another one even made it onto *The Herald's* website. *"If audience reaction is anything to go off of, then the highlight of the evening was the performance by the student band Three Lesbians in a Wheelchair, who once again did not disappoint,"* I read aloud at breakfast. "You guys are kinda becoming a big-ish deal now."

"I think we actually *might* be," Ethan said. "I've gotten like ten follow requests from people I don't even know."

"Wow," Victor dryly chuckled. "I wish *I* was popular."

"Vanessa even emailed us saying they had such a good night that we can stop over and pick up a box of brownies on the house," Ethan went on.

"Really? I didn't get that email!" Victor said as he whipped out his phone.

"SGB had this big Summer Send-Off event at The Commons last year," Tylor told us, "and part of it was this battle-of-the-bands type thing." He was able to eat with us because his professor for his Graphic Design class emailed them all saying that she awoke to a malfunctioning dishwasher and a kitchen full of water. "I guess the winners get like $1,000 or a semester's worth of free beer or something."

"Oh yeah, I've heard of it," Ethan nodded.

"You *have* to play it if they have it again!" I said with a bouncing leg.

"Oh wait, there it is," Victor breathed.

On a much more important note, Taco Tuesdays are apparently a thing at Percy's now. I learned about it when Victor chased Tylor and me down in the Quad after Macro to tell us instead of just texting us for whatever reason. Two tacos for $2 is the kind of shit I expect from an industrialized nation. I took two over to Ethan, because the people you love are the people you buy tacos for. "I must've been a good boy," he said as he chowed down on them at one of the high tables. "What'd I do to deserve you?" he asked with his head resting on his fist.

"I have a theory," Tylor chucked, "but I'm not gonna say it out loud because it involves penises."

At least one other person posted a pic of the double rainbow arcing across the sky over the football stadium on their story. *"If god hates gays then someone explain this shit,"* Victor captioned his.

March 29

It's funny how the news can't stop mentioning that the latest mass shooter was trans, and by 'funny' I mean 'it pisses me the fuck off.' Why does it matter how they identify? Why don't they point out that cisgender shooters are cisgender? Or white, or conservative, or men for that matter? Maybe I should start doing that every time there's a tragedy, like how members of my family like to point out things that Black people do while trying to tell me they aren't racist. *Nothing against cis, white, conservatives,* but...

Meditations has become my new bible. It's been *infinitely* more beneficial than the actual bible has ever been for me. I'll read over the parts I highlighted when I'm eating alone or while waiting for class to start. And I think it's actually helped me a little—I don't find myself sitting there at any given moment and worrying about what other people think of me as much as I used to. What they think of me is on *them,* not me. Don't get me wrong—I still do it, but it's progress.

Kade was taking some Kade-time, so Victor and I found ourselves spending our Wednesday evening at the planetarium again. The third time's not as stunning, but it's still nice to watch when you want to think about your own false sense of significance. We walked over to the frozen yogurt place on Main Street—*"Ew, Jesus Christ! Froyo!"*—but didn't head right back to our rooms just yet. Like it does every time I go past it now, the maintenance road behind Hostetler Field House drew my eye to its dumpsters, and my mind to the crime committed there three Sundays ago. I keep thinking about the others' reactions when I said that the guys who beat up Denver deserve to get beat up as retribution—*especially* Victor's. Sure, not wanting to hurt people is an admirable trait, but I would've thought that he of all people would have wanted them to pay.

"Do you remember when I said that the guys who beat up Denver should get beat up?" I finally asked him after talking myself up to say it.

"I do," was all he said.

"You said 'no comment.'"

"I did."

"Why? I picture you delivering vigilante justice on homophobes and racists and other assholes," I said, getting a laugh out of him. "I mean, you certainly let that bigot stool sample in the Quad have it when he was here. So do you not think those guys should get what they deserve, or what?"

He stayed silent for so long that I thought I'd crossed a line. Only after he tossed his trash into a can outside of Novak did he finally say, "Come sit." He hoisted himself up onto a retaining wall in front of the dorm, where I joined him. I passed the moments by creating faces out of the widows and archways in the front of Brubaker Auditorium across the parking lot. "Have you ever done something you aren't proud of?" Victor asked with hands folded in his lap.

I laughed a sarcastic laugh through my nose. *You don't even fucking know.* "Yeah?"

His shoe's heels bounced against the wall like a heartbeat. *Duh-dum. Duh-dum.* "I beat someone up in high school once."

"Like in a fight?"

"No," he said to the space in front of him. "I jumped them."

My head jerked towards him so fast that I almost gave myself whiplash. *What? Why? Am I friends with a hitman?*

"I already *told you* I'm not proud of it," he said as he twisted the string of his drug rug around his finger, "so please hold your judgements until the end."

"Sorry. Okay," I said as I resumed eye contact with Brubaker.

"So there was this girl at school who was a grade below me," he began his story. "She was on the shyer side, mostly kept to herself. I don't know how he found out, but this one guy found out that she was a lesbian. Or I guess I should say is a lesbian. Unless it was just a phase, like the rest of you kids."

"I feel like I already know how this goes," I muttered.

"She already got picked on because people thought she was kind of weird, but once *that* got out, people made her life hell. People would knock books out of her hands, knock her lunch tray off the table. Nonstop snide remarks. Somebody even put *bugs* in her locker. And that was just the stuff I *knew* about."

I swallowed. "That's horrible," my small voice sympathized.

"I tried to make friends with her, but she didn't trust me, and I don't blame her— she probably thought I was just trying to get close to her so I could humiliate her.

So then fast forward to our school's Halloween festival. You know, games and food and costumes and shit. People spiking the punch and graffitiing things. I was helping set up for the 'haunted school' when I figured out how I could get back at the guy who made her life hell." *Cue dramatic music.* "I knew exactly who it was too —the class Vice President, star of the basketball team, and one of the most popular guys in school. Wore those huge stud earrings that douchebags wear."

"Sounds like our pretty boy Aiden," I said as I twisted my own stud. "What'd you do?"

"Remember that part when I said how I beat someone up?"

"Oh, yeah."

"He had a spot in the woods beside our school where he and his friends would go and get high," Victor went on, "so I grabbed a mask and a baseball bat and waited there for him, hoping he'd show up to pregame before heading to the festivities. And could you believe my luck when he actually did? *Alone?*" His story legit made me gulp. I could almost see the flashlight under his chin. "I thought it was a good plan. Nobody would think anything of someone in a mask at a Halloween party. They'd think any screams were just part of the vibe."

"See, this is *exactly* why I don't do haunted houses," I said as a chill ran down my spine.

"I watched him, waiting until I could tell his senses were getting fuzzy enough that he couldn't fight back properly," he recounted with his hands clasped together in the space between his legs. "He went down easier than I thought he would. The look in his eyes once he realized it wasn't a prank made me almost let him go, but then I thought about how if *he* were the one standing over that girl, or Kade, or anybody else he thought was an easy target, that he wouldn't have just let them go." He swallowed. "I don't know what happened, but I couldn't stop swinging at him." He turned to face me, his eyes *wide* with terror. "You need to understand Trevor—I could've *killed* him. Like, I *legit* almost *killed* him."

I put my arm around his quivering shoulder. "But you *didn't* though." My own eyes went wide. "Right?"

"No. But at some point I must've realized what I was doing, because the bat was in the creek and the mask was in the trash and I was running as fast as I could," Victor said. "I wasn't running so I wouldn't get caught—I was running to get away from the monster I saw, but I couldn't get away from it because the monster was *me.*"

I pivoted to put my hand on his shoulder. "Listen to me Victor—you are *not* a monster. Maybe you did *one* bad thing, but how many *good* things have you done for other people?"

"I put him *in the hospital,*" he croaked like he'd only just then realized what he'd done. "*My* conscious actions put somebody *in the hospital.* Do you know what it's like to be *afraid* of yourself? To not know if somebody you care about might accidentally set you off and make you lose control?"

"But you didn't just act out of nowhere," I tried to reason with him. "There was a *reason* for what you did."

"That doesn't make it *okay*," he practically snapped before softening up. "I started meditating after that. I took a vow of nonviolence too. Not like an *official* one, but I promised myself I'd never hurt or, even wish harm, on someone. So if you're wondering why I don't think the guys who beat up Denver should get beat up in return, that's why."

"Props to you on that," I complimented him. "Forreal. I know *I* wouldn't be able to do that."

"Trust me when I say it's been a challenge at times," he chuckled. "That's partly why I don't eat meat either. I don't want animals to have to suffer because of my choices. Not that I'm judging you if you do."

My brain digested what he'd told me. "What's-his-name didn't think the girl put somebody up to it, did he? Like he didn't try to go after her again or anything?"

"Oh no. Everybody figured she didn't have anything to do with it. But she ended up switching schools just to be safe."

I nodded slowly before sliding down off the wall. "My ass is starting to get wet from sitting on this."

"Oh *dad*," he laughed as he hopped off after me. "You can just tell me to shut up. I won't be mad."

I was still so absorbed with his story that sliding down The Railing didn't even cross my mind. *Why are you so surprised, Trevor? We all have our secrets, don't we?* Forreal though, what is it with deep talks and cross-campus walks? "Listen," I told Victor, "I know you're ashamed of what you did, but you can't let your past define who you are."

"Yeah, I know."

"What's done is done. No amount of wishing that things had gone differently can change any of it."

"Oh, don't think that I don't know that," he said seriously. "But you know what? I *do* let my past define me, because I've shown myself what *not* to be like, and what *not* to do. My past is part of what motivates me, if that makes sense."

"It does," I nodded. "Like, there aren't many people who I want to *be* like, but there are plenty of people who I *don't* want to be like. I take all the traits and behaviors and attitudes that I hate, and work myself around those. I call it dis-inspiration."

"That's actually not a bad idea," he admitted.

"Of course it's not. When do I ever have a bad idea?"

"Let's see..." He put up a fist to start counting them off, but came up empty.

"Yeah, that's what I thought," I laughed through my nose.

March 30

LOCK HIM UP! LOCK HIM UP! LOCK HIM UP!

As much as I try to shun political news, I couldn't help it today. "I never thought I'd see the day," Kade grinned as he made popcorn for us.

"They're just being *so mean* to him," I said mockingly, though I wouldn't be surprised if nothing even comes of it, because you can apparently get away with anything when you're a rich white man.

"The sad thing is that none of this will change anyone's mind," Ethan shook his head.

"Fucking *sheeple*."

After we saw and heard our fill of that, we finally got around to playing the game Kade brought from home, *Istanbul*, while drinking tea and listening to a YouTube video of somebody playing an oud. "Didn't you say this was chestnut tea though?" I asked Kade after he'd called it 'chai' for the second time. "Why do you keep saying 'chai?'"

Victor laughed through his nose. "Like Confucius said, the difference between a chestnut and a walnut is how long you edge for."

Kade grabbed his head like it was splitting apart. "*Çay*, not *chai*. Jesus. Like the Turkish word for tea?" He grabbed a Post-It note to literally spell it out on before sticking it to my face. "Forreal Eth, how do you have any brain cells left after spending so much time with him?"

"Oh, I don't," Ethan smirked.

Kade scared me when he called me later on, because he *never* calls me. "Stop what you're doing right now," he said urgently.

My muscles locked. "What's wrong? Are you okay? Did something happen to Victor?"

"No. Go make some popcorn and sprinkle a packet of ramen powder on it," he said gravely. "Hashtag faded."

It took me a good ten seconds to finally speak. "Don't ever fucking do that again," I chuckled with relief as I got up to go to the cabinet. "We don't have any popcorn. And we're out of ramen too."

"Oh," Kade said like I'd let him down. "Well, like the holy bible says, I guess you're just fucked then."

March 31

Alas, this too shall pass.

This morning when Ethan and I went into Patnick for breakfast, there was a balloon tied to Paul's register that read 'HAPPY RETIREMENT.'

"Are you retiring?" I asked her as I handed her my ID for apparently the last time. She responded with a grunt that I took to mean *'what the fuck do you think?'* "Congrats! I'll miss you though," I said.

"Yeah, it won't be the same without you," Ethan smiled.

And then for the first and only time ever, I heard her speak actual words. *"Aww, that's so sweet,"* she croaked without looking at us.

I like to think she drove off with a cigarette in her mouth and a middle finger in the air as students dove out of her way as she sped away. They should erect a statue of her in front of Patnick, complete with a cigarette sticking out of a throat stoma. *'Here worked Paul, whose count of IDs she dropped on the floor was surpassed only by the cartons of Camels she smoked.'*

 4. POV: You're turning up at 370 Rock and you just connected to the speakers

April 1

You know how you freak out when you hear an obscure song that you like playing out in the wild? That's how I felt when I saw that *Real Life*, which I enjoyed so much that I recommended it to Zoe to feature as Proud as Halle's book of the month, on fliers around campus as their featured book for April. Go the fuck ahead.

Kade threw me a curveball after class when he asked me if I wanted to go check out the fish fry at the church on Main Street, and I threw myself a curveball when I agreed to it. Ethan and Victor, citing a litany of reasons not to join us—"What happened to the whole voting-with-your-dollars thing?"—opted for lunch at Zukoff instead. "I don't know what it is with churches always having the best fish sandwiches during Lent," Kade wondered out loud.

"Because Jesus blesses them himself," I said matter-of-factly as I wrinkled my nose at the dogwoods we passed. They're blooming all over campus so the whole place just smells like cum.

We didn't get to try the fish sandwiches though, thanks to the guy standing in front of the church trying to hand out tracts to people. "Did you know that it's possible to live once again after you die?" he asked us with a creepy grin. Kade turned and walked into the street without a word, where he almost got hit by a car. The acolyte turned to me with an expectant look.

"Uhh, *je ne parlais pas anglais*," I said before 180'ing back to the corner, where I waited for Kade.

"So I guess *that's* not happening," he said once he'd crossed back over.

"That person almost hit you!" I said like a Mom.

"Listen, I'd rather *literally* walk into traffic than listen to somebody try to tell me about Jesus," he said. "Besides, they stopped. Nobody's hurt. Nothing's broken."

My boyfriend and my friends and I went on a side quest to Brew 22 after lunch —"Well *that* didn't last long," Victor smirked when we joined them at their table in Zukoff—to pick up the box of brownies Vanessa had promised them, avoiding any churches along the way. Ethan dropped them off in 341 Kessler so they'd last until we went out to 370 Rock later on, because we figured they'd probably taste *amazing* while high. We borrowed Tylor's Frisbee for a game of disc golf since it was nice out, but it wasn't too long of a game though because yours truly accidentally threw it into the pond.

"I *told* you I was bad at it!" I said while Kade howled from the ground.

"You're even worse than *me!*" he screamed.

I wasn't even upset at having to drive to Wally World to get a new one because it gave us an excuse to not be inside. Kade's upbeat playlist was perfect for a windows-down drive. There wasn't much else to get since we haven't even been back for a week and are all pretty stocked up on things thanks to our parents, though you can never have enough mac and cheese cups or PopTarts—or toilet paper, apparently. "We're only gonna be here for like another month!" Victor scolded Kade as he grabbed the cubic meter of toilet paper out of his roommate's hands and put it back on the shelf. "We do *not* need all that!"

"We can always throw some into some trees and get a felony!" Kade said.

I let out a long exhale. "I can't believe we'll be a quarter of the way through college in another month."

"*Stop* dude," Kade said as he begrudgingly took an 8-pack of toilet paper instead. "I don't wanna think about it."

"Sophomore *AF*," Ethan said.

"And yet I *still* don't know what I wanna do with myself," Victor muttered.

We weren't in the mood to resume our game of disc golf when we got back—which I was fine with, since there were more people on the course, and all I needed was for a bunch of Heteros to see my gay, unathletic ass throw another Frisbee in the water—so we just hit up Percy's for dinner, went to see the Theatre department's production of *Hedwig and the Angry Inch* on a whim, and then just chilled in 222 Swafford before heading out for the night. "Don't forget that somebody has a birthday coming up soon!" Victor reminded us with a shit-eating grin.

"Oh, I remembered," I said smugly. "I have a reminder set on my phone."

"Ooh, look at me!" Kade said as he put his hands up and made a face like Butt-Head. *"I'm Trevor and I set a reminder for everything! What do you want, a fucking medal?"*

"I only brought it up because I was thinking it'd be fun if we had a roast," Victor said. "Like if we all took turns roasting each other?"

"Why do that when we can take turns spit-roasting each other?" I laughed.

"Why have a spit roast when we can have a pot roast?" Ethan asked. "Emphasis on the pot."

"Getting to talk shit on y'all?" Kade said enthusiastically. "Yes fucking plea—" He trailed off at the sound of chanting outside. We listened, hearing it get closer and louder until it was on the sidewalk right underneath the window.

"There's not another protest, is there?" I asked as I started to my feet.

"Oh," Ethan smiled, "I bet it's for the Autism Speaks fundraiser they're having at the Field House."

I sighed in relief. "Oh, good." I think it's awesome that the university promotes autism *acceptance* rather than just autism *awareness*. It's the same thing with Black History Month and Women's History Month—you can *know* about them all you want, but then what can you actually *do* to make progress?

On 10 p.m. trips down to the vending machine during the first month or so of living here, I'd see groups of guys going out, stoked at the promise of getting drunk and/or getting their dicks wet, and I'd be both envious of and intimidated by their confident exuberance, wondering what they had in their backpacks, never thinking that I'd someday be one of those guys with his own group of friends. We stopped by 239 Axworthy so Kade could grab one of the bottles of booze his sister had left for him over Break, and by 341 Kessler so Ethan could grab the brownies.

370 Rock was *bumping*, even more so than usual. Kade played bartender for us since none of us were in the mood to get high in the basement. "Ew, you know I hate vodka," I whined when he pulled a bottle of raspberry vodka out of his backpack. "Why'd you have to grab *that*?"

"You just think everything's for you," he faked me out before saying it again in the same cutesy voice he talks to his dog in.

I turned to Cameron, who was pouring himself a drink with stuff that wasn't vodka. "Can you make me one too please?"

"Sure thing, broski," he smiled. He gave me the one he'd already made, and watched me taste it as he whipped up another.

156

"Ooh, it's good!" I said to it, pleasantly surprised. "What is it?"

"SoCo Amaretto Lime."

"Just like the song," I said mostly to myself.

"You know Brand New?" he perked up. "I fucking *love* Brand New."

"I used to play the hell out of them last semester," I said. "Victor actually got me into them. It's good Fall music."

We started talking about music, and I let him scroll through my library. "This is some good shit!" he said. "Go ask if you can put it on!"

I raised an eyebrow. "Is that allowed?"

"I mean, the worst that they'll do is say no," he chuckled.

Buoyed by his encouragement, I asked Alex if he could hook me up. I put on the playlist I'd made in case I'd ever get the far-flung chance to play DJ, and held my breath, waiting for the collective groan of the vibe being killed. But instead...

"I forgot about this song!"

"Who's this by?"

"Yo! This used to be my *shit!"*

"Never heard it, but I fuck with it."

"Who's got the sticks?"

"It's fucking *lit."*

"Is this *your* music?" Ethan asked me as he pointed to the ceiling.

"Does the pope shit on little boys?" I smirked. "Like Stalin said, he who controls the music controls the party."

"Welcome to the party then, fam," Kade laughed.

I'm not sure how it came up, but I found out that Cameron actually used to be roommates with Bradley from Proud as Halle their freshmen year. "Let's just say I'm happy that Chance's roommate didn't mind me being over there all the time," he laughed as we all smoked some loud hookah.

"I don't blame you," I rolled my eyes. "How'd the two of you meet anyway?"

"I was at the grocery store one day waiting for the shuttle to make its round, not knowing that it was done running for the day, and he offered me a ride back to campus. We were talking and all I could think was, 'is this guy hitting on me?' It turns out he was," Cameron smiled. "He gave me his phone number before dropping me off, I got the balls to text him, and the rest is history." He shrugged with a smile. "He's been living in my head rent-free ever since."

"That's adorable," the romantic in me said sincerely. *I hope Ethan and I are together long enough for me to end my stories of how we met with 'and he's been living in my head rent-free ever since.'*

It wasn't until my boyfriend lifted the lid off the box of brownies that I realized how much I'd been looking forward to them. "The body of Christ," he said to each of us as we reverently took a piece of Templar treasure before he went around to distribute the rest.

"Hey, you know what this brownie and I have in common?" a thoroughly-zooted Victor asked us.

A thoroughly-zooted me shrugged. "I'd lick frosting off both of you?"

"Now, now," he smiled as he wagged a finger at me. "No, we both like getting baked." He laughed to himself as he took another deliberate bite.

I frowned. "Did you *ask* it?"

He looked up at me. "Did I ask it what?"

"Did you *ask* the brownie if it likes getting baked?"

Victor looked down at the brownie like he'd never seen one before. "No, I didn't." He stared at it until he sounded like he was about to start crying. "*God,* I'm such an *asshole.*" And then a little while later he asked us, "Do you think they have a bakery in Amsterdam or somewhere that sells brownies and cookies and stuff with weed in them?" as he watched Andrew disembowel a cigarillo.

Kade and I exchanged glances. "No Victor, I'm sure *nothing* like that exists."

"*Especially* not in Amsterdam."

"Oh, okay," Victor said. "Well if they ever make one, their logo should be…" He was quiet for so long that I thought he forgot what he was talking about. "Our brownies aren't the only thing getting baked." We were laughing so hard that we were on the floor. "What?" Victor asked like he missed a punchline.

"It took you that long to come up with *that?*" I shrieked.

"And don't you mean a *motto?*" Kade howled.

Victor turned to go like he was hurt. "Whatever."

I went after him to apologize and to tell him how good of an idea it was when I remembered that pretty much everybody there had been in other countries just last week on Spring Break. I listened to stories of Costa Rican nights, of Dublin pubs, of Roman pizzas, of Prague's cobbled streets winding in the shadows of medieval towers. My mouth would've been watering if it wasn't so dry.

"We got drunk with our professor every night," Cameron said. "This one girl took a shot of absinthe and puked."

"Italian boys are *so* fucking hot," Luca pined.

"I saw it and thought, *is that a bag of loose tea?*" Henry said about a souvenir bag of penis-shaped pasta he'd bought.

"Anybody who comes up to you and just starts talking to you wants your money," Alex rolled his eyes.

"I *swear* there was rum in that ice cream," June said adamantly.

Ethan set down his drink at the first notes of a Troye Sivan song, pulling me away from the stories to dance with him. "Did you put this on your playlist just for me?" he smiled.

"Nope," I said as we pressed our fronts together, "I put it on *because of you*." I was thinking about seeing if he was in the mood to disappear somewhere when Kade asked if we wanted to join him downstairs for some rips off of someone's bong.

"Is that what you kids call it these days?" Ethan laughed, reading my mind.

"Lemme go take a piss first," I smiled.

"Go piss girl!" Kade called after me.

Somebody not being able to hold their alcohol meant that I had to go use the upstairs bathroom, and I had to laugh when I squeezed past Andrew and Sonia's discussion about whether human civilization would revert back to 'the age of gods' when people used religion as a means to control other people. Like, *we there fam.* I took some drunk mirror selfies before leaving the bathroom, and let the breeze from an open window on the landing cool my face. I almost jumped back when I realized someone was sitting out on the roof, alone, hugging their knees to their chest.

Victor turned at the sound of me sliding the window open. "Oh, hey."

"What are you doing out here?" I asked. He didn't have a drink or a joint with him.

"Just looking at the stars." He sounded like he'd sobered up some, which was kind of weird, because he usually goes hard until he can barely function.

"Mind if I join?"

"Go for it."

The part of the roof I found myself on was on the side of the house, away from anybody out on the front porch or back patio. I laid back on the shingles, resting my head on my hands. *What if the night sky is just some kind of covering, and the stars are just holes in it letting in the light of whatever's on the other side of it?* "So what made you wanna look at the stars tonight?" I broke the silence.

"I dunno," he shrugged. "Why does anybody ever look at the stars?" He flipped his hood up and laid back to join me. We stared up at the sky, its authenticity making up for its lack of exaggerated eye-catchers that the planetarium provides. *Nothing like an intimate moment with the universe.*

"I think about that Pale Blue Dot picture a lot ever since I saw the poster of it in your room at your house, and what Carl Sagan said about it," I said. "Like, this is it. This is all we have. It makes you realize just how insignificant everything really is."

"Right?" Victor agreed. "But nobody gives a shit. We're literally *killing* our planet and we're killing each other, and nobody who can do anything to stop it fucking *does* anything about it. We destroy forests out of greed, we genocide animals because we can do it efficiently, we pollute the oceans because it's convenient, we keep people in poverty because it's somehow profitable." He groaned and grabbed his head. "It doesn't have to be this way. Why does it have to be this way?"

"You *did* watch *Don't Look Up*, right? And *Avatar*?"

"Yeah, but it still pisses me off."

I exhaled, sorry that I ruined his moment of peace. "Have you ever read any Stoic philosophy before?" I tried to change gears.

He shifted his bent knee towards Polaris. "Unh uh. Why?"

"It seems like something you'd like. It's about fate and the natural order of things, how nothing is inherently good or bad, but prescribed by the universe. It's the way we perceive things and react to them that's good or bad."

"I have a few problems with that logic," he frowned.

"I just thought it kind of went with how we think everything revolves around us when we're just a part of an *infinitely* bigger picture that doesn't give two shits about what happens to us. Like we're constantly on the brink of catastrophes and wars and pandemics and we act like we'll never go extinct."

He chewed on that. "Okay, I gotchu."

As good as bong rips sounded, deep conversations with people like Victor is the kind of stuff I live for. I let Ethan know I'd be down soon so he wouldn't think I ditched him, but not to wait for me. "Do you think there are parallel universes?" I asked Victor. "And also, do you want a sip of this?"

"Absolutely. And sure." We passed my SoCo Amaretto Lime back and forth. "Do you think there are?"

"Uh huh. I like to think there are other Trevors out there who took all the chances I didn't take and who grew up in different circumstances and stuff like that. It helps me when I'm feeling depressed and bad about myself. Like somewhere out there, my family was always accepting of me, and I met Ethan years ago."

"Yeah, I think a lot about what my life would look like if things had gone differently," he nodded. "I saw a theory online that said every person shares the same soul. Like, as soon as you die, you're born as somebody else, and you repeat that until you've lived the lives of every person to ever exist."

"*Sheesh*," I said as I propped myself up. "What about animals?"

"I don't know. Maybe. I *guess* animals have souls?"

"I don't see why *not*."

"I mean, I doubt souls are part of evolution. So either *everything* has one or *nothing* does."

"So do you have to live as every blade of grass too then? And every flower and leaf?"

"Maybe."

"*Goddamn*. That's a long existence."

"And that's just what's on *this* planet. Maybe you have to live out the existence of everything that has existed and everything that will *ever* exist."

"Okay, we need to talk about something else," I chuckled uneasily. "Why do you think we're here?"

He laughed out loud. *"That's* what you consider a step down?"

"I mean, is it impossible that this is all just accidental? Or intelligent design?"

He considered his answer. "Do you know what the chances are that a kid will have green eyes if his parents both have blue eyes?"

"I dunno," I shrugged. "I just always assumed that one of the parents would have to have green eyes."

He pointed to his own right eye. *"One percent.* So no, I don't think anything's impossible."

My toes curled and uncurled inside my shoes. It was almost like he was asking me to ask him. "Victor, can I ask you something?"

"You're gonna have to go get me a drink before I can think about kissing you."

I turned to him. "Wait, forreal?" *Good job Trevor, now he knows you'd low-key be up for kissing him.*

"April Fool's!" he chuckled. I groaned and dug for my phone to see if it was indeed after midnight. "What'd you wanna ask me though?"

My chest throbbed, my breaths heavy. I almost made something up. "I know this is absolutely *none* of my business, so don't feel like you need to answer if you don't want to, but why do you live with Kade and his family?" I managed to say. "What happened to your parents?"

'Why don't you mind your own fucking business?' he could've said, or, *'I don't wanna talk about it.'* But instead, "They're gone."

"Oh," I said as my asshole clenched. "Gone as in...?"

"Gone as in they're dead."

"Oh," my small voice said as my asshole retreated deeper into my body. I was going to leave it at that, but he went on.

"My moms were visiting their friends down in—"

"Wait—*moms?* You had two moms?" My asshole relaxed as the picture in his room of him as a boy with the two women with him streaked across my mind.

"Yeah? And?"

"Nothing! That's awesome!"

"Thanks?" he chuckled. "It was always funny to me how people reacted when they found out, but that's just the way it always was for me." He turned back to the night sky. "My parents taught me that all families don't have to look the same, and to be proud of ours. But they also told me there will always be people who are afraid of others who are brave enough to be themselves. They taught me to question with curiosity, and to understand instead of to judge. They taught me to never take shit from anyone because of who I am or who I grow up to be, and to stand up for the people who *do* get shit because of who they are."

So that's how, in the first hour of April on the side roof of 370 Rock Hill Road, more pieces of the puzzle of Victor fell into place. "So...what happened to them?" I asked, not realizing he had a tear running down the side of his face. Victor crying is one of those things that I can't imagine, like Patrick Paul being a sports announcer. "I'm sorry, I didn't mean—"

"No, it's okay." He took off his glasses and took a breath. "They were in Orlando for a bachelorette party, and they went out for drinks afterwards." He pressed his thumb and finger to his eyes. "They went to Pulse," he choked out. "They were at Pulse the night of the massacre."

My asshole disappeared like a black hole had caught it. *"Oh my god,"* was all I could say before I started crying too. Victor let me pull him into a hug. Neither of us had ever seen the other cry before, and neither of us held back. *"Oh my god. Victor, I'm so sorry. I can't—"* What could I even say? I had nothing. There were no words. So I just held him and let him grieve. He's like the third person I've ever shared shoulders to cry into with.

"I tell myself," he said between sniffles, "that they were the first ones killed, since they were found near the door. That one moment, they were enjoying the night, having a good time, and the next, they were dead before they knew what was happening." His words from just a few minutes before echoed in my mind. *"Yeah, I think a lot about what my life would look like if things had gone differently."* I played out the scenarios of the last time he ever saw them. *Did they tell him they'll see him in a few days? Did he say goodbye back? Did he tell them he loved them?* I thought about the other universes out there where Victor's moms couldn't make the bachelorette party, or went out to a different nightclub, or had left a minute earlier— where they're the ones he spends Christmas with, where they're the ones sending him care packages, where they're the ones calling him to talk about his day, where they're the ones moving him into his dorm, where they're the ones watching him accept his diploma and thinking *'we're so proud of you honey.'*

"I was staying with Kade while they were away," he said in a steadier voice. "It was actually his parents' idea to adopt me." *How do you break news like that to your son's best friend? How do you sit him down without getting hysterical and tell him that he's never going to see his parents again?*

"You didn't have any other family?" I asked.

"I do, but they're conservative as all hell."

I was both surprised and embarrassed to hear myself chuckle. "Say no more."

"It was a win-win for everybody," Victor went on. "For me, for Kade, for his family, for my family who would've had to put up with me." His weak smile faltered. "I still have nightmares about it. I'll be back in our old house and my parents will be making dinner or cleaning, but they're full of bullet holes or their faces are destroyed." I tried not to think about that image as we stared up at the uncaring blackness. "I wonder what they'd think about me. I mean"—he chuckled sarcastically —"how could anyone be proud of their loser of a son who has no game and who likes to get high and who doesn't know what he wants to do with his life?"

"Victor, have you *met* yourself?" I said as I turned to face him. "So what if you smoke sometimes and haven't been with a girl yet? And *nobody* knows what they wanna do with their lives at our age. You're just figuring things out, which I think is better than rushing into something and regretting it when it's too late."

"I mean, I *guess*," he reluctantly said. "But it seems like everyone else has their lives so much more together than I do."

"So? There's so much more to you than that," I said with conviction. "Do you know how much I look up to you? It's a fucking *privilege* to be friends with you."

He looked at me like he might start tearing up all over again. "Do you really mean that?"

"Abso-fucking-lutely. I wish *I* was raised the way *you* were raised."

"I think you turned out pretty good though," he said.

"My parents just taught me how to be *polite*—I had to figure out just about everything else on my own, and I don't just mean my sexuality." I crossed my arms over my chest. "I can't even *begin* to conceive how hard losing both your parents so young could be though," I said maybe stupidly. *How can life be so unfair? How can life be so uncaring?* "You wanna talk about putting things in perspective? Being face-to-face with the universe has *nothing* on losing somebody close to you. You see other people doing their own things, going to work or out shopping, and you wanna grab them and shake them until you get some sympathy out of them. *'They're gone, goddammit, they're GONE, how do you not care that they're GONE?'* You wonder why time hasn't stopped, how the world hasn't stopped spinning."

He looked at the space above me, at the trees and chimneys beyond us. "Who'd you lose?" he asked after a few moments.

Without any intention to, I told him about Ryder. I showed Victor that he's not the only one who's had to live with the pain and the unfairness and the abruptness and the emptiness—'The After,' as I call it—that he's not the only one who wishes that they existed on another branch of the tree of their life's possibilities, wishing that their life could have avoided that *one* swerve.

"I never knew," he managed to say in a cracked voice. "I feel so bad for you and your family for having to carry that. I couldn't imagine what coping with suicide is like."

"No, you probably can't." *And you sure as shit wouldn't feel bad for me if you knew that I was just another one of his bullies.* "But I don't wanna sit here and go back and forth about how the other one of us had it worse."

He wiped his eyes. "Definitely not."

We laid together in a way that would've made anybody sus of my fidelity to Ethan. "So your tattoo of The Tower..?" I started to ask.

"Yep," Victor nodded. "That was my Tower moment." I wanted to ask him to pull down his pants so I could see it in its true context. "I got a tarot reading done just for fun at a Renaissance fair like a month before it happened, and I figured that the woman who did it was just being all theatrical when she warned me about disaster and woe."

"So do you think they like actually work?" I asked.

"Work, like predict the future? Probably not. But I've never been able to totally convince myself that it was a coincidence. I have my cards just for fun now, but for a while I was low-key obsessed with them. I took them *everywhere* with me. Every night before bed I'd whip it out, and then afterwards I'd pull out my tarot cards."

You never know how much you need a good laugh until you get one. We howled and tossed on our backs, and I actually grabbed onto Victor because I was afraid he'd roll off the side of the roof. "*Ohmygod* did I need that," he laughed as he took off his glasses again to wipe his eyes for the hundredth time.

"A heart-to-heart, or some comic relief?"

"Both. You're the first person at school I've told all that to."

"You're just spilling all kinds of secrets," I half-joked.

"Perks of being my best friend," he smiled.

I stared down the sky, not thinking about the stars or Ryder or Victor's moms, but all the talks that he and I have had, how much less profound my life would be without him in it. "Yeah, I'd consider you my best friend by now."

"Really? More than Ethan?"

"Ethan's in a different league. Sure, we have our intimate moments, but I have no obligation to you or anything, if that makes sense."

"*Rude*," he smirked. "I know what you mean though. It's kind of the same with Kade. He's my brother and we've always been there for each other, but sometimes..." He sighed. "Sometimes I feel like I just can't talk to him about some things. Is it bad of me to say that?"

"I don't think so," I shook my head. "Everybody's in our lives for different reasons. You can't expect one person to be everything for you." Is it bad of *me* to say that?

"*Sheesh*. You're so wise. You're like a Buddha covered in burned hair," he misquoted *Anchorman*.

"That's not how the line goes," I laughed.

"Whatever you say, best friend."

We helped each other up to go in, but not before I asked him one last question. "You and Kade have been each other's main characters for like half your lives, right?"

164

"Yeet."

"What'll happen when you two eventually go your separate ways?"

I couldn't tell if he'd never really given it any thought before, or if it's just another inevitability that he tries to avoid dwelling on. "I'll worry about that when it happens. Until then, I'm just gonna enjoy being with him while I'm able to." He was just about to open the window when he stopped to turn to me. "You wanna know why I think we're here? I think this is all just an accident, and we're gone before we know it. Life is shorter than we think. You've gotta just smell the flowers while you can, because every day is all we have."

"You really *should* look into Stoicism," I said. I took one last look up at the sky before climbing in after him. "They're out there somewhere, aren't they?"

He looked back up and nodded like there's nothing he's more sure of. "Yeah, they are."

You would've thought that there was a search party out looking for me from the way Ethan grabbed onto me once my best friend and I made it back to the party. "Where WERE you?" he practically shouted. "What were you *doing?*"

I gave Victor a sideways smirk. "It took some convincing, but I managed to talk Victor into letting us double-penetrate him."

"Yeah," Victor snorted, "I said I wouldn't take either of you unless I got the package deal." *God, how I love a good double entendre.*

Talking with Victor sobered me up in more ways than one. I couldn't sip my water for more than a minute without looking over at him and thinking about the trauma he's endured, and how he's one of the strongest people I know.

2 a.m. rolled around, but the party showed no signs of stopping. "Hey Trevor," Cameron nudged me. "You know what a good song to kill the vibe to get people to leave would be?" He nodded to the bottles of SoCo and Amaretto.

I smirked and nodded a slow nod. "I think I sniff what you're smelling."

The song wasn't even on for a minute before people started throwing back the rest of their drinks, cleaning up their trash, and grabbing their stuff on their way out.

April 2

Okay, so I guess they're not dogwoods.

"They're not *dogwoods*—they're Callery pear trees, you fucking chode," Kade corrected me after I said how the dogwoods reek. "Fun fact—the seeds have cyanide in them."

"I had to explain to the RHA advisor what a chode was the other day," Ethan chuckled. "My phone fell out of my pocket and I called it a chode and he was like 'what did you say?'"

"I had to explain to my advisor what the gooch is," Victor said. "He asked me if this Wednesday would be a good day to meet to pick out my classes and I said 'that's gucc.'"

Ethan convinced us to go to the RHA/CPB rave event last night instead of turning up at 370 Rock. He was also the one who suggested that we do ecstasy, which I thought was a joke at first. "Now *that's* an idea I can fuck with," Kade said in our window booth at Ginny's. "I wonder if Alex knows where we could get any?"

"What if I don't wanna do ecstasy?" I basically whined.

Kade laid his phone face-down on the table. "*Shit*, my bad. I shouldn't have assumed. Would you be interested in doing drugs tonight?"

"Not really," I said meekly.

"Well that's too fucking bad," he said as he picked it back up. Feeling high-key peer-pressured and a little betrayed, I gave Ethan a look that begged him to change his mind.

"If you don't want to then you don't have to. I'll do whatever you want to do," he said, though the half-smile forming on his face told me what he *really* wanted to do. "But it *would* be fun though."

So that's how we ended up at 370 Rock, but not to party. I looked longingly from Anubis to the bottles in the kitchen as Kade pounded down the steps from the second floor like he was being chased. "I got 'em," he said excitedly as he patted his front pocket.

"Have fun, boys," Alex called after us with a grin and a wave.

Since Ethan and Kade weren't doing anything to make me feel any better, I slowed to keep pace with Victor. "Have *you* ever done this before?"

"Nope," he shook his head. "I did accidentally do meth once though."

That One Time I Accidentally Did Meth: An Autobiography by Victor Morozov.

Ethan spun on him. "How do you *accidentally* do meth?"

"I was at a party and I thought it was molly! How was I supposed to know the difference?"

"You're lucky you didn't get hooked on that shit!"

"Says the one who likes to do MDMA," I rolled my eyes.

"It was *one* time," Ethan said defensively. "And ecstasy isn't the kind of drug you get addicted to."

"Whatever," I muttered, staying quiet as we crossed the west side of campus towards Hostetler to let him know I was annoyed with him.

"You know I don't mean to come off as not caring," Ethan said as he hung back to put his arm around me. "It'll be fun. You'll see." He pecked my cheek.

166

"If you say so," I sighed.

We could feel the pounding bass through the walls of the Field House before we even made it inside. "RHA tries to have their events on Friday or Saturday nights to give students who don't like to go out something to do," Ethan explained to us. "And to try to deter students from going out and making bad decisions." Given the contents of Kade's pocket, the irony was unparalleled.

The large roll-up doors were kept open for ease of access as much as they were to keep the place from overheating. The far end of the court had a stage with a big screen behind it where the DJ stood, with speakers and lights mounted on stands and rigging around the room. Some organization was smartly selling glow sticks from a table by the door. Students weren't allowed to bring their own drinks in—for obvious reasons—but the bottles of water they provided were all we needed. Huddled in the bathroom at the deserted end of the building, Kade shook the little baggie into his cupped palm and handed each of us an ocean-blue tablet with a happy face etched into it. I stared down at it like it was the nuclear codes. *It looks like a kid's vitamin. I can't believe I'm about to do this. Do they make ecstasy tablets shaped like Fred Flintstone?* I closed my fist around it, hoping it would be gone when I opened it again.

"You're sure you wanna do this?" Ethan gave me one last chance to back out. "If you don't—"

"Yes," I said, more unsure than I've ever been about anything. "I don't wanna ruin anyone's fun." I caught him giving me a look in the corner of my eye. *Besides, I don't wanna have to listen to my friends talk about something else that I missed out on.*

On Kade's count, we threw our heads back and washed down our time bombs. "Well, speak now or forever hold your peace," Victor said as he stuffed his water bottle into his back pocket. "And by that, I mean try to make yourself throw up."

Back on the floor of the Field House, I was too overwrought to function. I just stood there as Ethan said hi to some House Council and RHA people. *Why couldn't we have just shown up drunk? Why couldn't we have asked Alex for some weed gummies?* "Do you feel anything yet?" Ethan asked me.

"Yeah, fear and regret," I said.

He gave me a concerned look. "Why? What's wrong?"

I turned my full attention to him. "Are you being forreal right now?" I chuckled bitterly. "I feel like you guys just wanna enjoy yourselves so bad that you don't even care what I want or what I'm comfortable with. I didn't even wanna do this, and now"—*because of you,* I stopped myself from saying—"I've done drugs, like *real* drugs, and instead of being able to *enjoy* myself, I'm just standing around waiting for god-knows-what to happen."

Ethan stared at me blankly. He could've said, *"Fine, go back to your room. Nobody's making you stay here."* But instead, he offered me his hand. "Come," he smiled. I took it and he led me into the crowd, where he brought me to bounce, then move, then eventually dance with him. *How can I stay mad at him?*

"I didn't mean to snap at you like that," I finally said. "I'm—"

"No, don't apologize. *I'm* sorry." He draped his arms around my neck. "You're right. You were nervous and I was being selfish instead of sensitive."

I hugged him back. "I'm still sorry though. I wish I wasn't so nervous about things all the time. I'll try to stop being such a poopyhead."

"You're not being a poopyhead," he smiled before leaning in for a kiss. "So here's the thing about it though—there's nothing we can do about it now. But whatever happens, I'll be right here with you. You trust me, don't you?"

"Of course I do," I said like I couldn't believe he'd think otherwise.

"My best advice would be…whatever happens, whatever you feel, don't try to fight it," he advised me. "Just go with it. Just let it take over." *Well that's reassuring.* I was anxious as all shit, but I was determined to have an open mind. I mean, the others do and they always seem to have fun. My neon-yellow necklace and bracelets floated between people while I waited for the countdown to hit zero, interpreting every feeling as the start of it. *Is this what it's like once you've been bitten by a zombie and didn't save the last bullet for yourself?* The anticipation was *killing* me.

"Are you sure Alex didn't just give you some candy or something?" I asked Kade after maybe a half hour. "I still don't feel anything." 15 minutes later though, I was singing a different song.

"KADEwhattheFUCKdidyougiveme?" I hissed through gritted teeth as my fingers dug into his shoulders.

Nothing—*nothing*—could have ever prepared me for the assault on my body and senses. The flashing, strobing lights were explosions, the bass an earthquake pressing in on me. Is it possible to experience PTSD for a carpet bombing run from a past life? But the freakiest part was what was happening *inside* of me. My body came alive—not just functioning, but *alive*. My networks of wiring pumped thunderbolts into every part of me. My skin became tectonic plates. My chest, an unstoppable engine. My brain, scrambled and fried. I tried to remember when a piece of gum got into my mouth before I realized it was my tongue that I was chewing on. I've never felt so energized in my life. *I need to move.* I was starting to freak out. *Ineedtogetthefuckoutofhere.* I forced myself through bodies so I could escape, but only once I was outside did I realize what I was trying to escape from was the thing alive inside of me. *This is why people gut themselves. This is why people gut themselves.* I was about to start climbing a tree when Ethan's voice caught me like a lasso. "Don't run off like that!" he said with fear in his face.

"I just had to get out of there," I nearly panicked. I wanted to peel my burning skull away from my skin. *How have my eyes not fallen out yet?* "Is this what this is *like?* Is this supposed to be *fun?*"

The bugs under his own skin made him fidget and twitch. "I told you that you just gotta go with it."

"How am I supposed to *go with it* when I'm freaking the fuck out?" I ricocheted in place. My fingers flexed like a malfunctioning claw game. It's a good thing I didn't make it to Main Street, because then I would've seen a Skeleton in bunny pajamas with a basket of Easter eggs and things would've gotten *real* bad. "Can we walk somewhere?"

Ethan and I powered across the Quad and the byways of campus. I felt like sprinting. I was deciding whether I wanted to heave one of the boulders or tackle the rock climbing wall in Overholt when my phone found itself in my hand. "I need to call Logan." He answered on the third ring. "Hey Logan what's up I hope I'm not interrupting anything."

"Wh—"

"So long story short Ethan suggested we do ecstasy and then Kade got some from his sister's friend who goes here but I guess he's all of our friends by this point and there's this event going on that's like a rave or something *that's* why Ethan wanted to do it but anyway I didn't wanna do it at first and I'm still kinda iffy about it but then it hit me and *holy fucking shit* is it unreal please don't judge me I don't know if you've ever done it before but oh my god you can feel it *inside* of you and it's almost like the music is *inside* of you it's the weirdest thing I've ever felt you just wanna move around and I *get it* now why people do this stuff at actual raves it all makes sense now and I *wish* you would've been here this weekend for this because honestly it's starting to not be as bad now and I think it's better when you're with more people doing it and you're one of my favorite people but I promise we'll still have fun when you come up next week—"

I couldn't shut up. I don't think I've ever talked so fast in my life. I heard him trying not to laugh the whole time, going "uh huh" and "yep" and "I bet" and "go ahead!" "It sounds like you're having a good time then," he said when I finally took a breath. Ethan took breaks from his boxing match with nobody to jump up onto a bench or to drop and do a few pushups. I finally let Logan go as Ethan and I made our way back to the Field House, which locked our eyes with its light show going on inside its open doors. I tripped and fell on some steps, getting up unfazed like an android.

Maybe it was because I was over the initial shock, but the rave wasn't as overwhelming when we went back to it. I didn't make eye contact with anyone though because I was high-key paranoid that they'd be able to tell that I was on drugs. *How many other people here are on something?* I felt more uneasy than anything, like I was crouching on a wobbling longboard on the edge of a cliff—I had to stand up, but I was too afraid of getting thrown off. *Just surrender to it,* I heard Ethan's voice say amid the frenzy in my brain. *You can do it. You won't fall. You trust me, right?* I closed my eyes and tried to force reset my mind, like a mix between mentally taking a deep breath and making my ears pop. I opened my eyes and couldn't believe what I saw and *felt.* Everything was good and incredible and *alive.* I relinquished control of my body and let it submit to the music, let it bound up the steps to race around the second-floor track, let it be amazed at what was happening in the room below. *This is what it means to be alive.* My body leapt back down into the phenomenon of the crowd and lost itself. *I can't believe I get to be a part of this.* I almost drowned when I ripped the cap off a water bottle and crushed it into my mouth. *Trevor Huffman, 19, of Swafford Hall, needed to be resuscitated by emergency services after going right the fuck ahead,* the police blotter would say. I found myself talking to anybody and everybody—people I recognized, people I'd never seen, it didn't matter. I bumped into Zane from Creative Writing, who I'd barely ever spoken to, and who was soberly enjoying the night.

"What's up buddy?" I said as I pulled him into an enthusiastic hug. He looked somewhat happy to see me until I whispered *"I'm on ecstasy right now"* into his ear. He kept his eye on me as he backed away.

An explosion of light lit up Ethan's face, and my jaw dropped. "What's wrong?" he asked me with a smile like he already knew. Another strobe showed me the stars in his eyes—those wonderful, wonder-filled eyes, eclipsed by portholes to the universe.

"Your eyes! You should see your eyes right now!"

"They probably look like yours do!"

The crowd parted for me as I darted for the bathroom. The sink grasped my fingers as I leaned over it to get lost in the cosmos that had swallowed my own eyes. *I am Trevor Huffman. I am love. I am the universe. And I can do anything.* That's why the stuff is illegal—society would be a lot harder to manage if everybody knew that they were manifestations of the universe.

Ethan appeared beside me in the mirror and I turned to hold his face. "I am the universe, and I love you." We tried kissing with our eyes open, but got weirded out.

I'd totally forgotten my friends were even there until we came across Victor punching his fists into the air, drenched with sweat. Kade was nearby, dancing with some girls like they were all possessed. None of us needed to speak because we spoke through our movements, like disciples of some New Age thing. The music got more on-point as it played—MGMT, CHVRCHES, A Place to Bury Strangers, the remix of "Pursuit of Happiness," and Passion Pit, which makes *way* more sense when you're high out of your mind. Even the stuff I didn't recognize kept the vibe seamlessly flowing, but Shazamming them didn't even cross my mind. Once-in-a-lifetime nights like that are meant to be just that—once-in-a-lifetime. *Ichi-go ichi-e.* Sure, we could all go to another rave and pop pills and listen to the same music in a year from now, but where will we be in a year? Who will we be in a year? I know a lot can change in a year because *I've* changed a lot in the past year. We might not even be friends anymore. Ethan and I might not be together anymore. Victor and Kade might have gone their inevitable separate ways. One of us could be dead. That's just the way it works. Ceteris paribus doesn't apply to the human experience. The only thing I can be sure of is that I can't be sure of anything. *"You've gotta just smell the flowers while you can, because every day is all we have."*

So as the four of us abandoned ourselves to the music together, for one night—as if it was the only night I'd ever have with them—I celebrated the family I got to spend it with. I looked from Kade to Victor to Ethan, all of them caught up in euphoria, all of them oblivious that in that moment the person who owes so much of who he's become to them was thanking the universe for letting the trajectories of their lives intersect with the path of his—the same person who was well aware that *yes, this too shall pass.* I wanted them to know how much of my life I've let them take up, how I couldn't have asked for better friends, how they've been giving me the best time of my life without even knowing it, how I hope the day never comes when we're just acquaintances who knew each other once upon a time. But those are the kinds of things you can't say because people will think you're on drugs—which, to be fair, I was.

I'm not sure if it actually happened or if I imagined it, but at one point—maybe hours later on the comedown—we stood tucked together in a circle with our arms around each other's shoulders like we were pepping ourselves up for a sports play. *"I love you guys. I love you guys. I love you guys,"* I affirmed, chanting as if in prayer.

April 4

TFW when you think you're watching an ad for cologne but it ends up being an ad for Velveeta.

In today's news, I made awkward eye contact in class with Zane, Ethan formally announced his candidacy for RHA President, and we met Paul's replacement, Pencie. Yes, Pencie. If people don't start calling her 'Pencil' behind her back by the end of the week, then this isn't NHU. You can actually understand her and she doesn't smell like an ashtray, so she's going to have to step up her card-dropping game if she wants to deliver that authentic Patnick dining experience.

Later on once I was back in 222 Swafford for the night, Tylor asked me if they could talk to me about something. "If you tell me that you got abducted by aliens again," I chuckled, though I was worried they were going to say they changed their mind about Logan coming down.

"No," they laughed. "No, it's not that."

I bookmarked my place in *Americanah*. "What's up?" *Whatever it is, it must be serious*. Their face reddened and they were taking deep breaths.

"Oh god," they said as they wiped their hands on their pants. "This was a lot easier when I did it in my head. Is this what coming out to people feels like?"

My mouth fell open. "Are you *gay*? Because if so then I have questions."

"No!" they laughed nervously. "No, I...I just wanted to ask you if you could start referring to me with they/them pronouns."

I blinked. *That was it?* "Yeah. Yeah, of course."

They smiled with relief. "Thanks."

"No, thank *you*," I smiled back. "Am I the first person you've told?"

"Yeah. I figured since you have to live with me, you should be the first to know."

"Wow, I'm honored. Forreal, I am."

Their hand found the back of their neck. "I was like, 97% sure you'd be cool with it, but part of me was still worried how you'd react."

"You're one of the coolest people I know, and the way you identify isn't going to change that," I said. "And referring to you with different pronouns isn't something you *ask* people to start doing, that's something you *tell* people to start doing."

Instead of responding to that, they just started laughing. "No, I'm not laughing at you. It's just like, *that's* what I was so worried about?" they chuckled. "I didn't think you being supportive would feel so...relieving."

"Right? And for me hearing you say that, it's like, *this* is how other people feel when I come out to them? *This* is what I've been so afraid of?" I smiled. "And I'm sure I'm gonna trip up, so please call me out if I misgender you or make you feel *any* degree of uncomfortable."

"*Please*," Tylor rolled their eyes, "we've been calling each other 'Mom' all year. But it's an easy thing to get tripped up on though. This'll be new for me too."

"It really *isn't* though," I said. "Maybe the first or second time, but after that there's no excuse." Repubes say that kids shouldn't be 'exposed' to something 'too difficult' for them to understand like someone wanting to go by different pronouns, yet they expect kids to accept that god is three distinct, separate beings, while at the same time being one single, absolute being. "What about 'ze' and 'zir?' Can I use those, or would you prefer not?"

"Go for it, if you're feeling extra French," they chuckled.

"Okay, you just unconvinced me," I laughed. "Oh my god, I can't *wait* for you to tell Victor. I bet he'll get you a cake or something."

April 5

Forget Christmas. Forget my birthday. Forget Thanksgiving. Forget Halloween. Forget New Year's. The best day of the year, no contest, is that first warm sunny day when you *know* that Spring's here, when you can *feel* it in the air, when the trees and bushes are popping with buds, when people are walking around outside without a purpose. Today was that day. *It's like campus awoke from its collective hibernation,* I thought as I ate my Zukoff lo mein in the Quad in shorts and watched footballs and slacklines and skateboards, listening to music pour from open dorm windows. Campus was so alive it was distracting.

I had to spend the afternoon at work in Rosenberg. I contemplated quitting.

I went back to 239 Axworthy after dinner—"Thank you for being you," Victor told Tylor with a hug after Tylor came out to the others as nonbinary—where Victor had me proofread his RA application. "You're good with grammar and all that stuff," he said to me with an expectant look with his Mac in his hand.

"How perceptive of you," I smirked as I reached for it. He nervously watched me read it over. "I think it's good!" I said after I'd proofread it.

"Forreal?" he asked like he didn't think so.

"Forreal. There are a few things I'd change structurally, but other than that..."

"Work your magic."

I didn't even know that he'd done most of the stuff he put in it—*'offer to tutor classmates,' 'help fellow residents acclimate and familiarize themselves with campus life,' 'volunteer for hall activities.'* "Did you just make shit up for this?" I half-joked.

"Nuh uh! Swear to god!"

"Well then I think you have a damn good chance at getting it," I said as I handed his Mac back to him. It hit me that I hadn't gotten him anything for his birthday, so I browsed for a shirt with a message on it for him while he read over it again before submitting it.

What was supposed to be an evening of board games turned into watching montages of grisly death scenes from the *Resident Evil* series on YouTube while we waited for the arrival of our pizza that Victor, high off of accomplishment, ordered for us. "We'll start playing once it gets here, I swear," he said as he let the next video in the queue play.

"I'm gonna go make some tea until then," Kade said as he got to his feet. "And by 'make tea,' I mean 'furiously masturbate into all your drinks in the fridge.'"

"Love me some extra protein," Victor chuckled before answering his incoming call. "Hello? Yeah. Sounds good, I'll be right down." He hung up and hopped to his feet. "Pizza's here. BRB," he said as he stepped into his slides and kicked the stop under their door.

I was trying to decide if the block of wood with nails sticking out of it sitting on Kade's desk was a project for class or just for fun when the sound of something breaking—the kind of sound you hear and you just *know* something's wrong—sent me to the doorway. Kade's broken mug lay on the floor beside Kade, who was writhing and convulsing like he was getting electrocuted. *Hoh my fucking god.* I moved so fast that I swear I teleported.

"Kade? What's wrong?" *Is he having a seizure?* "Kade?" *What if it doesn't stop?!* "Please say something!" I pleaded. His eyes rolling back into his head sent me into panic mode.

"HELP!" I yelled, so scared that I started to tear up. *Why the hell did this have to happen when Victor was out of the room?!* "SOMEBODY PLEASE HELP ME IN HERE!" All I could do was carefully try to cradle his head and beg the universe to bring Victor back. My head snapped to the door when a voice from the hallway answered my call.

"Hello? Did somebody say they needed help?"

"YES! ROOM 239! THE DOOR'S OPEN!" A girl slowly pushed it open, and her jaw dropped at the sight of us.

"Ohmygod, is he okay?" *Does he LOOK okay?!*

"No, I—I think he might be having a seizure!" She pushed the nearest chair out of the way and crouched beside us. "What should I do?" I asked as the water kettle went off.

"I—I," she sputtered, "I think we just have to wait for it to pass."

So that's what Victor walked in on. "What's—? Oh *fuck!*" He dropped the food onto the table and ran to grab a pillow to place under Kade's head. "There, make sure his head stays on it," he instructed us. Once Kade's movements became less spastic, I filled him and Nice Girl in on what happened. "Jesus *Christ* am I glad you were here," he said to me before turning to Nice Girl. "Thank you, Tanika. You didn't have to do this."

"I didn't really do anything," she downplayed herself, but the fact that she even showed up wasn't lost on us, and her just being there with me helped keep me calm—however calm you can be when one of your friends is short-circuiting and you can't do anything about it.

Kade finally stilled, and after a few moments his eyes swiveled around the room before resting on us. "Wha—what happened?" he asked like he'd just woken up. "Why am I—" he frowned at the floor.

"You had a seizure," Victor breathed seriously.

Kade stared. "W-what?"

"You had a seizure," he repeated. "Trevor and Tanika made sure you were okay." Kade looked from me to her and back like we were about to start torturing him.

"I don't remember *that*," he said in astonishment. We helped him sit up, and he pressed his palm to his head. Victor was getting him some water—I guess that's what you do whenever anything happens to anybody—when a knock at their door startled us.

"Is everything okay?" Monique asked from the threshold. "I got a call from somebody who said they heard some yelling about somebody needing help?"

"Yeah—" Victor scratched his head. "Yeah, Kade slipped and broke his favorite mug," he said with a glance down at Kade's broken mug. "And Tanika was going by and checked to make sure he was okay." Tanika nodded to back him up. He wasn't lying, but I felt like Monique could tell there might've been more to the story. She left once she made sure that Kade was okay—"Just make sure to give the Health Center a call if anything starts to hurt"—and Tanika stuck around until Kade was able to stand on his own. "Really, thank you again," Victor said sincerely, making her blush. "Would you like a piece of pizza before you go? You sure deserve one."

"Sure thing," she said like she was unsure of herself. "But no thank you, I have a gluten allergy."

Since there was a reason we'd ordered it in the first place, we sat on the floor together and picked away at the pizza in silence. I'd forgotten how hungry I even was. "I'm s-sorry guys," Kade apologized to a spot on the floor.

"Why are you apologizing?" I frowned. "You couldn't help it!"

"Yeah, but...you still h-had to see it," he mumbled. "A-and deal with it."

I gave his knee a little shake. "I'm just glad you're okay."

"*I'm* just glad nobody c-called the police over it," Kade said.

"Why?"

"Because the polio—the *police*—responding to a mental health episode is how people end up getting shot," he spat.

I left it at that so as to not upset him further. "Has that happened before?" I gently asked.

Kade nodded. "Uh huh."

"It's not like...epilepsy or anything, is it?"

"No, but that'd make sense, wouldn't it?" Kade answered cynically. "Of course the one with mental problems would go and have a seizure. Why shouldn't he have epilepsy too?"

"Shut up! I'd *never* thought that!" *What, does he think he's a freak?* "I'm sorry, I didn't mean to come off like that."

"You're good. I'm sorry for getting s-snappy about it."

"No, you have every right to get snappy about it," I said sternly. "You're clearly used to hearing stuff like that, and you shouldn't have to. Everyone says how they care about mental health, but then they go and make assumptions about people and it's not okay. Look at me Kade," I said, commanding his attention. "It doesn't matter to me what you have going on, or what you think you have going on, or what I think you have going on—you're one of my best buds, and I love you just the way you are."

The corners of his mouth turned up just a little. "Thanks, Trev." He set down his plate before my torso caught his arms as he fell into me, perhaps appreciating how he has people in his life who don't mind his self-perceived flaws—people who can see him at what he thinks is his lowest and his most vulnerable and say, *yeah, he's one of my best friends, and I wouldn't have him any other way.*

April 6

I love how the Repubes down in Tennessee who are all about free speech are so eager to start expelling their fellow state representatives who are joining students protesting at the state capitol in favor of stricter gun laws in the wake of the latest school shooting—school shooting number 13 this year, for those of us keeping track. *That's* 'disorderly conduct' but January 6th was a tourist visit? Kiss my goddamn dick.

I met with Dr. Averescu today to pick out next semester's classes. With the exception of Quantitative Reasoning—the fancy way to say 'math'—they're all classes I'm looking forward to: 20th Century American Fiction, Writing Creative Poetry, Rise of the Modern World, and French II, which I'll have with Victor again.

"I think I've asked you this before," she said to me from across her desk towards the end of our meeting, "but remind me why you want to pursue an English degree? What's your game plan, if you have one yet?"

I swallowed. "Well, I've been so inspired and moved by literature, so I guess what I'd *really* like to do is something that inspires other people through literature the way it's inspired me, almost like paying it forward."

"This is *your* life, Trevor," she said more seriously than anything she's ever said in class. "You don't owe yourself to anybody but you. The last thing you want is to realize a couple decades from now that you've been settling for less than what your heart wants."

"No, I know," I quickly said as I played with my stud. "I think that's what I really wanna do though. At first I thought of being a teacher or a professor, but now I'm leaning more towards being a writer, as stupid as that might sound. Assuming that Chat GPT doesn't antiquate English degrees."

"I don't think it sounds stupid at all," she said. "Imagine if every writer thought that what they were doing was stupid, or if they listened to the people who told them that they were wasting their time."

I sniffed what she was smelling. "That's true."

"I'm only asking because the next time you sit down to sign up for classes, it won't be with me," she went on. "I accepted a job at the University of Michigan starting this Fall."

"You're leaving?!"

"My husband and I both agree that nine years in New Halle is long enough for us. There's a life to be lived, and a small town like this isn't the place for us to live ours."

I let myself fall back into the chair. "You're like one of my favorite professors," I said like it would change her mind. "I'll miss having you as an advisor, and as a mentor. Congrats though."

She smiled. "Hearing students tell me that I've made an impact on them is what makes this job so fulfilling for me. I'll certainly miss having you in class, and our after-class chats. And I don't say that to just any student."

I pulled on my fingers. "Thank you."

"You're bright and you're talented, and you see things in a way most people don't. You have a gift, and don't ever let anything get in the way of you using it."

"I won't," I said with an inflated ego.

She saved the changes to my academic profile with a *click*. "So do you have any fun plans for the weekend, if you don't mind me asking?"

"My buddy from back home is coming down for the weekend."

"That'll be a fun time," she smiled, filling in the blanks on her own.

"What about you?"

"Oh, I'm making a bolognese for a Slow Food event tomorrow night," she gently swiveled in her chair. "And then there are some things around the house the buyer wants taken care of before they sign."

"That sounds...fun," I said as I stood to leave.

"It's interesting to see how you start to enjoy things you never thought you'd enjoy as you get older," she said. "And Trevor? I hope you know that you don't *need* a degree to be a writer."

"I know," I smiled from the doorway. "I'm here for more than just a degree, and I don't mean just getting turnt."

So that's how I had to explain to my advisor what 'getting turnt' means.

April 10

Like it was prophesied, my phone *pinged* with a *'Victor's b-day on chewsday get crunk lololololol,'* although we sure as hell didn't wait until Tuesday to celebrate.

Ethan and Kade had to meet with their own advisors, so it was just Victor and I who journeyed together up to Swafford Hall's 4th floor to meet his supposed one-time weed dealer, since Victor didn't want to keep mooching weed off of Alex or Eren. "What's up man," Victor casually said as 408 Swafford's resident let us in. "This is my bro, Trevor."

"Caleb," Caleb said as he gave me an up-nod. He actually kind of reminds me of Victor a little bit, if Victor had brown hair and didn't wear glasses and had more of a reserved personality and smelled like root beer-flavored candy.

"Hey," I nodded back.

Nothing in Caleb's single room smelled of weed—no Bob Marley stuff, no marijuana leaves, nothing with green and yellow and red stripes on it—although I guess the 'FEED YOUR HEAD' poster could be taken ambiguously. Victor traded Caleb a wad of folded bills for a brown paper bag that he tucked into his backpack.

"How much did you get?" I whispered to Victor once we were back out in the hallway.

Victor looked over his shoulder. "A few grams and five brownies," he said in a low voice.

"Five?!"

"Yeah? One for each of us—me, you, Kade, Ethan, and Logan."

"Well that was considerate of you to think of Logan," I said as I pulled out my phone to see if I had any texts from my hometown friend. "Do I owe you anything for it?"

"Just a night to remember—or not," he smirked.

I would've hung with Victor, but I felt like I had to tidy up 222 Swafford at least somewhat for Logan. It didn't take him long to park once he got onto campus since Fridays and Saturdays are the best time to find a good spot. "This is *way* overdue," he grinned as he hugged me. He'd stuffed his clothes, his pillow, a blanket, and our air mattress that Ethan didn't get to sleep on into his enormous hiking backpack. Mom and Dad say that they love me, but the fact that they included a bag of those big, shitty, waxy jellybeans in their care package of Easter candy for me that they sent up with Logan makes me think otherwise.

"Hells yeah it is!" I beamed. "I'm glad you made it down!"

Logan took in the dorms like a visiting high schooler, and the doors in my hall turned his head like he's never seen so many of them in one place. I introduced him and Tylor—I told him Tylor's preferred pronouns beforehand to avoid any awkwardness—before he peeped our room like he was moving me in. "Thanks for letting me stay, by the way," he said to Tylor.

"Hey, any friend of Trevor's is a friend of mine," they smiled.

Logan laughed through his nose. "You wouldn't be saying that if you knew some of the people he used to hang with."

I shot him a look. "Yeah, *used* to."

Tylor's eyebrows shot up. "Oh *really?*"

"Most of the rooms are suites like these," I off-ramped. "Ethan lives in a traditional dorm and has to share a bathroom."

"Where is he anyway?" Logan asked. "I figured you two were constantly joined at the—"

"He's picking out his classes for next semester. He should be done soon," I said just as my boyfriend texted me to let me know that he was on his way over.

Ethan and I gave Logan a tour of campus, walking him from Swafford to Bixby to Old Main to the Alumni Amphitheater to the Quad to Overholt and back to Bixby. "This is the railing I like to slide down." "That's where we did ecstasy." "That's Ethan's building." "That's the gym where the concert's gonna be."

"This looks *nothing* like the college campuses you see in movies," Logan said as his head swiveled.

We hit up Percy's for dinner instead of Patnick, since I wanted Logan to actually enjoy his visit. We found Victor slouched in a chair in the lounge area, with his roommate nowhere in sight. "How's it going? I'm Victor," he introduced himself to Logan. "He/him."

"Logan. He/him as well."

"Trevor's told me all about you. All the bad things, of course," Victor said with a smirk my way.

"No way!" Logan gasped. "He told me all the bad things about *you* too!"

"Isn't Kade with you?" Ethan asked.

Victor rolled his eyes. "He's on one of his many thrones at the moment," he nodded over to the bathroom that Victor and Tylor destroyed after downing some Double Nuclear Wings.

"Our other buddy Kade likes to do this thing where he's always taking a shit," I explained to Logan.

"It's like a party trick," Ethan muttered.

Logan and Victor made small talk while we waited for Kade to join us. "Finally," I said once he emerged. "Here he comes."

"So I'm taking a shit right?" Kade said to us, too focused on the invisible ball he was holding with both hands to notice Logan. "And then I start thinking—"

"Kennywood's open," Victor nodded down to Kade's jeans.

"Oh shit, good looks," Kade said as he zipped up his fly. "But has anybody ever befriended a group of crows and trained them to attack their enemies? Like, can't they recognize—"

"It's called a *murder* of crows, you cuck," Logan cut him off.

Kade looked up at Logan like he'd been slapped. They faced each other like they were about to duel. "Well well," Kade drew out in a formal tone. "You must be Logan. Your reputation precedes you."

Logan smirked. "And you must be Kade. I too have heard of your exploits and escapades." They kept leery, unbroken eye contact as they shook hands for a comically-long amount of time. "I should warn you, I've wrestled wild animals to the ground. I wouldn't think twice about breaking your legs if you become a bother to me."

"As could I." Kade pulled himself close to Logan, who didn't flinch at his proximity. "*As. Could. I.*" He stared Logan down for another second before spinning on us. "Are you guys done standing around with your thumbs up your asses? Let's go, I'm fucking *hungry.*"

"Just to be clear," Ethan smiled as Kade marched on ahead of us, "they've never met before, correct?"

"Correct," I nodded.

"Five bucks says they make out before the night's over." We shook on it.

I thought that Logan had gotten along well with Ethan, but he clicked so well with Victor—who made a point to show Logan his name on the list of Double Nuclear victors—and even more so with Kade that I was legit starting to wonder if they'd been Snapping and messaging each other on Instagram for months. Watching them all talk and laugh like they hadn't just met made me wish that I could make friends that fast.

"I figured we'll be chilling in your room, so we can do the roast there before we head over to Overholt," Victor said to me before explaining to Logan, "We're all gonna roast each other, like shit-talk roast."

"Why roast each other when you can spit-roast each other?" Logan smirked, making Kade almost spit out his raspberry tea.

We took turns shitting on the birthday boy back in 222 Swafford, where Kade fired the first shot. "I was gonna start with a joke from *Awkwafina is Nora From Queens*, but I know Victor wouldn't get it," he said. "I also can't make any jokes about pussy, because he doesn't get any of that either."

"He drums on things so much that he makes Trev's nervous tics look normal," Ethan roasted two people with the same flame.

"I don't even wanna know what he does to that poor stuffed shark of his at night when he's alone and all hornt-up," I smirked. And then we took turns on each

180

other after we were all done with Victor, but I was high-key eager to hear what they came up with to say about me the most.

"When we first met, I was like, 'is this guy flirting with me?'" Kade recalled. "But nope, apparently he just really likes to chew his lip."

"He'll pick out which shoes to wear like he's picking out a starter Pokémon," Ethan joked. "It's like, Jesus, we're just going over to Patnick." He pecked my cheek before giving it a pinch.

"He talks about how he doesn't have a stick up his ass but then he'll button the top button of his shirt," Victor said.

"You'd think he lives with three other people by how much he talks to himself," Tylor laughed.

"Multiply however nerdy you think he is about something by like four, and that's how nerdy he really is about it," Logan chimed in. It was all so on-point that they all had me in tears right alongside them.

Victor and Kade swung by 239 Axworthy to change clothes for the concert, and their fits made it clear that the rest of us were not dressed for the occasion—Kade had on Victor's plaid blazer and a t-shirt that matched his argyle socks, and Victor looked sharp as hell in suspenders and a pork pie hat like he was about to break into song in a black-and-white movie. Bodies strayed towards Overholt like shrapnel in reverse and coalesced into one big-ass line, where we bumped into Calvin and his friends. "Man, everyone's here!" my floormate flashed his toothpaste-commercial smile as he gave each of us—even Logan—a backhand-smacking, palm-raking, fist-bump of a handshake. "I didn't think so many people liked RBF!" He said that basically every Music major was there because seeing a live horn section outside of an orchestra makes them feel validated. And I didn't think this many people were into ska, I thought as we helped stifle the gym's basketball-courts-turned-concert-venue. I've never seen a more eclectically-dressed crowd before—you couldn't look in any direction without seeing blazers, suspenders, denim vests, flat caps, plaid shorts, studded belts, combat boots, you name it. It was like a family reunion for Chucks and checkered Vans.

The opening band was a ska band from Pittsburgh who played covers of Less Than Jake, Streetlight Manifesto, Goldfinger, and other A-list ska acts. The crowd's enthusiasm for them was lukewarm, but they went wild when Reel Big Fish took the stage, and even wilder once they started playing. But the skanking though. You could tell who the ska concert veterans were from the way they swung and kicked in place. It was the most fun concert I've ever been to, no contest. I don't think it's possible to listen to some upbeat ska and not be in a good mood. Do you know how many of the world's problems could be solved if everyone just listened to more ska? Do you think there'd be a war in Ukraine right now if the people in the Kremlin started their days off with some ska?

"Fuck, can Chadwick Patterson skank," a sweaty Victor said between songs as he loosened his tie with a glance over at Fedora Guy from Open Mic Night who was there, who'd jerked and hooked in a clearing of onlookers like he was fighting off a colony of bats.

"Grandpa used to skank!" Kade fake-sobbed into his hands. "But not like grandma though. That woman used to shake her ass up the wall like a *spider."*

We rode the current of the crowd through the gym and out the front door after the show ended. "You could *not* have picked a better first ska show to go to!" Victor yelled to Ethan from a foot away.

"What ugly music," Kade scowled. "Jesus didn't hang on the cross so you kids could listen to this shit on Good Friday. No offense," he said to Victor. "I'm kidding. Forreal though, ska shows are the fucking *best."*

We split for our own dorms so I could get Drunk *Jenga* and so Victor and Kade could get their respective substances, and I wasn't surprised to see that they didn't bother changing clothes when we met them outside of Axworthy. "Did you bring your brownies?" I asked Victor as I flicked my eyes at Kade's bag. "And where the hell's your birthday crown?"

"I'm saving them for tomorrow night. But don't worry though," Victor said as he patted his pocket, "we're still gonna get rigatoni," he smirked. "And I'll wear the crown tomorrow. When do I ever get the chance to go out looking so snatched?" His fit earned him a few looks on the walk over to Rock Hill Road, though I'm sure people just figured he had a thing for Frank Sinatra.

"Now," I said to Logan as we came upon 370 Rock, "I *will* warn you that most college parties are full of obnoxious Heteros and are so crowded that you can barely move. And *sometimes* the music is bad, but it's usually horrible."

"Good to know," Logan said flatly.

"This *isn't* one of those parties," I grinned.

"Oh good," he smiled, "though I kinda got the feeling that it wasn't from the hammer-and-sickle flag in the window." We spilled into the house, and his eyes landed on a vodka bottle with a spray nozzle for a cap sitting on the end table right by the door. "Yep, I'm liking this party already," he chuckled.

Don't ask me why, but the party felt like a college party from 20 years ago—a party of half-unbuttoned shirts, beer bottles, smoldering ashtrays, and *Uno*—the kind of party that The Strokes made music for. And Logan wasn't the only first-timer there—there were like half a dozen people there I'd never seen before. *Maybe it's Bring A Friend Night, and Logan just happened to come down on the right weekend?* My dick perked up a little when I recognized Jimmy from Miles' party last semester, the one who looks like he's from an emo band and who turned me on to chocolate vodka mixed with orange juice, and who's apparently also gay. "I was at a party and went to use the bathroom and walked in on him blowing somebody,"

Ethan chuckled, making me laugh, and also making me wish that I would've known that back then so I could've asked him if he would've wanted to come back to Miles' room with the two of us. *Take a seat, Trevor.*

Kade walked me through packing a hookah bowl with a flavorless shisha—"Oh no, not the *zag*," Alex laughed—as somebody named Greyson looked on. "Everyone, the ass is now fat," Kade declared as he carried it out to the patio. "I repeat, the ass is now fat." Despite his enthusiasm for a fat ass though, he didn't stay out on the patio for long, nor did Logan or Ethan. Through the kitchen window, I saw Victor holding a pretzel rod like a cigar and saying something to make Charlotte laugh, Logan and Luca getting 40 ounce bottles duct-taped to their hands and grinning like it was the most fun they've ever had, Kade and Greyson smiling and nodding in conversation against the kitchen counter while sharing a bag of chips. I looked from Anubis to the window and back again before setting down the hose to enjoy the party with my friends, which is how parties are supposed to be enjoyed. That, and somebody lit up an actual cigar and it fucking *reeked*.

In my sunglasses, I played the familiar role of one who documents but is undocumented, present but unseen, taking individual instant pictures of Ethan and my friends posing with the JFK portrait, doling out ageless shots to their subjects like souvenirs, like a bequeather of moments. Logan and I teamed up in pong against Kade and Greyson, who had a four-game winning streak going. Both teams had only one cup to go, and every missed shot only upped the tension. People gathered to watch, and I was saucy enough to feel cocky. "Now wouldn't it be a shame," I said as I wet my ball in one of our cups, bouncing it on the edge of the pool table. "Wouldn't it be a fucking *shame* if this ball were to land right in your cup, just like this?" I looked Kade in the eyes as I made my shot, sinking it dead-center. The room exploded. Logan and I gave each other forceful high-fives, and I ran around the table to yell in Kade's face exactly what he'd yell in mine if it were the other way around. *"Who's titty now? Who's titty now? That's what I fucking thought! Sit your ass down! Sit your ass down! Sit your ass down!"*

People trickled up to the second floor, but I didn't think too much about it until I caught sight of Ethan following Jimmy up as Andrew helped me rebuild the Drunk *Jenga* tower. The minutes passed before I let my curiosity take me up after them. I knew that neither of the male voices in passion behind Matt's door belonged to Ethan, so I let them be. I heard a handful of people talking in low voices behind Alex's door, which I timidly pushed open after peeping Ethan and Logan through the keyhole. Alex waved me in, and I shut the door behind me before taking a spot on the floor in the circle of people between my boyfriend and my hometown friend. I was wondering if we were going to play Spin the Bottle until somebody named Peter pulled out a bong that looked like something from a Dr. Seuss book, like what a bong would look like if it was high. He poked at some tacky-looking stuff and crème brûléed it with a butane torch, and was zooted as soon as he took a hit of it. Linh went next, holding her head with a "Holy fucking *shit*." Jimmy's dab hit knocked him on his back. Poor Ethan learned the hard way that you *aren't* supposed to pull the little bowl off of it when you take a hit. Alex leapt up and was out the door like the place was on fire while Ethan sucked on his finger and thumb.

"What made you think that was a good idea?" Logan asked, probably sounding more patronizing than he meant. "Why would you grab something that you just saw him hold a flame to?"

"I don't know," Ethan whimpered with a tear in his eye as I rubbed his back. "I just thought you did the same thing you do with a bong." Alex reappeared with a bag of frozen pearl onions that he remedially wrapped Ethan's hand in.

Knowing what *not* to do, I sucked when Peter gave me the go-ahead and immediately felt the storm clouds of dumb hedonism roll through the inside of my head. I've never gotten so high so fast before. Logan, Alex, a girl with tattoos on the backs of her hands, and Victor each got steamrolled one after the other like the countries of eastern Europe before the rising tide of communism. People *had* to have known what we were up to from how we came downstairs all at once like a horde of zombies. We splintered off to play Drunk *Jenga* or to smoke hookah or to watch pong or to eat frozen mozzarella sticks right from the box. I caught sight of Kade leaving with Greyson without saying bye to us, which upset Victor.

"He's probably going to take a squat in the cucumber patch," he said spitefully, though he took his own mind off of it when he started whining about wanting another tattoo.

"So what'd you think?" I asked Logan an hour or so later as he and Victor and Ethan and I made our way down Rock Hill Road.

He beamed as he threw his arm around my shoulder. "Best fucking night I've had in a *long* time."

I'm so used to Ethan staying in my room on weekends that it felt weird leaving him off at Kessler. Logan and I tried and failed to be quiet in 222 Swafford even though Tylor wasn't there. I don't know how running the air mattress pump at that hour didn't get us in trouble. From our own beds, we ate Easter candy and did impressions of memes from middle school until we were sore from trying to not laugh too loud. We were too busy having fun wasting time together back then to realize that moments like those are what make up growing up.

"I miss us," I finally said as I rolled onto my side to look down at him, thinking about that scene at the end of *Superbad* and wishing that the two of us never drift apart. "I miss being able to hang out whenever we want, and doing stupid shit all the time. I miss you, fam."

"I miss you too," Logan said. "It's weird not having you around. But that's how things work. Not everybody's meant to always be in your life all the time."

"You've always been my best friend though. My friends here don't have what we have."

"Yeah, they have a long way to go if they're tryna replace me," he chuckled.

Waking up without Ethan in my bed made me think it was a weekday for a second and that I was late for class. I forgot Logan was on the floor and almost kicked him in the face when I got up to pee.

The two of us waited outside of Axworthy for my friends to meet us so we could head over to Ginny's for breakfast. I kept forgetting that Logan wasn't Ethan as I watched people doing yoga in the grass, and had to keep stopping myself from holding his hand or rubbing his thigh. "I take it Kade's still asleep?" I asked Victor when only he emerged.

"Dunno. He could be," he said briskly as he walked ahead of us. "He never came back last night."

Logan didn't catch his tenseness. "It's wild that you guys get to do that every weekend," he shook his head, still hungover from the crossfade.

"It's not like that *every* weekend," I told him as I texted Kade. "I only went out to like four or five parties last semester."

"And whose fault is that?" he asked. "Just because you don't go out doesn't mean the parties don't happen. But if tonight's anything like last night, I won't be mad about it. Just saying," he smirked.

Nah man
I'm gonna grab breakfast with Greyson
You guys go ahead 😊
love youuu

We found Ethan balancing himself atop the retaining wall out front of Kessler, walking heel-to-toe. "Kade's not coming?" he asked after greeting me with a good morning kiss.

Victor snorted. "I'm sure Greyson's making him."

Ethan furrowed his brow. "Greyson's making him come to breakfast?"

"No, cumming. Greyson's making him *cum*. Ejaculate. Climax."

"Oh," Ethan said. "So...should we ask him if he wants to join us?"

"I'm not waiting around for him," Victor said. "If he's gonna put meat before mates, then fuck him." Ethan and I exchanged startled looks. *Oh Victor, just wait until you start getting laid. We'll never hear from you again. Logan'll tell you.*

Victor's cynicism subsided at Ginny's, where Logan was enjoying the morning-after college breakfast experience way too much. He looked around like he was on the set of his favorite movie. Overhearing other people's escapades and sexcapades from the previous night—naked laps, beer bongs, backseat encounters on the Drunk

Bus—always makes me feel like I'm missing out on things. I kept thinking about what Logan said about parties happening with or without me as I watched him dig into his Uncle Happy Time Breakfast Special, but Ethan's hand working its way up my thigh under the table kept me from thinking about it for too long.

Since the coffee at Ginny's didn't do the trick for him, Victor pulled us into Brew 22, where we each ended up getting a coffee. I told Logan all about Three Lesbians in a Wheelchair after one of the workers greeted Victor and Ethan like they were regulars. "Well now you can check 'get breakfast at the local diner' and 'get coffee from the local coffee shop' off your list of college-y shit you wanted to do while you're here," I said to him while we waited outside with our cappuccinos.

"I'm having a great time," Logan said cheerfully. "I'm about to transfer here."

I raised an eyebrow at him. "You've been here for one day and you wanna move here?"

"*You* wanted to come here before you ever even visited," he pointed out. "I *do* wanna transfer somewhere though. I've been looking around at schools for a bit now." And I don't blame him—as good as being home is, home isn't where character growth happens. "You and Madi and Ian and everyone else were smart to get away. I would've too if I could have afforded anything other than community."

"It's not your fault! This shit's *expensive.*"

Ethan joined us on our bench, squinting at the daylight through his glasses. "Do you play disc golf?" he asked Logan. "There's a course that goes all over campus. Today would be a nice day for it."

"What if *I* don't want to?" I asked.

"You just don't wanna play because you threw it in the—" Ethan stopped to smirk at the sight of Kade making his way up the sidewalk across the street, alone, and in his clothes from the night before. "Well look who it is—HEY SLUTMUFFIN!" he called through his cupped hands, turning more than a few heads. Kade looked around and smiled when he saw us before dashing over to the coffee shop.

"How was breakfast with *Greyson?*"

"I bet they had it in bed."

"A nice big sausage, with that white gravy."

Kade's smug grin only widened. "We *did* have sausage, and hashbrowns, and orange juice. We got McDonald's and took it back to his place."

"So yes to all of the above," I muttered to Ethan.

"Well if it isn't dollface," Victor said when he joined us with his own to-go cup. If he was still annoyed with Kade, he didn't show it. "Did somebody have a good night?"

"You could say that," Kade said simply, though the mirror pic he put on his Snap story of his bare, scratched-up back said he definitely did.

Logan got to see 239 Axworthy while Kade showered and changed—"You play the *drums?!*"—and then got to see campus from the top of the hill behind Bamberger Stadium as we played our way through the disc golf course. The five of us packed into my car to make a spontaneous thrift store run afterwards since it felt wrong to stay inside on a nice day with Logan there—that, and Victor wanted to hit up a Mexican restaurant for an early birthday dinner. Logan was happy to snag a hacky sack from the thrift store's toy section, but *nowhere* near as thrilled as Victor was when he found a cajón. "I've always wanted one of these!" he said as he hugged it like it was dear to him. Kade wore a bucket hat with orange and pink leaves printed all over it as he shopped, and almost accidentally stole it when he forgot he had it on when we went to leave. The Mexican place, Amigo's, made up for its lack of an original name with the quality of its food. The salsa was even better than Aldi's, and the burrito I got might've been the best burrito I've ever had, packed with pork *adobo* and pineapple and peppers and rice and topped with some kind of cheesy sour cream. My mouth wouldn't stop watering.

Back on campus, Logan tossed and caught his hacky sack again and again. "Anyone wanna kick this thing around like punks?" So that's how we became those people on a college campus playing hacky sack, which I don't think I've ever seen anyone doing here before.

"Forreal though, I don't think I've ever seen anyone here playing hacky sack," I said, looking to the others to back me up.

"You have now," Logan smirked as he juggled it between his heels. "The legend will be passed down from freshmen class to freshmen class how once upon a weekend, a mysterious, and dare I say stunning"—I rolled my eyes—"young man appeared to reintroduce the noble yet bygone sport of hacky sack to NHU, only to never be seen again."

"I *hope* he's seen again," Victor said as he sent it clear into the grass.

We pregamed in 222 Swafford, and by 'pregamed' I mean we put on *Ferris Bueller's Day Off* while Victor played his cajón while the rest of us plus Tylor played cards. Logan didn't mind just listening to the rest of us talk, because I know that college life fascinates him the same way California fascinates me. We all laid our hands on top of each other's and solemnly swore to turn the fuck up before heading out to 370 Rock.

Since we wanted to let Logan experience it, and since it'd been so long since we'd done it ourselves, we rode the Drunk Bus over to the far side of campus instead of walking over. I was low-key let down by it—there was somebody with a traffic cone they'd jacked from somewhere, but that was about it. We might've actually been the ones who looked like they were the most ready to party, with Ethan in his thrift-store shutter shades, Kade in his bucket hat, and Victor with his cajón and plastic crown and drawstring bag that smelled like dryer sheets. But watching the other riders laughing with each other hit me with the feeling of FOMO I used to get when I'd see other people going out to parties before I started going out, even though we were on our way to the most fun party I know. *Maybe we should do something crazy and tag along with them instead, and go to some regular-ass party like college kids are supposed to go to. Are we missing out on the quintessential college experience by not being basic?* I kept my thoughts to myself while I followed the king for the night down Rock Hill Road to number 370, where I left any regrets about not doing something different at the door. *And who knows, maybe those other people saw us and thought that they were the ones missing out.*

We rhymed the night before for about an hour before Victor caught my attention and nodded towards the bathroom. "Please tell me we're playing Soggy Biscuit," Logan said as I shut the two of us in with Victor, Ethan, and Kade. Any hopes he had of playing Soggy Biscuit were dashed when Victor opened his bag to dole out a pot brownie mummified in plastic wrap to each of us. *I wonder if you can get high from licking the brownie batter off the spatula?* We debated about what components of a sandwich made it a sandwich—"Wouldn't a hot dog be a taco then?"—while we eroded away at our brownies.

"Okay, real talk though," Logan said as he licked crumbs off his finger, "if the world was going to end and you were the only one who could save it, would you?"

"Ooh, I just finished that one this past week!" Ethan said, referring to *We Are The Ants*. "Of course I would." Victor nodded in agreement.

"It would depend on the day," Kade shrugged as he balled up his wrapper. A knock on the door saved me from having to answer, because I honestly don't know if I would or not. Ask me again after we stop trying to dig for water on Mars and start feeding people who are starving here on Earth.

I'm sure people saw the five of us leaving the bathroom together and probably thought we were having a circle jerk. Under the red, green, and blue laser lights, we smoked some loud hookah on the living room's pool table and its newest burn mark, which yours truly put there when I tried to de-ash the coals and accidentally dropped one. In my defense, it was hard to see.

"Don't sweat it," Alex assured me later on when I fessed up unsolicited. "The first rule of hookah smoking is whatever surface you're smoking on *will* get burned."

Logan took a puff of the hookah and scowled at it. "Is this supposed to taste like shit?"

"Well there's weed in it," I said, "so..."

"You're smoking *on top* of having an edible?" he laughed out loud. "Have you ever *had* an edible before?" The three of us shook our heads except for Kade, who nodded. "Dude, you guys are gonna be so fucking *gone.*"

"Isn't that the point?" Kade grinned.

I was admiring the gauges Kade had in of alien heads on tie-dye backgrounds when I realized I hadn't seen Greyson at the party. "I bet you can't wait for Greyson to show up, huh?" I razzed him.

"Nah," he shook his head, "he told me he's collabing with another guy for his OnlyFans tonight." Resisting the urge to ask him if *he's* on Greyson's OnlyFans, I just let the hookah smoke cloud my imagination. *Maybe Ethan and I could make an OnlyFans for some extra cash?*

In what was easily the artsiest moment of my life, I found a copy of Allen Ginsberg's *Howl* on a bookshelf and called for the music to be paused so I could do a reading of its titular poem—which I'd never actually read before because it's like the longest poem of all time—in my sunglasses while Victor freestyled on his cajón. The whole house gathered around to listen in a haze of smoke and stupefaction. Andrew sat right up front, watching me in his own sunglasses with his mouth hanging open like I was a prophet. I got as far as the part about cock and balls, which made Logan snort, and then I started laughing, laughing so hard that I collapsed into a chair. The music was on again by the time I'd calmed down.

Worried that getting crossfaded would kill me, I played games and floated from room to room and from person to person without drinking anything. The last thing I distinctly remember was Kade pointing at people and shouting, "He gets a tentacle up the ass! He gets a tentacle up the ass! Everybody gets a tentacle up the ass!" like he was casting spells. And then the brownie hit.

Apparently I do this thing when I'm really fucking high where anytime somebody says literally *anything* around me, I buckle over with my hands on my knees and laugh up at them, exactly the same way, every time. *"Guys,"* Kade announced with a finger in the air, looking like a mix between Hunter S. Thompson and the kid from *The Breakfast Club* in his bucket hat and Clubmasters, "I'm fucking *faded* right now."

I doubled over with laughter. "Oh my god, you *are!*"

"Will you fucking *stop* that?" he laughed at me, which only made me do it again, and harder.

"Fam," a drunker-than-I've-ever-seen-them Tylor said as they put their hands on my shoulders, making me hiss with laughter, "you high as *hell* right now."

"Hey everyone!" Logan yelled like the place was about to get busted. "It's Easter! Happy Easter!" Everyone groaned, except for me, who was the only one laughing.

"Gives a new meaning to Easter grass, huh?" somebody chuckled. Three guesses what my next move was.

The rest of the night was a series of chronologically-dubious vignettes. We made marbled paper in the hookah smoke with a laser pointer. We danced like we were background dancers in an '80s workout video. Tylor mixed black rum with hot sauce and drank it through a veggie straw before seeing how many veggie straws they could fit in their mouth. Victor tried to make a pan flute out of veggie straws and just ended up blowing spit on people. Ethan ate sugar cubes like they were candy. I shotgunned a whole can of whipped cream. Alex grilled cheese curls. Kade talked dirty to a bagel and ate out its hole. Logan went around reciting the same incantation in Spanish to everybody while waving around a lit incense stick. Cameron offered everybody a sip of juice from a glass he held with both hands and told them it was the blood of Christ. Andrew kept asking if anybody wanted to do acid with him. Tylor spilled an entire drink on themself and we had to convince them not to take off their clothes. June, Charlotte, and Sonia pulled Ethan upstairs to give him a makeover. Victor told us that he had something really profound to say about peanut butter but then forgot what it was. Eren legit almost started choking while playing Chubby Bunny with marshmallow Peeps. Kade was walking around like Edward Scissorhands and slipped on a stick of butter. June, Charlotte, and Sonia brought Ethan back downstairs in eyeliner, smudged dark purple lipstick, and one of June's cloche hats. Every time a new incense stick needed lit it was like the changing of the guard. Like nine of us stood in a circle and tickled each other's palms with our fingers, swaying from side to side like when they sat around the tree in *Avatar*.

"I think we just did a fucking rain dance," it took Victor like five minutes of giggling to say.

We went to Sheetz, where we had an *unimaginably* hard time ordering food. We raced down the slope by the Arts Complex. Logan tried to slide down The Railing after seeing me do it and flipped off it backwards. I called Ethan to make sure I said goodnight to him. Victor found a random fake potted plant sitting on a rock and just took it. Kade laid down on the sidewalk before I told him he was going to get arrested and pulled him back up. Logan accidentally swallowed toothpaste and Tylor kept telling him he was going to die. The three of us said goodnight to each other for like 20 minutes before we finally laid down to go to sleep and conked *right* the fuck out.

I'd never woken up still high, but I was so out of it when I got up to piss that I was practically stumbling. I stared at myself in the mirror and tried to remember why the hell I had dark lipstick on my face and neck. The hangover had me so weak that I actually *fell back to sleep*.

"Are we gonna go to that breakfast place again?" Logan asked once we were mostly awake.

"Well," I said to the pic on Kade's story of Victor putting his tongue between the 'V' of his fingers next to a passed-out Alex, "it can't be breakfast since it's like 1 in the afternoon. And if you're seriously thinking about transferring here, then you need to experience the most fundamental of NHU institutions—*Patnick*."

As if it wasn't already an off morning, we found an ambulance parked outside of the dining hall, and watched as they wheeled out a white kid strapped down to a stretcher who was yelling in some Asian language. "Maybe that was Andrew on the tail end of his acid trip," Logan joked.

I walked over to the granite pew of a bench that Victor and Kade were sprawled out on like they were still weak from the night before. "Do you know what that was all about?"

"Wait," Victor said sternly as he swung himself up. "We need to talk about something first."

"Okay?" *Please don't tell me I tried to kiss him or anything.*

He reached into his pocket and handed me a folded-up piece of paper. I opened it to read 'ASS-EATING CLUB MEMBERSHIP CARD. VICTOR J MOROZOV, VICE PRESIDENT' in my own handwriting. "Care to explain?" he asked as he struggled to not crack up.

"I got *nothing* fam," I laughed.

"If I'm the VP, then who's the prez? Ethan?"

"I don't *know!*"

Kade raised his hand. "I nominate myself for President."

Not only is Ethan not the President of the Ass-Eating Club, he's apparently not even a member. "Can I start an opposition ass-eating club?" he asked as he dispensed himself some cereal. The omelet station had already shut down, but Logan wasn't upset over it—like me the first time I'd eaten there, he couldn't believe all the food options. We told him all about Paul and did our best impressions of her while we ate.

"Well *I* am fat and happy," he smiled as he leaned back to put his hands over his stomach.

"Oh, give it like six minutes," I warned him with an evil smirk.

"What's in like six minutes?"

"That was only *part* of the Patnick experience," Kade leered.

Logan figured out what the other part of the Patnick experience was by the time we got back to the dorms. "I'm legit afraid to fart right now," he said as he walked like he had a broomstick up his ass. I gave him my ID and door code so he could face the limits of his mortality in privacy while we waited out in the floor's common area for him to finish. "How have none of you died of explosive diarrhea yet?" he asked with an appalled look when he found us afterwards.

"You get over it eventually," I said like a sophomore. "Do you have my ID?"

He felt his pockets. "*Fuck.*" I had to be that guy who had to call the RA on duty because I got locked out of my room.

We walked Logan to his car when it was time for him to go and traded hugs like he'd been friends with everyone for years. But who are your friends if not the people you go right the fuck ahead with? "This weekend's already like one of my top two favorite weekends," he smiled. I could tell that he didn't want to leave.

"The pleasure was all *ours*."

"You gotta come back down fam!"

I gave him a heartfelt hug. "I'll see you in like a month."

We watched him drive off as a different person than the one who drove down, one refined by questionable decisions. Because isn't that how you grow? "Well that was a fun time," Victor said.

"I don't know about the rest of y'all," Kade said, "but *I* got shit to catch up on."

"Yeah, samesies," Ethan nodded.

Victor snorted. "More like *boyfriends* to catch up on." He wasn't wrong—after a weekend of *zero* alone time with each other, Ethan and I pleasured each other like one of us had just gotten back from a Peace Corps deployment. We didn't even hear Nate at 341 Kessler's door until it was too late. Our eyes widened in panic. With nowhere to go and only a literal second to act, I pulled the sheet over us just as Nate looked up from his phone. His face turned beet-red before he walked right the fuck back out. Ethan and I just stared at each other in horror.

"Oh *shit*," he chuckled, though he was the only one of us who thought it was funny. I'd be lying if I said that I wasn't worried about Nate being so weirded out at the sight of two guys having sex that the fragile asshole that lives inside all straight guys will surface in him and start giving us a hard time, regardless of how cool he is with us gays. Between that and not being able to stop thinking about this past weekend—which might have quite possibly been the most fun weekend of my life —I couldn't focus on my studying, which meant that I had to bullshit most of my answers on my U.S. Military History test. The best times of your life are the ones you never even think of posting pics of. *Ichi-go ichi-e.*

After French let out, I joined Victor on his side quest to pick up a package from the mail center before getting lunch. I played dumb as he wondered who it could be from, and looked surprised when he opened it at our table to reveal a shirt that read 'IF THIS FLAG OFFENDS YOU THEN I'LL HELP YOU PACK' with a Progress flag on it instead of the typical, obtuse American flag. "Yo!" he grinned as he held it open. "I *love* this!" He changed shirts right there in the dining hall. "Which one of you did this?"

I limply raised my hand. "*Guilty!*" It earned him a few compliments and at least one raised eyebrow before we even left, by which point he was in a totally different mood. He was downing the rest of his pop when something on his phone made him start choking.

"Put your hands up!" Ethan said as Kade slapped his roommate's back. "Look at the birdie!"

"What, did A Day to Remember break up?" Kade half-laughed.

Victor wiped his eyes as he hacked out a few more coughs. "I got an email saying that my RA interview is *tomorrow?*"

April 11

So I guess they took a poll once where they asked people if they'd rather lose their right to vote or their right to bear arms if they had to choose, and an unsettling amount of people in the South said they'd be willing to lose their right to vote if it meant keeping their guns. Maybe I got something mixed up, but isn't the whole fucking *point* of being able to bear arms to protect the right to vote? But by all means, let the people with an assault rifle fetish not vote anymore so the country can maybe make some actual fucking progress.

We made sure to wish Victor a happy birthday on his way back from his Acting class. I played decoy while Ethan and Kade hid behind some bushes. Victor was too focused on me pretending like I was going to try to tackle him to notice the other two sneaking up from behind until he was caught in their bear-hugs. "Happy birthday you *big beautiful bitch,*" I said when I joined in.

"Stop!" Victor laughed. "I gotta get to my interview!" We sent him off with a push, making him trip over himself. He gave us all the deets at dinner.

"It didn't feel like a job interview as much as I thought it would," he told us over trays of $2 tacos. "It was basically just a conversation and some hypothetical questions, like *how would you handle a conflict between two roommates? How would you foster a sense of community while enforcing the rules? Tell me about a floor activity you would hold on a $20 budget. How would you comfort a resident feeling homesick? How would your current roommate describe you?*"

"I actually emailed them the answer to that one," Kade said.

"You got it," I grinned at Victor. "There's no way you didn't get it."

"I don't know," he said, though I could tell he was thinking the same thing. "I don't wanna harvest my resources before the dice get rolled."

I was eight sentences into *The Life of Pi* when Ethan called me, sounding more stunned than anything. "Okay, so I just got back from work, and all of Nate's stuff is gone. *Gone.*" He showed me his half-bare room to prove it.

"*What?*" I gasped. "Why?"

"I don't know!"

"He probably moved out."

"No *shit* he moved out," Ethan chuckled. "I mean I don't know *why* he moved out."

"He didn't give you a heads-up at all?"

193

"Unh uh," he shook his head, sounding low-key hurt.

I bit the inside of my cheek. "You don't think he got so weirded out from walking in on us that he switched rooms, do you?"

"I mean, that makes *sense*. But he couldn't stay for a few more weeks?" He shook himself out of it. "Whatever though. You know what this means, right?"

"You get to walk around your room naked and sleep naked?" I chuckled.

"Well *yeah*, but I was thinking more about putting the beds together so any cute guys can sleep with me whenever they want," he winked.

"It'll be a different guy every night," I joked.

His mouth fell open. "Just for that you're driving me to Walmart to get some bigger sheets! *And* buying me dinner on the way back!"

"I hope you like the McDonald's value menu," I chuckled.

He laughed a *boy-you-got-balls* laugh. "Oh, are you lucky you're cute," he smiled.

**STOP WHAT YOURE DOING
GO MAKE SOME STRAWBERRY MILK AND THEN
MAKE HOT CHOCOLATE WITH IT
IT'S LIKE EATING A GODDAMN CHOCOLATE
COVERED STRAWBERRY
SON OF A BITCH**

April 12

I wonder what would happen if the Earth just stopped spinning, like abruptly? Would gravity hold everything down, or would it all go flying off? That should be the ending to a movie. Not an apocalypse movie, but just like a regular-ass detective movie or something.

On my way out from History, I passed a group of visiting high school seniors just as one of them said that they should all take a selfie under the "tunnel." "It's called an *arbor*, you uncultured little shit," I said from behind my sunglasses without a glance their way. *Welcome to New Halle, son.* And you know what else I saw in the Quad? People playing hacky sack. And they weren't any of the kids visiting either—they were students who actually go here. There's no way it's a coincidence, but I'd rather eat an oyster than tell Logan that he started a trend.

RHA campaign season must be shifting into high gear, because fliers telling people to vote for Westley popped up in all the high-traffic areas of campus, and

Ethan came into Rosenberg to print out his own that he'd made himself. "Do you think having my face on them is kind of obnoxious?" he asked his own smiling face.

"Unh uh," I shook my head. "I think it'll help if people can put a face to a name and vice versa. Besides, now everyone will get to see that cute face." I winked him a kiss. "And besides, you already printed them."

"Some of us still have over $20 in printer money that'll expire in a month," he laughed, "so I can always print more." *Some of us? More like all of us.*

I haven't had an evening this low-key in a *long* time. Ethan has all his usual Wednesday evening stuff and doesn't want me going to the store without him. Tylor has class. Kade's seeing *Edge of Seventeen* with Greyson at Bixby. Victor just told me he's "busy," which means he's probably trying too hard with a girl on his floor. Calvin and Theo's and Nikole and Elisha's doors were both shut, and they're the only people on the floor I'd want to hang out with. If it was last September, I would've been happy staying in and jacking off all night, but now I hate having to be by myself when I see people studying together, hanging out together, even going to the gym together. I guess I could read or play Switch or go to the planetarium, but I'm not really in the mood for any of those.

I wonder if Caleb's in his room?

April 13

So that's how Tylor found me lying in my bed with the lights off, in my sunglasses, high as hell off an edible I bought from Caleb, listening to Kid Cudi through my AirPods, thinking about how all the spaghetti in the world could very well be beings from other dimensions that've been spaghettified and happened to end up somewhere that's good at capitalizing on things.

April 14

I wish we would've met years ago, you said to me,
Even if it was just a memory to hold onto
Of a boy at the beach who left my heart fluttering once upon a time.

April 15

Well I hope everyone enjoyed Spring, because Summer is here—it's been in the 70s every day, and the sun hasn't stopped shining.

Ethan and I made a trip to Wally World after he got done with work for some king-sized sheets, a pillow for me, and two blacklights to put on the wall over his bed. "Too bad we'll only get to use them for a few weeks," I said over dinner at Amigo's.

"Yeah, but then we'll have them for our room next year," he smiled. Every time I think about getting to share a room with him and a suite with Kade and Victor, I get hit with a jolt of excitement. I can't fucking *wait*. "Oh! And I found out what happened to Nate!"

"*Hmmm?*" I articulated through a mouth full of enchilada. "Do *tell*."

"He didn't move out because of us," Ethan said. "I heard from my one coworker, who heard from her little, whose friend is dating one of Nate's friends, that he got *expelled*."

"*Expelled? What?*"

"Yeah, I guess he refused to cite any of his sources on a paper and got expelled for plagiarism."

"Well that sucks," I said, half-sincerely. "*But,*" I raised my eyebrows at him.

"*But,*" he raised his eyebrows back at me. So that's how I finally got to spend a night in Ethan's room.

The warm sun sang to us as we stepped out into its brilliance the next morning. I don't know if it was because it was Friday, or because the weather was fucking *beautiful*, or because I'd just spent a passionate night—and morning—in my boyfriend's bed, or maybe all of the above, but I was in a *fantastic* mood. *Sitting in class would be an actual waste of the day.*

"Are you doing anything important in your classes today?" I asked on the way to breakfast.

Ethan screwed up his face in thought. "I don't *think* so? I think they're just regular-ass classes. Why?"

I shrugged. "I'm thinking about skipping mine."

"Oh? Why?"

"Why not?" I gestured around. "It's a beautiful day, and I feel like it would be better spent if we went and did something."

He raised his eyebrows. "So *I'm* supposed to skip class too?"

"*Yeah*, or else it won't work."

He grinned the smallest grin. "Okay, let's say I do skip. What would we do? Go to the nature trails? Go down to the outlets?"

I pretended to think about it. "I was thinking maybe going down to Pittsburgh?"

"Pittsburgh! That's kinda far from here, isn't it?"

"Like an hour and some. So we'd have to leave kind of soon-ish if we wanna make a day of it," I said, even though it wasn't even 9 yet.

He breathed in and squinted up at the sky. "Okay, you convinced me," he chuckled. We swung by 222 Swafford for a breakfast of PopTarts and to trade our backpacks for my keys and my camera.

Ethan's sunny day playlist made the drive down brighter and the air rushing in through the windows that much more invigorating. He Googled things to do instead of drinking in the skyline like I did when I lost my Pittsburgh virginity. "There's an *aviary?*" he gasped. "Would you wanna check that out?" he asked me with an eagerness I couldn't say no to.

I've never seen Ethan so stoked to be somewhere before than when we pulled into the aviary's—which turned out to be the *National* Aviary—parking lot. He was like a kid at Disney, watching stern-looking eagles surveying their enclosures, little penguins swimming around their pool, condors with wings as big as a person, birds the size of golf balls flitting from tree to tree, toucans with humongous bills. I'm not into birds like he is, but I'd be lying if I said his interest and enthusiasm didn't rub off on me a little. Between the fetidness of some of the wetter rooms and the birds being right there with you, Mom would've *hated* it.

Ethan left with a thrilled smile and a souvenir shirt. "Now where to?"

"I don't know about you, but I'm getting hungry," I said. Conveniently for us, there was a place within walking distance that was like a Zukoff-style food hall with different stations. We ate outside in the shade of an umbrella, where Ethan leaned back in his chair to look off into the nearby park from behind crossed arms. "You're not *full* already, are you?" I asked, though his banh mi sandwich was so packed with toppings that I wouldn't have blamed him.

"Nah, I'm just appreciating the day," he smiled. His sunglasses caught the sun as he looked around at the sky and the trees. "Skipping class to do this was a good idea. Good looks, babe," he said as he bumped my foot with his under the table.

"Making deviants out of boys is what I do," I smirked as I tapped his foot back. I scrolled around on a map of the city as I sucked my drink down to the ice cubes. "It looks like there's another park down at the tip of the triangle. You wanna check that out?"

"Since when have you started calling your dick 'The Triangle?'" he asked, making me almost choke. "Forreal though, what triangle?"

After a nerve-wracking drive through the city's central business district, we made our way into the park, which was buzzing with life—bikes and hoverboards whirred by, a girl was getting some photos taken, some guys played catch on the chalk outlines of bygone forts, a cart sold snacks and cold drinks, a kid marched around a flag mounted to a chest harness he wore, somebody named Trevor gave somebody named Ethan a piggyback ride for the 20-or-so feet I could carry him before almost toppling over. From the fountain at the tip of the peninsula, I took in everything—the 'IRON CITY BEER' billboard sitting atop the ridge like the Hollywood sign, the giant satellite dish of a stadium that looked like it was either about to put on a bomb-ass light show or beam you up to the mothership, the rivers teeming with watercraft of all kinds, the golden bridges flanking the trees and the buildings like wings.

Our interwoven fingers sat on the edge of the fountain as we enjoyed its refreshing mist. "I'm probably gonna get sunburned," I said as my eyes followed some day drinkers on a tiki hut boat circumnavigating the horn of Pittsburgh.

"Samesies. But I'll take getting sunburned if it means getting to enjoy the day with you," Ethan said. "And here I was ready to sit in class—"

"Wait, hold that pose," I said before snapping an instant pic of him. His smile and his shades added to the lo-fi Cali vibe that instant pics taken on a sunny day tend to have. We watched the clouds before heading back across the park with our locked hands swinging between us, which was apparently too much for one person to handle.

"Don't you fuckin' look at me, boy," he growled. "I'll fuckin' kick your *ass*." I wasn't even looking at him, but telling me in a raised voice *not* to look at you is one sure-fire way to get me *to* look at you. I picked up the pace and prayed that he'd leave us alone if we got far enough away.

"Wait, was he talking to *us*?" an apparently oblivious Ethan asked me.

"I *think* so," I muttered.

"I just figured he was on the phone or something," Ethan said as he looked over his shoulder.

"Don't look!" I hurried us on. I was rattled at first, but it got kind of funny as we shit-talked the guy's fragile masculinity. I kept half-expecting to run into him everywhere we went for the rest of the day though.

Ethan said he wanted to see Pitt's campus, which made me nervous for obvious reasons. "I ended up applying there," he told me as we made our way back to my car, "but it was just a *little* too expensive for me."

"Lucky for me—no offense," I chuckled as my mind started going down the rabbit hole of Ethan going to Pitt and ending up with Dillon.

I showed Ethan the Cathedral's gothic abdomen before taking him up to the top floor. Back on the ground, we checked out the towering dorms and guys in sleeveless shirts as we walked a few blocks down the street before looping back towards the Cathedral to soak up the afternoon in the open grassy plaza it watched over. I don't know if nobody had class or if everybody just skipped or what, but there were people fucking *everywhere*. The most crowded I've ever seen the Quad on even the most beautiful of Common Hours is just a *fraction* of how many people were scattered across the grass. You'd think there was a concert or a sit-in or something. And what people weren't sprawled out on blankets were passing a Frisbee or a football or spiking a ball down onto a little trampoline. "It's called *Spikeball*," Ethan said like a Kade. "We have a set in our building that I've seen people rent out and play in the courtyard."

We used up the rest of the film in my camera on instant photos of each other lying in the grass or posing on benches. "I'll trade you my 'Ethan with a dandelion behind his ear' for your 'Trevor looking cool under a tree,'" he said as he held them like playing cards. And after we traded, we threw them down like *Pokémon* cards in battle—using only the most sexual-sounding moves, of course.

As much as I wanted to take Ethan somewhere to eat in the neighborhood that Kade and Victor took me to when I visited with them, I wanted to go somewhere with Ethan that I hadn't been to, somewhere that would make the day unique to *us*. "I remember Kade telling me about a place that has Korean food and empanadas," I suggested. "I wonder if it's anywhere around here."

Ethan's eyebrows shot up. "I mean, even if it's *not*."

For as international as Pittsburgh is, I guess there's only one place in the whole city where you can get Korean food and empanadas. The neighborhood effortlessly made itself my second-favorite neighborhood of the city, thanks to all the Progress flags draped in windows, hanging off porches, stuck to car bumpers, pinned to backpacks. Everybody looked like they ate organically, and all the businesses seemed like they were unique local ones. Every storefront had a water bowl out on the sidewalk for all the dogs that people were walking. I felt like a hipster. I felt like I was in Seattle. We passed an outdoor barbecue place with picnic tables and yard games, a place where you can make your own candles, and a pinball cafe—"I can play pinball in my dorm for free"—before we found ourselves in a gift shop of sorts, where I picked up a few pins and an art card that read 'Another World Is Possible.' It was a little above my price point, but the stuff is all made by local artists, and the store donates some of their profits to causes that make conservatives cringe— because after all, we vote with our dollars. If I hadn't already gotten Victor a birthday gift, I would've totally gotten him a Ruth Bader Ginsberg coffee mug. Ethan bought a pair of 'Pretty Decent Boyfriend' socks, reminding me with a grin how his "sock game is apparently shit." At Korean & Empanada Place—which is about as big as 222 Swafford—we each got an empanada and split an order of fried chicken nuggets that were unlike any chicken nuggets I've ever had. The prices were borderline lavish, but the food was *beyond* worth it.

The only other store on the street that Ethan wanted to check out was a socially-conscious, Industrial-style version of Bath & Body Works. And it wasn't the kind of place that only women and effeminate men shop at—they had soaps and washes with actual masculine fragrances like cedarwood and bergamot instead of the typical shit that's marketed to capital-S Straight guys with a fragile sense of masculinity, like gunpowder and motor oil. Ethan had me hold the body wash he bought while he went to use the all-gender bathroom, and I was perusing the impulse buys up front when a picture clipped to a board behind the front counter made me double-take so hard that I almost snapped my neck.

It was the same exact picture Victor has in his room at his house of him as a kid with his parents at the aquarium. I popped my eyes back into my head before asking the cashier as casually as I could, "Is that picture from the aquarium here in Pittsburgh?"

She followed my eyes to see what the hell I was talking about. "Oh! Yeah, that's the aquarium at the zoo here," she smiled politely.

"Is that family of yours?" I asked without caring how intrusive or cringe I sounded.

"Nah, those were our old neighbors." And then after a moment, "They're the ones who actually started this store."

"Oh really?" I asked, *high-key* curious.

"Yeah," Mila—as her chalkboard name tag read—said. "We were those neighbors who were always over each other's houses and doing stuff together—dinners, cookouts, day trips, all that jazz. I even remember when they were talking about opening this place."

"Do they ever come in to help work the place?" I asked. *Maybe she knows something that Victor doesn't, and his parents have been alive this whole time.*

"Oh no, they've been dead for a few years now." She frowned like she had a hard time believing it. "Actually, I guess it's been *several* years now."

"Oh, I'm sorry to hear that," I said as I played dumb. "And is that their son?"

"Yeah. His friend's family took him in. I can't even remember the last time I saw him."

"Were you friends growing up?" If she thought a random-ass stranger was asking her weird questions, she didn't show it.

"He was a few years younger than me, so we never played together or anything," Mila said, unaware that the person she was speaking to and the kid in the picture have been there for each other through some of our best, worst, scariest, deepest, and most vulnerable moments. "They were so proud of this store that they built out of nothing, but you should've heard the way they used to talk about him. They used to call him their reason for living."

I stared at the picture until it went fuzzy as Victor's words to me on the side roof of 370 Rock seared across my mind. *"I mean, how could anyone be proud of their loser of a son who has no game and likes to get high and doesn't know what he wants to do with his life?"*

I just nodded before turning to the front windows. "I'm gonna go wait outside for my friend—I mean, boyfriend." I just stared at the pavement from a bench out front, too shooketh at what I'd just stumbled upon to even think about the unfairness of life, where the boyfriend in question found me a few moments later. *Like, what are the fucking chances that we'd end up here of all places?*

"Sorry, my contact was being an asshole," Ethan said, blinking like he was trying to make me believe him. I handed him his bag, and as much as I was bursting to tell him what had just happened, it's not my place to tell Victor's story. Walking down the sidewalk on autopilot, I made zero attempt to be present in the moment. *Was the store Victor's moms' full-time job, or just a side hustle? Were they well-off, or did they make sacrifices to make it happen? Did Victor hang around in the back, playing his DS or doing homework like the kid at the Chinese buffet? Or was he always over Kade's house? Was Kade his neighbor too? Did they leave the store to Victor, and he's secretly the kingpin of the most environmentally-friendly apothecary in Pittsburgh?*

On another note, I was yesterday-years-old when I discovered that stir-fried ice cream is a thing. It's ice cream, but like hibachi. They better not put a place like that in Bixby next or else I'm going to be so fucking broke.

**We know you hate us mom, but if you could find it
in your heart to turn up with your kids tonight**

**Can you find it in your heart to milk this cock?
Jk luv u**

"As much as I'd enjoy going over to 370 Rock," I said to Ethan as I pulled into a spot in the Swafford-Axworthy-Walcott lot later on, "I also wouldn't mind keeping the day's impromptu momentum going." I mean, I can't really complain about missing out on things when I go out to the same party over and over.

Ethan bit the inside of his cheek. "Well then let's go out to a different party then," he smiled. "Just the two of us."

Having convinced me that we can have fun without it, Ethan led us towards Southway Apartments without Drunk *Jenga* or anything else in tow. "Whose place are we going to anyway?" I asked as we hung a right onto a road I'd never been down.

"No clue," he said matter-of-factly.

I raised an eyebrow. "So we're just gonna walk into some random party?"

"Pretty much," he smirked. I opened my mouth to voice my concerns before shutting it. *You know what's not attractive, Trevor? Constantly worrying about shit.*

He steered us towards an unimpressive-looking house that reminds me of the one from the *American Football* album cover that had an obvious party going on behind its curtains. "This one looks as good as any, don't you think?" Ethan said, undeterred by the guy standing outside the door.

"Who do you know here?" the doorman asked as we approached.

"We're friends with Sam," Ethan said simply.

He eyed us up with a sip of his flask. "Three bucks a pop."

I reoriented myself with the typical college party—the congestion of people, the nasty-girl rap, the capital-S Straight guys. The fact that we weren't supposed to be there made it more fun for me, like it was a game and I had to play a part in order to stay in. And I played it well—I talked to whoever happened to be near me, and anybody I even remotely recognized got a "What's up buddy?" like we were already friends. I guess the key to doing anything is to just do it confidently, like Ethan had demonstrated.

"Would I be correct in thinking that there's no Sam here, and you just made a lucky guess?" I asked in the kitchen as we cracked open some vodka seltzers.

Ethan nodded. "You'd be correct."

There actually did end up being a Sam at the party after all—he made up half the pong team challenging the team who'd been ruling the table that we found ourselves near. "Good looks," I congratulated him when he sank a shot and finished off his drink.

"Here, play for me while I get another drink from my partner," he said to me as he started to walk off with his plastic cup.

"*This* partner?" I asked stupidly as I gestured to his teammate.

"*No, my partner* partner," he laughed. *Is he gay?* I half-assed my shot so I could get a look at Partner Partner, and I'd be lying if I said I wasn't disappointed to see that it was a girl who pecked him on the lips—not that I necessarily thought he was *cute* or anything. It's funny how I think I'm so gender-inclusive but then I assume people are gay when they talk about their 'partner.'

Sam and Pong Partner broke the other team's streak and gave them shit as they left the table. "Come back when you learn how to throw!" Pong Partner berated them.

"And *thanks* for stopping by," Sam added in a cool, clear voice fit for a radio show that made me freeze.

"Oh my god," I gasped. "You're DJ Twinkle Toes. From WXNU."

He grinned. "And what if I am?"

My face lit up. "I *knew* your voice sounded familiar! I used to listen to your show all the time! Monday, Wednesday, and Friday, from 12 to 2!" I added to prove my devotion. "It was like the soundtrack to my first semester!" I didn't tell him that my first semester was my only other semester.

"Glad to hear you liked it man," he said sincerely. "Sometimes I like to think that I'm Jesus and music is my gospel." I could've kissed him.

"This is my boyfriend, Ethan," I said instead. "He plays at Open Mic Night at Brew 22. He kills it every time."

Ethan tugged his arm out of my grasp. "I can *speak*, you know."

"Dude! I thought I recognized you!" Sam said, shaking Ethan's hand and patting his shoulder like he'd just met a local celebrity. *I* was low-key salty that he was all over Ethan when Ethan didn't even say anything about how good his radio show was. "You and your band are the only reason I go anymore! Are you gonna end the year with a bang?"

"I don't know if I'd call it a *bang*," Ethan said as he tried to suppress a smile, "but yeah, we'll be playing on Monday. We'll save the bang for the Summer Send-Off," he grinned.

My mouth fell open. "You're playing the Summer Send-Off?"

"Yeah? I didn't mention that?"

"*No!*"

"Oh," he chuckled. "Well, we are."

I spent the rest of the night in an exuberant mood, shotgunning seltzers and laughing with strangers when I wasn't stealing kisses with Ethan. We moved to the music together before he started going to town on my neck. My hands grabbed his hips and he pressed himself up against me. "*That ass is making me wanna do bad things to it*," he purred, making me moan through closed lips. We found our way to the wall, where we sloppily made out.

Another thing I'd taken for granted at 370 Rock was Ethan and I being able to dance together or make out without anybody caring. But as a guy who looked like a Lumberjack major reminded us, we weren't at 370 Rock. "Hey, take that somewhere else," he said sternly, but not in a threatening way. "Nobody wants to see that."

"Of *course* they do," I chuckled like it was obvious.

"You just mean *you* don't wanna see it," Ethan pointed at him with a drunken smile. "Maybe just don't look at us then."

He turned to go, and that could've been the end of it if I'd kept my mouth shut. "And how about giving us a smile before you go?" The guy looked shocked more than anything, but he still had me feeling uneasy. Even Ethan gave me a surprised look. "Was that too much?" I asked sheepishly.

"Maybe we should disappear for a bit, just in case," he said as he led us to the back door. *Just in case he's going to get his friends to help him beat the shit out of a couple of faggots.* The cement slab of a back patio was a cluster of drinks and cigarettes that were being the appropriate level of loud. "Good job at not taking it too seriously though," he smiled.

Around the side of the house, I slammed the rest of my drink and tossed the cup into the grass—which I still feel bad about doing—before Ethan and I picked up where we left off. We made out against the siding until a sound I couldn't discern grabbed my attention—a meaty sound, like somebody falling to the ground over and over. We peeked around the corner to see a fight going on in the front yard—two people were throwing punches at a third, burlier guy who was almost too drunk to land a hit. His fist met one of their jaws, sending him to the ground. Another person joined in, and then another, and then people started running to join in all at once like it was magnetic. We watched the fight snowball into an all-out melee.

"I think that's our cue," Ethan said as we and some others started backing away.

The wall-shaking bass came to a stop as somebody cut the house's music. 'EVERYBODY OUT!" a voice bellowed. People *poured* out of the house before dispersing in every direction. A guy even felt the need to jump through one of the first floor windows. Not out—*through.* I bolted through the back gate and down the alley after Ethan, remembering how the last time I ran away from a party that was about to get busted was with Dillon, who I'd kissed on a dare a half hour beforehand, and who I'd spent most of the following half hour with in a walk-in closet.

Ethan slowed to a stop only once the house was out of sight and we couldn't hear any angry yelling. "Well that was fun," I panted when I caught up to him.

"Can't say that I've ever seen that happen before," he grinned before pulling me into the shadow of a detached garage. The wail of a siren pulled our mouths apart yet again as the trees and houses flashed red and blue from the lights of a responding police car. We stumbled back onto campus like two drunk lovers not fleeing from anything—back to Kessler and up to room 341, where we finally got to finish uninterrupted.

April 16

Does anybody know where people get the statues of Mary they have in their front yards? Is there some kind of Catholic store somewhere or do you have to order one from The Vatican or what?

Getting down to the last few weeks of the semester means that everybody's starting to feel the weight of projects and presentations and papers, but that sure as shit didn't stop us from enjoying the day. Professors should really take the weather into consideration when assigning homework, like Dr. Sutcliffe having Kade's class read all of *Silent Spring* by Monday. Like, who has time for that on a weekend like this?

Ethan and I met up with Victor to grab McDonald's for breakfast to-go to eat outside, while Kade and Greyson hung back in Kade's bedroom to do sinful things with each other. Or maybe Kade was making him learn a board game, I don't know. We stuffed our faces with hotcakes and McMuffins and told Victor all about our day in Pittsburgh—leaving out the part about his mom's store, of course. "And then last night we just went to some random house party," Ethan concluded.

Victor raised an eyebrow. "Just some random house party?"

"Uh huh," Ethan nodded. "A fight broke out and then we ran away. Did you guys go to Alex's?"

"Yep. And then the three of us went back to our room," Victor rolled his eyes.

Campus was littered with students enjoying the weather by any and all means. Even Kade, who had a boy in his bed and the room to himself, couldn't let such a gorgeous day happen without him. At his own suggestion, Victor drove us to some hiking trails that wind through the woods and run along a stream that the more outdoorsy NHU students like to frequent. Ethan and I recounted our Pittsburgh adventures to Kade on the way, who listened like he didn't live there. "Didn't I *tell* you that that Korean and empanada place would be fabulous?" "I almost actually came in my pants the first time I had that ice cream." "My mom got shit on by a bird at the Aviary once." "Yeah, *no* clue what the kid with the flags is all about." "Wait, so you *didn't* go to Randyland?!"

Somebody at the Aviary had told Ethan about an app that identifies birds by their calls, which is to say Ethan's phone stayed in his hand the entire time. "That's a cedar waxwing!" he'd gasp as his foot would catch a root. The trails led us past gigantic rock formations, trickling waterfalls, a million signs telling you not to swim in the rapids, an old watermill, and a covered bridge that was swarming with people in 'Historic Covered Bridge Society' lanyards.

"Don't these people have anything else to do?" Kade grumbled as we went back to an infinitely-less crowded lookout along the water. "Like, go home and look at your stamp collection."

"Ah, the fine art of philately," I smirked.

We looked out onto the stream from our vista, where I let the sound of the running water relax me.

"Wait, isn't that the fancy way to say sucking dick?"

"That's *fellatio*."

"Why do fellatio when you can do philately?"

"Why not do *both*?"

"I like my dicks the way I like my stamps—licked."

"Licked and sticky."

"Grandpa used to philately!"

"But not like—"

"I'll fucking hit you if you say it."

Back on campus, we threw a Frisbee around with Tylor and Amina and Jaxon, and took turns taking my longboard for a ride until we walked/rode to Subway for dinner. We ended the evening with a listening party for the new Waterparks album that we'd each refrained from listening to on our own so we could hear it together for the first time. We had to keep restarting songs because we'd start talking too much and wouldn't be able to fully appreciate the music.

It's going to be hard for there to be a party to top last weekend, which we already started referring to as 'The Weekend.' We started off the night at 370 Rock in a downstairs kind of mood, rolling joints and playing blacklight pong and *swearing* that the highlighter graffiti on the door was moving before migrating back upstairs. We smoked on the patio until it started to drizzle, which was when Victor learned a valuable lesson: *don't* pick a hookah up by its stem. He was halfway to the door when the glass base fell off and shattered on the cement.

"Oh my *fucking* god. I am so sorry," he told Alex so gravely that you'd have thought he was at a funeral. "I swear I'll pay for a new one."

"It's just a vase, man," Alex told Victor as we helped clean up the pieces. "We'll just use something else until we can replace it."

Victor crouched down with a hand broom. "I feel like such a dick," he muttered.

"Really, don't worry about it," Alex told him. "I've actually had this hookah as long as I've been in college," he reminisced. "I got it at a smoke shop like a week into freshman year, back when you only had to be 18 to buy tobacco products. My old roommate and I used to smoke it by the window." He let the shards fall from the dustpan into the trash can with the sound of a car accident. "It's too bad it didn't make it to the end." The look on Victor's face had me *dead*.

"Hey, at least it wasn't the nice one," I said to try to make him feel better. "At least Kade wasn't there to see it." Kade found out anyway though, because you can't see a hookah with a half-quart milk jug for a base and not ask questions. We smoked out of our now-shatterproof hookah in the living room, where the laser lights and Pink Floyd anesthetized our minds.

Victor learned the hard way that smoking weed out of a hookah while watching a laser show and listening to *Dark Side of the Moon* can apparently be enough to push you past the Point of no Return. "Has anyone ever thrown up from weed before?" he asked with difficulty after fighting to stand up, wearing the look of somebody who *knows* they're too drunk. "Like, they got so high they puked?"

"Dude, you're *not* gonna puke if that's what you're asking," Alex assured him as his own head lolled. "I don't know *anyone* who that happened to." But there's a first for everything, after all—five minutes later, Victor came back from the bathroom looking like me on my most sleep-deprived days.

"So remember how you said you never met anybody who puked from weed before?" he said like they were his dying words. "Hi, I'm Victor." He tried walking and stumbled sideways into Luca.

I went over to hold him up. "We should get him back to his room."

"*How* are we supposed to do that?"

"Where's Kade at?"

"*Probably* getting his peen wet."

"Fuck *off.* I'm right here."

"Just let him crash here."

"I want my *bed*," Victor whined obstinately.

Matt called a friend of his whose sorority was doing some kind of DD service to come pick Victor up. We helped him to the car like a great-grandma and stuffed him into the backseat. "Remember," I smiled through the rolled-down window as Kade struggled to buckle the two of them in, "if they *don't* know, they *won't* know."

Kade frowned at me. "Know what?"

I shrugged. "I dunno."

"Fam, you lit as *shit* right now."

I guess I must've not looked too hot myself if Ethan had to ask me if I was okay. "You look a little..." he trailed off.

"I'm just gonna go hang out in the bathroom for a minute," I nodded loosely. "Just in case." I shut myself in and lowered myself near the toilet, closing my eyes and hoping that it would pass.

I stirred to the sound of birds. The translucent windows glowed with light. Discombobulated, I forced myself to sit up. *Did I just sleep on the bathroom floor all fucking night?* I reached for my phone to try to make sense of things, but the only message I had was from Kade saying **Guess wo just thrre up out the window of a moving vehicle.** There was, however, a Post-It note that had fallen on the floor that read '*Went to Ginny's and the store. Didn't want to wake you guys. Help yourself to anything except the leftover kebab.*' I blinked and read it again. *Guys, like plural?*

The creaky hallway floorboards screeched in the absence of any and all noise in the house. It was so quiet that it was eerie. The rooms were bizarre with warm, natural light. Being alone in their house felt wrong. I figured the other person the note mentioned must've left already because I didn't see anyone passed out anywhere and the beds were empty. I downed a glass of water, went back into the bathroom to take a piss, and nearly jumped out of my skin when I saw Ethan asleep in the bathtub under a throw blanket with a pillow. *How did I not see him before?* I sat on the edge of the tub and gently stroked his hair as I took him in. *My god is he adorable*, I thought just before I let out a tub-rumbling fart. He stirred, opening his eyes just a smidge. "Good morning, beautiful," I said as I leaned down to give him a kiss on the forehead.

"Morning," he said with a sleepy smile. "How do you feel?"

"Not great. But not horrible either. You?"

"Other than sore as hell? About the same." He pulled the throw blanket off himself. "Did you give me this?"

"Nah, it was already there." *Maybe that's why they call it a throw blanket—you throw it over people who are passed out.* "Why'd you sleep in the tub? That *couldn't* have been comfy."

"Oh, it wasn't. I wanted to make *sure*"—he trailed off in a yawn—"I wanted to make sure you were okay in here." I guess the people you love are the people you sleep in a bathtub for.

"You could've been cute and slept with me by the toilet," I chuckled.

"No thanks," he winced as I helped him up. "What time is it?"

"Like, 12:30. 12:42. Why, do you have a date?"

"Yeah, with the others. We have to practice before Open Mic Night tomorrow."

I laughed out loud. "You think Victor's gonna be able to practice after a night like the one he had?"

"I'm not worried about him. It's the rest of us who need the practice."

I furrowed my brow. "What do you mean, 'the *rest* of you?' Isn't it just you and Kade?"

"Uh…" He rubbed the back of his neck like a Trevor. "Amina may or may not be playing with us too," he smiled.

My mouth fell open. "Forreal? Why didn't you tell me?"

"Because I like surprising you?" he responded like it might've been the wrong answer.

I declined his offer to sit in on their practice, and found myself getting lost in the house's library of records after he left. One thing led to another, and soon my fingers were sticky with shisha, and the speakers were popping to life with The Beach Boys, Donovan, and The Zombies like it was 1966. I opened the windows so I could still hear the music when I took Anubis out onto the front porch. Nobody told me *not* to make myself at home, nor did anyone care when they found me like that. All they said was to not eat the kebab.

The four of them grinned at me like I was making the walk of shame as Matt pulled up along the sidewalk. "You're still here?" Andrew asked as I let him into his own house, carrying bags from what was likely their last Wally World run as NHU students.

"Should I not be?" I asked, suddenly worried that maybe I *shouldn't* be.

"Nah, I don't care," he said as he brushed past me.

"It's been a while since *this* was on the turntable," Matt complimented my choice in music. "And also good morning."

"Is cupcake feeling better?" June asked.

"Whatcha smoking?" Alex asked as he brought in the rear.

"Just citrus mint," I said as I went in to help put stuff away so I didn't look like a total mooch.

"I can't believe you slept on the bathroom floor all night," Andrew laughed. "I've never even done that."

I just shrugged. "Why go away to college if you're not gonna pass out on a bathroom floor?"

"Was Ethan still in the tub when you got up?" June asked.

"*Yeah.* I told him he should've slept on the couch!"

"So did I," she said in a sing-song voice. "He kept saying he didn't wanna leave you. It was actually hella cute. Andrew's never done that for me."

"Because I've never *had* to!" Andrew said to the can he placed in the highest cabinet.

Alex showed me a pic he took of me slumped over on the tile like I was dead. "So what flavor's next?" he asked once the groceries were put away. "I can get the coals started."

Matt popped the cap off a lukewarm cold brew. "*I'd* be up for a bowl."

My fingers found my stud. "Uh...I know this looks rude, but I was actually going to get going once this one was done."

Alex scoffed. "Well isn't *that* convenient? He wants to dip as soon as we get back."

"I swear! I've already been smoking for three albums!"

"Go 'head!" Andrew called from the dining room as he laid a shirt out on the table and plugged in an iron.

"I'm just kidding," Alex told me, though I low-key felt like he *wasn't.* "You probably have shit to do."

Victor sent me a screenshot of the apologetic text Alex sent him last night after he got sick, and I can't stop laughing at how gone Alex must've been when he sent it.

Duck I have Loan sma
Small
You guys weren't big, honestly
earnt my intention to fuck you
Normal
You just went TOO AHEAD

April 17

Today's been rainy and in the 50s, which is to say Summer's over and it's Spring again. Welcome back!

We swung by Bixby after lunch—"Sutcliffe was telling us about palm oil today, and dude? Holy *fuck*"—to register for the Rainbow Run this weekend, which *isn't* a Proud as Halle-sponsored race like I initially thought it was—it's just a run, but you get covered in some kind of color powder as you go, which I guess is the whole appeal of it. "It's not like a *marathon* or anything," Ethan told me when he tried to convince me to sign up. "Lots of people just walk." He said he *has* to help out with it since RHA's cosponsoring it with CPB, although nobody's actually making him. And speaking of CPB, the elections for its and SGB's offices are this week. I voted for all the names I didn't recognize as a fuck-you to the popular ones.

I knew the last few weeks of the semester would be full of bittersweet moments, and today was the first—the last Open Mic Night of the year. It feels like the first one just happened, back when I went on a whim and when Ethan was just some guy who played a pop song. Tylor, Nikole, Elisha, and I got to Brew 22 as early as we typically do and it was already standing room only. It was like being at a frat party. *There's no way we're not violating some kind of fire code.* A few people were even standing outside at the open fold-open front windows. I'm not saying that everybody was there to see Three Lesbians in a Wheelchair, but I'm also not saying there wasn't any correlation, especially after they made it onto Twitter and *The Herald's* website. '*As you can see,*' Dr. Jurado would say as he'd draw a graph of it, '*the crowd gets bigger the more fucking fire the music gets, proving a direct relationship between the two.*' And now that I have a face to go with the persona, I feel like I've seen Sam/DJ Twinkle Toes at every Open Mic Night. Every act gave some version of "thanks for all the support this year" when they were done. The Improv Club people gave a stage-worthy bow after their performance. Chadwick Patterson went to tip his fedora and accidentally flung it at a girl sitting up front.

"Don't stop supporting live music, of any kind," Matt said after his 7-minute acoustic epic.

Finally, to a level of applause that only strengthened my theory, Ethan, Victor, Kade, and Amina made their entrance from the back where they must've changed clothes—the guys were dressed in thrift-store suits and ties like they were about to play at prom, and Amina wore what has to be the most beautiful dress she owns. She looked like she was ready to sing opera. "Hello," was all Ethan said. It was the first performance he didn't need his phone for. Victor *clacked* his sticks together and they went right into it.

Ethan had told me that they were going to play songs by a band I'd never heard of, and he was correct. It was bright, lively, and low-key dreamy, like dream sequence music. Kade provided the backing vocals again, which always surprises me, even after all the times I've heard him sing. Victor sounded bumpy and staggered, but that was just his mastery of the drums. Amina took over during the breakdown at the end on Kade's electric guitar, electrocuting the room with her EMP pulse and sending needles of ice into our spines. Ethan may have been the one singing, but he wasn't the star of the show this time—they really felt like a *band* instead of just Ethan and his supporting musicians. I loved his and their past performances, but this one blew me away.

"I'm gonna go ahead and guess that there probably aren't many Parekh & Singh fans in the crowd?" Ethan asked the room after the applause quieted down. "Yeah, I didn't think so," he chuckled. "Anyway, we're Three Lesbians in a Wheelchair, and if you've seen us before, you'll see that we have a new member—Amina Hadid on guitar!" He gestured to Amina, who smiled and traded Kade's guitar for her own Common Hour-seasoned acoustic.

"The pleasure's all mine," she said genuinely.

"Now, before we get into the next one," Ethan went on, "I just wanted to thank you for all the support over the year. I know it sounds cheesy and you've been hearing it all night, but it *really* does mean a lot to me. I've always heard people say how college is the place where you get to discover yourself and get exposed to new things, which is true, but I think it's also the place where…" He took a breath. "I'm gonna get personal for a second, if you don't mind." *Like we have a choice*, I smiled. "I already knew who I was before coming here, but I was never allowed to be that person back home. Coming to NHU and having the opportunity to finally be the most authentic version of myself, for really the first time ever—whether I was making a family out of the friends I wish I'd met years ago, or being able to hold hands with my boyfriend without worrying about what anyone would think, or just being able to play music I love to a room full of people—it's an experience I wouldn't trade for anything." He actually earned himself another round of applause. I already know his story, but I'd be lying if I said that hearing it again didn't choke me up a little. "So I guess what I'm trying to say is—as small of a thing as these Open Mic Nights might seem to you, they're a place where I feel like I belong, so thank you for giving me somewhere that I can fit in. Sorry for rambling. This last one's called 'Ghost.'"

The tone couldn't have been more different from the first song. It was slower, subdued, classy, and a little jazzy. Like the previous song, Kade's voice lent it an ethereal vibe, but unlike the previous song, this one was all about Ethan—but to Ethan, it was all about me. There had to have been over a hundred people there, but I was the only one he sang to. He made the rest of the room disappear. His earrings twinkled and his adoring eyes pierced mine, breaking contact only to glance down at the keys. The sudden feeling that he wanted to do the song just to sing it for me caught my chest like a hook. *I love you way more than you know, Ethan.*

If the audience was let down by the band for not ending their run of performances with a bang, they certainly didn't show it. A handful of people gave them standing ovations. One of the fake decorative flowers from a vase on one of the tables landed on the stage, and then another.

"Thank you for making this so much fun for us! I'm Ethan!"

"I'm Victor!"

"I'm Amina!"

"And I'm Kade!"

"We're Three Lesbians in a Wheelchair, and we'll see you at the Summer Send-Off!"

Victor leapt up to take the mic. "And vote Ethan Eastwood for President!" he said with a wave. People went up to the stage to congratulate them and even to take selfies with them. I had to stand around and wait for several minutes before I could get a chance to see them. "Well *hello* handsome," I said with my arms around Ethan's neck.

"Don't we look *hot?*" Victor said as he gestured down at himself. "We thought we might class it up for the last one."

"Did you like it?" Ethan asked me.

"I was expecting something crazy, but that was *perfect,*" I smiled. Ethan lit up like my approval was all that mattered.

"Really? I was hoping you'd like it," he said almost shyly.

"I'm sure some of your female fans were disappointed to hear you talk about your boyfriend, whoever *that* lucky devil is," I smirked.

"Send them my way," Victor said. "Girls are wild about drummers. It's science." I had to stop myself from making a joke about him being an anomaly to any such science.

Alex and his housemates found us and congratulated the band as we congratulated Matt on his last-ever Open Mic Night performance. "Afterparty at our place!" Alex joked, I think.

We loaded up Victor's shithead car before grabbing some drinks and pastries to take to one of the recently-vacated tables, where I kept getting lost in the thought of their band playing at the Summer Send-Off. "Forreal though, anyone wanna come chill at our place for some hookah?" Alex asked when we finally got up to put our mugs in the bin for dirty dishes. I caught Victor raising an eyebrow, and so did Andrew.

"It's a Monday night," he told his housemate. "I'm sure they have shit to do."

Victor got in his car to drive their stuff back to Axworthy, while Kade started to head down Quincey Street with Ethan and me. "You're not riding back with Victor?" I asked Kade.

"Just because I ain't going to *their* afterparty doesn't mean I'm not going to my *own* afterparty," he laughed through his nose as he loosened his tie. "I'm staying over at Greyson's place."

"So what, Victor's gonna have to take all your stuff up to your room by himself?"

"But *will* he though?" Kade smirked as he crossed the street without looking back.

So that's how I ended up trying to keep amps and electronic drum set parts and a loaded guitar case from falling off of the luggage trolley that Victor pushed down their hallway. "How were you gonna do this by yourself?" I asked, pissed at Kade for leaving his brother to do it himself.

Victor just shrugged. "It would've just taken longer and I would've been swearing more. You're not staying over in Ethan's room tonight?"

"No, I am. I'm gonna head over there after I leave here."

"I can drive you over if you want," Victor said. "I have to move my car out of the 15-minute spot anyway."

I held my fist out for a bump once we got to their door. "You the real MVP, fam."

"No, *you* the real MVP."

April 18

Today at Common Hour there was a fraternity renting out its members for the day for a fundraiser, like if you need someone to do your laundry or go pick up dinner for you or give you a ride somewhere. I wonder how many people rent out somebody just to try to sleep with them? That's literally how porn starts off—not that I've ever watched porn.

You know how you'll sometimes find yourself doing something and you're like *remind me again why I'm doing this?* Long story short, I told Kade I'd go over to Greyson's apartment to get his wallet that he'd left there, and all I could think about the whole way there was how I was being set up to get pranked. *Why can't Greyson just meet him somewhere?* And then Kade 'letting him know I was on my way' was him sending me Greyson's number so *I* could let him know when I was there.

"Hey Trevor!" Greyson gave me an up-nod from the doorway in gray sweatpants and a tank top, which is probably the same way he greets all the other boys he takes back to his room. And the fact that he had to take me back to his room to give me Kade's wallet instead of just handing it to me at the door 100% convinced me something was up. "I don't know how someone goes all morning without realizing they don't have their wallet on them," he said as I followed him down a cinder-block hallway past closed door after closed door. It was like they took one of the traditional dorms and removed all sense of community from it— there was a cork board near the door advertising some town events and things people were selling, but that was it. "He seems like he can be a little scatterbrained."

"I guess he can be at times," I admitted. "I love him though. He was the first best friend I made here."

"Only ever just friends?" Greyson smirked as he unlocked his door.

I raised an eyebrow. "Yeah?"

The rooms are single studios that are as white and as blocky as the hallway. I'd be constantly trying to sleep with people too if I lived there, assuming I wouldn't succumb to insanity from the isolation. I don't know why they even bother going over to Kade's room when Greyson lives in a literal sex dungeon—at least two of the bedposts had handcuffs dangling from them, and I swear there was some kind of harness under the bed. I eyed up the nightstand, not even wanting to know what kind of kinky shit he had in there.

Greyson picked up Kade's wallet from the kitchenette counter and passed it to me. "Here you go. And no, I didn't take all the money out of it."

"Like Kade ever has cash on him," I smiled as I slipped Kade's smiling face into my back pocket. "Do you *like* living here? I mean, I'm not the most sociable person, but I feel like I'd get lonely after a while."

"It can at times," he shrugged. "But it was cheap compared to other places, so..."

"I'm sure the privacy's nice though," I said, immediately wishing I hadn't.

"Yeah, it is," he smirked as he glanced around his own room, probably thinking about all the sexcapades it's seen. "You and Ethan are together, right?"

"Yeah? Why?" I asked, unsure if I felt more territorial or just uncomfortable.

"No reason. Just curious," he shrugged. "And a little jealous." *Okay, that's my cue.*

"I'm actually gonna go swing by to see him at work to say hi...on my way to class," I lied.

"Sure thing. Let me walk you out." He let me go first, probably so he could check out my butt and mentally undress me. "If you and Ethan ever wanna make my place a little less lonely for me, just hit me up." I've never been so happy to get away from a guy's room before. I didn't say anything about it to Kade when I swung by Arrowood, but I told Ethan all about it over a Thai tea.

"It was *so* uncomfortable," I concluded.

"It was just uncomfortable because we're together," Ethan smirked. "What? You're telling me you wouldn't hit that if you were single?" he asked.

214

"I don't *know*," I said defensively. *Greyson's deep brown eyes and smooth skin—my hands lifting his shirt up and off his chest.* "I mean, I—I don't know!"

"I'm *kidding*," Ethan said as he pinched my cheek, though I'm not sure if he was. *"Would you ever be interested in a* minage uh twah?" he leaned over to ask.

"I don't know," I frowned. *With Greyson? Probs not. With Jimmy or Miles or Dayton or Roman? Probs.*

Ethan didn't pursue the topic. "So you know how next week is RHA election week?" he asked as he sucked up the rest of his boba pearls.

"Uh huh."

"I totally understand if you don't want to," he said, which made me brace myself, "but I really need to get my name out there as much as possible, and I was wondering if you'd be willing to campaign for me?"

I tried not to wear my thoughts. "Campaign how? You already have posters up."

"I know, but I'm worried that might not be enough. Maybe you can mention it to your floormates, or before class starts, or at Lit Club maybe? It would really mean a lot."

I let my puffed cheeks deflate. "Yeah, I can do that."

"Thanks babe." He reached over to squeeze my hand. "I know it's not your favorite thing to do."

"No, but what kind of shitty, unsupportive boyfriend would I be otherwise?" I asked as I bumped his foot under the table. "I could even see if Tylor or Kade or Victor would wanna go around my building with me."

"Yeah! It won't be as bad if one of them were with you," Ethan nodded. "And I did ask Kade and Victor too if they'd be willing to do it too, in case you're thinking I'm just asking you."

"Kade probably did his whole *'that's-none-of-my-business'* thing," I chuckled.

Campaigning wasn't as awful as I thought it would be, which I guess is one perk of always overthinking things—they're never as bad as you think they'll be. "So are you gonna give a spiel before class starts?" Tylor asked me after I told them about it while we waited for Macro to start.

"Everybody probably already got the message from overhearing us talk just now," I said in a low voice like everyone in the class wasn't right there.

Tylor crossed their arms. "I'm gonna tell Ethan you didn't do it for him."

"You do it then!"

"I'm not the one he asked!"

I tried to inconspicuously glance around the room. Everyone looked like they'd rather be doing *anything* else than spending a relatively nice Tuesday afternoon sitting in an economics class. I cleared my throat. "Excuse—"

"Stand up," Tylor hissed.

I begrudgingly stood. "Excuse me everyone." I tried to pretend that nobody watching me had eyes. "I just wanted to say real quick to those of you who might live on campus"—my eyes followed Dr. Jurado as he walked into the room—"that the election for the Residence Hall Association board is next week, and I just wanted to give a shoutout for Ethan Eastwood, who's running for President. You should go vote for him." My face felt like hot salsa as I dropped back into my seat and I gave Tylor an *are-you-happy-now?* look. *That was so fucking cringe.* I expected to hear scoffs of *'who cares?'* and *'RHA's fucking lame,'* but the only person who had anything to say about it was Dr. Jurado.

"You heard Trevor—go vote. Vote anytime you have the opportunity to. You might not care about whatever it is or think your vote doesn't make a difference, but it does." He took a bite of a banana he brought in with him. "How do you think anything happens around here?" he asked as he waved it around the room. "If it wasn't for people like his friend wanting to do anything, then you'd have these university numbskulls running everything." He looked right at me. "Thanks for letting us know. Best of luck to your friend."

"See how hard that was?" Tylor whispered as Dr. Jurado kicked off class with the customary price and quantity graph.

Bolstered by Dr. Jurado's support, I did the same thing at Lit Club. "How many of you live on campus?" I asked the room from The Stool—which, yeah, might have been sacrilege, but it got people's attention. Nikole and Theo and one other person raised their hands. "Oh shit, never mind then," I said as I stepped down.

"What he *means* to say is to tell all your on-campus friends to vote for Ethan Eastwood for RHA President," Nikole spoke for me as she gave me a look.

The rest of the night saw Victor and Kade—"He just wants to go around giving campaign pitches because he hopes he'll meet someone who can make him pitch a tent"—and Kade's bass following me around Swafford's floors to talk to strangers, which is probably one of the most un-Trevor things I can think of, but the people you love are the people you overcome your fears for. And Victor and Kade even did some of the talking without me asking them to, which I wasn't about to complain about.

"My boyfriend's running for RHA President—it's the board that oversees all the House Councils—and it'd mean a lot to him and to us if you'd consider voting for him in next week's election."

"Are you tired of fuckboys always running the show? Ethan Eastwood for prez."

"Do you have a moment to talk about our lord and savior and future RHA President, his holiness Ethan Eastwood?"

Despite Victor's protests, we only stuck to knocking on the open doors. "Think about all the potential voters we're missing!" he said.

"Think about all the people we'd be pissing off for interrupting their night," I said, thinking about how I hold my breath whenever I get a knock on our door at home and wait for whoever-it-is to go away.

"It honestly doesn't matter who wins," Kade shrugged as he played an unplugged Chili Peppers bass line. "We'll all still be property of the State anyway."

I figured we'd be met with lots of blank stares and annoyed body language, but I was surprised not only at how many people actually knew who Ethan was—which was only like four people, but still—but how many people were actually interested in the election. Some residents even had questions for us, questions that just got more difficult when I'd bring up gender-neutral housing.

"Is this Ethan just some guy, or does he have any relevant experience?"

"How will he build and improve relationships with the other campus organizations?"

"Would an executive board under his leadership fairly represent the diversity of its constituents?"

"That's not really up to him to decide," I said as I tugged on my collar.

"What would gender-neutral housing look like? Would it be confined to a specific dorm? Because if so, that's discrimination."

"Why should I want a cis guy make decisions for a trans girl like myself?"

"Say we do get gender-neutral housing—if my roommate gets a sex change, will I still have to live with him, her, whatever it is they'd be?"

"I'm sure that guy's a fucking Ally," Kade scoffed as we walked away.

I called it a night after one girl held us captive with questions and scenarios for like ten minutes before finally letting us go. "This is like a goddamn job interview," I complained.

"Welcome to the world of public service," Victor said flatly.

April 19

I always used to think that coming up with names for paint colors would be kind of a fun job, but then I thought about having to arrange them by color and put them in order, and now it just sounds like the worst case of analysis paralysis ever.

We did something crazy today and got breakfast at Ginny's on a Wednesday. It was actually busier than I thought it'd be, and it wasn't all just townies either. "Yeah, we came back from class and you were in Ethan's room eating a big thing of pudding," I told Kade my dream as Ethan snickered. "And I said to you, 'tell Ethan what you told me about Wyoming.'"

"Wyoming?" Kade laughed.

"Yeah. And you laughed to yourself and were like, 'Oh yeah, up there we call them the Shkeets.'"

"The *Shkeets*? What the—?"

Victor jumped up from his seat so quickly and so violently that he even startled people at other tables. "You're fucking *shitting* me," he breathed with wide eyes.

"What? What happened?"

"*I got it,*" he said. His hands hit the table with a cutlery-rattling *slap*. "I fucking GOT it."

"What, chlamydia?"

"An RA position!" He scooped up his phone to show it to us like an eye exam. "I'm gonna be an RA!"

We just stared as it sank in. "Holy *shit* dude."

"Are you fucking forreal?"

"Congrats fam! I *told* you you'd get it!"

Victor couldn't not grin as we shook his shoulder and ruffled his hair. "I just got the email and, well, here—" He read the email like it was one of Willy Wonka's golden tickets. "*Dear Victor, we are both pleased and excited to offer you the position of Resident Assistant for the 2023-2024 academic year. Out of the hundreds of qualified and competent candidates, we have selected you to serve and represent the students living on campus. On behalf of the Residence Life team, congratulations! You have been assigned to...Portis Hall?!*" he squinted. "That's like, far away as fuck from Novak! I'm gonna have to walk across campus to come see you guys!"

"If I can make it over from Kessler," Ethan said, "I think you can make it over from Portis."

"And now you don't have to anymore since Trevor moved in with you," Kade said under his breath.

I gave him a look. "*Me*? I didn't—look who's talking!"

"Dad and Dad, both of you shut up right now or I'm running away," Victor said. "I guess I shouldn't be complaining about it though."

"Yeah, you should be proud of yourself. Forreal, congrats dude."

But like the passing of Ruth Bader Ginsberg—rest her soul—the *now-what?* eclipsed the news. "So I guess we're gonna have to find a new roommate then?" Ethan spoke our minds. But lucky for us, the universe had our backs.

"Whattup buttercup?" I answered Logan's call as I stepped into one of the staff rooms in Rosenberg.

"Fam!" Logan beamed. "I got in!"

I laughed through my nose. "You've been with Sara for *how* long and she just *now* let you—"

"*No*, I got into NHU! I just got my acceptance letter!" he beamed as he held up a paper-sized envelope. "I'm transferring!"

"Shut the fuck up," I gasped. "Are you forreal?"

It turns out he wasn't just saying things when he said he wanted to transfer when he was here visiting—he'd been hustling for grants and scholarships for months, and applying to schools all over the northeast. "I'm looking forward to getting out of here," he said. "Not that I hate it, but I just don't wanna be one of those people who live their whole lives in the same place." He shook his head with a smile. "You know, I used to not understand why you didn't just go to school here, but I get it now."

"I'm happy for you man, really. I'm already pumped for it," I smiled. "We're gonna have so much *fucking* fun."

"I know, right? Not gonna lie though, I'm nervous about the whole roommate thing. I don't wanna have to room with some weirdo."

I almost knocked myself over. *"Dude!"* I laughed at how perfectly things were falling into place. "Victor *literally* just found out he's gonna be an RA so he won't be able to live with us anymore! We need another person to take his place!"

Logan blinked. "Like I said, I don't wanna have to room with some weirdo."

> So I think I solved our roommate problem
> **LOGAN IS TRANSFERRING HERE IN THE FALL!**
> **Can he live with us?**
> **Can we please keep him?**
> **I promise I'll take him on walks**

I told Logan who to contact while I left work early to power-walk over to the Residence Life office before it closed for the day to explain our situation in person to somebody named Maria. "We'll need the written agreement of your other two roommates," she just said when I stopped to take a breath. "They'll need to log onto their housing portal and electronically give their consent." Kade and Ethan and I had everything finalized by dinner.

"Maybe I can still live with you guys," Victor said as he played with his bowl of some kind of bean chili. "I can sleep on the couch."

"That'd make you a pretty shitty RA," I laughed. "Ethan and I are gonna put our beds together, so I'm sure there'll be room for one more," I bounced my eyebrows.

"Dude," Kade gasped, "let's put *all four* of our beds together!"

Kade split for Arrowood from Patnick, leaving Victor and me alone for one of those cross-campus talks. "You don't seem super thrilled about being an RA," I said.

"No, I am!" he said quickly. "Believe me, I am. It's just that...now that the initial excitement is gone, I'm starting to think about other things."

"Such as?"

"Such as how Kade's been my literal brother for almost seven years now, and how I'm gonna have to get used to him not being right there all the time," Victor said somberly. "I knew it'd happen eventually, but I feel like it's happening so fast all of a sudden."

"Life moves fast sometimes," I paraphrased Ferris Bueller. "Look how fast it's moving for Logan—this morning he didn't know where he'd be going to school, and now he has to accept the fact that he'll be sharing a bathroom with Kade."

"God help him," Victor chuckled as he crossed himself. "But it's not even the thought of you guys having fun without me that scares me—it's that we'll eventually drift apart from not being physically close."

I raised an eyebrow. "We don't live together *now* and we're like best friends. It's not like you're going to a different school." I didn't say we aren't going to drift apart though, because that—as I learned the hard way—is something I *can't* promise.

"Yeah, I know, but..."

"Different doesn't always mean bad," I pointed out. "Adapting to new situations is part of the human experience."

"*God*, you're so deep."

"That's what the bishop said to the bishop."

I met Ethan outside of Malik after the RHA forum let out to walk over to Kessler with him and the rest of his House Council, though the two of us hung back to let the others go on ahead of us. "Anything new with the gender-neutral housing proposal?" I asked him.

"No," he sighed. "I don't think anything's gonna come of it this year. But we *did* pass a vote to change 'two weeks' in the RHA constitution to 'fortnight.'" I couldn't tell if he was trying to be funny or not.

"So is Hunter gonna have to switch rooms then?"

"No. My RA said since it's almost the end of the year that they're just gonna let them stay where they are. But it's gonna mess up their living arrangements for next year."

"That fucking sucks," was all I said.

"That it *does*."

I didn't know what to follow that up with, so I pulled a white-people move and changed subjects. "I was talking with Victor on the way back from dinner. He said he's worried that we're gonna stop hanging out with him since we won't be living together, and that we might start drifting apart."

"It's not like we're just gonna totally *forget* about him," Ethan scoffed. "How's that any different from how it is now?"

"That's what I told him," I said in a sing-song voice.

We hit up the vending machines for some iced tea before going up to 341 Kessler, where I dropped onto Ethan's/my bed. "You know, with all this unused furniture, I probably *could* just move into your room," I half-joked as my eyes drifted across Nate's old furniture.

"How would you get into the building?" Ethan asked. "Or the room? Not that I'm trying to talk you out of it."

"I'll just flirt with the DA while I slide on by," I smirked as I watched him drop a few pieces of colorful paper into a small tin inside one of his desk drawers. "What are those? Do you make crafts in RHA?"

"Oh, no. They're comments."

"Comments?" I repeated.

"Yeah. There's a comment box that gets passed around at the meeting and people can write whatever they want on the pieces of paper, and then they get read at the end of the meeting," he explained.

"Like, *snarky* comments?"

"I mean, they *could* be," he chuckled.

"And you collect them?"

"Just the ones that get written about me," he said like he was almost embarrassed by them.

I blinked. "Okay, wait. Back up. *What?*"

He just laughed. "Somebody wrote a comment about my new shoes after I'd gotten them, and then more people started doing it, and then it just became a thing." He showed me the tin and scraps of paper inside.

"Can I read them?" I asked, *immensely* interested.

"Have at it," he said as he passed it to me. I crossed my legs on the floor and picked them out one-by-one.

'A day with Ethan is like a day in paradise'

'Ethan is the coolest'

'I wish I was Ethan's roommate so I could watch him sleep'

'If at first you don't succeed, you're obviously not Ethan'

'Ethan is the hero this university NEEDS'

'Ethan is so cute'

'Dear Ethan, I hate you. A lot. Love, Bailey'

'And god said, 'Let there be Ethan''

'If people were rain, I was a drizzle, and Ethan was a hurricane'

'I didn't know I could see something as beautiful and sexy as Ethan in glasses'

'Ethan's eyes are looking extra blue tonight'

'But, soft! What light through yonder window breaks? It is the East(wood), and Ethan is the sun'

'The things I'd give for a night with Ethan'

'The fault in our Ethans'

'I was thankful for Ethan this Thanksgiving'

'Ethan is the ray of sunshine that fills the world with unicorns and rainbows!'
'Ethan starts the day with a bubble tea made from the tears of his enemies'
'ETHAN FOR PREZ 2048'

"So what I'm getting out of this is that there are a lot of people who wanna sleep with you," I laughed. *And I can't blame them.* "So wait, you're this popular"—I picked up a handful and let them flutter to the floor—"and you're worried you're not gonna win the election? You have a ton that flat-out say 'Ethan for President.'"

"Most of them are from the same few people every meeting! Remember your theory about the 'loud minority?'"

I waved him off. "Oh, hush."

"And even if not, this is just one group of students. And they see Westley just as much as they see me. He goes to the meetings too, remember?"

"*Okay.* And does he get comments like this?"

"*No.* But comments don't mean shit when you have the full support of SGB vouching for you."

"That doesn't mean people *like* him," I said. "You can at least talk to people without looking like you just shat yourself."

April 21

Have you ever *really* stopped to think about all the alternate universes out there where there are other versions of yourself being way better versions of you than you'll ever be? It's like, *really* fucking depressing. But hey, at least tech genius Trevor and cyberpunk vigilante Trevor are living it up somewhere out there.

I was yesterday-years-old when I learned that 4/20 is basically a holiday among college kids. There were more empty seats in class than usual, and way more weed references than usual. There's no way that Dr. Jurado didn't go home and get high as hell after class. I also didn't think that I'd be the one of our friend group who'd be the most eager to celebrate the day it was intended to be celebrated. And here I thought Victor was the stoner out of us.

"You know I absolutely would," he told me at lunch with a wince when I asked if he wanted to get baked later, "but I have a workshop with the other first-time RAs that I have to go to." He gave me an apologetic look. "I'm skipping Improv Club if that makes you feel any better."

"I'm gonna celebrate it with Greyson," Kade said at dinner before reminding me that April 20th is also Hitler's birthday.

"I'm going to the CPB meeting for the Rainbow Run with the rest of the RHA e-board after work, but after that I'll be down!" Ethan said enthusiastically.

Since I already had his number from when I got that half of a brownie for myself last week, I asked Caleb if he had any gummies I could buy off him. "Thanks for pulling through on such short notice," I felt cool saying to him as I let 408 Swafford's door close behind me. I traded Caleb my cash for his zippy bag of gummies that I folded up and stuffed into my back pocket. I didn't know if I was supposed to just leave or stick around so as not to look rude. "So, have you been celebrating the day?" I asked, making even myself cringe.

"No? I *had* class," Caleb chuckled. "I'm about to head over to my bud's place though. He's making a water bong." And then he sideswiped me when he asked, "You wanna come light up with me on the way over? I cut through the woods to get there and I know a good spot." *That's the kind of thing I'd say if I wanted to make out with someone before murdering them.*

"I mean...sure," I agreed. "But why though? I like barely even know you."

He shrugged. "You seem cool. Victor seems cool. It's a holiday. I'm feeling generous."

"I can drive you over and we can smoke in my car if you want, if smoking in the woods would be risky." *Now that sounds like the kind of thing you say to someone if you wanna make out with them—not that I necessarily do.*

Caleb raised an eyebrow. "A random parked car would look even more sus."

I followed him towards the Ski Hill and into the trees. We stuck to the trail for a bit before he led us off into the undergrowth. *I'm glad I didn't wear my white Vans,* I thought as I stepped gingerly onto the soft, wet ground. "Here it is," he said when we came upon a kind-of clearing with a fallen log. *He could kill me right here and nobody would ever know.* But instead of a machete, he fished an Altoids tin out of his backpack. And instead of mints, a row of joints lay tucked inside the paper. He held one in his mouth as he scrolled on his phone. "My buds and I always start every smoke sesh with the same Sublime song." Once his Sublime song was playing, he lit the joint and took a hit. "You can come and sit, you know," he chuckled as he held it out to me.

Trying not to think of the bugs, I joined him on the log. "Ohh, this actually tastes *good,*" I said after I'd hit it. "Like, it almost has a bit of flavor to it."

We passed it back and forth while we talked, listening for rustling leaves or a snapping twig. A Tame Impala song shuffled on next, which kind of sounds how The Beatles would sound if they were still making music. I don't know if the quality of the taste of the weed has a direct relationship to the effectiveness of it, but that shit *hit* me. Or maybe it was the fact that we smoked another one after the first one. Caleb held his phone next to an ant to see if it would start dancing.

"So wait," I said in regard to another Sublime song that came on, "so he smokes...infinity plus two joints?"

Caleb stared at the invisible equation floating in the air a few inches in front of his face. "Yeah? I think? I dunno, math was never my thing, so…"

"Yeah, me neither. And that was *before* they started throwing imaginary numbers at us."

"Yeah, like eleventy-twelve," Caleb said, stony-faced. "Or 42."

We started talking about classes and hometowns. He's a PoliSci major from Snow Shoe, Pennsylvania, which is like an hour and a half east of here and looks as boring as it sounds. "No wonder you wanted to go away to school," I said as I squinted at it on Google Earth. "There's like fuck-nothing there!"

"Dude," he smiled at me with lazy eyes, "have you *seen* where we go to school? There's fuck-nothing *here* either."

"Yeah, I guess," I said before I started rambling. "I wonder why I'm even here sometimes. Like, I'm a city boy. I *like* civilization. I need to be *around* civilization."

Caleb laughed through his nose. "Why the hell *are* you here then?"

"I dunno. It wasn't super expensive? And the English program was supposed to be good?" I shrugged like it might've been the wrong answer. "Sometimes I think about if I'd gone to Pitt with my ex instead of here." I looked off into the trees. "We'd probably still be together."

"Shit fam, sorry to hear that things didn't work out."

"No, don't be. If I'd gone there, then I wouldn't have met my friends or my current boyfriend. He blows my ex out of the water." *Ha, blows.*

The smallest smile crept across Caleb's face. "I always like finding out who else is gay."

I turned to him before I could stop myself. "Are you gay?"

"I dunno. I know I'm definitely at least bi."

"Oh, okay. Cool." In another universe where Trevor is single, that's about when he and Caleb start making out. And then they might—"Hold on! 42's not an imaginary number!"

We laughed so hard that we almost fell off our log. I laughed so hard that my stomach hurt. I laughed so hard that I actually sobered up a little.

"That was *perfect,*" Caleb wheezed as he clutched his sides.

"Why don't we hang out more?" I asked as I wiped my eyes.

"Uh, because I've seen you for a total of like five minutes before today?" he pointed out as he checked his phone to read the text he'd gotten.

"That's fair." Though it's actually bullshit—my first five minutes of meeting Kade left me wanting more of him.

Caleb shot off a text before making sure he had everything. "Well, I'm gonna carry on my way," he said as he zipped up his bag. "I don't wanna get there too late."

I pulled out my own phone to check the time, half-afraid I'd have four texts and a missed call from Ethan. "Yeah, I'm gonna bounce too." We returned to the path and went opposite ways. "See ya man. Thanks for the smoke."

"Yup. I'll see you around."

It wasn't dark out yet, but the sun-burying hills made the woods unnerving enough for me to nope the fuck out of there. The sky bled with ink by the time I was back on the streets of campus, where Ethan's text telling me that his meeting was finally done found me. I studied my face in my phone's camera to make sure I didn't look too high, though I couldn't come up with an excuse to give him as to why I was already high if he'd be able to tell. I found him sitting on the wall in front of Bixby near the waterfall, but he saw me coming before I could sneak up on him. *Oh my god, that smile.* "Hey babe," he greeted me with a kiss. "How was your day?"

"Not bad," I shrugged. "It was just a regular old Thursday." *For the most part.* "How about yours? What made your meeting take long?"

"Well," he took a breath, "*we* were under the assumption that RHA would be paying 30% of the cost of the Rainbow Run and that CPB would be paying the rest. But then their advisor was trying to tell us that we were responsible for 35%, which, sure, we could do if the rest of our budget wasn't already allocated for the rest of the year. And then Shannon started bringing up all kinds of petty shit, like who's gonna transport the color packets the morning of, and who will—" *I like how he keeps saying 'we' and 'our,' like he already knows it's gonna be his organization. And who's Shannon? It's such a nice evening. What would Louis Pasteur think about his role in the creation of 4/20 as a weed holiday? How spicy would shit have gotten if a group of students threw President Norwood off the top of Old Main when those protests were going on? How many people are using weed as an aphrodisiac tonight?* "Are you listening?"

I snapped my head back to him. "Sorry, I kinda zoned out."

"Something on your mind?"

"More like my mind is on some *things*," I accidentally said out loud.

"Huh?" He stopped to study my face like it was an optical illusion. "Are you high?"

"I may or may not be," I slowly said, shamefaced at being found out.

"What—? *How*—? Did you *smoke*?"

"Can I lie?" I asked, which probably just upset him.

"No."

I sighed. "Yeah, I smoked. In the woods, with Caleb. After I bought the gummies for us, he asked me if I wanted to smoke with him."

His confusion turned to hurt. "But I thought we were gonna get high together?"

"We still can. I have the gummies with me."

His hurt turned to irritation. "You couldn't have waited for me to get done?"

"I figured if I was just sitting around—"

"So even though we had plans to get high together," he said as he dropped to one of Zukoff's outdoor tables, "you went ahead and did it without me? With some guy you've met only one other time?"

I didn't try to sit next to him. "*Twice*. And what do you think we did, kiss or something?"

"*No*, and I'm actually hurt that you'd think that I'd think that." His face showed it, too. "It's the idea though—I was hoping to make a date night out of it. I knew today was gonna be a long one for me, and I figured a good way to end it would be to relax with you and just enjoy the night, but I feel like you put what *you* wanted to do over what I wanted *us* to do."

Instead of telling him that I'd basically said the same thing to him after we all popped molly, I sat beside him to put my arm around him, which only made him get up. "But we still can!" I said, feeling like a total ass.

"You're not *listening* to—" He shook his head. "You know what, I can't have a serious talk with you when you're like this." *He can't even look at me, that's how bad of a boyfriend I am.* "Maybe you should just sleep in your room tonight."

"No, no no no," I panicked. "I'm sorry. You're right, I was—"

"Can we please just talk about this tomorrow?" he said more than he asked. "And you realize it took you until *now* to say that you're sorry?" he added with a cynical laugh. *Yeah Trevor, you self-absorbed prick.*

It was a struggle to not tear up. He was right—he'd been thinking of us, but I was thinking only of me. "I mean, if that's what you want..." Even if he had changed his mind, I didn't deserve to spend the night with him. "Do you want me to leave the gummies with you in case you—"

"No," he said firmly to the ground.

He didn't pull away when I gave him an apologetic peck on the cheek. "I really am sorry. I love you." He just looked up at me with sad eyes.

I tortured myself the whole way back to Swafford, which was even easier to do since the euphoria part of the high had passed. *I don't blame Dillon for leaving an asshole like me. Maybe he left because he was tired of being treated the way I treat people. I wouldn't blame Ethan if he left me too. I don't deserve him. And he certainly deserves better than me. He didn't even say 'I love you' back. He didn't even say 'I love you' back. He didn't even say 'I love you' back. He didn't even say 'I love you' back.*

Tylor could tell something was up as soon as I swiped myself into 222 Swafford. "You're not staying over Ethan's?" they asked me.

"No," I sniffled. "We kind of had a fight."

"*Shit*, I'm sorry to hear that," they said sincerely. "I *was* planning on spending the evening in the nude though, so I hope you don't mind," they said to try to lighten my mood. I forced the weakest smile as I stared up at the ceiling. I felt cold and empty, and the only person who could warm me didn't want to see me. *The people who came up with the idea of hell got it all wrong—being forsaken by god has nothing on being forsaken by the people who you love.*

"Why are we okay with hurting the people we love?" I asked the ceiling.

In the corner of my eye, I caught Tylor looking up from their notebook. "I think we get used to them and lose sight of how much they really mean to us," they answered after a moment. "But the people you love are the ones you're willing to let yourself be hurt by. But if you let yourself get hurt over and over again, then you're just stupid."

Their words ran through my mind over and over until they were all I could think about. I remembered the part in *The Perks of Being a Wallflower* about how we settle for someone we think we deserve even when they're not good for us, and how Ethan might someday come to realize that he *doesn't* deserve me and that he *could* do better.

I know you probably don't wanna hear from me but I'm texting you anyway because I'm not gonna be one of those people who let their pride get in the way of us.
I'm really sorry. I know it probably doesn't mean anything to you, but I am. It was selfish and wrong of me to disregard what you wanted and you don't deserve that.
I really wish I could cuddle with you right now because that's the only thing that would make me not feel like a piece of shit but I know I don't even deserve that
I love you so much 😭😭😭😭😭😭😭😭😭😭😭😭
I hope we can still get breakfast tomorrow 😭

The blinking ellipsis I kept checking for never materialized. I wish he'd just tell me what an asshole excuse of a boyfriend I am instead of ghosting me. I let the water rain down on me without even feeling it before I actually started showering. I thought about having a gummy or two to try numbing my mind, but seeing a text from Ethan set my pulse racing. I think I got a cardio workout in the second it took for my face to unlock my phone.

Come on over 😊

Old Trevor, in some silly act of penance, would've insisted on staying put or would have even ghosted Ethan back, but thankfully I'm wiser and less dramatic than he was. And from the way Ethan hugged and held me instead of making me ask for his forgiveness, he showed me that he's the kind of person who refuses to let his pride control him either.

"I'm sorry babe," I said with teary eyes as I thought about how the night could have very well ended with me not being able to breathe in the smell of his body wash.

"I'm sorry too," he said into my shoulder. "I feel like I was being dramatic."

I made sure my eyes were dry before I had to face the DA, although I'm sure she'd seen her share of bleary-eyed kids, given the day. "Why do we do this to each other?" I asked him as we laid on his bed with my head on his chest. "I never *want* to hurt you or make you feel bad, but I do it anyway and I don't know why. I hate myself for it."

"Don't say you *hate* yourself. Nobody's perfect," he said as he twirled a finger in my hair. "Every couple has their fights. They're not gonna make posts about it on Instagram though, so we're made to believe that love is supposed to be this perfect thing, and if it doesn't feel perfect then you're apparently doing it wrong. But love's messier than it looks, and sorting out the messes is what makes relationships stronger. Yeah, it hurts and it sucks, but it helps make us a stronger couple." Or to put it another way, in his own words: *If I didn't have forever in mind, then I wouldn't be wasting my time.*

Our chests rose and fell together for a minute or ten. "Do you know what made me text you tonight?" I broke the silence.

"What?"

"I was wallowing on my bed and all of a sudden this Stoic thought hit me—not something I read, but rather something I figured out on my own."

"Oh?"

"I thought about how everyone who's ever died—or, I guess I should say *most* people who've ever died—went to bed the night before, and never in a million years would they have thought it was the last time they'd do it. And there's no guarantee that tonight couldn't be the last night for one of us."

"Stoicism 103," he smiled into my hair as he squeezed me tighter. I fell asleep in his arms, which isn't too hard to do after you've come down from a high.

I woke up in only my underwear, but I didn't remember undressing. "Did you have your way with me after I passed out?" I joked after he woke up.

"You *wish*." He wormed his arm underneath me. "I figured you wouldn't wanna sleep in your jeans."

"You figured correctly." I stretched and let my arm fall over him. "How late did you stay up?"

"Not *too* late. I actually *did* have a gummy though," he said sheepishly. "I put in my earbuds and then it was 1:30."

"You know, unexplainable lapses in time are a sign of getting abducted by aliens," I smiled. We lay with our noses less than an inch apart from each other's. "How about we do tonight what we were gonna do last night?" I asked him. "No friends, no parties, just us."

"That sounds *perfect*," he grinned. "I wish you didn't have to go to class."

"Don't *you* have to go to class?"

"Not my first one. My prof emailed us saying she wouldn't be in today."

I thought for a moment. "Fuck it then. If you don't have class, then I don't have class."

He gasped. "Skipping two Fridays in a row? I'm telling your mother," he said as he booped me on the nose.

"I said I was only skipping my first one! And go ahead, see if I give a shit," I dared him as I rolled on top of him.

April 23

Ethan's neighbors probably thought we were going at it for a second time on Friday night when we were actually just *super* baked and moaning at how good the milkshakes we got from McDonald's were. You know that part in *The Perks of Being a Wallflower* where Charlie says how he had a milkshake that was so good that it scared him? *That's* how good those milkshakes were. "I wish *I* could make you moan like that," Ethan said to me with a laugh, though he *did* have me moaning earlier on. The night's vibe was one of Christmas lights, *House of Balloons*, and nude instant photos. We peaked as we were having sex, and it was like having sex for the first time all over again—the kind of sex you can only dream about having, the kind of sex that makes you believe in magic. I think I might've had an out-of-body experience. There are some people who spend every single weekend night like that, and I can't really be mad at them.

As much as I would've liked to have spent the whole morning naked in bed with Ethan, we met up with Kade and Victor at Ginny's. "So what do you guys think?" Kade asked us halfway through breakfast.

"They're good," I said, "but I think I like the blueberry peach ones better."

"Not the *waffles*, you chode," he groaned. "What I *texted* you." I thought he was high out of his mind and just saying things, but I guess he was serious when he said that he and Victor were going to do acid with Andrew and June and Alex, and if we'd be interested in doing it with them. I was glad that Ethan kept what he wanted to do to himself so as to not pressure me.

"How long do we have to think about it?" I asked without trying to sound like the idea scared the shit out of me. *Like, haven't people jumped out of windows and shit while tripping?*

Kade shrugged. "Until they get back from whatever they're doing."

"He said the trip lasts for like twelve hours," Victor added, making me start choking on my second-favorite waffle, "so we were gonna do it right after they get back."

"Twelve *hours!?*" I coughed.

"And they said because of how it works, it'll feel even longer," he casually added. I gulped. I was more scared than excited, but I was more curious than scared. I wanted to experience firsthand what made the 1960s what they're remembered for, what made The Beatles go from *A Hard Day's Night* to *Magical Mystery Tour*. A small voice in my head whispered, *if you don't try acid in college, then why are you even here?*

I nodded. "Yeah, okay."

"That's what I was hoping you'd say," Ethan grinned.

I guess acid's harder to get than ecstasy because we had to pay up for our doses—in the form of $50 of the cheapest food from McDonald's for everybody. Ordering that much food after you just ate makes you legit feel disgusting. "We're gonna wanna have it for later, in case we forget to eat," Alex told us as he stuffed it all in the fridge. "And trust me when I say you do *not* wanna try ordering food while you're tripping."

Andrew opened a zippy bag so tiny that it shouldn't have been allowed to exist, and tipped the pinky-nail-sized postage stamps it held into his palm before offering one to each of us. I looked down at it, not even caring what the since-perforated original image on it could have been. "Are we supposed to chew it?" I asked.

"Just put it under your tongue and let it dissolve," Andrew said as he did just that.

We smoked with Anubis on the patio as we waited for it to hit. I tried my best to keep an optimistic attitude since having a stick up my ass usually doesn't do me any good. Don't get me wrong though, I was still nervous as shit. I was glad that Matt doesn't do drugs anymore, because having a responsible, clear-headed adult around made me feel more at ease. We hit the seniors with questions about it, all of which they answered with a "Just wait," or "You just have to wait and see."

And then "Colours" by The Avalanches came on, and the only existence I'd ever known came to an irrevocable end in the most wonderful way.

Thank fucking god I'd already tried ecstasy, because if yesterday would've been the first time I felt every part of my body pumping to life, I would've been freaking the fuck out. It energized me like ecstasy, but not like let's-go-karate-chop-a-tree energized. But unlike ecstasy, it cracked open my mind and let me properly see the world for the first time. It was like I'd been living my entire life in sepia and I finally got to see all the colors—the billions and billions of beautiful colors. It's like I was seeing everything for the first time all over again with innocent, childlike fascination. I ran my hand across the concrete like I'd never felt anything solid before. I turned a rock over in my hand, felt the veins of a leaf, dumbstruck that I've walked this Earth without ever appreciating what a miracle each of them are.

You hear about people taking acid and start seeing dragons and shit that isn't there, but I didn't have any of that. Instead, everything that was already there was what changed—or rather, I saw everything for what it all truly was, everything that an inhibited mind kept me from seeing. Instead of a yard full of grass, I saw every individual blade in sharp definition. Leaves gave off visible vibrations. My own skin even felt like it was its own entity instead of a part of me—which, I'm not going to lie, thinking about being trapped inside it almost made me freak out. The grass, the leaves, the flowers, the trees, the clouds—everything was *breathing*. And I could *hear* all of it. Every surface undulated, flowing with currents of energy and life. Everything was *alive*. Everything *is* alive. Everything was tinted purple. *The world is a wonderful place, a living, breathing creature. Benevolent, loving Mother Earth.*

Religion went out the window. Science went out the window. Nothing was no longer unknown. Every mystery of the universe made clear, unquestionable sense. Art became foolish. Money became laughable, and civilization a joke. The beginning and end of everything is this—that the universe is love. Out of everything in existence, love is the only thing that matters—love, a chemical reaction our brains concocted to mean something to us and to make us feel something. *Dr. Sutcliffe was right all along—in the beginning we were all beings of pure, unbounding love, capable of anything. But people lost sight of that. They found that love isn't profitable. Love doesn't give people power. Love doesn't control people. But ignorance does, as does fear, as does hate. And that's why this is illegal—if every person came face-to-face with the being of pure, unbounding love that they are, that would be the point where humanity swerves—the point where we would begin to build a better world, to right the world that we've wronged.* The more I thought about it, the closer the darkness crept in on us—darkness that waited in the slightest shadows, in the cracks in the patio, from the open windows. But because I'm a soul with limitless potential, I only had to think of the beauty and the love in the world, and the darkness retreated. I remembered the words of the prophet Martin Luther King, Jr. and I almost started to cry—*"Darkness cannot drive out darkness; only light can do that. Hate cannot drive out hate; only love can do that."* And then I thought about that thing that plays at the end of *Minecraft* about how everything you experience is just the universe speaking to you, and the part that goes *"and the universe said I love you because you are love"* put tears in my eyes.

The song ended.

"Trevor!" Kade gasped at one point, looking like some misshapen character from an Adult Swim show. "What's wrong with your face?"

I felt it in a panic. "What? What's wrong with it?"

Kade pointed at me. "Doesn't he look like Humpty Dumpty?"

"Oh my fucking god, he does!"

"Holy *shit* dude!" Ethan laughed, his own eyes and teeth glowing in the dark in the daylight. Every song that came on never wanted to end. I checked my phone a few hours later and couldn't understand how only 20 minutes had passed. *Is this how we cheat time?*

The atmosphere was different inside the house—not *bad*, but not bright and happy like outside. I watched a kaleidoscope endlessly unfold on the ceiling. A malevolent force sat lurking in the corner, but I knew it couldn't hurt me because evil cannot hurt love. I stared at myself in the bathroom mirror like I was an extraterrestrial until my face got so warped that I didn't recognize myself. Soap bubbles at the bottom of the sink looked up at me like a million eyeballs. I found Victor in the back corner of the living room standing inches away from a life-sized bust of Julius Caesar on a pedestal that I'd literally never seen before. *Am I legit hallucinating right now?* It drew me to it, past the corporeal shadows. Standing right behind Victor, I stared into the empty white eyes that examined my fears and my sins. It was like when explorers in the jungle stumble upon some cursed totem that makes them go insane. I felt like it would swallow me. "Surrender yourself unto he," I muttered, making Victor's soul leave his body for a moment. We backed up until the couch caught us, where we held each other without ever taking our eyes off of his.

What insects there were outside floated through the air like motes of dust. "Just so you know," I announced to the others as the benign world embraced me again, "Slenderman is in the house."

We decided to go on an adventure. Walking away from the house was like going on a spacewalk. I felt like if we'd go too far from it then some tether would snap and we'd be lost forever to nonexistence. It was majestic though. Walking down Main Street was like a trippy music video. I could hear the vibrations coming from the dancing trees and buildings. I wanted to jump but was afraid to, because I was worried I'd just keep going up and up into the apocalypse-colored sky and never come back down. *Why are people so afraid to see the world like this?* A woman was pushing a baby in a stroller towards us and as we got closer and closer, the baby's face kept getting uglier and uglier, but I couldn't look away from it. One of the stores had a bunch of pinwheels displayed out front like aliens. And then there were all these people planting saplings and flowers all over town like cultists, and I remembered that it was Earth Day after I saw a flier advertising a town-wide Earth Day event. "Guys," I said like I was about to start crying, "it's Earth

Day today." *Why isn't it the most important day of the year?* I started to think about how we treat the Earth like shit and I almost teared up. Why do people spend the effort—and hurt other people along the way—to get to any kind of paradise after death when paradise is right here? Was this world the promised heaven once upon a time before people came and ruined it? I wanted to weep for the world—for the world it once was, and for the world it could be if only we would choose love over fear.

At the park, I put my hand in the fountain and let the water run over it like I'd never experienced water before. *The world is full of this stuff and nobody even cares. Why does nobody care what a miracle this is?* I wanted to show people handfuls of water and start preaching the gospel of water if I wasn't so paranoid about them finding out I was on drugs. We ambled across the empty sand of the volleyball court like astronauts exploring the surface of the moon.

We demolished the food we got earlier as our auras of love kept the darkness at bay. "I don't even feel hungry," Kade said with wide eyes as he microwaved a burger in its wrapper, "but I feel like I probably should eat something so I don't die." It might have been just a cheap microwaved burger, but it tasted so phenomenal that it shouldn't have been possible. And then I thought about the incessant holocaust going on to make cheeseburgers possible and I almost wept.

"Well now I know potatoes have feelings too, so I don't know what to do anymore," Victor said as he stuffed his mouth with fries like they were about to disappear.

There was only one part of the trip that almost got bad. It was just Victor and I and the darkness clinging to the walls like mold. I was taking a piss when a super-weird song by The Doors started to play. *Holy fuck holy FUCK.* "Victor!" I yelled. "Turn it off! *TURN IT OFF!*" I ran from the bathroom with my unwashed hands over my ears to shout at him to turn it off while he struggled in horror with whoever's phone was hooked up. He finally just yanked the speaker's plug out of the wall, which felt like the world coming to a stop.

The comedown wasn't a simple decline-and-you're-done like weed or alcohol, both of which seem like a waste of time anymore. It would spike, and then go back down, and then go back up, over and over. I rewatched a video I took of a blank, unmoving ceiling. Alex sent me a pic of me at the park sitting in a wooden beach chair so large that my feet didn't even reach the edge of the seat, staring up at the sky at whatever had me transfixed. I still can't believe the whole thing all happened in just a single afternoon and evening—eleven incense sticks to be exact. I don't think I can ever look at the world the same way again, which all seems nonsensical when I think about it now. How the hell can people be lawyers and accountants and CEOs when the world is here and waiting to be experienced? How can people settle for such a meaningless existence when they can do *anything*?

Ethan had to go help set up for the Rainbow Run early this morning, leaving me alone in his bed, and as cozy as I was, I didn't want to stay inside and let another beautiful morning go by. But I didn't leave the room without looking around and imagining what it's going to be like to live together and have a room that's *ours* —disagreeing over where things will go, discovering that our tastes clash, discovering that we do indeed get on each other's nerves. I can't fucking wait.

I took a Danish and a coffee from Brew 22 around town with me as I looked at everything through unscaled eyes and with an unclouded mind. The trees and grass didn't look like they were breathing, but that doesn't mean that they weren't. 370 Rock was still asleep, though I exchanged pleasantries with a guy in a bathrobe on the porch next door clutching his head and holding a cigarette. I stumbled upon an old church on the edge of town that I couldn't help but stop and admire—a stone, ivy-grown building surrounded by weathered headstones and an iron-and-stone fence that perfectly complemented the morning of birdsong and blossoming flowers. I wound my way back to 222 Swafford, where Tylor and I put on the whitest clothes we had for the Rainbow Run so we'd get as colorful as possible. Victor and Kade and I tried to describe the things we saw and felt on our trip to Tylor with an apostolic zeal as we walked over to the starting line in the parking lot behind Richter Music Hall.

Just about everybody there looked identical in their sunglasses and white sleeveless shirts, so it was a little hard to find Ethan. His job at the event was to be one of the people throwing packets of powder at the participants as they'd go by. "Yeah, I had to help get an ass-ton of these set up along the route," he told us with a nod to a huge plastic bucket loaded with color packets.

"*Had* to," I said with air quotes. "Would you get in trouble if you hit Aiden Fuentes right in the face with one?"

He thought it over. "Probs."

Kade pointed to the bucket of color packets. "Can you steal a few of those so we can shoot them out of my slingshot later?" he asked Ethan.

Tylor laughed out loud. "I *forgot* about that thing."

The crowd had swelled to like a million people by the time Ciara and Jayden, the CPB President who has a California personality, got up on a platform and gave the kind of hoo-hah you'd expect before setting us loose. The air exploded with music and neon clouds that colored people and parking lot alike. Volunteers with handheld cannons fired staggered volleys into the runners. *Music video idea: trench warfare, but the artillery shells and grenades are packets of color powder with whatever band playing right in the midst of it.* I blew Ethan a kiss as we passed him, feeling bad that he couldn't do it with us. Tylor and Victor kept pace with Kade and me instead of taking off at their normal speed. People jogging and even just walking made me feel not too out of my element. We were *covered* in color before we even made it past Patnick.

"*Dude*—imagine doing this on *acid*," Kade laughed.

Ethan and the other volunteers got to run the course after everyone else had finished, but it was kind of pointless if you weren't getting blasted with color powder. "You barely got any color on you!" I said when he joined us at the finish line.

"Yeah I did!" he said as he showed me the little bit of powder on his shirt.

"Inadequate," I said before taking off my shirt—"*Yes please!*" Victor squealed—so I could shake some of my color off onto him. So that's how Ethan found himself surrounded by four bare-chested folks snapping their shirts over him like the lead-up to some kind of locker-room porn.

"Okay—OKAY," he laughed. "*Stop!*" Just when he thought he was as painted as he'd be, Kade took a color packet from each of his pockets and clapped them together over Ethan's head, engulfing the five of us in a smog of blue and purple. We were shaking it out of our hair for *hours.*

April 24

I hope that we get to see stats of our life when we die—breaths taken, miles walked, times blinked, times you said the word 'the,' shits taken, webs shot, all that. Not that it would matter, but it'd still be fun just to see.

It's been two days and I still don't feel back to my pre-acid-trip self, which isn't necessarily a bad thing. I was reading that what's called 'the afterglow' can last for weeks, though I'd personally be okay with it lasting for the rest of my life just to remind me that there's more to things than what I can perceive.

The RHA election polls opened today and run through the end of the week, and the results will be announced this Sunday at the final RHA event of the year, which is some kind of dinner/banquet/dance thing. There are four people running for President, and the fact that I've never even heard of one of them before shows what kind of campaign they're running. I asked Ethan who his choices would be for the other positions and just voted for them since he'll have to work with them. And speaking of elections and Presidents, take three guesses which SGB President got voted in for a second year.

After thinking about it and brainstorming ideas, I finally decided I'm going to get a tattoo. Nothing fancy, just one single word—"unless," from *The Lorax.* On top of its call-to-action message, it resonates with me on a personal note too. I've accepted that my high school years are over and that I could've spent them better, but I'm determined not to let my college years be a repeat of them. The next few years of my life can be as boring and as uneventful as I make them...*unless*. I'm going to get it in typewriter font, right over the scars on the inside of my wrist. Victor's going to get one too that Kade drew for him—a skull with a flower in one eye socket wearing a crown with a cigarette between its teeth.

"You don't even smoke though," I said.

"Oh my *god* mom," Victor rolled his eyes. "It's called *art*."

Since neither Kade nor Ethan were in a tattoo-getting mood, Victor and I got Taco Bell for lunch before taking our designs around town for quotes. The town of New Halle has like four tattoo parlors, each one kept in business by waves of premature brains drunk on the freedom of not having to listen to their parents anymore. We decided on New Halle Ink, which we were biased towards from the start thanks to the Progress flag in the window, but we wanted to explore all the options. Bright and bohemian, its macrame plant hangers and shelf of take-one-leave-one books made it seem like it should be down in Pittsburgh instead of up here in its namesake. The person who took our deposits for appointments for this Friday has gauges that made Kade's look like pinholes.

I took my longboard out for a ride and put on the 'vibing at college' playlist I made back in September, but it didn't hit the same way like it used to. Campus isn't the same as it was—I know where all the sidewalks lead now, and the buildings hold memories for me. I'm a part of it, and it's a part of me. And I'm not the same person I was back then either. People really aren't kidding when they say that college is the most transformative time of your life. If I've grown as much as I have and if I've experienced as much as I have in just the past seven months, then I'm fucking *stoked* to see what College Graduate Trevor is going to be like.

April 25

So I finally got around to trying popcorn with some ramen powder sprinkled on it, and it legit might have been the best popcorn I've ever had. Like, why have people been keeping this shit a secret? Wake the fuck up, America.

Ethan and I were planning on starting *Stardew Valley* yesterday evening after dinner in 341 Kessler, but a surprise phone call ruined those plans for us. "It's probably just spam," Ethan said as he accepted the call. "Hello? I think you might have the wrong number, I didn't order anything. Nope. Sorry. No problem, bye." He set his phone down with a frown. "Well that was weird."

"What?" I asked.

"That was someone from Domino's telling me they're downstairs with my pizza. I didn't order a pizza."

I furrowed my brow. "That *is* weird."

"You didn't order me one without telling me as a prank, did you?"

"Who do I look like, Kade?" I chuckled. *We should totally order Kade a pizza without telling him just to mess with him.*

Ethan laughed through his nose. "That actually does sound like something Kade would—" His ringing phone cut him off. "Hello?" he answered it. "Yes, I'm *sure* I didn't order anything." He raised an eyebrow. "I mean, if you say so. Okay, I'll be right down." He hung up and let his phone fall to his bed. "He said they can't take it back, and asked if I just wanted it."

"I mean, you can always throw it in the fridge and have it later," I shrugged.

"That's what I'm gonna do. Ain't nobody tryna pass up a free pizza," he chuckled as he stepped into his slides. "BRB."

After five minutes, I told myself he was trying to figure out with the delivery guy how the mix-up could've happened, or he bumped into someone he knew. But when five minutes turned into ten, I started to worry. *There's no way it should be taking this long.* I went down to the lobby to see what was up, and found him sitting in an armchair, holding an ice pack over his eye as the RA on duty and another student stood by. There wasn't a pizza box in sight. "Babe, are you okay?" I asked him, and I audibly gasped at the sight of dried blood under his nose when he turned. I was kneeling at his side in an instant. "What happened? Did you fall down the steps or something? Where's the pizza?"

"Yeah, *this* is from tripping down the stairs," he said, his voice dripping with a sarcasm I'm not used to hearing from him.

"Well *I* don't know what—"

A campus police officer showed up just then, shutting me up. I listened as Ethan filled him in on what had happened just a few minutes prior. "I thought it sounded kinda sus when the delivery guy said he was waiting outside of the side entrance instead of the main one," Ethan shook his head, cursing his own naivete. He went out to meet the driver, and some people—"definitely at least two, *maybe* three"—grabbed him, pulled a pillowcase over his head, laid some punches into him, then threw him to the ground before running off. Anthony, the other guy who was with us, told the officer he saw them take off as he was coming towards the building, and he hit the emergency button before going to help Ethan. *And there I was, doom-scrolling on Instagram.*

The officer, whose badge read Previn, listened while he scrawled down both Ethan's and Anthony's accounts of what happened. Neither of them could give a description of the assailants other than they were dressed in all black with their hoods up, and the camera the RA checked didn't show anything more than that either. "It sounds like you were targeted specifically," Officer Previn said to Ethan. "Can you think of any reason why someone would want to do this to you?"

"I mean, I'm running for RHA President," Ethan said slowly like he was inventing a reason. "I guess it's a little competitive, but I didn't think it was the kind of thing you get assaulted over." Officer Previn nodded, but he saw the way I was holding Ethan's hand in both of mine, and perhaps drew his own legitimate conclusions.

"I can't believe this," I said to Ethan in a low voice while Officer Previn asked the RA and the DA some questions. "I'm so sorry this happened to you."

"Sorry for what?" he scoffed as he flipped his ice pack over, giving me a glimpse of his bruised eye. "It's not your fault." He says that, but if I kissed him or held his hand or danced with him in front of the wrong person, then it might as well be my fault. My mind ran through all the homophobes I'd encountered at NHU, trying to think of who it could've been. Whoever had done it, I wanted to pull a Victor and make them hurt for what they did, though I know Ethan of all people would be appalled if I ever did something like that.

Officer Previn clicked his pen and flipped his notepad shut. "It's not a lot to go off of, but we'll do what we can to try to identify them," he said to Ethan. "Now since this isn't an emergency, the school won't notify your parents or guardians without your consent."

"No, that won't be necessary," Ethan said as politely as he could.

"Okay then. I'll walk you over to the Health Center. The rest of you are free to go."

"I'm going too," I said immediately. Yeah, no way this guy doesn't know we're gay for each other. I thanked Anthony before we left, glad that there are people who aren't afraid to step up or step in and do something to make sure someone's okay if they need help, like when Tanika came to my aid when Kade was seizing up. People saw us getting escorted by a campus police officer and probably thought we were delinquents. All that the student worker at the Health Center—who wasn't Devon, thank fucking god—did was give Ethan an ice pack and some ibuprofen, which was exactly what the RA did. Officer Previn even offered to walk us up to 341 Kessler, but a protective, pissed-off boyfriend was all the security Ethan needed.

Safe in his room, I wrapped the ice pack in a hand towel and held it up to Ethan's eye to give his arm a rest. He winced as he put another to his bare, bruised chest. "I feel so bad," I said like speaking too loud would cause him more pain. "I should've gone down with you."

"When have you ever gone down with me just to grab a pizza?" he said flatly.

"I haven't, but I will from now on," I said adamantly. "Does the RHA President get a bodyguard? I'll take the job if you get elected."

Instead of responding to that, he just closed his uncovered eye. "What am I gonna tell the others when they ask why I have a black eye?" he asked after a moment.

"I'd just tell them the truth," I offered as I rubbed his back.

"Yeah, I probably will." He sighed. "I just can't believe that something like that happened to me again."

My hand froze. "What do you mean, again?"

He took a breath. "One of my baseball teammates from back home figured out I was gay—I guess from seeing me checking out the other players—and let's just say that he *violently* told me that if he ever caught me ever even *looking* at him again, he'd fuck me up and tell everybody my secret."

My hand found my mouth. "No."

"I honestly thought he was gonna rape me," he said in a shaky voice. "I quit the team the next day—my school team, I mean. I joined a regional travel team and just made sure I didn't look at anybody for longer than a second."

I set down the ice pack so I could hug the beautiful soul that he is with tears in my eyes, eyes that teared up for him, for Ryder, for Denver, for Kade, for Will, for Victor's parents—for all the people who have to live at the mercy of an ignorant and hateful world, who were punished simply for being themselves. I know I've said it before, but cishet people who who say they don't get why Pride is a thing or how being openly queer can be an act of courage can sit the fuck down and shut the fuck up.

"And then after that happened," Ethan went on, "I started to think again that maybe being gay *is* a choice. Maybe if I just tried harder to like girls, then I'd fix myself. That's when I tried the whole fake-girlfriend thing." *Fix, like he could just rewire himself.* "And then once I couldn't even get off to girls in porn anymore, I figured I was so broken that not even god could fix me, or that I'd let myself go so far that he didn't *want* to fix me."

"I know the feeling," I empathized. "But no more trying to fix yourself. You're the only Ethan Lucas Eastwood to ever exist, and you're perfect the way you are."

He smiled a painful smile. "Do you know how much easier my life would've been if I'd been hearing that all along?" He kissed my cheek. "I love you so much."

I kissed his forehead. "I love you so much too. Nobody will hurt you again as long as I'm around." *That's* a promise I can make.

We cuddled on his bed in silence for the longest time, my fingers lightly stroking his chest. "I'm gonna tell my mom about me," Ethan finally said.

I propped myself up. "Really? Are you sure?"

He laughed through his nose. "Of course not. But I have to. It's so overdue. I can't keep living a lie anymore. I can't keep making myself small for the comfort of other people."

"When are you gonna do it? When you're home for Break?"

"Nah, before that," he shook his head. "I wanna give her some time to digest the fact that she has an abomination for a son before she has to live with me."

I hugged him. "It's not gonna be easy, but you'll be so happy you did it. And whatever happens, I'll be there for you. If you have to come live at my house, I'll make it happen."

"Thanks babe," he smiled, perhaps thinking what it would be like to finally live a life free from fear.

April 26

Dr. Davis reminded us that our Final essay for Black Lit is due by next Wednesday "at midnight"—so Tuesday-going-into-Wednesday midnight, or Wednesday-going-into-Thursday midnight? We have a lot of balls to call ourselves the greatest country on Earth when we still can't figure this shit out.

Ethan's sunglasses hid his black eye on the way to Patnick, and he even kept them on inside too until Kade said that he looked like an asshole. "I'm not really in the mood for any jokes about it," Ethan said dejectedly as he took them off, "so please don't."

Kade actually gasped. "I wouldn't joke about that," he said tenderly.

"That looks *bad*," Victor winced. "Did you get in a fight or something?"

"Can we wait until we're sitting down?" he asked with his head down, aware of at least one person staring. *Are the people who did it here right now, admiring their work?* He filled the other two in once we were back at our table with our food. "So I don't know if it was because I'm gay or running for President or both, but yeah," he concluded with his arms folded on the table.

Victor thought. "I wonder if it could've been the same guys who attacked Denver?"

"They got expelled, remember?" Kade said. "Besides, if there *was* a gang of asshole homophobes preying on us queers, I'm sure I'd make for a pretty easy target."

"Well, whoever it was, they had your phone number, right?"

"*Obviously.*"

"So it was either somebody you know, or...or somebody you know *betrayed* you!" Victor said like he was at a murder mystery dinner. He asked so many questions and voiced so many theories that I thought he was going to start putting together an evidence board.

"Give it a *rest*, dude," Kade finally said, catching Ethan's miserable eyes. I *hate* seeing him like that—it's almost like he's not himself. Between getting beat up, having to walk around with a black eye, the thought of coming out to his mom, and the RHA election—all on top of our impending Finals—I don't blame him for being out of character. It almost feels like we had a fight and haven't totally made up yet.

"So I was listening to WXNU at work, and a Ginger Root song came on," I said when I called him later on to try to put a smile on his cute face.

"I've never heard WXNU play Ginger Root before," Ethan said, though I could hear the *'okay, and?'* in his voice.

"And then out of everything that DJ Twinkle Toes—you know, Sam, from that party—could've said, you know what he said?"

"What'd he say?"

"He said there's a very talented band called Three Lesbians in a Wheelchair who actually played a few Ginger Root songs at Open Mic Night"—Ethan perked up at that—"and that anybody who wants to hear them play live again should be sure to catch them at the Summer Send-Off next weekend." *Oh yeah, I guess that's stressing him out too.* "You guys got called out on the radio! I've never heard a student band get called out on the radio before!"

It took him a moment to speak. "I, um…" He gulped. "We actually decided that we're *not* gonna play at the Summer Send-Off." My expression slid off my face so fucking hard I'm surprised it didn't put a hole in the floor. "We won't have the time to practice." He stared at my speechless face before cracking up. "I'm *kidding!* Of course we're still gonna play!" he laughed. *There's the Ethan I know.* "We've been picking and practicing songs. And Kade and Victor's friend Derrick is gonna come up and play with us too. I guess he can really shred on guitar."

As pumped as I am for their Summer Send-Off performance, thinking about my poor boyfriend kept me in a sad mood for most of the rest of the evening. I wanted to do something for him to lift his spirits—not just a cute gesture, but something that'll make him genuinely light up—but I kept coming up blank. I was sitting in an extracurricular lecture about how the Civil War is still ongoing when an idea hit me, something that I *know* he'll love. I got up and left so I could get started on it, stopping at the bookstore to buy a big sheet of poster paper that I unrolled on the floor of 222 Swafford. I stared down at it, trying to think of what to write.

"Are you taking an art class over at the elementary school?" Tylor joked when they came back from their evening Film class.

"Yeah. I need to pull my grade up, so I thought I'd make a collage for extra credit."

They stared down at the paper alongside me. "Forreal though, what is it?"

"Something for Ethan."

"But what *is* it?"

"A big piece of paper," I smirked.

"What are you *putting* on the big piece of paper?" they chuckled.

"If you'd shut up for five seconds and let me think," I laughed, "then maybe I could come up with something. And also can I borrow your rainbow Sharpies?"

Tylor groaned an exaggerated groan. "I *guess*. As long as you don't let them dry out."

"I *won't*, mom."

20 minutes later, I stood back to admire my work just as Ethan texted me that he was done with RHA. It's cheesy, but I know that he'll love it—and that's all that matters.

April 28

So you know how I said acid makes you feel like you're experiencing everything for the first time? I think it's the same thing with listening to music while high from weed—it's like you're really *hearing* it for the first time. And then you pat yourself on the back for having good taste, because go the fuck ahead.

For their last event of the year, Swafford, Axworthy, and the other four dorms on the street all pooled their money and resources together to hold one big Block Party. And despite Ethan not living in any of those halls, he worked a shorter shift so he could help them get set up for it. I grabbed some balloons from the bookstore after Macro let out—I quadruple-knotted them so as to not repeat my Valentine's Day snafu—and took them, along with the sign I'd made for Ethan, to the blocked-off street, where setup for the event was already underway. I found him talking to another dorm's e-board member with his back to me, and I held the sign open and waited for him to turn around. He lit up at the sight of me, but my sign caught him off-guard before he could get a word out.

'THIS MIGHT BE GAY
AND IT SEEMS KINDA CLICHÉ
I DON'T HAVE A BOUQUET
BUT CAN WE SOIRÉE?'

"Are you...asking me to be your date to the RHA banquet?" he finally asked.

"Uh huh," I nodded with a grin. "You said that the biggest thing you missed out on in school was a guy you like asking you to be his date to something, right? And didn't you say there were always balloons when you pictured it?" I jerked my wrist to make them bounce. I could've done it in one of our rooms, but he's had to always

242

watch it happen to other people, and I figured that it was time that other people got to see it happen to him.

He looked from me to the sign to the balloons and back without a word. *What if he'll be too busy helping out, and now I just look stupid?* But then he lit up like you wouldn't believe it, pushing the sign away to hug me. "Oh *babe!* This is the sweetest thing anyone's ever done for me!" Ethan pulled away to meet my eyes. "But this isn't really the kind of event you *ask* someone to like that. It's not like a formal or anything."

"I don't care," I kept on grinning. Over his shoulder, Other E-Board Member gaped at us like I'd just proposed to him.

Ethan took in the sign again, bubble letters and Sharpie sketches and all. "I hope you aren't expecting this to be fancy or anything," he said to my sorry excuse of a champagne glass. "It's just gonna be finger foods and stuff."

"That's okay," I smiled. I gave him a few more moments before asking, "So?"

"So what?"

"So is that a yes or a no?"

He pulled down a balloon to boop me on the head with it. "Of *course* it's a yes, you goofball." He planted another kiss on me. "I'm gonna go put these upstairs in the office for now," he said without explaining what office.

"Do you need help setting anything up?" I spontaneously offered.

"No, you don't have to," he said as he wrestled to untie the balloons from my wrist.

"It's not a problem. I don't have anything super important to do."

"I mean, if you *really* want to. I think there's still some stuff in the office that has to come down." He gave up and went to hunt down a pair of scissors. "You wanna come see the RHA office?"

I was surprised to learn that anybody can swipe themselves into Malik's front door, though I guess they have to be able to if they need to visit the RHA office or want to attend one of their meetings. The meeting room is nothing but rows of a dozen-or-so tables in a semicircle facing another, lone table at the front of it. The RHA office, on the other hand, is basically just a way more cluttered version of Kessler's House Council office. *I guess this RHA stuff isn't as big of a deal as I've been thinking it is,* I thought as I took in the shelves of old trophies, a random hulking safe sitting in the corner, and certificates and posters and notes that may or may not have been comments from the Comment Box taped to the wall. "Is that gonna be your drawer unit next year?" I asked as I nodded to the one with Ciara's name spelled out in alphabet magnets on it.

Ethan didn't debate me on it, surprisingly. "Yeah, it will," he smiled.

His good mood unfortunately didn't last though, thanks to event prep stuff not going as smoothly as he would've liked. "The DJ better get here soon," a stressed-out Ethan muttered as he checked the time, "or we won't have any music when it starts."

"So then there won't be any music when it starts," I said. "It'll be okay." I think he took my calmness as indifference, which didn't do anything to help. He was still tense even after the DJ—DJ Twinkle Toes if you can believe it—showed up and started to set up.

"Don't tell me this is all the whipped cream we have," Ethan said as he dug around in a cooler so big that you could've stored a corpse in it.

"Elena said they put everything they got in there," Jamal, Gladby Hall's president, answered.

"Mother *fuck*," Ethan swore. "This isn't gonna be enough."

One of the posters I saw in the RHA office about going out of your way to make someone's day flashed across my mind. "I can run to the store real quick," I volunteered.

"No, don't," Ethan protested in a gentler tone once he saw what he'd driven me to do. "We can work with this."

I put a hand on his shoulder. "It's okay, really."

But making sure they had enough whipped cream for whatever the hell they needed whipped cream for wasn't the only reason I drove to the store—I swung by the McDonald's drive-thru on the way back to get something that I hoped would put a smile on Ethan's face. I made a beeline for him without even setting down the bags of cans of whipped cream, and held out my surprise for him with a goofy grin. "What's this?" he asked like he'd never seen one before.

"A milkshake," I said.

"For what?"

"For you." I nudged it towards him. "Because you're stressed out and you seem like you could use a milkshake."

He looked at it for another moment and pulled me into a hug. "You went all the way across town to get me a milkshake?"

"And to get more whipped cream."

"That you'll be reimbursed for, by the way," he said before he sucked up some Oreo pieces. "*Mmm.* Yeah, I needed this," he smiled. He pecked me on the cheek. "Thanks babe."

I grabbed him by the shoulders and steered him towards a bench. "Go take a break. I can help with this." He went without a fight, watching me with his elbows on his knees as he slurped his shake.

"You were right," he told me after he threw the empty cup away. "That did the trick."

Once DJ Twinkle Toes got the music pumping and once people started showing up, Ethan finally relaxed and started to enjoy himself. The halls and other organizations taking part in the event all had their own tables of different games and food and crafts set up along the road.

"Prepare your anus," a voice said in my ear. I turned to see Kade holding a can of whipped cream and Victor juggling cornhole bean bags behind him.

"Eat my ass like a sundae, *dad*," I said maybe a little too loud. "And I didn't know you could juggle!"

"There are a lot of things you don't know about me," Victor said mysteriously. "Now who's tryna violate these cornhole boards?"

We played cornhole, played Plinko, ate walking tacos, made tie-dyed t-shirts, pied RAs with plates of whipped cream—"*I'd totally cream pie the guy second from the left*," Kade whispered—and swung at piñatas. "My therapist would say it's a bad idea to hand me a weapon," this one girl from my building who I've never heard speak before said as she choked up on the baseball bat, "but what he doesn't know won't hurt him." I traded an *oh-shit* look with the donkey.

"Is Westley even here?" I asked Ethan once I realized that I hadn't seen him.

"He's at the Block Party over at *The Commons*," Swafford's VP Aimee rolled her eyes from the nearby popcorn wagon she was working. *Is the last Thursday in April Block Party Day or what?*

"He's not even at his own building's last event?" I scowled.

"What a fucking *chode*," Victor said with a tongue blue from a snow cone.

DJ Twinkle Toe's/Sam's music was so on-point that I ended up Shazamming like half of the songs. "I'm not taking any requests," he said as I approached the table. I guess he didn't remember me from the party.

"Nothing I could request would slap as hard as this stuff," I admitted defeat. "What genre is this even?"

"It's mostly indie pop—it's my favorite sunny weather music." I think it might be *my* favorite sunny weather music too now.

"I'm *absolutely* looking this stuff up later," I said as I peeped his screen.

Sam actually gave a surprise pitch for Ethan's campaign when he took a pause from the music to ask if everybody was having a good time. "And if you haven't already done so, vote Ethan Eastwood for RHA President! And be sure to catch his band, Three Lesbians in a Wheelchair, at the Summer Send-Off next weekend!"

"Wow, *someone* has friends in high places," Victor said.

"More like high friends in places," Kade chuckled.

"It's not *my* band though," was all Ethan muttered.

"Have you gotten the chance to practice for that yet?" I asked them. "The Summer Send-Off?"

"Individually, yes," Kade answered. "Together, not so much. We're gonna try to get on that this weekend."

"What about Derrick?"

"He picks things up pretty quickly," Victor said. "We'll run through it all together when he comes up next Friday, and probably the day of too."

"We still haven't decided on which two songs we wanna play, so we're just gonna practice a handful and see which ones fit the vibe when the time comes."

I couldn't not grin. "Have I mentioned that I can't fucking wait for it?"

We hit up ladder ball, ring toss, giant Connect Four. Ethan and I shared cotton candy while we watched the Color Guard's performance. I'm not *saying* that it was Kade and Victor who did it, but they were nowhere to be seen when a water balloon fell from the sky and landed right in the middle of it.

"It wasn't us!" Victor insisted when I asked him about it. "Kade went back to our room!"

"Why, did he have to take a shit?" I laughed.

He shook his head. "He asked Greyson earlier if he could spend the night there, but Greyson told him that he had to go home for a family emergency. But then he saw on Greyson's Snap story that he has another guy over at his place."

I sucked my teeth. "*Oof.* What a fucking *dick.*"

"I know, right?" Victor breathed. "So yeah, he went back to the room for some Kade-time."

As bad as I felt for Kade, I didn't want to let my sad and angry thoughts keep me from enjoying the rest of the Block Party. It was supposed to be over at 8, but there were still a lot of people sticking around, even after Sam had torn down. I wasn't ready to call it a night yet, and neither was Victor.

"I kinda wanna go check out the Block Party at The Commons," he said like the idea would upset me.

I considered it. "Yeah, I actually wouldn't be against that," I nodded.

"I'm having fun just playing this," Ethan said from his game of Spikeball when I asked him about it. "And then I was gonna help clean up."

I felt my shoulders slump. "Oh, okay."

"You guys can still go without me," he chuckled.

"You're sure? I don't wanna leave you here."

"You're not *leaving* me here," he insisted with a smile. "Go on, go have fun with Victor."

I pecked him on the lips. "Thanks, I will."

There were so many other people trickling into The Commons that I almost forgot it was a weekday. "You know, this is the first time just the two of us have ever gone out anywhere," Victor said.

"Yeah," I said after thinking for a moment, "I guess it is. But does it really count as going out though if we won't be drinking?"

"Who said anything about not drinking?" he laughed. I've never been a Thirsty Thursday kind of person, but I guess there's a first for everything.

The police presence there told me that The Commons' Block Party was a *party*. You'd have thought it was the last party of the year. The wide-open yard between the buildings was a sea of revelers, with a cup or can or bottle in every hand. One of the more popular DJs blasted your typical, god-awful party music across the entire place at a deafening volume. *I guess if you live here and are trying to study then you're just fucked.* Between that, the alcohol, and the food trucks, it made the House Council Block Party look like some dopey school carnival on the last day of 3rd grade before Summer vacation.

"I wonder if Nikole's here with What's-Her-Friend?" Victor asked as his eyes followed either an order of nachos or the girl carrying them.

"Now *why* would you care if Nikole's here?" I smirked.

> **Wattup girlfriend**
> **You at the commons?**
> **Holla at ya boy**

I might perhaps be at the commons
I might also perhaps be slightly drunk

Nikole met us at the door to Hayley's building—"*Hayley*, that's right"—and gave us drunk hugs before she led us up to her apartment. "It's been a hot second since we've hung out," she said as we rounded a flight of stairs. "And we literally live across the hall from each other."

"We've been going over this friend of ours' place like every weekend," I explained.

"He also moved into Ethan's room, so there's that," Victor razzed me.

The only other people at Hayley's place were another girl named Kayla and a guy named Damien. She introduced them to Victor and I, and we all did a shot together before heading down to the complex-wide party with a Dave & Buster's flask filled to the *brim* with strawberry rum, some hard seltzers, the rest of the bottle of strawberry rum, and a can of Sprite. Hayley and Kayla and Damien stuck with us for about two minutes before going off on their own. Nikole and Victor and I roved through the crowd, stumbling upon a game of volleyball, a dead pig being roasted over a fire, and the apartment's pool, which was almost as dense with people as the cement around it. We watched girls in bikinis splash water at each other from the shoulders of guys with toned chests who were probably itching to fuck them. *What do they think this is, July? That water's gotta be* freezing.

"Assuming that at least half of the people in the pool have already broken the seal," Nikole asked us, "what would you guess the piss-to-water ratio is?"

"Come on, you know I'm not good at math," I whined. And then I remembered how hard Caleb and I laughed when I realized he'd said that 42 is an imaginary number, and I started cracking up about it all over again.

"Jesus, are you *that* drunk already?" Nikole asked in astonishment. "Good god." She and Victor caught each other's glance and laughed.

"No!" I said. "I only had"—I pinched an inch of air beside the top of the can—"this much!"

"Wow, you're quite the cheap drunk, huh?"

Like Sam had done, the DJ at The Commons also gave an unexpected pitch for the RHA election. "And for all you freshmen here, don't forget to vote for Westley Westwood for RHA President!"

The three of us traded looks. "Westley *Westwood?*" Victor said. "Are you *kidding* me?"

"It's like the battle of the cardinal directions," Nikole said as she poured more rum into her Sprite.

We hit up one of the food trucks, because when has anyone who's drunk not wanted to eat? I scarfed down my walking taco while Victor took concerningly small bites of his veggie hot dog with an empty stare. "You okay fam?" I waved my hand in front of his face.

"Yeah," he shook himself from his thoughts. "I just got this urge to go to a state fair all of a sudden," he said deadpan, which made Nikole start uncontrollably giggling.

"Oh, who's the cheap drunk now?" I accused her.

"Is there even any Sprite *left* in there?" Victor asked her. "If you just keep adding rum to it and drinking it, won't it eventually just be all rum?"

"*Huh.*" She held out the can to look at it. "I guess that would explain why it doesn't taste like Sprite anymore."

We ended up back near Hayley's building, where we saw a girl who was bent over and retching, which was kind of funny until we realized it was Kayla. Damien held her hair back in case she did end up puking. And only Chadwick Patterson, *only* Chadwick Patterson, would be standing there beside them, too absorbed in telling them a story to even take a puff of the cigar he had.

"And I told him, 'dude, *don't* cut against the grain!'" he said, seemingly sober and not caring that nobody was listening to him. "But the idiot didn't wanna listen, so of course he split his wood, just like I said." He shook his head. "You'd think it's common sense, but I guess not." Even after Kayla finally *did* hurl, he just took a step back and kept on talking. He only wandered off after Damien and Hayley carried her off, which was our cue to disappear too.

"I didn't know somebody could be so passionate about whittling," I muttered.

"I'm sure you could find someone," Nikole said absentmindedly with a look over at Hayley's building. "I should probably go make sure she's okay."

"I can come make sure she's okay too," Victor offered. I snorted and tried to pull it off as a cough.

"Nah, I think we'll be good," Nikole declined.

"Will you require an escort back to your building later?" he went on, making even me cringe.

"Nah, I'll probably just crash at Hayley's," she said with a polite smile. "Have a good night guys."

I managed to wait until we were outside the perimeter of the apartment complex before giving Victor shit. "You can't take a hint, can you?"

"We were so close to kissing though!" he groaned.

"*When?* Where the hell was I?"

"In line for the porta potty."

"Oh," I nodded.

"Yeah," he went on, "we were watching the DJ stage, and the lights and everything made me feel like I was at a concert. And then I imagined that Nikole and I were at our favorite concert together. And then I said something and we both laughed and it really felt like we were about to kiss. It would've been so romantic." He sighed, though he seemed more happy from getting so close to his goal than he was crestfallen from missing it. "I wanted to try again. That's why I offered to help take Kayla back upstairs."

"Yeah, we could tell," I rolled my eyes. "We can ask her if she wants to come out to 370 Rock tomorrow and you can try again?" I shrugged. "But maybe try not to act so thirsty this time?"

"I wasn't *acting—*"

"Hold that thought," I said as I pulled my ringing phone out of my pocket. "Kade's calling me. Hopefully he's drunk."

"I *hope* he's not."

I answered and put it on speaker. "Hey slutmuffin."

"Trevor?"

"Yeah?" I chuckled. "Who else would it be, you chode?"

"I don't know," Kade said without making a chode joke. "Where are you? Is Ethan or Victor with you?"

I caught Victor's eye. "No, it's just me," I said, wondering if Kade would say anything that he otherwise wouldn't if he thought I was alone. "I was at the Block Party at The Commons and now I'm on my way back. I *am* a little sloshed though, so...why, what's up?"

"Sounds like a fun time," he said like it wasn't. "I just took a walk around campus to get some fresh air and to think about things." He paused. "I don't know if

Victor told you, but Greyson and I aren't seeing each other anymore. Not that we were ever really *together*, but..."

"I know what you mean," I said, only then remembering what had happened. "And yeah, he did mention that. I'm sorry about that, fam. You must've really liked him. You were over his place a lot."

"Yeah," he breathed. "I don't ever get romantically involved with people for more than one night unless I really think we could be a thing. But *I'm* always the one who gets dumped, the one who gets ghosted, the one who's always being told 'I don't think things are gonna work out,' or 'it's not you.' It's *always* me—why else can't I ever have a lasting relationship? Once people realize how fucked-up I am, they're *gone*."

Instead of trying to tell him that he's not, I tried the opposite. "I think falling in love is just finding somebody as fucked-up as you. Not *you*, but in general."

"*You're* not fucked-up. Ethan's not fucked-up."

"Everybody has their own issues," was all I said.

"Maybe." And then after a moment, "Did you ever think about how ridiculous it all is?"

"What, somebody telling you how special you are to them when they actually care way less about you than you thought they did?"

"That, but also just *everything*. Existence. Everything you know is all just inside your head. The love you feel for another person, the calmness you feel when a song hits just right, all of your dreams and thoughts—every emotion you've ever felt so strongly that it just *consumes* you is nothing but a chemical reaction in your brain interpreting externals."

I saw Victor nodding out of the corner of my eye. "Yeah, I've thought about it before."

"And your brain, the thing that makes each of us *us*, is just a freak result of improbable evolution," Kade went on. "We're such miraculous accidents, and yet we treat each other like shit, like other people don't matter."

"Isn't it bullshit?" I nodded.

"But *do* we really matter though? Like, imagine how little space you occupy on the planet, and then how little space Earth occupies in the entire *universe*. And time?" He laughed out loud. "Try to imagine how much time has existed before you were born, and then how much time will exist after you die. In the scope of all things, we truly do *not* matter. We could all cease to exist and nothing would even notice. We're just a blip in time and space. I've almost gotten panic attacks thinking about it."

"Yeah, I don't blame you," I said with two fingers on my temple. "Also, *how* high are you right now?"

"Oh, I don't know. However high up the water tower is."

Victor and I traded looks before turning to the water tower at the top of its hill. I furrowed my brow. "What do you—?"

"*Oh my god,*" Victor gasped, the alarm in his voice and his starkly ashen face saying it all. "*Oh my god. We need to get there right now,*" he said, already on the move.

"Is somebody with you?" Kade asked sternly.

"No. No, some people were just walking by."

"Oh, okay."

Victor turned around to look me dead in the eyes. "*Please keep talking to him.*" I nodded. Not being an ear for Ryder contributed to him doing what he did, and I'll be damned if I ever make the same mistake again.

"So wait, did you climb the water tower?" I asked Kade, trying to sound more curious than some of the most scared I've ever been in my life.

"Yep."

"I don't believe you."

"I did! Here—I turned my flashlight on. Can you see it? I'm aiming it towards The Commons." Sure enough, a small, bright light appeared against the tower's dark silhouette. It could've been just another star.

"*Oh fuck. Fuck, fuck,*" Victor swore ahead of me. "*Please god, not again.*"

"Yeah, I can see it. Is there a ladder or something you can climb?"

"Uh huh."

"You're way braver than I am," I tried to say like I wasn't jogging and on the verge of panicking. "I'd never be able to make it up there. I'm *terrified* of heights."

"Oh, you wouldn't like this then. I wish you could see this view though. I wish I would've come up here sooner. You can see all of campus, and town. And the trees just go on and on. And the *stars.*"

"It's the highest point in town, right? Isn't it higher than the radio tower?"

"No, I think the radio tower's a little higher." I started thinking about if being at the top of the radio tower would microwave your brain when Kade asked, "Did you know that I had a twin when I was born?"

"*What?* No?"

"Yeah. He only lived for a few days though."

"*Wow,*" I blinked. "That's...unfortunate."

"Yeah," he said bitterly. "I always think about why it happened to *him* though. It could've just as easily been me instead. He would've gone on to have a life, and I would've just been another neonatal death statistic. But *why* though? Why am *I* the one who's still here?" If it was anything to joke about, I would've said something about how the universe must've figured that two Kade Oakleys would've been too much for it to handle.

"Because...existence is cruel?" I offered. "And we should count ourselves as lucky to have made it far enough to be able to realize it?"

"But *should* I pity my brother for never getting to experience the joys of life? Or should I envy him for never having to experience the pains of it? Sometimes I wish it *was* me instead of him. Do you know how much pain I would've been spared?"

"I mean...yeah, there's a lot of pain in the world. But don't the good things make it all worth putting up for?"

"That's the grand question, isn't it?"

Victor and I reached the bottom of the hill, but the water tower was still a ways up. "I always wondered what it would've been like to have a brother to grow up with," Kade went on. "Maybe if I had someone to talk to and someone to listen to, then maybe I wouldn't have ended up as fucked-up as I am."

"Isn't everybody fucked-up in their own way though? I mean, I've been depressed, I'm an insomniac, I have ADHD, I have anxiety. I know what it's like."

"Yeah, so you see what I'm saying."

"But you have Victor though! Didn't you say he's your soulmate instead of just your brother?" And then a random-ass thought hit me. "Have you ever thought that maybe he's the reincarnation of your biological brother?" I turned to Victor to catch his look. *Dude*, he mouthed. I just shrugged.

"Woah," Kade said. "That *would* be crazy. I guess it's not *impossible*, though."

"Of course it's not! Maybe that's why you two click so well, because you were always meant to be in each other's lives!"

He was silent for a few seconds. "I never thought of that."

And then before I could think about it, I said, "Did you know I used to have a brother too?"

"*Really?*" I could hear the surprise in Kade's voice. "Wait—*used* to?"

"Yeah." My eyes squeezed themselves shut. "He killed himself."

"Oh my god," he gasped. "*Shit* Trev. I'm—I'm so sorry to hear that."

"His birthday would've been next weekend," I went on. "He felt lost in the world too. He listened to so many people tell him in different ways that the world would be a better place without him in it until one day he finally came to believe it."

"*Trev,*" was all that Kade could say. "*Fuck...*"

"Trust me, however much you're hurting is *nothing* compared to how much the people in your life would be hurting if you took yourself out of their lives. You can never understand how much of their lives they let you take up. The world's been cruel to me too, but we've both pushed through. And look how far we've come. Your brother would be proud of you. Your brother *is* proud of you."

"What's there to be proud of? I'm just—" He stopped speaking. "Wait, is that you coming towards the water tower?"

"Yep!"

"Who's with you?"

"It's your brother!" Victor forcefully said into my phone.

"You said Victor wasn't with you!" Kade shouted. "Was he listening the whole time?" I kept my eyes on the faint glow of Kade's phone however-many stories up above us. The only phones that should be up that high are the ones belonging to water tower workers and Straight guys doing Straight-guy shit.

"Yeah, and it's nothing I don't already know!" Victor said almost angrily.

"But I thought you were at The Commons? Why are you here?"

"To make sure you're okay!"

"Well then you wasted your time! I've never been okay and I'll never be okay! You can't help me! Nobody can help me!"

"No! Don't say that! You don't believe that and I know it!"

"I do too believe that!" Kade said like he was annoyed with us. "I'm broken beyond repair and nobody can save me."

"Don't say that you're—"

"You think I don't know myself?" Kade yelled.

I almost dropped to my knees, petrified because I truly did not know how the situation would end, and because how it would end would be partially up to me. "I know what it's like to feel broken, to feel like nobody can fix you," I said like I was begging him to believe me while I fought to hold myself together. "And you're right, nobody can fix you. Because you're *not* broken."

"You're not broken, Kade," Victor reaffirmed.

"The bands that my brother loved always sang about how it's okay not to be okay," I said before Kade could get a word in. "I know what it feels like to be crushed under the weight of all the bad thoughts, to wanna give up just so they'll stop. But they *do* stop. You just have to be strong. And I know how cliché it sounds and I know you're tired of hearing it from your parents and your therapist and other people who don't know what it feels like, but *I* know what it feels like."

"Maybe they stop for *you*, but not for *me*," Kade scoffed. "Or at least the threat of them doesn't. They come whenever they want, and when they do..." He didn't need to explain what it feels like to succumb to the mercilessness of your own mind when it's out to get you. "And when I *do* make it through a day, thinking that it couldn't get any worse than that, another day comes along and proves me wrong. And I'm so *tired* of fighting it. I just want it to *stop*. What kind of existence is it to be more afraid of life than to be excited by it? To be afraid of what you might do to yourself?"

I gave myself chills when I remembered what he said to me during one of our first deep cross-campus talks when I asked him if he'd ever thought about killing himself. *'I almost have to make a conscious effort to stop myself from doing it.'*

"It's like I'm living with a bomb strapped to my chest," Kade went on. "Do you know what it's like to wake up every day and not know if you'll be able to bear it? Can you imagine waking up every day and knowing that it can be the scariest day of your life?"

"No, I can't," Victor answered him. "But you know what the scariest day of *my* life was? The day I found you in the garage. I was so fucking *terrified* that I'd have to face the world without you, that I'd have to face a world without you in it." He was trying so hard to keep it together that he was shaking. *I guess that's what he meant by 'again.'* "I *knew* what I was signing up for by befriending you and I've *never* regretted it. I'm *more* than willing to put up with it if it means getting to have you in my life." It wasn't a declaration—it was a plea. "I'll put up with it all. I'll help you through it all even if it kills me, because that's how worth it you are to me." *And if that's not love, then I don't know what is.*

"Why would you want a mentally unstable—"

"*Stop.* Just *stop,*" Victor cut him off. "I know you inside and out, Kade. I've seen you at your lowest. I've talked you through whatever was on your mind. I've listened to you and I've let you cry on me. I've held you whenever you just needed someone to hold you and tell you everything's gonna be okay. And not *once* did any of it *ever* make me wanna stop being your friend, make me wanna stop being your *brother!*" he yelled through watery eyes. "I love you, and nothing about you can ever change that. I don't care how broken you think you are—you're worth all of your brokenness. You're so fucking worth it."

Kade's voice was weak when he finally spoke. "Do you really mean that?"

Victor took off his glasses to wipe his eyes. "If you were broken to pieces, I'd still love every last piece of you," he said to my phone. "I'd take a bullet for those pieces. *That's* how fucking worth it you are."

The agonizing silence drew on and on and on and on. "Guys," Kade finally breathed like he'd been holding his breath. "I'm so sorry guys. I'm not doing this."

"Not doing *what?*" Victor asked urgently. "What aren't you going t— NOOOOOAAAGGHH!" He split apart the night with a scream that would've curdled my blood if the light from Kade's phone plunging from the top of the tower hadn't already curdled it.

You always hear about your life flashing before your eyes, but you never hear about other people's lives flashing before your eyes. All the big moments of our friendship played like a montage, but I could've had those experiences with anybody who I chose to let into my life. It was his quirks and idiosyncrasies that hooked my gut—the way he caught my eye with a smirk that first day in History class, how he's always smiling like he has a joke on his lips or knows something that you don't, the easy look of focus in his eyes when he spins pottery or strums his bass, how he slaps his knee when he laughs, how he laughs until he cries or has to hold onto you for support or rolls around on the ground, the seriousness with which he plays a board game or brews tea, his absolute lack of a filter, how he closes his eyes in utter contentment when a song hits just right, how he plays with his food, how he always has to slide a card off the table to pick it up because his fingernails are so bitten-down, how all the things I started saying just to make fun of him have become a standard part of my vocabulary—all the things I would've never gotten to experience if I'd befriended anyone else in his place, all the things I suddenly couldn't imagine not having in my life anymore.

His phone hit the ground.

"It was just my phone!" Kade yelled down to us. *It was just his phone. He's okay. It was just his phone. It's gonna be okay.* I don't know when I'd dug my fingers into Victor's shoulders. The only sounds from the two of us were our own sniffles. "Okay," Kade called down after what could've been a week. "I—I'm gonna come down now."

In what was easily the most suspenseful moment of my life, I watched the shadow that was Kade slowly descend through the cage surrounding the ladder. Neither Victor nor I cared that I was hugging his neck from behind, shaking with relief.

Kade dropped the last several feet to the base of the tower, where he lowered himself to the ground with the grace of someone who'd just reentered Earth's atmosphere. We let him have his space as he hugged his knees. He swallowed before finding his quivering voice. "I'm s—I'm *sorry* you had to—" He looked from Victor to me and back, like he'd only just then realized what he'd done, before he started full-on *wailing* into his palms. *"I don't know what the fuck's wrong with me!"* Victor tackled him into a hug, and I watched the two brothers furiously cry into each other as I let out my own tears I'd been holding in.

"The only thing *wrong* with you," Victor choked out, sounding angry and petrified and relieved all at the same time, "is—why would you—you—what were you—*why?*"

"I know, I'm *sorry!* I'm so *fucking* sorry!"

"Do you know how fucking scared I was? Don't ever do that again!"

"I don't *want* to! I just wanna be *normal!*"

"You *are* normal! *Nobody's* normal! There's no such thing as being normal!"

"Pick one already!"

They cried with their foreheads pressed together and into each other's shoulders. They couldn't look into each other's faces for longer than two seconds without burying themselves back into each other.

"Nobody's normal," I sniffled as I knelt beside them, sitting back on my feet. "You know every flaw about yourself, so of course you're gonna think you're the only person that has anything wrong with them. But *everybody's* fucked-up, and

255

everybody tries to hide it," I said as I tried to keep my voice steady. "You wanna talk about not feeling normal? That's like the story of my life."

"Maybe. But you don't go trying to jump off a water tower whenever somebody rejects you." Kade stared at the ground between his shoes with horrified eyes. "We weren't even seeing each other for three weeks, and I go and do this? Isn't that so stupid? Am I always gonna be this stupid?"

"No, but there are more ways to hurt yourself than just physically. I used to be unkind to my mind, and it was unkind right back to me. And then after feeling rejected and like you don't belong for so long, not feeling *anything* starts to sound pretty appealing."

Instead of responding to that, Kade slowly said, "You said your brother felt like he didn't belong either. What did you mean? It's okay though if you don't wanna... talk about it."

I closed my eyes and sighed. "The short version is he was trans and people weren't okay with it and he hanged himself."

"Jesus. I'm so sorry," Kade turned away from me. "I feel so fucking *selfish.* I didn't think that that could've been a trigger for you. And I couldn't imagine what that was like—for you, or for him." *No, I'm not the one you should feel sorry for. Besides, you wouldn't feel sorry for me if you knew the things I'd said about him, sometimes to him, just to look cool in front of the people who I thought were my friends and everybody else who chose fear over love.* Kade looked up at Victor. "You won't tell Mom or Dad, will you? Please don't tell them."

Victor laughed out loud, but not in a good way. "I *should.* But I won't. I *really* should though. But I'm not going to." I think he was trying to decide for himself as much as he was trying to make a point to Kade. "We're brothers. We need to be there for each other, and I need you way more than you think."

Kade pulled at some grass before flinging himself onto Victor without warning. "I don't know what I'm gonna do without you next year," he said quietly.

"It's not like I'm going to a different *school!* Just because we won't be sleeping in the same room doesn't mean you won't have people to take care of you. Trevor and Ethan will be there for you. And you'll have Logan too!"

"Pfft. Logan will switch rooms after a few weeks of living with me once he sees what I'm *really* like."

"Oh *please,*" I scoffed. "If Logan can still be friends with *me* after all these years, I think he'll be able to put up with you." And then we all started to laugh. We laughed like we'd forgotten what it felt like to laugh.

"But forreal though," Kade said, "I feel like I'm such a burden to everyone. Like, I feel like I should be apologizing to everyone for having to put up with me and all my shit."

"The Kade Oakley I know would never apologize for who he is," I snapped.

Victor nodded before turning to Kade with a stern look. *"Kade,"* he said like Kade was a child standing next to a broken vase, "you *have* been taking your medicine, haven't you?"

Kade rubbed circles in the grass with his hands. I could feel his face flush from where I sat. "I *might've* been skipping them."

"Kade! Come on!"

"I know! I'm sorry! I—things seemed like they were going so *well*. Not just with Greyson, but in general. And I guess I thought I could get by without them for a day or two. Or three."

Victor clasped Kade's hand with both of his own. "Please, *please* promise me you won't try going without them again."

Kade looked more ashamed than I've ever seen him. "I promise." He sighed. "I just hate being so dependent on them all the time though. Is this what the rest of my life is gonna be like? That I won't ever be okay without them?"

"Maybe it will be," I answered. "Life might have you backed into a corner every day."

Kade gulped.

"But you have people who care about you. You don't need to face it alone. *None* of us can face life alone."

"Yeah," Victor nodded. "Do you think I'd be able to do any of this"—he waved in the direction of campus—"without you guys around?"

Kade gave Victor a look. "What do *you* have to worry about? You're so much stronger than I am."

"Are you *shitting* me right now?" Victor chuckled. "Do you think there's nothing that keeps *me* up at night too? Do you know how many times my brain tries to tell me that I'm a failure and that I'll never be good enough?"

Kade's eyebrows shot up like he was seeing his brother for the first time. "Do you really feel that way about yourself?"

"*Hell* yeah. But you know what motivates me to ignore it all and push through it? *You*. You're the toughest person I know."

"Really?"

"Kade, only the toughest people can go through what you go through every day and still come out smiling and cracking jokes."

My hand rested on Kade's back. "We're in each other's lives for a reason, and I don't think that being too afraid to be open with each other is one of them. It's something I need to get better at too. I don't care if I have to make time for you every night—I'll do it if it means being there for you."

"Oh my *god*, you sound like my therapist," he chuckled. He hugged me with a sniffle. "Okay. I'll start trying, if I need to." He laughed at himself. "Who am I kidding—of *course* I'll need to. But you'll be sorry you offered though," he smiled before abruptly pulling us into a hug. "Forreal though, thank you," he said in a voice above a whisper. We all hugged for a few more moments before he let go to look around in the dark. "On another note, do either of you know where my phone went?"

We scanned the ground with our own flashlights. "Here it is!" Victor said. "Oof, big yikes though."

"What? Is the screen cracked?"

"You could say that." He handed Kade his phone, shattered screen and all.

"Big yikes is right." Kade turned it over in his hand. "Can I borrow your car tomorrow to go get a new one?"

"No," Victor shook his head. "I'll drive you."

"I can go by myself. I'm not gonna drive off a bridge or anything."

"I don't think that you would. But I'm still gonna drive you."

"I don't want you to go out of your way for me any more than you already have."

"I don't care."

"What about your classes?"

"My classes can miss me for a day."

"But why—"

"Kade," Victor shut him up, "when someone you care about scares you like that, you realize just how much of a miracle every second you get to spend with them is." And isn't that the truth? It sucks that we never realize it sooner.

The two of them hugged for the thousandth time that night. "I love you Vic. I don't say it enough, but I fucking love you."

"And I love you too Kade, no matter what you think of yourself."

"Can we sleep in the same bed tonight?"

Victor hesitated. "I mean, if you want to," he chuckled.

The three of us, closer and more sober than we've ever been, trudged back towards campus and to our dorms, where my two best friends may or may not have platonically shared a bed. I wanted to spend the night in their room too, to sleep on their floor for no reason other than to stay close to them, to cradle Kade's sleeping head in my lap with a love for him so unshakable that they'd have to pull me away from him. No, you never realize how much of other people's lives they let you take up, but you also never realize how much you let them take up in yours either.

I didn't tell Ethan about any of that though when he asked me how the rest of my night went when I saw him at lunch. "We met up with Nikole at her friend's place and just hung with her for a while before heading back," was all I said. The story we came up with as to why the other two needed to go get Kade a new phone was that he was so upset over the whole Greyson thing that he yeeted it and broke the screen, which Ethan didn't question.

"Yeah, I'd be throwing my phone too and more if that ever happened to me," he said from behind crossed arms.

April 29

'April 25—Campus police responded to a call for an assault outside of Kessler Hall. The case is currently under investigation.' I'm still fucking seething over it.

Instead of coming along with us when Victor and I went for our tattoo appointments, Ethan hung back to try to get some work done for his Ethics in Media final project. Kade tagged along with us though, which made me feel good. Even though he seems okay now, I'd be low-key worried about him if we'd left him alone. Is that bad or assuming of me? I didn't know if I was supposed to pretend like last night hadn't happened, but thankfully he was busy downloading and logging into all his apps on his new phone on the walk over to New Halle Ink.

We checked in for our appointments, and I killed some time in one of the poetry books in the waiting area while Kade showed Victor how much faster and smoother his phone is than Victor's. Lauren, my artist who has an effervescent personality, called me back first. I studied the drawings pinned to the wall—pocket watches, wolf's heads, crystals, hearts and daggers, outlines of other things—while she shaved and cleaned my wrist. *I can see Kade being a tattoo artist.* The disinfectant was cool against my skin, and the smell reminded me of formaldehyde and how I was the only kid in Biology class who couldn't bring themselves to slice open a dead animal.

I started having second thoughts about the whole thing while Lauren filled a thimble-sized cup with ink and adjusted her gun's settings—you know, the permanency and all. But you know where I'd be if I let all my second thoughts scare me away? Living back home, going to community college, and existing instead of living. Victor and Kade would be friends with some other guy, and Ethan would be with somebody who's more confident. But as I looked down at the purple stencil overlaying my scars—almost like a word on a piece of lined paper—I knew that it was what I wanted.

Victor's description of getting a tattoo feeling like a razor on your skin wasn't entirely inaccurate. I winced when the furious needle started piercing my skin. "Nutritious and delicious," Lauren said cheerfully. I got used to the feeling as she worked, but I still couldn't bring myself to watch. Not that tattooing a single word takes very much time, but Lauren's congeniality made the session fly by, especially once we started talking about *Stardew Valley*, which Ethan and I still have yet to play.

"It sounds kinda like *Minecraft*, and I'm low-key afraid I won't be able to stop playing it," I confessed.

"Oh, you totally won't," she smiled.

Victor's conversation with his artist, Mik, turned passionate once they started talking about the backwardness of conservatism and the harm that religion can cause. Kade even got up to join in from their cubicle's doorway. "Like, I don't give a *fuck* if it makes sense to you or not," I heard Mik staunchly say. "It's *human rights.* There's fucking *nothing* to debate."

"Yes!" Victor vehemently agreed. "Thank you! Exactly!"

Lauren was done before I knew it, dabbing up what few droplets of blood there were. I stood before a mirror to examine the newest part of me from every angle. "I love it," I grinned.

After paying for the tattoo and some aftercare ointment, I took my plastic-wrapped wrist to the couch where Kade sat, sketching in a book he'd brought along to pass the time. "Was it as bad as you thought it'd be?" he asked me.

"Is *anything* ever as bad as I think it's gonna be?" I laughed as I glanced at his drawing—a cartoon-style volcano with eyes, vomiting lava with all kinds of other shit going on around it. It looked like something I'd see on Redbubble. "Have *you* ever thought about being a tattoo artist?"

He lifted his pencil from the paper. "You know, yeah, actually. I've never tattooed before, but I can draw, and I like doing it." He shrugged. "I dunno. Maybe someday."

"I mean, you already pierce people," I chuckled, making him snicker. "You seem like you're doing better today," I said casually and cautiously. "Has today been a good day for you so far?"

"*Any* day is a good day after a night like last night," he said. "But yeah, I feel better. Victor's gonna start keeping me accountable with my meds."

"That's good to hear," I smiled. "I can check up on you too, if you want."

"Please do. I won't turn down any help," he said to his sketch. He paused, his eyes drifting across the floor. "I'm still so ashamed of myself though. I *know* I can't do it on my own, but I keep trying to anyway. I'm *literally* Einstein's definition of insane."

"I mean, if we wanna be technical," I said. "Being forced to be dependent on something fucking *sucks* though, doesn't it?"

"*That* it does," he said without looking at me. "I hope you don't think less of me after seeing me like that."

I slapped his leg harder than I meant to. "Of *course* I don't. If anything, seeing you at your most vulnerable just makes me appreciate you that much more."

"I hope you get this sappy with Ethan."

I shrugged. "I try."

Kade showed me more of his drawings, sharing the inspiration and his thought process behind each of them until Victor emerged with plastic wrap around his upper arm. "I forgot how badass getting a tattoo makes you feel," he grinned.

I waited until Ethan joined us in 239 Axworthy to gently peel the plastic wrap off my wrist—"Let's peep that shit, fam!"—like the tattoo might come off with it, like it was a price sticker I was trying to perform a clean kill on. My skin was red, tender, and almost felt like it was burning. The word itself bulged out like it was stamped from the inside.

"It's like Braille, but with lines instead of dots," I said.

"You mean like *words?*" Kade laughed as he hopped out of his chair. "Anybody wanna accompany me down to the vending machines for some snicky-snacks?"

"I'm good," I passed.

"I could go for a snicky-snack," Ethan said as he got up to join him.

Alone with Victor, I brought up something he'd said the night before that was 100% none of my business, but that had been gnawing at me ever since. "Victor," I said to the floor, "last night, at one point you said to Kade, 'don't do this to me *again.*'"

The way Victor looked at me when he finally turned to me told me I'd struck something serious. "Kade's always had his ups and downs, but 2020 put him in a bad place—a *really* bad place." *Didn't it for all of us?* "It was that Summer. I got up one night for a glass of water, and I heard noise from the garage." He swallowed. "Both cars were running. He was in a sleeping bag on the floor with his headphones on. He'd stuffed towels under the door and taped plastic over the vents."

My breath caught in my throat. *"Holy shit." He actually tried to—?* "Did his parents ever find out?"

"Unh uh," he shook his head, hugging his knees. "He *begged* me not to tell them, and I promised him I wouldn't because I didn't want him getting put in a mental hospital—which, sure, it was pretty selfish of me, and sure, it might've been the wrong thing to do. But I was afraid. I *wanted* to tell them, to tell *somebody*, to make sure he got help. But I wasn't about to betray his trust after so many other people had already lost it. So I did whatever I had to to let him know that I was there for him." *So what you're saying is that you're the reason why he's still here?*

"Shit," I breathed. I wanted to ask him more, but didn't know what, or if it was even my place to ask. Kade and Ethan returning to the room with bags of Takis and potato skins put an end to our moment.

"So the two of us were just talking about possibly getting a felony tonight," Kade said to us. "You guys in?"

Victor just stared at him. "You wanna go out tonight?"

"Oh, not just that—I wanna turn the fuck up."

"You're *sure* you wanna go out tonight?"

"Why wouldn't he wanna go out tonight?" Ethan asked.

"Yeah, why *wouldn't* I wanna go out?" Kade glared.

"Because..." Victor said as he rubbed the back of his neck like a Trevor. "Because why go out when we can have a circle jerk right here?"

We spent the rest of the afternoon playing games and listening to Victor's post-hardcore playlist while I appreciated the miracle that Kade is—how I'm able to sit on his floor with him, able to talk and laugh with him, able to make jokes with each other, able to enjoy music together. I couldn't stop thinking about Victor finding his brother trying to end his own life, but I'd happily take having to relive that horror over and over again every day if it meant never finding my brother after it was too late.

We piled into Victor's shithead car to make a run to the store for mixers and snacks to take to 370 Rock later on, where Victor told us about all his other tattoo ideas without any of us asking him. I legit couldn't stop admiring my own. I kept my hand twisted so my wrist faced outwards to show it off, low-key waiting for somebody to nudge their friend and nod at it. *Take a seat, Trevor.* "So what you're saying is we could've gotten a bag of Takis like ten times bigger than the one in the vending machines for only twice the price?" Ethan chuckled in the snack aisle.

"Economies of scale, son," I flexed on him. Kade smirked and gave me an up-nod.

"*Son?*" Ethan scowled/smiled. "What are we, bros?"

"Bros who get each other off."

"Can we make it three of us?" Kade asked.

"I wish *I* had bros who'd get me off!" Victor fake-cried into his palm.

We picked out pop like our choice would go on our transcripts. "What do you guys think?" I asked. "Cherry vanilla Coke, or strawberries and cream Dr. Pepper?"

"Where the fuck do we live, Sudan?" Kade scoffed. "Get *both* of them. What was the point of dropping the atomic bombs if we're not gonna live in excess?"

"Too *soon!*" Ethan called him out.

"It was like 80 years ago, it's not—" But then the song that started playing over the store's speakers shut us *all* right the fuck up. We all stared up at the ceiling with our mouths hanging open.

"Are you fucking *shitting* me right now?"

"Is this real life?"

"*Wallows?*"

"I've *never* heard Wallows playing out in the wild before." It felt *so* much better than hearing a song I like on WXNU. I felt so pumped up that I could've skipped through the store.

We stopped at Subway for dinner on the way back, which was the first time I ever traveled to the Subway in New Halle by car. I played with my stud while I ordered to try to get a compliment on my fresh tat out of the snack assembling my sandwich. The four of us were talking about why dentists tell you to brush your teeth when they'd be out of a job if everybody had clean teeth when *another* Wallows song came on in Subway and knocked us out of our booth.

"*Two* Wallows songs? Within a half hour of each other?"

"What is *happening?*"

"Is Wallows *mainstream* now?"

"So hold on," Ethan turned to me with a smirk. "According to your definition, anything that plays on the radio is considered pop music. And *also* by your definition, all pop music is shitty, correct?"

I rubbed my neck, knowing where he was going. "Well, not *all* of it."

"So then according to the transitive property of mathematics," Kade took over, "would Wallows not be considered shitty music?"

"*No!* No math!" I begged him as I clutched my head as an excuse to not answer his question. *Is everything I know wrong? Or is the stick still that far up my ass?*

We took some of the refreshments we'd picked up over to the Quad for an outdoor showing of *Knives Out* before we got ready to head over to 370 Rock with my neighbor from across the hall, since I felt bad for never inviting her to come out with us. "So let me get this straight," Nikole said in the dining room of New Halle's best-kept secret, "*this* is the party you guys have been coming to all semester?"

"Pretty much," I said, feeling bad all over again.

"I'm actually high-key jelly. This is my fucking *vibe.*"

"You should've been here for *The* Weekend," Ethan grinned as he wiped some rum and cherry vanilla Coke from his mouth.

"Well you're here now," Victor said enthusiastically. He literally wouldn't leave her side all night.

"Dude, you're trying too hard," Kade said to Victor while Nikole was hitting up the bathroom. "Needy and desperate *isn't* an attractive look. Play hard-to-get and see if she makes the effort."

Victor looked like he'd been told he had to shave his head. "But what if she *doesn't?* I don't wanna let the chance slip by!"

Kade groaned. "And this is why you're single," he muttered.

I turned to Ethan. "Did I do a good job at playing hard-to-get?" I asked. He started laughing so hard that he started coughing.

"You're kidding, right? You came in to see me at work like every day!"

"Maybe I just wanted coffee!"

"*Bull-fucking-shit* you just wanted coffee," Victor laughed out loud. "You used to talk shit on people who'd get coffee all the time!"

"I *seent* it," Kade said.

Ethan drew a finger up my chin. "Just admit it, you were a simp for me."

"I was a *total* simp for you," I said before we shared a passionate drunk kiss. "Still am too."

Ethan told everyone who asked about his black eye that a box fell off a shelf in his House Council closet and hit him in the eye when he went to get something down. "I accidentally punched myself in the face one time while trying to start a lawnmower," Alex chuckled.

"I had to wear an eyepatch in 3rd grade for like a week once," Luca said.

I checked in on Kade while he and I watched a game of Flip Cup from the sidelines. Victor and Nikole might as well have been sitting on the same chair. "How're you doing?" I asked, and he knew I didn't mean how turnt he was feeling.

"I actually feel really good," he nodded. "So good, that it's weird to think that that all happened just last night." And the way he smiled told me he wasn't just saying that. "Isn't it wild how that works, how you can go from being so bad one day to so good the next, and good to bad?"

"Yeah, it is." For as much as I like to say how into Stoicism I am, so much of my mood is still dependent on externals. *That's* something that'll take a lifetime of learning for me to master, if ever. "We just have to take it a day at a time, and shut off from the world when we need to," I said, earning a nod from Kade.

The two newest pieces of ink in the house kept earning Victor and me compliments all night. Victor kept his sleeve rolled up like a douchebag to show it off. "Dude!" Nikole exclaimed. "How did I not see that before? That's fucking *sick!*" She admired it up close. "Can I touch it?"

"Yeah, go ahead," he nodded almost eagerly.

She felt his raised skin, glistening with ointment. "The lines are so *sharp*," she said, probably making him hard. The more the night went on, the more he wouldn't shut up about her.

"I might try holding her hand if we're sitting together," he told me at the kitchen counter. "But then does that look like I'm trying too hard? Maybe I'll just put my arm around her. Or maybe—"

I squeezed my eyes shut. "Dude—I will *punch* you if you don't shut up," I scowled. "You're overthinking it. Just make a fucking *move* already." I know that I can be cringe and anxious around guys who break my scale, but holy *shit*.

He and Nikole found their way downstairs, where Eren, Linh, Andrew, Ethan, and I were getting rigatoni by various means. Nikole gave the bowl to Victor without hitting it when it got to her. "I'll pass. My mouth always tastes gross every time I try smoking."

"Yeah, I don't really like it either," Victor said. He looked at the bowl with longing as he handed it to Eren without taking a hit.

Ethan and I managed to not start laughing until they got up to check out the stolen-door-turned-pong-table half of the basement. "It's *never* been *done!*" he snickered as he collapsed into me.

"*And* I'm *the simp?*" I giggled.

264

Crossfaded, we ended up on the patio with a bunch of other people who gradually filtered back inside until it was just Nikole, Victor, Ethan, and I, all sitting in awkward silence. "Oh, can you show me how to make that one drink you like?" Ethan asked me with a wink. "The one with the SoCo?"

"Oh yeah! It's pretty easy to make."

The two of us went inside so the two of them could have the patio to themselves. We slid between Kade and Alex's conversation about conspiracy theories—"Like there's a *reason* why we never went back to the moon!" Alex gesticulated—and into the bathroom to watch Nikole and Victor through the open window with the light off. They sat with their legs pushed up against one another's, talking and laughing low enough that we couldn't hear them. *"They better fucking kiss,"* I whispered.

Nikole put her hand on his thigh, a gesture that he returned.

"Oh shit!" Ethan grinned.

They smiled and looked into each other's eyes in a way that only ends one way —or two ways, apparently.

The screen door tore open.

"Where'd the third plane go? Where'd the third plane go? Where'd the third plane go?" Kade urgently asked them. "Do *you* know where the third plane went? Cause *I* sure as shit don't. Where'd the third plane go? Where'd it go? Where'd it go? Where'd it go? Where'd it go?"

Ethan and I covered our mouths to muffle our laughter at how *pissed* Victor had to have been. We ran back to the kitchen, where everybody was cracking up at Kade, who was taking up the whole doorway to the patio, repeating the same question over and over without giving anyone a chance to answer him.

"Where'd the third plane go? Nobody fucking knows, because it *wasn't* a plane —it was a *cruise missile!"* He turned to go before spinning back to point at them. "Bush did 9/11, Roosevelt did 12/7, Johnson did 11/22! And has *anybody* seen where the hell my cigarettes went?" He walked off, leaving Victor looking embarrassed and Nikole with her face in her hands, though they both looked like they were trying not to laugh. Nikole muttered something to him, stood up, and took him by the hand into the house, through the kitchen, and up the stairs.

Ethan met my shocked look. "Go the fuck ahead!"

"Finally!"

I'm not sure what they ended up doing, but Victor's hand landed on my shoulder like eight minutes later. "Dude!" he laughed like he'd just won the lottery. He took me over to the record player to tell me all about what happened without me even asking, but I listened anyway because I'm a good friend.

"Go 'head!" I slapped his back. "Did you parallel park? Did you put the wand in the chamber of secrets?"

"Parallel park?" he laughed. "No?"

"Did you bust a nut?"

"No, but—"

"Did you put your hands up her shirt?" I purred into his ear. "Did she push you down onto the bed and pump that dick of yours? Did she wrap her lips around that throbbing cock? Did she ride the cum right out of you?"

"Oh, fuck," Victor bit his lip. "I—I gotta go." He tried to hide the tent in his shorts as he made for the bathroom and shut himself in.

Nikole found me before she left to head over to another party that one of her friends was at. "Tell Victor I said I'll see him later," she said as she hugged me goodnight without giving me any hint of whether she enjoyed her encounter with him. Victor was in disbelief when he came back out and found out she'd left.

"What?" he said like she'd broken protocol. "Where'd she go?"

"One of her friend's apartments. Up the hill from here, I think."

"What if I wanted to go with her? I would've at least said bye."

"Maybe you coulda if you weren't all hornt up."

He screwed up his face. "I wasn't trying too hard, was I?"

I ran my hands down my face. "I can't fucking take you."

"Said the bishop to the bishop," he said without skipping a beat.

With Nikole gone, there was nothing keeping Victor from going right the fuck ahead. I could tell he was getting pretty fucking fried from how loud and handsy he was being. Fast forward to him sitting cross-legged on the floor with a big plastic cup of water and a 5-gallon Kmart bucket—a harsh reminder that you can always go too ahead.

I crouched in front of him and put on my best Patnick Paul voice. "How ya doin' hun?"

He just shook his head without looking up.

"Do you think you're gonna be sick?" I asked in my best Trevor voice.

He shrugged, still looking down.

"Do you wanna go back to your room?"

He nodded. I got up to find Kade slouched in an armchair, looking pretty zonked himself. "Hey, Victor said he wants you to take him back to your room."

"Oh does he?" Kade smirked.

"As in he's in the slumps."

"Oh. Okay." He heaved himself out of the armchair and grabbed onto me to keep himself from falling. "Maybe..."

"Maybe I should walk you both back?" I finished his thought for him.

He smiled a zooted smile. "You're the best, fam."

Ethan was elbows-deep in a game of *Telestrations* when I found him to tell him I was gonna bounce. "Hey, Victor and Kade aren't feeling well, so I'm gonna walk them back."

"Those kids," Ethan laughed. "You want me to go with you?"

"No, you stay and have fun. I'll let you know when I'm on my way back, and I can meet you outside your building?"

"Sounds good," he said as I bent down to give him an almond-liqueur kiss.

To a nearsighted person who didn't have their contacts in, Victor strolled a straight line. "I just want my *dick sucked!*" the cranky child in him whined.

"Have you ever tried doing it yourself?" I asked him.

Kade threw up his hand. *"Guilty!"*

Victor rolled his head at me. *"You* like sucking dick, don't you Trev?"

"You're too drunk to consent, remember?" I grinned at Kade behind Victor's back.

"Fuuuck, that's *right,"* he pouted. "Why's it so hard to get *laid?"*

"Just go hump your shark when you get back to your room," I chuckled.

"It's not the *same,"* he whimpered.

April 30

Do you know how much it'd suck to get stabbed with a trick knife that gets stuck and actually goes into your chest? I'm not sure if I'd be more pissed or more overwhelmed by the irony of it if it ever happened to me.

It's also been 0 days since I've had an actual nightmare. I dreamt that I was walking Kade and Victor back from the party and we took a shortcut through the woods, where I discovered the hard way that Kade was a werewolf. And then Victor got dragged away by these vines that were going under his skin and drinking his blood—which is to say you can bet what my next story will be.

I hung out at the desk for a minute on my way back into Swafford to ask Nikole how she liked the party. "So what'd you think of 370 Rock?"

"I loved 370 Rock," she said. "I wish there were more parties like that around here."

"Right? Regular parties are ass after that."

"They're all the same shit! Unless it's a Theatre major party." She chuckled to herself. *"Those* are a fucking vibe."

"Victor seemed like he had a good time," I smirked.

She shot me a serious look. "Why? What'd he tell you?"

"Nothing!" I chuckled. "Just that you two made out."

"Yeah, that was about it."

"Five out of five stars?" I half-joked, hoping for his sake that she'd give a good review.

She made a face like she was trying to get something out of her teeth with her tongue. "I don't know."

"Why? Was it bad?"

She stood up to look around the lobby to make sure he wasn't around. "You can't tell *anyone* I said this."

My eyes mentally widened. "I won't."

She leaned over the desk, so close to me that I thought *we* were about to kiss. *"It was like kissing a fish,"* she whispered.

I let out a loud, head-turning laugh. *"What?* What does that even *mean?"*

"You know, like…" She let her mouth hang open in an 'O' and shook her head from side to side with her eyes closed. I slid to the floor and was *howling.*

"Stop!" I screamed. *"You're joking!"*

She wiped her eyes from laughing at me laughing. "I swear to god!"

Clutching the counter for support, I hoisted myself up. "I *can't—*it *hurts!"* I've never wanted to tell anybody something so bad before.

Since the others were busy practicing for the Summer Send-Off, I put on an indie pop playlist and spent most of the afternoon working on my paper about how the Compromise of 1850 contributed to the outbreak of the Civil War, and then chipped away a little bit at *Homegoing.* And despite my protests that I wasn't a resident of either Kessler or Draper, Ethan insisted that nobody would care if I was at the two hall's joint last event of the year—a Block Party, if you can believe it, held in Kessler's donut hole of a courtyard—though I think he just wanted to rope me into helping set up for it. "You could've just walked in," he said when he met me at the door. "How do you think the Draperites are getting in?"

"I don't *know!* So what, anybody can just come in and wander around? How is that even safe?" He didn't even have to sign me in.

"Trust me, I heard the same question a thousand times when we pitched it at our House Council meeting," he rolled his eyes.

Thankfully there wasn't a whole lot to do, because I've learned that implementing events isn't my thing. "Do you actually *enjoy* doing this?" I asked as I helped Ethan get some things out of the House Council office. "Putting together events, I mean?"

"No, I like doing it!" he smiled. "I think planning things and making them happen is fun! You kinda *have* to enjoy it to be in House Council," he laughed.

"Yeah, until things don't go right and you start flipping shit," I chuckled, earning myself a slap. "Do you think you'd wanna be like an event planner or something? Like, maybe in the music industry? Promoting concerts and shit like that?"

268

"I've thought about it."

"And?"

"I'd *love* to do that," he smiled. "I get excited just thinking about it—bringing music to people and knowing that *I* helped make it happen."

"Do you think that might be what you wanna do with your life?" I asked.

His phone rang before he could answer. "Hold on, my mom's calling me. Hopefully it's a quick call," he said with a swipe. "Hi Mom. Oh, it's going—I'm just helping to get set up for a House Council event. Yeah, I can talk. Why, what's up?"

I poked around the office while I waited, letting my eyes land on the spot where Ethan and I used to blow each other. "They *told* you?" Ethan practically yelled, making my head snap to him. "They told me they weren't gonna tell you!" He mouthed *'they told her I got beat up!'* to me. "No. Because! I didn't wanna have to tell you if I didn't *have* to," he chuckled. "Yeah, pretty much." He slouched into one of the chairs and let himself swivel as he told her what happened. "Yeah, I'm okay now. I have a nice bruise under my eye though. I don't, no. I mean, unless somebody I'm running against wants to knock me out of the race by *literally* trying to knock me out, then I don't know," he smiled. "I don't! I'm *not* lying! The campus police officer who talked to me said—" His mouth fell open as he brought himself to a stop. "*What?* That doesn't even make sense! Why would I be the target of a hate crime?" he said uneasily. "I just *said* I don't know. *No*, I'm not dealing *drugs*. What would I not be telling you? That's what *I'm* asking! Mom, I—no, I—I already said—" He looked like he was in pain. "Why would I do—please, let me speak. I told you—Mom, *please*—" He grabbed a handful of his hair. "Okay! *Yes*, I think I know why!" He let his eyes close, opening them to look into mine with a determined look. *I can do this,* they told me. "I know why."

I laid my hand on his shoulder on my way out, letting the door shut behind me so he could have his privacy. I pretended to read the fliers pinned to the board in the hallway while I tried to eavesdrop on him having the hardest conversation he's ever had to have. "Revelation", the Troye Sivan song from *Boy Erased*, popped into my head, since it seemed like the appropriate song for that moment in the soundtrack of Ethan's life.

"Mom...there's something I've been wanting to tell you for a while," Ethan said instead of going for the old *Mom-I-have-a-brain-tumor-just-kidding-I'm-just-gay* trick. "You know how people would always ask me why someone as handsome and as talented as me didn't have a girlfriend? Well, there's something I've known about myself for a while now, and it's time you knew too. You probably already know what I'm gonna say, but I need you to hear me say it. I'm..."

Go on. It's just two words. Yes, I know they're the hardest two words you'll ever say, but there's nothing you owe to yourself more than saying those two little words.

"I'm gay, Mom. I'm gay."

And just like that, Ethan's life swerved into uncharted territory. Maybe it'll get easier, or maybe it'll get harder, but all I know is that he's free now.

I heard him sniffle. "Yes, I'm sure. I've never been so sure of anything before. My whole life, I guess? *Nothing* happened, it's just the way I am," his voice cracked. I wanted to go in and hold his hand for him, but it was something he had to do on his own—that, and I was locked out. "I'm still the same *person*. I'm still your *son*. So to answer your original question, somebody probably didn't like seeing me and my boyfriend holding hands or something." And then his tone switched from nervous to annoyed. "*Yeah*, I do. And I love him. He's kind, he's sweet, he's everything I could ask for and more. Nobody's ever treated me the way he does," he said, making my heart well up the same way it used to those first couple weeks after our first kiss. "His name's Trevor. Oh my god *Mom*, I'm not answering that. Use your imagination! Yeah, they do, and they still love him. Because I *met* them. It's *not* a choice, Mom. No, it's *not*. Okay then, let's say it *is* a choice—do you really think I would've chosen to not be straight? Why would I *want* a more difficult life? Why would I have wanted a life where I'm not allowed to be myself? A life where I had to watch everybody else get to be allowed to be in love when it was forbidden for me? No, you tell *me*. Oh my god, please don't, I'm so past that. Oh, believe me, I did. I used to pray to god every single night, in *tears*"—his voice cracked again—"*begging* him to make me straight, *pleading* with him that I'd do whatever it would take just to be *normal* and to have a normal life. And he didn't do shit."

I frowned an angry frown at the bulletin board, remembering all the sleepless nights I spent trying to bargain with somebody who I was told over and over loved me and would always be there to listen to me. *My god, my god, why have you forsaken me?*

"So what, if the bible said 'thou shalt not write with your left hand,' then would left-handed people be getting persecuted? Yes it *is* the same thing. Some people are born left-handed and some people are born gay, that's just the way it is. You realize that one of the ten actual commandments says not to work on the Sabbath, but I don't see people burning down stores for forcing people to sin by working on the Sabbath. Yeah, *exactly*, it *is* ridiculous. No, I don't. Not anymore. For a number of reasons. No, but it certainly *contributed*. Because I could be the most devout person —I could pray and read my bible every single day, and go to church every Sunday, youth group, even *witness* to people—but then I won't be allowed into heaven because god decided to make me gay and damn me from the start, regardless of what I did or how hard I tried? That's a pretty dick move. *Oh* yes it is."

Coming out as gay is hard enough, but coming out as not believing in god in the same conversation? *Sheesh*. But why is that even a thing? Why is believing in something different, or nothing at all, such a big deal?

Ethan's tone went from annoyed to indignant as he took control of the conversation. "No, I don't wanna hear that. What do you *mean*, how could *I* do this to *you*? Do you think we would've been having this conversation if I'd been raised in an accepting environment? Of course I appreciate what you've done for me, this has *nothing* to do with that! So what, is your love for me contingent on me liking girls? Am I a total disappointment to you now? Are you never gonna look at me the same way again? Are you gonna disown me? Trevor had a brother who committed suicide because his parents didn't accept him for who he was either—is that what you want? Would you rather have no son instead of a son who's different from who you thought he was? I can give you his parents' number and you can listen to them tell you how they'd do *anything* to have him back. No, I'm not apologizing. I'm *done* apologizing for who I am or what I believe. And if you don't like it, then don't come pick me up. I'll live with Trevor. At least *his* parents can accept me for who I am. I have to go now. Because I have an *event* to get ready for. I'll talk to you later. I'm hanging up now. Okay? I love you. Bye."

My teeth were clamped down on my tongue so hard that I don't know how they didn't bite it off.

The door finally opened and he walked out like he was in a daze. "You did way better than I did," I said as he walked past me towards the nearest couch to drop onto it.

"I can't believe I just did that," he said like he was emotionally drained.

"Did it go how you thought it would?"

"More or less."

I couldn't tell if he was about to puke or cry. "How do you feel?"

His face buried itself in his hands. "I've never felt better," he croaked.

I sat beside him and rubbed circles on his back. "Doesn't it? I thought the school wasn't gonna tell them though, unless...do you think Officer What's-His-Face reported it as a hate crime and then they had to tell her?"

"I don't know," he said apathetically. I felt him shaking, the kind of shaking that comes with gentle sobbing. He looked up at me with glossy eyes. "It feels so *liberating*." I cradled him as he wiped his nose. "It feels like I've been carrying the biggest weight for the longest time, and now it's *gone*."

"You should be so proud of yourself. *I'm* so proud of you. Today's the day that your life truly begins." I kissed his cheek. "Are you nervous about going home now?"

"A little. It's my stepdad who I'm more worried about. But as long as my mom has my side..." He trailed off, perhaps thinking about how there's a very real possibility that she won't.

"Well, whatever happens, it's done. Like you said, you can just move in with me if you need to." And then I beamed at him like he was glowing. "You can do anything now, you know. You're unstoppable."

"I know," he smiled, but it disappeared as soon as it arrived. "I'm sorry for bringing Ryder into it. I shouldn't have said that, but I wanted to scare some support into her."

"It's okay. He was the kind of person who would've been glad to know that his death gave someone the opportunity that he didn't get to have."

"*Hopefully* I have the opportunity."

"You do. You just made sure of it." I gave him a loving shake. "We should probably take the rest of this stuff out. People are gonna think we snuck off to blow each other."

"They're just jealous," he laughed.

The Block Party was way less formal than my own building's event, but that didn't make it any less fun. The food was just chips and snacks and bottles of water and cans of off-brand pop, and Kessler's House Council Treasurer DJ'ed the event with their own speakers and subwoofer. Residents chalked a four square court onto the herringbone bricks, which promptly attracted a line of students. Games and crafts—"I haven't made sand art since vacation bible school"—came to life on tables along the perimeter of the courtyard, which offered *superb* acoustics for the music. Even the residents who stayed in their rooms hung out at their open windows, making the whole thing feel like a tightly-knit inner city neighborhood. It was the most block-party Block Party I'd been to all week. I was low-key nervous when Ethan introduced me to the GAs—the graduate assistants, who oversee all the RAs in their own buildings—but even they didn't care that I, a Swaffordian, was at their event. Jen, Kessler's GA, said she was happy to "finally" meet me. "I might've mentioned you a few times," Ethan admitted.

"A *few* times?" Jen laughed. Ethan just smirked at me and shrugged.

The two of us watched a game of oversized chess play out from one of the metal benches. "Thanks for being my emotional support this past week," Ethan said as he laid his head on my shoulder. "I honestly don't know how I would've gotten through it without you."

"I mean, what kind of shitty boyfriend would I be otherwise?" I chuckled.

"The boy I loved asked me to be his date to the banquet," he listed off, "I'm feeling good about the election, the Summer Send-Off is coming up, and I finally came out to my mom."

"What was that last part?" I asked.

"I said I finally came out to my mom."

I squinted at him. "*Huh?*"

He raised his voice at me. "I *said* I finally came out to my mom!"

"Say it louder."

He smiled as he caught on. "I came out to my mom!"

"Now stand up and say it!"

He stood up on our bench and spread his arms out to shout "I CAME OUT TO MY MOM!" to the sky, earning himself a couple claps and a cheer.

Kade texted me to ask me what our dinner plans were—**Unless of course ass is on the menu**—so I held off on grabbing any real food after the event. I was on edge the whole time we were in Taco Bell, waiting for Wallows to start playing like a gunshot.

"So what's the move tonight?" Victor asked us. "The usual? Drugs? Felonies?"

"Ooh, let's evade taxes," Kade said.

"How about some punk shit?"

"Let's drive around the Christian college and play porn real loud!"

"Let's stay up all night," Ethan suggested.

"All night?"

"All night," he repeated.

"May I ask *why*?"

He shrugged. "I dunno. Pulling an all-nighter was one of those things I always thought I'd have to do when I came to school. I almost feel like my freshman experience won't be complete without one."

"So you *do* know," Kade smirked. "But yeah, I haven't had to pull one either, actually."

Victor was the only one not sold on it. "That'll be kinda hard, won't it?"

"*You're* kind of hard."

"I *wish* I was kind of hard," he joked. "What are we gonna do though? Getting drunk or high will put me right to sleep."

"I guess games and movies then?"

Everdell was right up in Ethan's room, but they opted for the wider selection available in 239 Axworthy, which worked out because that's where the caffeinated tea is. "In the name of the father, the son, and the holy ghost," Kade blessed us as he sprinkled the wet tea infuser over us.

We paid resources and placed meeples until after midnight, taking a break to hit up the pool and foosball tables in the rec room. And then we walked to Sheetz, where we spent the equivalent of the cost of a new vinyl record on energy drinks. "Here's to another seven hours," I said as we toasted.

"Oh Jesus *Christ*," Victor mumbled as he wiped a trickle of Monster from his chin.

The only sober people on Main Street, we energized ourselves for the long night ahead. "I might be totally making this up," I said, "but doesn't nicotine help you stay awake?"

"No, it can," Kade answered. "Why do you ask?"

"Just wondering," I said while I tried to figure out how to ask my follow-up question without sounding too eager.

Kade gave me a sideways look before he and I slowed to a stop. We abruptly pointed finger guns at each other. "Are you saying what I think you're saying?" he asked.

I raised my eyebrows. "Puff puff?"

We passed only two other sauntering wayfarers on Quincey Street on our way to Rock Hill Road. "Is it rude to not go to their party and then just show up this late?" Ethan asked.

"Fam," Kade chuckled, "we *are* the fucking party."

There must've been a memo that we missed, because 370 Rock was *dead*. "We're on the right street, right?" I asked its dark windows.

"Did they all go out somewhere *else*?"

"Why would they—" I stopped speaking when I heard music faintly playing from around back.

Like the trespassers that we were, we snuck around the side of the house, towards the bushes and tree branches dancing in the light from the tiki torches. From our shadowy vantage, we saw Matt sitting alone with Anubis' hose in one hand and his phone in the other, listening to something that sounded like a mix between jazz and reggae from a little Bluetooth speaker. I was thinking about how to announce ourselves without being weird when Kade crept closer and made a quick, loud slurping sound. "Jesus fucking *Christ!*" Matt choked as he nearly yanked the hookah over. "*Goddammit.* How long were you guys standing there?"

"Like literally ten seconds," Kade laughed. "Where's everybody else?"

"They're at the bar. It's Luca's birthday."

"Oh," Ethan smiled. "Well happy birthday to him."

Kade narrowed his eyes. "Why would they wanna go out to the *bar* when you guys already have the best parties?"

Matt shrugged. "For old time's sake I guess? Maybe they saw that senior bucket list thing *The Herald* always puts out a few weeks before the end of the year and got sentimental? That, and they probably wanted to steal a cup one last time."

"You didn't wanna go with them?"

He raised an eyebrow at us. "Oh yeah, because going out to the *bar* is my idea of fun," he said sarcastically. "It's just not my thing anymore."

Victor wasn't convinced. "Even if it's *not* your thing anymore, shouldn't you be trying to make the most of the rest of your time here before you graduate?"

"I know what I like and don't like," Matt said simply. "Why aren't *you* guys out somewhere?"

"We're staying up all night," Ethan said, like staying up all night just for shits and gigs is something people do all the time. "Drinking will just make us sleepy."

"And besides, where else would we go other than here?" Victor said.

"Well, do you wanna smoke then?" Matt asked. "I can get another bowl going."

The four of us traded looks. "I mean, we don't wanna *intrude*."

"But if you're *offering...*"

Matt damned the detritus of coals to die in the tray while Kade packed a new bowl. "That ass is now fat," he announced when he returned to the patio with it.

Matt's music was all reggae, but not Bob Marley or Sublime reggae. "*Ooh! Ooh!*" Kade exclaimed like his prostate was getting massaged when one trumpet-heavy song came on. "I *fucks* with this. I fucks with this *hard*." He fucked with it so hard that he was frowning. "Who *is* this?"

"*This* is Rebelution," Matt answered. "Them, SOJA, Snarky Puppy, and Pacific Dub make up most of my nighttime hookah smoking playlist. We used to spend *so* many nights out here smoking while listening to them and just talking about shit. There's nothing like a good late-night hookah conversation."

Kade's choice in tobacco—guava—paired well with the reggae and tiki torches. Victor was still hung up on the fact that somebody about to graduate wanted to stay in by themselves on their second-to-last weekend as a student. "But don't you wanna make as many memories as you can? Aren't you gonna *miss* all this?" he asked Matt like he had a stake in it.

"Of course I'm gonna miss it, but I've made my peace with it. A lot of people think it's just the end of something, but they forget that it's the beginning of something too," Matt stroked his goatee. "I think that's why we're afraid of things like death—we're just afraid of what we're familiar with coming to an end."

Victor blinked. "That's the deepest shit I've heard all day."

"Well excuse *me*," Kade scoffed.

We talked about the universe, the world wars, *Pokémon*, and why microwave companies keep putting popcorn buttons on microwaves when literally every bag of popcorn specifically tells you *not* to use the popcorn button, but my mind kept going back to what Matt said about a senior bucket list. Yeah, it's cute and makes you reflect on everything, but what, you check everything off and then all of a sudden you're ready to graduate? And what if you never did any of those things? Does that mean you threw away your time at college? I'm sure I'll probably visit all the places on campus and around town that hold meaning for me and get all sentimental when my time comes, but that doesn't mean I'll be ready to face the real world. I handled graduating high school *way* better than some of my classmates—which I guess would've been hard for me too if I actually had friends and was involved in things—but I *like* it here. How will I spend the rest of my time on campus when I can count on two hands, one hand, one finger, the number of days I have left before I leave this place for good? And what if I could count on two hands the number of days I have left to *live*—how would I spend *that* time?

"Would you live your life differently if you knew you were gonna die?" my thoughts finally ruptured out.

"I don't know how to break this to you," Ethan said, "but you're dying as we speak."

"You know what I mean," I half-scoffed. "Like, if you got diagnosed with a terminal illness and found out you only had a few months left to live."

"I don't even wanna think about it," Kade said immediately. "I mean, I can't *help* but think about it though. I know I sure as shit wouldn't be going to class."

"But who's to say I *won't* be dead in a few months?" Ethan pressed me. "I could develop a terminal illness, or get hit by a car the next time I cross the street."

"Patrick Paul almost hit me with her car once," Matt said.

"I mean, it has to happen to *somebody*, and there's no reason it shouldn't happen to me," Ethan insisted. It hurts to think about, but it's true. Maybe if we were all mindful of our own fragility, then maybe we'd be nicer to each other and to ourselves. "I don't know how I'd spend the rest of my time, but I do know that I'd be pissed with myself for not living more for myself," he said to the hookah. "That'd I'd have spent most of my life lying about myself for the convenience of other people."

"But you're doing something about it though," I nudged his leg. "You came out to your mom. That's a good start."

"Oh go the fuck ahead!" Victor practically yelled as he jumped up to hug him.

"Good for you fam," Kade patted his knee.

"Yeah, I still can't believe I did that," Ethan smiled. "But I think we get so comfortable and content with our lives that we're afraid to change things up or try something new," he went on. "But only doing what's easy in life makes for a pretty boring life." The background I'd set for my Mac last Summer to remind myself that I was making the right choice by going away to school flashed across my mind—'*Life begins at the end of your comfort zone.*'

"It'd be more of a mindset shift for me more than anything else," Victor said as he twirled the string of his drug rug around his finger. "I mean, I'd still drop out and tell my Acting professor to shit and fall back in it, but I feel like I'd appreciate the world more. We take so much for *granted*, like breathing. It's such a miracle to be able to take a breath and know that you're *alive* because of it, but we just assume we'll just keep on breathing forever." I became conscious of my own breaths, of my heart and lungs working nonstop to keep me alive, and how miraculous we all really are. *Short story idea: everybody has a digital counter on their chest, and every time they take a breath it goes down by one.*

"I kinda felt like that when we were on acid," Kade said. "Being able to see and appreciate everything for what they were—I mean, are."

"Same," I nodded. "It's a shame that it has to take either dying or drugs for it to happen though, or to be mindful of the time we have."

"I will say, acid is the one thing I never regretted doing," Matt said. "I think it permanently changed my outlook on things, and for the better."

Our mortality and the ghosts of psychedelics rose with the smoke. Kade exhaled a cloud of it through his nostrils like a fog machine. "You know what's scary to me?"

"Clowns."

"Okay, besides *that.*"

"Running out of toilet paper?"

"Thinking about how there's a skeleton and meat inside of you?"

"Not knowing when you're gonna do something for the last time," Kade said. "Like, someday you'll do something or go somewhere and it'll be the last time you ever do it, and you won't know it." *That's* the kind of thing that can give you a panic attack, because the day will come when I laugh with Kade for the last time without knowing it, have a heart-to-heart with Victor for the last time without knowing it, kiss Ethan for the last time without knowing it.

"I can do you one better," Ethan upped the ante. "How many times have you *already* done something for the last time without realizing it? Like, my mom used to take me to this park in our neighborhood, and I'm sure the last time we went felt just like any other time."

"I know what you mean," Victor nodded. "I remember hanging out with one of my friends like a week before our first day of high school. But then he found new friends and we never hung out again. We still texted sometimes, but yeah, it was never like it used to be."

"There was a toy store back home that we used to go to," Kade told us. "We went one day and found out they'd closed down. I threw a tantrum, obviously."

"It's kind of a dumb example," Matt half-smiled, "but there was a day when I was done playing *Animal Crossing* for the day and I never picked it back up."

"No, that's not dumb! That's exactly what I mean!"

I just nodded, thinking about when Dillon and I saw *Jurassic World* in the theater without knowing it would be our last date night to the movies. I tried to remember the last night he and I spent together, how I held him without ever stopping to think that we could ever have an expiration date, and certainly not how fucking imminent it could be.

We heard music stop playing from somewhere nearby as parties shut down and drunken voices moved down the street. "I guess maybe I should get into the habit of treating every moment like it could be the last time it happens," Victor said like a character in some story with a moral. But ever since I learned the phrase *ichi-go ichi-e*, I know that everything I get to experience *is* the last time it'll ever happen, because every moment only ever happens that one single time.

If I ever write a book, this will be the Vonnegut-inspired quote I'll put in it—whenever you're high off of life, or love, or the beauty of the world, remind yourself that *this too shall pass.* When you feel alone in the world, and like you don't matter, and like you're ready to leave this world behind—*this too shall pass*. When you laugh with friends until you cry—*this too shall pass*. When you say goodbye to a loved one with a hug—*this too shall pass*. When life doesn't let up and does everything it can to keep you down—*this too shall pass*. When you lose sleep over somebody in the best possible way—*this too shall pass*. When you lose sleep over somebody in the worst possible way—*this too shall pass*. When your mind is at peace—*this too shall pass*. When you watch the sunrise—*this too shall pass*. When you get to wake up every morning next to that one person who's become your whole world—*this too shall pass*. When the person who you've let become your whole world becomes so ordinary that they're just another part of your life that you take for granted—*this too shall pass*.

The smoke came out in flavorless wisps, but we declined Matt's invitation for a third bowl. "We don't wanna keep you up any longer," Kade insisted as he got up with a stretch.

"I'm glad I got to enjoy your company," Matt said as he rested the serpentine hose on Anubis' spout and hit the power on his speaker. "It's a shame that I only got to know you guys over these past couple of months. I wish I had friends like you when I was a freshman."

We checked our phones as if Old Main's clock faces weren't towering right above us. "I actually don't feel too tired right now," Victor said as he crushed his empty can.

"Do we wanna watch a movie in my room since it's like right here?" Ethan offered. "There's room for all of us, and no sleeping roommates to disturb."

"Well there goes my dream of having three other guys in my bed," Kade pouted.

We tried to remember all the movies we watched together, and tried to come up with a good one to end the year with. "You know what I'm in the mood to watch?" Victor asked.

"Nikole getting undressed?"

"Ha ha," he said mockingly. *"Interstellar."*

"He didn't say no," Kade whispered to me.

"I haven't watched *that* in a hot second," Ethan said.

"It's nice and long," Kade smirked. "You gotta really stretch yourself out for it."

We didn't see a single person in Kessler's halls. All the closed doors made it feel like one of the suites. Victor and Kade took in 341's rearranged furniture as they slipped off their shoes. "Why'd your roommate get expelled again?" Victor asked. "Didn't he stab his girlfriend or something?"

Ethan laughed. "If that's code for refusing to cite sources on a paper, then yes."

Victor snapped his fingers. "Oh wait, I was thinking of someone else."

Kade let the double-twin bed catch him. "So *this* is where the magic happens."

"I bet *you'd* like to be a part of the magic, you dirty little queer," Ethan teased him.

"*Oh-hoo!*" he squealed from the bed. "Somebody's making me moist!"

"Yourself?"

The only other time I'd seen *Interstellar* was when I was ten, so I didn't know what the hell was happening, or anything about Timothée Chalamet except that he had my attention. Despite Victor saying he didn't feel tired, it only took like a half hour for him to stand up and yawn. "So remember how I said I was up for watching a three-hour movie?" he asked, earning himself glares from the three of us. "I actually don't think I can do it. I'm gonna head back." We promptly gave him shit for it.

"What do you *mean* you can't do it? *You're* the one who wanted to watch it!"

"Just keep watching and if you crash here, then you crash here."

"Sit your ass back down."

Victor obeyed, and lasted another 12 minutes before capitulating. "*Bed...*" he growled as he made for the door like a zombie. "I need my *bed.*"

"Let us know when you get back," Kade said as he unpaused the movie.

I started feeling sleepy by the second hour, but it held my attention, and by the end of it my mind was blown open more than it's ever been, except for that one time I did acid. "What'd you think?" Ethan asked me.

"*Shush,*" I silenced him. *Can an ant understand the laboratory it found its way into? Could it begin to comprehend the space station it can't ever realize is even there? And yet we humans are so adamant that we know everything when there are things that exist alongside us—right before us—that we can't even fathom?*

"He just *shushed* me!" Ethan said to an apathetic Kade.

"Holy *fuck* was that long," Kade said as he got up to stretch. "It did the job though." He nodded to the window. "Sun's starting to come up."

I walked to the window to take in the warm glow starting to bathe campus, from Old Main to the football stadium. "Would anybody be up for a walk?" I asked.

"A *walk?*" Ethan asked like he couldn't believe me. "Where?"

"To the hill behind the football stadium. We can watch the sunrise from up there." They just stared at me. "We have to walk that way anyway!"

"*You* do," Ethan yawned. "*I* need to get some sleep if I don't wanna be a wreck later on."

"What was that thing you said earlier about only doing what's easy in life?"

He ran his hands down his face with a groan before swinging himself up off his bed. "*Okay,* let's go."

Campus was more alive than I expected it to be at 6 a.m. on a Sunday morning, though the only people out were either on a run or doing yoga. By the time we reached Bamberger's parking lot, the sky was singing so loud that I could almost hear it. Drowsiness and dewy grass made us stumble us as we hurried up the hill. The daiquiri sky had given way to a fuzzy navel orange by the time we reached the crest, announcing the greatest show on Earth. *Any moment now.* It was the kind of morning you dance to, the kind of morning Christ returns on. The goddess itself finally peeked over its creation—the endless sky, the ocean of trees, all us reverent Romantics surrendering themselves in the face of its glory.

"Why isn't there a sunrise-watching club on campus?" I asked as I shielded my eyes.

"You just started it," Kade said from behind me.

We hung around for a while to take some Instagram-worthy pics. "Yeah, this was a good idea," Ethan admitted. "I like never get to see the sun actually *rise*."

"How geocentric of you," Kade said as he drank in the panorama. "The Middle Ages Catholic Church would be so proud."

But like all things, the moment had to end. "I really *should* go back and get to bed though," Ethan said. "Are you gonna come back with me?"

"Nah, I think I'll stay here just a little longer and then just crash in my room." I gave Ethan a kiss and Kade a nod. "I'll let you know when I get up." I watched the two of them dwindle down the hill before turning back to face the morning. Without even caring that the grass was still wet, I folded my legs beneath me and stuffed my hands into my hoodie's front pocket, sitting at attention to take in everything before me, and I saw that it was good. I dwelt on the miracle that we get to experience and be a part of, and how it all too shall pass. I closed my eyes and let a truth wash over me, like Moses on Mt. Sinai. *"That you are here,"* I mentally quoted Walt Whitman, *"that life exists, and identity, That the powerful play goes on, and you may contribute a verse."*

I awoke several hours later trying to figure out why I was naked before remembering my ass was wet from sitting in the grass. I guess I was too tired to even put on dry underwear, not caring if Tylor got any revealing views.

Did you guys stay up all night?
Might anybody be awake yet?
I'll take that as a no
I'm getting breakfast if anybody's interested
When the fuck you guys getting up
YARGH
This sucks

Victor and Ethan were already done with their smoothie and wrap from Percy's by the time I joined them. "Um, this table's for well-rested people only," Victor said when I went to pull out a chair. Ethan got up and took a few steps before smiling and sitting back down.

"That's discrimination," I said, giving Ethan a kiss before digging into my boneless wings. I randomly thought about Victor kissing like a fish and I had to choke back a laugh. "I take it Kade's still asleep?"

"Please—he sleeps in until noon when he goes to bed at a normal time," Victor chuckled. "And why are you eating those with chopsticks?"

"Why *aren't* I eating them with chopsticks?" I said to my wings.

"I don't know how you guys stayed up *all night*," Victor said as he watched me from behind crossed arms. "Weren't you tired?"

I just shrugged. "I'm a seasoned insomniac." I gave up on trying to use the chopsticks and just started spearing my wings with one.

"Oh, I'm *still* tired," Ethan laughed as he checked himself out in his phone's camera. "I think I might lay back down for a while after we leave. I look like hell." I had to stop myself from giving him shit over not helping set up for the banquet when all he's been doing for the past two weeks was helping set up for events.

Outside of Bixby, Ethan parted ways with us to head back to Kessler. "*You're* not gonna go back to sleep, are you?" Victor asked me, which made me laugh out loud.

"One does not simply 'go back to sleep.' Like, it's physically impossible for me."

"Do you wanna take a walk around or something then?"

We wound our way through a trail in the woods—we stumbled across a random-ass clearing that I never knew was there that the Pagan Order on campus probably goes out to to do their stuff in—and eventually found ourselves resting by the pond in the shade of a tree. "I think this is one of my favorite spots on campus," I said as I thought about all the times last semester when I used to sit at its edge to read or write or think or just listen to music.

"Yeah," Victor nodded. "It's a good spot when you need somewhere to ponder. Get it? *Pondering?* By the *pond?*"

I just laughed through my nose, trying to think of how to tell him about Ethan and I happening upon his moms' store in Pittsburgh, and that would've been the perfect moment to do it. But it felt like something I wasn't supposed to know though, like it was supposed to be a secret of his. I'd been rehearsing what to say over and over—how I saw the same picture that he has in his room back home, how Mila at the store said she used to be their neighbor—all leading up to what I'd really been wanting to tell him, that *yes, they'd be so proud of you, despite whatever you think about yourself. How could anybody not be proud to have you as their son?* But I couldn't bring myself to do it. For as much as I preach opening up to each other and making ourselves vulnerable to each other, I couldn't do it. Instead, I asked, "Do you wanna check out the RHA banquet with me? I'm gonna go either way."

"Anything to keep me from going back and staring at my notes," he said as he pushed himself up. We swung by our rooms to change into button-down shirts without coordinating it. "Would you believe me if I said Kade's *still* asleep?" Victor told me when he met me back outside.

I laughed through my nose. "Yeah, actually."

"You wanna go up and pee on him?"

You'd think with a name like 'A Blue Carpet Affair' that the banquet would be a black-tie event, but it felt more like a cocktail hour at an unassuming wedding reception. I was wrong in thinking that the only people who would be gathering in the big event room on the top floor of Bixby would be House Council members and RAs and GAs and RHA members, because the place was actually pretty packed. Maybe everybody was just that sick of studying. Victor and I were debating on whether to hit up the food tables or the selfie station first when Ethan, dressed like he was getting his senior picture taken, found us. "How was your nap?" I asked him.

"Not bad," he smiled, though his eyes told me he could've slept longer. "I'm already looking forward to going back to bed though."

The food was even more low-key than I was expecting it to be—but let's be real, what college freshman is going to complain about a free meal, even if it is stuff like fruit salad, pigs-in-a-blanket, and sandwich rings? *"And* there's agua *fresca?"* I gasped. "That's boujee as shit." And it wasn't just one flavor, either—there were like *five,* and they never ran dry.

The three of us stuck together, taking pictures in comically oversized sunglasses and hats, but I didn't forget that Ethan and I were technically each other's dates to the whole thing. While he and the rest of Kessler's House Council waited their turn to take group pictures, I made my way over to the DJ table to request a song that I knew Ethan would like, thanks to the video he'd uploaded a year or so ago of him playing it. And was I surprised to see that Sam was DJ'ing the event? Yeah, actually.

"You're just a man in high demand," I greeted him. He stuffed his bruschetta in his mouth so he could give me a fist bump.

"Yeah, I guess so," he said like he was surprised by it too.

"Are you taking any requests?"

"Only if it fits the vibe." The vibe was a 50/50 mix of hip-hop and Frank Sinatra-esque jazz.

"'Kissing a Fool' by George Michael?" I asked.

He gave me a knowing smile. "It's already in the queue."

"Love it. Thanks, man," I said as I walked off, even though he didn't actually do anything for me.

I learned just how well-known Ethan is from how many people came up to him to say hi and good luck and all that. And I guess Kessler's GA Jen wasn't joking when she said that Ethan talks about me a lot, because people were even telling *me* how glad they were to meet me. "I almost feel like we're a celebrity couple here," Ethan laughed, flashing me back to prom when Dillon told me how we were probably the most popular couple there as he smiled that smile that I used to get so drunk off of. I was too infatuated back then to realize that I was always just something for him to show off. "What, don't you think so?" Ethan asked, shaking me from my thoughts.

I saw Westley coming over to us just then, which saved me from having to either lie or talk about my ex. "Here comes your opponent," I muttered.

"Ethan, Trevor. Howdy," Westley said like he was in good spirits. "It's good to see you both here."

"Hey Westley," Ethan responded. "It's good to see you here too." I couldn't tell if they were being genuine or fake.

"Nice event, huh?" Westley looked around at the room before glancing at Ethan. "You know, Trevor, when I saw Ethan's bruise at RHA, I told him that he shouldn't let his boyfriend hit him like that." *Wait, what the fuck?* "I mean, how can he run an organization when he can't even stand up to his own boyfriend?"

"What the *fuck*?" I scowled. "I'd *never*—"

"You look like you haven't been sleeping too well either, Ethan," Westley spoke over me. "Wait—don't tell me you've been losing sleep over this," he chuckled.

Ethan just glared at him. "I'll tell you whatever you want me to tell you if you'll leave us alone."

"*Whatever* I want?" Westley stroked his chin. "Okay, how about you tell me that you'll forfeit the results if you win?" *Oh please.*

"You must not be too confident in yourself if you're resorting to *that*," I snapped.

"Whatever you wanna tell yourself," Westley smirked. "I'll see you later—or not." He walked off just as Victor and his fresh plate of snacks found us.

"So I'm *pretty* sure there were two people in the same bathroom stall, and I'm pretty sure they were—" He registered the looks on our faces. "Yikes, what happened?"

"Just some fucking Slytherin, and not the good kind," I said as I put my hand on Ethan's shoulder. "Do you wanna get some air?"

Ethan just nodded. "Air sounds good."

We stepped out onto the rooftop terrace, where we took in the view of downtown campus. *There's no way Westley didn't have something to do with what happened to Ethan.* "Don't let him get to you," I nudged Ethan as we leaned on the railing. "You kept your cool way better than I would've. I would've told him to fuck the fuck off."

"Trust me, I'm not. There's just a lot happening—Finals, practicing for our set on Saturday, the thought of going home." He breathed in as he gazed across the buildings of the Quad. "I just can't believe Westley," he shook his head. "Like, how fucking full of himself *is* he? That's *exactly* why I never wanted to be friends with the popular kids in school. I *never* wanted to be like that."

"And that's why I love you," I pecked his cheek. "Well, that and some other things. But can we please talk about how he was acting like a 12-year-old?"

We laughed at each other's impressions of Westley and hung around outside until we finished our snacks. "I wonder if my date is going to ask me to dance at all," Ethan asked nobody in particular as he licked some ranch dressing off his finger.

"I was waiting until we were finished with our food!" I said.

"Okay, well..." He gestured to the empty plate.

I bowed and extended my hand to him. "Would you like to join me on the dance floor?"

He took my hand. "I would."

Victor folded his paper plate like a taco and dropped it in the trash. "Anybody opposed to people thinking we're a throuple?" he said with food in his mouth.

Being totally sober meant that it took like six songs for me to start dancing. We were taking an agua fresca break when my song came on. "Oh *hell* yes," Ethan said as he pulled me by my arm back onto the dance floor. "I *love* this song." I smiled to myself. *Go the fuck ahead, Trevor.*

Anybody who had a problem seeing two guys slow dancing forehead-to-forehead together kept their assholery to themselves, not that we were the only queer couple there. I opened my eyes to see Ethan's staring back into mine. "This is really nice," he said.

"The whole thing, or just us?"

"Well, both, but I meant just us. This is like the prom experience I never got to have."

"Well then, mission accomplished," I smiled.

He pulled back to look at me. "What do you mean?"

"I asked you if you wanted to be my date to this, and then I requested this song for you so we could slow dance together, because I wanted to try to give you the prom experience you didn't get to have."

He stopped moving so he could hold me tight. "I don't know what I did to deserve you," he said into the side of my head.

We didn't speak as we orbited in place so we could enjoy our once-in-a-lifetime moment together. Everybody and everything else disappeared around us. I thought about the alternate universes where Trevor and Ethan are dancing together as each other's dates to prom, where they're dancing together at their friend's wedding, where they're dancing together at their own wedding. I fought to not tear up. *You could never begin to imagine how much of my life I've let you take up, Ethan.* His own wet eyes told me that perhaps he too was thinking about the same things. *"I can't even say that it was everything I ever dreamed of, because I could've never imagined that it could've been with someone like you,"* he whispered when the song ended. I wiped his eyes for him before kissing him slowly. *"I love you so fucking much."* We just stood there and held each other even as the next song totally killed our vibe.

"I wish you could've seen yourselves out there," Victor said tenderly when we rejoined him. I started thinking sad thoughts about how he's probably never gotten to dance with someone he loves.

Ethan's phone started to ring, and the color left his face when he saw the screen. "Oh *shit.* It's my mom." My eyebrows shot up. He looked from me to Victor and back like he was waiting for our command.

"You should probably answer it," I said.

"I *really* don't wanna answer it."

"Well don't then. I know if it was me though, I'd rather just get it over with."

Ethan squeezed his eyes shut and took a deep breath before answering the call. "Hello? Hi Mom. Yeah, I'm good. Hang on, let me go somewhere quieter. Yeah, there's this end-of-the-year—" The people he pushed himself through drowned out his words.

I gave Victor a concerned look. "I get the feeling she's not calling just to figure out when they're coming to pick him up."

Time moved so slow that I was starting to think I was on acid again. I couldn't do anything other than stress-eat cheese and crackers while thinking about the conversation he was having. I kept checking my phone only to see that not even a minute had passed. I finally went out to check on him, but didn't see him anywhere. I was wondering if he ran away to start a new life somewhere until I spotted him sitting by himself at the far end of the atrium, watching the evening sun sink through the windows. He turned to me as I approached, looking like he'd been crying. *Oh no. Oh no no no no no no no no.* I slid into the seat beside him on the couch to let him collapse into me.

"She said she still loves me," he sobbed, shaking, wetting my shirt with his tears. My chest bounded, soared. I was so happy for him that I could've cried too. *Happy tears. Fantastic tears. It's going to be okay.*

I pulled him off of me to look at him in the face, glistening eyes and sad smile and all. "I'm so happy to hear that," was all I said.

"I can't believe it," he choked out. "All this time, I thought she was gonna say..." *You thought she was gonna say that you're no son of hers. You thought she was gonna force you to repent. You thought she was gonna throw you out of the house.*

"People can surprise you sometimes," I told myself as much as I told him. "You can be yourself at home now," I nudged him.

"It's gonna be so weird," he sniffled. "I can't wait."

We watched the golden-hour campus deepen in color under the setting sun, at least one of us thinking about how sunsets and life can both change before your eyes without you ever even realizing it. "She *did* say that my stepdad isn't thrilled though," Ethan said.

My fingers glitched as I caressed his back. "Is that what you expected?"

"More or less."

"He's not your dad though. Fuck what he thinks."

"Yeah, but I still have to live in the same house as him though."

"At least you have your mom on your side," I pointed out. "Having someone there who support you makes all the difference." Just ask me, ask Ryder, ask Kade, ask every other person who's ever felt like they don't belong.

"She also said she's looking forward to meeting you," he turned to me to smile. "When they come to pick me up."

"I'm looking forward to meeting her too," I smiled back. "When exactly are they coming to get you?"

"*Exactly?* Like, down to the millisecond?" he smirked. I just gave him a look. "My last exam is Thursday morning, so I guess in the early afternoon?" I counted down the number of days I have left with him before we'll be separated for the Summer. *Eleven days.*

"Are they gonna announce the election winners soon?" I asked.

"Probably. I guess we should head back in."

We returned to the banquet with our hands clasped together, and found Victor vacantly nodding along as Chadwick Patterson was telling him about the proper way to string a crossbow. Ethan and I stood by, catching Victor's eye and trying not to crack up. Chadwick only shut up when Victor finally just walked away.

"Would you believe that all I said was 'what's up?'" Victor chuckled before turning to Ethan. "So...how'd that go?"

"Better than I ever thought," Ethan said like he was about to start laughing.

"I'm so glad to hear that—forreal," Victor smiled just as Ciara asked the room for its attention from the stage set up at the far end of the room.

"Is it okay if I go find the rest of my House Council?" Ethan asked me. Even though *I* was his date, it only seemed right to me that he should share the moment with the people who'd been with him since the beginning.

"Yeah, of course." I sent him off with a peck. "You got this." He looked at me with a lip-biting grin before disappearing into the crowd.

Ciara, decked-out in a dress and heels, thanked us all for coming, thanked the people who made it all possible, all the usual speech stuff. "And now," she said as she gestured off to the side of the stage, "please help me in welcoming NHU's Director of Residence Life and the advisor to the RHA executive board, Frankie Biddercombe."

With a name like Frankie, I expected their advisor to either be a 77-year-old woman or a 31-year-old gay guy who still thinks he's a twink, but from his glasses to his plaid shirt to his bowtie, he fit the vibe of what I thought college professors would look like before I actually met any. "Greetings, ladies, gentlemen, and other esteemed folks who either bend or transcend the gender binary," he started off.

"I like him already," I muttered to Victor, who nodded.

"Like Ciara said, my name is Frankie. Being the Director of Residence Life is like being Santa Claus in a way, because I know about all the times any of you have been bad. I don't care if you're good though." He shot us a smile. "Thank you for spending your last relaxing Sunday of the year here with us. I saw all the hard work that went into this event, so I know how much the students who put it together appreciate you being here." I expected him to go into a commercial about how wonderful of an organization RHA is and how we should all think about getting involved with it, but he didn't even mention it after that.

"I'm sure that most of you, if not *all* of you, have heard somebody say to you how your years at college will be the best years of your life—how they're the years you learn things about yourself, the years you discover new things, the years you broaden your worldview, the years you build lifelong friendships." *Check, check, check, and hopefully check.* "But that isn't true," Frankie said with a finger in the air and a twinkle in his eye. "Your college years have *the potential* to be the best years of your life. Your college years have *the potential* to be the years you discover new things, and so on and so forth. Because you can't sit around and expect everything to just happen! You need to go out and *make* it happen." He pointed around the room at us. "Your years at school are only as good as *you* make them."

"Because you see, your time here at NHU is like a day at the theme park," he went on. "You and your friends spend the day at the theme park because you want to have fun and have a good time with each other, but just because you *go* doesn't mean you're *guaranteed* that. What happens to you once you're inside is all up to *you.* You could just stick to the rides you know you like, or you could try something new. Maybe you ride all the big roller coasters, or maybe you wait while your friends ride it because it's too scary for you." *Gulp.* I swear his eyes lingered on me as he said it. "You could play all kinds of games and win prizes, or maybe you don't play any games. You could eat French fries, or you could eat a funnel cake. It's all up to you. 10,000 people can be at the park at the same time and each and every one of them will have a different day."

"Now, since I assume that most of you are either freshmen or sophomores, I ask you this—how will you spend your time here? Will you take advantage of your time, or will you let your time take advantage of *you?*" My wrist drew my eyes down to it. *Unless.* "And of course I'm not just talking about your years here at NHU —every year has the potential to be the best year of your life, just like every day has the potential to be the best day of your life."

"Now enough of me! Enjoy the food! Enjoy the music! Enjoy each other! And enjoy the rest of the evening!" he concluded. The applause that followed him off was definitely more authentic than the applause he walked on to. *Where the hell was that kind of pep talk when I was in middle school?*

Ciara returned to the front of the stage. "Thank you for those words, Frankie. As always, your wisdom is invaluable." Frankie gave a *what-can-I-say?* shrug from where he stood. "Now, over the past week, you've all—hopefully—cast your votes for your RHA e-board members for the next academic year, and I'm happy to say the results are in," she smiled. "I'm not gonna give a speech or anything because I know we all have stuff to do, so I'll get right to it."

Frankie passed her an envelope from the stack that materialized in his hands. "Your next RHA National Conference Chair is—"

One at a time, she announced the winner of each position. Different pockets of people cheered their friends in celebration. *This forreal is just a popularity contest— and in that case, Ethan's about to flex on everybody.* Each of the Vice-President-elects and the cute, preppy-looking Parliamentarian-elect made their way to the stage through successive rounds of applause for a congratulatory hug from Ciara before lining up on stage.

"And finally," Ciara smiled as she opened the last envelope, "the President of your next Residence Hall Association is..."

At least four assholes in the room were securely fastened shut.

"Ethan Eastwood!" she happily shrieked.

"YES!" Victor and I whooped as we high-fived. Ethan's House Council erupted around him, and the cheers and backslaps that followed him to the front told me that it wasn't even a tight race. Even the genuine excitement Ciara hugged him with gave away which of her protégés she was partial to. The President-elect joined his new board of colleagues, accepting hugs and handshakes from them. He smiled into the room like it dazzled him. I didn't know where Westley was, but I would've loved to have seen the look on his face.

Ciara presented the officers to the room. "Give it up for your RHA Executive Board for the 2023-2024 year!" It would've been the perfect confetti moment, but I guess nobody wanted to deal with *that* mess. I thought about all the students living on campus who won't have to change their living arrangements because of their gender identities, all the future students who will face one less form of discrimination because once upon a time there was a President of some student organization who fought for a more inclusive campus. *Campus is gonna change for the better, all thanks to you, Ethan.*

Like it was Open Mic Night, Ethan thanked his supporters as he made his way back to his biggest fan, who congratulated him with a kiss that might've been a *little* too passionate for a room full of people. "Hap-py birth-day, mis-ter pre-si-dent," I sang sensuously.

"But it's not my birthday!" he laughed.

I put a finger to his chest. "But *you're* the President now."

"Not yet I'm not! I get sworn in on Wednesday!"

He got whisked away to take like a million pictures with current and future e-board members alike. I pulled out my phone to break the news to Kade without caring if he was asleep or not and saw that he'd texted me just a minute beforehand.

Dude
So it was like 7:10 when I got into bed
And when I opened my eyes it was 7:18
And then I realized it was 7:18 PM
☻☻☻☻
I literally just slept all fucking day

May 1

Ten more days before Ethan will be missing from me.

Ethan sent me a screenshot of the official election results this morning, and his margin of victory over Westley was 58 to 34, which was the biggest of any seat!

In other news, I had to delete my AP News app for the sake of my mental health after I read that a guy in Texas shot and killed five of his neighbors because one of them asked him to stop randomly firing his gun. People say it's their civil liberties to be an asshole and that it's their freedom to own a gun for every cell in their body, but what about the rest of us? Are the freedoms of a few more important than the freedoms of the many, like the freedom of not having to live in constant fear for your own safety and well-being? The freedom from persecution? The freedom to be yourself? Life, liberty, and the pursuit of happiness? Do none of those matter anymore? I can't fucking take this country anymore. Remind me again why people who live in the mountains and wear tin foil on their heads are the crazy ones? I'll take being ignorant if it means being mentally stable.

The others were shooketh when I told them at lunch that I'm done with the news. "So what, you don't wanna be informed anymore?" Victor accused me.

"You sound like a libertarian," I fired back, making Ethan snort. "I'll just get all the important news from you guys."

"You're doing exactly what the Illuminati wants you to do," Kade said. "You're becoming a sheeple."

"I'm not becoming a *sheeple*," I scowled. "How about I give *you* shit when you stop doing something that's not good for *your* mental health?" *That* shut him up.

"What if you only check it like once a week?" Ethan suggested. "Or don't let it get to you?"

I laughed out loud. "You're telling *me* to not let something get to me?"

"Imagine if all the people who've changed things for the better had stopped their work because they read something they didn't like," Victor persisted. "If anything, getting upset should spur you into doing something about it."

"I mean, yeah, but what can we do other than vote and get involved with groups on campus, which—correct me if I'm wrong—*none* of us are part of." Their silence told me I had a point. "I can be the most informed person out there, but being informed by itself isn't good for much."

"You're right," Victor admitted. "I could be doing more, and I'm not."

"College students have a lot going on," Kade said.

"Not *really* though. Not *me* anyway."

"What if we agree to make an effort next semester?" Ethan suggested. "We can each join a group and hold each other accountable and motivate each other, like gym buddies?"

Kade sat up. "Do gym buddies still jerk each other off?"

We laughed and promised to make the commitment to get more involved. I'll probably give Proud as Halle another try since Bradley and his friends will be graduating, but I'm sure there'll still be someone who will accuse me of not being gay enough.

Ethan scared me when he called me later on while I was at work, saying "I'm fucking *livid*" as I answered.

"Oh no," I said nervously, praying that I wasn't the one he was livid at. "What's wrong? What are you livid about?"

"We just got an email from SGB telling us that we can't play at the fucking Summer Send-Off!"

My jaw dropped. "What?! Why?"

"Here, let me pull the email back up. I mean, I think it's pretty fucking convenient that Westley, the acolyte to the organization that's putting it on, loses the election to me, and then we get this the next day. Here it is—*'After further consideration, we regret to inform you that your group does not satisfy the requirements to perform at this year's Summer Send-Off event.'* Like, what fucking requirements? Like, what the fucking shit?" he practically yelled. I'd never seen him so angry before.

"So you think it's a retaliation thing?"

"I mean, I don't know why else. Why the fuck would it be an issue all of a sudden?"

I had nothing. "Do the others know?"

"Yeah, that's how I found out. Victor texted me in all caps."

I sighed, feeling so defeated for them, and helpless that there wasn't anything I could do. "So what are you gonna do?"

"I don't fucking know." He ran his hand through his hair. "I guess *not* play at the Summer Send-Off."

Feeling defeated turned into feeling pissed—pissed at how not having the right connections to the right people gets you left out and left behind. Isn't that what Dr. Jurado told us on day one? But does that mean we have to just sit back and eat it?

"Okay," I said. "Fuck 'em then. Have your own concert."

Ethan blinked. "Have our own concert," he repeated.

"Yeah. Set up in the Quad or on the roof of Bixby or somewhere. You don't need SGB's blessing to put on a show." *I* wasn't even sure how serious I was being, but Ethan didn't shoot me down.

"*Okay,*" Ethan said, "say we wanna play our own show. We don't have the proper equipment or anything."

I bit the inside of my cheek. "Maybe we can see if Sam or anybody from the Music department can hook us up?"

Ethan still wasn't sold. "Even if they do and if they can, it's *five days* away. How would we get the word out? How would we get people to come to our shitty-ass show instead of the *Summer Send-Off?*"

"We can get Sam to mention it on the radio! We can get Amina or Kade to make posters, we get people we know to tell people *they* know! It'll be just like campaigning again!" *How is he not stoked for this?* "You wanna be a concert promoter someday? Here you go. Here's your practice."

His silence told me he was really thinking about it. "What if people don't show up?"

I gave him an *I'm-done-with-this* eye roll. "Look, you can either put on your own show, or you don't play anything at all. But I think people will come. Forget everything that people know *you* from—remember how big the crowd was at the last Open Mic Night? They'll be so fucking stoked to hear you guys play a whole-ass concert!"

He turned it over in his head. "*Goddammit,*" he finally smiled, "I guess we have some work to do then."

May 2

Nine more days.

Whoever decided that May should be Mental Health Month must've been a student, because it's too convenient that it coincides with Finals. "I wish they had therapy dogs on campus all year round," Victor said after we and literally every other person on campus paid them a visit in Bixby during Common Hour. I wonder if the therapy dogs get overwhelmed and stressed out from having to see so many people, and then need their own therapy session to unwind from it?

For as imperative as they're *rapidly* becoming, we neglected studying for Finals in favor of an evening of Domino's pizza, Siouxsie & The Banshees, cold brews, and the occasional cigarette break, but I think we have a pretty decent plan. The Quad was out of the question as a concert venue since 24-hour Quiet Hours is in effect there as well, and a concert is considered "loud, boisterous, or disruptive activity." The roof of Bixby obviously wasn't allowed, and Bamberger was a no-go since we'd have to pay a *very* pretty penny to use it. The Alumni Amphitheater would be cool, but I doubt it was built to withstand earthquakes. Kade was actually the one who had the idea for the field hockey field. "The noise shouldn't be a problem, since it's literally on the edge of campus," he said.

"And it's on the way to The Commons!" I said. "People will literally have to pass by it to get there!"

"Who do we ask to see if we can use it?"

"Oh! I think I might know," Amina said as she opened her Mac. "Here, help me figure out how we wanna word this…" Whoever she emailed was on top of their shit, because we got their blessing within the hour.

"Okay, but what about a stage?" Victor asked. "The Theatre department might have something, but it's probably just some shitty little platform."

"Lemme ask Ciara," Ethan said as he reached for his phone. "If there's anybody who has a ton of connections, it's her."

"Do you remember that band that played at Homecoming? *They* played on a stage."

"That's right!" Ethan gasped. "CPB has a stage!"

I raised an eyebrow. "Do you really think CPB would undermine its parent organization's event?" It turns out that not only they would, but they *gladly* would. CPB's Vice President of Programming, Carter, has been going to Open Mic Night all year, and has been one of Ethan's fans ever since his first performance.

"*I am indignant over the way they treated you, and frankly I'm almost embarrassed to be associated with them at the moment,*'" Ethan read Carter's email aloud. "He said yes they have stage, and yes we can use it for 'free-ninety-nine.'"

Victor and I traded looks. "Free-ninety-nine?" he asked.

"Free-ninety-nine," Ethan smiled.

The aspiring graphic designer enthusiastically took it upon herself to create a poster to put up in the high-traffic spots around campus. "Holy *fuck*," Amina said to her laptop. "*Two* posters from Printing Services cost $55?"

Kade gave her a confused look. "Why wouldn't you just print them yourself from the digital media studio in Arrowood?"

She stared at him before laughing to herself. "Goddammit Kade, you're a genius."

"Are you allowed to use that stuff for personal use?" the stickler in me blurted out.

"When has anyone ever gotten anything done by following the rules?" Amina asked me as she met Kade's high-five.

"And doesn't SGB *own* Printing Services?" Ethan chimed in. "Aren't we trying to shove it up their ass anyway?"

"Guys," Kade grinned as he grabbed his head, "we're *actually* fucking doing this."

"And what about Sam?" I asked. "We can see if he'd be willing to give you another shoutout." I emailed him—"*I'm the guy who asked you to play 'Kissing a Fool' at the RHA banquet*"—to ask if he'd be "interested in helping an underdog crusade against the establishment," and if so, if I could meet up with him to fill him in on the deets.

"So what would you need from me?" Sam asked after I'd explained our situation to him today at Common Hour at the table in Rosenberg where he'd set up shop with his laptop and a wreck of notes.

"Honestly, just getting the word out would probably be the biggest help," I said as I pulled on my fingers. "So if you could like, shout them out? Maybe like every day? But I know WXNU is funded by SGB though, so I don't know if it would be like a conflict of interest or something."

"Yeah, I can do that," Sam nodded. "And I don't care if it's a conflict of interest or not. I'm on Team Ethan all the way."

I could've hugged him. "Thanks. That'll be huge."

"How big is this thing gonna be?" he asked.

"As big as we can get it, I guess. The bigger the better."

"Love it. Do you need any equipment? Speakers? Anything?"

"I mean, they have their own amps," I said, realizing how dinky it sounded. "And Victor'll have his real drum set too."

Sam leaned back and crossed his arms. "I can hook you up with whatever else you need. And if I don't have it, then I can probably get it." *Ah, the old blank cheque.*

I blinked. "You're *sure?* I mean—*yeah*, that would be...*wow*." He had me give him their email addresses so I wouldn't have to keep being their messenger.

"Perf, I'll see what I can do," he said. "Thanks for letting me be a part of this, by the way."

I put my chair back at the table I stole it from. "Why are you doing all this for us?" I asked him. "I mean, the radio announcements are one thing, but letting us use your stuff, and getting stuff for us?"

He laughed through his nose. "Let's just say that you guys aren't the only ones with a vendetta against SGB." Like Dr. Jurado did indeed tell us, it's all about who you know. And since things have always come easy for SGB, they've forgotten what a determined group of students are capable of—students who've been itching to give them a big middle finger.

"We're hitting up Taco Tuesday after this, right?" Tylor asked me as we waited for Macro to start later on.

I raised an eyebrow. "Does the pope shit on little boys?"

They smirked. "You think Jurado will wanna go with us?"

I wouldn't have considered it if it was any other professor, but the guy has 'Riviera Maya' written all over him for Christ's sake. But going with some random-ass students though? "I don't know." I shrugged. "What the hell though—the worst he'll do is say no."

Class felt like one of those scenes from an '80s high school movie of some boring-ass class that nobody wanted to be in—nothing against Jurado's classes. The vibe was one of chewing gum, doodles, a clock that you could hear ticking, pencil mustaches, and jeans washed so light they could pass as a glacier. "Come on, guys," Jurado said, "I know you're all ready to be done and get out of here for the Summer, but you're almost there. I know you can do it," he encouraged us before turning back to the board. "Now, suppose that all the nations bordering the South China Sea relinquish their claims to the region. How might that affect the rates of a bed and breakfast in Algeria?"

"Can we have class outside?" a voice from somewhere a couple desks ahead of us asked instead of answering.

Instead of automatically saying no, Jurado walked over to the window after a moment and looked down at the Quad. "Will you *promise* to pay attention if we go outside?" he asked. We nodded furiously, and he exhaled through his nose before smiling a resigned smile.

So that's how we got to have class outside. Students in the other rooms watched us on our way out, jealous that there were people who got to leave the building and that it wasn't them. Out in the Quad, Jurado led us to the gazebo, where we settled on the seats and on the floor, making the lone student who was already there pack up their stuff and leave. I thought everybody's attention span would tank, but we all seemed to be even more focused, and were actually getting into his lesson like we had a stake in it. *Is this the next breakthrough in academic instruction?* Conservatives will call it being lazy.

At the end of the period, Tylor and I hung back while the others radiated away from the gazebo after thanking Jurado for class. *"Ask him,"* Tylor urged me.

"Why do I have to?" I whispered as I watched Jurado head back towards Ebersol.

"You're gonna miss him!" Tylor said in a sing-song voice.

Cursing Tylor for their forced lessons in personal growth, I caught Jurado before he got too far away. "Excuse me, sir," I called before I could chicken out, feeling high-key awkward. *Who asks their professor to grab dinner with them? Students who wanna sleep with them, that's who.*

"Trevor!" he smiled. "What's up?"

"We—Tylor and I—we were gonna go grab some tacos from the Student Center, and we were wondering if you'd like to come with us." His silent stare only upped the awkwardness. "Tuesdays are Taco Tuesday at Percy's Grille."

Jurado just blinked. "You're asking me if I would like to go get tacos with you?"

"Yes sir. You get two tacos for $2." Behind me, Tylor nodded.

"How long have they had that?" Jurado asked like he was upset.

"I wanna say for like maybe a month now?"

Jurado let his hand fall against his side like he was ready to storm off. "And you've been keeping this a secret from me this whole time? *God,* you kids need to tell me these things!"

"So...is that a yes?" I asked.

"Yes, it's a yes! When are you going?"

"We were gonna head over there now," I answered with a small smile.

"I'll be right down—let me grab my stuff from my office," he said. I swear I heard him muttering to himself as he marched off.

Tylor and I waited for him to return, and led him up to Bixby like we were taking an older family member somewhere new. One or two students gave him a wave that he returned, greeting them by name. At Percy's, he ordered his tacos like a dad ordering a Happy Meal. I thought about offering to pay for his, but figured that'd be weird.

"I'm sure my son'll be here every Tuesday next year," Jurado said as we found a table. "He would've been coming this year too, had we *known* about it," he said with a roll of his eyes.

"Does your son go here?" Tylor asked.

"Not yet. He'll be starting in the Fall. It'll cost him like ten bucks since I work here." I could almost see Dad materializing over Jurado's shoulder and giving me a glare. "So is this your way of thanking me for giving you your best class of the day?"

"Nah, we were gonna ask you anyway," I said. He raised an eyebrow at me. "I swear! We talked about it before class even started!"

"We actually did," Tylor backed me up. "But yes, it was the best class of the day."

I was low-key worried there'd be a lot of awkward silence, but Jurado's so easy to talk to, so real, and so down-to-earth. He asked us about ourselves, and not just what we're majoring in or what we want to do with our lives once we're out of here. He listened intently as we told him what we like doing and how we spend our time. He didn't look fazed when I mentioned that I have a boyfriend. He seemed to enjoy hearing how we're more than just one-dimensional students in one of his classes probably as much as we enjoyed hearing that he's more than just an NPC in our own lives. I can only dream of spending my 20s the way he did—on top of the things he'd already told us in class, he spent his junior year studying abroad in Barcelona, dug wells in Sri Lanka, almost got arrested in Tijuana, and backpacked through the Andes. "I would've worked as a fisherman on the Red Sea too if I hadn't bumped into this girl at the bus station."

"Your wife?" I guessed.

He nodded. "I canceled my plans, we started dating, and got married a few months later."

I sat back, the romantic in me glad to hear a good love story. I'm jealous of people who fall in love so authentically and so quickly without any plans to do so. Like, what does it feel like to meet somebody and *know* that you're going to spend the rest of your life with them? And what does it mean if I've never felt that? Is there somebody out there who would totally bowl me over if I met them, who would leave me captivated with a single 'hello?' *Somebody already* did, *you pube. Remember?*

I was surprised that Jurado remembered or even cared about the campaign pitch I gave for Ethan in class. "Did your friend have his election yet?" he asked me.

"He's actually the boyfriend in question," I smiled. "But yeah, he ended up winning it!"

Jurado slapped his palms on the table. "Good for him! What was it for again?"

"He'll be the President of RHA—the Residence Hall Association. It's the group that oversees all the House Councils."

"I used to be in House Council when I was an undergrad student," Jurado said. "The treasurer, if you can believe it."

Tylor smirked. "I never would've guessed."

"So yeah, he's becoming kind of a big deal on campus," I talked Ethan up. "He and our other friends started a band for Open Mic Nights at a coffee shop in town, and now they have kind of a fanbase on campus."

"Oh really? What kind of music do they play? What's their band name?"

"Mostly covers of obscure-ish alternative songs. And they're called"—I couldn't keep a straight face—"Three Lesbians in a Wheelchair."

Jurado choked on his food, turning more than a few heads with his hearty laugh. A piece of something that he coughed up almost hit me on the arm. "I love it!" he said as he wiped his eye. It took a few more coughs and a drink of his unsweetened iced tea for him to calm down.

"They were gonna play at the Summer Send-Off event this weekend, but they got kicked out because SGB didn't like that he won the election," Tylor filled him in. "So they're having their own concert instead at the field hockey field."

"My son would probably like them. He hates anything that plays on the radio."

"Between that and liking tacos, I feel like I'd get along with him," I chuckled. *And bonus points if he's cute.*

Instead of responding to that, Jurado looked off into the dining area like he wanted to say something but wasn't sure if he should, tapping his fingers on the table. "What I'm about to say is something I typically reserve for upperclassmen."

I held my breath. *He's gonna tell us he shoots porn and wants to know if we'd be actors for him.*

"My wife and I are having our end-of-the-semester party at our house on Friday night, and I would love it if you could come if you're not gonna be up to anything." *Wait, WHAT?* Tylor and I exchanged glances to make sure we heard right. "It won't be a bunch of 50-year-olds just sitting around or anything, if that's what you're thinking." *That's exactly what I was thinking.* "It's always a fun time."

"I'm not sure what our plans are yet," I answered for us, looking at Tylor like they were a cue card.

"Well, think about it. I'll forward you the invite. And I *get* it if you don't wanna come," he said like he could tell we thought it sounded stupid. "If one of my professors had ever asked me that, I would've said no and then laughed with my friends about it while we got drunk off of hooch."

We both laughed with him. "Yeah, we'll see what we're up to, and let you know either way."

"Seriously though, no pressure if you don't want to," he said as he pushed out his chair. "Well, I'd love to sit and talk more, but I can feel those jalapeños starting to fight back, and I didn't bring any Tums with me. Enjoy not having to take antacids while you can." We tossed our trash and bumped elbows with him. "And thanks for asking me to tag along. I enjoyed talking with you two."

"Sure thing," I said. "And I enjoy listening to your stories too, even if they make me feel pathetic about myself."

"Oh shut up. What are you, 20?"

"19," I corrected him.

"Oh *please*. The rest of your life is a blank canvas. And no matter what anybody ever tries to tell you, *you're* the one holding the brush. Don't ever forget that." He winced and put a fist to his chest. "Just heartburn," he assured us.

"Go get your Tums," Tylor teased him. "We'll see you in class."

So that's how we not only got to enjoy a taco dinner with my now-favorite professor, but also got invited to his house party.

"Okay, I *100%* thought he was gonna ask us if we wanted to blaze it with him," Tylor laughed after Jurado and the two of us went on our ways.

"I mean, he pretty much *did*."

The lowering sun blinded us as we left Bixby. "So are we gonna get one of those sorority taxi things to take us there and pick us up later, or what?" Tylor asked.

"Wait, you wanna go?"

"Do you *not*?"

"I dunno. Won't it be weird? He said it's gonna be mostly upperclassmen. We're probably not gonna know anybody."

"That's what you *do* at parties—you go and you meet people. It's called socializing. You should try it sometime," they said, making my nostrils flare. "You've been going to the same party over and over all semester. Try something different." *Life begins at the end of your comfort zone.*

"I guess," I caved.

"Besides, look how much fun he is in class. *Now* imagine how much more fun he'll be at his own party where there aren't any rules."

May 3

POV:

You're full on cheese cubes and *pâté* and *gougères* and Dr. Le Marque's homemade *bœuf bourguignon* from the year-end potluck the French Club hosted, listening to the surf rock that the interning WXNU DJ has an affinity for under a tree near Devlin's greenhouse, letting your eyes wander past your book for a moment to appreciate the warmth of the sun and the verdant grass, the trees alive with birds and the flowers alive with insects and the campus alive with people, and how they're all only possible because once upon a time a star formed and fragments coalesced around it into a planet that somehow got water onto it that gave way to life, and millions of years of evolution later, here you are. And considering how many other planets that are without water or that are just a little too close or just a little too far from their stars, it's pretty fucking amazing that I'm able to be here and consciously appreciate it all.

As promised, Jurado emailed Tylor and me the invite to his 'Spring luau.' *I hope the party's as colorful as the invitation.* I crept his address on Maps and saw that he actually lives just down the road from downtown New Halle. "It doesn't say anything about bringing a guest though," I said apologetically to Ethan, who was all for me going.

"That's okay," he smiled. "I'll just go to 370 Rock with the others. It's not like we're gonna die if we're not at the same party. We'll still have Saturday night."

Last night was the last Lit Club meeting of the year, which meant there were more snacks than usual. It *is* kind of a lame club, but I enjoyed it, and it got me out of my room. It's where I met Miles. I'm not sure if I'll stick with it next year or not though. I guess I'll have to see what else I end up getting involved in. For my last hurrah from atop The Stool, I channeled Malcolm X to promote Three Lesbians in a Wheelchair's reactionary concert, though Amina's posters did a *way* more bad-ass job at getting the word out. She made them last night, and Kade helped her print them and put them up around campus this morning. The one I saw in Bixby's front windows literally stopped me in my tracks. I was expecting a flier, but it was a poster—a legit concert poster for an *actual* band. She arranged black-and-white cutouts of herself, Ethan, Victor, Kade, and Derrick in action on their respective instruments on top of one another so they look like a Great Wave about to crash over the red-tinted buildings of campus, with a mushroom cloud and lightning bolts collaged in the background. 'THREE LESBIANS IN A WHEELCHAIR' explodes from it in sound-effect-in-a-comic-book font, with the time and place in speech-in-a-comic-book font closer to the bottom. I don't know who SGB has making their posters, but the official Summer Send-Off one looks like it was made from a PowerPoint template next to Amina's.

"What do you think?" the creator herself asked me when she caught me gawking at it.

I forced myself to look away from it. "This is *incredible.*"

"Thanks," Amina said as she admired it beside me.

"How long did this take you?" I asked. "Have the others seen this yet? Where'd you get the pictures?" My questions made her chuckle.

"I just took them from Instagram and YouTube. And it was like after 1 a.m. by the time I finally finished."

"*Woah,*" I said to the poster. By the time I finally pulled myself away from it, a couple other people had stopped to check it out.

"Guys, you gotta peep this shit," Victor said in the video he put on his Instagram and Snapchat stories. *"Is this fuckin' legit or what?"* He zoomed in on himself, furiously brandishing his sticks behind his drum set. *"I look like a goddamn ROCKSTAR."* Ethan, Kade, Tylor, Alex, Miles, Sam, and everybody else who I follow who's a fan of theirs shared it on their own stories too. I even overheard someone in Patnick asking their friend if they saw how "there's gonna be another band coming to campus this weekend." *Those SGB fucks are going to be sorry they ever disqualified them,* I smirked.

May 4

May the 4th be with you. And also with you. Let us pray.

"Now I know you're all excited for the Summer Send-Off this Saturday," Sam said between songs during his radio show, *"but did you know there are actually two concerts happening this weekend? I know, I know, what a time to go to New Halle, amirite? NHU's own Three Lesbians in a Wheelchair will be putting on their own show this weekend, so if you're looking for them at SGB's event at The Commons, they won't be there. I repeat, Three Lesbians in a Wheelchair will NOT be playing at the Summer Send-Off, but all us fans of theirs can see them play their own entire set this Saturday at 1 at the field hockey field. It's on the way to The Commons too, so you don't even have an excuse not to stop by!"*

The tattoo itchies that Victor warned me about are here. I never wanted to scratch the hell out of something so bad before. "Try slapping it," he advised me. "That sometimes helps."

"But I've been getting my wrist slapped for most of my life!" I joked, though it's not really that funny, especially when I was conditioned to do most of the slapping myself.

I figured I'd do something adventurous and visit the buildings I hadn't been in yet, just to say that I've been in them—not all at once or anything, but like just taking a detour through one on the way back from class. I checked off Old Main, which you'd think would be part of orientation, and Vollmer Technical Science Hall, which has more dead-ends and apparently less bathrooms than you'd think. I gave up on my series of side quests after a door in a stairwell in Rafferty spit me out right into a classroom as class was going on.

"You know that used to be a dorm, right?" Tylor laughed when I told them about it later in Macro. "That's why it has a weird-ass layout."

Anybody hoping that class would've been outside again was disappointed. The two of us hung back to let Jurado know that we'd be at his party. "Great!" he said as he clapped his hands together. "I'm looking forward to seeing you both there!"

"Do we need to bring anything?" I offered. "Snacks, or...?"

"Nope," he shook his head with a polite frown, "just your Hawaiian shirts. We'll have plenty of food and drinks."

I was last-night-years-old when I went to an RHA meeting for the first time so I could see Ethan get sworn in. The forums are open to anybody, but let's be real, the only people going either *have* to go, or are from other organizations looking for a co-sponsorship. Since I was neither, I got more than a few *who's-he?* looks, though a couple people I'd met over the past week did say hi to me. I'm not sure if I was surprised to see Westley there or not, who I pointedly avoided looking over at in case we made weird eye contact.

"You don't wanna come with me?" I'd asked Kade earlier. "You don't wanna be there for one of your best friend's proudest moments at NHU?"

Kade just scoffed. "And sit through an hour-and-a-half long meeting that I give zero shits about? I'd rather castrate myself." He shook his head after a second. "Actually, no I wouldn't. But I have better ways to spend my time." And he wasn't saying that to be snarky or anything—Finals Crunch is here, and it's not like I don't have any work to get done. But I still made time to make it to the RHA meeting to support my boyfriend, who I didn't tell I was coming.

"What are you doing here?!" a thoroughly-surprised Ethan asked me with a hug.

"I came to watch you get sworn in," I smiled.

"But don't you have a paper to work on?"

"I'll work on it later," I said. He raised an eyebrow at me. "I'll stay up later if I have to!"

"Isn't getting that done more important than this though?"

I gave him my best puppy-dog look. "Just say it, you don't want me here."

"Oh my god, stop," he smiled as he booped me on the nose.

Kade was right about the meeting being a waste of time. It was like listening to a noise machine teach geography. It was like going to Lowe's. I was bored in like thirty seconds. It wasn't even a real, listening-to-debates, voting-on-amendments kind of meeting—it was just a recap of the banquet and where the year-end budget stands and stuff like that, though there was a girl from the Blue & White Society who sang a short motivational song about finishing the year strong. Even the swearing in of the sharply-dressed incoming e-board members had me trying to hide my yawns, but it was a big moment for Ethan that I wanted to be there for.

"I, Ethan Eastwood," he repeated after Ciara with his hand on the gavel, "as the President of RHA, swear to represent and always act in the interest of the residence hall constituency, to maintain the integrity of the RHA constitution, and to uphold the mission and values expressed therein." His newest Instagram post is of Ciara holding the gavel out to him like she was proposing to him while the other new and outgoing members looked on in exaggerated astonishment.

After the meeting adjourned, Kade and Victor joined the President and me for a celebratory trip to Taco Bell. "I need a study break anyway," Victor said. "My eyes would've fallen out of my head if I had to read about language fallacies any longer."

"Fallacies, like the ancient Greek hero?" I asked like a Victor. Kade was too busy taking a selfie with The Skeletons dressed in graduation regalia and accepting their diplomas to make the phallus joke I was waiting for.

We ordered an unhealthy amount of food for four people, but I feel like we all deserved it. "Hey Trev, 'you know you want me,'" Kade read off a sauce packet.

"Well then," I said as I grabbed one, "'things just got real.'"

"Guys," Victor said, "'I crave myself. Is that wrong?'"

"Oh my god," Ethan said as he let his phone fall to the table. "Guys—a band playing at the Summer Send-Off called Frottage Cheese just asked me if they can open for us at our show." Every part of that had us laughing and slapping each other's shoulders like Heteros.

"Are you fucking forreal dude?"

"Sheesh fam."

"Frottage Cheese? I fucking can't right now!"

We still weren't over it by the time we finished eating. "These Frottage Cheese people must either really hate SGB or really like you," Victor said to Ethan.

"I'm not the only one in the band though!" the unofficial frontman said.

"But you're the face of it! You already had the fanbase before we came along." Victor waved a shaka sign between himself and Kade. "Ain't nobody coming to see us."

"I'd come to see you," I encouraged them.

"Oh, we know you would," Kade winked at me.

May 5

Two too-blue eyes and lips that are
Always spilling the perfect words
Keep you wrapped in me
Long after the slow song ends.

May 6

Five more days.

I picked up a copy of *The Herald* to scan the police blotter—'*May 2—Borough police responded to a call on Picketts Road about the theft of a screwdriver by a male actor on a pedal bicycle*'—at breakfast, and was surprised to see my boyfriend's face smiling up at me from the front page. 'RESIDENTS, MEET YOUR NEW E-BOARD,' the headline read, above a picture taken from the RHA meeting the other day.

"You legit kinda *are* becoming like one of the most popular people on campus," Victor said admiringly after he'd read the article on the newly-elected RHA e-board, which was more about what RHA had done over the past year rather than the members themselves.

"Quit inflating his ego!" Kade pounded on the table as his and Victor's phones went off at the same time. "Derrick said he's just leaving our place now and is on his way," he said after reading the text.

"What's he getting from your house?" I asked.

"Uh, Vic's *drums?*"

"He packed up your drums and loaded them into his car by himself? How big is his car?"

"He's done it before," Victor said simply. "And he drives an SUV, so..."

As much as we wanted to just hang out, we all desperately had studying to do —Victor and Kade especially, since they wouldn't be getting any studying done with their friend visiting. Tylor and I took a study break to make a thrift store run since we didn't know how serious Jurado was being when he told us to bring our Hawaiian shirts to his party. The thrift store's Hawaiian shirt department didn't have anything in my size, but the one I got doesn't look too bad with a t-shirt layered underneath. We were going to get a phallic-shaped statue of some ghost-looking thing as a joke gift for Jurado for inviting us—"Why get him that when we can keep it for ourselves and have some fun with it?"—but found a colorful Day-of-the-Dead-looking skull for him instead, which meant we also had to stop at the dollar store on the way back for a gift bag so we didn't look broke-ass. I could hear faint drums and bass coming from the direction of the Ski Lodge as we parked, but I couldn't make out the song. We went back to our studying in 222 Swafford until the others were finished practicing so we could all meet up for dinner at the foremost dining hall in town.

Derrick must've changed his look sometime since the videos on Victor's YouTube channel were shot, because he legit looks like an H&M model. His skin glistened like it was oiled. *This guy's in a Robotics Club?* He gave Tylor and me each a mating display of a handshake when we met them outside of Patnick. "Wassup, wassup," he said in a voice that was way softer than I expected.

"How's it going?" Tylor asked like the chill person they are.

"Your reputation precedes you," I said like someone with a stick up their ass.

"We were gonna just have pizza delivered to the Ski Lodge, which you apparently *can* do," Victor told us as Pencie swiped us in, "but we didn't want to eat without you. And we wanted *him* to feel the Wrath of Patnick."

"It's cool," Derrick shrugged. "I've been having the Pitt Shits until two days ago."

I waited until Derrick wasn't right there to ask Kade if Derrick works as a model. *"No?"* Kade laughed. "He works at Best Buy. I'm telling him you said that though."

Jurado's invitation said his party started at 7, so Tylor and I waited until like 8:20 to call one of the sorority DD taxis. We weren't even in the car for five minutes when it pulled up to a house set apart from the others with a million cars parked outside. It reminded me of the kind of house in the woods that a group of hornt-up 20-somethings go to spend a weekend in only to get massacred. "I *guess* this is the right place," I muttered.

"Wouldn't *that* be a vibe?" Tylor said as they peered past me out the window. "If we showed up at the wrong place?"

"Could you imagine?" I laughed, although it actually *wouldn't* be that funny, since shooting people who accidentally wander onto your property is apparently the latest trend here in the great U.S. of A-holes. Like, you just wanted to shoot somebody.

A ground-level deck with strings of pineapple lights hanging from the wooden railing wrapped around the entire house and was scattered with people who were all older than me smoking and socializing. From what I could see through the windows, the place looked pretty packed, which just upped my uneasiness. We arbitrarily picked one of the screen doors to enter through, and found ourselves in a great room that seemed to take up most of the house. The party was easily as colorful as the invitation—between the beachcomber hats, garlands of fake hibiscus flowers, and plastic hurricane glasses, I forgot that I was in New Halle for a moment. It was probably the only party on May 5th that wasn't a Cinco de Mayo party, even if the food felt more 'fiesta' than 'luau.' My eyes swept the room for anybody I knew, and we must've looked lost because a nearby girl approached us. "Hi! Glad to see you could make it," she said like we were floormates. *Do I know her from somewhere?* "Are you some of Julian's students?"

"If Julian would happen to be Dr. Jurado," I winced, "then yes."

She stood on her toes to look around the room. "I *swear* I just saw him—oh, here he is!" As happy as I was to see Jurado, it was nowhere near as happy as he was to see us.

"Tylor! Trevor!" he exclaimed as he shook our hands. "Glad you came! And I love the shirts!"

"We're happy to be here," I said genuinely, already feeling like the place was warming up to me. I held out the bag with our gift. "We got a gift for the house as a thank-you."

"Oh! You didn't have to!" Jurado said as he set down his drink to take it. He admired the skull from all sides, having only good things to say about it. "Isa!" he called across the room. "Look at this!" He disappeared for a second, reappearing with a woman at his side. "This is my wife, Isabella. Isa, these are two of my students, Tylor and Trevor."

"It's a pleasure to meet you," she greeted us warmly.

"You as well," Tylor smiled.

"I love your home," I said like an Ethan.

Jurado showed her the skull. "Look what they brought for us!"

"This is *beautiful*, boys," she said as she took it.

"*Tylor goes by they/them*," I heard her husband whisper to her.

"Ohmygosh, I'm so—"

"Don't worry about it," Tylor downplayed it, though I'm sure they've got to be so sick of being misgendered.

Jurado looked around the room before taking the skull over to the fireplace, setting it on the mantle beside some kind of large decorative stone that looked like a Mayan calendar. "It looks good there," I said like my opinion mattered.

Jurado drooped a fake lei over each of our heads like he was giving us his blessing to enjoy the party. And they weren't the cheap, itchy, shitty ones the Health Center uses to promote safe sex. "Help yourself to whatever you want," he invited us. "There's food all over the place—the pork's been on the smoker since last night— and the drinks are in the kitchen. Let either one of us know if you need anything," he said before letting himself get sucked into another conversation.

Tylor and I checked out the food options, which were scattered all over the place—the dining table was crowded with aluminum trays, and every surface had at least one bowl of snacks or a plate of *antojitos* and *tapas* that someone had brought. I could stand anywhere in the house and be within arm's reach of some kind of food. And Jurado wasn't lying when he said it wouldn't be all 50-year-olds— most of the guests looked like they were students. "Not gonna lie," I said, "I was actually expecting this to be way more lame."

"Yeah, samesies," Tylor nodded. "Wanna go see what bevvies there are?"

The Jurado's kitchen had to have been the most densely-populated room in New Halle. We squeezed through bodies to the far counter, where a Hong-Kong skyline of liquor and wine and juice bottles sat open and violated. Cans and bottles of beer lay buried in ice in a tub on the floor. "When he told us to get ourselves a *drink*," I said as I watched people light their cigarettes on the lit stove on their way out onto the deck, "did he mean a *drink* drink?"

"He didn't say *not* to," Tylor said as they reached for a bottle of rum.

I took my daiquiri and plate of *tacos al pastor* over to the pair of couches in front of the fireplace, where the girl who'd welcomed us was sitting with another girl who had a woodpile of Spanish rice on her plate. "So do you know most of these people?" I tried my hand at small talk as I took a seat across from her. "Or did you feel as out-of-place as we did when you arrived?"

"Oh no, I know some people here," she chuckled. "I don't think I introduced myself, but I'm Jolie."

"*Enchanté* Jolie," I smiled. "I'm Trevor, and this is Tylor." Tylor waved as they sat.

"And I'm Hannah," Spanish Rice Girl smiled.

"That's my sister's name too, but with no 'H,'" Tylor told her. *So is their sister's name Hanna, or Annah?*

"How have we lived together this entire time and I only just now learned that?" I asked them.

"Are you two roommates?" Hannah asked before Tylor could give me a smart-ass answer.

Tylor draped their arm over my shoulder. "We're lovers, actually." It took every fiber in me to not spray my drink all over the place.

"Oh, okay!" Hannah said as she probably tried to figure out which of us would do what in bed.

I scanned the room again, picking out Dr. Kershaw from the Business department, who gave us Jurado's evaluation, and who was wearing the same three-piece suit he'd worn then. I got up to get another drink, leaving Tylor and Hannah and Jolie to continue our debate over whether plantains are bananas or not without me. I found Jurado by the drinks, and I listened and laughed along as he recounted a story about how he was almost swindled out of $100 by a gang of schoolchildren on their most recent family vacation to Peru.

"Do you need another drink, Trevor?" he asked. "Everyone, this is Trevor..." He introduced me to the people who'd been listening. "What can I get you? Isa makes a mean margarita."

"Oh *hell no*—I mean, no thank you," I laughed. "I don't do tequila."

"Neither do I," he chuckled.

I nodded to his hurricane glass. "What are *you* drinking?"

"A zombie! You want one?"

So that's how I watched my professor eyeball pours before shaking up an alcoholic beverage for me, a minor. He speared a paper umbrella through a cherry to top it off. "Ta da!" he said as he handed it to me, expectantly watching me taste it.

"Woah is that boozy," I said with wide eyes. "It's good though, thank you!" *I'm gonna be so fucking hammered though.*

"Oh, and I want you to meet my son!" Jurado said like he just remembered. I grabbed Tylor and led them over to the bottom of the stairs where Jurado waited for us, standing beside a guy who made my dick perk *right* up. From his olive-green eyes to his thick, black curls to his square jaw, he was *gorgeous.* You know how some people are so hot that it almost makes you mad? *That's* how hot he is. "Trevor, Tylor, this is my son Elijah," Jurado introduced us. "Eli, this is Trevor and Tylor. Tylor uses they/them pronouns. I have them both in one of my Macroeconomics classes."

Eli gave each of us an up-nod and I managed to choke out a hello as I shook his hand. "How's it going?" he smiled.

"Their friends are in a band," Jurado went on. "They're playing a concert tomorrow."

"That's dope," Eli said. "Are they playing at The Commons?"

"Nah, they're having their own show," Tylor said. "It's a long story. It's at the field hockey field. You should check it out if you can."

"When is it?" Eli asked. "Maybe I'll stop by if it's after my game."

If Dad had ever had a party for his friends and favorite students when I was still in high school, I wouldn't have been anywhere near as chill as Eli was in the same situation. Let's be real, I wouldn't have even shown my face—I'd have just stayed in my room and gone hungry. It was a struggle to not follow them when Jurado led his erection-inducing son off to turn another guy gay, but I forced myself to peep the rest of the ground floor, which consisted of the bathroom, a guest-room-turned-laundry-room thing, a TV room, and a sunroom that doubled as a study. I found myself out on the deck to get some air, and out of all the people I could've ran into, what are the chances that one of them would've been Alex?

"Dude," he laughed out loud when he saw me. "Are you fucking forreal right now?"

"Ayye!" Tylor happily shouted.

"What the hell are you doing here?!" I grinned.

Alex fist-bumped each of us. "What the hell are *you* doing here?"

"Um, getting turnt? Why aren't you at your own place?"

"Because there's no *way* I'd miss my last Jurado party. My bud Khaleel already had to bounce, so I'm *hella* glad you guys are here."

"Okay," I said absentmindedly as I texted Kade **Alex is at our professors party!!** with a shit-eating smile.

"So why are you here?" Alex asked me again. "*How* are you here?"

"Jurado invited us," I answered.

"Jurado just up and invited you?" he asked like he didn't believe us. *Maybe this party's more exclusive than I thought?*

Yeah, we know 😊

Have fun, nerds

"Yeah? I mean, we took him to Taco Tuesday, so that might've had something to do with it. And also, what the hell is that?" I asked as I nodded at what I assumed was his drink until I realized it was topped with a glowing coal.

"A hookah," Alex smiled.

It may have just been a Mason jar with a hollowed-out, foil-wrapped half of an orange for a bowl with a notch cut into the side for the straw-turned hose, but it sure as shit did the job of a hookah. *Wasn't Alex the one who told me weed smokers are the best engineers?* I ogled it from all sides. "This—this is—" I struggled to say while Tylor snickered at me. "It's like the Berlin Wall of hookah smoking, and you're Mr. Gorbachev." I took a video of it in action to send to Kade. "Did you bring some shisha?"

"Unh uh, I used some of Jurado's."

I gave him a look. "Don't tell me Jurado has a hookah."

"Why *wouldn't* Jurado have a hookah?"

"That's fair. But why are you smoking out of a citrus fruit instead of the real thing?"

"Because I like to be a show-off sometimes," he shrugged as he took/sipped a puff from it. "Even if it's a pain in the ass to make. The smoke isn't that strong either."

"Can you show me how to do it?" I asked as I eyed up his feat of engineering.

Alex shook his head. "I'm fresh outta oranges."

"What about a pineapple? Could you make one out of a pineapple?"

"Yeah, if you find me a jar that big," he chuckled.

What in the actual FUCK is that

Wishing that I could also satisfy my oral fixation, we listened to Alex tell us about Jurado's parties as he sipped on a little bottle of Disaronno he kept in his back pocket. I guess Jurado has a party at the end of every semester, except the ones at the end of the Fall semester are holiday-themed. A Rebelution song shuffled on from Alex's phone sticking out of his shirt pocket, and as I looked from it to his hookah to the tiki torches, the idea occurred to me that maybe 370 Rock isn't necessarily a place as much as it is a state of mind. Tylor disappeared into the house to get some more food just as the host himself appeared from around the other corner, talking with another guy about his age.

"I really think that nobody should settle for less than 10,000," Jurado told his companion.

"Holy *shit*," the other man laughed. "And here I was gonna say 40, as in four-zero. *10,000* though?"

"Sure, why not? How can we call ourselves a free people otherwise?"

"And why stop there?" I asked without having a clue what they were talking about.

"Yes!" Jurado exclaimed. "And why stop there? Make it a million an hour!"

"*That's* more like it," I toasted him. "What are we talking about?"

"Minimum wage. I was saying how I don't think it should be less than $10,000 an hour."

Alex coughed almond liqueur down his chin. "Holy *shit*. That really *is* more like it!"

"Wouldn't that wreck the economy or something?"

"If the fucking Cheeto gets elected again then the economy's gonna get wrecked anyway," Jurado scoffed, "so what have we got to lose?" *He knows what's up*, I smirked.

"He's not gonna win," Alex waved the idea off.

"Work's just so...*demeaning* though," Jurado went on, shaking me from my worst nightmare. "We get one chance at life and we have to waste it at some *job* we don't even care about? Letting someone buy hours of your life for *seven* bucks a pop? Are you *shitting* me? Who the hell came up with *that?!*" He gulped his drink. "I can't wait to see how you kids shake up the workforce someday."

"Shouldn't minimum wage be like $30 an hour or something if it had increased in proportion with the rate of inflation?" I asked to try to sound smart in front of them.

"Something like that," Jurado's Friend concurred.

"And let's say you *do* land a six-figure career," Jurado went on. "Is your *life* really worth *that* little to you? I don't trust anybody who makes work their life."

"It's a shame," Alex said as he took a drag through his straw. "Sinful, really."

"I don't know how the cycle can ever end," I lamented. "People following their dreams isn't good for business. People doing what they were born to do isn't good for profits. So unless the paradigm ever changes, I guess we'll all just be damned to being slaves of the system, like that part in *1984* about how the future looks like a boot stomping on a human face forever." I shook my head. "I'm Trevor, by the way," I said to Jurado's Friend.

"I like the way you think, Trevor," he said to me. "And I'm John. John Sutcliffe. I teach in the Economics department too."

"Oh, I've heard all about you!" I practically shouted. "One of my best friends has you for class! He *raves* about you!"

"Glad to hear I made an impression," he smiled. "Who is it? Which class?"

"Sustainable Economics, on Monday, Wednesday, and Friday mornings. His name's Kade Oakley."

Dr. Sutcliffe laughed out loud. "*Oh* yes, I know *exactly* who he is. He's...how do I wanna say this...?"

"He says things that make you go 'what the shit?'" I offered.

"Yes, I'd say that's accurate."

"*Much* provocative," I chuckled.

"One time in class, he asked"—he looked around to make sure nobody was standing right there, confirming that we were indeed talking about the same Kade Oakley—"why we're able to have genetically-modified crops and animals, but not genetically-modified genitalia." I almost spit out my drink. Jurado was laughing so hard he had to hold onto the deck railing.

"I love this kid already!" he screamed.

"That's like right on par with the things he says *outside* of class," I said between laughs. '*This baby was conceived in a GMG-free facility,*' the future labels will say.

Dude
Sutcliffe is here too
IM GETTING TURNT WITH SUTCLIFFE

"And I see you've already met Alex," Jurado told me. "You've gotta watch yourself around this one."

I caught Alex's eye. "Oh, we've already been turning up together all semester. Is he one of your 400-level regulars or something?"

"I've had him in my class since last Spring," Jurado chuckled. "He idolizes me for whatever reason, so naturally he's one of my favorite students." He nodded to Alex's fruit hookah. "Is that one of your weed bongs?"

WHAT THE FUCKKKKK

The conversation went from how a million-dollar-an-hour-wage would revert us back to a barter system, to the inevitable robot economy, to what would happen if people had to eat money to survive, to what would happen to social safety nets, to ethical business practices, to when Jurado and Sutcliffe were in college. It turns out they were actually roommates their sophomore year and stayed friends this whole time. "I remember one time I borrowed his car without asking so my friend and I could have a race," Jurado laughed at the memory. "You were so pissed."

"Yeah, because you hit the curb so hard you blew out one of the tires!" Dr. Sutcliffe reminded him. I knew I was starting to feel the zombie from how much I was laughing at the thought of Jurado slamming into a curb and popping a tire. *'That's why they call it a zombie—because it zombifies you,'* Victor would say. But however saucy I was feeling was nowhere *near* how saucy Dr. Kershaw was feeling. He drank from a flask that never left his hand, and was getting so sloshed that he could barely walk straight. He tried other people's drinks without asking them, and told crude jokes that would've left even Kade just blinking.

"May I present the head of the Business department," somebody laughed after he'd shuffled off.

Tylor wanted a zombie too but I didn't know where Jurado went, so I tried making one for each of us myself. "Disclaimer," I warned them as I uncapped a handle of rum, "I have *zero* clue what I'm doing."

They took a sip and started coughing. "Holy *fuck* is that boozy!" they laughed. "Whew!"

We had somebody take our pic in front of a plastic shower curtain with a beach scene on it next to an inflatable palm tree like we were taking prom pictures. *I wish I would've brought my instant camera with me.* "You know what I just realized?" I asked Tylor.

"That there's churros?" they answered.

"There's no music at this party," I said curiously. "This is the first party I've ever been to that didn't have—wait, *what* about churros?" I had vaguely promised the others that we might make it over to 370 Rock at some point, but as I stood there with cinnamon on my fingers and chocolate sauce on my lips, I knew that that wouldn't be happening.

Jurado, in a beachcomber hat and with a drink that kept refilling itself like an Old Testament miracle, held out his arms from the landing on the open staircase until he held the room's attention. He thanked everybody for coming and said he hoped that everybody was enjoying themselves. "And if anybody sees Susan going for the wine again, please feel free to take it away from her!" The person who I figured was Susan, who reminded me of a large bird, laughed with her hand over her mouth.

"Like I do at the end of every school year," Jurado went on, "I'd like to recognize the students of mine who will be graduating next week, all thanks to their hard work and achievements."

One by one, he called each of them up and introduced them to the room, sharing what they meant to him before shaking their hand and sending them back down. And it wasn't just fortune-cookie stuff either—he recounted a specific memory he had of each student. *What will my future favorite professor say about me when my time comes?* I gave Alex a pat on the back when he returned to his spot next to me, looking like he was on a sedative that was kicking in. Right as Jurado took a breath to say his piece about Hannah, I spotted his hookah sitting on the floor in a nearby corner.

"Oh hey, there's the hookah!" I blurted out.

"Hey asshole, I'm speaking!" Jurado shamed me from his platform as a few people chuckled.

"Sorry," I laughed at myself. Listening to him celebrate stranger after stranger got pretty boring, so I welcomed his brief spiel about life that no speech to an outgoing class would be complete without.

"In a week from now you'll be leaving NHU for the last time," he said as he held onto the banister to keep himself up. "It'll be one of those rare, optimistically poignant moments of your lives. Yes, these years will always be dear to you and this school and all the people you've met along the way will always live inside you too, but don't forget that a piece of each of *you* will always live here at New Halle as well. Even after you're long gone from here, your legacy will help make this school the school that it will someday become, just as every student whose name has been forgotten has helped make it what it is today. NHU is only ever as great as the students who choose to study here. Campus is nothing but a reflection of the students who've made it their home. Without *you*, there is no *it*." The room was quiet, except for Dr. Kershaw hiccupping.

"There's a quote by Steve Jobs that I love—*'You appear, have a chance to blaze in the sky, then you disappear.'* Go out and change the world. Make yourselves be seen. Take up space. You are a gift from the universe and you can do anything." I could feel the ink on my wrist tingling, telling me, urging me, warning me, *unless.* "I'm so proud to have had the chance to call myself one of your instructors." *I* got a little choked up, and I wasn't even graduating.

Dr. Kershaw stumbled over to Jurado after he'd returned to the ground floor. *"Great* speech Jules, but imma get going," he slurred as he pointed to the wall. "Can I get my keys?"

Jurado shook his head with a *that's-cute* smile like a bouncer when you think you're getting into the club. "No you're not."

"I'm *fine*, I swear!" he said, though his nearly-crossed eyes said otherwise.

"You're staying right here, Greg," Jurado said, keeping calm even as Dr. Kershaw persisted. I popped pieces of bacon-wrapped chicken into my mouth as I watched their game of tug-of-war play out. Jurado finally just led him to the spare bedroom/laundry room and literally pushed him in and onto the bed, and pulled the door shut with a triumphant look.

"Is there a window in there?" a nearby girl asked him. "Because he *will* climb out of it."

"He's not climbing out of any *window*," Jurado waved her off. "He doesn't even have his keys."

You know you're drunk when you start drawing a map of the world without anybody asking you to. "Because fuck the Mercator projection," I said as I passed the paper around to show it off.

"*How* do you know where things are *at*?"

"Did you *memorize* this?"

"*Dude*—what if all the oceans are actually surrounded by *land*?"

"I'd like to thank the globe I got for my 5th birthday," I said like I was accepting an Oscar.

"It's too bad you don't put that much effort into your assignments," Jurado razzed me.

"I do if it's a class I care about," I shot back. "So where'd you get the hookah?"

"A friend of mine got it for us in Egypt," he said casually.

"Oh *shit*, that's *legit*! I thought you were gonna say you just got it at some store."

"*Most* of this is stuff people just gave us." He gestured to a wooden, canary-yellow giraffe head craning out of the wall. "You think I'd buy this shit on my own?"

"Do you ever use it?"

"The giraffe head?"

"No, the hookah!"

"Oh," he laughed. "Sometimes at parties."

"You mean parties like this?" I asked slowly.

"Look, I'd be for it, but I don't know where Alex went, and I don't play with it anymore ever since I burned a hole in the rug."

"That's fair. But you're in luck though," I said as I set down my plate and rolled up my invisible sleeves, "because I worked at a hookah lounge when I was in Morocco over the Summer."

I've never seen Jurado look so genuinely impressed before. "*Really?*"

"Nah. But I've watched my friend get it ready enough times."

Jurado and Tylor and Eli watched me sprinkle, pack, wrap, and poke while I called for supplies like a surgeon, letting the coals heat up right on the stove. Jurado moved the hookah to a table by an open window, where I topped it off with my freshly-packed bowl. *Kade would be so proud.* "It looks way more clutch when it's not sitting in the corner, *Dad*," Eli said.

"Doesn't it, *mom*?" I said reflexively before Jurado could respond.

Eli frowned as Tylor cracked up. "Did you just call me mom?"

"No," I said as I tried not to laugh. *Well that wasn't cringe.*

After a few minutes, the hookah was pumping out smoke like a Victorian-era textile factory powered by child labor. I offered Eli the hose and a hookah tip. "No thanks, I don't smoke," he declined.

"Neither do I," I said cockily as I took another hit. "Do you have asthma or something?"

"No, but I play baseball, and it'd probably be a little tough to run bases when you can't breathe properly." *Dear god, what I'd give to see him in a baseball uniform.* "And all the other health stuff in general."

"Makes sense," I said as I made a mental note to see if I could find him on Instagram. "My boyfriend plays baseball too."

"That's dope. Does he play for the school? I guess I should ask if he even goes here first," he smiled.

"Yeah, he goes here. He played club baseball back in the Fall, but he got too busy with other stuff this semester to do it again."

"I gotcha," Eli said just as somebody accidentally yet forcefully bumped into him on their way to get a drink they certainly didn't need. "I'm gonna move to the sunroom—it's getting a little too crowded in here." I took one more drag before laying down the hose to join him. *He hasn't said anything about a girlfriend yet.*

A handful of people were gathered outside of the room that Jurado had shut Dr. Kershaw in. I guess somebody went to check on him and he wasn't there. Eli and I saw that one of the windows inside was open as we peered past people looking around like it was a crime scene. We shared a smirk and my stomach fluttered.

The two of us were the only people in the sunroom. Eli sprawled out on the sectional while I took a wicker chair opposite him. I had to fight to keep my eyes away from the middle of his tropical-leaf print boardshorts. I imagined myself climbing on top of the chaise, on top of him. I crossed my leg over my other knee.

"My dad must really like you to have invited you," Eli said as he picked up a metal brainteaser puzzle within arm's reach like the ones Mrs. Costner used to keep in her classroom. "Most of the students he asks are juniors and seniors or grad students."

"I guess so," I said as I tugged on a shoelace. "He said you're going to New Halle next year. Do you know what you're gonna study yet?"

He exhaled through his nose with a shrug. "Honestly, I think it's all a waste. I feel bad for the kids who put themselves tens of thousands of dollars in debt just because they were told they have to. And a diploma doesn't really mean anything in the end, if we're gonna be real." *Like father, like son.* "But since my dad works there, it'll cost me like fuck nothing. It'd almost be dumb of me to *not* take the opportunity."

"But what are the opportunity costs of spending four years of your life doing something your heart's not set on?" I asked, using an economics term that I'm sure he's heard his dad use.

"Trust me, I've thought about it. But I think the experience will be good for me though."

"Yeah, I feel ya on that," I chuckled. "I assume you'll be commuting?"

"Nah, I'll be living on campus. Yeah it'll cost more, but I want the *full* college experience. Mom and Dad are on board with it," he said, answering my next question. "They think it'll be good for me to get out of the house and be *sorta* on my own. Don't get me wrong—they're cool as hell, but I have to get out from under their roof at *some* point, and I'd like to do it while I'm still young."

"True dat," I agreed, almost envious of how cheap it would be for him. "Do you know what dorm you'll be in?"

"I can't remember the room number, but I know it's in Swafford Hall."

I sat up. "That's the building Tylor and I are in!" *Maybe he'll get our room. Maybe he'll sleep in the bed I sleep in.*

We started talking about music. Eli's tastes are even more alternative than mine—he listed off who he's currently on a kick of, and I've only heard of maybe two of them. I pulled up *The Herald's* website to show him the video of Three Lesbians in a Wheelchair's performances. "Another friend of theirs came up for the weekend to play with them tomorrow too."

"Yeah, I'm *definitely* checking that out," he grinned.

"It's gonna be like an entire concert," I said. "There's even another band opening for them called Frottage Cheese."

A group of young women came in and settled on the sectional with their wine glasses, pushing Eli to the edge without even acknowledging him. He shot them a sideways glance before just getting up to let them take over. "You wanna move outside?" He *had* to have known I was into him by how eagerly I followed him. *You're such a simp, you know that Trevor? But what are you even doing? You have a boyfriend.*

The deck was empty except for a few guys talking and smoking cigars, ranging in age from grad student to retired. "Have you been down to the creek yet?" Eli asked me.

"What creek? There's a creek?"

"I'll take that as a no," he smiled. "Come on, I'll show you."

A set of wooden steps went down the hill, leveling out to a platform that overlooked the gentle creek. It was dark except for a string of garden lights. *This is where I'd take someone if I wanted to make out with them.*

"People have gone skinny-dipping in the creek before," Eli told me. "And I don't just mean students. I'm talking like *adults*."

"What are you saying?" I half-joked, hoping that his answer would be, *'Do you wanna try it?'*

"Just that from what I've seen at these parties, some people still haven't lost it."

"I hope I'm like that when I'm older," I smiled. "That the 19-year-old in me never totally dies."

We leaned our elbows on the wooden railing. We were standing so close that we could've kissed. *Go ahead, just touch him. Make it look accidental.*

Remember that part about you already having a boyfriend?

But Eli's so hot. And he brought you down here.

What would Ethan say if he knew?

Ethan's not here though.

You already told Eli you were taken.

Yeah, like that stops people.

How could you even think about doing that to Ethan? Do you want to hurt him like that?

Just brush your arm up against Eli's—

Some rustling off to our right startled us. Two people emerged from the rocks that led down to the water with heavy breaths, carrying wet towels.

"Hi," said the woman.

"How's it going," said the man.

Eli and I stifled our giggles as they trudged back up to the house. "That was *perfect*," I said as I gave him a playful slap on the shoulder. "Have you ever gone skinny-dipping in there before?"

"I have," he said smugly. "Have *you*?"

"Just in a hot tub."

"*That's* hot. With your boyfriend?"

"With my boyfriend at the time."

"Did you do stuff in it?"

I smirked. "We sure did."

He smirked back. "Hashtag *goals*. But I guess the creek will have to do for now." I felt my dick stiffening. *Go for it. Now.*

His phone *pinged*. "Hey, I'm gonna head out—my buddy's waiting for me out front." *What? No!* "We're gonna go meet up with this chick and her friend. Maybe I'll get to bring her down to the creek later if I'm lucky," he winked. *God fucking dammit, no!* "It was nice meeting you—maybe I'll see you at the concert tomorrow?"

I muttered a goodbye as I watched him take the steps two at a time, low-key hurt at how quickly he left. But can I really blame him when he has a chance at getting his dick wet? He might have been done with me, but I sure as hell wasn't done with him. I downed the rest of my drink and made my way down the path towards the creek, walking along its edge until I couldn't see any lights from the house or hear anything other than the running water. Getting murdered didn't even cross my mind. I untied my shorts and went to town on myself as I let my imagination run wild. *He takes me up to his room and locks the door. Our tongues wrap together as our hands explore each other's skin. I lift his shirt off and trace his sculpted chest. I feel his lubed-up head press against my hole before I let him in with a gasp. He grunts as he breeds me. He whimpers into his mattress as I make his bed rock. I try to keep myself from collapsing into him as I—*

I muffled my gasps as I shot onto the ground. The flipping sensation in my chest immediately turned to shame. I listened, but the only sound was of my own panting. I grabbed my cup and returned to the party. In the sunroom, somebody strummed an acoustic guitar as an older man played a pair of bongos. I played with the same metal puzzle that Eli had fidgeted with until I remembered I wanted to try finding him on Instagram. I pulled out my phone to see a series of texts from Ethan that made me feel like an absolute piece of shit.

Check your snap to see what youre missing 😄
I hope youre having a good night 🙂
Are you still coming over here after??
I wish you were here abbe
***babe lol**
I love you so much I dont know what im gonna do
without you over break
I dont say it enough but you mean so much to me
🥺🥺🥺🥺

Ethan's Snap was a video of Victor sitting on a stool, with one hand on the wall and the other on the counter like he'd fall off if he let go. *"Guys, I can't move!"* he laughed through his slits for eyes. *"I feel like one of those Chilean miners trapped in a mine and I can't move!"*

I let myself fall back into the lounge chair. *I can't believe I was actually thinking about making a move on Eli. Am I really that shitty of a person?* I sat there feeling ashamed of myself until I registered someone standing in front of me. "No pressure, but I'm ready to go whenever you are," Tylor said.

I heaved myself up. "I'm ready now."

We said bye to everyone we'd talked to who was still there. Isabella and Jolie gave us hugs, Dr. Sutcliffe shook hands with us, and Jurado gave us one-armed hugs. "I'll see you punks on Tuesday," he bid us farewell.

While we were waiting for our ride, I looked through the window to see some of the adults clearing the aluminum food trays off the table to set up a game of pong. *I really hope I'm still like them when I'm 50.*

Eli still hasn't accepted my follow request.

317

5. POV: You're at 'some loser concert' and it might be your favorite one ever

May 7

Four more days.

Ginny's was the busiest I've ever seen it, full of seniors checking another item off their senior bucket list. I feel like doing something for the last time and *knowing* that it's the last time you're doing it is the least authentic experience you can have of it—you're just trying to recreate and hold onto moments that have passed, moments that you got so caught up in that you forgot they're only once-in-a-lifetime.

At our large round table, Tylor and I traded stories about our night partying with professors for the other five's stories of what we missed at 370 Rock, but I'm glad that we did something different. "I thought it'd be pretty lame, but *I* had a lot of fun," Tylor said.

"Yeah," I nodded. "Forreal though, between Jurado and Sutcliffe—"

"Still *high-key* jelly about that," Kade grumbled as a jism of strawberry jam fell into his lap.

"—I'm about to change my major to Economics just so I can keep having them for class." I took a sip of my coffee. "Oh, and if anybody has a Dr. Kershaw for class, you might not see him again."

The others left Ethan and I off at Kessler, where my boyfriend took a Trevor-amount of time to pick out what he was going to wear for their concert. "Do you think this looks okay?" he asked me, wearing the tie-dye shirt he made at the OG Block Party that he'd cut the sleeves cut off of.

I clicked my tongue. *"Tattered jean shorts are a must for the young homosexual,"* I said in my lispiest voice. "Yeah, I think you look good," I said in my Trevor voice.

He laughed through his nose. "I could be wearing nothing and you'd still think I look good."

I'm not sure why I expected the two of us to turn heads as we headed over to the field hockey field when we just looked like two guys who were ready to take the sunny day on a date. "Hopefully they have the stage constructed by now," Ethan said as we left the dorms behind us.

I turned to him. "Constructed?"

'Constructed' was indeed the appropriate word, because one doesn't simply 'set up' or 'put together' a structure that could house a small house. "Oh my god," Ethan gasped, slowing to a stop as it came into full view.

I let his keyboard stand fall to the ground. "Please don't tell me that's your stage."

"I think that's our stage," he stared.

It bore down on us as we crossed the empty grass, grass that would hopefully be holding an audience of people before long. "Holy shit," I swore as my eyes traveled across the speakers hanging from the covered metal truss. "This is *infinitely* more badass than I was expecting." *This is the same stage that was set up at Homecoming? Why does it look so much bigger?* We found Sam up on the stage, directing the placement of the backline cabinets and amps while he hooked up the front speakers.

"Let's bring those a little closer to the drum riser," he said as he flapped his hands like an interior decorator.

"*Dude*," Ethan said to Sam with the world's widest grin, "This is...*amazing.*"

Sam bumped elbows with him. "I went as big as I could."

"No *shit* you did," I scoffed in a good way.

"*This has gotta be like a hundred grand worth of stuff,*" I heard Ethan say to himself.

I was too blown-away by the setup Sam managed to snag to see Derrick's car pull up. "Holy. Fucking. *Hell,*" Kade said with his mouth hanging open. "You're sure this isn't the actual Summer Send-Off?" Between his Clubmasters and his tank top, he looked like he was ready to take a drive down Pacific Coast Highway. Amina complimented his California look with a sundress and her own movie-star sunglasses. Derrick looked like he was about to shoot a cologne commercial in his unbuttoned shirt that showed off his toned chest.

"Dude! Have you *seen* this shit?" Victor shouted as he bounded up onto the stage with a bandana tied around his head. "This is fucking *legit!* I didn't think it was gonna be this big! And yeah yeah, said the actress to the bishop."

Two of Frottage Cheese's members pulled up in an old Isuzu flatbed truck with their gear strapped down like they were fleeing from something before the rest of the band showed up in a regular-ass car. Victor put together his drum set at the back of the stage while Frottage Cheese's drummer assembled hers on the riser. I don't know why they didn't just use the same set. Maybe it's like wearing somebody else's underwear. Sam played a potpourri of background music as more and more people filled in the grass, some with blankets and others with coolers. I got whiffs of a warm spot in the pool as I made my way over to the food truck that parked on the road alongside the field—which, good looks on their part—to get a peach iced tea and an order of nachos that I sure as shit didn't need.

319

Frottage Cheese's members checked the mics and tuned their instruments before nodding for Sam to kill his music. "How ya doing, New Halle?" the singer shouted to a lukewarm response. "Let's fix that right now." Their songs were all pop-punk—old covers, newer covers, a couple originals. And they were good too—just them alone not being at the Summer Send-Off made it that much shittier of an event. *Fuck SGB and their concert*, I thought as they brought the fucking house down with a cover of a Sum 41 song. Victor wouldn't shut up about how good their drummer was, but I think he just thought she was cute.

When their set ended a half hour or so later, Frottage Cheese's singer thanked everyone for coming, Three Lesbians in a Wheelchair for letting them play for them, CPB for the stage, and Sam for all his help. "I gotta go," Ethan said with a peck, leaving me with a pulse-racing smile. As soon as Frottage Cheese had torn down, Victor and Derrick started moving his drums up like a pit crew—Victor had painted 'END HETERONORMATIVITY' on the front of his bass drum—while Amina and Kade tuned their guitars. Ethan double-checked the mics before disappearing to take a pre-gig piss or something.

Victor giving his drums a few hits to make sure that they sounded to his liking turned into a series of beats that turned into a full-on solo. He shook the ground with his freestyle as Amina and Derrick and Kade took their places to bursting pockets of excitement. Victor brought his jamming to an end before taking a breath and banging out the iconic intro to "Feeling This." Kade had me worried though when *he* started singing instead of Ethan, who was nowhere to be seen. *Did he get locked in one of the toilets? Did he get sick? Did something come up at the last minute? Did his mom call him to say she changed her mind and he's not welcome at home? Did he get jumped and beat up again? Did he—?* But then right in time to take over the chorus, he strolled out and made himself the center of the show, turning every Open Mic Night performance into easy listening music. I don't care what he says about not being a performer—untie him from his keyboard and give him a stage, and he makes it his. He even hopped down off the stage to come right up to me to sing in my face with his finger on my chest, leaving me swooning. The instruments fell away, leaving Ethan and Kade and Victor to end the song in staggered vocals, before Derrick took the band right into their next song. "This one's for my boyfriend," Ethan said as he pulled down his shades just enough to wink at me. *Coming out takes a lot of different forms*, I thought as I beamed back.

After being just the band's guitarist, Amina finally got to show off her glamor and power. "Let's get you people moving," she said before she brought the concert a West-Coast vibe that we didn't know it was missing. I don't think it was possible for the SGB-sanctioned Summer Send-Off to scream 'Summer' any louder than my friends' concert. I hope there was a Cinematography major there capturing footage for a concert film. The band's rendition of "99 Red Balloons" started off sounding like

Nena's new wave version before switching to Goldfinger's punkier version partway through, and Ethan knocked us all off our feet when he furiously sang the last verse in German. I was so turned on that it wasn't even funny.

Calvin sideswiped me when he made a guest appearance for "Sun Tan." The crowd chilled and swelled like they were at a music festival. "Calvin Frost on the trumpet!" Ethan shouted. Calvin gave the crowd his toothpaste-commercial grin and held his instrument up like he was about to lead a charge. Ethan gave him a bro hug before he introduced the other members and thanked everyone who made it all possible before continuing to crush song after song. The crowd fucking *lost* it when Amina played her solo at the end of "Ms. California." Kade even whipped up a circle pit during "Empty Space," which he sang so Ethan wouldn't have to sing their last song with a shredded voice.

"I forreal can't thank you enough for being part of this," Ethan told the crowd as he ran a hand through his sweaty mess of hair. "I won't ever forget this. This has been unreal." He drained the rest of his water and wiped his mouth. "This is our last song! This one's called 'Pictures of Girls!'"

I grinned, thinking about the alternate universe where Trevor is confident enough to be in a band, and gets to sing one of his all-time favorite songs to a crowd of people—is what *could* have happened.

Chalk it up to being high off of life or caught up in the moment, but I found myself pushing my way through towards the steps off to the side of the stage. And then I don't know if time lapsed or what, but all of a sudden I was facing a thousand-person-strong crowd from the stage. I felt my smile falter. *Okay, there are WAY more people here than I thought.* The music fell apart. Ethan let the mic drop to the stage with that head-splitting noise that microphones like to make so he could hurry over to me.

"What's wrong?" he asked me with wide eyes like I was injured. The crowd started to murmur.

My grin returned. "I wanna sing this one. Can I sing it?"

His eyes only grew wider. "You wanna sing it?"

I nodded, never so sure of anything before. "Yeah."

His eyes narrowed. "You're sure?" he arched an eyebrow.

Kade, Victor, Amina, and Derrick were all staring at me. I felt a sea of eyes on me. "I'm sure."

I thought he might've been upset that I wanted to hijack his finale, but he couldn't hold back his smile. "Okay," he said as he retrieved his fallen mic. *No backing out now.* "So remember how I mentioned my boyfriend earlier?" he asked the audience. *Holy goddamn shit is this a lot of people.* "I think he loves this song even more than he loves me," he pretended to cry before handing me the mic and signaling to Victor to count them in again. *How do the words go again?*

Clack-clack-clack-clack!

So that's how I—introverted, anxious, has-to-talk-himself-up-before-he-makes-a-phone-call Trevor—sang one of my favorite songs by one of my favorite bands to a *field hockey field* full of people. On any given day I'm worried if the people walking behind me on my way to class think that I'm breathing too loud, and then there I was *singing* to them. From a *stage*. Nobody laughed at me. Nobody booed. People were having *fun*, taking videos, whistling at me holding notes I didn't know I could hold. I didn't recognize most of the faces smiling back at me, but I liked to imagine that everybody I'd ever met at NHU was there in the crowd just so they could see how far I'd come. I couldn't mimic Ethan's movements since he was at his keyboard, so I just did what I remember seeing singers in concert music videos do. I didn't even care if I looked stupid. I was no Ethan, but the girls standing smack up against the front were no less thrilled to have me slap their hands. Ethan and I sang the bridge back and forth to each other from across the mic with our faces inches apart. *I can't believe this*, his eyes said to me. *I know, isn't it crazy?* mine smiled back. I got to be a part of his most public kiss ever before he ran back to get on his keys. The band drew out the outro, crashing it to a deafening close. I almost passed out from the adrenaline rush.

"We're Three Lesbians in a Wheelchair!" Ethan bellowed over the roars and cheers. "We'll see you next year, New Halle!"

Kade flung his pick into the crowd. "Stay classy, New Halle!"

"And thanks for stopping by!" Victor said.

Kade glared at him. "*Stay classy.*"

Victor pointed a drumstick at him. "*Thanks for stopping by.*"

"*Stayclassy*," Kade coughed. Victor's crushed-up water bottle just missed his head.

I was at Ethan's side before Sam's music was even back on. "Best concert I've ever been to!" I was grinning so hard that it hurt. "You're like, *actual* rock stars now. And I can't believe I just sang in front of all those people!" I yelled as the shock of it only just then started to set in.

"Me neither! Go the fuck ahead!"

"Um, so yeah," Tylor called up to me from the edge of the stage, "who the hell are you and what'd you do with my roommate?"

Kade was ruffling my damp hair before I could answer. "*Where* in the actual *shit* did that come from?"

Victor ran over to grab me and shake me like a snow globe. "What the hell were you thinking?" he laughed. "What the hell's wrong with you? What even *was* that?"

"I don't know! I guess I was just really in the mood!" I said, making Kade spit out his water.

The crowd didn't swamp the stage like I half-expected it to. The band plays one song at Open Mic Night and people don't leave them alone, but then they play a full-on show and people bounce as soon as it's over? Maybe they were just that eager to get to SGB's event. A few people did come up for a few words though, but unfortunately for Victor, one of them was Chadwick Patterson, who mansplained to him—for lack of a better term—how different drums make different sound pitches.

"Last-ever party at our place starts right after this," Andrew said to us as we ferried equipment from the stage to Derrick's car. "Unless you have to *study* or something," he rolled his eyes. "I'm joking—if you have stuff you need to do, then please do that first."

"Oh yeah, like *that's* gonna happen," I sneered. *How could I concentrate on anything after* that?

Ethan found me once the band's stuff was all packed up. "Sam said that he and the CPB people can take care of the rest of this. So I think we're done here."

"Good, because I am extremely *turned-on right now,"* I said in a low voice. We stopped by 341 Kessler to unload Ethan's gear and a couple of other things before heading over to 370 Rock.

Since every other school's semester had already ended, there were people at 370 Rock from out of town who came to party with their friends one last time. We were that yard full of people having so much fun that it wallops you with a severe case of FOMO when you see it—a yard of cornhole, kiddie pools, and charcoal grills. The porch and patio flowered with people. *Everybody* was drinking—even Matt shuddered down a sip of somebody's orange pop and premixed Long Island Iced Tea. Victor and Tylor were those people drunkenly waving to the girls sunbathing on the porch roof across the street. It was like a party in a music video. *Life can't get any better than this.*

"I still can't believe you pulled off a whole-ass concert," I said as I stood ankle-deep in the kiddie pool. "Like, the fact that that all came together in like a week? And that *crowd?*"

Victor shrugged up at me with his shirt open. "What can I say? We're talented."

We started talking about music festivals, and I can't say I was surprised to learn that Tylor and Amina are the only two of us who've ever been to one. "I feel Lollapalooza's lineups are better, but the Bonnaroo crowd is way more chill," Tylor said.

"I went to Electric Forest last year, and holy *shit*," Amina sternly said.

"Can we please all go to one sometime?" I begged my friends like the drunk kid I was. "Can we please go to one and take drugs?"

There were about a thousand people in the kitchen, making and downing drinks. The empty bottles rang out in the recycling bin with glass-on-glass *shrieks.* Victor nudged me and nodded to a big Gatorade dispenser that looked like it had stories to tell sitting on the counter. "Why do I get the feeling that that's not filled with Gatorade?"

"It's not," said someone who kind of reminded me of Miles if Miles had pockmarks and didn't wear glasses and had a deeper voice. "It's my special jungle juice recipe. I call it 'The Stuff that Killed Kennedy.'"

Victor blinked. "The Stuff that Killed Kennedy?"

"Yep," he smirked. "Have some."

We filled our cups up about halfway and swirled them under our noses. "I always thought jungle juice was just everything leftover from the party the night before all dumped together," Victor said like a freshman. I gingerly took a sip, but couldn't taste anything other than pop and juice.

"I don't even taste any alcohol," I said.

"That's what makes it dangerous," Straight Miles smirked. *Dear god, he even has the same dimples too.* "There's three handles of liquor in there."

Victor coughed into his cup. *"Forreal?"*

"Think of it like a pot brownie," Straight Miles said before walking off. "One is all you need."

Victor and I took small sips so as to not go too ahead too fast. I could tell how potent the stuff was by how obnoxious I was feeling. "When I'm drunk I feel like I could take on the world," Victor smiled as we watched Ethan crack open and chug the King's can.

I snorted. "How much did you have to eat today?"

"Not much."

"Yeah, I can tell."

Kade got up from the game of Kings, stopping to look down into my cup on his way past. "Whadda *you* got, boi?"

"The Stuff that Killed Kennedy."

He gasped. "Too *soon* fam!"

"Hey, I didn't come up with the name! If I did then I would've called it The Magic Bullet or something."

"Dude!" he almost choked. "That's *way* too fucking soon!"

"You mean like the blender?" Victor asked.

Kade grabbed my cup to try it. "Is there even anything in here?" he frowned. "I don't taste shit besides Sprite and STIs."

"Trust me, there's *definitely* alcohol in here." Once he'd gone, I leaned back into the hallway to make sorrowful eye contact with Number 35 himself. *Sorry for the assassination jokes, Mr. President.*

It's okay, the *Time* magazine portrait of JFK said back to me. *Ask not why you should turn up, but how you should turn up.*

All the new faces made it feel like our first time at 370 Rock. It almost didn't even *feel* like 370 Rock. It might have been their last-ever college party, but it didn't feel monumental or anything. They didn't get a keg. They didn't hire a clown. Yeah, there was that voice in the back of my head reminding me over and over *this is the last time you'll ever get to do this*, but I was having too much fun to stop and think about it for too long.

We played Kings. We played pong. We played Flip Cup. We played Liar's Dice. Straight Miles got hotter each time I saw him, even with his arm around a girl. The stairs were a two-way street of people, couples, groups. I used up the rest of my instant film and handed out photos like party favors. The whole pool was warm from people lighting up wherever. People had two, three doses of The Stuff that Killed Kennedy and paid for it. Kade must've been so eager to get outside to smoke that he walked right into the back screen door hard enough to knock it right out of place.

"Is it just me, or does that juice got you feeling a little h-word?" was the last thing Ethan said to me before we disappeared upstairs together.

But I couldn't stop thinking about Ryder all evening, and I couldn't get him to go away.

Finally, while Ethan and my friends were busy watching Tylor try to pick up a cup to drink with just their teeth, I slipped away from the party to go up to the roof to spend some time alone with my thoughts. The luminous moon made the clouds glow, and although I couldn't see them, I knew there were trillions and trillions of stars up there behind them. *You're out there somewhere, Ryder. Can you see me from up there? Even among the secrets of the universe, can you hear what my heart is saying?*

A leg coming through the window scared the hell out of me.

"Oh shit," Alex swore. "I didn't think anyone would be up here. I can go back inside if you want." As much as I didn't want any company, Victor didn't tell *me* to buzz off when I interrupted him on the roof that night.

"Nah, you're fine."

He lowered himself beside me up against the wall of the house. "So I see you found my favorite spot when I need some time to be alone with my thoughts."

I nodded. "Yeah, it's a good spot for that." We sat in silence, tuning out the voices and the throbbing bass from the party beneath us. "So what thoughts do you need to be alone with?" I asked even though it was none of my business.

"Graduating," he breathed. "I've been dreading it and dreading it, and it's finally here."

I turned to him. "You're not excited or happy?"

"Not at *all*." His words came in forceful breaths. "I'm *scared*. I'm scared *shitless*. I've never been so scared in my life."

325

"Why?" I asked, though I had an idea why.

"*Because,* I don't know what I'm gonna do after this!" Alex said like he was trying to hold it together. "I don't have any *plans* for my life like everybody else does!" The image of Jurado putting a hand on Alex's shoulder and telling a room full of people how proud he is of him and how far he's going to go flashed across my mind. "I don't wanna leave this. I'm gonna miss it all so much." And I knew that 'it all' didn't just mean being a student and parties at 370 Rock.

"What about the others? Do they not wanna graduate either?"

"June and Andrew have some art residency in an old converted synagogue lined up, so their lives are already that much more put together than mine."

"What about Matt though? He doesn't really know what he wants to do either, does he?"

"Nope. And he's not even bothered by it." He laughed through his nose. "He's so *calm* about it and I don't know *how.* I've been doing nothing but freaking the fuck out about it." I remembered the hookah conversation we had with Matt when we stayed up all night last week, and the poem from *Interstellar* about raging against the coming darkness. "And besides," Alex chuckled spitefully, "he's ace, he doesn't drink, he doesn't get high. What's he gonna miss?"

"Um, his *friends?*" I frowned. "Student life? All the freedom that comes with it? *Staying up until 2 and sleeping in until noon with nobody to tell you otherwise? Trying new things? Going on side quests just to see where you end up? Finding where you fit? The experience of making your own way with the family you built along the way? All the same stuff you're gonna miss?* "Has college just been a way for you to get laid and fucked up?"

"Of course not. Most of the memories I've made here I've made while sober and soft, but I just feel like I didn't do as much as I could have done," Alex said to the shingles. "And now my chance is gone."

"Like what, getting involved with things?"

"*That,* and..." He uncomfortably shuffled his feet. "I never up and said it before... but I'm bi."

"Oh, that's cool," I said genuinely, even if I sounded unenthusiastic.

"Or maybe pan. I don't know. I just know I'm definitely not straight," he said with a strained voice like he was about to tear up.

"There's nothing wrong with not being straight!" I tried comforting him.

"I *know* there isn't, and that just makes me angrier at myself! I kept lying to myself about it until last semester, and then I only got the balls to experiment with other guys over Winter Break."

"Well at least you're learning to accept and love yourself!"

"Yeah, but I'm so *pissed* at myself for not accepting myself when I *started* school instead of *now.* I was always so afraid of what people would think about me, even my friends. And yeah, I *know*—if they're really my friends then they wouldn't care. I don't know. You know what I mean."

I nodded. "I do."

"I'm just so mad that being afraid kept me from making the most of my time here. It's like I've been holding myself prisoner. And now it's over." He swallowed. "Do you know what that *feels* like? You can't know, and you should be thankful you never will," he spat.

I let myself stew for a moment. "I know what self-hate is like though. And people in high school were *way* shittier towards me for being gay than anybody I've met here has been."

"That they were." He swallowed before turning to me. "Thanks for listening to all that."

"Don't mention it. And thanks for opening up to me about it."

"Sure thing," he said like he wasn't sure about it. "So what thoughts are *you* out here to be alone with?"

I wasn't in any mood to talk about it. "My brother," was all I said with a mouth full of cement.

"Do you miss him?"

"Uh huh." *You don't even know.*

"Does he still live at home?"

"Unh uh."

"Did he move out?"

I felt my bones stiffen. "He's dead, actually."

"Oh *shit.*" He sat up straighter. "Do you wanna talk about it?"

The stars held my eyes. *I can't do this right now.* "Not really. It was a couple of years ago anyway." *Like that would ever make any difference.* "I think I'm gonna go back in now."

He didn't follow me in. "I'm sorry," was all he said behind me.

There were less people downstairs, having either left or disappeared into some dead end of the house. "You good?" Ethan asked me, mistaking my glumness for drunkenness. "Do you feel okay?"

No. But I will eventually. I nodded and put on a good face for him. "Yeah."

He smiled. "Good."

I resumed my old role as a wallflower as Macklemore's "Good Old Days" echoed through the house, not because I felt shy or like I was out of my element like in days past, but because I wanted to make the last party at 370 Rock—*the* last party—last as long as possible. I watched Ethan and Kade and Victor and Tylor and Amina at their favorite party, wondering if they would've ever been friends if I hadn't introduced them to each other. I watched the newcomers, getting turnt like it was just any other party. I watched Matt and Andrew and June and Sonia and Luca and Henry and Charlotte and Eren and Cameron and Chance—the friends who won't be NHU students anymore this time next week—living it up with arms around shoulders and heads thrown back in laughter. And I thought of Alex alone on the roof, perhaps hugging his knees as he sniffled, sad that it'll all be over, but glad that it all got to happen.

I know all too well what it's like to want to hold onto a moment forever, but every moment is just that—a moment, and they're all meant to pass, just like all of us are someday meant to die.

The last in series of pics and videos on Andrew's Instagram story is one somebody took of him this morning looking like a total frat guy, standing in the yard with a wrecking ball of a recycling bag bulging with cans and bottles and broken-down boxes in each hand. 'Heracles slays a titan and takes its balls as a trophy, 2,023 BCE (colorized).'

May 8

A.S. (antescript, because P.S. is overused)—"Cigarettes & Saints" by The Wonder Years

Dear Ryder,

It's been a while since I've talked to you, but believe me when I say that there isn't a day that goes by that I don't think about you. I skipped class today because it's just a study day, but also because somebody would probably see me staring off into space and ask me if I'm okay. Because right now, I'm not okay.

Today's May 8th, which means you would've turned 23 today.

I know it doesn't mean anything now, but I just need you to know how fucking sorry I am. I still haven't made peace with everything I did to you, and I know I'll never forgive myself for it. I just fucking wish that you could've had 18 or 19-year-old me for a brother instead of the piece of shit you got stuck with.

Maybe we don't have souls, and maybe I'm just typing words on a screen that nobody will ever read because I tell myself it's going to make me feel better or make some kind of difference. But isn't that all that journaling is anyway? A form of self-therapy, like prayer?

Anyway, I just wanted you to know that I'm keeping you extra-close today. You'll probably be hearing from me again at some point. I'm not even going to try to pretend that I'll be able to put you to rest someday, because you were a part of my life, and you're a part of me I never want to forget. I'll keep you with me as long as I live. And then after that, maybe we can meet up? I'd love to see you again, and get to know the person I never took the time to understand. There's so much to catch up on.

Love, your piece-of-shit brother,

Trevor

May 9

Two more days.

Saying goodbye to my favorite professors wasn't the profound and heartfelt moment that I thought it'd be, like at the end of *Harry Potter* or some other boarding school movie. I knocked on Dr. Averescu's door to turn in my final assignment even though it was open, because that felt like the thing to do.

"Thank you, Trevor, for making class enjoyable for me," she said as she rose to bid me farewell for good. "If you ever need a letter of recommendation for anything, or if you just want to talk, you can always reach out to me."

"Thank you for everything," I said as the moment got heavy for me all of a sudden. "Good luck with whatever's next for you, and have fun with it." I was low-key disappointed that she didn't go in for a hug.

Jurado followed me out into the hallway after I'd handed in his exam. "We'll be having our 4th of July barbecue over the Summer if you think you'll be around for it," he invited me.

"As honored as I truly am, I live in Buffalo, so it might be a bit of a hike for me."

He just stared. "You know I don't invite just *anybody*, right?"

I played with my stud. "I mean, I could *probably* make it."

"I'm *kidding*," Jurado smiled. "It's just a cookout. Please don't drive down all the way from Buffalo just for that."

"I'll see how I'm feeling that day," I smirked, making him laugh.

"Now don't be a stranger next year!" he pointed at me. "Just because I won't have you for class doesn't mean you can't swing by. Maybe we can catch up over some tacos?"

"I'd like that," I smiled.

"Have a great Summer," he said as he patted my shoulder. "And be good! Or if you're gonna be bad, be good at being bad," he winked.

May 10

Twelve more hours.

Kade's Snapchat story has been full of things he scavenged from Axworthy's trash rooms. *"Why the shit would somebody get rid of this?"* he angrily asked a glow-in-the-dark poster of Absalom the caterpillar smoking hookah. *"Forreal people, check your trash rooms. Hashtag upcycle."*

I could've gone home today, but Ethan's keeping me here for one more night because I'm not ready to leave him yet. It's funny how we look for ways to kill time until we find ourselves living a day that we never want to end, and only then do we realize how wrong we've been doing things.

I put on *American Football*—that soundtrack of endings and beginnings, of the shifting of life's chapters, of memories and regrets, of all the things that make up what it means to be alive and to grow—while the two of us roamed the twilit campus that we made our home. The dorms, Bixby, Patnick, the Quad, the classroom buildings, Hostetler, the streets and sidewalks and all the grass in between—*this is where life happens.* I remembered exploring campus that first day or so after moving in, so worried about if I'd fit in and if I'd make friends, and if Ethan had thought about the same things as he moved in. *What things did you discover,* I wanted to ask him as we said goodbye to it all. *Do we have the same memories? When did you realize that this is where you belonged?* I let his hand slip away from mine so he could balance on a stone or a curb, feeling empty without him until his hand found mine again. I led us to the bench by the pond where I used to spend those September afternoons so we could watch the water catch the setting sun. I scratched our initials into it with one of my keys before we left, so now anybody who sees the 'EE+TH' inside of a heart will maybe wonder whatever became of those two people who were each other's worlds once upon a time on a rock hurtling through space.

We made love to The 1975 like it was our wedding night, like it was the last night we'd ever get to have together, feeling instead of speaking so we could memorize the landscapes of each other to keep with us over Break when the empty spaces in our beds are too loud to let us sleep. Because after all, what are we but two colliding tectonic plates? What is love but an earthquake?

May 11

With Tylor's side of the room bare and my belongings all packed up, I almost felt like I was leaving 222 Swafford the way I found it, but I knew that wasn't true—except for some pinholes in the wall, the next students to live their lives there will never know that that room watched a young man grow into somebody he never thought he'd become. But what do college dorm rooms do if not watch people grow? I quadruple-checked the drawers and cabinets for anything I might've missed, and loaded up my car before heading over to Axworthy. I helped my best friends carry their things out like a parent, trying hard not to tear up when everything they didn't send back with Derrick was finally crammed into Victor's shithead car.

"I know it's only for a few months but..." I trailed off when it came time to say goodbye, feeling like I'd start crying if I looked them in the eye. *But you two are my family, and I don't know how I would've gotten through the year without you. Yes I know that all things shall pass, and yes I should smile because it happened, and yes I should be stoked to see you again, but still.*

"I'm gonna miss you too fam," Victor finished for me.

Kade patted my back. "Maybe you can come down and visit over the Summer?"

We hugged, and they left me on the sidewalk to return to their other life, a life without me or Ethan or Tylor or New Halle or food that makes you almost shit yourself. *I know I don't need to tell you guys to have a good Summer,* I thought as I watched them drive off.

As I passed the Field House on my way to Kessler, I thought about the 370 Rock crowd and everybody else who was inside for commencement rehearsal, eager to step into the lives they've been preparing themselves for. But it was Alex my mind hovered on—how the scariest moment of his life is getting closer with every second, how the life he'd gotten used to and came to love was about to pass. I projected positive vibes his way. *Remember Alex, nothing ends without something else beginning. And who knows? Maybe it'll be better than you ever could've thought.*

I tried to keep my things somewhat sorted and organized when I packed, but Ethan threw his stuff together like the Red Army was closing in, smushing clothes and school supplies and cleaning supplies and food all together in the same bins. "I don't understand how you *still* aren't packed yet," I said as I tried not to get stressed out over it while I played *Tetris* with his things, recognizing a lot of the same swag I'd gotten from freshman orientation.

"I detect disapproval," he smirked as he rolled up his coffee mug in a pair of underwear. "I've been busy! I had Finals, I had to meet with Frankie, I had to make sure the RHA office is—"

"Okay, *yes*, sorry," I rolled my eyes. "How silly of me."

Both of our Summer Breaks sound like they're going to be pretty low-key. I didn't ask him if he thought he might be able to make it to Pittsburgh to visit with Kade and Victor too, because I didn't want him to feel left out if he couldn't. "I just plan on working as much as I can," he told me.

"That's not a break!" I protested.

"I need the money! And it'll keep me busy and out of the house."

I stacked the corners of his notebooks flush into the corner of a box. "Even though your mom's cool with you doing the gay?"

"I mean, yeah, *she's* cool with it. But I told you, it's my stepdad I'm worried about."

"You know, the more you talk about him, the less I'm looking forward to meeting him," I said. "And if things end up not being good at home, then I'll just have to come down and kidnap you."

"Only if it involves handcuffs," he smirked. He held up my copy of *The First to Die at the End*. "Can I take this home, or do you wanna hold onto it until we move in again? I didn't get to finish it yet with Finals and everything."

"Yeah, go ahead," I smiled, as much as I don't like entrusting other people with my things. I imagined Ethan taking a book down from a shelf in our future apartment and stretching out on the couch with his legs in my lap, and my chest soared.

We turned 341 Kessler from Ethan's room back into just another dreary cell. Doors and drawers shut with hollow echoes. He dug through his now-exclusive bathroom for anything he might've forgotten. "I'm gonna see if I can drop a deuce before they get here," he poked his head out. "I try to avoid rest stop bathrooms if I can."

"I don't blame you," I chuckled. "I'll keep chugging away at this," I said as I gestured to what was left of his bookshelf and desk.

"No, you deserve a break after all your help," he said before closing the door.

I kept at it anyway though because there wasn't anything else to do. I read over pages of notes and reminders scrawled on Post-Its as I packed up his desk, smiling at his folded-up copy of the set list from their concert. *The next time this box will be all unpacked will be when we're moving into our new room.* I found a sheet of paper folded in half underneath an organizer in one of the desk drawers, and opened it to see a list with items crossed off in pencil and different colors of ink.

-*make friends with people on my floor*

-*go to a football game*

-go to a play or musical

-go to a party

-make out with someone at a party

-avoid the freshman 15

-pull an all-nighter

"Did you make like a freshman bucket list or something?" I called to the bathroom door.

"I said I can get the rest of it!" Ethan's voice called back. I kept on reading, high-key interested to see what expectations baby-faced freshman Ethan had for his first year away at college.

-get involved with a club

-do karaoke (or something similar)

-attend a random lecture

-pledge to a frat

-dye my hair

-be open about my sexuality

-have sex

-find a boyfriend/fuck buddy

-have a threesome

-take an elective I normally wouldn't take

-find a boyfriend/fuck buddy

-do something reckless (but not too reckless)

-find a boyfriend/fuck buddy

-find a boyfriend/fuck buddy

Find a boyfriend/fuck buddy.

Find a boyfriend/fuck buddy.

Find a boyfriend/fuck buddy.

Find a boyfriend/fuck buddy.

It's crossed off.

I wasn't sure how I was still standing when I couldn't feel my legs. I looked at the paper until the words became hieroglyphs. Even after Ethan ripped it from my hand, I could only just stare at the space it had occupied.

"I told you to take a break," he said nervously. *And now I see why*, I wanted to say.

"You—did you...do all of these?"

He read it like he was seeing it for the first time. "Well, pledging to a fraternity isn't crossed off," he dodged, "so..."

My teeth clenched, my eyes squeezed shut until they saw stars. "I'm *talking* about—"

"The threesome was before we—"

"I DON'T CARE ABOUT THAT ONE!" I roared, making him jump and not caring what parents heard me.

"Babe, *please* stop yelling—"

"You're telling *me* to stop? Are we only together so you could cross something off your list?" I spat. "Have you only been putting up with me this whole time so you'd have somebody to *sleep* with?" It was like being on ecstasy all over again in that I couldn't stop moving—pacing, flexing my fingers, clutching my head. *Has our relationship been for show this whole time, like when I was the boyfriend Dillon liked to show off so he could feel validated?*

I've never seen Ethan look so hurt before. "Are you being serious right now?"

I almost couldn't look him in the eye. "Believe me, I really wish I wasn't."

"I can't believe you'd actually think that," he said in a small voice. "*This*—I made this at the beginning of the year! I forgot it was even there!"

"Please don't lie to me," I warned him.

"I'm *not* lying! I—"

"'Pull an all-nighter' is crossed off and that was like a week-and-a-half ago!" I shouted. "You didn't *fucking forget* about it!"

"Babe"—I shuddered at him calling me that—"*please* let me explain!" he pleaded as tears started rolling down his face.

"It better be a good explanation, because it looks like you've been using me this whole time."

"How can you say that?" he cried. "After everything we've done together? After all our dates, after—" *After slow dancing together? Cuddling and sharing earbuds? Valentine's Day and going out to dinner? Listening to you play songs for me? Spending my birthday together? Staying up late and telling each other our secrets? All the videos on my phone I took of you just being you that always made me grin like I was the luckiest guy alive? Whispering 'ichi-go ichi-e' into my ear as we danced hand-in-hand to "Champagne Supernova"? Yeah, that's exactly why it hurts so much.*

"You probably would've done the same stuff for anybody else who would've shown you attention," I said. "I mean, it's right there." I gestured to the paper lying on the floor.

"If I'd fallen in love with somebody else, then yeah, probably! But everything I did for you I did because I love *you!*" his voice cracked. I wanted so bad to hug him and hold him, to tell him that everything was going to be okay. "I fell in love with *you!*" *But do you even love me, Ethan? Did you ever actually love me, or did you just love having somebody telling you that they love you?*

The room started to spin. *No. No, not again. Oh my god, not again.* I grabbed onto a bedpost to keep myself from falling over. *This isn't happening. I can't believe*

I let this happen again. He reached for me and I took a step back. "Please get away from me," I growled, unable to meet his now-joyless eyes that used to captivate me.

"I just feel like we could both really use a hug right now," he sobbed, looking more miserable than I've ever seen him. *You don't know how much I want a hug from the Ethan I fell in love with.*

"I need to go," was all I said. *I need to get away. I need to get away from you.* I backed up and reached for my shoes.

"Please don't go, Trev!" he begged me with tears streaming down his face. *"Please,* I don't want this to be how we say bye to each other!" *I'm so fucking stupid. I'm so goddamn FUCKING stupid.* "I love you Trevor, you know I love you!" I shook myself out of his grasp, and pushed him away when he tried to hold onto me again. "I love you so *much,* I love you so *fucking—"* His words got lost in his sobs as he dropped to his knees to let us part on my terms.

My feet shot me down the hall, dodging parents and luggage trolleys without looking back. I didn't stop running until I was behind the wheel of my car, where all the anger turned into anguish. I screamed without caring who saw, screamed until I could only cry, sobbing harder than I had since the last time I found out that I meant way less to the person who I'd let become my everything. I would've wailed my fists on my steering wheel if I wasn't afraid of setting off the airbag.

I can't believe I didn't see it before. He wasn't allowed to be himself at home, so he decided he'd do whatever it took to make up for what he'd been missing out on. And in true Trevor fashion, I gave too much of my heart too quickly to somebody again without caring what would happen—except this time I *knew* what could happen, and I went and fucking let it happen again anyway. He even said at that glow stick party last semester that he was more interested in getting laid than getting into a relationship. I had to pull off the road twice because I was sobbing so hard that I couldn't even see. How much of his year was predetermined by a list? Did he even *want* to dye his hair, or did he only do it because it was on his list? And he didn't even legit *dye* it either, so what else did he half-ass just to check it off? I've seen how good of a liar he can be, so how much of all the things that he said to me while we were laying in bed together, or watching the clouds pass like moments, were just to keep me around? I made a promise to myself after Dillon that I'd never let myself become someone else's accessory again, but here I am paying the price again for being a fool. *Never again. Never. Again.*

Mom was trimming the bushes when I pulled up, and her smile faltered as soon as she saw my distraught face. "Oh honey, what happened?" she asked as the grass caught the clippers.

I just walked up and hugged her without even trying to stop the tears. My voice was too shredded to even speak from screaming along to Wallows' "Guitar Romantic Search Adventure" turned all the way up for most of the ride home. *Mom, remember how somebody hurt me that one time? Well, it happened again. I fucking let it happen again.* Not needing me to explain, she just hugged me back and gave me all the comfort I never got from her the last time.

May 12

I was about to text Ethan 'good morning' when I remembered that I didn't text him goodnight. I feel bad for leaving the way I did, but I was, and still am, in shock. I tried to stay hopeful as I answered his call. *It's just a rough patch, right?* But as we talked, the feeling that I tried to smother in my bed as affliction tossed and turned me only became more real.

"*Yes,* I went into the year hoping to find somebody who'd be able to meet my needs," Ethan tried to explain to me, looking like he'd slept even less than I did. "So I'm not gonna ask you to forgive me, because you were right—it's exactly what it looked like. But I never thought I'd actually find a real *boyfriend* along the way, somebody who'd sweep me off my feet and live in my head rent-free." Remembering how I used to feel the same way about him tugged at my heartstrings. *You told yourself you wouldn't be so eager to do it again, Trevor.* "And yeah, at the beginning of the year I thought that relationships were mostly about sex," Ethan went on, "but you showed me that there's so much more to being with somebody—things I never imagined I would've felt, things I would've never pictured for me and another guy if it wasn't for you." He fell apart and cried into his hands. "*You were the best swerve that ever happened to me,*" he sobbed, setting off explosions that demolished my insides. "If sex was all I wanted, then I would've just stuck with Tinder or Grindr and not bothered with the work that a relationship takes." *But hookups don't hold you afterwards and tell you things to make you feel special.* It's been so long since I fought to keep from crying in front of him—we always let ourselves be vulnerable with each other—that I'd forgotten how to do it.

"I want to believe you," I finally said, making his mouth quiver. *God, how I want to believe you. I wish you were my first relationship, so I could still be that naive and believe everything you're saying.*

"*Please* babe, you *have* to," Ethan said with sad eyes.

I didn't speak. I didn't shake my head. I just stared without seeing, thinking about the hard fact that things never last for as long as you think they will. *No. Stop thinking that.*

"We'll be okay," he pleaded. "Relationships aren't always smooth, but we'll get through this. Okay?" *Are you telling me that, or are you saying that to convince yourself?* Dillon taught me to not promise things that are out of my control, and I had hoped that Ethan would've been wise enough to not do the same. "We're gonna *have* to be okay before we move into our room next year."

"Maybe I should switch rooms with Kade," I heard myself say. "That way you'll be with him, and I'll be with Logan."

"*What?*" a horrified Ethan gasped. "*Why?*"

"I think it might be good to have some separation from each other." *Maybe I should try to switch rooms altogether?*

"Wh—" his voice cracked. "What are you saying?"

I exhaled. "I think maybe we should take a break from each other," I said without looking at him, almost ashamed of myself for even suggesting it.

"But we're already gonna have a break from each other all Summer!"

I shook my head. "Ethan—" The words caught in my throat. I swallowed, and it felt like I was swallowing nails. "I mean a *break* break."

His tears started flowing again. "*What?*" he gasped. "You can't be serious!"

I pressed my fingers to my eyes. "Don't you think that taking some time for ourselves"—*some time away from each other*—"would be good for us?"

"*No!*" he wept. Tears dripped off the tip of his nose. "I don't *want* time for myself! I want time for *us!* The thought of us being together again is the only thing that's been getting me through the last day!" *Us being together was never a guarantee,* I was scared to hear myself think. *No, you don't believe that. You don't believe that, Trevor.* "We're *gonna* get through this," he begged more than he said. "We've had our misunderstandings before and they've only ever made us stronger, don't you think so?" *I think that I wish I could just turn off my brain and forget that the last 24 hours ever happened, and fast forward to three months from now.*

"I don't know."

"Well," he sniffled, "you know how I feel. I'll do whatever I have to—*anything*—to make us work."

"I know." *Oh, how I know you would. But would you if I wasn't your first?*

"I love you Trevor, you know that, right? I'll always love you, and only you."

"Yeah," I said in a faraway voice, unable to bring myself to say the words back to him.

May 13

I've been having parallel conversations with Victor and Kade all day, who already heard Ethan's side of the story. Victor listened to me speak my thoughts out loud like a real friend—how upset and how hurt I am, how betrayed I feel, how I hate seeing Ethan like that too.

"I'm sure you've already talked about it, but you're *sure* it's not just a misunderstanding?" he asked me like the thought hadn't already crossed my mind 40,000 times. "To me it sounds like you two might just have crossed wires."

"Believe me, I wish that's all it was," I told him with my head hanging off my bed. "This feels like more than just a misunderstanding though." The thought of what else it could be watered my eyes. *I think I still love him.*

"I mean, I know how you can misread things sometimes," he said carefully. It wasn't what I wanted to hear, but he wasn't wrong.

"If this was the first time that I felt used by the person I loved, then yeah, maybe I would be just misreading it." I flipped myself over and sat up. "This just feels like...I don't know."

Victor looked off-screen. "Trev, I can tell you what I think all day long, but this is something the two of you need to figure out on your own. And I'm also like the *least* qualified person to be giving you relationship advice, so..." he trailed off with a weak chuckle. "But don't mistake me being unhelpful as me not caring. I hate seeing you two do this to each other, whether you mean to or not."

I guess he told Kade about our conversation, because Kade pretty much told me the same thing. "You're gonna think I'm just saying this," Kade said, wearing an apron as a pan of vegetables sizzled behind him, "but before the two of you even got together, I could tell there was something between the two of you, and you just clicked when you did get together. So it hurts me extra to know you're both hurting like this."

I didn't know what to say, with an apathy that scared me.

"I'm gonna tell you what I told Ethan," Kade went on. "Please make the effort to put aside whatever you *want* to think and talk to him—really *listen* to him. I know you can work it out. You're both mature people." He laughed to himself. "Relatively speaking, anyway."

May 14

Ethan and I talked. It's over. I can't believe that after everything, we're over.

May 15

Is this real life?

If this is what I want, then why can't I stop crying? Why do my insides feel like they're in a blender?

I remember reading something online once that said something about understanding why hurricanes are named after people.

Is this what it feels like to die?

May 17

I think I might be getting depressed again. Victor and Kade both posted clips and pics from the Waterparks concert they went to and I'm not even jealous. I just don't care.

I have to get used to all the little things that come with the aftermath of a breakup again, like doing my best to avoid the music we used to listen to, and random memories reducing you to tears all of a sudden. I got an email notification that he posted a new video because I forgot to unsubscribe to his YouTube channel. I didn't want to watch it, but I couldn't stop thinking about watching it. His curtains are closed, but I can tell it's still daytime. His room's a mess. I don't think he unpacked a thing—but then again, I barely have either. He didn't need to give an introduction or anything because his appearance says it all. He looks terrible—the circles under his eyes prove that he's been getting about as little sleep as I do on my most restless nights. But it's his expression of defeated sadness that unnerves me the most—the happiness and optimism that I fell in love with a lifetime ago are totally gone.

He started playing, and I would've recognized the song even if it wasn't in the title of the video—"Konstantine" by Something Corporate, the Tsar Bomba of post-relationship songs. I couldn't tell if it was more of a *I'm still not giving up on us'* or *'it was fun and you gave me great memories but we can never work out again,'* but whatever it was, the nine-and-a-half minute storm of emotion had me sobbing the entire time, filling all the empty space he left inside of me with nothing but pure agony. And if that's how I felt, then it's no wonder that he looks like he can barely keep himself together, like the slightest thing could break him. *You did this to him, Trevor. This is the person who you would've done anything for.* I tore books from my shelf, shattered a Lego model against the floor. I wanted to rip down my shelves, to throw things through the window, to punch holes in the wall until my hands broke. I threw myself on the bed and wailed into my pillow. I wanted to destroy myself just so the pain would stop, but he was already destroying me for me.

I remembered the promise I made to him the day he got beat up. *'Nobody will hurt you again as long as I'm around.'*

Is this how Dillon felt? Am I no better than the person who once destroyed me?

May 18

I had to call off again today. I was hoping that being at work would help take my mind off of things, but even when I'm there I have to keep dipping into the back to cry into a returned shirt.

I was looking for my copy of *The First to Die at the End* before I remembered that Ethan has it—or at least had it, because I'm sure he burned it by now. I threw away his birthday card to me, his Valentine's card, all the instant pictures of him, the magnetic poetry set he got me, even the Teddiursa stuffie, but the memories are what I wish I could get rid of the most, but to lose them would mean to lose who I am.

I know that this is how people grow, but why does the human experience have to be so fucking painful?

May 20

I can't stop Googling *'why does it hurt so much if i broke up with them,'* but it's nice to know that there are other people who know what it's like, even if it doesn't do anything to stop the hurting. *"And now you're just a stranger with all my secrets." "Loving you was the most exquisite form of self-destruction."*

May 21

I don't know why I didn't unfollow him on Instagram sooner. Seeing him sad would make me sad, and seeing him happy would make me sad. But am I really so self-absorbed to think that he wouldn't move on from me?

Somebody tagged him in a pic from a party last night, and at first I thought it was the wrong person. *I can see him changing his studs for hoops, but buzzing his hair? And wearing a crop top?* The eyes were what gave him away though. Those eyes will always give him away.

But what sent shockwaves through my chest was the other guy in the pic, the one whose leg he sat on. I stared at their laughing smiles until my head spun, the kind of smile that proves he was just using me. Because if he really loved me as much as I loved him, then he wouldn't be so quick to let another person have him.

I'm the one who wanted to end things. I'm the one who wanted to let him go. So why do I constantly feel like I'm going to throw up?

May 23

I ache to be repulsively drunk,
Anything to stop recalling
All the cool easy lies
You whispered to please me
That played like sweet music,
Never seeing the bloodstains on your tongue.

▶ 6. POV: It's summer break and you're trying to enjoy it but you don't know what to do with your life

May 24

It's been a struggle to not load up the Summer playlist that I've been putting together with all the Midwestern emo I've been listening to. I don't think music has ever made me cry so much.

I talked to Kade again, and I shouldn't have even wasted my time.

"Look, I *know* neither of you want this," he said, "so I'm telling you this as your friend—you and him need to talk and actually *listen* to each other, and—"

"*Kade,*" I groaned, "that ship has *sailed*. He and I are *done*."

"I think—" He stopped himself. "Actually, never mind."

"No, tell me," I said rudely. "I wanna hear what you think."

He blinked like he didn't want to say it. "Do you wanna hear what I think, or do you wanna hear what *you* wanna hear?"

"Tell me what you think," I taunted him.

341

He looked away from his screen and sighed, like he knew I wasn't going to like what he had to say. "I think you're being prideful," he said, making my nostrils flare. "I think you're being dramatic and making yourself out to be a victim without considering that maybe *you're* the one who hurt *him*."

"Why are you so quick to side with him when he's—"

"I'm *not* picking sides! He's my friend too! Or did you forget that?" he glared. "I love both of you guys! How do you think I like watching my two best friends tear each other apart? Have you ever thought about *that*?" *You know what? I'm not listening to this.*

"You know," I laughed scornfully, "I thought I could find a little support from you, but I guess that was asking too much."

I hung up.

May 25

I'll finally think I'm able to hold myself together, and then a song he introduced me to will come on at work or out in the wild somewhere, and take me ten steps back.

Maybe because he wanted to try to distract me, Logan asked me to help clean out his treehouse. It was like entering a time capsule from 2016—the chalkboard we used to dare each other to write swear words on still had graffiti and eraser marks on it, and torn-out pages from old video game magazines were still pinned to the walls. It's funny how that treehouse watched two happy-to-be-alive kids who used to play *Pokémon* inside of it for hours grow up and come back to smoke a couple bowls to try to forget about life. It's tempting to fall into the trap of longing for simpler or easier days or numbing yourself to escape from the current ones, but I'm trying to remember that that's not how to live life.

My phone roused me from sleep. I felt for it from the couch in Logan's basement. It was 11:37 a.m., and Kade was calling me. I silenced it and pushed my face back into the cushions with a groan. *He can leave a message if he really wants to talk.* And he did. Listening to it made me feel like shit for the way I talked to him. I called him back, rehearsing my apology as it rang. *Look, I'm sorry for lashing out like that. You were just trying to be a friend for me, and instead I—*

He was in his sunroom in a bathrobe when he answered. "Hi."

"Hello," I winced.

"Did I wake dollface up?"

I stretched. "Kinda."

"Sorry."

342

"Nah, you're fine."

"So...how's it going?"

I ran my hand down my face. "Look, Kade, I'm sorry for flipping out on you like that. I'm just—"

"No. You're just in a bad place and the stress of it got to you."

"Yeah, pretty much."

"I figured, which is why I'm calling you. Do you wanna come down and stay with us for a few days?"

So that's how, after lighting up the group chat with Victor and switching shifts with some people, I made plans to go down to their place for a long weekend next weekend to go to Pittsburgh's Pride parade. I don't know what else we're going to do yet, but I'll be happy doing whatever keeps my mind occupied.

After we hung up, Kade sent me some links to some videos and articles about ways to practice mindfulness.

Here are some things I do when I have a lot on my mind, which is basically all the time lol
I thought they might help you out
Love ya fam ♡

May 27

POV:

It's 12:14 a.m. and you're in your best friend's treehouse and you just demolished a whole bag of flour tortillas that he snuck in to get and he won't stop talking like Batman and you forgot how to lick and Bob Marley makes a lot more sense now.

May 28

So I think having the munchies is less about actually eating because you're hungry and more about searching for that *one* texture and flavor combo that just hits the fucking spot—which means that we need to figure out a way to deliver that orgasm for your tongue that doesn't involve you having to eat half the stuff in your kitchen. This is *exactly* the kind of shit we need to be funding.

I'm starting to wonder if Kade might've been right. *Am* I just being dramatic about all of this? I mean, how long and how often do college relationships *really* last? We weren't even together for five months—why am I making a big deal out of a five-month relationship that a part of me always felt was going to be temporary anyway? Don't get me wrong though, I never *wanted* it to be temporary. My god, did I want it to last forever, though nothing does. We were just in a new environment with our feelers out to see if we could find something we liked—as did Kade and Will, Kade and Greyson, Miles and Branden. Why did I think we were special? Was I being stupid or naive to think that we'd still be together after three more years of college?

Relationships that don't work out are just prepping you for *the* one. How else are you supposed to figure out what you do and don't like or want if you don't meet people and try things out? How else are you supposed to learn how to treat a relationship and the person you have it with? Yes I loved him, and yes I miss him, and yes I wish things could go back to the way they used to be, but wishing and wallowing has never helped me move forward. The healing process is just that—a process. My feet aren't going to pick themselves back up.

Was it really only five months?

May 31

POV:

You're finally having an okay day but then you go to put on a record and you find a note from your ex-boyfriend tucked in the sleeve.

Hi Trevor, the birthday boy with a nice toy,

Surprise! It's me. It's March 5. Happy birthday! You brought me home to spend the weekend with you. We just finished listening to this album and now you're in the bathroom. I know I've said it before, but I'll say it again to put a smile on that cute face of yours someday when you go to listen to this again—you made falling in love more magical than I ever thought it would be. I still can't believe this isn't a dream.

Until my birthday,

Ethan, who's not the birthday boy, but also has a nice toy (you're the one who said it!)

xoxoxoxoxo'

June 7

I got back home this morning from a five-day stay with Kade and Victor, and now I'm not really sure what to do with myself. I'd forgotten what being in such a good mood felt like.

The two of them had just gotten back from a trip to the grocery store when I pulled in their driveway. "Goddammit," Kade greeted me, "you couldn't have gotten here two minutes earlier and helped us carry stuff in?"

"It's good to see you again fam," Victor said like there'd been a recent death in my family. "I'm sorry about how things went with Ethan." He gave me an empathetic hug. "It makes me sad." *Things didn't just 'go'—it happened because of me.*

"Thanks," was all I said. He let go and we stared at each other for a second. *I don't wanna talk about it anymore,* I projected.

Sure thing, fam, his look said. He broke into a grin and rapid-fire punched my chest. "Real talk though, I'm so fuckin' pumped you're here!"

"Samesies," Kade said as he hooked his arm around me. "I'm actually *hella* happy to see you again."

"Well that would explain the erection pressing into my side," I said, forgetting what it felt like to be inappropriate.

He leapt in the air with his hands on his butt. *"Ooeh!"*

"There's the Trevvy I missed!" Victor laughed.

I handed them groceries to put away—"Cumin? More like cum *in!"*—since I didn't know where anything went. "Do your parents make you do the shopping when you're home?" I asked as I passed him a bag of tortilla chips as big as a Central American country.

"Oh *hell* no. I *loathe* grocery shopping."

"Well then what's all this for?" I gestured to the rubble of reusable shopping bags.

"We're having some friends over later for a pool party."

"How many friends, thirty? When does this pool party start?"

Kade smirked. "As soon as we get in the pool."

I don't understand how some people can have pools in their backyards and only ever go in for a quick after-work dip. "If I had a pool in my backyard, I'd be in it every day," I said to the clear, azure-blue sky from an inner tube that looked like a donut, complete with pink icing and sprinkles.

Kade grinned from his popsicle float. "Oh trust me, we *are."*

"Delightful *AF*," Victor said in rainbow Chubbies from the big watermelon slice he laid on.

It was an enviably relaxing afternoon of nothing to do and nowhere to go. The vibe was one of pool floaties, BENEE, and lime-flavored tortilla chips. Their dog Katie stayed outside with us, stretched out on a pool lounge chair in the shade of the umbrella. We discussed how the government limits how many pools the population can own—"Like liquor licenses!"—because economic output would plummet if everybody owned one. We tossed a foam football between us, whacked each other with pool noodles, and took turns seeing who could make the biggest splash from a cannonball. Kade was about to pass the football to Victor when he froze.

"Guys—there's a warm spot in the pool."

I sniffed for the telltale reek. "I don't smell anything."

"No, I mean there's *literally* a warm spot in the pool."

Victor and I exchanged glances. "*I* didn't do it."

"Don't look at me!"

We turned back to Kade, who grinned mischievously and put a hand in the air. "*Guilty!*"

"You're fuckin' *gross*."

Kade was about to say something back when he looked over my shoulder. "Behold! A maiden most fair appears! And by that, I mean 'the sluttiest bitch north of the South Side.'"

I turned around to see the only member of the Oakley nuclear family who I hadn't met yet, standing on the pool deck behind me in an oversized shirt that completely hid her shorts. "Who you calling a slut, slut?" she fired back.

Kade faked her out with the football. "I'll throw this at you. I'll fucking do it."

"Calm your tits." She focused her attention on me. "I don't think we've met. I'm Kelsey. I have the misfortune of being his sister."

Kade snorted. "You think *you're* the unfortunate one?"

"I love that I get to have you for a sister," Victor chimed in. "Best sister ever. Ten out of ten stars. Would recommend," he nodded with a smile.

"I'm Trevor," I said with a small wave, already feeling comfortable around her. "It's good to meet you too."

"*You're* the Trevor I've heard so much about?" she said genuinely. "I'm glad to finally meet the man himself."

I raised an eyebrow. "Oh?"

"These two almost couldn't shut up about you over Winter Break. Victor says you're his go-to for some deep talk." Victor gave me a *what-can-I-say?* shrug. "And you must have a *lot* of patience if you're still friends with *this* one after a year," she added as she shot Kade a look. He gave her two middle fingers.

346

"Go eat a shit. You think you could still get us those goods I asked you about?"

"Yeah," she nodded. "I *should* be able to get my hands on them this weekend."

"Perf."

She turned to go in before spinning back to us. "Oh, and I have something for you from Alex in my trunk that he gave me when we met up the other day. Remind me to give it to you."

"What the hell would Alex wanna give you?" I asked Kade as Kelsey made for the house.

"Dick," Victor said without skipping a beat. "I dunno. Maybe you left something there?"

"What'd you mean by 'goods?'" I asked Kade even though it was 100% none of my business. "Booze?"

"Pfft. She can get booze anytime." He waded over to me. "I didn't tell you in case it didn't happen," he grinned in a low voice, "but she said she could probably get us some shrooms. She said they're like acid, but brighter and don't take all day."

I was too eager to be polite. "Do you think she could get some for me too?"

"Does the pope shit on little boys? I already gotchu fam."

And then the not-so-irrational fear that they invited Ethan over too to try to get us to make up put me on edge. "So who else is all coming over?" I tried to ask casually.

"Just Derrick and some people from school. And don't worry, none of them are *total* Heteros," Victor assured me.

"School as in high school, or New Halle?"

"High school. Who from New Halle would—oh wait, never mind, there is one person from NHU coming." *Oh fuck. It'd better not be him.*

"Who?"

"You'll see. You'll be happy to see them though."

Kade laughed through his nose. "Not as happy as *you* will," he said to Victor. *Is it Nikole then? Wouldn't it be a vibe if it was Patrick Paul?*

We played some group pool games after Derrick and a few others arrived. I pretended I was having as much fun as they were while checking out the guys and being anxious as hell over potentially seeing Ethan walk through their gate. And then when a pair of arms hugged me from behind while I was trying to open a stubborn bag of chips without making them go flying everywhere, every part of me froze.

"Trevor! I didn't know you were gonna be here!" a girl's voice that wasn't Nikole's said. I let myself breathe.

"Amina! I didn't know you were gonna be here!" I smiled as I hugged her back. *Is it me, or is something different about her?* I didn't get too much time to think about it though, because I caught sight of Amina standing behind her. I let go to look from one to the other. "*Wait*, what the shit?"

Both Aminas laughed. "This is my twin sister, Jamila," the real Amina explained. "People get us mixed up all the time."

"And sometimes we trick people on purpose," Jamila smiled as she and her twin traded mischievous glances.

"Well you picked a good person to trick," Kade laughed. "Trevor's like the most gullible person on the planet."

"Am not!" I lied indignantly. "So wait, is she the person from NHU you invited?"

"Yeah? Who'd you *think* it was gonna be?" he asked like he legit had no idea. I was so relieved that I laughed out loud.

More and more people trickled in through the back gate, drowning out the music with their voices. There probably *were* close to 30 people there, and a couple of them had me thinking dirty thoughts. Kade manned the grill with a spatula in one hand and a mojito with home-grown mint leaves in the other, serving up burgers and kebabs that we skewered together for him. We tried to not look like we were having *too* much fun when Laura popped out to say hi once she got home from work, high-key worried what she'd think about a bunch of underage kids drinking at her house. But her and her husband surprised at least one of us when they joined the party themselves later on. Nobody thought it was weird that their parents were crashing the party, especially once they started facing off against pairs of us at the snack-table-turned-pong-table.

Kelsey disappeared through the gate and returned with a duffel bag patched with duct tape that looked like it'd been found on the side of the road. "Here, this is what Alex wanted me to give you," she said as she set it down at Kade's feet with a *clink* of metal and glass.

Kade slid out of his seat to kneel beside it. "Do you know what it is?"

"No, because I'm not nosy, like *some* of us," Kelsey zinged him.

Kade scoffed. "I *meant* did he tell you what was—" He unzipped it and his mouth fell open. "No *fucking* way." We crowded around to see what had shut him up. It was dismantled, but I still recognized the painted vase and the patterns etched into the brass.

"*Holy shit*," Victor gasped. "That's the hookah."

Yes, it was *the* hookah—Anubis, witness to the midnight conversations, the crazy theories, the endless records, the parties where I'd found a sense of belonging —that I was certain I'd seen for the last time. But like a ghost, there it was again.

"Look at all this stuff!" I said. Everything we could need was inside—hoses, a cube of coals, boxes and tins of shisha, a bag of mouthpieces, extra gaskets, a hotplate. "And he's just *giving* it to you?!"

"I guess," a dumbstruck Kade said. "You wanna fire it up?"

"Right now?"

"Do you think he gave it to us so it could sit in this dirty-ass bag?"

He set some coals on the hotplate and packed the bowl with a flavor called cactus fruit while we dug through the bag. "Hey," Victor said as he took out a sooty piece of notebook paper, "there's a note in here too!"

"Read it to me," Kade said. "My fingers are all sticky."

"No comment," he smirked before reading. *"Dear Kade, hopefully nothing's broken by the time this gets to you. We both know how careless your sister can be."*

"Ugh, rude," Kelsey scoffed.

"I was packing up my things," Victor read on, *"and when I came to this hookah, I wasn't sure what to do with it. Part of me didn't want to hold onto it anymore because it represents something to me that has passed, but I didn't want to just get rid of it either, also because of what it means to me. So in the end, I decided that I wanted someone who'd be able to appreciate it to have it, and you're the only person who came to mind. Trust me when I say that it's one of my most prized possessions. I've had it all through all five years of college, which have been the best five years of my life. I'd give anything to relive those five years again.*

Everything has to come to an end though, but as you and your friends reminded me, I have to learn to trust that everything will eventually be okay instead of being afraid of it. It may not be tomorrow, or even in a year, but everything will be okay. Trying to hold onto the past only keeps me from living in the present.

You don't need to thank me for this. I should be thanking you and Victor and Ethan and Trevor. My last year at NHU wasn't easy for me. Thinking about graduating kept me awake more nights than I'd care to admit, but you all gave me a semester of parties to remember, and for that I'll always be grateful. Believe me when I say that it was my favorite semester, and you guys helped make it so.

Isn't it funny how people can boomerang back into your life? It's still crazy to me that you used to just be one of my best friend's little brother.

So, before I change my mind about it again, I bequeath this to you. Whether it's at the parties you'll have at your own place someday, or just next to an open window in your dorm room when the stress of college gets to you, I want you to make fresh memories with it. I can't think of anybody who deserves it more. Thank you again, and best of luck with everything, Alejandro." Victor looked up from the paper. "Wow," was all he said. I almost teared up—it made me think of the thorough, closure-giving suicide note that Ryder never left us.

Kade washed his hands on a hunk of ice from the cooler before hunting for his phone. "He said not to, but I'm gonna thank him anyway."

And though we'll probably never step foot in 370 Rock Hill Road again, we carried on its spirit that night, as does any group of friends who turn up in the most authentic way possible. Anubis' raging water went unheard under the rumbles of the hot tub as we clouded the air. Everything was chill until some guy who'd never handled hot coals with a flimsy pair of tongs before tried to flip the coals himself and dropped one on the floor.

"*No!*" Kade yelped as it smoldered on the carpet. He frantically snatched the tongs from him to pick it up and drop it in the tray like it was a Japanese game show. "My mom's gonna *kill* us!"

"Kill *you*," Victor corrected him.

"Maybe she won't notice it since it landed on the black part? Here." I dragged a potted plant over a few inches to cover it up. "Look. Boom."

"But what happens when she goes to move it?" Kade panicked.

"You sound like me," I laughed. "Calm down. It'll be fine. Go in the hot tub and sit on a jet."

You'd have thought that Victor and Jamila were tethered together by an invisible hookah hose from the way the two of them stuck together—everywhere one went, the other followed, and it wasn't just Victor doing all the following. From the patio swing, I watched him flirt with her between rounds of Mao when talking was permitted. I caught him as he came over to get a couple of cans from the cooler. "You hoping to get a taste of some Lebanese food tonight?" I bounced my eyebrows.

"*Shut up!*" he warned me in a low voice before smiling. "I mean...yeah?"

"Do you only like her because she looks like Amina? Cause that's kinda fucked-up if so."

"*No!* Maybe I only liked Amina without knowing that Jamila was the one who I really liked!"

I furrowed my brow. "Isn't that like the same thing, but backwards?"

But maybe he was right though, because I've never seen him talking astronomy with Amina, showing her the stars with their necks craned skywards. "That one there's Polaris—there's the Big and Little Dipper," he told Jamila with their heads touching so she could see where he pointed. "And then over there somewhere is the Andromeda galaxy."

"It's so fascinating," Jamila said with their hands clasped together.

"*Five bucks says they hook up,*" Kade whispered to me from beside me at the table.

"No *way*," I smirked. *Not once she finds out he kisses like a fish.*

We played poolside poker under the light of the lights on the underside of the umbrella and along the deck railing. "Look fam," Kade nodded over at the patio with a grin. I turned to see Victor and Jamila making out on the patio swing. They pulled away to say something before getting up and heading inside together.

"No *way!*" I said happily. "Go 'head!" *He's such a good guy. I'd be honored to sleep with him.*

"Eat shit. And also you owe me five bucks. And also he has a full house," Kade said to the other players.

Just about everybody who hadn't left yet was playing another card game on the patio or had migrated into the game room, leaving me alone in the pool, drunk off of hard iced teas. Two boys were on the pool deck making out, the one straddling the other on his lounge chair. I don't know if they didn't know I was there or didn't care or what. I sank down into the water like an alligator and closed my eyes, imagining the three of us together in the hot tub, our hands and mouths exploring each other's bodies. I looked up to see them leaving the deck, one pulling the other by his hand to probably do stuff behind a closed door. I rubbed my lust below the water and debated whether I should try joining them or just get off in the pool. Kade appearing kept neither from happening.

"You're still in here?" he asked as he jumped in to join me.

"Yeah?" I said like I didn't have a hard-on. "Not all of us have a pool they can just take for granted."

"That's unfortunate, but it's also none of my business," he said as he pushed his wet hair out of his face. We let the water come up to our necks. *Just two bros sitting three feet apart in a whole-ass pool because they're gay as hell.*

"Vibe check?" I asked him.

"Ask me how saucy I'm feeling right now."

"How saucy you feeling right now?"

"Tzatziki," he said without skipping a beat.

I snorted. *"What?"*

"I just wanted to say tzatziki. How about you?"

"Uhh...that one with the 'W' that I can't pronounce. Wusta-chusta-busta."

"I gotchu," Kade chuckled.

We listened to the nighttime reggae and the voices from the party's new center of gravity. "We invited him to come visit too," Kade said out of nowhere. "Not at the same *time* as *you*, obviously. Maybe in a few weeks."

"Okay," was all I said. I watched my hands float on the surface of the water. "Why are you telling me?"

"I dunno. It kinda just came out."

"That makes *three* things," I said blankly. *Will they take him to all the same places they took me to?* "I really *am* sorry for snapping at you when I called you last week." You know you're drunk though when you start apologizing to people out of nowhere.

"Don't worry about it," he waved me off. "Breakups are tough. You weren't in a good place."

"Yeah, but you were just trying to be a friend, and I was making it hard for you."

"I *wish* you were making me hard."

I splashed him. "Get your mind out of the goddamn gutter."

He splashed me back. "But life's more fun when your mind's in the gutter!"

We heaved armfuls of water at each other. I wrestled a hold of his wrists. We stopped, and the water fell quiet. I relaxed my grip, and flinched as he moved his hand towards me. "Don't tickle me!"

"I'm not gonna tickle you."

I let his fingers find my chest and trace my collarbone. His touch aroused me, his wet hand making me think of all the times my exes and I showered together. I returned his caresses, breaking eye contact only to behold what we were doing. The back of his neck welcomed my hand. He didn't protest when I closed the gap between us to plant my lips on his. My dick was in full bloom.

I pulled away, seeing the waiting desire tucked in his heavy eyes. *"Am I making you hard now?"*

"Oh yeah."

We made out slowly, authentically, unlike the last time we kissed all those months ago on a dare. I found him under the water and held on. He worked me back, until we were hungry for each other.

"Have you ever done it in here before?" I breathed.

He glanced over at the patio, where some people were still hanging around and being maybe a little too loud for the time of night. *"Let's go inside."*

We dried ourselves off and avoided making contact with any eyes as I followed him up to his bedroom, where we left our friendship at the door. We covered mouths, buried faces into pillows, hoping nobody would hear us fulfilling each other.

"Why'd it take so long for that to happen?" my best friend asked me as we laid naked together in his bed.

"I don't know," I said, although being with Ethan probably had something to do with it. *"This isn't gonna make things weird, is it?"*

He stroked my hair, his face inches from mine. *"Not unless you make it weird."*

We made out some more before spooning, the alcohol and his arms and the *what ifs* lulling me to sleep. As much as I enjoy spending my morning cuddling with another guy, I didn't want anybody to know what we'd done. I pulled on my boardshorts and prayed that nobody else was awake yet as I tiptoed past closed doors and down to the basement.

I'm glad I only brought *Circe* with me instead of my Mac, because sunrooms and June mornings were made for coffee and reading. It was so relaxing that it was distracting, with all the plants, the trees catching the sunlight of the breaking day, the birdsongs—

He'd be able to name every bird, glued to the window like he was seeing birds for the first time. Am I just being a prideful, dramatic piece of shit? Did I really throw away one of the best things to ever happen to me? Did I get so used to him that I thought he was replaceable?

But he used me. I might be a lot of things, but somebody who lets themselves get used isn't one of them anymore. So if I wanted what was best for myself, then I had to do it.

Victor and Vince provided me with a welcome respite from my tormenting thoughts. I didn't see any regret or embarrassment in Kade's eyes when I caught them in the kitchen that first morning, and I know he didn't see any in mine either. If Victor thought anything of why Kade and I let him crash in the basement alone, then he didn't say anything about it—but then again, he might've been too high off of his own conquest to care.

"Jamila thought it was so sweet that I was with only one girl all freshman year," he said with a shit-eating grin while we had breakfast in the sunroom.

"Oh my *god*," Kade groaned/yelled. "Yeah, *one* time!"

"Like you were turning down girls left and right!" I razzed him.

After we ate and cleaned up from the night before, the whole family got ready for the Pride parade. I checked myself out in a full-length mirror, sporting a sleeveless shirt and literal head-to-toe rainbow accessories. *Would I wanna make out with me if I bumped into myself at the parade? Yes.* I blew myself a kiss.

"We haven't been this colorful since the Rainbow Run at school," Victor said as we painted stripes on our cheeks in front of the bathroom mirror.

"We haven't been this gay since that protest at school," I chuckled.

"I don't know what *you're* talking about," Kade said as he put on glossy purple lipstick in a hand mirror. "I was *born* this gay." His glow up was so good that it made me wonder if he's done drag before. His face practically shone, sparkling as much as his bejeweled 'CUMSLUT' collar he ordered for the occasion. Laura took our pictures like it was the first day of school.

I learned last year that Pride parades are some *prime* places to people-watch. On top of all the cute guys, there are the drag queens and kings, the rainbow-dyed hair, the dog masks, the 70-year-olds who made it that far. I didn't even care if any of the conventional gays were judging me for not being conventionally gay enough. A girl with rainbow bat wings loved our fits so much that she asked if she could take our pic.

As much as I'm into city blocks full of young, gay couples as the next gay guy, I can't see any of them without thinking about the universe where Trevor is taking Ethan to his first Pride parade, which is another thing that I just assumed I'd always get to do with him. Or the one where Ethan's at his first Pride with—god, *why does it still hurt if I'm the one who let him go?* We found a spot along the densely-packed boulevard to watch the parade. The onlookers stretched endlessly in either direction. I actually don't think I've ever seen so many people in one place before.

Aren't we kind of like an easy target for hate? I waited until Kade went over to go buy a rainbow thong to delicately ask Victor, "Being here doesn't make you nervous at all, does it?"

"No? I don't mind getting hit on, as long as—"

"Not *that*." I swallowed. "I mean, since...you know..."

He frowned at me. "I *don't* know."

I bit my lip. "About something bad happening at a place that's supposed to be a safe place for people to be themselves? Like what happened to your parents?" I winced.

"Nuh uh," he shook his head resolutely. "Absolutely not. Being too afraid to show up means that the terrorists win." He unfurled the flag he'd brought—his Progress flag from school that he'd Sharpied 'THE WORLD HAS BIGGER PROBLEMS THAN BOYS WHO KISS BOYS AND GIRLS WHO KISS GIRLS' on—and kept it waving in the air the entire time.

There was one person though who wasn't there to celebrate diversity and inclusivity, wearing a shirt with a bible verse on it and trying to hand out tracts. Like, what did he think was going to happen, somebody would see him and suddenly repent? But nobody chased him off. Nobody argued with him. We all just let him be, which is all that anybody who's there wants for themselves, or their friend, or family member, or partner, or whoever it is they're an ally to.

It's always bittersweet for me to see out-and-proud teenagers, and kids even younger than that, because I'm resentful that I didn't have the opportunity to be myself until recently—thanks to being surrounded by people who chose fear over love—but seeing them find acceptance and love just as they are makes my heart swell and my eyes well up with happy tears. *Someday there won't be a need for Pride parades anymore, just like how we don't need to demonstrate for emancipation or women's right to vote anymore. Someday, coming out will just be another thing of the past. Someday, an entire generation of queer kids will be the first to say they're in love with who they love, and that they are who they are, and they'll just be allowed to be, and the old order of things will pass away.* I'm envious that I didn't get to grow up in that kind of world, but I'm happy for all the kids that will. I might not even live to see that kind of world, but I'll do whatever it takes to help create it.

We parted ways with Kade and Victor's family to join the million other people at the festival at the park at the end of the parade, but we didn't hang around for too long since it was like Zukoff at Common Hour on steroids in hell. Only as we were leaving did it hit me that I'd been there before—Ethan and I walked through the same park together after going to the Aviary when we skipped class to drive down to Pittsburgh. And if the memory of that day gut-punching me over and over wasn't enough, I was about to screenshot the pic Victor posted of the three of us when the text beneath it made the bottom of my stomach drop out yet again. *Liked by EthanE16 and 24 others.*

I came down to Pittsburgh to get him off my mind, but he wouldn't stop popping up. All I could think about was the last song the band played at Open Mic Night, and how he looked me in the eyes and sang about how he's a ghost to me. He knows I'd see that he liked the pic. Is he trying to tell me something? Is that just me being full of myself? *We can still be friends, can't we? I haven't forgotten about you.*

No, Ethan. We could never be just friends—you can only either be everything to me or nothing to me. If you're not my whole life, then you can't be in it.

And whose choice was that, Trevor?

"Well now you don't have to go all the way out to LA to get your June Gloom," Victor chuckled as the smoke from the wildfires up in Canada hazed up the whole city as he drove us downtown the next day to the Arts Festival that Kade wouldn't shut up about.

"You're gonna *love* it," he told me for the seventh time as he drummed on his leg. And he was right—I loved it so much that I looked up "Buffalo art fest" to see if there's anything like it back here. Most of the stuff in the vendors' tents put a *what-the-actual-fuck?* grin on my face, and some of it just made me uncomfortable. But what is art but anything that gets a reaction out of you? I bought a couple of things that cost more than I would've normally paid, but you can't see a portrait painting of Ben Franklin wearing 3D glasses and *not* buy it.

"A real-life example of price inelasticity," I felt the need to tell the artist as I tapped my card.

The price of the food was *extremely* elastic though, so we left the festival—Victor with his two stickers and Kade with a canvas tote bag tucked with artwork—to go hit up an Indian place on the other side of the city that served the best Indian food I've ever had. And then we went on a side quest to the top of the ridge so we could drink in the most panoramic view of any city I've ever seen. I filtered the shit out of my favorite pic before posting it. We watched the city and the rivers below us breathe with people and cars and watercraft. My eyes lingered on the fountain at the tip of it all where Ethan and I sat and held hands once, unaware that we'd be strangers again in a month's time.

"Imagine living in one of these houses and seeing this view every day," I said to distract myself. "This has Buffalo beat so bad, it's not even funny."

Kade leaned his elbows on the railing. "I'm sure Buffalo's nice in its own way," he tried to downplay his hometown. "Though I'm sure this hits different when you haven't lived here your whole life."

We took a roundabout way back to their place so they could 'show me something.' "I need you to think of your current all-time favorite song," Victor instructed me. "That song that makes you turn up the volume and say 'go the fuck ahead' as soon as you hear it." Asking me to pick just *one* song would normally give me a case of analysis paralysis, but "Rollercoaster" by Bleachers had been energetically living rent-free in my head for days.

"Okay," I nodded. "I'm thinking of it."

He disconnected his phone to pass me the cord without taking his eyes off the highway. "Put it on."

His car *pinged* as it accepted my device. "Any specific reason why?"

"You know how *The Perks of Being a Wallflower* was filmed in Pittsburgh?"

My head snapped to him. "No! Forreal?!"

"Yeah," Kade said from the backseat. "But you know that scene when they drive through the tunnel?"

"Uh huh?"

He pointed ahead to a sign speeding towards us that read 'TUNNEL ½ MILE AHEAD.' My eyes went wide. *No* fucking *way*. "You're about to feel infinite," he grinned.

There wasn't a sunroof to stand through, but once the city exploded into being all around us—that city that never stops surprising me, that city that makes me fall in love with it over and over again—I felt more alive than ever before, never so happy to exist on this odds-defying rock at that moment in time. Because yes, the human experience hurts, and yes it's relentless, and yes there will be nights when you can't even cry yourself to sleep, but the people who become your family, and the times you share with them, and the music that's always there for you, and the promises of possibility make it all worth it to me. All I could do was stick my head out the window and laugh, grinning like an idiot because I got to experience that moment with the family I'd made. And even though moments like that don't last, I'm sure as hell going to keep making them happen while I can.

My ex said that we—people in general, I mean—give meaning to each other, that without each other there wouldn't be a point to any of this. I think he was right.

After a night of late-night swimming and philosophical smoking—"How much of yourself can you replace with robotic limbs before you're no longer considered you?"—we went out for breakfast at a place that had these crepes that were so delicious that I'd actually consider fighting somebody for one if it came down to it. We spent the rest of the day in their backyard, moving from pool to deck to patio while trying out a new psychedelic. Kelsey even took the day off to do them with us. "The weather's perfect for it too," she said to the cloudless sky as we split a frozen pizza with our own special topping on it. "Nice and bright." Her description of shrooms being like acid but more colorful and not taking the whole day was 1,000% accurate. And there couldn't have been a better place to do them than in a pool surrounded by trees and flowers.

Acid made me see and experience everything like I was seeing and experiencing it all for the first time, but shrooms just made me feel like I was dancing in the eternal pastures of paradise. Colors were more vibrant, and the music was downright sublime. The sun and the water embraced me in warm love. Everywhere I looked, the world beamed back at me. *You are my greatest creation,* it said to me. And all I could do was bask in its love—which was all it wanted of me—and feel the euphoria of getting to be a part of it. My mouth was actually sore from all the non-stop smiling.

After I had a spiritual experience with one of the trippier Beatles songs—"You look like you just discovered Islam," Victor laughed as I dropped to my knees to stare up at the sun with an open mouth—Kade and I left Victor and Kelsey so we could go talk to his herbs, and by 'talk to his herbs' we meant 'sneak up to his bedroom.' We gingerly kissed behind his closed door, breathing in each other's skin. We left our boardshorts on the floor. In his bed, I pulled away from him.

"Remember how you said it's only weird if you make it weird?"

His galactic eyes bored into my own. "It's weird, isn't it?" he correctly guessed.

Outside, Victor spun in place in the pool with his arms outstretched while Kelsey laid on her back on the deck, both of them beaming back up at the sun. Kade said he had to 'flavor-blast' the pool, which just ended up being him throwing different-colored pool noodles in the water. And when we started to come down, we simply made another pizza. We waited in the kitchen with it to make sure the house didn't burn down, watching each other's faces like they were Dalí paintings.

I explored the pool liner's design through a pair of goggles, the sun and the greenery above the water's surface making me feel like I was in the lush splendor of Babylon. The water hugged us until the evening sun cast the trees in one last lingering golden glow before it bowed out. The music was perfect, the pool was perfect, the sky was perfect. Feeling our own descent, we packed a bowl of citrus mint and smoked hookah while we reflected on the day.

"Why can't we do that every day?" Victor asked as he slapped his cajón, too caught up in his own thoughts to notice Kade's smoke rings.

Kelsey watched Anubis' effervescing water catch the mint leaves and orange slices that Kade had added to it. "What, drugs?"

"No. Well, maybe. I just meant enjoying life with no strings attached. I guess if it takes drugs to do it, then sure. Whatever it takes."

I shook my head. "Who came up with the idea of making people waste away their one life at some job instead of letting them enjoy it? I'd like to talk to them."

"Probably the capitalist swine overlords," Kade answered matter-of-factly as Vince popped out to dump some recycles. "Hence why we need a robot economy."

I savored the refreshing mint flavor as I exhaled smoke and nihilistic thoughts through my nose. "Such is the cost of economic progress, apparently," I rolled my eyes.

Vince laughed through his nose, earning himself a glare from Kade. "What?" Kade demanded.

His dad just shook his head, looking us over. "This is like a damn commune," he chuckled before going back in.

And then yesterday, wanting my last day with them to be a thrilling one—literally—my friends took me to the local amusement park. The funny part was that I never told them how deathly afraid I was of roller coasters. We got to the park minutes after the gates opened, just in time to see a coaster shoot a train of people *straight* up into the air with the sound of an otherworldly *WHRR.* "Are we gonna go on that one first?" I tried to ask casually as I watched the screams crest the erection of the coaster.

"We will," Victor assured me. "But we should get the big ones out of the way before the lines get too long." I gulped. *Well fuck me.*

I tagged behind them, taking in the games and the food stands. Frankie's speech from the RHA banquet blared in my mind. *'What happens once you're inside the theme park is all up to you.'* Maybe roller coasters aren't all as scary as I've been thinking they are, I thought as we passed some tame-looking wooden ones. *Or maybe they are,* I thought as a serpentine trail of steel in the sky ahead of us stopped me in my tracks. I shielded my eyes to look up at it. "Holy *fuck.*"

Victor turned back to me with a wild grin. "I know, right? It's some Cedar-Point-level shit."

I couldn't tell them I didn't want to ride it—I didn't want to ruin their day by making them sit around with my scaredy-cat ass. The coaster stared me down, mocking my insecurities like a Horcrux trying to save itself. *Look how pathetic you are. 12-year-old girls will ride me, but you won't? You're worthless and weak. I hope you like being everybody's bitch, because that's all you'll ever be. Have fun watching life from the sidelines, you wimpy little twink.*

I remembered tagging along with guys from school to go to Six Flags and stupidly thinking that I'd have fun with them, but every time they headed for a coaster, I'd make some excuse to not join them—*"My stomach kinda hurts,"* or *"I feel like I gotta take a crap."* I'd just walk around by myself until they were done, jealously watching other groups of friends laughing and having the time of their lives. *Look how much fun they're having,* I'd beat myself up. *Why can't you be like them, Trevor?* It was just another thing for me to torture myself over, another thing that made me different from them.

But this is now.

And then I remembered the laptop background I took to school with me, that affirmation that reminded me I was making the right decision. *"Life begins at the end of your comfort zone."* Fists clenched, jaw set, I scowled back at the coaster. *Get with the times, you pig shit.*

"Let's fucking do it," I said.

As bold as I was feeling then, listening to screams and watching the trains corkscrew and invert at harrowing speeds in the shadow of the coaster's monumental figure made me start having second thoughts. *I can't fucking get out of line.* And then once we were buckled in, I left any and all confidence I had on the ground.

One sure-ass way to confirm you're afraid of heights is to lay with your back almost flat in an open car with barely anything between you and the ground hundreds of feet below you. I almost started praying. *Am I really putting my life in the hands of a seatbelt and a restraint?* "Holy fucking shit. *Holy* fucking shit. *Holy* fucking shit," I repeated with my eyes glued to the track's vanishing point. You couldn't have paid me enough to look down over the side. Victor and Kade whooped and clapped without even a twig up their asses. *Anybody who's ever died on a roller coaster—or rather out of a roller coaster, I guess—started off their ride exactly like this.* Hill after hill of the coaster's track sank below us. My knuckles were white.

"You okay fam?" Kade asked me when he saw the look on my face.

I gulped. "Is now a bad time to tell you I'm fucking *terrified* of roller coasters?"

Victor's glasses-strapped head appeared in the gap between the seats in front of us. *"What?!"*

"Oh shit," Kade bit back a laugh, but not in a making-fun-of-me kind of way. "You're gonna be fine," he reached over to pat my knee. "It's gonna be fun," he smiled. I nodded, not at all feeling any better about it.

At the top of the roller coaster, I could hear the windless air. Time slowed. It would've been serene if we weren't so fucking high up. I could see over every other ride. I looked down on the hills, the river, the swaths of buildings. For a second, I wasn't even afraid. *What if we kissed at the top of the…*

And then the velocity yanked us forward—*fast.*

"Holy SHIIIIIT!"

The ground hurtled towards us before we got thrown to the side and launched back towards the sky, twisting so many times that I didn't know which way was which. I didn't dare let go of the harness. But somewhere on that ride, my screams from fear turned into screams from the thrill of it. It was my first time ever being on a roller coaster, but the feeling felt so *familiar* somehow, almost like flying. And by the time our train slowed to a stop, I was laughing. I couldn't stop laughing. *Go the fuck ahead, Trevor!*

"So *why'd* you wanna go on this if you're terrified of roller coasters?" Kade smiled with his hair all blown back.

"I didn't! And you should see your hair!"

"You should see *your* hair!" he laughed.

Walking on solid ground felt so weird after that that I was almost stumbling. *That's what I was afraid of this whole time?* We stopped to howl at the photo of ourselves mid-ride—Victor's face was red from the rush, Kade looked like he was about to projectile vomit, and there I was, conquering one of my greatest fears. I almost bought a picture to commemorate the day, but I know I won't ever forget it— that, and I didn't want to spend $30 on it or have to carry it around all day. Kade almost got us thrown out for trying to sneak a pic of the screen.

"Which one's next?" I eagerly asked.

We rode every coaster in the park. We went on rides I wasn't sure I'd live to see the end of. I screamed myself hoarse. We ate loaded French fries. We ate deep-fried Oreos. We threw rings onto bottles in exchange for Pokémon stuffies. We bought souvenir hats that look like squids. We stayed until the park closed. It might have actually been the most fun day of my life.

Our last ride of the night was the behemoth that I baptized myself on. I watched the spinning and speeding lights of the other rides as we climbed higher than any of them. Everything else we did during my visit—the pool party, the Pride parade, the Arts Festival, doing shrooms—those would've happened regardless. *But this? I did this. This happened because of* me.

The train slowed as it climaxed. In the dark, I could just see Victor grinning beside me. "This is it fam. Make the most of it."

The *clack-clack-clack-clack-clack* of ascent went quiet, and the train lurched forward. I put my hands in the air as I let myself fly towards the ground and back up again. I may have been alive for 19 years, but I was yesterday-years-old when I stopped letting fear run my life.

June 10

POV:

You and Logan and Parker Tam are hotboxing in Parker's car in the cemetery and Parker drives you all to Wendy's because you got the munchies *real* bad and the girl at the window *has* to know you're all fucking baked because you can't stop giggling and then Parker's dog walks across the room and Logan asks if the dog just danced and then you start cracking up at the empty Wendy's bag because it looks like George Washington in the crinkles and then all of Mt. Rushmore and then you go *back* to Wendy's where the *same* girl is at the window again and then you almost DoorDash a bottle of ranch dressing because you forgot to ask for some and then you wake up in your own bed with *no fucking clue* how you got there.

June 15

I fucking hate these "June is dedicated to the sacred heart of Jesus" billboards that show up every year. Why is June dedicated to the sacred heart of Jesus and not any other month? Could it be because June is also Pride month? This pissed-off queer thinks so. Don't even fucking get me started. Like, haven't the Christians already done enough to try to oppress us?

There's a quote attributed to Leonardo da Vinci: *"Once you have tasted flight, you will forever walk the earth with your eyes turned skyward, for there you have been, and there you will always long to return."* In other words: what does getting a tattoo, bottoming, and going on a roller coaster all have in common? You enjoy it one time and then you can't wait to do it again.

Madi and Logan couldn't get over the fact that the kid who used to be too afraid to even look up at a roller coaster was the one who dragged the three of us to Six Flags yesterday. I led the way to the gates with a spring in my step and eagerness in my smile.

"Forreal though, who even *is* this guy?" Madi asked Logan.

"Fuck if *I* know," Logan just laughed.

I pulled us from coaster to coaster like a gay dude on a college campus full of guys who doesn't know where to look first. "I can't believe I used to be so afraid of these!" I laughed after our fourth one of the day. I must've been feeling extra saucy, because I let them talk me into going on the big fucking tower of swings. *"Holy shit,"* I breathed as we rose higher and higher into the air. *Maybe this one wasn't such a good idea.* For as fast and gargantuan as they can be, at least roller coasters are on a track—sitting in a chair freely hanging in the air is a different story. I was afraid to look at anything, and closing my eyes made me nauseous, so I just pretended I was watching everything zip by through a car window. And then if that wasn't terrifying enough, the ride fucking *stopped.*

Don't ask me why being that high up and not moving was worse than being that high up and spinning in a circle, but it was. Maybe because there's nothing to distract you from the fact that you're in a seat with stories and stories of empty air beneath your dangling feet, with only a bar holding you in? I don't know. All I know is that I was freaking the fuck out.

"*Oh my god. Oh my god,*" I hyperventilated. "*Holy fucking shit. Holy goddamn fucking shit.*" Madi didn't bother hiding her fright either, and *that's* saying something. I don't know how Logan was holding up, because I wasn't about to turn around and jostle the chains that were keeping me alive.

Being that high up with your mortality staring you in the face makes you realize some things about your life. *I haven't been living my best life. I've just been existing instead of living. I've been taking for granted all the days that I get to experience, the breaths I get to take, the music that makes my days brighter, the connections I get to have with the people I care about. And even though I pushed him out of my life, I still love Ethan.*

I've been trying to tell myself otherwise for weeks, but I can't keep lying to myself anymore—I still love Ethan. I've always loved him. I've never stopped loving him, even when he made me feel betrayed, even in spite of the things I'd said. I would've called him right then and there to apologize to him and admit what an asshole I've been to him if I wasn't afraid of dropping my phone, even if just to hear him say *yeah, you are an asshole, now fuck off and don't ever call me again.* I wanted nothing more than to talk to him, even just leave a voicemail, anything to let him know that he still means something—*more* than just something—to me. Kade was right about everything he said to me on the phone. I just can't believe it took that long, and being in that situation, for me to realize it and wise the fuck up. Suddenly, I wasn't afraid of just dying anymore—I was afraid of dying before I could tell Ethan how I really felt, whether he wanted to hear it or not.

We might have been stopped for maybe only a couple of minutes, but the ride couldn't have started back up soon enough. I was too busy fumbling with my phone to even register what the ride operator said as we touched back down to Earth. I thanked myself for all the times I stopped myself from deleting his contact info—*see, I still cared about him*—as I tapped it with a shaky finger.

I'm sorry Ethan. I'm so fucking sorry. I know I was the worst boyfriend ever, but you still mean the world to me and I've done a shit job at showing it. I don't know what the hell I was thinking, but I still love you, and I always have no matter what I said. I want to love you forever. I know I don't deserve to even be talking to you, but I'd do anything to be a part of your life again, and I get it if you don't want anything to do with me, but oh god do I—

"Hello?" a woman's voice answered. "Trevor? Is this Trevor?" *He still kept my number.*

"This is Trevor," I said, high-key confused. "I'm trying to reach Ethan. Is he—is he there?"

"He's—" She hesitated. And then she started sobbing.

June 16

A.S. (antescript, because P.S. is overused—"Not Now" by Blink-182

Dear Ethan,

It's hard to believe that I've only been here for two days, but it feels like one continuous, restless night. And even after two days, I'm still not used to seeing you with stubble—but yet I'm used to seeing your face beat up. Isn't that some shit? The doctor's optimistic though that your vision should fully recover, but I guess we'll have to wait and see.

Everybody keeps saying that it's rare for a coma to last for more than a few weeks, which I was happy to hear, because I always just assumed they lasted for years and years. But since I think in worst case scenarios, I'm still worried that you'll be in a vegetative state until somebody eventually pulls the plug decades from now. And apparently the longer somebody's in a coma, the less chance they have of coming out of one, at least with a fully functioning brain.

I couldn't believe your mom when she told me what happened. Trust me when I say that I got here as fast as I could, not that that would change anything. I still can't believe this real life. I know some parents—or in this case, stepparents—can be unsupportive of their queer child, but I never thought one would actually be so disgusted by them that they'd take a baseball bat to them. I don't want to believe that you and the other guy you had in your room were doing anything, but your beer-drunk, now ex-stepdad did, and just the thought of it was apparently too much for him to handle. And here I thought you were spending your Summer living up the life you'd been so long overdue this whole time.

I have to say, you talked up your mom to be way worse than she actually is. I pictured some Fundamentalist nut who doesn't watch TV or listen to music on Sunday, but it was actually her idea to let me stay at your house. She said it feels so empty with only her in it. You should see her face when she talks about you. She'll be telling a story about when you were little and misbehaving, and then she'll start breaking down because no matter what you thought of yourself or what you thought she thought of you, you'll always be her son and nothing could ever stop her from loving you. She and I have cried together so many times. She told me how upset you were when they came to pick you up and how you had tears in your eyes the whole way home. She said she's never seen you so sad about something before, and for so long. It scared her how unlike yourself you were. *"He's always been a caring person, but I never saw one person mean so much to him,"* she told me.

I finally got to see your room, although under circumstances I could've never imagined. I thought I wouldn't be able to bear to even look inside it, let alone step foot inside. But then I got swept up in the life you had here. I couldn't help but feel like I'm looking through a dead person's things. There's so much I didn't know, so many little details about you that never came up. Like, how did I not know how into *Stranger Things* you are? I want you to tell me everything about you, I want to ask you questions until you're sick of them. But accepting that you'll never speak to me again is turning out to be way harder than I thought it would be.

I called your phone just to hear your cheerful voice telling me to leave a message. And before I even knew what I was doing, I did. There's got to be at least five voicemails on your phone of me apologizing or telling a story or just rambling. They're kind of like journal entries. They're my meditations.

Have you ever heard this Blink-182 song before? I can't stop listening to it, picturing what the music video for it could be:

You—your spirit, your consciousness, your ghost—are standing here beside me, watching me cry over you, watching me plead with you to wake up, watching me tell you all the things I wish I would've told you when I had the chance to, watching me tell you about the future I dreamt of for us, watching me apologize to you for treating you the way I did, watching me apologize for taking you for granted, watching me telling you to stop holding on and move on to whatever's next, because this cruel and painful world is no place for a pure and loving soul like you.

And you, suspended somewhere between being dead and being alive, are trying to tell me that you *want* to wake up, that you don't want me to leave your side just yet, that you forgive me, that you want a life with me in it, that although you've seen the universe and yes it's pure and yes it's more beautiful than you ever imagined, you're not ready to go yet because there's so much of the world you still want to experience.

And all the while, scenes from the time we got to share together play like a montage: us meeting at Starbucks, us laughing over games with our friends, me teaching you to longboard, our first kiss, saying 'I love you' to each other for the first time, me cheering for you at Open Mic Night, you playing the piano for me and me only, playing hooky to spend the whole day together, me watching you make a rock star of yourself at the concert. And after all that, *all* of that, me pushing you out of my life. And I can't tell who's singing to who. It's like we're trying to talk to each other, but only one of us can hear.

But I know that's just me being full of shit though, because why would you want a life with me in it when you can do so much better?

We had so many good times together, but the ones I can't stop tormenting myself over are the ones that never got to happen—watching you play baseball, writing you erotica for a birthday gift, wearing matching couples costumes for

Halloween, spending Christmas or New Year's with you. But now those are just more dreams I'll have to save for when I'm asleep. And thinking about somebody else getting to do those things for you and with you—who gets to see your face light up, who gets to hear the song of your laugh, who treats you the way you deserve to be treated—hurts me so fucking bad.

I saw a board game all about birds and I teared up right in the store because I know how much you'd have loved it, and there aren't many things that made me happier than seeing you happy. I just can't believe how goddamn self-absorbed I was that I never stopped to consider how painful the aftermath of us was for you. Why do I always treat people like this? Will I ever stop being a piece of shit?

I've been thinking about life a lot. You told me over Winter Break how we were an eighth of the way through our college careers, and now I'm a quarter of the way through it. Everything that happened in the past year I get to do only three more times—or rather, I only have three more chances to do it. I know you well enough to know that if we were still together and something happened to you, you wouldn't want me to stop living just because you couldn't anymore—you'd tell me that there's more to life than just you, and that I wouldn't be being fair to myself. And I'd want the same for you too if it were the other way around, though I know you wouldn't need anybody to remind you to live. It's just that the world's going to be that much harder to navigate knowing that you aren't out there somewhere brightening it up.

So I'm going to try to do better. I'm not going to waste my time anymore. I'm done watching my life pass me by. Can you believe that I went on a roller coaster? And I *like* them now?

I just want you to wake up though. You don't deserve this. You never did *anything* to deserve this. And you never deserved me. All I want for you is for you to wake up and be happy and be with somebody who treats you like a fucking *king*. And yeah, the thought of you spending your life with somebody else—somebody who's actually worth all the hurt that they'll cause you—fucking kills me. But I love you, and I want the best for you, even if that means a life without me in it.

But please come back though. There's that *one* guy out there whose world you'll totally make just by being in it, and who'll give you the life you deserve. Don't come back for your family or your friends, but do it for him. I'm so jealous of him. He doesn't know what's in store for him.

I love you so much Ethan. I'll always love you, even when you want nothing to do with me. I'll keep you with me for the rest of my life. You'll never understand how much of my life I've let you take up.

Forever yours,

Trevor

July 3

POV:

You're watching *Everything Everywhere All at Once* and the guy says to his wife in one of the alternate universes where they're not married how he wishes he could've had a life with her, and you remember how the person you love once said how people give each other meaning and how life is only as good as the people you share it with, and you're sobbing because you could've had a life with him if only you hadn't taken him for granted.

July 22

The afternoon-baked city calls my name, tempts me,
One glimpse of adventure and I'm gone—
I grab my camera and my desire and I ride,
Driving after life, chasing down the promises
Waiting in the sleeves of secondhand records,
Clinging to the noodles of midnight ramen bars,
Scratched into the sides of weathered benches,
Scrawled in the lines of crosswalk poetry,
Drifting through the vibrant air of sun-beaten parks,
In the episodic company of those other hungry souls
Who yearn to drag it out and dance with it, unrelenting,
Until the rising day set us loose all over again.

-golden hour

July 30

I think the meaning of life is this: that you make the most of it while you can—or something like that, but more profound-sounding. Marcus Aurelius knew it, Walt Whitman knew it, Ferris Bueller knew it, Victor knows it. The whole getting-the-stick-out-your-ass-thing still applies though, just to be clear.

Years from now, when gas masks have become a part of our faces, we'll fondly look back and laugh at how everybody lost their minds over this *one* airborne toxic event. It still kills me how the country shut down over five COVID cases, but then nobody gave a shit when it was all over the place. Hopefully the anti-maskers will be against gas masks in the future when the air itself is noxious, because that'll actually solve a lot of this country's problems—aside from the noxious air.

My life feels like one of those poignant, optimistic scenes at the end of a movie where the main character knows things aren't going to be the same anymore, but not necessarily in a bad way. The song in the soundtrack for it would be "Quarter Life Crisis" by Judah & the Lion. I'm not saying that my story is at an end, but it certainly feels like there's a beginning on the horizon, and there can't be a beginning without some kind of ending.

In another month I'll be back at NHU, where somebody named Zander Flynn, who I can't find on Instagram, has been assigned as my new roommate. Kade and Logan and I agreed that if he turns out to be a pain in the ass or a capital-S Straight guy, we'll gaslight him until he moves out.

I read through both of my journals for the first time, and holy fucking *hell.* I made myself laugh, I made myself cry. I was predictable, I was surprising. *I remember laughing so hard at that that it hurt. I forgot about that! Jesus Trevor, how could you be so stupid?* But I don't know if I'm going to keep journaling though. I really haven't felt the urge to write down everything that's been happening to me recently. I think I might start doing something crazy and just try to live my life instead of trying to record it, and I feel like I've been doing a pretty good job so far.

My Summer started off rough, but I'm not going to spend the rest of it wallowing in my misery and getting high to numb my feelings. I know that obsessing over 'could haves' and 'would haves' and 'should haves' aren't good for anything except keeping me from moving forward. After Ryder's death, I used to listen to the soundtracks of the games we grew up playing, wishing I was 8 years old again. After Dillon broke up with me, I dug canyons in my records and wished we were still in each other's lives. And you know where both of those got me? Fucking *nowhere.*

Don't get me wrong though—I still miss Ethan. Oh *god*, do I miss him. I miss the *shit* out of him. I'll go from 100 to a total wreck in a moment. I'll be making French press and then remember how he used to call it "rich-people coffee," and then all of a sudden I'm crying on the counter because he didn't deserve anything that happened to him, including me. He finally got the chance to be himself, only to get punished for it.

This is going to sound bad of me, but I think seeing him in the hospital and being unable to live his life has motivated me to try to do a better job at living mine. His mom's been giving me weekly updates on how he's doing, which have all been the same until the latest one. My heart leapt when she said he started opening and closing his eyes, but that's apparently just a normal automatic reaction for the 'post-coma unresponsive state,' which can last from months to years. She said the doctors said he'll likely make a full recovery, but I hope it doesn't take years.

I've been writing more short stories. I almost gave myself a panic attack while working on the one about the sub that went down to see the Titanic and got lost on the ocean floor. I've been toying with the idea of making a blog to post them, but I'm not sure if I'm ready for that just yet.

I purged most of my books. Years of finds from thrift stores and garage sales and library sales and bookstores left me with an accumulation of history books and classical literature that I knew I was never going to read. Let's be real—they were decorations, decorations owned by someone with a stick up their ass. I have Google if I ever want to read something historical, and I'll go to the library if I'm ever overtaken by the urge to read Jude the Obscure. I ended up getting way less cash for ten boxes of books than I was expecting, but now I have a handful of stuff that I actually want to read. I can't believe I've been holding onto all that shit this whole time when there's stuff like Tomorrow, And Tomorrow, And Tomorrow that I could've been reading.

Dad and I got to spend some father-son time putting up a wall shelf system to replace my bookcases, since I didn't need them anymore. The fake plants, my camera, my record player and records, and my Arts Festival buys all give it the indie-kid vibe that I'm going for. And speaking of indie music, I've been listening to so many random indie pop playlists—even more than the music in my own library— that I'm at the point where I can actually recognize a decent number of artists.

I dug out my bike for the first time in forever to hit up the bike trails around different parts of the city. And instead of just sticking to my neighborhood, I've taken my longboard to the Waterfront and the parks along the lake. I've never actually taken the time to explore the city I've spent most of my life in. It's funny what places you stumble across when you just go out and look, especially when you're not looking for anything in particular. I've discovered two new bookstores, a new record store, a new Indian restaurant, a tea and coffee house, and like 90 new thrift stores. There's a huge flea market that pops up once a month that I never even knew about, and we went to the big food festival too. We even almost drove to Toronto just for poops and giggles, but Logan couldn't find his passport card. And if he or Madi are busy or don't want to come along with me, then I just take myself on a date, because life's too short to not show yourself some love. And when I'm not out exploring or doing something new, I've been trying to rediscover the joys we tend to overlook in all the little things. I think about all the things I'd miss or the things that I wish I could do just one more time if I lay dying—everything that I have the opportunity to do, but never *do*—like catching lightning bugs, or playing *Scrabble* with Mom and Dad, or going out for ice cream, or flying a kite, or even just going on a walk, and I go ahead and do them. I even got an industrial piercing just for the hell of it.

Because here's the thing: we can chalk it up to chance or fate or coincidence all we want, but our lives are made up of moments that *we* make happen. And those moments become days, and those days are what make up the rest of our lives. And in the grand scope of everything, our lives are nothing more than a series of passing moments—unique, unrepeatable, once-in-a-lifetime moments. We're only at this theme park called life for one single day. *Ichi-go ichi-e, hoc quoque transibit.*

I've spent far too many moments making myself into what other people want to see at the expense of who I am or what I want. The more I try to please other people, the less that my life is my own. I may only be 19 and think that I have my whole life ahead of me, but for all I know, most of my life could have already happened. Whether it lasts for another 60 years or only another week, I'm not going to sit by and just watch it pass me by. There will only ever be one Trevor Bentley Huffman, and being anything less than the most authentic Trevor Bentley Huffman ever would be a waste of a life. Because the day *will* come when my life will pass, and when that day comes I want to go knowing that I lived it the best that I could. And that's up to nobody but me. The word inked on my wrist serves as a reminder of that.

But beyond the upcoming school year, I don't have a clue what my future looks like—hell, who knows what the upcoming school year will even look like? And I'm okay with that. I may not have a plan for my life, but I've never felt better about it. I'm just going to keep trying to find my way and look for the right people to make the journey with while enjoying the ride. I said I feel like I'm on the cusp of something, which means there must be something I'm leaving behind. Because like death, like heartbreak, like going away to school, there's never an ending without a beginning, just like how there's never a beginning without an ending.

Because what is life anyway but an endless series of endings and beginnings?

. . . .

A.S. (antescript, because P.S. is still overused)—"Expert in a Dying Field" by The Beths

Dear Trevor,

I need you to listen to me. The year is 2031. The spotted lanternfly population has exponentially exploded over the last few years and has decimated the world's food supply. You always heard that the wars of this century would be fought over oil or technology, but nobody could have predicted that NATO would be the ones invading Ukraine for control of its grain production, but here we are. You need to start preparing now if you want any chance of surviving. Nobody ever thinks they'll be the ones to witness the extinction of humankind, but the apocalypse has to happen to somebody, doesn't it?

I'm kidding—as far as I know, anyway. The Earth's climate *is* in uncharted territory though, so we'll see.

I was going through some old documents and came across the journal you kept during your freshman year of college, and all I can say is holy *hell* did the feels hit me. It's not like I forgot about it or anything, but reading it through your eyes as it happened brought that year back to life in a way that memories often fail to do. I put on some Brand New and Motion City Soundtrack while I read, and all of a sudden I was 18 again and living in a small town in western Pennsylvania, when the first breezes of Fall were rustling the yellowing leaves.

You said at the end of your last journal that you wanted to live your life instead of trying to record it, and I'd say you've been doing a pretty good job, since you haven't kept a journal since then. So let me bring you up to speed on what's happened in the meantime, starting with your sophomore year:

Your new roommate Zander will come off as shy and almost too nerdy at first, but he'll turn out to be pretty cool. You and Kade will be his mentors, giving him and Logan sophomore tips, forgetting that the two of you were just freshmen yourselves only a few months prior.

Between living on the other side of campus, having duty shifts, having desk shifts, and getting involved with the Theatre department, Victor won't be around as much as you thought he was going to be. He'll still make time for you and your friends, but the dining halls will end up being where you'll see him the most, talking about how easy it used to be to just hang out.

You'll think you'll never go to another party as fun as the ones at 370 Rock Hill Road, but Tylor and Amina and Jaxon's place on Southway, Nikole and her friend's apartment at The Commons, and Theo's apartment next door to the one Miles used to live in will all prove you wrong. Because 370 Rock isn't a place—it's a state of mind.

But you won't spend every weekend at their places, or even out at a party. The four of you won't even be opposed to just spending the night in every now and then, sometimes sipping on whatever liquor you'll have Tylor buy for you.

Logan will join you and Kade for rainy Saturdays of *Axis & Allies*, but it won't take long before he'll come to find his own friends and his own place in the college microcosm—trying out Improv Club with Victor, the Gamer's Guild with Kade. That's not to say he'll forget about you, but don't expect him to always be hanging around your room. Life happens outside of it, and he'll be sure to not let it pass him by.

And you won't spend as much time keeping to yourself either. You'll run for Novak's House Council Treasurer and somehow win. You'll get a job as a tutor. You'll go to events on and off campus. You'll go to the gym a handful of times with Victor. You'll still go to Lit Club for a while, but you won't go back once you discover how much better you click with the student staff of *Crane* magazine after submitting one of your short stories to it for publication. You'll give Proud as Halle another chance too, and finding it to be more bearable than it was before, you'll actually get involved with it. And it's there that you'll meet Micah.

But as much as you'll want to make it work, you'll find that the things you love in him are only the reflections of somebody else you once loved. It'll hurt to let him go, but keeping him to yourself like that isn't fair to either of you. It'll be the same story with Hollister too. And after him you'll tell yourself you're done with love, because there's only one person you want to be with and you threw him away. Instead, you'll settle for being friends-with-benefits with Kade when you're lonely and not seeing anybody, and you'll spend inebriated weekend nights in the beds of one-time conquests, struggling to remember the next morning how you got there.

And whether he knows it or not, Ethan's mom will give you status updates on him along the way. *"He's been in an irritated mood today but that's normal." "Today he was able to walk around on his own." "He asked me if he knows somebody named Trevor."*

You'll turn 20.

Logan will ask one day why you're all going to school in the middle of nowhere, which is a thought that crossed your minds more than once. Like Dr. Averescu realized, there's a life to be lived, and New Halle, Pennsylvania may not be the place to live it, in spite of all the good times you've had there and all the memories it's given you. Because every place in your life—just like every person in your life—is in it for a reason, and not always for the long run. So after weeks of research and admissions and applications, you and Kade and Victor will get accepted to Pitt, while Logan will get into CMU. You'll uproot your lives to start a new one together in Pittsburgh, because life's only as good as the people you spend it with.

It will be a homecoming for Kade and Victor, and it will be a kind of homecoming for you too, because Pittsburgh—the city you first fell in love with on a chilly November day a lifetime ago—is where you belong, even if it took a couple of years of a life somewhere else to figure it out. A sense of finality will hit you when you move out of your parent's house for the last time. You'll watch the 'Welcome to New York' sign shrink in your rearview, and you'll remember the ending of *Winesburg, Ohio*, thinking about all the things in West Seneca that you'll miss, but excited at facing the adventure that is life and the pursuit of dreams.

Your first apartment will have no central air, two bedrooms that you'll share in pairs, and you'll have to walk a block to do your laundry, but the four of you will make it your own, rounding out the furnishings with yard sale finds and whatever you can find on the curb. You'll crowd around your kitchen table for every-other-Friday-night Chinese takeout or whatever Kade made for dinner. The occasional extra folding chair or two will make an appearance when any of you are seeing somebody you want to introduce to the rest of the house.

You'll be amazed at how backwards New Halle was compared to the city. Walking down Forbes Avenue, you'll wonder how you managed to survive for two years with only six options for okay food—not that you'll be able to afford to eat out or order out all the time. You've never been frivolous with your money, but being on your own will certainly make you think twice about what you buy. Everything from bubble tea to stir-fried ice cream will become a luxury. And any hopes you'll have of Mr. and Mrs. Oakley helping their sons out with all their new expenses will quickly go out the window. The four of you being totally on your own will be a scary new reality, but you'll survive, though more broke than you've ever been. That first year in Pittsburgh is going to be rough, I'm not going to lie. Sure, Mom and Dad will help you out a little, but $100 will suddenly be *way* less than it used to be.

Your money and Logan's money and Victor's money and Kade's money won't belong exclusively to each of you anymore, but to all of you. Kade will find that out the hard way when he buys a new board game as a housewarming gift that could've bought dinner for a week. You'll frequent the museums because your student IDs will get you in for free. You'll rotate pizza places depending on when they have deals. You'll all get onto the same phone plan. Most of your clothes will come from thrift stores. There will be concerts every other night all over the city, but the only ones you'll go see will be in the basement of whichever house parties are cool enough to have basement shows. You'll pay $1.50 to see movies that Mom and Dad probably paid a buck to see in some dingy theater 20 years ago. The four of you will pool your money together for rent and shopping trips to Aldi. You'll earn yours from the kitchen at Chipotle, bringing home leftover burritos for dinner until you're sick of them. You'll deliver for DoorDash even when you never feel like it, until you discover that being a Lyft driver is more profitable, but at the cost of a

Friday or Saturday night with the boys. Kade will even end up selling his car, memorizing the bus schedules for the common good.

Making small talk with your neighbors will eventually turn into them inviting you to join them when they have friends over and have backyard barbecues. So that's how your family will grow to include Gabe and Coleslaw and Maya and Amir, and their friends will become your friends too, who will help you make your home in the neighborhoods beyond Oakland, in Bloomfield and Lawrenceville and Squirrel Hill. You'll take your studying to the same tea house that Kade and Victor introduced you to. Grabbing groceries from the Asian supermarket will be nothing out of the ordinary. The outdated bowling alley will be where you'll meet Gianna and Sebastian.

And all the while, there will be texts from Ethan's mom. *"He was asking about you again."*

You'll turn 21.

For as long as you've been looking forward to it, the celebration will be pretty low-key. Tylor will drive down to stay for the weekend, the first time you'll see them since the end of your sophomore year. They and Kade will take you out for drinks, an instant photo of the three of you legally drunk to commemorate the night.

Kade will take a semester off for mental health reasons and end up not going back. He'll apprentice at a tattoo shop instead, where he'll be only one of two people who aren't trans. But his side hustle is where he'll shine—working in the studio of one of his professors from Pitt, who will help him get some of his works shown at a few small exhibitions.

Since the four of you will be able to afford something a little nicer by the time it'll come time to renew your lease, you'll move into an apartment on the north side of Oakland. You'll finally have your own bedroom, and the living room won't be in the kitchen anymore—but hang onto those window air conditioners. Amir, Maya, and Coleslaw may not be just a property line away anymore, but your place will still be a second home to them.

Your junior and senior years will be what you always wanted college to be like when you first went away to it—the same experience you had hoped that befriending Alex and Andrew and June and Matt would be a steppingstone to. You won't have 'parties' as much as you'll have 'some friends over for drinks'—which isn't to say that you'll never play Drunk *Jenga* or pong again, but there will certainly be an uptick in discussions about literary theories. You, Kade, and Logan will spend no small number of weekends getting tipsy and smoking Alex's old hookah and talking about world history. You and Amir will bounce books off of each other, diving into things you used to think only the most progressive of students bothered to read. And thanks mostly to Kade and Gianna, your apartment will find itself pervaded with Art majors and Film majors and Philosophy majors and corduroy pants and middle-shelf wine. Your Pittsburgh friends—most of whom won't even be from Pittsburgh—will introduce you to underground music scenes and B-horror movies and postmodern art. They'll take you to dive bars and basement raves and record-store concerts of local artists. You'll invite them over to listen to readings of your latest story. To this day, you still talk about the Halloween and New Year's parties you all used to throw.

Isn't it funny how you never realize how good the days of your life are until you find yourself longing for them?

Ethan's mom will call you to give you what will end up being her last status update. *"He said he wants to talk to you."*

The sight of him and the sound of his voice will almost be too much for you. It will be all awkward small talk and avoiding the glaringly obvious. *"Do you know who ended up becoming President?"* he'll ask.

Your nostrils will flare, remembering how you cried when it sank in that 77 million people of this country chose fear over love, when it hit you that so many people's lives were about to become unnecessarily harder. *"Fuckstick fucking is,"* you'll spit. *"How have you not heard about that?"*

"I know about that," he'll roll his eyes. *"I meant the RHA President. Who did they end up making the President of RHA instead of me?"* You'll stare at him and then you'll laugh, laughing in disbelief that *that's* what he cares about. And he'll laugh too, and you'll realize how much you missed that laugh.

"I remember us," he'll shift. *"I remember everything."*

Your face will flush. *"I wouldn't want you to forget. You deserve to know what a piece of shit I am."*

"You talking to me right now shows me that you're not a piece of shit. We just didn't end well."

"I'm sorry. I wish you could know how sorry I am for how I treated you."

"We had a lot of good times," he'll say.

"Do you think you could ever forgive me?" you'll ask before you can stop yourself.

It'll take him a moment to answer. *"I don't know."*

"Do you think something could ever happen between us again?" you'll go on.

"I don't know," he'll repeat.

You won't hear from him again until you get a package in the mail from an address in Rosemont, Pennsylvania. It'll be your own copy of *The First to Die at the End*, the book you lent him back when you were still together.

"I finally finished this," the note inside will say. *"I figured you'd want it back."*

The story of Trevor and Ethan could've ended there, but you'll text him for the first time in years—just a simple thank you, but the fact that you sent it will end up meaning everything. Because that's how you'll start a conversation with a number you long ago gave up on ever hearing from again.

At Kade and Victor's insistence, he'll catch a bus to visit to see your place and to see what your lives have become, and to come to Sebastian and Gianna's Friendsgiving dinner. You almost won't be able to give him a hug like the others when he arrives. The only two not wine drunk at dinner, he'll ask you if you want to take a walk around the block for some fresh air. Part of you will expect him to tell you to stay out of his life, and the other part will hope that you and him go back to your apartment to reacquaint yourself in the most intimate way. Neither will happen—the two of you will simply just talk, catching up like any old friends, not realizing until just then how much he was missing from you.

"So what are you gonna do now?" you'll ask him.

"I guess I'll just go back to New Halle," he'll say, the words hurting you more than you'd expect them to.

Since everybody will have jobs, he'll only spend one night on your living room couch.

The day after he goes back home, he'll text you. **I put up a new video. You should watch it.** You'll remember the last video he put up and how he sang out of anguish—anguish that you had caused him. But the new one will be a song that he discovered through you once upon a time, back before either of you could ever know that it would eventually become your song—"Understand" by Hippo Campus. His voice will crack and his eyes will tear up for anybody in the world to see, but he'll sing for only one person. And that person will watch, and you'll sob, sobbing because after everything and after what you did to him, none of it should be happening.

"I forgive you," he'll say when you call him afterwards, your face still wet. "I'll always forgive you, because nothing you could do could ever make me want to stop trying."

"Why...how could you want to forgive me after the way I acted?"

"Sometimes you just have to be on a bus riding away from somebody to realize how much they mean to you." Because isn't that what love is? When your brain gives you a thousand reasons not to, but you only need that one from your heart to make you dive in headfirst?

So that's how you and Ethan will get back together.

He'll transfer to Pitt too, since everyone he knew at New Halle will either be two years ahead of him or will have moved away. He'll transfer his life from Rosemont to Pittsburgh, where his life was already waiting for him in the form of the three people who've always loved him just as he was. His mom will watch the moving van carry her son away to the life he always deserved, perhaps penitent that she herself helped keep him from it for so long. Nobody will mind another person and their belongings moving into your already-cramped apartment, because Ethan's the kind of person you just can't help but make room in your life for.

You'll turn 22.

Like all other things, college will pass. Like when you graduated high school, the regrets of the things you didn't do while you were in college will hit you all at once. All the people who will have jobs lined up for them before they graduate will make you think more than once that you must have done college wrong somehow, but you'll come to realize that you had the most Trevor-Bentley-Huffman college experience ever, and nobody else can say that.

Like so many other things in your life, Summer vacation will become just another has-been. You'll all take a vacation to Kade's relatives' house in Huntington Beach, California to celebrate graduation. Seeing the coast from a drop top will be everything you ever imagined, but after seeing all the places in the pictures that made you so envious of it in the first place, you'll realize that maybe southern California isn't everything you'd always mentally chalked it up to be.

Except for not having classes or research papers, your post-graduation life will feel mostly the same for a while. You won't land a good job all of a sudden. You and your roommates will still have to be smart with your money. Most of your Pittsburgh friends will still stay local, but Logan won't be one of them. Already having gone to three different schools in three different places in four years, he'll move to Chicago for a job that opened up through his now-fiancée Natalie. If one measures success by how much money they make, then he's well on his way to becoming successful, and god knows he deserves that after the childhood he's had.

So it will be Ethan instead of Logan who will ride in your passenger seat when you head back home for the holidays, or to his hometown to visit with his mom for a few days.

You'll turn 23.

Aware that life can catch up to you when you least expect it, you and Ethan and Kade and Victor will try to make the most of your time together, remembering that every moment you get to share is truly only once in a lifetime. You'll go to concerts and festivals around the city. You'll save up for road trips to Cedar Point, Hershey, D.C., Bonnaroo. Staying roommates won't even be a question when you move into the house you currently rent, which will get even bigger once Victor leaves.

After years of practicing lucid dreaming, he'll just be gone one day and nobody will ever hear from him again. Your theory is that he finally succeeded in astral projecting and never looked back. I'm kidding.

His job bartending at a gay bar might have let him bring home covetous amounts of tips, but that's not his purpose. As he's always done, he'll try to do as much political good as he can. If there's a rally or demonstration going on somewhere in the city, he'll be there, even if just to counter-protest. He and your city council member will be on a first-name-basis with each other. With a Public Policy degree to his name, he'll move to Harrisburg, where he'll find new roommates and land a job interning for Senator Hammond's office, working to help her become the state's first female governor.

So that's how Victor's and Kade's lives will take diverging paths, and the day each of them had once feared will come to pass.

You'll turn 24.

Ethan will work his butt off to graduate a year early, but his degree may not have even been necessary. While pursuing his dream of being a music event coordinator, he'll cross paths with Sam—formerly WXNU's DJ Twinkle Toes—who will already be established in the field, and who will introduce him to the right people, getting him involved with work where he can. Although Pittsburgh will come to publicly know Ethan as the guy who performed a duet of "Same Love" with another local artist in the park after one of the city's Pride parades, his contributions to the local music industry will be all behind-the-scenes. He'll shake hands with all but the biggest of artists. When Wallows comes through Pittsburgh on tour, he'll pull some strings so you can meet them in person. Don't even try to prepare yourself, because there's absolutely nothing you can do.

You'll turn 25.

Your downtown office job will pay so well that you'll have more money than you've ever had. You won't be able to afford whatever you want, but you'll be able to live comfortably without constantly being frugal. But then one day you'll wonder if going to bed before 10 p.m. so you can get up early to do something you aren't passionate about is really the best thing you can be doing with your life. You'll find yourself in a place you thought you'd never be in—working a meaningless job that brings you nothing but a paycheck. And you'll remember one time at your old job in New Halle University's library how you found something laying in the printer about how the next Michelangelo is writing invoices because it's easy and pays the bills.

So you'll quit, taking a job as an editor instead. It'll pay way less, but you'll find it more fulfilling, and it'll even turn out to be a step in the right direction. Thanks to the people you'll meet and realizing that your life is up to nobody but you, your first collection of short stories—years and years in the making—is set to be published this upcoming February.

You'll turn 26.

Kade will meet Elias, a friend of a friend of a friend who's in town from Copenhagen, at one of his exhibitions. Kade never said that the move there would be temporary, and from the Instagram posts you'll see and from the occasional postcard you'll get, you know he won't be coming back. He's happy and he's in love

—but more importantly, he has somebody who loves him back enough to make him their whole world—and if there's anybody who deserves that, it's him.

So that's how you and Ethan will suddenly find the house to yourselves.

Adulting is the weirdest thing you'll ever do. You'll enjoy shopping for candles and throw pillows and kitchen utensils. Not only will you develop a taste for pasta salad, but yours will be a staple at every cookout. You'll enjoy doing yard work because it'll be *yours*. And just wait and see how your tastes in music change. A lot of what you used to listen to won't play from your speakers as often anymore, but when they do, they'll take you back to another place and time—like when you'd have the wind in your face and snow in your shoes but you wouldn't even care, because you'd be on your way to the other side of campus to see the boy you were crazy about, the same one who's been living in your head rent-free ever since—and you'll know that you've lived. And you'll have Ethan by your side to make the adulting journey with you. You'll play Kade's *Catan* game that he left behind, the edges of its cards brown from being handled. You'll get an espresso machine, and he'll make you designs in the foam like he used to so many years ago. The two of you will go on a side quest on the way up to your parents to stop by New Halle University to let the memories flood back. Some things will be different, like the new Asian bistro in the Student Center, but a lot things will still be the same, like both of your initials inside of a heart that you carved into a bench once upon a time.

And then one night when you're both stoned, eating Chex Mix and listening to *More* on vinyl after sex, you'll go to ask him, *"Do you think we'll still be doing this when we're 70?"* But you'll choke on your words and you'll have to fight back your tears, because it will be at that moment when you'll finally comprehend what it means to have forever in mind, what it means to actually get to share the rest of your life with the person who you've let become your entire world.

But Ethan will beat you to it. The two of you will take a vacation to the beach— the same beach where your paths may have crossed years before you ever even met—and get up early one morning to go down to the shore to watch the sunrise. *"Do you remember that Dr. Seuss quote you told me back when we were first dating?"* he'll ask as the water laps your feet. *"'You know you're in love when you can't fall asleep because reality is finally better than your dreams?'"*

"You remembered that?" you'll ask.

"Of course," he'll smile. *"How could I ever forget it?"* You'll think he's just creating a romantic moment, one that you would have remembered for the rest of your life even if he hadn't gotten down and pulled out the ring—and no, it won't be a Ring Pop like the two of you always joked about using. *"I still can't get over that I get to be in the dreams of the guy who was always in my own,"* he'll say as you both start sobbing. *"I want you to keep me awake for the rest of my life."* Victor will cry when you'll ask him to officiate the ceremony.

The answer you'll give people when they'll ask how the two of you met will be that you met in college, as if it was as simple as having class together and getting the balls to ask him if he wanted to get coffee. Love in the long-term is messy though. Don't expect it to always be as cute and as Instagrammable as when you first started dating. You'll get upset with each other and argue over the smallest things and say hurtful things on purpose, but then you'll remember that there are millions of universes out there where Trevor and Ethan aren't even in each other's lives and how you're fortunate enough to not exist in any of them.

And now you're 27.

Don't take life so seriously that you forget to enjoy it. You're only here for this one time. I'm proud of you for figuring out the whole getting-the-stick-out-of-your-ass thing, and especially so early on.

Don't care too much about what other people think. Living for the comfort and convenience of other people is one of the most sure-fire ways to ruin your life.

Don't take people you care about for granted, because someday they won't be in your life anymore, often with little or no warning.

Don't take moments for granted, because each and every one will only ever be experienced that one time.

Don't fall into the trap of thinking that your best years are behind you. Yes, New Halle was fun, and those first years of you and your friends trying to make it on your own in Pittsburgh were fun, but everything is, has, and will ever be only what you make it. Don't ever wait for the perfect moment to come to start living and appreciating life.

Don't settle for less than your passions if you don't have to. Leave that for the people who've forgotten how to dream. Life comes at a cost, and any life that costs you your happiness isn't worth it.

Don't let other people's lives make you feel like you're not living yours the 'right' way. You're doing you better than anybody else ever could.

Don't be afraid to take chances. The regrets of the things you didn't do and the chances you let slip by hurt so much worse than the mistakes you do make.

There's a life waiting for you out there, and it can be anything you want it to be if only you make it happen. I can't wait to see what the next one you create for yourself looks like.

Love,

Trevor

RESOURCES

As someone who struggles with/has struggled with anxiety, depression, self-love, and just being happy in general, it was important to me to give some of the characters in this story the same struggles, because readers whose minds aren't always kind to them need to see that they're not alone. It's okay to not be okay.

Trans Lifeline: Call 877-565-8860, or visit translifeline.org

The Trevor Project: Call 1-866-488-7386, text 'START' to 678678, or visit thetrevorproject.org

988 Suicide & Crisis Lifeline: Call or text 988, or visit 988lifeline.org

Crisis Text Line: Text 'HOME' to 741741, or visit crisistextline.org

ACKNOWLEDGEMENTS

In the acknowledgements section of a book called *Dojo Dilemmas* by Joseph Cucci, the author says that he was worried what people might think of him after publishing his book. I was also worried at first what people would think of me after reading my story, but then I remembered that life's too short to always live for the comfort of other people. Besides, anybody who has a real problem with it probably voted for Trump multiple times and doesn't have any room to talk about what is and isn't moral.

Reading paragraphs of names in the acknowledgement sections of books made me think that I may have done the writing process 'wrong' somehow. Self-publishing this book means that I had no editor, agent, etc., nor was I part of any kind of book club that gave me encouragement—but that's not to say I didn't have my own fan club. Endless thanks to Dalton Dornish, Ricki Rumbaugh, Courtney Becker, Destiny Chamoun, and Jeffrey Brandle, whose enthusiasm, support, and suggestions for this story—even in its unrefined versions—helped make it possible.

The proper thing to do here would be to name every person I met at Slippery Rock University, because every person who made an impression on me during my time there made it into this story in one way or another. (So yes, if you were at SRU between the Fall of 2012 and the Spring of 2015, you could very well have been the inspiration for a character or line in this story!) But, that would be a lot of names, so here are the ones who deserve it the most: DJ Wolfarth, Collin Burke, Jim Kovacs, Aaron Kollar, Tyler Malorni, Sarah Hammond, Tanner Lewis, Danielle Wolfe, Tommy Wolfe, Kelly Williams (Jelly Fladden), Tom Williams, John Riggio, Tyler Hahn, Bob Calabrese, Nate Smith, Kyle Perza, Jess Horgos, Jackie Metcalfe, Mike Capo, Ashley DeWitt, Mindy Hood, Becca M., Paula Mims, Cole Vecchio, Walker Martz, Matt Eichler, Casey Carreiro, Darryl Andrews, Zach Rapp, Jamie Peace, Carl Izzo, Bronte Soul, EJ Christopher, Ray Scalise, Patrick Beswick, Dr. John Golden, Dr. Aaron Cowan, Dr. Joseph Alessi, Dr. Thomas Daddessio, Dr. Jesus Valencia, Dr. Rhonda Clark, and of course, Boozel Jake.

And even though they weren't part of my SRU story, it'd be wrong to not give a shout out to Tyler Wagner, Josh Butler, Jon Sammel, Connor Rudge, Nicole Bell, Nick Quinn, Brandon Cannon, and Dr. Julian Gallegos from CCAC.

Thank you to all the bands and artists who helped bring this story to life and who have always been there for me. This story would not be what it is, nor would I be who I am as a person, if not for the music you've made. You change lives in more ways than you know.

Thank you to the WSRU and WNHU college radio DJs (New Halle University's college radio station was originally named WNHU until I discovered it was already a real college radio station), and to the people who compiled all the YouTube playlists of relaxing Nintendo music, for giving me my favorite music to write to.

Thank you to all the authors who've inspired me with their stories and who've given me books to get lost in—Stephen Chbosky in particular for writing *The Perks of Being a Wallflower*, without which this story would not exist.

And because I love him and can't pass up the chance to embarrass him, thank you Dalton. Even though you were so unimpressed with the first draft that you didn't read the entire thing in a single day (just kidding), I literally would not have been able to dedicate myself to writing this if not for you tackling chores and giving me space and time to work on it. The people you love are the people you do dishes for. I love you more than you know ♡

And I'd like to give a shout out to myself, which I feel is something authors should do more often. Writing a book takes *a lot* of work, time, and dedication. The fact that I managed to write this whole thing without losing motivation is almost miraculous. So, Ryan: go 'head! I'm so fucking proud of you.

And of course I'd like to thank you too, because what's a story without an audience? Out of all the books out there, you chose to spend time with *this* one, the one that *I* created. I hope you enjoyed reading this as much as I enjoyed writing it. I hope you discovered something new, whether it be an artist or a different way of looking at the world. But if you take only one thing away from this story, let it be this: the world will never get better unless we start choosing love over fear.

Ryan Wagner didn't major in English or Creative Writing, nor was he any kind of Fellow at his school. The last piece of fiction he wrote before this story was a one-page assignment in 10th grade. He's just a guy who had an idea pop into his head one day and who never gave up on it. He enjoys music that slaps, dumplings of all sorts, fish tacos, books written by people who don't have a stick up their ass, video games, and tabletop games, among many other things. His dislikes include people who don't know how to drive, entitled white people, and perforations in cardboard that don't perforate, also among many other things. He lives in Pittsburgh with his fiancé and their dog.

Ryan in 2025
(Photo credit: Dalton Dornish)

www.ingramcontent.com/pod-product-compliance
Lightning Source LLC
Chambersburg PA
CBHW011142100726
47899CB00010B/3145